Liz Ryan's Novels

'Liz Ryan understands not only a woman's heart but a woman's mind.'

Terry Keane, Sunday Times (Ireland)

'Captivating . . . Brings a freshness and verve to the boy-meets-girl story. The Ryan twist on fictional romance invests the rosy garden of love with some of the sharpest thorns.'

Justine McCarthy, Irish Independent

'Vivid and witty . . . great charm.'
Brenda Power, Dublin Sunday Tribune

'Immensely readable.'

San Antonio Express News

'Will delight the reader who has already devoured Maeve Binchy.'

Liverpool Echo

'Liz Ryan is smart and funny and she writes well.'
Irish Times

Also by Liz Ryan in Coronet Paperbacks

A Note of Parting
A Taste of Freedom
The Past is Tomorrow
The Year of Her Life

About the author

Liz Ryan has been a journalist in Ireland for many years, and a regular contributor to many magazines and radio programmes.

Blood Lines

Liz Ryan

CORONET BOOKS

Hodder & Stoughton

Copyright © 1995 by Liz Ryan

First published in Great Britain in 1995 by Hodder and Stoughton
First published in paperback in 1995 by Hodder and Stoughton
A division of Hodder Headline
A Coronet paperback

The right of Liz Ryan to be identified as the
Author of the Work has been asserted by her in accordance
with the Copyright, Designs and Patents Act 1988.

8 10 9 7

A CIP catalogue reocrd for this title
is available from the British Library.

ISBN 0 340 62456 6

Printed and bound in Great Britain by
Clays Ltd, St Ives plc

Hodder & Stoughton
A division of Hodder Headline
338 Euston Road
London NW1 3BH

Acknowledgements

For my late father John Greenhalgh, who taught me to read and to love books.

This first one of my own was aided and abetted by many wonderful friends: Sue and Frank, Helen, Gerry, Nell, Tom, Clare, Pat, Noelle, Sarah, Collette, Brendan and Aine, Sheila and Dominique, all of whom deserve haloes for their patience. Also my brother Rob, his wife Lorraine and my mother Lil.

For the loan of their invaluable photocopiers, my thanks to Michael Hogan, John Saunders and Vere Wynn-Jones. Also, to my long-suffering colleagues at *The Evening Herald* and especially to my editor Michael Denieffe, who so generously granted leave of absence.

For faith, advice and support even when I least deserved it, I am greatly indebted to Peter Carvosso, Michael Brophy, Jane McDonnell, Anne Harris, Rita Hughes, Carolyn Caughey, Maeve Binchy and my marvellous agent Richard Gollner.

Part One

1

Eamonn Laraghy was a big man, in every way. His six feet two inches rose from the ground like the trunk of an oak tree, solid, sinewy, unarguable. He could, and frequently had, put the fear of God into anyone fool enough to try to cross him, flattening them with a mere gathering up of his eyebrows. In any dispute, his reputation for physical power preceded him, often ending hostilities before they began. Above all his fearsome attributes, it was his voice that nailed his victories for him: a booming farmyard roar that the local people claimed was a force more frightening than a Kansas cyclone. None had ever seen a Kansas cyclone, but they nearly all had a brother or sister or cousin who had. When Eamonn was angry, as he was now, he could be heard half a mile away.

"I forbid it and that's final! The end of it, now!"

He chopped a large meaty hand through the air and came dangerously close to striking his adversary, immobilised before him like a hypnotised rabbit. A navy vein popped out on his forehead and the flinty grey eyes snapped sparks. Eamonn did not like to be challenged, much less resisted, here on his own turf where his word was law. By God it was.

Provided they were not personally embroiled in these confrontations, Eamonn's farmhands enjoyed them immensely. It was like going to a boxing match without having to pay in. Blood was not actually spilled, as a rule, but the atmosphere was much the same. Around the periphery of the house and gardens, grins came to several faces as Eamonn's furious shouts whirled out on the dancing December wind.

But no smile touched the resolute countenance of his daughter. For the first time in her life, Kerry Laraghy was determined to stand up to her father and get her own way.

"I'm sorry, Daddy, but you are no longer in a position to forbid anything. Today I come of age and there is nothing you can do about it. I'm going to Paris and that's that."

Eamonn stopped in mid-tirade to draw breath and stare, bewildered, at his only daughter, the lovely girl who had been the apple of his eye from the day she was born. He adored her, completely, utterly and without reservation, and until this moment he had had no reason even remotely to suspect that his sentiments were not reciprocated. Right from the start, from the day his tiny infant first smiled up at him, they had claimed each other exclusively, investing all their considerable affections in the recognition that they were two of a kind.

And now, here she was, turning eighteen only this very morning and already flaunting her independence provocatively. Eamonn was totally baffled, and deeply hurt.

"But, Kerry, what about the farm, the estate, the horses? I thought we had an understanding? I thought ye *wanted* it all?"

Mention of the horses would, surely, bring her to her senses. They ran as fast and far through her blood as they did through his own; for generations the love of their horses had been both a Laraghy strength and a Laraghy weakness.

But Kerry stood unmoved.

"Of course I do, Daddy. I just don't want it now, this minute. It's too much, too soon! I want to live a little first. Go to Paris with Brian in January, have fun, stay till I've flung my fling. I'm too young to take on all this! *Look* at it!"

With a burst of exasperation she flung open the wide French windows, grabbed her father and propelled him across the room until he stood squarely in front of Ashamber, all nine hundred lush green acres of it, glinting in the wintry morning.

Out on the Italian terrace, the first rays of sunlight stretched luxuriously along the length of the winking mosaic, down the wide steps and on out to the little lake beyond, where even now in winter the willows wept and whispered. In summer the lake was ringed with misty mauve aubrietia and wild exuberant bluebells; but today a frost hung over it fine and delicate as a baby's lacy shawl. To either side of the lake lay the formal lawns, their roses clipped and furled in wait of warmer weather, and beyond this again the bubbling brown river separated the gardens from the estate proper, with its tiny boathouse and banks of cherry trees, which in spring intoxicated Kerry with their thick foaming blossom.

It was all very lovely. But it was not the gardens that tied Kerry to Ashamber, Eamonn knew. It was the hundreds of acres of rippling grass expanding beyond that, where as a small child she had often wandered lost for hours on end, contentedly weaving her daisy chains while half the staff went mad with worry, fearing her fallen into the river and drowned.

Their fears never materialised. The child never fell into anything worse than a haystack, never got kicked or bitten by any of the horses, never got caught up in the blades of a threshing machine. It was as if she were a part of Ashamber herself, gathered into its arms and assured of a safe berth there. Vividly Eamonn recalled her first riding lessons in the paddocks, on a fat placid pony called Mick which subsequently carried her to precocious success in local gymkhanas. After that there was no stop to her gallop, and as the child grew into a girl she seemed to bond with the very land, riding out across the endless acres at first light each morning, red hair blazing as wet clods of the rich black earth flew up into her tingling face, her mare Zephyr snorting with the sheer exhilaration of it all.

That Kerry would take over Eamonn's role at Ashamber was understood from the first. Eighteen had been settled on as the age at which she would start training with him, learning all there was to learn about producing Derby winners. Over the years she picked up much of it haphazardly, forking hay and scrubbing tack in the long holidays, but only now was her formal education to commence. And only now, seemingly, had she decided she didn't want it. Eamonn was aghast.

With a sudden renewed burst of anger he slammed the windows shut and marched his infuriating daughter to a sofa, on which she sat down, defiantly waiting for him to recover his composure. Grabbing a chair, he slewed it round to face her, seating himself astride it, his beefy arms incongruously akimbo across its elegant mahogany back.

"So, what the hell do ye want then, Kerry? Ye don't want Ashamber, is that it? Don't want to become a trainer after all? Don't want to build up the breeding with me either, don't want anything to do with any of it?"

She saw that his rage disguised his pain, and met his gaze anxiously, sudden conciliation in her larch-green eyes.

"Oh, Daddy, don't be silly. You know I do. All I'm trying to say is that I have my whole life in front of me. If I don't get out and see something of the world before I bury myself here, I'll – I'll explode!"

"It's that infernal brother of yours. I might have known it. Yer meddling blasted twin causing more trouble. He's put all this madness into yer head, that's what."

Kerry couldn't and didn't deny it. Since embarking for Paris three months before, Brian had phoned and written constantly, filling her head full of tantalising tales of the City of Light until now she just had to see it for herself. His departure had been saluted with a final oath from Eamonn, who after years of arguing his son's choice of career, finally washed his hands of the whole sorry business.

Not that Eamonn didn't love his son. Of course he did. But the boy was so quiet, so remote, it was like shadow boxing. Not for an instant could he envisage Brian running Ashamber, much less making a go of it. The lad was simply cut from a different cloth – his mother's cloth. And so Eamonn grunted in disgust as Brian went off to Paris to study, apprentice himself to Yves St Laurent and hotly pursue a young French girl called Lucienne de Veurlay. Lu and Kerry had befriended each other at Sylvermore, the Galway boarding school charged with teaching English to the one and manners to the other, and Lu had come on a summer visit to Ashamber. Felled like a sapling, Brian had fallen madly in lust and, he insisted, love.

Eamonn continued to ridicule Brian's obsession with fashion, but with rare tenacity Brian stuck to his guns, and was now making unexpected headway with both his guru and his girlfriend. Maeve, his mother, was torn between regret that her son had not gone to college and delight in his choice of Lucienne. Brian's equable temperament might have produced such a fine lawyer, or a doctor . . . fashion was not the same thing at all, not even quite respectable from what she heard. But, on the other hand, Lu was a most charming girl whose father owned a vast vineyard in the Loire, and that made up for much.

"Yes, Daddy. Brian does have a lot to do with it. But I would have gone anyway – if not to Paris, then someplace else. It's 1968, Dad, I don't want to miss what's left of the swinging sixties! Anyway, wouldn't you prefer me to have fun for a while, and then come home ready to settle down, rather than be cooped up here all miserable and frustrated?"

Yes. Yes, he would. Eamonn had to admit the truth of that. Furious as he was to find his plans thwarted, Eamonn was not a fool. Through the mist of rage he perceived that Kerry had a point. If he held her here, against her will, she would never be happy, never settle properly into the management of Ashamber; nor was it his wish to imprison his beloved daughter against her needs and instincts. Far better to let her go to Paris and get it over with . . . fondly he recalled his own youthful sojourns, in Tipperary on his mother's family farm. Only a rural backwater, but what a paradise it had been!

For several moments he said nothing, turning the thing over in his mind like a coin in the pocket of his tweed jacket. Kerry suspected he had been wearing the same one all his life, its rough fabric as warmly familiar as her own skin. She had the wit now to stay silent, leaving him to see the sense of her argument for himself.

"All right then." His voice was gruff. "Since ye seem to want it so badly, ye can go."

In a single leap she was off the sofa and hugging him tightly, green eyes sparkling with relief.

"Oh, Daddy! Thank you! You're so good to me, such a sweetheart!"

Eamonn coughed, mortified. It was a rare day indeed that anyone called him a sweetheart – even, he reflected wryly, his own wife. Especially not his own wife. But Kerry's hugs and kisses made up now, as they invariably did, for whatever was lacking between Maeve and himself. Reluctantly he allowed a grin to etch itself into his ruddy features.

"Ah, sure, love, don't I only want what's best for ye? Would I ever refuse anything ye really wanted?"

No. He never had and never would. He understood her, Kerry knew, as well or maybe better than she understood herself. He hadn't spoken to Maeve for weeks after Maeve sent her to Sylvermore, and even all these years later Kerry still felt the chill it had caused between her parents. Not that there hadn't been a chill to begin with. But Kerry had no idea why; it was the one subject she dared not broach, not even to her father although it consumed her with curiosity.

She hugged him again, twining her arms around him as she exuded gratitude and excitement, and Eamonn returned the embrace with equal affection, noting as he did so how the child's spindly body had lately filled out. What had once been skinny was now slim, no longer a target for teasing, no joke at all.

"Only – only there's one thing I'll ask of ye, Kerry."

"What, Daddy?"

"I want ye to tell me here and now, honestly, when and whether ye really intend to come home." His voice was raw.

Come home? But of course she would. Home was Ireland, and Ashamber, and the horses; Paris was just a joyride, a breather before reality. That he could even think otherwise upset her instantly and painfully. She was not a girl to break her word or her bargain.

"Look, Daddy, it's December 27 now. I'll go right away, with Brian when he goes back in January, and be home by summer. By July first, say. How does that sound?"

That sounded fine. Terrific. Once a date had been fixed he knew she could be trusted to adhere to it. His smile clinched the deal and they settled comfortably back into the sofa to iron out the details which, he saw, she had already well worked out in her head. In fact she'd had the advantage from the start, springing the whole plot on him from what was obviously a long-considered position, giving him no chance to marshal his own thoughts on the matter. Clever girl. What an heiress she would make, one day, to all that he had built up in the course of his fifty-four long, tough years. All that the Laraghys had built up over six generations.

"And now, missy, if we can put all this talk of Paris out of yer head for a minute, there's another little matter to be dealt with."

"Oh? What's that?"

"Come with me and see."

Dutifully she got up and trotted out behind him, across the ancient flagstones of the vast hall, down the two hundred-year-old stone steps with their historic indentations, on around the gravelled driveway to the side of the house, where there stood a ramshackle collection of sheds, garages, outhouses and storerooms.

With undisguised pride and pleasure Eamonn threw back the doors of one of the garages to reveal her birthday gift: a long, low, white Mercedes 380-SLC convertible. Delivered a week earlier, it had been hidden away amongst the spades and hoses and cobwebs until this moment, a moment he wanted to share only with Kerry. The car might come from both her parents but its recipient, Eamonn jealously liked to feel, was his and his alone.

For several moments Kerry said nothing at all, staring spellbound as if it might vanish, a figment of her notoriously fertile imagination. But it didn't. Sleek and shiny, it sat there with its grey leather seats wrapped in plastic, its keys dangling alluringly from the ignition. Over the years her birthday gifts had been more than generous, even by the standards of such wealthy parents: they included her mare Zephyr, a diamond necklet one year and its matching earrings the next, and the hand-tooled Mexican saddle she had so devoutly desired when she was fourteen. But this – this was magnificent. For once she was lost for words, an aching lump rising to her throat and tears, absurdly, invading her astonished green eyes. It was more than a car. It was an acknowledgment of her maturity and her independence. In this she could, and would, go anywhere and everywhere.

"Daddy. Oh, Daddy."

Eamonn's grin seemed to stretch right round to the back of his head.

"Well, milady, since ye want to see the world, ye might as well see it in style, eh?"

It was barely six weeks since Kerry had passed her driving test, one of the various goals she had set herself since leaving school in June. To her outrage she failed the first attempt, with a heartfelt recommendation from the examiner that Miss Laraghy curb her taste for reckless speed before applying again. Fuming, she took it a second time at a steady 30 mph and passed – but there would be few roads travelled at 30 mph in this.

"Omigod. C'mon, Dad, get in – let's go and get Brian!"

Brian was due into Dublin airport at noon. Deeming it tactful to accept a Christmas invitation to the château of Lu's parents, he had promised to spend his birthday and New Year at home instead, and Kerry had intended to pick him up in Eamonn's old maroon Jaguar. But this was something else again. Brian would be knocked dead.

But reluctantly Eamonn shook his head. It was nearly eleven, and at that time he met his wife daily in her blue drawing room where they went over the accounts and discussed business with the singlemindedness of two generals mapping out battle strategy. On that, at least, they were agreed. Ashamber took precedence over any number of personal considerations, and this was the one encounter with Maeve that Eamonn did not dread. Far from it; he heartily admired her acumen and farsightedness, even if she did make him feel like a child accounting for itself to the school principal.

"Sorry, love, but ye know what yer mother's like if I'm late. Off ye go and get him yerself. Just let me see if ye can handle that car, and then I'll wave ye off down the drive."

It was more than a drive, it was an avenue nearly a mile long, and Kerry would be out of sight long before she reached the wrought-iron gates that had guarded Ashamber for two centuries. After that, an easy spin up to Dublin, where the traffic might be a bit more – oh well – Kerry assured herself, if everyone else could do it so could she. Kissing her father's cheek, she opened the door and slid behind the wheel as Eamonn marvelled on what the miniskirt was doing for his leggy daughter these days.

In a flash, the engine was purring and Kerry was grinning up at him, hugely pleased with herself.

"Don't worry, Dad! I can do it. Tell Mummy we'll be back in time for lunch – and about the Paris thing, OK?"

With a miraculously smooth switch from clutch to accelerator, she was out and away, leaving Eamonn bemused behind on the gravel. So he was to be the one to inform Maeve of Kerry's plans, was he? With the distinct impression that he'd been somehow left holding the baby, Eamonn laughed and scratched his balding head as he stomped back indoors.

In the new car, Kerry fiddled with an alarming array of dials but couldn't locate the heater. No matter: the top was up and the blood in her veins had never felt more fired. Deliriously she fumbled till she found the radio, tuned into Caroline where the Stones were painting it black, and set off to claim her brother.

In her blue drawing room, Maeve Laraghy's eye lit idly on a glass paperweight, round and heavy, cunningly filled with entrapped violets and a solitary lily of the valley. Often she gazed at it and wondered whether the flowers were real. Certainly they looked real, but then how could they survive? Perhaps they had been treated somehow, glossed or sprayed or waxed in some clever attempt at immortality.

Her cool white hand stretched out to pick up the paperweight, the glass cold and solid against her neat, taut fingers. She turned it over and over. They couldn't be real. Could they? There was only one way to find out.

Maeve's calm face reflected nothing at all of what she was thinking, the thought that was not nearly so terrible as it had been the first time. She would like to open the paperweight to inspect the violets. She would like to open it by cracking it in one swift clean stroke on Eamonn Laraghy's skull, that strong, thick, hairy skull that reminded her of a coconut, brown from the sun and wind, fuzzy, with just the same degree of impenetrability. A coconut, pure and simple.

She sank into the embossed cushion of the chair at her desk, inexplicably drained after the row she had just overheard, the heated voices of Eamonn and Kerry raised in conflict. Her husband did not, and never would, know how much he terrified her. That pair of steel-grey eyes that rolled and snapped like ball-bearings, that awful roar . . . the grim ghost of a smile twitched across her lips. She knew her own restrained tones drove him mad, he could not abide the low-pitched, modulated speech she deliberately adopted in all her dealings with him. It still took him by surprise, after all these years; he still expected an adversary to shout back just as Kerry had now. How could you have a satisfactory argument with a woman who never raised her voice? She had the advantage from the outset, and to this day he never understood how or why she did it. But he hated to engage her in combat. Rather a full-scale row with all the stable hands, lads, drivers, managers, the lot, than that.

But today, at any rate, they had nothing to fight about. With a small sigh she put down the paperweight and dismissed the overheard altercation. Evidently it had been resolved. On the Chippendale desk, four neat piles of paperwork awaited her attention. Maeve was the financial backbone of Ashamber; she did all the accounts, supervised every transaction, vetoed Eamonn's every extravagance. She loved the ruled columns of figures, all entered in blue ledgers in her small precise hand, and she relished her encounters with the tax inspector the way other women enjoyed drinking champagne, in their bright new hats, at the racecourse on Derby day. She won every year, hands down.

Monetary skills came as easily to Maeve as swimming to a fish. In another, later era, she might have been an entrepreneur or even a tycoon, sending shivers down the spine of the stock exchange. It was her misfortune to have been born rather too early, in the winter of 1920, but even here at Ashamber her success was gratifying. She didn't take the spectacular risks that Eamonn's racing cronies loved to take so flamboyantly, but she saw a shrewd investment immediately.

If Eamonn was the heart of Ashamber, Maeve was the brain. The work occupied much of her time, gave her great satisfaction and engaged her attention exclusively, apart from her duties as a mother and society matron. Once, before her marriage, Maeve had liked to play the piano, to read the works of John Stuart Mill, Bertrand Russell and Maynard Keynes; she had had a mind straining at the leash. But not now. Now, she avoided any such distraction, any indulgent reverie, anything at all that might bring her to wonder why on earth she had married Eamonn Laraghy.

Only once had she been honest about it. The day before the wedding, nervous and emotional to an unprecedented extent, she admitted to her mother that she was marrying for money. A business transaction, pure and simple. In exchange for taking her out of small-village life and genteelly impoverished Protestantism, Eamonn got a dutiful, attentive and competent wife; a fair deal all round. Maeve's widowed mother had not been destitute, but she had been poor, and in a way it was worse to have a very little money than none at all.

If you were really poor, people took care of you. The Irish, North and South, liked to see people a step lower on the ladder than they were themselves, affording them a rare opportunity to be top dog, superior, the donor instead of the eternal alms-seeker. You could abandon yourself to poverty, almost, make a career of it, secure in the knowledge that nobody would let you starve.

But if your family had had money and let it slide away – ah, that was different. That was careless. You were not a sad case then, you were merely a mess. It was up to you to sort things out as best you could, and at twenty-nine Maeve had known that "out" meant a man. Immediately. Any older, and she would be on the shelf for the rest of her life, knitting cardigans and tucking her mother's shawl round her chest down all the dreary days. There was little demand in the Northern town of Lisburn for ladies of declining fortunes and advancing years who could explain the principle of supply, demand and curve with a clarity that cut clean through a man's ego.

It was precisely this ability, which she had not then been devious enough to disguise, that had ruined both of her early relationships. It was a major disappointment for a chap to take a blonde little chit of a thing out to a meal or a party, only to find that she wanted to do nothing but talk. Talk about things he had never heard of, to boot, economic theories

as remote as the man in the moon. There were plenty of
girls who could do better than that. Maeve knew she had
frightened off both Peter and James, and that if she was
going to improve her lot at all, she would have to relegate
her own interests to second string. Moreover, she would have
to move outside her own small Northern Protestant circle and
consider a Catholic. A Southern Catholic, if necessary, from
the Republic's side of the border.

Maeve was not conscious of the bitter twist to her lips as
she sat here now contemplating all this, nor did it occur to
her that she was committing that cardinal sin against her
own rules, daydreaming. With her chin on her knuckles she
leaned on her desk, still focusing on the heavy paperweight.

Not that she hated Eamonn, exactly. She simply disliked
him, men in general, all men if she were honest, for coming
between herself and her ambitions. They appropriated unto
themselves all that was best in life and handed, with condescending smugness, the dregs to their women. *Their* women.
The babies and the domesticity and the grind that most
women accepted with gratitude. Maeve knew she was lucky;
she didn't have to cook and clean all day, she had the
chance to exercise her mind if only in the service of her
husband, who happened to need a first-class accountant. Not
because she had had a chance to go to university and develop
herself, or to the London School of Economics, a mecca she
had once dreamt about the way other women dreamt of
balmy nights in the South Seas.

One thing she would say for Eamonn Laraghy, even now:
he never questioned her intellectual ability. Perhaps he recognised from the start what an asset it would be, or perhaps
he had just decided to overlook it since she was otherwise so
suitable. She was gracious, more sophisticated than the local
girls with whose rustic charms Kilbally seemed exclusively
endowed, and she would fit in very well at the helm of a
business whose affairs, in 1949, were beginning to flourish
dramatically. Foreign fillies were all very well for weekends,
but Eamonn knew he needed a wife who would look and act
the part, entertain with diplomacy, dress with chic, handle his
big busy household without bothering him over every petty

little detail. His was the "real" world, and a wife must manage her indoor empire quietly, invisibly.

Her opportunities, it seemed, all revolved around men, around their requirements and Eamonn's in particular. So unfair, so absurd: there must be thousands of women burying their abilities and ambitions under piles of laundry. It was a terrible waste, and Maeve's puritanical mind hated waste. But, having made her bargain with Eamonn, she stuck to it quite literally for better or worse, moving immediately upon marriage to Kilbally, converting to Catholicism, making the right friends and even insisting on regular church attendance. Eamonn hated that, but was forced to tag along for fear people might think his marriage in trouble, which it was soon enough anyway.

Signs of the rift were quickly spotted in such a small place and caused any number of minor complications that irritated Eamonn and galled Maeve intensely in the beginning. Finally he dropped out of church altogether, but she had to go the whole hog, holier than thou, holier than everyone, unwittingly showing him up for the heathen he was. It did not occur to him that there were worse things she could have done too, once safely married to him.

She could, for starters, have salted away an immense amount of money. He never would have noticed; but you didn't bite the hand that fed you, and Maeve despised people who welched on their debts. She didn't deal with them, commercially, and saw no reason to operate differently in a marriage that was, essentially, a business.

Or she could have settled into a life of leisure, like so many of the horsey wives, busying herself with just a little charity work for appearances' sake, to justify the clothes and the jewellery, the beauty treatments and the travel. But to Maeve money simply meant security, status and a position of some authority. It gave her great pleasure to sanction her husband's expenditures, made her feel in control, and nineteen years later it was still a heady feeling.

Children did not enter much into Maeve's scheme of things, although she had known there would have to be some, of course. But it seemed to her that the more you could afford to have, the fewer you did. Poor people's houses teemed with children, rich people's were full of space and quiet. It had been a relief to discover the advent of twins, two for the price of one as it were, all her duty done in one swift swoop. The pain of the birth was appalling, and she made up her mind never to repeat it.

But she was a competent mother, nonetheless, everyone admitted that. She consulted with teachers and dressed the twins beautifully, saw to it that they had music and elocution and dancing classes, a pony apiece for their fifth birthday, little parties with their friends in the rose sitting room. The children were groomed and disciplined and vaccinated, and unanimously agreed to be a credit to her – though it was unfortunate, she privately felt, that Brian had got all the good looks, while Kerry was cursed with such very red hair and a quirky temperament which, in her teens, began to terrorise all the local boys. As yet, Maeve could not think of a single young man who would or could be expected to put up with Kerry.

The villagers thought it odd that the Laraghys had stopped at only two children. Funny how rich people so often did, it was a mystery how they managed it . . . but then Mrs Laraghy was already in her thirties, and very figure-conscious, and Eamonn always had had an eye for gamey, buxom girls . . . Maeve heard the murmurs, and learned to let them wash over her like the tide over a rock.

In the early days when the twins were still babies, Eamonn had been an enthusiastic husband. Whenever he had to go abroad, as was frequently the case, he invited his wife to come with him; she need not watch the racing if it didn't interest her, but couldn't she have fun, shop, socialise? No man intent on mischief would have issued such candid invitations . . . but he had long since given up.

She was relieved. She didn't enjoy the disruption of routine such excursions entailed, she didn't like her husband's loud boisterous friends. Most of all, she didn't like the renewal of marital relations that seemed to be part of the "fun", the excess of alcohol and then his clumsy sexual advances. Eamonn was never aggressive, but he was persistent, and it had taken him a long time to get the message. Like many women of her generation, Maeve had no idea that there could be such a thing as a skilled, tender or considerate lover and, despite his premarital roisterings, neither had Eamonn. Stoically they soldiered on in bed, like army recruits on skirmish manoeuvres, until the arrival of the twins put a respectable stop to the whole unsatisfactory business.

Eighteen years, already, since that dreadful day in the labour ward? Mildly astonished to think of how long ago it was, Maeve fingered the gilt inlay of her desk, tracing the indented leather with her index finger. Where was it all going? Round and round in circles, with the horses in the fields? But for her daughter it would be better. Kerry would never have to sleep in the same bed as a man who was a mere second best to the London School of Economics.

She jumped as there was a loud knock and Eamonn marched into the room instantly upon it. Knocking he had learned, but waiting was an art beyond him.

She winced as his wet boots tracked across her glossy parquet floor; he winced too as the Chinese rug shot from under him, depositing him with a jolt on the small antique sofa on which he both looked and felt ridiculous. Would the woman never get a decent sofa in this room, never pin down that damn carpet? Apparently not. As was his blunt way, he came straight to the point.

"I've given Kerry her birthday car. She's gone off to meet Brian in it, thrilled to bits with herself."

Maeve felt a twinge. He might have waited, so that she too could have shared in their daughter's pleasure. But – too bad, too late. It was a long time since Maeve had shed any tears over spilt milk.

"And here's something else. She says she doesn't want to start in on the horses with me just yet. Wants to go back to Paris with her brother after the holidays, spend six months gallivanting there first."

With belated caution, Eamonn paused to assess what effect this news might have on his wife. On the one hand, it was a change of plan, and Maeve liked things to run according to schedule. But on the other, she had never approved of the tacit understanding that Kerry would start training racehorses as soon as she turned eighteen. This, he supposed, was a reprieve of sorts, and might please her.

Evidently it did. With not inconsiderable relief, Eamonn detected the glimmer of a smile in her reply.

"Well, she'll certainly have my permission to do that, Eamonn, and yours as well I hope. The girl is very young. She needs to spread her wings a little before taking on anything as onerous as Ashamber."

He nodded. "Aye. That's what she says herself. I suppose I can see the sense of it. I've told her she can fire away, with me blessing, provided she comes home and knuckles down at the end of it."

"Good. I'm very pleased you're being so reasonable."

In fact Maeve felt another tiny twinge. Could the girl not have come to her first? No. Always her father. First in this, first in everything. Even though she knew Brian gravitated more to her, it still hurt, just a little.

Looking down at her diary, an idea struck her.

"Eamonn – our New Year party on Saturday. Why don't we make it a send-off party for Kerry? It's all organised already, but we could invite some extra people, make it bigger, more glamorous, give the girl a first taste of what to expect in Paris."

Glamorous. Eamonn knew what she meant by that. He'd have to wear his monkey suit, smile at any number of idiot women and pretend he could still dance like a teenager. Oh, well. If it would bring a smile to that cold face of hers, and please Kerry into the bargain, right, so be it. He shrugged.

"Aye, Maeve. Whatever ye think, whatever."

Sergeant Mulligan had a problem. He did not, as a rule, like to give tickets to locals. People zooming through from Dublin on their frenzied way to Cork or Limerick, yes. They deserved tickets, the speeds they went, on roads built for horse and cart. And what there was in Cork or Limerick to be rushing to anyway, Sergeant Mulligan was at a loss to understand. It made more sense when they went racing through in the other direction. But local people, whom he had known since they were in short pants, and only ever exceeded the speed limit in case of dire emergency, well, he would let them off the once.

But this was the most blatant offence he had ever encountered. Kerry Laraghy, of course, he might have guessed, her licence only a wet weekend under her belt and doing the ton already. She had nearly knocked him off his bike as she shot to a halt at the crossroads where he was waiting for the lights to change, and Sergeant Mulligan felt life had dealt him a short enough hand already without gratuitous homicide attempts on it. It was bitterly cold and starting to snow, and he was not amused.

Besides, it seemed to him that there was something not quite right about the whole situation. Here he was, a grown man nearing sixty, out on a freezing December day with only a pedal cycle to his name, while this mere child sailed around in a flashy white Mercedes with an insolent grin on her kisser, not the slightest hint of repentance anywhere about her. It was time somebody put a stop to her carry-on. He took out his notebook.

"Well now, madam, and what have we to say for ourselves? Doing one hundred miles an hour here in the middle of main street, in wet conditions, a menace to yerself and everybody else?"

Beside her he could see the brother, the infinitely nicer, quieter twin. But of course she was the one in the driving seat where her besotted father had idiotically placed her the day she was born. A brazen little hussy.

"Was I really, Sergeant? Well, what do you know! Isn't this car just wonderful?" Naughtily, incredibly, she closed one eye and winked at him. "It's my birthday present. I'm eighteen today. You're not going to give me a ticket, are you?"

The smile was huge, the tone wheedling, and Sergeant Mulligan's pen shook slightly, unaccountably, as he poised it over his pad. That was a scandalous shade of lipstick she was wearing – with scarlet gloves, to match! Resolutely he put the tremor down to the cold.

"I most certainly am, Miss Laraghy. You can wipe that cheeky look right off your face, and learn some respect for your elders while you're about it."

Belatedly he thought of the case of fine, single-malt whiskey her father sent him every Christmas, the most recent batch only three days ago. Oh, well. By next year this would be long forgotten, and once he had started to write the ticket he could not undo it. Irritably, he tore it off.

"Here you are now, take your medicine and don't let me catch you driving like that a second time."

Kerry felt a shaft of concern. Daddy wouldn't mind, of course, but Mummy would lecture, make a mountain out of this molehill, maybe even impose limits on driving. Damn!

Ungraciously, she snatched the ticket.

"Oh, right so Sergeant, ruin my birthday if you must. But I think it's terribly mean of you . . . after that lovely whiskey my father gave you, too. He'll be furious."

Rolling up the window, she wrenched the car back into gear and shot off. A spray of muddy slush flew up and drenched Sergeant Mulligan to the knees of his navy-blue uniform. The crack about the whiskey stung, and he was uncertain who the object of Eamonn's threatened ire might be. A great pity, he told himself sorrowfully as he remounted his bicycle, that she was turning out so badly. Her mother was such a lady. But the father had her spoiled rotten. Buckets of money but no breeding whatsoever, no class at all. A great shame, altogether. Pulling his cape back down over the handlebars, the sergeant headed back to the station with an unsettling feeling of disappointment.

Brian made no attempt to restrain Kerry as they continued, at a speed not noticeably decreased, into the Kildare countryside. Eagerly she chattered on about joining him in Paris, and he thought how welcome she would be; he missed his sister very much. But first he had news of his own to impart, and hoped she would be equally glad to hear it.

"Kerry, you'll never guess. I've proposed to Lu, and she has accepted me. We're going to marry."

"Marry? Oh, Brian!"

Oh, no. Not at eighteen! They were far too young. Lu was supposed to be for fun, not for life. Try as she did, Kerry could not disguise the horror that whisked across her face.

"Kerry – aren't you pleased for me? For us? I know you think you're going to lose your twin now, to a foreign country and a foreign woman. But I would have had to settle there anyway. I want to get to the very top of the fashion business, and I know now I can do it. Lu is sure of it." Gently, he laid a hand on her arm. "It's not that far away, Kerry. And I'll come home often, always be in touch, run like a spaniel whenever you whistle."

Solemnly, he leaned across to kiss her cheek, his sallow skin brushing her freckles, his profile similar but far more symmetrical.

Kerry felt a cold sick clench in her stomach. This wasn't how things were meant to go at all. Lu was a nice girl, but somehow she seemed so much older than Brian, so assured, sophisticated, purposeful. He couldn't possibly marry her, at eighteen! It was ludicrous.

"For God's sakes, Brian, you haven't got her pregnant, have you?"

He laughed. They did not share their mother's attitude to sex.

"No, I haven't. But Lu's parents are agreed, and we're living together anyway, so why wait?"

Ah. It was Lu's idea. Kerry sensed it instinctively. Lu, with her deliberately broken English, her fey astute charm, had determined to have Brian from the first moment she saw him. He was handsome, talented, heir to a fortune, an extremely eligible young man.

"Does she really love you, Brian? Are you sure?"

"Naturally. She said so herself. That's when I proposed."

He smiled a helpless, most appealing smile, and Kerry saw that her brother was hopelessly smitten. He looked like a toddler clutching a lollipop, and she did not know whether to laugh or cry.

"Brian, I can't offer you my unreserved congratulations. You're far too young if you ask me. But since you haven't asked me, and since I'm your twin who adores you, then I'm happy for you. Provided you know what you're doing."

He beamed. Even if he did not yet have her approval, her good wishes meant a great deal to him.

"And will you – uh – help me get round Mother and Dad?"

"I'll try. But I've been a bit of a shock to Dad today myself. I'd keep his glass filled up during lunch if I were you."

He nodded, and shuddered as the car ploughed deeper into the twisting lanes, nearer and nearer to Ashamber. Maeve, he thought, would not object, but Eamonn's unpredictable rages were legendary. There would be hell to pay if this family reunion were mismanaged. In Paris, getting engaged had seemed such a logical, grown-up thing to do, whereas here, suddenly – but here, he had Kerry. His sister could work miracles with Eamonn, and despite her misgivings he knew he could rely on her to do her best this time. Always, since childhood, they had been loyal, devoted, fiercely united in any adversity.

On and on they sped, past the leafless trees, ominous black silhouettes against the gunmetal sky, until there it was: Ashamber. Grey, square and sombre on this winter's day, it stood sentried by the long line of ash trees that gave it its name, serried and precise all the way up the winding avenue. Brian looked at the orderly line of gaunt trees and braced himself as if for the firing squad.

Eamonn's drink crashed from his hand, the crystal tumbler splintering unheeded on the floor as he leapt to his feet, purpling with rage. It took a lot to make him drop his drink.

"Yer *what*?!"

"Engaged, Dad. To Lucienne." Brian's voice was low and very meek.

"Lucienne?" Eamonn pronounced it something akin to Loose End. "And who the bloody hell might she be?"

"Oh, Dad, you remember. She was at school with Kerry, and you met her last summer when she came here to visit."

Eamonn stared at the boy, this son of his who was a complete mystery to him. Off to France first, to make frocks no less, and now getting married he said. There wasn't a whit of sense to any of it.

"Brian, listen to me. Yer a boy, not a man. Ye know nothing whatsoever about women or marriage, and ye'll not marry this

– this person, or anyone else, until yer twenty-five at the very least. Is that clear and understood?"

His bellowings could be heard all over the house, Maeve knew, as she sat silently at her side of the lunch table, trying to reconcile pride in such an excellent choice of fiancée with fear that Brian was indeed much too young. Even now, in the teeth of his father's fury, the boy's face was ashen.

"But Dad – we love each other – we—"

Eamonn's hand cut through his stuttered protests like a butcher's blade, slamming down on the table with such force that several more glasses juddered to the floor.

"That's *all*, sir! I won't hear another bloody word about it!"

Kerry saw her brother flush, and desperately wanted to throw her arms around him. But that would only shame him further; and besides, their timing was off. Eamonn was still reeling from her own news, and taking it out on Brian. Unfairly so.

"Oh, Daddy, he does come of age today, and Lucienne is a very—"

"Nor ye either, madam! Ye've caused enough havoc yerself for one day. Get out of me sight, now, the pair of ye!"

They had gone too far, too soon. Swiftly, Kerry beat a retreat.

"All right, Daddy. We'll leave you and Mummy to think it over. It's only an idea, you know. Brian hasn't bought a ring yet or anything." She shot him a warning look in case he had done exactly that. "We're very sorry if we've upset you, especially after my lovely birthday present."

Was there a car for Brian, too? If so, Eamonn was perfectly capable of shoving it into the river. Tentatively, she embraced him, and then her mother, who accepted the gesture as if it were a delivery of frozen beef. Maeve's physical response to her children had always been minimal, and as she drew back Kerry glimpsed for the first time some clue as to where her parents' difficulties might lie. Strange bedfellows: but that was not a thought into which a daughter delved too deeply. Or at all.

Wearily, Maeve sighed.

"Oh, for goodness' sake, Brian has only just got home. Let's not have a row already. Eamonn, calm yourself. Brian, darling, drop the subject."

Surprisingly, they both did as they were told, Eamonn subsiding like a sanded flame, Brian struggling to regain his dignity as Maeve distributed a thin smile evenly between them.

"Let's discuss something more immediate. Our New Year party. Your father and I have decided to make it special this year, to celebrate your coming of age and to send Kerry off in style. The oak panelling and the flagstones have such superb acoustics, we can have a little orchestra and string lights in the trees, maybe even get a rock group for your friends . . . h'mmm?"

A rock group? Maeve had not yet even mentioned Kerry's departure directly to her, but clearly she must be pleased. Such spontaneity was unheard of, even if conciliatory gestures were not. It would take some organisation to upgrade the party at this short notice, but if anyone could do it, she could.

Diverted, they waded into these warmer waters. But Eamonn was breathing heavily, and on Brian's face there settled a look of sullen rebellion such as Kerry had never seen before.

2

Impatiently, Brandon Lawrence drummed his fingers on his rosewood desk, waiting for two things to arrive. First, a cloud of Chanel No. 5, and then his wife.

Not that he looked forward to smelling the one, or seeing the other. He looked forward to the plane which would then bear them, and him, from Heathrow home to Ireland. He looked forward to leaving this plush, stuffy office, and he looked forward to leaving his plush, stuffy home out in Richmond. In the absence of their parents, his two small sons would be officially in the care of their maternal grandmother, Patricia, but Brandon knew that their nanny would cope while Patricia gaily got on with her bridge and her friends. He would miss his sons over the weekend, but he would not by any stretch of the imagination miss any other component of his domestic scenario. A whole weekend away from it was worth almost anything, including this damnblasted party to which Marianne was dragging him.

But the party was in Ireland, and that destination was what he was looking forward to most devoutly of all. Left to his own devices, he would have quit London years ago, and gone back there for good.

But Brandon had not been left to his own devices since the day his elder brother, Alex, waved goodbye, went off to a motorcross rally and died in it. Such tragedy was not unusual in the Lawrence family, but Brandon had felt a cold frisson as he watched Alex's coffin lowered into its grave, taking his own carefree youth with it.

His father, Dermot, was not a man who panicked easily. Over the centuries numerous of his ancestors had perished in all manner of stupid, self-inflicted and frequently spectacular disasters, and Alex was merely the latest on a long list of foolhardy casualties. He was lamented, but he was not indispensable. Accordingly, Dermot summoned his second son into his study five days after the demise of the first.

There ensued not a dialogue but a monologue. Dermot was very sorry, he flatly stated, but Brandon was going to have to abandon his marine engineering studies, take over the family business at London headquarters, and Alex's place at the helm there. The place which he, Dermot, would still occupy were it not, regrettably, for his gout.

Brandon gasped: Dermot continued.

No more bachelor fun. At twenty-two, a man needed a wife. A wife to replenish the family's traditionally inexhaustible supply of sons. Brandon would marry, sire a first boy, buckle down to corporate life in London, and he would do it all now, this year.

"No!" Brandon's heart and mind had cried, but he was not overly surprised to hear himself say yes. Yes, sir. Dermot Lawrence was not a father; he was a patriarch and a tyrant. He demanded obedience and he got it, because otherwise life became a hell not worth living.

And was all this, now, worth living? Brandon had to assume that it was, since everyone seemed not only to think so but to admire his success, envy his good fortune. At thirty, he had a pretty wife, two healthy sons, a hectic social life and a company mushrooming to the awesome proportions of a nuclear explosion. Originally a small crystal industry founded in 1802, it was now an international conglomerate incorporating the export of linen and seafood, leather and whiskey, to destinations where in turn cosmetics were produced, newspapers published and media interests acquired. Brandon, in every sense, had made it.

I have it all, he thought, and I hate it all.

No. That's a lie. I hate this job, this city, and this mountain of money that buys everything except freedom. But I don't hate my boys, and I don't hate my wife. I only – only – only what?

I only pity her, that's what. She's a good wife, a devoted mother, a super hostess. She does everything she was hired

– married – to do, and that's why I pity her. She has looks and style, but she has no ideas of her own, no identity. She's a clone of ten thousand other married ladies out there, and she bores me to tears.

Does she find me dull, too? Sometimes I think she does. That's all I've ever been let be. If only she'd say so, if only honesty were as important as duty, and appearances. If only she'd hit me over the head with a hammer. Then I could hit her back, and we'd have grounds for divorce. But being boring isn't a crime, for which people deserve prison . . . this *is* a prison, though. We've served seven years already, of a life sentence; people do less for murdering their fathers. I wish I *had* murdered my father.

But I didn't. I did my duty, to him, and now I'm doing my duty to her, to the children, all these employees, everyone, except myself. And what, in God's name, am I going to do next? Go to the opera, and the ballet, and the board meetings, for the rest of my days?

Go barking mad, preferably. There's a history of that, in my family. Some did their duty, but some did a runner. I wouldn't be the first. But then, where would I go? And where would that leave everyone else? I wish I could do it, but I can't. I simply can't. I'm not being noble, or heroic, or selfless. I'm being realistic, cowardly and selfish. I'd never get custody of the children, or another penny from Dermot, or that house when he dies. I want the children, and I want that house. It's my only link with Ireland, and some day I'm going . . . Where in hell is Marianne? We'll miss the plane.

But Marianne Lawrence was not in the habit of missing planes, particularly ones carrying her to parties. Even as Brandon consulted his watch, there was a whiff of Chanel No. 5 on the air, upon which his wife wafted in bodily moments later. Looking up, he had to admire what he saw.

At twenty-nine, Marianne carried her years lightly. Dark, svelte, swathed in furs against the evening chill, she peeped out at him like a well-tended marmoset. Above her deep violet eyes, a curl bobbed on her forehead as she bestowed a per-fumed kiss on her husband, purring with pleasure, touching his face with one small, gloved, proprietorial finger. At her

age most women would sooner cut the curl off than attempt
to carry it off, but somehow the girlish affectation became
Marianne admirably. As London became her, far better
than Ireland ever had; here she bloomed like a rare orchid
in an exotic hothouse, gracing Harrods with a presence
that shrivelled instantly at Hollyvaun. But she could bear that
horrible house when, as now, there was a party to compensate for having to stay there.

She stood back and swept her gaze over Brandon like a
metal detector. How attractive he was, still! Thirty-one next
summer, but taut and limber, even if it was tension instead
of squash that kept the weight at bay nowadays. His blond
hair was thick, the eyes blue . . . moody blue, admittedly,
but then Marianne never had been quite sure what went on
behind them. There was a reserve in Brandon that nobody
could penetrate. But physically he was a fit, attractive man
– if only he wouldn't frown so, cultivating wrinkles for the
future. If only he'd look a bit more pleased to see her.

She plumped out her lower lip in the moue she knew was so
fetching, and was rewarded with a brief smile as he stood up,
stuffed his briefcase with paperwork and bade his secretary
goodbye. Louise was the most efficient of secretaries, well
able to manage while her boss made yet another of his endless
trips to Ireland.

Not just Ireland, Brandon thought as he held the door for
his wife. I'm going home, Marianne. That's what Ireland
means to me, as London never has and never will. You
loathe the place, but I love it, and some day I'll get back
there, with or without you, once and for all.

Hollyvaun will be cold tonight, and quite possibly Dermot's
welcome will be too. But a time will come when he'll be
gone and I'll have possession, way out under the Wicklow
mountains on that black bottomless lake that terrifies you.
There's no social whirl there, despite the sheep and the
butterflies – but there's peace and quiet and clean fresh
air. There's my boat, on that lake, waiting for me. Waiting
for the day when I can hoist sail and cast off.

Until then, I'm sorry, Marianne. Not just for myself, but
for you. You were an innocent sacrifice on the altar of my

father's autocracy, and I was wrong to allow it. But we never grew to love each other as I prayed we might, and now our only hope is to change course. Not today, and not painfully if I can help it. But we can't go on this way. It's the wrong way, and we're lost. Sooner or later the wind will change, and when it does you and I are going to move in very different directions. I can't make it happen, but I can prepare for it, and be ready to leave as soon as it does.

"Catch, Kerry!"

Wearing nothing more than a towel, Kerry stretched out an arm still wet from the bath, caught the beribboned parcel and a glimpse of Brian's brown eyes before her bedroom door slammed shut.

Her birthday present. As eagerly as a child of six she ripped the ribbons off, and the crackling red paper, hopping first with curiosity and then delight as its soft contents unfolded into her arms. A slim, shimmering sheath, its night-navy spangles winking up at her in the firelight, indigo, royal blue, sea green, emerald: slowly the sleek tube fell to its full length, a creation light years removed from the amber taffeta she had been planning to wear tonight. Not a girl's dress, but a woman's. Her very first.

Eileen was agog. "Try it on, miss, try it on!"

Impatient, but gentle with the delicate gossamer fabric, Kerry shimmied into it and flew to the mirror with a sharp intake of breath that had nothing to do with the fit – and yet, everything. Standing shocked before her she saw a tall, stunningly sexy young woman shining like a mermaid in an undulating wet skin that flowed round her body like a river round a bend. Each tiny sequin picked up and threw off a lighted sliver of the rich fabric underneath, gleaming at a new angle with every move she made.

"Oh, miss, it's – it's indecent!"

Clearly the transformation was too much for Eileen, and Kerry giggled, then laughed outright.

"Good old Brian! He knows what a woman needs before she knows it herself. That fellow's going to make a great designer someday."

"If he doesn't go to jail, for making things like that."

"Oh, he didn't make this, Eileen. The label says Courrèges. Brian won't be let put any of his designs into production for ages yet. Come on – help me put my hair up, and find some accessories!"

Impatiently Kerry sat down at the dressing table of her yellow bedroom, a warm cheerful room in the west gable filled with books and photographs, lotions and potions, white wicker furniture and a clutter of girlish bric-à-brac. Maeve's neat elegant hand had never been allowed near it since Kerry was twelve and insisted that all the fine French furniture be removed, sold, burnt, whatever, and tonight by the combined glow of lamp and fire it remained the same snug haven it had always been. Dubiously, Eileen set to work, braiding Kerry's thick red hair, twisting it loosely up on to her head, leaving stray wisps and tendrils to wander at will down the nape of her neck.

It was like painting a picture. Next came Kerry's diamond necklet and earrings from previous birthdays, and then makeup, a dusting of ivory powder which failed to hide the freckles sentried across the bridge of her nose; sepia eyeshadow and darker mascara and finally a slick of lipstick on her wide, well-defined lips. Silver high-heels, a pair of evening gloves filched by Eileen from Maeve's collection, and Kerry stood up to view the finished canvas.

Electrifying. A knock out. Instantly excitement tingled in Kerry's veins. Here, visibly, was the end of her girlhood and the start of she knew not what, as heady as champagne. She would taste that too, officially for the first time, its bubbles fizzing and bursting on her tongue as the fireworks shot skywards to welcome 1969. Tonight, she would dance all the way through to the dawn of her beckoning future, and she could hardly wait.

On the landing, Kerry stopped to survey the scene below. Already the chamber quartet was playing Vivaldi in the huge stone hall, under the Christmas tree and the towering crystal chandelier that cascaded down like Powerscourt waterfall, reflecting each burnished instrument. Stretched in front of the white marble fireplace, Fionn, Eamonn's favourite of his four wolfhounds, appeared to be snoozing peacefully but was, she knew, keeping a close weather eye out as the first guests handed their wraps to Eileen and her husband Paddy.

Standing in a little knot Kerry could see several of the country's leading horsey figures, whiskey in hand as they caught up on common interests. Vincent O'Brien, a greater trainer even than Eamonn, with his wife Jacqueline; Victor McCalmont and his wife Bunny; Pat Taaffe, the shy jockey who had ridden Arkle into history back in '64, and an Indian maharajah who owned a fine stud nearby, resplendent in cummerbund and pearl studs. In the years to come, many of these people would be important to her, Kerry knew. Not friends, necessarily, but vital contacts, colleagues and working associates. Eamonn had roistered among them for years, a hugely popular figure with his hearty smile and rich baritone voice that enlivened all their many parties.

Every New Year's Eve, here in his own home, he would sooner or later burst into song. "The Derry Air" or "The Rose of Tralee", all the Percy French melodies with which he could make the rafters ring. As a child Kerry had listened entranced from this very spot, her flannel nightie curled round her toes as all the men joined in, flooding the house with their strong, deep voices. She would have new friends, henceforth, as she moved out into a wider sphere but always her roots would be here at Ashamber, in the world her mother manipulated so easily, the world her father breezed through so vigorously.

Maeve looked superb tonight, as slim and soignée as in the wedding photographs of nearly twenty years before, gracefully welcoming the guests who had come so far to this party, a much more glamorous affair than their usual homey festivities. But it was for Eamonn that Kerry felt a sudden twinge of deep affection as she spotted her father, pumping several hands simultaneously, playing the role of genial host that came so naturally to him, perspiring liberally as the ballroom filled up with people and music, noisy and hectic, just the way he liked things to be. Eagerly, she ran down the stairs to join him.

Eamonn's face lit up as it always did for her, before he blinked, stood back and stopped dead in his tracks, quite forgetting the man whose hand he had been shaking.

"Mother of God! Is this me little girl? Well, well. Well. What – what on earth has happened to ye? What have ye done to yerself?"

His ruddy flush of surprise was half admiration and half nostalgia as he absorbed this gorgeous young woman who, up to an hour before, had been his gauche, gangly teenager.

"Hot stuff, eh, Dad? Brian gave it to me. What do you think?"

Whatever Eamonn thought was lost in the welter of compliments that numerous other men immediately offered, their eyes full of naked admiration and, she recognised as a woman does, lust. A happy glow began to burn in her as she chatted with them and with her father, offering new arrivals a warm welcome as she played joint hostess with her mother. It was the first time, it dawned on her, that she had ever been acknowledged as a woman instead of a child, and it was fun. Great fun, much easier than she had expected, just an amusing game really once you picked up the rules. Demurely she dropped her eyelids, smiled, murmured, and began to flirt with a coyness that made Eamonn laugh.

"Ye bold hussy," he whispered to her, "ye don't fool me for one minute, missy. Ye'd take a horsewhip to any of these men here quick as ye'd look at them, if they didn't flatter ye up to those eyelashes fluttering away there like a pair of butterflies."

She giggled. It was like a masquerade, playing a charade of somebody other than herself, an evanescent part of this airy evening. Somebody touched her left elbow and she turned to find Brian, a smile of pure pleasure melting across his face as he surveyed his elegant sister.

"Well, madam, I'm delighted the dress fits so well."

That was an understatement and she knew it. Leaning over she thanked him with a kiss, thinking how heart-stopping he looked himself in his evening suit with the black dress bow deepening his dark eyes. They were not identical twins, but tonight for the first time Kerry felt they were equally attractive. But was it the last time that she would have Brian all to herself?

With a pang she realised how soon now she would lose the brother to whom she had always been so close. After six months in Paris she would relinquish him to his future there, and to Lucienne. That he would marry Lu she did not doubt, although for the moment he was tactfully avoiding the subject and had been duly presented with a car just like Kerry's except that it was black. But if hers represented freedom, she thought, Brian's represented something else – the full weight of his father's power and money. Eamonn rarely interfered in his children's lives, but there was no doubt that he still controlled them.

At this moment, however, Eamonn was mopping his brow as he chased after a waiter with a drinks tray, and Brian took his sister's hand, led her on to the dance floor and twirled her the length of the waxed parquet with visible pride. Then her friend Debbie's escort cut in, one young man after another, all the friendly local chaps she had known since babyhood. Breathlessly she danced from one to the next until, flushed and dizzy, she reeled at giddy speed into arms she didn't know at all.

"Oh!"

It was as if a safety net had broken her fall from some dangerously high wire. Gasping, she clutched at the lapels of the tuxedo to steady herself, her face flaming against a starched white shirt, her wide eyes briefly glimpsing a strong, calm face much older than her own.

"I'm sorry, I'm dancing far too fast, I'm sorry."

He did not immediately reply, catching her as she stumbled, his composure absorbing her confusion in a way that was embarrassing.

"Had you better sit down?"

She nodded. "Please. Out on the terrace. I need some air."

The man took her hand and steered her outside, into the cold that slapped her smartly across the face, and sat her down on a hard wrought-iron chair under a tree threaded with tiny pink and white lights.

"Better?"

"Yes. Much. Thank you."

Her heart was beating like a gong, her legs jellied, and

she could think of nothing further to say. Silently he sat down with her, and from something in his mien she felt an inexplicable scrutiny, thirsty as it was impolite. Prickling, she backed away. .

"Why are you staring at me? Is my lipstick smudged? What's the matter?"

Nothing was the matter. Nothing, Brandon Lawrence thought, had ever been more idyllic than this lovely, lovely girl, playing at grown-ups, dressed to the nines for her party. A girl who looked everything that Marianne did not, radiating a fresh innocence he had long forgotten could exist, in anyone.

He became aware that he *was* staring, rudely, and wrenched his eyes away. Dimly he perceived Marianne dancing inside, gliding by the glass doors on the arm of some debonair escort, smiling at the man with eyes round and purple as pansies. He did not care if she should glide off the edge of the planet. But this girl's tone told him that perhaps he had offended her, and about that he did care.

Before he could construct a redeeming sentence, she spoke again.

"Do you just inspect people, or have you a civil tongue in your head?"

"I'm sorry. May I ask who you are? Who you came here with?"

Her laugh crackled brightly in the dark. "I came with Brian Laraghy."

Brandon's heart sank to the bottom of the green pool of her eyes. Brian Laraghy. Young, handsome, just right for her. Of course.

"Brian's my brother. We live here." She extended her hand in its long velvet glove. "Kerry Laraghy."

His relief was that of the last man into the Titanic's last lifeboat. Brian Laraghy's sister. Abruptly, his mind cleared.

"Ah, yes. The daughter of my hosts, I believe. I'm Brandon Lawrence."

Solemnly she took his outstretched hand and shook it, and again they lapsed into silence, shadowed in the soft aura of the light from the trees. As Kerry's breathing slowed and her vision focused, she saw before her a most striking man;

not nearly so gorgeous as Paul McCartney, nor as wickedly sensual as Mick Jagger, and much older than both – but a man, decidedly, with *something*. Something delicious. Her whole body glowed from his touch, savouring the feel and smell of his skin, the timbre of his voice. A voice like a sheepskin jacket.

"Are you all right now? Feeling better? Would you – would you like to dance again?"

Like Daedalus, Brandon implored providence to preserve his wings lest they melt so close to the sun. When she nodded, reality evaporated, and when she smiled, her smile dissolved his very fingerprints.

"Yes, please."

Eagerly she stood up and his eyes slid down from her wide red mouth to the hollow of her throat, to the curve of her body in its spangled sheath. Standing also, he was riveted, entranced.

What could he say to her? There was nothing about this willowy young woman remotely like any of the other women he met at parties, and he felt as nonsensically shy and awkward as a schoolboy on a first date. With a candour that was as endearing as it was unexpected, Kerry surveyed him appreciatively.

"What an attractive man you are! I'm glad I fell into your arms, since I had to fall at all. Is that the wrong thing to say?"

It was, of course. He was an adult, not one of the boys she was supposed to be with, and she wasn't sure whether she was even allowed to dance with him. But what the hell! She'd have a go, and see what happened.

Forgetting his invitation, Brandon remained motionless, gravely charting the planes and angles of her face as intently as Columbus charting the Atlantic. He did not want to rejoin the party; but if he stayed here with this girl, he would not be answerable for his behaviour. Reaching for her hand, he felt it brush against his wrist, and its fortuitous touch electrified him. It was a gesture Marianne could have practised for a thousand years without ever achieving its unrehearsed, unforgettable effect.

High in the winter sky, a white moon gleamed like a coin

spun in the night, the distant stars glimmering on its edges caught in the metallic mesh of its light as they nestled on their bed of black velvet. In just a few more moments it would be midnight and the first day of Kerry's new, independent life. Flushed and suddenly, piercingly happy she walked with Brandon back through the open French windows and into the music, letting him carry her away on *The Blue Danube* until it eddied to a stop and the violinist came to the edge of his dais, bowing and wishing them all A Happy New Year.

From nowhere, two sharp tears stung her eyes as the church bell rang out down in the village, a cheer went up and her father and brother came to kiss her, taking her hands as they joined in singing "Auld Lang Syne". She hardly knew what she felt as everyone linked arms and sang their way round in a circle, but she sensed the moment crystallise in time, locked into her memory like a rare jewel in a vault. Later, in other years to come, she would take it out and polish it, behold its beauty anew as it lay perfect and enshrined like an icon in some cold church grotto.

It was a long time later before Kerry conceded defeat. Brandon Lawrence was not coming back. She had thought he would, that he must, but he did not. The showering fireworks were all extinguished, and back out in the dark of the terrace she couldn't see him anywhere. Disconsolate, she ran her mind over what details Brian had supplied: the Lawrences, Mummy's friends from Wicklow, one of the relatively sane branches of a notoriously eccentric outfit dominated by a despot called Dermot. There had been a brother who drove himself to perdition in a motorcross rally, but now there was a wife. A wife called Marianne. Children, too, small boys named Christopher and Harold.

It was absurd, but Kerry's night lay shredded before her, and she found herself shivering in her filmy dress, freezing. She turned to go back inside.

"Hi."

He materialised like a ghost, an incongruous ghost carrying two glasses of champagne.

"Thought maybe you could use this?"

He sounded hopeful, and apologetic – as well he might be. Truculently she snatched one of the glasses and downed its contents in a single gulp. And then, to her utter mortification, she hiccupped loudly.

Oh, God! How awful. He would think she couldn't even hold her drink. Blushing furiously, she struggled to retrieve the damage, but too late; he was laughing aloud.

"Oh, dear! I see we're not quite used to champagne."

"No. OK. I admit it. I'm only eighteen, not a hardened boozer."

Her defiance only made him laugh the more, and the mention of boozers – her father, by all accounts, could drink Lough Allen dry if ever anyone should have the good sense to replace its waters with whiskey. But he'd better not make fun of her if he wanted to – wanted to what? Coming closer, he took the glass from her hand and clasped it in his own.

"Listen, Kerry. I have to tell you that you're the loveliest, liveliest creature I've ever seen. I wish with all my heart I could ask you out, see you again tomorrow night. But I can't. I'm married, and I have two young children."

She was pleased. Like her parents, she expected honesty from everyone, and respected it enough to come clean in return.

"I know. It's a pity, frankly. You're much nicer than all those silly boys in there."

"Am I?" Why he should be flattered he had no idea, but he was.

"Yes. You are. What a funny thing your name should be Brandon and mine Kerry. Mount Brandon is a mountain peak in County Kerry."

Her prim schoolgirl's tone made him smile again, but he felt as if she had raised him up on top of that peak, enthralled as he contemplated the view, resisting the dangerous sense of vertigo. He *couldn't* resist: in one stride he was wrapped around her, holding and kissing her with a violent vigour he'd forgotten he possessed.

It wasn't the romantic thing she'd thought a kiss was. It was stunning, shocking, a powerful onslaught that unbalanced her, made the fine hairs on the back of her hands stand up as she slid them around him, under his jacket, digging her fingers so tightly into his back that she was appalled.

It was her first kiss. Her first real kiss, from a real man, nothing to do with youthful fumblings at all, a solid thing that left them both speechless. Many moments elapsed in silence after they drew apart, until Brandon recovered himself and was horrified.

"Oh, Kerry, I'm so sorry. I had no right to do that. You must forgive me."

"Forgive you? But I thought – I thought it was wonderful!"

"It was. But I had no business to do it."

She wished he'd do it again. But he stood back.

"Your name suits you perfectly, Kerry. You're every bit as wild and magnificent as Kerry itself. Captivating, superb."

Captivating? Magnificent? Me? She was as amused as she was amazed.

"Well, that makes a change! At school they called me less charming things. Awkward. Irresponsible. Impossible."

Thinking of the nuns in Galway, Kerry winced. Christ. This was the very sort of situation they had so direly warned against.

Brandon winced also, realising that she was fresh out of the convent. That wouldn't have stopped Alex, or Dermot, from doing the disgraceful things he wanted to do himself. But the family's traditionally lax morals were one pattern he could break, one legacy he could reject.

Yet he could not walk away.

"Oh, Kerry – I find you altogether magnetic, can't think how to stay away from you, can't stand the thought of never seeing you again. Don't you feel it too? Didn't that kiss hit you the way it hit me?"

It had. By God, it had. But she'd better not add any more fuel to the fire.

"Luckily, Mr Lawrence, the problem solves itself. I'm leaving the country. The day after tomorrow, for Paris."

He choked down a laugh. To her, Paris would be the ends of the earth. To him, it was an hour away.

"I'll be gone for six months," she continued firmly, "so there you have it. We'd better say goodbye right away."

They certainly had. Mummy would read the riot act if she caught her out here with this married man, an extremely nice man but one, unfortunately, entirely outside her orbit. Like Ashamber, he was simply too much, too soon. A pity, but it couldn't be helped.

Brisk and direct, she extended her hand, and Brandon hesitated.

No. Don't do it. Don't even think of drawing this innocent girl into the web of your marriage, the pain of the eternal triangle, yet another family scandal . . . leave her alone, for your own sake, for everyone's, but especially for hers.

He grasped the hand.

"Yes, I'm so sorry, Kerry, but you're right. Paris is a long way off." Leaning forward, he kissed the top of her head. "You'll grow up fast there. It's a fabulous place, but don't let it swamp you. And if ever – you need – a friend, let me know. My wife is well acquainted with your mother, after all."

Anything, he thought. Anything, to keep sight of her. But she bit her lip, and frowned.

"Need you? Why would I? Brian will look after me. But mostly I can take care of myself."

Her sure young independence touched him. If he didn't go, right now, he would gather her up and kiss her again, and again, and then—

"Good night, Kerry. Goodbye."

In one stride he was down the steps and gone. She did not attempt to detain him, nor even return his adieux. In just two more days, she would be in Paris, all thought of him forgotten, the new year filling up with other adventures, other people.

Overhead, the moon was still bright and scrappy as it sailed between the swaying trees, and in the distance she could hear the soft snorting of a horse somewhere, a mouse scurrying inside a bale of rustling straw, the muffled laughter of departing guests. How lovely it was, this serene, secure home of hers . . . the man was merely a ripple on its tranquil surface, a ripple that would fade out and disappear.

But Kerry felt a small ambivalent pang. Life was pushing her one way, pulling her the other now that France was actually imminent: enticing her to stay here and yet forcing her to go. She wanted to become a woman of the world and yet she wanted to be Daddy's girl; she loved her mother but could not in honesty say she *liked* her; she wanted Brian to be happy with Lu and yet remain her twin, her touchstone.

And then there was Ashamber itself, its old grey walls so strong and enduring, as comforting as they were challenging. Soon, tonight's revellers would all be gone and the house would settle back down into slumbering hibernation, its ballroom silenced and its beating heart laid to rest. She thought of her mare Zephyr, drowsing peacefully in her dusty stable, of the deserted cobbled yards and the sweet musky barns, she smelt the odours of leather and wet grass, saddle soap and bran bins and apple pies, all jumbled together on lucid spring mornings and smoky autumn evenings . . . was she mad, even to think of leaving?

Possibly. Probably. But she couldn't stay here for ever. She had to make her move, and make it now.

3

The plane soared into the sky and Kerry watched Ireland drop away from her like a patched-up overcoat, one that was warm and familiar but heavy and cumbersome too. She exhaled a small sigh of relief. Up, up and away at last! Gleeful excitement flashed through her every fibre, and as soon as the plane levelled off and the bar opened, she ordered champagne with, Brian noted, an unusual note of authority in her voice, comically imperious.

He eyed her curiously. What had got into her, these last few days? She was skittish as a newborn colt, leaping this way and that, bright-eyed and unnervingly volatile. Maeve had made it plain to him that he was to take charge and care of her, but it would be like trying to mould quicksilver, a reversal of roles he did not relish. Pleased to have her with him on the one hand, he wondered on the other whether he should have encouraged this expedition quite so enthusiastically after all.

Unbuckling her seat belt, Kerry sat up and twisted her head to have a good look around her. But none of the other passengers looked remotely interested, or interesting, and she found their indifference baffling as they were catapulted through the intense azure stratosphere. But it was so exciting! Even for those who travelled frequently, could the miracle of flight be any the less astonishing, the vast tract of blue sky any the less piercing? And they were going to Paris, the most desirable destination in the world!

Here and there some passengers were already accepting drinks, and from the galley the clatter of trays was audible. Curiously Kerry watched people calmly begin to eat their lunch, but even as she wondered, the stewardess arrived with her champagne and she took it with a grin, pouring the whole thing into a glass before Brian had even opened his. Lifting it aloft to admire the rising bubbles in the sunlight that poured through the window, she downed three-quarters of the liquid and sat back with an oddly detached, expectant look.

Brian stared.

"What on earth are you doing, sis, guzzling like that?"

"Practising, Brian. I'm practising how to drink. The other night, it made me burp like a pig. But I reckon if I keep trying I'll get used to it."

She beamed at him triumphantly. "See. Not even a tiny burp this time. I'm getting better already."

God almighty! How would he ever restrain her, when they got to France and its oceans of wine? Since he'd been living there he'd become accustomed to alcohol, handling it with the same quiet ease he did most things, but if Kerry went on like this she would be lethal as a cruise missile. Eyeing her nervously, he made a mental note to enlist Lu's help immediately upon arrival.

Lu and Maeve had had a chat over the phone last night, and Brian was heartened to hear his mother calmly discussing wedding plans, in total contrast to Eamonn's bullheaded rantings. But Lu would manage even him in due course, if Maeve and Kerry chipped away at him too, there would be a wedding, this very year . . . Happily, Brian's thoughts meandered off down this rosy path. What a wonderful wife Lu was going to make.

Kerry's thoughts, also, were on Lucienne de Veurlay. Already, it seemed that her future sister-in-law was on much better terms with her mother than ever she had been herself, joining Maeve in the life they both seemed to regard as an acquisition and management campaign. First the man, the key to the safe, then the house, the furs and jewels, the status and cachet that went with the whole caboodle . . . an endless list of assets to be catalogued.

Kerry had never been sure how Lu did it. But from the start she had shown some knack, some instinct for flirting and alluring. Assiduously she had worked on it, polishing herself up until she gleamed like a diamond, developing her best points to camouflage the weak ones. Long after her English was fluent, her accent remained fetchingly French, a weapon in the armoury that captivated first boys and now men.

But Kerry suspected that Lu, like Maeve, secretly rather despised men, cultivating them cleverly and pragmatically to further their own ends. Love, to them, was a four-letter word, too vulgar an emotion to be entertained, and Kerry clearly remembered the nights when Lu would sneak back into Sylvermore after illicit dates, laughing as she dissected the latest feather in her cap with an analytical eye as cold as it was compelling.

As for Maeve – only in the last six months, since she'd had more time at home, had Kerry begun to watch and think about her parents' relationship. Never as a child had she witnessed violent scenes, but neither had she felt any great warmth between the two. Maeve treated Eamonn almost as if he were just one step above his dogs, patting him on the head if he were good, but subtly conveying that he was generally a mess and a nuisance. Her condescension made Kerry ache for her father, who seemed to accept his lot so mildly. It was all wrong for such an extroverted, warm-hearted man, and thinking of it now, she feared suddenly for Brian. He was quite unlike his father, but Lu and Maeve had a lot in common.

But then, everyone's parents were a mystery, and never did behave with any logic. Snapping out of her reverie, Kerry extracted a cigarette from a slim silver case and lit it with what she hoped was cosmopolitan panache. Like drinking, smoking was a current experiment; but before she could show off at all, the no-smoking light came on and she realised with a jolt that Paris was already in sight. With a squeal of excitement she pressed her nose to the window.

"Oh, look, Brian! I can see Sacré Coeur! And the Eiffel Tower! Look, all the roofs are red!"

Brian smiled, experiencing the pleasure of returning to his spiritual home. How innocent his sister was . . . her education had been so strict, her mother such a martinet, that in most ways she was still a child, no matter what the gown from Courrèges might say to the contrary. He would enjoy being her mentor, showing her all the wonders of his favourite city, provided of course Lu could keep some kind of lid on the girl. Getting into any more trouble with Eamonn was the last thing he needed.

Beside him, Kerry jigged in the seat as Paris flew up to meet them, looking huge and busy and crazy as it whirled below the banking plane, and then they were hurtling down the runway at a speed that was petrifying, awesome, thrilling.

Lu was waiting to meet them, waving through the glass screen of Le Bourget's arrivals terminal. Brian spotted her immediately and fumbled agitatedly, in a most unexpected flap, through customs, his nervousness taken for guilt and all his bags searched. But finally they were out, and Kerry was touched to see how eagerly the two fell into each other's arms, hugging and chattering incoherently. Momentarily forgotten, she stood back to survey Lu: the cropped cluster of blonde curls, the wide hazel eyes, the almost scientifically sculpted cheekbones. At her neck she wore a knotted chiffon scarf, just so, its imperial red matching the shade on her lips, a smooth study in savoir-faire.

Kerry giggled, thinking how the girl matched the landscape at Sylvermore, with its neatly clipped fuschia hedges. But Lu's petrol-blue suit from Chanel was pure Paris. The wretched girl could be nothing else *but* a model, Kerry thought with rueful consciousness of her own flaming shag of red hair and the freckles spilling across the bridge of her nose. Curt, someone had once called it; a *curt* nose. Kerry wasn't quite sure what that meant.

With a little shriek Lu abandoned Brian and came to embrace her, planting four consecutive kisses on her cheeks in the flamboyant gesture that had, in Ireland, been the only one that ever appeared out of place.

"Kerry! It is so wonderful to see you! Let me look!"

Lu stepped back and absorbed her school friend in a single glance that annulled, instantly, all Kerry's aspirations to glamour. She thought she had dressed for Paris, with worldly chic; it was apparent that she had not. Her fine wool coat was well cut, yes, her boots of glazed Italian leather, her gold stud earrings from Cartier and a Christmas gift from Lu herself. But the impact was not quite enough. Almost, but not quite. Some vital ingredient remained to be drawn out and developed, like a tangled red curl teased into an elegant chignon. Lu laughed and shook her head prettily.

"Well – I do love the gloves! Come on, let's find the car. I had to park ages away."

"You mean miles," Kerry returned tartly, attempting to redress the balance of some invisible little battle she had not even known she was fighting.

It was a longish drive to the rue de Vaugirard, and Kerry sat silent in the back of the Citroën as the lovers kissed and canoodled in front, lost in their private world. Their pre-occupation freed her to concentrate on the sights and sounds of Paris as they sped by in a beckoning blur, and she was struck by even the ordinary, everyday buildings, so stately, so tall, so – so what? So arrogant, that was what. These were buildings sure of their own worth, dignified, grandiose, unlike anything she had ever seen before. Everywhere there was light and space and symmetry, greenery peeping even in January from among the bare branches of the trees. The streets were so wide, the traffic so aggressive, the people so full of vitality as they rushed along the pavements, in and out of the métro stations with their quaint green iron arches.

How could such mundane edifices look so lovely? It was just like the postcards, all the *colonnes de Morris* plastered with bright haphazard posters, their cylindrical surfaces blaring colour, the whole city ablaze with it. A city to be young in, to fly high and free in, and Kerry was so enthralled she was speechless all the way to wherever they were taking her. It occurred to her that she had no idea where that might be, when the car abruptly drew in.

Decanting her passengers, Lu cruised away in search of parking, and Brian grinned sheepishly.

"Sorry. We didn't mean to ignore you. But we hadn't seen each other for a week!"

"Oh, I didn't mind. Come on, Brian, I'm dying to see where you live!"

He pressed a buzzer and the heavy gate in front of her

swung open on to a paved courtyard. Stopping at a concierge's desk, he exchanged some words of remarkably fluent French for a hefty set of keys, while Kerry received a glance that made her feel like a cat slinking in by mistake. Picking up their luggage, Brian led the way to a doorway and up the first of what felt like twenty flights of stairs.

In fact it was six, but Brian was oblivious of their steepness even with all the bags; he couldn't wait to show Kerry his splendid home-from-home. Unlocking a door at last, he flung it open and showed her inside.

"Well – what do you think?"

Used as she was to the affluent loveliness of Ashamber, Kerry stopped nonetheless in surprise. Here too was an impressive abode, but quite different, its splendour sleek, streamlined, regal. In fact, the apartment belonged to Lu's parents, Claire and Lionel, and its décor had nothing whatever to do with Brian. But that he regarded it with a proprietorial eye was immediately clear. Dropping the luggage he took his sister by the hand and led her from room to room, and Kerry felt the strange sensation of being led through the pages of an interior décor magazine.

She couldn't fault it. But she couldn't say she liked it either. For his sake, she tried.

"It's really beautiful, Brian."

That was true. In its impeccable good taste, the place was classically beautiful, richly painted and gilded in tones of white and gold, perfectly fitted and draped and swagged, the stiff upright chairs dispersed just *so*, the embossed wallpaper marching from room to room like a regiment of soldiers, the massive beds canopied as if for royalty.

"We sleep here, in the main bedroom, except when Claire and Lionel are in town. You're in the guest room next door. It's all ready for you."

Indeed it was, right down to the matching white soaps in the antiseptically tiled bathroom. Kerry felt as if she were in a hotel, that she should register somewhere.

"Do – do Claire and Lionel mind my staying here, do you think?" After all, she had never met them. But Brian just beamed.

"Certainly not. They're delighted, they regard you as practically family now."

"Am I? Are you really going to marry Lu, Brian?"

He turned and looked at her frankly.

"Yes. Yes I am, Kerry. I know you feel a little uncertain about it, that I'm too young, but you can't choose the exact moment in life when you'll meet the right person. If she happens along early, well – you don't send her packing and tell her to give you a call when you turn twenty-five. I would have thought you, above all people, would be in favour of seizing the moment?"

She grinned. That was, as a rule, one of her few steadfast principles. Whatever life threw up, you grabbed and made the most of. So why couldn't she shake off this uneasy feeling about Brian's great good fortune in finding the perfect wife? Even as she asked herself the question, the answer came with it.

Perfect. That was the problem. Lu was so perfect, just as this apartment was perfect, her pedigree was perfect, everything was so overpoweringly perfect. Kerry felt the weight of all the perfection as if it were another bag to be hauled up the stairs. But she could not articulate it to her besotted brother.

"So – so how are you going to convert Daddy?"

"I don't know yet, Kerry, quite honestly. But I'm relying on you to help me. He always listens to you."

Kerry felt Brian's keen gaze, and knew he was disappointed in her. Her first attempt to intercede with Eamonn had not been the *tour de force* he had been hoping for. Not at all.

"I'll try again, Brian. That's all I can say. I'll do whatever seems best for you."

It was not quite the response he expected. It lacked her usual galloping enthusiasm. But, for the moment, it would have to suffice. With a shrug, he dropped the subject of his marriage.

"Go and get comfortable, sis. When Lu gets back and we've all had a shower and a drink, we'll get dressed up and have a night out on the town. What would you like to try?"

"Try?"

"Well, there's French, of course, or Vietnamese, or Greek, Italian, Moroccan, Creole . . ."

She was nonplussed. Such ethnic variety, in the Ireland she had just left, was unheard of. She had thought he was going to say there was steak, or fish, or chicken.

"I – I – oh, Brian, don't tease me! You know I haven't a clue! What do you recommend?"

He busied himself with unpacking while she yanked off her boots, caught sight of herself in a mirror and decided to have a shower right away.

"How about Procope?" he called at length, shouting over the hammering jets of water.

"Procope?" It sounded to Kerry's ears like some awful broth one might give to an invalid. Complan, sort of.

"It's the oldest restaurant in the world, Kerry. It's been in the rue de l'Ancienne Comédie since 1686. You'll love it."

"Oh. OK, then! Let's go there."

She felt the tiniest twinge of disappointment. Creole sounded so much more adventurous, or Vietnamese . . . she wasn't sure about somewhere so heavily historic. But, as always, he was trying to please her, and that was what counted; in due course, she would sample all of Paris's more exotic wares under her own steam.

"And afterwards, Lu and I will show you the city by night, it's wonderful, we'll take you up the Arc de Triomphe and the Eiffel Tower and to Montmartre, up in the cable car . . ."

Cable car? That sounded like fun. Brightening, Kerry emerged from the shower and planted a damp kiss on Brian's cheek. Already, it was clear to her just how much in love with Lu her brother was – but she, Kerry, had prior claim. If Lu were half as clever as she thought she was, she would do well to remember that.

Kerry never forgot that first night in Paris. Everywhere they went there was magic in the air, shooting electric shocks through her senses like a hallucinogenic drug. Never had she seen such a blazing panorama as the Place de la Concorde with its hundreds of burning lights, all ablaze as if specially for her; never had there been anything like the foaming fountains of the Hôtel de Ville, their jets bursting skyward into thousands of shattering shards of water as she gazed, awed, up into the crystalline night sky.

Under the towering majesty of Notre Dame, Brian pointed out the belfry where, he asserted, the ghost of Quasimodo wandered the shadowy buttresses, weeping for Esmeralda, and from the top of the Eiffel Tower she felt the whole structure sway sickeningly, and laughed with giddy bravado. In the cable car that carried them up to Sacré Coeur she thought she *would* be sick, as it swung up above the quivering lights of the city, but when she got out she stood mute and transfixed before the luminous white beauty of the Basilica, as dreamy and exotic as the Taj Mahal. To their surprise, there was a steel band from Martinique pounding music out over the sloping terraces, even on this icy night, gathering other tourists as the sound palpitated across the sleeping roofs of Paris, and everybody clapped as a group of limbo dancers eddied low under a metal bar, their sinuous black bodies pliable as ectoplasm, urged on by the stamping, whistling crowd as coins showered about their hands and feet.

Lower and lower the limber, laughing dancers writhed, down and down until they were horizontal, snaking tentacles of the night, and then out and up in one triumphant motion to riotous applause. Enthralled, Kerry watched them do it over and over again, until she became aware of being separated from Brian and Lu, and wandered out to the balustrade to look for them. Far below, Paris lay spread out to infinity, out to the horizon where a plane darted busily amidst the stars, far away en route to some distant land, its winking red light pricking a droplet of blood from the night. It was so silent out there, she thought, like a city on another planet, unknown, awaiting the explorers. What would she find there? Almost, she did not want to know. This moment was wonder enough.

Below the balustrade, Brian was kissing Lu. Kerry saw them from where she stood; a long kiss, full of love and passion, oblivious of everything but itself. The stab of loneliness, of exclusion, that she felt evaporated instantly, like steam off a filly, and she turned back to the panorama before her, thinking how Brandon Lawrence had kissed her with just such a passionate intensity. But he was in London now, or Wicklow, or wherever; and she, Kerry Laraghy, wanted to be nowhere but here, seduced by this sorceress of an enchanting city.

Caroline Somerville-Norton would strangle Marianne Lawrence, she decided, if she twirled that spoon in that cup of tea once more. Just one more twirl and her friend was a dead woman.

"Marianne! For pity's sake stop doing that!"

"Doing what, Caro?" The violet eyes were vast with innocence, the voice slightly petulant.

"Playing with that damn tea, is what! You haven't touched it, you haven't eaten a bite – what on earth is the matter with you?"

Caro was annoyed. As a rule the girls enjoyed their afternoon teas together immensely, gossiping and giggling here at the Ritz, their shopping heaped about their feet, the piano tinkling agreeably in the corner. Not today. Today, Marianne was driving her nuts.

"Oh . . . nothing. I'm sorry."

Like a scolded child Marianne obediently put down the spoon, lifted the fine china cup and took a genteel sip. And then, to Caro's horror, she replaced it in its saucer with such a violent shudder that the flatware clattered loudly together. Slowly, unthinkably, her eyes filmed over with tears.

Get her talking, Caro told herself swiftly. Get her talking before she actually starts crying into the blasted fairy cakes.

"Mari, what is it? Come on, *out* with it!"

"I'm so sorry, Caro." From her black clutch bag Marianne fished a small handkerchief and dabbed discreetly at her eyes. "But I think I am going to have to tell you. I can't stand it any longer."

"Stand what?" There was little in Marianne's life, that Caroline knew of, to be "stood" with any need of heroic valour.

"Brandon. His behaviour." Marianne's lower lip trembled like a falling leaf. "It's just terrible, Caro. Just so absolutely terrible, I can't take it any more."

"Take what? What's he done?" Caro was mystified. Her friend's husband was the envy of their whole set, a delectable man, the original textbook catch – and a nice, decent human being into the bargain. Oh, a bit serious at times, maybe, a little preoccupied, but certainly not the kind who gave a girl any trouble. She had always considered Mari to be singularly blessed in her marriage.

"He's – he's *changed*, Caro! He's just not the same any more." Marianne sounded like a little girl, bitterly complaining that her ice cream had melted in the sun, and Caro bit back a laugh.

"Oh, come on now. People don't turn into ogres overnight. Is he all tied up with his work, or what?"

"Ye-es, that's part of it. I never see him any more. He's at that wretched office morning, noon and night. It's so bad for the boys. They see so little of him, it's a wonder he can remember their names."

"But Marianne, Brandon *is* a very busy man. He has a huge company to run. It's part of the price you pay for him."

"I know that! But it's been different since we came back from Ireland after New Year. It's not just his work that's distracting him. I can tell. It's something else."

"What?" A terrible suspicion began to dawn on Caro.

"That's just it. I don't *know* what. He's become so moody. So remote. We never talk about anything any more, he won't take me out anywhere, he won't – he won't even sleep with me, Caro." Marianne's voice dwindled to a whisper.

Caroline sat back on her spindly velvet chair and considered. Well, what do you know. Brandon Lawrence. She never would have thought he was the type. But then, what man was not, when you came down to it? Really they were just animals, the whole lot of them, even the most plausible ones. She hated to disillusion her friend, but the obvious truth of the matter didn't seem to have percolated through Marianne's feathery head. It would have to be spelled out to her in black and white.

"I'm afraid it sounds to me very much as if he might be having an affair, Marianne."

To her surprise, Marianne did not burst instantly into tears. She looked down, picked an imaginary piece of fluff off her powder-blue bouclé suit, bit her lip and nodded almost imperceptibly.

"Yes. That's what I think too."

Caro looked at her in bewilderment. The woman was nearly thirty, for crying out loud, this Jackie Kennedy lookalike with her bouffant black hair and her big mauve eyes. If she knew what was wrong, then surely she knew what to do about it?

"Well, then, Mari, you're going to have to take things in hand, aren't you? Right this very minute, we're going to have to go round to Harrods and Janet Reger, get you some gorgeous new lingerie, sexy stockings, perfume, the lot, aren't we?" Caroline sighed to herself. She had thought their shopping complete for the day. Her feet were killing her.

"I've – I've already done all that, Caro. It didn't work."

"What? Are you sure? Have you given him enough time? Did you get the kind of thing he really likes?"

"Oh, yes. Lots of silk and lace, buckets of fresh perfume, the works. I'm telling you, he didn't even notice."

Christ. This did sound ominous. Caro considered further.

"Have you any idea who it – she – might be, Mari? If you knew what, or who, you're up against, you'd have a very useful weapon. You have to fight fire with fire, you know."

"All I know is, it isn't anybody obvious. It isn't Louise, for starters."

Caro nodded, unsurprised. Brandon Lawrence was not the sort of man to go for that old cliché, with the secretary. Who, then? Mari said it had started after they came back from Ireland, about six weeks ago . . . so . . . Was the woman in Ireland, then? And if so, how was Brandon managing to see her?

"Has he been back to Hollyvaun since then, Mari?"

"Once or twice. Not often, or for long."

Oh. That seemed to rule that out, then. It must be somebody new, here in London.

"Mari, I hate to say this, but I think you're going to have to put somebody on him. It's the only way. You'll have to have him followed."

Marianne swallowed nervously, fiddling with her charm bracelet, not looking at her friend.

"I – I – oh, Caro, I hate to think of doing that. It's like *spying* on him."

"That's exactly what it is, Marianne! That's the way the system works! They cheat on you, you spy on them."

"You really think there's no other way?" Marianne's voice fluttered hopefully.

"No. I don't. You're going to need evidence, you know, if it comes to court."

"Court? Oh, but Caro – we're Irish, we married in Dublin, divorce is out of the question! And besides, I don't *want* one!"

Well, no. Brandon was the kind of man you hung on to, if at all possible. To divorce him would be to throw the baby out with the bathwater. But it was a salutary threat, none the less.

"No, but he's not to know that, Mari. If he is into anything worse than a fling, you must confront him with chapter and verse. Otherwise he'll just deny it flat out – they all do. And then they go right on doing it. You have to be prepared to say you'll get a separation, at the very least."

For several minutes Marianne sat silent and miserable, thinking. Of course Caro was right, but Brandon was such a wonderful husband . . . or had been, up to now. The last thing she wanted was to lose him, or even to alienate him, to have any ugly scenes.

"Marianne! Do you hear what I'm saying to you?"

She jumped guiltily. "Yes, Caro, I do. I'm just thinking it over, that's all. I really do hate to . . ."

"Oh, for heaven's sakes, Mari! You're not the first woman this has happened to. How do you think everyone else deals with it? If you don't find out who, where and when, he'll just bluff it out and there'll never be an end to it."

"Yes. Yes. You're right, of course. I will – I will do what you suggest."

Caroline leaned over and patted Marianne's hand consolingly.

"Take it from me, kiddo, you're doing the right thing."

In Ireland it was a harsh winter's night. Here and there Eamonn could hear the howl of a dog in some faraway field, then another, and another, each picking up the cry in turn and passing it on until the cacophony reached an eerie, incessant wail. They sounded more like wolves than dogs on nights like this, he thought, and knew that in the morning there would be angry farmers out counting the bodies of their dead lambs. Then a visit from Sergeant Mulligan, to him and to anyone else known to keep dogs, but nothing would ever be proven, no dog would ever be shot. But he made sure that none of his would ever need to be. Throughout the lambing season they were kennelled at night, on long chains in a barn from which they could not escape.

Except Fionn. Fionn stood beside him now, almost level with his master's hips, and would remain in the vicinity all evening. Then he would sleep in front of the dying embers of the fire in the hall, as every night, his huge hulk as frightening to strangers as it was comforting to the household. Eamonn bent a little and ran his meaty hand through the dog's long coat with affection.

"Well," he asked aloud, of himself as much as the dog, "what should I do, eh? Should I chance the risk, do you think?"

Fionn looked up at him adoringly and rubbed against his leg. Even with two sweaters bundled under his ubiquitous tweed jacket, Eamonn shivered slightly. It was one hell of a cold night, it would freeze for sure. He should go inside, now. Not that it would be much warmer there, after he'd consulted with Maeve. God only knew what she'd say; something short and biting, no doubt, designed to make him feel a fool.

But he'd stand his ground on this one. Resolutely he turned on his heel and stamped up to the back door that gave into the kitchen, Fionn trotting behind, his tongue lolling a little, paws padding evenly on the thin layer of frost already underfoot. As he let himself in, Maeve sat chatting amiably with Neville McCormack, head man on nearby Cushla stud, elbows on the table as she cupped a mug of tea in her small, delicate hands. Funny, to see her with such a man in such a pose, with so uncouth an object as a mug, but Eamonn knew her behaviour was deliberately adopted. She looked fetching tonight, in a roomy white angora sweater and pale grey trousers. Since

Kerry had taken to trousers, Maeve had too, but really, he thought wryly, she had been wearing them for years.

Neville liked Maeve, and she enjoyed the snippets of news he fed her – who was buying what stock, who was visiting which trainers, who was entertaining whom and why. It was a harmless liaison, and Eamonn liked to see his wife on friendly terms with the neighbours, giving them tea here in the kitchen where they felt at home. In the early days, it had been all cucumber sandwiches and bone china in the rose room, but Maeve was smart enough soon to see the error of that. Oh, the ladies liked it, naturally, but the men had squirmed uncomfortably when they arrived in their Wellington boots on wet days, dripping their way across the glossy floors and rich rugs. So now she fed them here, with ordinary tea from a big pot and thick slices of Mary's plum cake, and a tumbler of whiskey, neat, the way the men liked it. Such visits were the only time, Eamonn reflected, that he ever got a decent cup of tea in his own home.

They had not noticed him come in as they chatted intently, about cover fees by the sound of it. The Maharajah had recently sold his stud, throwing prices into uncertainty and effectively demolishing the cartel that had obtained for years. Eventually Maeve looked up, and shivered.

"Do shut that door, Eamonn, there's a draught."

Not a naturally warm woman, Maeve recognised nonetheless the importance of having an ear to the ground, of picking up information which, cleverly deployed, could make or break an important contract. Many of Eamonn's international successes, he knew, had emanated from conversations here in this very room, coups that had greatly enhanced his standing as far away as Europe, India and America. It was not from owners, but from their senior employees, that Maeve learned what was really happening in the racing and bloodstock world, and somehow or other nobody ever seemed to have twigged her system.

Eamonn would have liked to reward her efforts, but could think of no way of doing it: its fruits seemed to be their own reward. Sometimes he gave her a token of his unspoken gratitude, a pearl pin or one of the oil paintings of which she was fond, but her thanks too were token. Once, when he had won a big training commission in the teeth of ferocious competition, he had thrown his arms around her in spontaneous delight, beside himself with joy. It was a major step in Ashamber's growth, entirely thanks to her. But she had stiffened in his arms, found an excuse to extricate herself and escaped to the blue drawing room she knew he hated. He had not tried again.

He was glad, now, to find McCormack here with her. It would be more difficult for her to reject his idea out of hand if an impartial third party were present. A referee, so to speak.

"How are you, Neville?" He thrust out his hand and the other man shook it, half rising in greeting with a broad smile. Eamonn's jovial manner made him easily the most popular of the six men who had controlled Ashamber for close on two hundred years. He took a mug from a hook on the wide oak dresser, poured himself tea and sat down at the table. It was the only room in which he was not required to remove his boots, and Eamonn's comfort in the kitchen was consequently complete.

"I've been thinking, Maeve," he began conversationally. "About Blue Heaven. A fine young creature, wouldn't you agree?"

There could be no dispute of that. Blue Heaven was one of the most promising colts Eamonn had ever trained, a potential winner of many a Classic race. This year, as a three-year-old, it stood every chance of taking the Derby, both British and Irish, and with luck maybe even the Prix de l'Arc as well. Unsure what her husband was driving at, Maeve nodded.

"So," he continued eagerly, "what would ye say to letting Kerry have a crack at it, eh? Letting her cut her teeth on Blue Heaven? She wouldn't be in time for the Derbies, of course, but she'd have the whole summer before the Arc – with me supervising her, of course."

Both Maeve and Neville froze in their chairs, mugs halfway to their mouths, unable to believe their ears. Had Eamonn lost his reason? Would he seriously let a teenager loose on such an animal? Andrew Stockton, its owner, would go simply and certifiably mad. The thing was utterly, utterly preposterous.

"Eamonn – is this some kind of joke?"

"Not a bit of it. I think the girl should start with the best, that's all. She can't miss with that fellow. And then think how encouraged she'd be, how many new commissions we'd get!"

Slowly Maeve replaced her mug on the scrubbed oak table.

"Are we to take it, dear, that you've been drinking again?"

Typical. Exactly the response he'd expected. Eamonn turned to McCormack to recruit support.

"Listen to that, Neville. Where would we be without these women to keep us on the straight and narrow, eh? What's your view of the matter?"

McCormack sensed trench warfare in the air. He had no wish to be caught in no-man's-land.

"Yes – well – Kerry is very young, is she not? And the animal very valuable? Would you not start her on something safer, Eamonn – on Sushi, say?"

Eamonn's colour rose. Sushi, indeed. Sushi couldn't win an egg and spoon race on Laytown beach.

"Well, now, and where would I be without you all to keep an eye on me bank balance for me? Has nobody any faith in me daughter?"

"That's just the point, dear. You're letting a personal relationship interfere with a question of business. Kerry has no experience whatsoever, it would be sheer irresponsibility to let her near a horse of that calibre. You just let her stand on her own two feet, now, and she'll be grateful to you for it."

"But Maeve, where's she to *get* her experience?"

"On less crucial animals, Eamonn! Not on some priceless pearl you want to drop into her lap!"

McCormack decided it was time to go. His wife would have supper ready. Eamonn was annoyed to see his potential ally stand up and pull on his waxed green overcoat.

"You're not leaving, Neville?"

"Sorry. Sally will . . . uh . . . you know how these women are, Eamonn. Don't want hot tongue and cold shoulder for supper."

With what he hoped was a conspiratorial grin, Neville was gone, his tea unfinished on the table. Belligerently Eamonn eyed Maeve and started on another tack.

"Tell you what. I'll underwrite the whole thing meself. If we lose the Arc, I'll compensate Stockton out of me own pocket. How's that?"

"Eamonn, listen to me, and don't interrupt until I've finished. First and foremost, you are going to train Blue Heaven all year, you and you alone. Under no circumstances am I having you risk Ashamber's reputation in this reckless way. For another thing, you're not talking about some private slush fund. You're talking about *our* money – company money, in effect – and I will not have you gamble one penny of it on such monumental stupidity. And finally, you know that horse is going to win this year no matter who trains it, but if by any miracle Kerry were involved, think how disappointed she'd be when her next ones didn't do half as well. It's a completely insane, artificial way to try to start her career, and if she turned out to have no real ability thereafter, she'd be the laughing stock of the entire industry."

"No ability? But the girl is me own daughter, Maeve, it's in her blood! I just want to give her her first break, make sure she gets quality animals from the start, and after that she's on her own."

Maeve looked at him, with lacerating shrewdness.

"No, Eamonn. You don't just want this for her sake, at all. You want to make her an offer she can't refuse, invest so much in her that she'll be trapped. You want to find a way to lure her home, nail her down and hijack her whole future. Don't give me that fatherly concern act. It's the sheerest selfishness I've ever heard."

Stunned, he reeled so far back she almost felt sorry for him. But inexorably she finished her argument.

"Has it ever occurred to you that Kerry might find something else she wants to do with her life?"

It had. It was a nightmare that haunted him constantly. But if she knew she had Blue Heaven to look forward to . . . Breathing rapidly, he leaned across the table.

"She promised me she'd come back and she will! She said herself it's what she wants!"

Maeve heard the high cracked note in his voice and looked away. She couldn't bear it when Eamonn started getting emotional. And she hated it even more when his emotion clouded logic.

"Eamonn. The girl is eighteen. It's unfair to – to try to kidnap her like this! Let her enjoy Paris, explore her options and learn a little about life. Then she can make her own mind up."

The finality rang tight in her voice like a metallic thread. Eamonn recognised it and knew that the matter was closed, would never be mentioned again. If he went ahead and let Kerry train the horse, Maeve would never come to see it run, never applaud its victories, punish them both with her silence for years, for an eternity of indifference. Even had he won the battle, he would have lost.

Gripped with a sudden, invasive anger, he flung back his chair and strode round to her side of the table, torn between twenty years of rejected love and the past ten minutes of mounting hatred.

"I'll do exactly as I please, Maeve, with me own money and me own daughter – both got by the sweat of me own brow, for that matter!"

He was immeasurably satisfied to see her whiten to marble. But she made no reply, her eyes fixed on the door by which Neville had just left. His fist crashed down on the thick oak.

"Did ye hear what I said to ye, Maeve? I'll do exactly as I please here in me own home with me own family, and if it makes a hole in yer neat little books, that's just too bloody bad."

Still she said nothing. Eamonn felt his blood pressure rocket, and the terrible urge to do something violently irretrievable. But still he stared down, still she looked steadily away from him, intransigent. In one swoop his hand cleared the table of all that stood on it, cups and jug and plates flying in all directions, splintering on the flagstones amidst a confusion of milk and tea and sugar, crashing across the room, cutting through the knot that constricted his heart. Now he could breathe. In two strides he was out of the room, slamming the door with such force that Fionn began to bark savagely.

Outside, the cold air quenched his fury rapidly, and he felt the first flash of mingled shame and sorrow. One way or another he paid every time, win, lose or draw. Only for Kerry were such contests worth it, and it was years since he had truly lost his temper. For a moment he stood panting, gulping down the cleansing air. Kerry. He would give anything to see her, he missed her so much, so painfully.

Maeve couldn't be right about her not wanting to come back. Of course she would. She had promised him, and he knew her deep atavistic attachment to Ashamber. In the summer she would come running up the steps into the hall, throw her arms around him, her eyes sparkling to see him, home where she belonged.

But now – what? Alone, bereft, Eamonn stood irresolute, wondering what to do. The idea of spending the night here, under the same roof as that woman, revolted him. It just wasn't the same at all without the twins, it wasn't a proper blasted home in any sense. Then, gradually, his head cleared, his rage faded.

Helen. Of course. He would go to Helen. She would know what to do. Seconds later, he was backing his old maroon Jaguar out of its garage, ripping up the gravel as he reversed until he realised there was something in his way.

Fionn. The damn dog stood there patient as Job, waiting for him to open the back door and let him in. Nobody was going anywhere on a night like this unaccompanied.

"Oh, bloody hell! Come on then boy, get in, get in."

In one bound the shaggy creature was in and stretching comfortably along the length of the back seat.

As he roared off down the drive and out on to the winding country lane, Eamonn cast his mind back to the first moment he had begun to doubt the wisdom of his marriage to Maeve. He could pinpoint it exactly, only six months after the twins were born. Six months. I did try, he reassured himself now as he had then. I gave her plenty of time. After all, a man's only human, and I only asked. But Maeve had propelled herself to the verge of hysteria, her voice for once shrill, her composure strangely shattered.

"Never again, Eamonn, never! I'll never have another child, ever, do you hear me? Do you?"

He heard all right, and suspected he had heard the end of

it too. So be it. He certainly wasn't about to rape his own
wife. But he was more hurt than he'd ever have thought it
possible to be. He knew she was grasping at the difficult birth
to rationalise something else, something deeper. Somewhere
along the way she had withdrawn from him, silently resigned
from the sexual side of their marriage. Why, he did not know:
they were not days in which such delicate matters were
discussed. But it felt fundamental, and final. For months
thereafter, he tried to woo her back, with less hope, less
enthusiasm each time, beating his head against a brick wall
until finally he lost patience and stamped away to his fields
and stables, exasperated. The devil take it. At least he had
the two children, that she could never take away from him.

And he had Ashamber, a thriving enterprise that was
immensely satisfying. Ascot, Longchamps, Saratoga . . . his
colts, fillies and geldings won at all of them. Only the magic
double eluded him, a winner trained *and* bred by Eamonn
Laraghy. Although breeding had been the original *raison
d'être* of Ashamber, it was in the formation of novices that
he excelled – up to now. Now, they were all performing like
Olympic gymnasts, his name and money were made, and it
was time to hand the lunging reins over to Kerry.

Henceforth, he would breed and she would train, a
formidable duo, alchemistic and invincible, until the day came
when they would achieve that double, enshrine Ashamber in
legend. Then – then what? Eamonn couldn't see round the next
bend on their road to glory, couldn't see any way to further perpetuate the Laraghy name. Kerry would marry, he grudgingly
supposed, but even if her children had talent they would have
some other name. God *damn* Brian and his bloody frocks!

Never, ever, did Eamonn admit that he loved his daughter
more than his son, but he did. A terrible distinction, between
his two cherished children, but there it was. He could no more
help it than he could help the falling rain or the course of
the river as it flowed through the meadows. In her was
embodied all that he held dear, an extension of his own
self – and soon, now, she would be home. Only five more
months to go. Cheering at the very thought, Eamonn put
his foot to the floor and sped on towards Helen. He hadn't

phoned, but Helen would be very happy to see him, for the simple reason that she always was.

Helen Craigie was a widow, and a merry one as Eamonn often irreverently laughed. Forty-eight years old, she was the mother of two grown children: Paul who worked in a Dublin bank and Antoinette who was a nurse in San Antonio, Texas. Living alone in a suburban cottage on the outskirts of Dublin, with only a small pension to call her own, she was arguably the happiest, most comfortable, agreeable and relaxing woman Eamonn Laraghy had ever known. Her blue eyes never failed to crinkle up with delight when she saw him, her pink cheeks dimpling with pleasure as he hugged her tight, barrelling into her little house and seeming to fill the whole place with his bulk. She never came near Kilbally, only twenty miles distant, never overlapped into his life there in any way, perfectly contented to see him when she saw him. That had been their arrangement for nearly ten years now, they were the only two people who knew of it, and it suited them both ideally. The comfort they drew from, and gave to, one another was immense.

Several times over the years Eamonn tried to set Helen up somewhere more comfortable, feeling she was entitled to at least a modicum of the luxury enjoyed by his legal wife, who contributed so infinitely less to his happiness. But always Helen refused. She would take nothing from him, no apartment, no money, no jewellery, nothing at all. The only tangible thing she did accept, freely and gladly, was the occasional trip abroad, when he had race meets to attend in France, Britain, Italy. Then, they would take separate flights and meet up in their hotel, laughing like runaway children as they fell into a big double bed, in which they replenished all on which their respective spouses had sold them short.

It had taken Helen a long time to forgive Jack his crass stupidity in getting killed in a traffic accident, an accident entirely attributable to his own negligence; he had simply dashed across a road without looking and been hit by a bus. After his death, life had been bleak for a long time, and for that she was inclined to hold him responsible. But gradually she shook off her sorrow and her pointless recriminations, met Eamonn and slowly, deliberately, picked up the threads of her life. A capable, affectionate woman, Helen needed a man in that life, but only in the physical sense. Otherwise, she could perfectly well take care of herself.

Never in a million years would she have allowed, nor even wanted, Eamonn to abandon his wife and family for her. She was no homewrecker. Seeing that there was much to be glad of in things as they stood, Helen simply accepted them that way, reckoned on seeing Eamonn once or twice a month, and left well enough alone. It worked beautifully.

She was sitting quietly watching television and knitting a matinée jacket for Paul's impending first baby when she heard the hum of the Jaguar in the driveway. It had its own distinctive purr that she always recognised. Dropping her knitting, smoothing down her tan-and-cream-checked dress, she automatically patted her wavy brown hair as she hurried out to let him in.

"Eamonn! Darling!"

He gathered her up into his arms and hugged her tight, beaming down at her, Fionn lolloping behind him as the dog invariably did: love me, love my dog. She returned his embrace and pulled him in out of the cold, to the small, simple sitting room where the fire crackled and blazed companionably.

"Tea, whiskey, a sandwich? What would you like, darling?"

"Yes. Exactly, Helen. I'd like tea, whiskey and a sandwich. And you."

He bent to kiss her forehead; she was a good nine inches shorter than him.

"Well, then, you've got the lot! Come on, sit down, give me your jacket and tell me all about it."

He blinked, then laughed. Even after so many years together he was still surprised by how well she knew him, how she almost always guessed when he had something on his mind. He tried not to burden her with anything extraneous, anything to do with his work in particular, which would and usually did solve itself. But his family life – and hers – were a shared topic on which they often exchanged advice to mutual benefit, seeing things more clearly from the outside. Most recently, their absent daughters had been a common topic to mull over. Helen missed Antoinette every bit as much as Eamonn missed Kerry, but with far less immediate hope of seeing her again.

The last time they had met, it was Brian's wild marital schemes that had brought Eamonn bounding to her doorstep, beside himself with outrage, and Helen had shared in his misgivings if not his ire. Her own son, Paul, was only twenty-two and far too young, in her view, to be an expectant father. She counselled patience and caution: but neither, she knew, was a quality outstanding in Eamonn's volatile make-up. Now, she saw instantly, it was something else again, something probably to do with Kerry. Eamonn fretted dreadfully about the girl.

Over the food and drink she got it all out of him, the plan involving Blue Heaven, and Maeve's total resistance to it. But, to his surprise, Helen sided with Maeve.

"She's absolutely right, dear, if I may say so. You _are_ trying to hijack the girl, and parents who clip their youngsters' wings usually end up alienating them."

"Alienating? Helen, it's Kerry I'm talking about."

"Just the same."

Slowly, carefully, she spelled out her thoughts on the matter, reasoning him round as far as she could. But he was stubborn, and it was uphill: even when he had to admit the sense of what she said, he would not give in. Long after midnight, deciding to call it a day, Helen stood up, turned to him and took his hand in hers.

"Tell you what. Let's sleep on it."

With a tenderness known only to her, he too stood up and took her other hand.

"Helen Craigie, you are the cleverest, loveliest woman in the world. Come on. Let's do just that."

Arms around each other, they made their way up the stairs to Helen's downy double bed.

That same night, twenty miles over the Northern border, in Maeve's home town of Lisburn, a man was shot dead.

Twenty-six years old, a diabetic, the father of a newborn son, Andy Lazenby was found cold and hard as stone, face down in a ditch with a plastic bag over his head, or what was left of it after the bullet entered the back of his skull and exited through the bridge of his nose. Next morning, the rigid body was discovered and scooped up by two young paramedics, who strapped it onto a stretcher before returning briefly to the ditch to vomit violently into it.

The *Belfast Telegraph* carried ten front-page paragraphs on the murder, the stricken widow, the orphaned infant and the investigation now to commence. In Dublin, the *Irish Times* carried six, as did the *Independent*, and in London the dailies ran two or three.

Two days later, Andy Lazenby was buried in a hillside ceremony attended by an extraordinarily large crowd. Many of those present did not personally know the milkman, popular though he was; they went along simply as a repudiation of the evil that was sweeping into and destroying their community.

Responsibility for this death was proudly claimed by the IRA, and soon, in the emerging new pattern of things, a Catholic would in turn be killed by the UVF. And then another Protestant, a soldier or maybe just a random retaliation; and then another Catholic, and so on, and on, and on. The mourners of both persuasions were at a loss to pinpoint when or how it had all started, back in the mists of history, but for nearly a year now it had been raging out of control, and they were terrified.

Where would it end? Would Britain clamp an iron fist down on her troubled province? Would the Irish Republic start reiterating its old claim to the disputed, misbegotten territory? Would there be civil war, tearing the whole island asunder, ripping marriages and families and whole communities apart like a tornado? Catholics and Protestants, Nationalists and Loyalists alike prayed for a solution, soon, to be implemented by the politicians who held their lives so literally in their hands. But they were not optimistic. Britain was so blindly apathetic, Ireland so small and scared, that they felt like a bone torn between an elderly boxer and a nervous chihuahua. Plus which, there seemed to be a distinct limit lately to the power of prayer.

4

Whistling, Kerry kicked her way down the rue de Vaugirard past the Luxembourg Gardens and up into the rue Racine, the blazing blue day billowing around her like the sails of a schooner, unfolding a panorama of colour and sound and smell, lifting her spirits high as a kite.

God, it was good to be alive on such a day! To be taking her first big bite out of life and finding it delicious. In her outsized Aran sweater and a mauve miniskirt, a leather duffel bag slung over her shoulder, Kerry hummed to herself as she stopped to buy a bunch of sunny yellow daffodils, again for a bag of crunchy green apples, yet again to inspect a silk shirt in a shop window.

Should she buy that too? The milky, opalescent sheen of the grey silk lured her into the tiny boutique where she fingered the soft fabric and melted into instant acquiescence. This was how she had always wanted to shop, at random, without Mother being sensible at her side, without having to account to anybody. Fishing out her wallet she paid the assistant and stood watching admiringly as the parcel was wrapped up in the way Parisiens seemed to have perfected, with a pretty giftwrap, a lot of extravagant blue ribbon and an artistic flourish.

The two young women exchanged smiles of pleasure and Kerry went on her way, Simon and Garfunkel's new song on her lips as she floated down the street, enjoying the long walk, glad to be by herself for a change. She knew Paris well enough now to wander round without getting lost, to read signs and notices in windows, ask directions without ending up in Monaco. Her French was coming on in leaps and bounds. For that, she reluctantly admitted, she had Lu to thank. And for a lot more besides.

Within a week of her arrival Lu had taken Kerry well in hand, signing her up for one course after another, starting the education which, she insisted, would stand to Kerry all her life. But only after a ferocious row. At first, Kerry rebelled furiously, fighting shy of what she knew was Maeve's influence, a vicarious attempt to control her even from almost a thousand miles away. It started with the fashion shows which, Lu insisted, Kerry should attend.

"You have looks, Kerry, you have money, it will be no time at all before you have entrée into all the most amusing circles. So, you must prepare, *non*? Tomorrow you will come with me to Dior and watch the show, you will see how to walk, how to carry a dress to best advantage, how to put the finishing little touches, OK?"

Lu smiled across the kitchen table where they sat having a late-night coffee.

"No, Lu! I'm not interested in goddamn couture! And I'm perfectly capable of dressing myself, thank you very much, I can do up my buttons just like a big girl!"

"That, right now, is all you can do, Kerry. Do you know the difference between a Dior and a Balmain? Does a silver pin or a gold brooch go better with your winter coat? It is perfectly useless to have this wonderful Irish wool if you do not know what to do with it, *chérie*."

"I don't *care*, Lu! I'm not a bloody Christmas tree, to be decked out in season! I like to shop at random, off the peg, and fashion shows bore me silly."

"And it is not just *la mode*, Kerry. You must learn many other things. You will enrol for a language course, a cookery class, a wine workshop . . ."

"Lu, are you mad? We have a staff of dozens at Ashamber! And while I'm here, Paris is hardly short of restaurants."

Lu was at the end of her rope with Kerry. The girl was a savage.

"Kerry, when you return to Ireland to start running Ashamber with your father, you won't be a girl any more.

You will be a businesswoman, expected to give and attend many lunches, dinners, parties. It won't be all horses and jeans and mud. Lots of it will be meetings, conferences, travel. Men do not simply buy a horse, you know. They buy a slice of success, and you must offer it to them on a silver salver, very prettily dressed up, or they will shop elsewhere."

Dimly, Kerry saw the sense of that. The business *was* expanding overseas, she would have to compete on far wider a territory than her father's. Damn, damn, damn. This super-cilious Frenchwoman had something she had not, an ability to look at everything objectively and realistically. And yet Lu seemed to know also the difference between selling a product and selling oneself. It was a fine line which, Kerry had to admit, would need demarcation in the predominantly male bloodstock business. It did, she supposed, mean learn-ing all the gracious arts and skills that France could offer, burnishing them up like racing trophies. Men had tricks in trade of their own. She would have to acquire her own little arsenal of smiles, after all.

"Very well. I'll go to the show tomorrow. But not cookery, not wine! Wouldn't some sort of quickie hostess course be enough? There'll always be other people to do the cooking and pour the wine."

"No, Kerry. You must learn to distinguish good food from mediocre, choose it, discuss it, cook it. A woman in your position will be expected to be knowledgeable about many things, and if you are, people will have greater faith in your knowledge of your business. You will acquire an air of authority."

"Yes, well – we can't all have your single-mindedness of purpose, Lu."

Kerry knew she was being rude, petulant, in this deliberate dig at the girl who had determined to have her brother from the first day she set her beady eyes on him. But still Lu argued unflinchingly on, resolved to ingratiate herself with the woman soon to be her mother-in-law.

"Kerry, shut up and listen. Do you simply want to waste your time here, or do you intend to do something useful with it? It's time to start dealing with life, not just enjoying it like a little girl in a sweetshop!"

"I want to *live* it, Lu, not deal with it."

"But you must exercise some control, or it will control you! Your staff will never respect you if you can't manage them, and you will never respect yourself if you can't order and discipline your affairs. Now, let's have no more of this. Next week I will take you to Fauchon, to Goldenberg, Androuet, Caviar Kaspa and all the markets. We will enrol you in a good course in gastronomy. Then wine. You will learn the difference between a Sancerre and an Alsace, a Burgundy and a Bordeaux, and by the time you meet my father at the wedding I will expect you to be able to discuss his vines with him knowledgeably."

"And when might that be?" Kerry pouted sulkily.

"September 10."

So, it really was on, then? Kerry still didn't know that she liked the sound of it, any more than she liked the sound of this Draconian régime. Who the hell did Lu think she was, anyway? What was this rubbish about silver salvers? Who cared about any of this stuff the French took so seriously, with their inflated arrogance? Did being French automatically make Lucienne de Veurlay an expert on everything? On the other hand, if she didn't do as Lu suggested, what *would* she do? She had six months in which to have the time of her life – but how, exactly, and with whom? Maybe she would meet some new people on these courses, maybe some sense of purpose would not be an altogether bad thing . . .

"Oh, all right. You win. I'll do all this dreary stuff, if you really think it'll be useful later on. But I'm still going to have fun."

"I guarantee it. At night, we will go out on the town, to clubs and cafés and jazz bars, we will introduce you to all our friends and find you a nice amusing boyfriend, a different one for every night! Wait and see."

And so, surprisingly, it had turned out. Lu saw that it did: Kerry was the kind who would turn mutinous if she didn't get the promised carrot to crunch. Within weeks, she was enrolled in five courses, making friends with her fellow students and with the large circle in which Lu orbited effortlessly, trailing Brian in her wake like a bedazzled satellite. But only at night. During the day, Kerry noted, he slaved single-mindedly at the salon of Yves St Laurent, engrossed in his work to a degree of which she had never before thought him capable. Lu tracked his progress, but never disturbed him.

One day, Lu steered her into YSL to pick Brian up for lunch. But when they arrived he was still busy, and Lu got into conversation with an acquaintance, leaving Kerry to tap her foot impatiently as she sat waiting on a little gilded chair. Things were hectic, with doe-eyed models running around half-naked, blowing airy kisses to one another, surreal in their skin-sucking lamé trousers and exaggerated make-up. To Kerry they looked like a bunch of fluttering narcissists, yet she marvelled at their utter confidence . . .

Suddenly, there was a volley of hearty oaths from inside the atelier she couldn't see. It was as if she were suddenly back home in the stables, listening to a stable lad berate a recalcitrant horse.

A door opened, and an olive-skinned youth emerged, glaring from under a tangle of rampant black curls, his vivid blue eyes flashing like ambulance alarms. Round his neck and wrists swung a cargo of junk jewellery, moving with him as he sailed across the salon with more grace than Kerry had ever seen in a man, muscular as an athlete but lissom as a dancer, volcanically angry until, abruptly, he caught sight of her. His beautiful face filled with such a wide, open, instantly endearing smile, such quick vitality that Kerry stared: what an exquisite creature!

"*Qui êtes-vous?*"

Despite the smile Kerry caught a note of challenge in the question, and bridled.

"I'm Kerry Laraghy, and whatever it is you're angry about, I didn't do it. I'm only waiting for . . ."

"Brian! You're Brian's sister! But such a beauty, I could light my cigarette on that hair!"

Beauty? It was a word Kerry could not associate with herself. Even as she turned to see which of the models he must be referring to, the youth marched up to her, took her

by the shoulders and kissed her firmly on the face, not once
but twice.

Three times! Four! The nerve of him! She struggled to find
words adequate to her indignation, but already he was calling
out to Brian and Lu as they arrived, laughing at her ruffled
feathers.

"*Alors, OK, mes enfants, allez!* We must celebrate the
arrival of this *coquelicot* in style. You will all be my guests
at the Flore for lunch. A magnificent lunch, for a magnificent
demoiselle!"

Composedly, Lu made the introductions.

"Kerry, this is Yves Tiberti. One day you will read his
name on every label from London to Tokyo."

"You mean, after the Laraghy label?"

There. She had said the wrong thing, already. But this
upstart looked like he could use the wind taking out of
his sails anyway. She glared at him, and he grinned at her,
unabashed, his eyes running riot over her in a way that made
her blush hotly. With mock officiousness, he hustled everyone
out, collecting two more friends as he went, exclaiming in
gravelly tones quite at odds with his lithe physique. He had
a voice that sounded like coal being scrunched in a grate. But
evidently he spoke English, after a muddled fashion that made
her laugh as he flamboyantly led the way out.

A couple of streets away, a bright pink 2CV was parked,
a large dent in its front bumper. Brian whispered to her that
there had been an accident lately, involving a tree in the Bois
de Boulogne; Yves was a notoriously reckless driver. Now, a
parking ticket sat neatly folded under the car's single wiper.

"Again, Yves?" Brian's tone was despairing.

"*Mais oui, mon ami!* I need a dozen more to create the
world's first paper ballgown, made entirely from parking
tickets! Come on, get in, get in!"

The doors were flung open and his thick dark eyebrows
commanded them all to obey; they were, Kerry thought, two
of the straightest, most compelling eyebrows this side of
creation. How could anyone ever work with this man and
hope to retain their sanity? Something about those eyes,
those eyebrows, shepherded her straight inside their owner's

soul, so that she wanted to fight her own suggestibility, but couldn't find a single reason to.

Somehow they all crammed inside the tiny car and held their breath until, miraculously, it started. Sitting on her knee Kerry found a little creature who reminded her of a leprechaun.

"Hi. Yves never bothers with introductions, and this dreamy brother of yours never remembers. I'm Zoe Zimner."

The girl produced an impish smile, and Kerry felt glad to be among friends of her own age. What did this Zoe mean about Brian being dreamy? That he was handsome, or that he had a head like a sieve?

"I'm Kerry Laraghy. You're American, aren't you?"

"Yeah. Native New Yorker. Just six more months, and then Uncle Sam claims me for his own."

By the time they sputtered to a halt outside the Café de la Flore, Zoe had told Kerry all about herself. Nineteen, a college drop-out, consumed with a burning need to design sportswear ("ski suits, swimwear, riding britches, tennis dresses, the works"), she was the daughter of an apparently outstanding American fashion photographer, of whom Kerry had never heard.

"He didn't marry my mom until I was eight years old. Pity. I used to have such fun when everyone was on their case, when there wasn't a priest, rabbi or minister in all of New York who'd marry them."

"Why not?" Kerry had a new and keen interest in lovers thwarted by circumstance.

"Cos there would have been gang warfare at the wedding. A Jew and a Catholic, can you imagine – both families in mourning for their lost child? The hate vibes would have blown the roof clear off St Patrick's cathedral. So finally they eloped, got hitched on a cruise ship somewhere off Cuba, by the captain. There was hell to pay when they got back."

All through lunch Zoe prattled on, her short life apparently as crammed with incident as Yves's promised sandwiches were now bursting with meats, cheeses, salads, olives and all manner of delectables. Laughing and chattering, they washed them down with white wine (Sancerre, Lu informed Kerry, pointedly), and then, inhaling a pungent Gauloise, Yves chivalrously offered to sacrifice his afternoon's work to show Kerry Paris.

"Oh, Yves, would you really? There's so much I haven't seen yet, and it's such a bright clear day, I have a guidebook . . ."

"Throw it away, *chérie*, and I will show you the Paris of Yves Tiberti." Brian raised a laconic eyebrow at that, and muttered to Kerry that Yves was in fact Breton, a blow-in from the wild west. Solemnly Yves raised a hand for silence.

"We will have no jokes, please. Despite my origins I understand Paris perfectly, and am ideally qualified to show it to Kerry, because I understand pretty girls even more perfectly."

Again, everyone laughed, and Zoe smiled at her new friend.

"Go with him, Kerry! He's great fun, you'll have a marvellous time."

"Yes, I will. Why don't you come too?"

Zoe grimaced in the direction of the sixth member of their group.

"Daniel. Keeps my nose to the grindstone. Which as you can see has already worn it down considerably."

Kerry giggled. Zoe's nose was indeed short, like the rest of her, but sweet. Daniel looked calm, quiet, professorial in spectacles.

"Is Daniel your boyfriend?"

"Yep. My minder, too. He bosses me round just like Lu—"

Zoe's sentence skidded to a stop, but mentally Kerry finished it, and was disconcerted. She didn't like to think of her brother as being putty in anybody's hands, and he certainly wasn't in his father's. How had Lu got such a grip on him?

They gathered up their things and went their separate ways. As good as his word, Yves propelled Kerry off on their odyssey, and took her to an entirely new side of the city – a steamy, seething side whose existence she had never suspected. On foot, on the métro and on buses, they went to the historic Marais, to the ethnic markets of the rue Mouffetard, to the sizzling North African cauldron that fermented out in Belleville. It was far from the glamorous itinerary she would have expected of Yves, but it was riveting.

Oh, she thought, how fabulous, how beautiful! I'd never have found any of this by myself, discovered such variety, heard such stories. Why did nobody ever tell me about these Chinese shops, these Jewish delis, Arab bakeries? There's a new curiosity in every corner. I've been to the Île St Louis before, but never to this witches' café full of cats and crucifixes . . . oh, it's weird, wonderful, I'm hallucinating!

His delight mounting with her own, Yves trekked on and on until darkness fell, talking, waving, laughing as they toured the zinc bars, seedy places in which he fed her peculiar drinks and marvellous anecdotes until her head was whirling.

"Enough?"

"No! More! More Paris, more everything!"

Giddily they fell out into the night that neither of them would ever forget. Everywhere Paris glowed like a gorgeous jewel, brilliant with the light that spilled over the golden dome of Les Invalides, the Bastille's winged God of Liberty, the silhouette of the Opéra, the surging waters of the Seine. Paradise, she told Yves, and he promptly showed her the Élysée Palace. It was a fascinating experience, from which she returned quite light-headed, starstruck as a child in Aladdin's cave.

After that, all six became increasingly close-knit, meeting often for casual drinks and, every Saturday, lunch at the Café Cluny next to the little museum of the same name. It was less expensive than the Flore, and Kerry was glad; the rest of them were supported by affluent parents, but Yves seemed to have nobody, living a precarious existence in the large, ramshackle apartment he shared with Zoe and Daniel on the rue St Antoine. Often, when Lu and Brian wanted privacy, she went over there, and came to love the place with its lively buzz, its big windows forever open on to the warm spring air. Frequently she stayed overnight, on a sofa or on the floor, after a hectic evening spent dancing barefoot to the music of the Antilles. At the centre of things, Yves held court amidst a fluid procession of friends, mostly foreigners, his perpetual curiosity piqued by Italians, Africans, South

Americans, anyone and everyone his charm could seduce into a kind of permanent party.

With reckless generosity he entertained them all, and when Kerry rashly expressed a wish to visit Maxim's, promptly took her there. Lu warned her in advance to discreetly pay the bill, but he caught her as she fumbled to do it, and reddened furiously as he snatched it from her. He worked part time as a barman, he insisted, and could afford to treat her. But Kerry knew that he could not, and felt profoundly sorry for what she had cost both his pocket and his pride.

But today Kerry's mind was on other matters as she made her way to the Cluny to meet the group for lunch. After three months in Paris, she had discovered so much, realised how much more there might be – must be – in a world infinitely bigger than the one she had left. How could she possibly go back there now that . . . oh, hell's bells!

Her shoe was stuck in a grating, in one of the metal grids which encircle every tree in Paris. Crossly, she bent to release it and the heel came away in her hand. Oh, damn! She wasn't far from the Cluny, but she could hardly hop all the way there. There must be a heel bar somewhere – in the métro, maybe? Lots of the bigger ones had them.

Muttering, she stuffed the heel in her pocket and hobbled off to the one she could see from where she stood. Sure enough, there was a heel bar, and she sat swivelling on a stool as she waited, inhaling the dry chalky smell of the métro with pleasure.

Down the tiled corridors with their big square posters, Parisiens hurried about their business, in and out through the clanking turnstiles, the distant klaxon of the trains coming like music to Kerry's ears. She loved this underground world, the purposeful vigour of it all.

And then, from a point that must be down on the platforms, there *was* music coming to her ears. Music that rose and fell in eddies so familiar she gasped, transfixed as though by an arrow. It couldn't possibly be. But it was – "The Rose of Tralee", sung in a clear tenor voice so unmistakably Irish that for one wild moment she thought it was Eamonn's. But of course it was not; her father had never set foot in the métro in

his life, and the idiocy of the thought made her giggle. Even
when Eamonn was roaring drunk, he didn't sing in the streets,
much less fly to Paris to disgrace himself.

But undoubtedly somebody, somewhere, was singing one
of his songs. She must find out who, and why. Snatching her
shoe, she ran to the ticket window, bought one and shoved
her way through to the source of the sound as rudely as any
native.

And there he was. A busker in jeans and an Aran sweater
much like her own, only frayed across one shoulder by the
strap of his guitar. The jeans were patched and faded, his
sneakers thin and pathetic on this chilly day in mid-March.
Oh – of course! It was St Patrick's day, March 17. That
was why he was playing an Irish song. To her amazement
Kerry felt a lump harden in her throat as she thought of her
parents at home, missing them for the first time, briefly but
acutely. Cursing herself for an emotional fool she stood there,
floundering in the flow of the music as it swirled down the
tunnels of memory, carrying her back to those achingly sweet
nights when, as a small girl, she had sat sucking her thumb
at the top of the staircase, listening to her father sing below
as his friends joined in all the rousing choruses, their voices
flooding the house like golden honey.

For what seemed like hours she watched the busker, incredulous that he should have the power to so stab at her
heart, impaling it on the thorns of this song as if he personally
had grown and plucked that very rose. As his voice swelled
and burst upon the final crescendo she gaped at him like a
snake before a charmer, mesmerised.

"So our Irish eyes aren't smiling today, no?"

She jumped back. It was as if a mannequin in a shop
window had spoken.

"And our tongue is out of order too?"

He was speaking to her. In English, with an Irish accent.
Speaking to her.

"I – oh – I – how do you know I'm Irish?"

"Well, now, let's see. Is it the red hair? Or the green eyes?
Or those little freckles that won't go away? Or that surprised
look you'd never see on a Parisien face?"

"I – no – well, I haven't been here long, I come from Kilbally, I just didn't expect – why were you singing that song?"

She knew she was babbling, but couldn't stop herself.

"Why?"

Now he stared back at her, his amused expression giving way to a puzzled frown.

"Is there any particular reason why I shouldn't sing it? What's wrong with it?"

"Nothing. Nothing at all. It's just that it's – it's my father's favourite song. You – you don't expect to hear it in the métro St Michel."

He strummed his guitar idly, surveying her from head to toe.

"Homesick, are we?"

"Homesick?" Until this very moment she had hardly thought of home at all. "No. Not in the least. I'm staying with my brother. And his fiancée."

Far away at the back of her mind Maeve's voice sounded its warning bell: never speak to strangers. Especially not scruffy ones like this. But he spoke to me first, Mother.

"Ah. I see. Odd girl out. Brother loves fiancée. Fiancée loves brother. Nobody loves poor little sister."

"What?"

"You know . . . lovebirds billing and cooing in their corner, kid sister ignored on the sidelines. The gooseberry syndrome."

"How dare you! My brother is my twin and he loves me very much."

This was ridiculous! She realised he was laughing at her, his brown eyes dancing. Brown eyes dark as a turf bog . . . the brown bog of Allen, wild, treacherous, unpredictable.

"So, what's a nice Irish girl like you doing here? Being serenaded by buskers, without even giving them a centime?"

Oh. Of course. She should give him some money. She rummaged for ten francs, held the coins out to him. He did not move.

"Don't you want it? I can't just throw it in your guitar case."

"Why not?"

"Because . . . because I've talked to you. It would be rude of me."

"And Mummy taught her little girl always to be polite, did she?"

She couldn't fathom such sarcasm. She was merely trying to thank him, at his own request, for playing a lovely old ballad. Irritated, she flung the coins in the case.

"Here. I have to go now."

He bent to retrieve the money, and counted it.

"This would just about buy us a coffee apiece."

His eyes crinkled humorously, his brown beard parting over even white teeth as he smiled and flung back his ponytail, but something in his compact physique denoted a challenge.

"Sorry. I haven't much change on me. And one hardly writes cheques for buskers." Her tone was cool.

"I wasn't being sarcastic, so there's no call for you to be. I meant – just that I'd like to buy you a coffee. It's been a long time since I met anyone from home."

She hesitated, scrutinising his dark, weatherbeaten face, hoping she didn't look as uncertain as she felt. There was some faint aura about the man that frightened her.

"I can't. I'm meeting friends for lunch. Sorry."

"Lunch, huh? Well, I haven't earned quite enough for that yet. Only been here half an hour. Too bad."

She felt a mixture of relief and unreasonable disappointment. For the life of her she could not say why she didn't want to walk away, but she didn't.

"But – but it was very kind of you to invite me for coffee. Maybe some other time? Do you always play here?"

"Depends. I move around. But if you're passing by again, well, the offer still stands. OK?"

"OK."

She smiled at him tentatively, and he smiled back. A smile that all but split the stones of the walls, stopped the trains of the métro with a squeal of their brakes. The sensual power of it took her breath away, hit her like a punch in the stomach. Oh, dear Lord. Why had she misunderstood about the coffee?

Why couldn't he let her pay for lunch? But she sensed that even to suggest it would be a mistake.

His whole stance was so aggressively independent, it left her no choice but to shrug with feigned indifference.

"Bye, then."

"Bye."

He readjusted his guitar and began to play again. Not for her, but for the other people in the tiled tunnel. There was a finality about it, and Kerry knew he would not play an Irish song this time. Nor did he: it was "Eleanor Rigby". She had been dismissed.

Darragh de Bruin was twenty-two years old, and in a state of revolt. It was a common enough state for his age and generation, but he could not seem to get beyond it. The catalysts were predictable: education, politics, religion, family, all the indulgences of the late luxurious sixties that his friends managed gradually to outgrow. They simply diminished such things to manageable proportions, but he could not. Like a nuclear arsenal they stockpiled in his mind until he was ready to explode with the raging injustice that seethed within him. It ticked like a time bomb in his brain, and made him acutely unhappy. Why couldn't he grow up and settle down like everybody else? Why, why?

Earnestly he identified and rationalised each object of his panoramic anger. But for every one he slapped down, two more rose up to fill the gap. The environment, the economy, Vietnam, racism, anti-Semitism, the social system, irrational practices and attitudes of all descriptions laid constant siege to his soul. It was a soul only very recently evolved, and still in a fragile condition.

His father, a major in the Irish army, had drawn up a strict military plan for his family's upbringing, and it was executed with precision by no less authoritative a mother. It had worked admirably on Darragh's two older brothers and two younger sisters, but somehow skipped him completely, bypassing him like a badly aimed bullet. His parents bridled: the boy was neither the usurped eldest nor the spoiled baby. There was no reason why he should prove so difficult. Until he was eighteen, they kept him tightly in check, and then, with no warning whatsoever, he woke up one morning with a mind full of questions. Not sensible questions with scientifically verifiable answers. Just questions. His family's inability to move from the military to the metaphysical rattled them badly, and Darragh, for the following three years, had not been a popular young man.

"He'll grow out of it," his mother predicted, as if his discomfort were childish clothing that had become too tight, and to please her Darragh tried. One did one's best to please one's mother, particularly this mother. But it was no good. He was clearly close to becoming a black sheep.

But life went on. He finished university as a point of honour, graduating with a disappointing BL and a profound sense of dissatisfaction. After intensive study of the law, he felt stifled by its dry rigidity, quite unable to go down the dusty road to becoming a barrister. The summer of 1968 shattered his few remaining illusions, and after the assassinations of Martin Luther King and Robert Kennedy he strummed his guitar endlessly up in his room, until finally his parents' nerves snapped.

"Out. Get a job, earn a living. That'll make a man of you. We've done our duty."

They were surprised, but not sorry, when he immediately packed his few clothes and dog-eared books into the trunk that had once accompanied his father to the Congo, and disappeared. His allowance was cut off, father and son spoke no more, and an occasional postcard thereafter was the extent of inter-familial communiqués.

In Paris, Darragh's spirits lifted. He rented a minuscule apartment out in Ivry, with a long window looking down over the suburb's summer dust, and savoured the smell of croissants that rose from the bakery below at six sharp every morning. But he did not buy any. He simply holed up here, turning things over in his head, refusing to come up with a plan of any kind. He had had enough of plans. Determined to stage his revolution thoroughly if at all, he slept by day, read by night, ate breakfast at noon and lunch at seven. He made friends with the girl across the landing, Monique Laclos, and in return for English lessons she tutored him in French.

His quick, keen mind was trained to absorb information, and he made rapid progress, finding in the sonority of this new language a sensual pleasure that improved, he found, his ability to play his guitar. Where else might music now lurk, waiting for him to find it? And what else, for that matter, lay hidden from his senses in the thick opaque folds of his education? It became imperative to find out.

Almost obsessively, he began to explore the art galleries, museums, theatres, libraries, churches, monuments and parks. The things that he found there enthralled him; never had he experienced such a sense of wonder, startling and insatiable. The frustration of being unable to discuss any of what he learned, with his new French friends, drove him almost mad until he met Monique. She solved that problem, but his savings were running out, and until Ireland joined the European Community he could not acquire a work permit. Busking came to mind as an ideal way to survive, to develop his musical skills and assert his independence. He could play when he chose and where he chose, and meet new people into the bargain. The intimate, claustrophobic atmosphere of the métro drew people to him: foreigners sniffing out local colour, rival buskers come to criticise, Parisiens amused by the novelty of his repertoire. It was warm and dry, too, with acoustics as good as any auditorium. He was aware that he had never played so well, not just handy ballads but other things as well, folk and jazz and even some classical experiments. One night, an acquaintance took him to a club in Montmartre, where he heard Françoise Hardy live for the first time. The husky tigress clawed at his senses and left them raw. Time and again he went back, to hear Barbara, Georges Moustaki, Serge Reggiani and Jacques Brel, all the *chanteurs* whose electric intensity shocked every nerve in his body.

Over endless coffees and cigarettes and marcs he began to get under the skin of his adopted country, to understand its habits and manners, language and culture. Politics, too. The riots of May in the month before he arrived were a subject that fascinated him; he read and talked about them incessantly until he could almost feel the water cannon

and the truncheons, climb up on the barricades as valorous
as Danny Cohn-Bendit himself.

And yet, something was wrong. Some hunger devoured
him, some nameless thing that was perpetually irksome, a
riddle that made him throw wide the windows of his studio
at nights, breathing deeply as though the answer might come
on the breeze. He had a natural aptitude for maths, but this
problem wouldn't come out right no matter what way he
approached it. Determined to wrestle it into submission,
he set himself to assuaging every desire, no matter how
fleeting the whim. He drank wine, he walked miles, he
read Proust to half-blindness, and still the gnawing need
for he knew not what remained.

Sex. That must be it. He needed a girl. Right, then. Wildly
he laid siege to Monique, the first one to hand, and applied
himself to studying sex as if it were Euclid.

Monique was pretty, with tanned smooth skin and a blonde
ponytail that bobbed appealingly, and she was a little in love
with him. When he kissed her on the cheek, the night she
finally felt he had mastered the subjunctive, she was ecstatic.
Shyly she kissed him back, and he took her in his arms and
kissed her properly, at length, with an ardour that rather
scared her. Her apartment was as small as his, and the
move from the table to the bed was brief. He made love to
her for most of the night, fiercely, and again with a lighter
touch next morning. They parted with friendly smiles and a
mutual feeling of joyful release, and Darragh decided that
his fondness for Monique had definitely increased. She was
terrific – but still not what he was searching for.

Confused and ambivalent, he showered, dressed and went
off to play in the Luxembourg Gardens until a *flic* threatened
to arrest him for breaking the bye-laws. But, more than a
month later, when he was least expecting it, he found his
answer.

He knew it the moment he saw the coltish girl staring at
him in the métro, transfixed for some reason that was not
clear.

Sweet Jesus, he thought, how exquisite. Look at those eyes.
That mouth. Look at the way she's looking at you! Don't miss

a beat, now, don't hit a false note, the music is holding her.

His lungs were hurting when he finally hit the last notes and the girl seemed to come out of her trance. He had not the faintest idea why "The Rose of Tralee" should have this effect, beyond that the girl was obviously Irish. He would have given anything to meet her properly, to get talking with her, and it stung when she put him down with her money and her cool sarcasm. When she walked away, he wanted to yell aloud, to run after her. But she would come back. She had to, as surely as day followed night.

His certainty bordered on the cosmic.

Everyone was having a terrific time at lunch, laughing raucously at some hilarious story of Yves's, including Kerry who hadn't heard a word of it. Her responses were automatic, but her reverie so obvious that gradually it sobered everyone, and the conversation drifted on to a more serious note. Brian and Yves began to discuss fashion, sensing that they were both getting clearer now about where their future lay.

Brian was edging, slowly, into evening wear, making up his mind to specialise in flowing romantic gowns that would be timeless, translucent, eternal. Yves was just the opposite, all keyed up into short, snappy, clever little numbers that would make their wearers think, talk and laugh with their witty originality. One day, Brian saw, Yves would be a world-class designer, a unique phenomenon – if, that was, he didn't blow it all and end up a kitchen porter instead.

Already, his ability on a good day was breathtaking. But on a good day, Yves liked to do more than draw or pin swatches on dummies: he liked to live it up, to embark on long lunches from which he rarely, if ever, returned. Surrounding himself with a wide and eclectic circle, he released his enormous energies into any number of diversionary activities, and was frequently rebuked at the salon. Everyone warned him he was treading a tightrope, but then he looked so tragically repentant, so comically downcast, that over and again he was forgiven for "positively, absolutely the last time", and he would shoot off at another tangent the very next day. Discipline was not his strong suit.

But today, Kerry could not care less if any of them wanted to dress their future clients in dustbin liners or biscuit boxes. Her expression was glazed as she dimly heard Zoe calling for coffee, Lu admonishing Daniel for something, Brian talking heatedly with Yves, his brown eyes full of unusual . . . brown, just like the busker's . . .

"So, sweetie, who is he, h'mm? Come on, tell Uncle Yves all about him, and I will decide if he is good enough for you!"

Trust Yves to spot that she had become excluded. He edged closer to her and put a concerned arm around her shoulders, and Kerry was unable to rebuff him.

"Oh, Yves, how did you know—?"

"Easy, *chérie*. Only a man brings that look to a woman's face. If you have found a nice one, I am very happy for you."

Affectionately he hugged her, and Kerry gazed at him, taken aback. More than once, she had thought that . . . that she might be falling in love with Yves. He was so unfailingly kind, taking her everywhere, giving her little gifts; flowers, books, a pair of mittens one weekend when they had all gone to try their hand at skiing in the Alps. She knew what even such small things cost him, and grew fonder of him every day.

But they never kissed, other than in greeting, and she sadly came to the conclusion that she mustn't be his type. Often he took her by the arm, but he never held her hand, and in clubs at night they danced almost exclusively together, but went their separate ways thereafter. If only she were cute, like Zoe, or sophisticated, like Lu! It had become first puzzling, then painful – and now – here he was saying that he would be happy if she had found somebody else!? Clearly, he cared very much about her. But not for her.

"Happy for me? But I thought – thought – maybe – oh, I don't know what I thought, Yves! It's just that you – you're so good to me, so kind, I like you so much—"

Something in his face made her stop short, and he laughed. But it was not his usual insouciant laugh, she thought; it had a bittersweet edge.

"Oh, Kerry. Don't tell me – don't tell me that Brian hasn't told you?" His smile had the most curious twist to it.

"Told me what?"

Abruptly, the smile vanished altogether, and he looked at her with unprecedented seriousness, taking his arm from about her shoulders.

"Kerry, I am not a man you should think anything about at all. Not in that sense. I am – I prefer – I am happier in the – with – with other men, Kerry."

"Other men?"

She was nonplussed, her eyes wide in genuine innocence. Kilbally had never yet produced such a thing as a homosexual man, certainly not for public consumption, and Yves's explanation left her merely mystified. Across the table, she was aware of Brian detaching himself from the chitchat and turning to them, a look of combined guilt and sadness shadowing his face.

"Yves, it's all my fault. I meant to tell her, but I just couldn't seem to find the right moment. I'm sorry." He reached for Kerry's hand. "And I'm sorry for you, too, *chérie*. I should have done it at the start, and not embarrassed Yves into this."

The two men caught each other's eyes, but neither spoke, the rest of the group quietening as they realised what was happening. They all knew! Kerry saw it instantly and felt a crimson flush creep up her neck, fan out across her face. What a fool she was! And now they all thought she had fallen for Yves, a gay man far beyond her reach. The shame of it whipped her into quick retort – too quick.

"Oh, of course it isn't Yves! It's a busker I met in the métro!"

She shot what she hoped was a disdainful look at Yves, and he shrank back, hurt. A long, hollow silence followed, until Zoe defused it.

"A busker, in the métro? Oh, Kerry! You shouldn't be let out on your own!"

Assorted emotions scudded across Yves's face before his sparkle suddenly returned as if a switch had been thrown. Circling his fingers around a mock guitar, he began to strum the imaginary instrument and sing bawdily, an outrageous passage from one of the rugby anthems. Even respectable

matrons lunching at other tables smiled surreptitiously as he
stood up and serenaded the whole group, his blue eyes full of
mischief, his manner that of a medieval minstrel, doffing an
invisible cap and bowing low at the end of the performance.

Cackling, they broke up. It was nearly three, they all
had things to do. Far more important things than ask
Kerry about this unlikely busker. Evidently the whole notion
was too risible for words, literally, they thought she was
joking, and dispersed with callous indifference. Furious with
herself and with them, Kerry tugged on the red leather gloves
that had so incensed Sergeant Mulligan.

I'm sorry about Yves, she muttered under her breath, and
I don't know how I'm going to make it up to him. But I'm not
joking about – about whatshisname. I don't know his name.
But I've never been more serious in my life.

Even from his eyrie on the fourteenth floor, Brandon was
sure. It *was* the same car. A beige Ford Cortina, completely
ordinary and unremarkable, except that it had been down
there in the parking lot every day for three weeks now. The
same beige Ford he glimpsed occasionally in the rear-view
mirror as he drove to or from work, the same one that drove
off to lunch if and when he did. A terrible thought crossed
Brandon's mind.

Kidnappers. An industrial kidnap of which he, Brandon
Lawrence, was the target. They were going to demand a
ransom so large no insurance company would pay it, even
were he insured against such a thing, which he was not.
Nobody was ever kidnapped in Ireland, and in London the
thought had simply never entered his head. But now – now
he had better move – fast.

Swiftly Brandon crossed the room, picked up the phone and
tersely instructed Louise to get him the police.

Half an hour later, Detective Sergeant Charles Galloway sat
in the button-back leather chair on the other side of the rosewood desk, taking copious notes and the whole thing, Brandon
was glad to see, very seriously. He had arrived in plain clothes
in an unmarked car, with two other officers who now sat by
the window, eyes trained on the vehicle far below.

"Very wise to ring us, sir, very wise indeed. You can leave it to us now. Just go about your normal business and we'll report back to you in no time at all."

Brandon showed them out and they disappeared as discreetly as they had come, but his anxiety did not. What if . . . if it was not just himself they wanted, but Marianne as well? The children? His blood chilled at the thought, but his lips set like a steel trap. Nobody was going to touch his family. Admittedly, he did not see nearly as much of Chris and Harry as he should, but he loved them dearly, deeply, nonetheless. He allowed himself a small laugh. If the kidnappers wanted a member of his family, he would offer them Patricia. They would not kidnap a second time.

But Chris and Harry – they were his heirs, his flesh and blood, and over his dead body would anyone touch them. Not that it would be dead, he hoped. Again, he picked up the phone, and dialled his friend Louis Burford.

"Louis? Brandon. I need some information. What security firm do you use?"

Louis was relieved. Relations between Britain and Ireland were becoming more strained every day. It was time a man in Brandon's position took stock of the situation, and precautions. But why now, today?

"There's a car been tailing me, Louis, for nearly a month. Didn't want to say anything until I was sure it wasn't coincidence. But it isn't."

Louis was aghast, only slightly mollified to hear the police had been called in, and showered a salvo of advice down the line.

"Yeah, yeah, I will, Louis. Thanks. Call you later."

Hanging up, Brandon went back to the window and peered down again. The car was still there, but now it was surrounded, its doors open, a man standing beside it, talking to a figure that looked like Galloway. Whoever he was, he was cornered. Minutes later, the man was bundled into another car and driven away, evidently under considerable protest.

It was over an hour later before the call came.

"Mr Lawrence? Galloway here. We've got your man – and your answer, I'm afraid."

Afraid? Of what? Brandon felt a thick slice of fear lodge itself in his gullet, and braced himself.

"It isn't a kidnap, sir. It's – ah – it's your wife, sir. It appears she's hired this man to – um – to follow you. He's a private investigator. His name is Robert Farleigh. Perfectly legitimate."

"My wife?" Brandon didn't follow.

"Yes, sir. For whatever reasons of her own, I'm afraid she has engaged this person to – er – keep watch on you. He's even been abroad when you have, on the same planes in some instances."

Marianne? A private investigator? Brandon was bewildered.

"You mean that this man is going about on a perfectly legal pretext? That he's *spying* on me? On my wife's instructions?"

"Yes, sir."

Brandon swallowed hard, thanked the man and hung up in a fury so white he hit a parking meter as, moments later, he wrenched his Saab out into the London traffic.

It was a fifty-minute drive to Richmond. Brandon did it in thirty. The hall door slammed so violently behind him that Patricia, in the morning room, clutched her chest and shrieked.

"Marianne! Mari-anne! Get your butt the hell out here!"

No answer. The goddamn bitch was skulking in here – he raced into the morning room and slammed full force into his mother-in-law.

"Where is she?"

"Good heavens, Brandon, what's going on? What kind of way is that to address my daughter?"

"Fuck off, Patricia."

She recoiled, open-mouthed, shocked as if by an electric fence, and even in the midst of his anger Brandon smiled grimly. He'd been wanting to say that for years. But full marks to the woman, she recovered swiftly, and made him wait for his answer. Normally her son-in-law was the quietest, politest of men.

"She's taking a bath, since you ask so nicely."

He ran up the stairs and into their bedroom, smelling immediately the heavy scent from the bathroom. Without knocking he flung open the door, bursting in just as Marianne was about to step into a deep steaming bubble bath.

Gripping her by one wrist, he whirled her round, panting.

"So. My wife spies on me, does she? Hires a PI to mind her husband for her while she's out gallivanting, does she? And now perhaps she can tell her dear husband what the hell she thinks she's doing, can she?"

Flinching as he spat each word at her, his grip like pliers on her arm, Marianne whimpered with fright.

"Ow – ow – Brandon, let go of me! You're hurting me!"

His grip tightened. "I'll let go of you when I have the truth out of you."

Her eyes welled with tears.

"And you can forget the waterworks, Marianne. I want an explanation, a full and very frank explanation, and I want it now. *Tell* me!"

His face was alabaster, harder than she had ever seen it. With her free hand she brushed away the first tear as it spilled down her cheek, humiliated that she should be caught like this, naked and defenceless. In a suitable outfit she would have been able to aim for a lot more control of the situation.

"All right, Brandon. I will tell you." Weeping despite herself, she sank down on the edge of the bath.

"I hired Mr Farleigh because I suspect that you're having an affair, and I wanted to know who the woman was. Is."

"An affair?" Abruptly his tone switched from enraged to baffled. "What do you mean? What kind of fool are you? I'm not having an affair with anyone!"

"But – but you must be! You're never here, I never see you and neither do the children, even when you are here you don't listen to us, you don't seem to care about any of us any more. There *must* be somebody else."

Her voice was the voice of a small, lost child. As suddenly as he had burst in and seized her, Brandon released his wife, stood back and stared at her as if at a slightly crazed woman he was meeting for the first time.

"Oh, my God, Marianne . . . is that what you really think? And if it is, why didn't you tell me? Ask me about it?"

"Why? Because what would be the point, Brandon? What

adulterous husband would ever own up, just like that?" She rubbed her wrist and lifted her head high enough to meet his stony eyes. "Would you have? Do you, even now?"

She was not surprised when he evaded her gaze, staring vacantly into the clouds of steam on the wall behind her.

"No," he replied eventually, dully. "I don't own up, Marianne, because there's nothing to own up to. I haven't been seeing anyone else. No one at all."

He sounded sincere. Equally perplexed, they looked at each other. And then he seized her wrist again, pulled her to her feet and pushed her into the bedroom, tearing off his tie and jacket, loosening his collar and breathing hard as he flung her against the bed.

"But yes, my dear wife, there is somebody else. Somebody I haven't seen, but been thinking a great deal about while you've been dragging me round your parties and dinners and whatnot. Somebody who might mean more to me now than you ever try to, if I let her. But you needn't worry. She's in France, well away from the both of us."

"I knew it! You have a woman! You lied to me, Brandon! You have got a floozie! Some little French tart, a trollop!"

He hit her so hard the blood spurted down her chin and over her breasts in rivulets as she sank to the floor, instinctively covering her face against the next blow.

But it did not come. When she dared to uncover her eyes it was to see him sitting on the bed, his head in his hands, sobs choking out from between his fingers. Marianne had never seen Brandon weep before, and it surprised her how steadily she was able to get up and go to him, put her arms round him and pull him to her, gathering his crumpled face into her spattered shoulder as if he were a small boy wounded in a corner fight.

"Brandon. I think we have some talking to do. A lot of talking."

5

Sunday was an eternity Kerry thought would never end. If she didn't get back to the métro St Michel, she would combust with frustration. But he would not be there today, it would be too quiet with too few people about – and besides, she had committed herself to a spring picnic in the Bois with Brian and Lu.

They were discussing the wedding, holding hands on a rug on the grass, a picture of happiness, as Kerry sat savagely pulling blades of grass to shreds. It seemed she was to be bridesmaid.

"And so, you will have to start the fittings, Kerry. I have asked Brian to design my dress, and yours. His first official commission."

Lu smiled brightly, and the significance of that dawned on Kerry. Brian Laraghy was to do Lucienne de Veurlay's wedding dress. Lu, the daughter of a leading wine producer, one of the best-known models in France, the toast of *le tout Paris*, was entrusting the most important dress of her life to her untried, neophyte fiancé. She worked at Dior, she could have got it there at cost, but no; she preferred to marry in something by this unknown young student. It was a major act of faith.

Kerry had to admit she was pleased.

"That's a wonderful idea, Lu. The wedding photographs will be in all the papers and society magazines. Brian couldn't buy that kind of exposure for any money." She turned to her brother. "So make sure you do a good job of it, Brian! You won't get a second chance!"

Brian grinned, but somewhere behind his eyes she thought

she saw the tiniest trace of sadness, or wistfulness, something slightly diluting his happiness.

"I'll do my best, Kerry. But – we're wondering – would you do us a favour?"

She nodded unhesitatingly.

"Would you phone Dad and try to reason with him again? His blessing is really very important to me. To us both."

Kerry smiled wryly. Here, for once, was something Lu could not manage or manipulate. In recent weeks their relationship had been quite cordial, yet Kerry felt the need of caution in it; somehow their schoolgirl adventures had become real, and serious.

"Yes. Of course I will. But I can't promise any results. In fact Dad may well eat the face off me."

"Oh, rubbish, Kerry! He adores you. You know he does. You can wrap him round your little finger if you try."

They thanked her profusely, but Kerry's smile was apprehensive. She still did not think that Eamonn was about to authorise the marriage. And she wondered that Lu would allow her to be put in such a dilemma, caught between her father's anger and her brother's disappointment. Could she not simply go straight at the thing and telephone Eamonn herself?

But already Lu had moved on to the question of the guest list.

The métro St Michel bobbed into view at last amidst the teeming throngs on the boulevard, barely fifty metres away now. Kerry's heart lurched. What if – what if? Now that the moment was at hand she was petrified, hot and cold at once, her stomach shrinking and her breathing shallow. By the time she reached the entrance her panic was such that she had to stop and grip the iron rail for support, her palm clammy in its glove. She was shaking from head to foot.

"*Ça va, mademoiselle?*"

The voice was solicitous, concerned. A passer-by thought she was unwell. Turning to stammer thanks and reassurance, she found herself staring into two brown eyes full of ironic amusement. Oh, God. Oh, no.

"What's the matter? Are you ill?"

There was anxiety in his question. She gulped a lungful of the crisp air and tried to speak normally.

"No. No. Fine. Been running, that's all."

"Really? But there are plenty of trains. Every few minutes."

He knew why she was here! The bastard was making fun of her again. Mortified, she glared at him. What was *he* doing here, for that matter, muffled up with his guitar in its case over his shoulder? He was supposed to be down in the métro, not waiting to catch her out up here in this excruciatingly embarrassing position.

"Yes, well, I'm in a hurry – have to meet someone."

The moment the lie was out she regretted it. Now she would have to leave him a second time, go off to meet the fictitious someone. Pride before a fall. Dammit, she could not do it again!

"Ah. Lunch with the brother, is it? Another nice little bistro, an apéritif, a chat about the wedding?"

"Wedding?"

"Yes, well, if he has a fiancée then I presume he is getting married? Or is that just my bucolic Irish interpretation of some much more sophisticated scheme?"

She laughed, slightly hysterically.

"No. Yes. No. I mean, yes he is."

"Good. It's nice to know our quaint native customs haven't entirely deserted us in this howling Babylon."

He swept a sarcastic arm down the boulevard and smiled at her. She groped for some response, but nothing came.

"So, you're all right then? What a pity you're in a hurry this time too. I've saved up the price of lunch since Saturday."

She took a deep breath. "Look. It doesn't matter. I can call to cancel my rendezvous. If you've saved up the money then the least I can do is accept your invitation. But I really don't expect you to pay for me."

He appraised her grimly, inspecting every stitch she wore.

"H'mm. Let's see now. Ebony earrings, leather gloves, leather jacket, possibly Italian, designer jeans . . . I'd say men have been paying for you all your life, lady. Or are you by some extraordinary chance the managing director of IBM?"

She flushed and stared down at the ground. Why was he so belligerent, again? She had done nothing to deserve it. After a moment his eyes softened.

"Sorry. That was rude of me."

"Not rude, really. Just condescending and nasty, like you were before."

"Was I? Sorry. Guess I'm just a crude busker with no manners at all."

"Oh, for chrissakes! Are we going to argue, or are we going to have lunch? What did you ask me for, if you didn't mean it?"

Her snap of anger was real. Enough of this.

"Yes. Yes, we are. Come on, then."

He turned on his heel and strode off, leaving her to follow, feeling both repelled and oddly attracted by his brusqueness. Rounding a couple of corners they came to a small café with faded lace curtains in its tiny window, the name Émile scripted over the door, two workmen in denim overalls sharing a carafe of Pernod and water at one of the round red-chequered tables.

"Not quite your usual standard, perhaps, but mine."

Without further ado he ordered Perrier while she struggled out of her jacket, not helping her with it, not holding the chair for her, asking instead for two menus and a *jeton* for the phone.

"You'll need to cancel your date with your friend, I take it?"

"Oh – yes." Kerry thought quickly. She was due at her French class at two thirty. She would go to the phone and cancel that.

"Who were you going to meet, anyway?"

"Oh . . . it was a group thing. They won't miss me."

"Yes, they will."

"Why?"

"Because you're so incredibly lovely. You'll be missed the way the *Mona Lisa* would be missed from the Louvre."

His tone was so matter of fact, it seemed to have nothing to do with a compliment. In recent weeks, Kerry had had more compliments than in the rest of her life put together, but still didn't know what to do with them. She shied away immediately, unnerved.

"How many women a week do you say that to?"

He frowned into his Perrier and looked offended.

"None at all. I've never seen a woman who looks like you, though I'll grant you Paris is full of lovely women. You have some kind of energy in your face, that's all. It appeals to me, it's very striking and it's my definition of beauty. Purely subjective. I'm not an expert on the matter."

Belatedly, she fell back on Lu's methods.

"Thank you. I'm flattered, then. My name, incidentally, is Kerry Laraghy."

He slapped the table and laughed.

"I forgot! I'm Darragh de Bruin."

With a prim nod she went off to phone the language school. By the time she returned, his prickly mood appeared to have mellowed.

"I'm very glad you came back to the métro, Kerry. But I knew you would."

"How?"

"Instinct. You have to have faith in your own instincts and intelligence. Two essentials. Mine told me you'd be back. But if you hadn't come, I'd have found you anyway. I'm sure the Irish embassy keeps its visiting little rich kids on file."

He flashed her a white, brilliant, disorientating smile that threw her totally off balance. But she wasn't amused.

"Why are you so aggressive, Darragh de Bruin?"

"C'mon, Kerry Laraghy, relax! I'm just teasing you! Here, take a menu, pick something and tell me about yourself. What are you doing in Paris?"

"I'm taking six months off before I start my career. My father trains horses, and I'll be joining him in the business. But I wanted to see a bit of the world first."

"Ah, yes. Eamonn Laraghy, isn't it? I've heard his name. In his fifties and at the top, right? Are you looking forward to working with him?"

Was she? Yes. Naturally, she was. Yes. No. Maybe. One day.

"Well . . . I guess I am. I love the place, love the horses.

But I just felt a little, you know, pressurised. I needed time
to think."

"So. You sit around all day and think?"

Was he mocking her again? But he looked quite interested.
She felt unexpected gratitude to Lu for providing her with a
raison d'être.

"Certainly not. I study French, and wine, and cookery, and
grooming . . ."

"Grooming? That should come in handy, right enough,
when you rejoin your horses. And when will that be?"

"July." She snatched the menu he proffered, insolently.

"I see. Tell me something. If you weren't your father's
daughter, do you think he'd hire you?"

"I – yes, of course he would. I've grown up with the
business, I know it inside out. But if I weren't his daughter,
I might not want the job. My father can be a rather difficult
man."

She leered slightly at him, to indicate what she thought of
difficult men. But he ignored the tiny barb.

"How so?"

"He's excitable. Bossy. Flies off the handle, has to have
everything his own way."

"But you can manage him, is that it?"

"Yes. Usually." She grinned a reluctant, crooked grin. "And
what about you? What brought you here?"

He sighed as the waiter brought their steaming plates of
pasta, a bowl of parmesan and a carafe of rough red wine.

"To be perfectly frank, I don't know. Getting out from
under family pressure, I suppose, like you. Exploring. Trying
to work out some kind of framework for my life. Trying to
figure out how to contribute something to people, to society,
before I start taking anything out."

"Oh." She was nonplussed. Usually people said they were
trying to paint in Paris, or meet a millionaire rock star at the
Crazy Horse. His obscure candour perplexed her.

"So how are you going about that?"

It was well into the afternoon by the time he had finished
telling her, or trying to, haltingly, and she emerged from
the discussion as from a scalding shower. Never had she

suspected, much less identified, the terrible gaps, the yawning holes in her education, her imagination, her culture, her ideas, her whole life. She simply didn't *have* any ideas, she saw, like a child realising it is in a class too advanced for it.

Nothing, nobody he mentioned meant anything to her. Monet, Manet, Degas, Redon; Lawrence, Russell, Hegel, Shostakovitch, Klee, Genet, Simone de Beauvoir – nothing. A total blank, mere words she had seen on paper but never absorbed. All she could think of was how to get away from him, how to slink back invisibly to the sanctuary of Lu's apartment and hide, sit there burning with shame and ignorance.

It wasn't her fault that she knew nothing of art, or music, or literature, or botany . . . or anything at all. Was it? She could not apply herself to that, she was so busy keeping up with the conversation, not for his sake but for her own. Through his eyes a painting separated into its different dimensions, opening out into a mind game. A walk in a park became a floral festival, an ecological adventure, possibilities whirling through it like autumn leaves. A sonata was a celebration, a synthesis, music was not a fleeting pleasure but an integral part of everything. She didn't dare confess that she did not know the difference between a sonata and a concerto, a Monet and a Modigliani.

But he sensed her unease and slowed down, leading her through a maze of dissertation and speculation, going back to the beginning when she found herself in a blind alley. He had a map in his mind, and gave her directions, but left her to follow them for herself. It was like walking on ice – exciting, but frightening too. She knew she would make a false step eventually, and flounder, and that he would laugh at her even more acerbically than before.

But his discourse simply led into this uncharted territory as easily as water slipping down a precipice; there seemed to be no other way it could go. It was the lack of reference points she found so undermining. Everything seemed to turn to chalk and dissolve as she touched it, turn into something else that she couldn't grasp. And yet it was a compelling panorama that he painted, a vista with breadth and depth, without horizons, without absolutes. He saw, he

felt, he thought, he tried – and evidently he needed someone to
do it with, some kind of sounding board. But not her, surely?
She was just a girl fresh out of school; he was four years older,
a college graduate. When he stopped for breath he would
realise that, and be disappointed in her, deceived. For now,
he interpreted her silence as – what? Agreement? Languor?
Boredom? Her cheeks flamed with the awful mortification, the
revelation of her directionless life. But still his voice rolled
across the empty meadows of her mind, his eyes sparkling,
compelling. He was so fervent.

She did not want to leave. The stimulus buzzed in her
brain, making of it a magnetic field, alive with a new force of
irresistible intensity. It was as if a dam had been broken and
a cataract poured into every crevice, swamping her, carrying
her away. But there was no question of going with the flow.
She was totally out of her depth.

"Thank you so much for a very interesting afternoon,
Darragh. I've enjoyed it, and learned a lot from it. But I
have to go now."

The light quenched in his face, the urgent verve fell in his
voice.

"But why? Where? Don't, Kerry. There's something I
wanted to show you."

Letting her jacket fall back on the chair, she decided to be
honest with him.

"Look. This has been one of the most fascinating afternoons
I've ever spent. You've given me enough to think about
that I'll be busy for months, and it's been wonderful to
meet someone with so many new ideas. But I know *nothing*,
Darragh! There's no point in even pretending. I couldn't
begin to engage you on your level. And as for wanting
to show me something – well, you must realise that my
opinion is completely worthless. I'm just not equipped to
judge anything. And it's you, yourself, who have shown me
that."

He looked up, and for a few long moments said nothing.
Then he took her hand and clung to it like a lifeline.

"But Kerry, that's just the point. You have a blank canvas.
It's set up there on an easel waiting for you to fill it in. You

can put anything you like on it, make the brush strokes go any way you want. That's why I've enjoyed talking to you so much. You don't know anything about anything, but you're curious, so eager to learn, experiment. Your opinion *does* matter, because it's fresh, free of prejudice and therefore honest. Don't leave now!"

She hesitated, uneasy, unable to touch bottom.

"Darragh . . . oh, I can't. I'm ashamed of myself. It's dreadful to realise I've read nothing and seen nothing, been nowhere at all. I'd like to crawl into a hole and disappear."

"Kerry, don't be absurd! I don't expect you to know anything, you're too young – how old are you, exactly?"

"Eighteen."

"There you are. At eighteen I knew even less. But you'll see. This city – all cities – are full of people and places crammed with information, ideas, energy. I've only dabbled, it's ridiculous that you should be frightened away. I want to discover things *with* you."

There was no doubting his sincerity. He searched her face, anxiously looking for some kind of response, acquiescence. But the girl was not a fool. She was intelligent enough to admit to ignorance. Hardly likely, therefore, to succumb to flattery. But it wasn't flattery. He wanted her terribly.

"Why?"

"Why? Why do I want you to stay? Because you're interested, that's all. You don't follow all of what I say but you try to, your enthusiasms incline naturally to mine . . . maybe you don't realise how refreshing it is for me to meet someone who at least listens, who doesn't look at her watch and find a polite excuse to leave."

A thought struck him.

"You *don't* want to leave, do you?"

The authority drained from his voice, leaving it suddenly shy. He should have taken her to see a film, or window shopping . . . she was just the same as Monique, as all the girls. Another mistake.

"No."

Her voice was low, her tone neutral. But it was enough. His eyes filled with such relief that she could not but smile, with such unreserved frankness that he wanted to shout, jump on the table, burst into song, shake Émile by the shoulders till his teeth rattled. It was a smile like a sunrise.

"You'll come with me, then?"

"Yes. If you promise not to patronise me. I feel fool enough already."

"Stop knocking yourself, Kerry! You're a young woman with the whole world in front of her, that's all. You should be dancing in the streets, you'd have such a wonderful time on the way."

She looked at him gravely.

"Thank you, Darragh, for that advice from the elderly."

They both laughed as he helped her on with her jacket, wrapped her scarf warmly round her throat and paid the bill with a grin that left Émile suspicious. Had somebody left the wine off it?

Outside, the afternoon was lemon ice, lending a translucent pallor to the passing, anonymous faces. He took her hand in his and was astonished when she did not resist, apparently determined to shed, right now, whatever artifice it was that girls usually employed. In the low winter light her profile was clear, contemplative.

"You're not a busker for lack of anything else, are you?"

"No. I'm a lawyer, officially."

"Family?"

"An army."

"Where are we going?"

"To the Musée Rodin."

"Where's that?"

"Rue de Varenne, near the Hôtel des Invalides."

"What's in it?"

"Rodins."

"Oh."

They walked briskly. Kerry could not tell whether it was the exercise, or the wine, or the tingling cold that lit such a little flame inside her, diffusing warmth in all directions. She was excited, but not in the jittery way that preceded a party, or a trip, or a keen day's hunting across the dangerous walls and ditches of Kildare. It was a slow-burning, concentrated sensation that made her at once deeply contented and acutely alert.

"Let's get some *guimauves*." She loved the chocolate marshmallows.

They stopped at a stall and bought a bag from a toothless old man in a beret, and she was gratified to hear Darragh negotiate in a French far more eloquent than correct. Good, she thought, there's one thing I can do better than he can.

They sat down on a bench to munch the *guimauves*, and he laid his guitar on the ground.

"Aren't you going to play today?"

"No. Not now, anyway. Maybe later tonight."

He smiled vaguely, but her heart sank. Somehow she had envisaged spending the rest of the evening with him. But how? Where? Even if she could work out the details, it was unthinkable. Brian would worry, Lu would lecture . . . and yet it had seemed somehow inevitable. If not at her place, then his, anywhere, it didn't matter.

"Where do you live?"

"Ivry."

It was a long way out, on the southern fringe of Paris, not far from Kremlin-Bicêtre which she knew to be an unsalubrious neighbourhood. Even Yves hadn't taken her there, which made her itch to go.

"In an apartment, or with friends, or what?"

"If you could call it an apartment! It's just a studio, one room with a kitchen and bathroom, approximately the size of one of your horse's stables, up on the sixth floor. A friend had it, and I moved in when he moved out."

Good. He could hardly have a girlfriend cooped up with him in one room. Not that that was any of her business . . . but still she was glad it was only one room.

"Oh, Kerry, look."

He put his hand on her arm and pointed with the other to a very old lady tottering down the street in their direction. She was frail and bent almost double, whether from deformity or against the cold it was impossible to tell. One hand clutched her ragged collar to her throat while the other held a pathetic bag that swung impotently by her side. Her breath came in

long, slow whistles, and as she came nearer Kerry saw a
rheumy tear tremble in the corner of one pale eye. Impulsively
she jumped up and thrust out the bag of *guimauves*.

"Here – please – take these. And this."

She held out a fistful of money from her pocket. The old
lady stopped and gazed at her, uncomprehending.

"Please, take them. *Tenez, tenez.*"

She understood. Wordlessly she took the money and the
bag, looked at Kerry for a moment, nodded and shuffled
off.

Kerry sat back down, feeling the old lady's misery cut a
little strip out of her happiness.

"Oh, Darragh. How awful. Somebody should – oh, I don't
know, there should be some sort of care for poor people like
that."

"I didn't know the rich cared so much about the poor."

His tone was acid and it burnt.

"All right! I admit I'm rich, or rather my father is. But that's
not a crime, my crime! I've only just left school, I didn't make
the world, it's not my personal wrongdoing."

"It's everybody's doing, that all adds up to something like
that."

Of course it was. Hers and his and everyone's. But it was
unfair of him to blame her for it, when all she had done
was try ineffectually to help. From the distant past came
a memory of Maeve, debating one summer's evening with
the local curate, explaining how much charity work she did
while he explained how it was people like her who made it
necessary. The curate, then, had been accusing precisely as
Darragh was now.

"So what should we do? Forget the Musée Rodin and go
enlist with the Red Cross right away?"

He looked at her sidelong, and suddenly stood up, irritable,
impatient.

"Let's go, Kerry, or it will be closed."

It was virtually a command. Obediently she got up and
followed him, but she was seething. How dare he!

He set off so fast she had to run to keep up. She tugged
at his sleeve and looked with frank anger into his face.

"Hey. Don't stamp off like that. If anyone's to blame for poverty, it's you."

"I beg your pardon?"

"You. You men who run the world, and make such a bloody shambles of it. You have the power, and you abuse it. Muck everything up."

Politics, his favourite subject. But not now, when he was so angry he would not be objective. He knew he was being peremptory and nasty, making her pay for his failure to be first to approach the old lady. He resented, he realised, not her quick sympathy but his own hesitation. At this rate he would lose her very soon, antagonise her as he seemed to antagonise everyone.

"Sorry. You're perfectly right. It is a shambles."

She continued to stare at him for a long moment before permitting him a smile. "My mother would hate to see the company I'm keeping."

I'll bet, he thought, I'll bet. With an abruptly possessive gesture he slipped an arm round her waist and urged her to hurry. It was twenty minutes before five, and closing time.

Kerry scarcely had time to take in the sculptures that roamed wild in the grounds of the Musée Rodin as Darragh led her swiftly inside to his goal. But immediately she felt the power of the place, a strength emanating straight from the stone, from *The Thinker* and *The Burghers of Calais* and *Balzac*, old men and young men and men being made to say she knew not what at the hands of their creator. These were no mere statues, they were living beings released from their matrix, and Kerry wove a path through their jungle disturbed and uneasy.

Still she was unprepared for the sight that finally confronted her, hit her so hard she recoiled in shock. It was Rodin's *Kiss*: an organism so alive, so beautiful, radiating such perfect purity that she was immobilised. In each other's arms, the two tender young lovers fused, locking out all else, melting into a privacy that denied yet compelled the beholder, their love flowing from one to the other in velvet flux, suspending the ions of the air trembling on the lips of some invisible paradox. Each was strong but timid, erotic, the

context of the other, integral and entire. For an infinite length
of time Kerry stood transfixed. Then slowly, tentatively, she
edged a little closer, and the lovers moved with her. She
ached to touch them, they were so human, yet so elusive,
real and unreal all at once. From every angle their supple
undulating limbs cleaved closer and closer, one to another,
deeper and deeper in taut passion until she could bear to
intrude on them no more. Their kiss was a violently intimate
thing, sacrilegious to see so displayed. She wanted to weep
for them.

"Well?"

Darragh's voice was quiet, but it rang in her mind like a
shot. She twitched, but did not reply, and he brushed his
fingers against her hair, felt its electric charge, her whole
being quiver and leap away from him. Intuitively he quit the
room and left her alone.

Why, Kerry breathed, why do I feel like this? She hardly
knew how she felt. Stunned, her senses shocked as disinfect-
ant shocks a raw wound, but oddly quieted too, soothed, her
nerves bathed in a cool, healing balm she had not known
she needed. Her eyes clung to the little statue, her heart
profoundly touched by the lovers, pinned on the brink of
fulfilment, trapped in the plight of their own incarnation. It
was heartbreaking, an exquisite happiness that encompassed
and strove to conquer its intrinsic tragedy. On and on she
stood, mesmerised and unmoving until a distant bell clanged
and splintered the tableau in fragments.

The caretaker came, mumbling in French, and she realised
she must leave. Where was Darragh? She had not even seen
him disappear. With a last involuntary look she broke free
and went to find him, her soul churning, lingering behind.

He was sitting on a bench in the garden, his hands in his
pockets, moody and detached. Without a word she touched
his shoulder and he stood up, leading her away with her
face buried in his duffle coat. The stone stare of *The Thinker*
followed them out through the petrified garden and into the
hushed dusk, and for nearly an hour they walked on, together
but separate, each pursuing a silent path of thought that
required no explanation or justification. Around them the

bustling body of Paris wended its way home and left them alone in the night.

It seemed to be understood that they were going to the apartment out at Ivry, and that Kerry would cook dinner for them there, try one of the recipes she had learnt, a steak Diane perhaps, with asparagus and a good bottle of rich red Burgundy. Then some cheeses, a Gruyère and a chèvre and a strong robust comté . . . what came after that she wasn't sure, but they would talk at any rate, talk endlessly about statues and paintings and poetry and music, and maybe even horses until the illuminations of the distant city's landmarks were extinguished one by one.

That she could cook anything was an idea so far-fetched it made Darragh laugh, and she was indignant, incensed at his leering scepticism. She would show him, by golly. Laughing, he hugged her; she was adult and infantile by turns, sassy and yet so innocent, enchanting. In a supermarket they bought what food they needed, although privately he did not expect that they would ever eat a bite of it. Almost eight hours after lunch, he was hungry again, but his appetite was for her, not for her textbook repast. He could devour her right now, he thought, and she stifled a shriek as his hand slipped under her jacket, down into the waist of her jeans, grazing her back, dropping further, exploring.

Shocked, she pulled away and turned to remonstrate with him. This was not how people behaved in public. But she couldn't wait to be alone with him.

He wasn't classically beautiful by any means, in the careless way that Yves was beautiful, but there was a steeliness in his body as in his mind, hard and compact, a texture that was intriguing. Only Brandon Lawrence had ever had such an effect on her, reminding her of how her body fused with a horse's as the animal raced on a dawn wind, flying over the fields and ditches with a beat that made her blood thunder in her temples. But now, she could hardly remember what Brandon Lawrence looked like.

As they entered the apartment, laden with groceries, her eye lit on a stack of wood carvings piled high against the opposite wall. Odd carvings of nothing in particular, boats and animals and children's toys, small pieces of furniture, African masks; but if Darragh had done these, then he was an even better carpenter than musician. However, she had not come here to discuss the décor. She felt such lust for him, it made her head swim, her muscles melt.

Nonetheless, when he locked the door behind them she knew a frisson of fear. Did he just not want to be disturbed, or would he keep her here, against her will? She didn't know this man at all, she had not told Brian where she was, Christ almighty . . . but there was no going back now. Nor did she want to.

Without a word he packed away the food in the kitchen, returned to her and slowly, systematically, stripped her of every stitch she wore. Her jacket, her sweater, the blouse underneath, which he undid one button at a time, bending his head to lick and nuzzle at her breasts as he exposed them to his sight and touch. Then her jeans, kneeling in front of her as he removed the belt and undid the zip, peeling them away like the skin of a soft ripe fruit. Then her underwear, and at last she was naked before him, quivering, gasping as he slid a finger into terrifying new sensations.

His own clothing was a quicker, simpler affair, flung off into a corner as they surveyed each other in silence, and he put his hand on her shoulder to lead her, she thought, to the narrow bed. But he did not. Instead, he pushed her down onto the wooden floor, and lowered himself immediately on to and into her.

She expected it to hurt, the first time. But not this much. As his weight crushed her shoulderblades down into the rough wood she cried out, and again as he penetrated her, but he did not soothe or caress her. Instead, he raised himself up on his hands, staring intently into her open eyes, and set up a strong, fast rhythm that made her wince with pain, tears stinging her eyes.

It was agonising, it hurt so much, she thought she would die as he thrust harder, faster, deeper and deeper into her. It was a long time before her cries of pain turned to whimpers of pleasure and she decided, finally, that she would die of that instead. But only when he felt her shudder and dissolve beneath him, heard her actually yell aloud, her face contorted and her fingernails impaled in his back, did he allow his body to take over from his mind, his control to break loose. With a terrible groan, sweat pouring into his eyes, he collapsed on to her, clenched his teeth and shuddered violently.

So drained that speech was impossible, they lay there for fully twenty minutes afterwards, glued to each other, smiling, suffused in the soft warm afterglow. Her eyes dilated to a dark emerald green, she gazed into his, gently twisting a strand of his long hair round her finger, her lips brushing his face and neck, the smooth skin under his thick beard.

"Not bad for a beginner, huh?"

"Not bad."

His own eyes were so filled with surprise, joy and sheer exhaustion, they were almost black. Monique had never left him feeling like this.

"A beginner?" Suddenly he repeated the term, its import dawning on him. So that was what all that shrieking at the start had been about – it was her first time, he was her first man. He had simply assumed otherwise, but now he saw that he had done so without reason. She was just a young girl, fresh from a country where virginity was the norm at eighteen. Touched, he kissed her nose. And something struck him.

"You – you're not on the pill?"

She shook her head, unperturbed, sleepy.

"No. I've been on a tight leash instead, up to this. But it'll be OK. I'll find a doctor tomorrow, go on it first thing."

He gripped her grimly.

"You sure will, lady. This is a studio, not a nursery."

Nodding acquiescence, she returned his embrace. I could love this girl, he thought. But he did not say it.

Joy, on meeting Darragh de Bruin, was not unconfined.

Brian mustered a wan smile and hastened to confer, privately and anxiously, with Lu. Lu took one look at the tattered, bearded man and informed Kerry that this was not the type of person her parents, Claire and Lionel, expected to entertain at their apartment. Zoe spoke to him for about half an hour, shook her head and expressed surprise that so little time had gone by.

"What do you think, Yves?"

Yves picked up the fork with which he proposed to tackle Kerry's *coquilles St Jacques* and gazed intently at her through its tines.

"Put it this way. These potatoes, *chérie*. They are light and fluffy, yes? Moist, mouthwatering, a joy for all the senses?"

"Certainly."

"I rest my case. You can produce marvels, when you try."

Sagely, he bit into a morsel, and Kerry stared at him, aggrieved.

"You mean you think Darragh is – dry? Heavy?"

"Did I say that?"

"No, but you meant it, you sod. Well, we can't all be flighty will o' the wisps like you, Yves Tiberti. Darragh may not know a pink bolero from a blue peplum, but I find him extremely exciting and interesting, and I won't hear another word against him."

Nor would she, from anyone. But, conscious of the unease that descended, unfairly and inexplicably, whenever she introduced Darragh into their group, she spent more and more time alone with him, and got to know him much better as a result. Impossible to define the exact moment at which she fell in love with him, but she did, dreadfully.

July loomed, and she was at her wits' end.

"Darragh?"

He looked up from the small, complicated wooden boat he was carving and motioned that she might fill his empty beer glass.

"Yes, Kerry?"

"How – how long do you plan to stay in France?"

"Not much longer. I signed up with Voluntary Service Overseas last Christmas. I'm going to Africa in September, to work in a developing village in Senegal."

"Africa! Oh, how exciting! Why didn't you tell me?"

"Why would I? You're going back to Ireland, aren't you?"

His casual tone flattened her heart like a steamroller, but

she supposed he was only being sensible, had not wanted to
cast a shadow over their time together. How lucky he was,
and how free! Dismally she thought of Kilbally, where her
own narrow path inexorably led, and then of Africa, of which
she had lately heard so much from Yves's immigrant friends.
Africa, where the sun shone and the wild elephants roamed
. . . God, even they were freer than she was!

It isn't fair! I love Daddy, but he's asking too much of me!
I want to see more of the world, I want to go on wandering
and learning, I want everything this man can offer me!

Would he offer it, if I asked?

"Darragh?"

"Mmm?"

"We're well suited, don't you think?"

"Quite well, yes."

"What would you say if – if I said I'd go to Africa with
you?"

"I'd say your father would take his shotgun to us both."

"But if I could get round him?"

"Could you, do you think?"

Airily, she beamed a confidence she did not feel.

"Oh, yes. I always – usually – do. Anyway, I'm an adult
now. He can't force me to do anything I don't want to. And
I don't want to work with him, not now anyway, not until –
how long are you going to Africa for?"

"Two years, minimum. Maybe three."

"That's great. Ideal. I'll be twenty-one then. That'll be time
enough . . . you'll be going back to Ireland too then, won't
you?"

"I suppose so. But I don't make long-term plans, Kerry."

"Not even . . . not even for me?"

There, she thought frantically, with a rush of mixed panic
and relief. I've called his bluff. He'll have to put his cards on
the table. If he says no, I'll go home. But if he says yes . . . Oh,
he must say yes. He loves me. I know he does. He's never said
so, but Irishmen are the strong, silent type where emotion is
concerned. He'd take me with him to the ends of the earth.

Half-amused, half-annoyed, Darragh reflected. A woman
had not been in his calculations at all. But then, he had

never met one like this before, so keen to do everything, try everything, taste every flavour. And such a stunner in the sack, now that she had grasped the nettle . . . the kind of woman it would be a great pity to lose.

Losing was not what Darragh did best.

"Tell you what, Kerry. I'll go home with you in July and we'll talk to your parents. I'm older than you, they'll listen to me, I'm sure."

Yes! She was just a child in their eyes, but he was a grown man.

"Oh, Darragh! Africa! It's wonderful! You're wonderful!"

"Kerry, Africa is amazing, but it's not wonderful. It's poor, it's dirty, it's . . ."

"It's divine, and I'm going to adore it! I adore *you*!"

Do you, he thought, immensely gratified. Do you, indeed?

"Oh, my God, Brandon, look at this!"

Marianne pushed her sunglasses up on her head and held out her newspaper to her husband. It was the *Irish Independent*, more than two weeks old, but even here in the Aegean summer sun Brandon could never quite switch off. It was vital that he read all the financial pages, particularly after a winter so stormy, a spring that had been fraught with uncertainty. But unlike Marianne he did not read the gossip pages. Dozing comfortably on his deck lounger after a big breakfast, he opened one eye but did not take the paper from her. It would not be the kind of news he would deem important.

"What is it, darling? Read it to me."

"It's the Laraghys – you remember, Maeve and Eamonn in Kildare, we always go to their New Year party? Well, you'll never believe it, but it says here that their daughter has run off with a pauper, got married in Paris three weeks ago and is planning to go and live with him in Africa! Can you imagine? Poor Maeve, she must be distraught! And Eamonn has cut the girl off without a cent, they've had the most awful row, it says."

She passed the paper to him and he grabbed it from her, paling under his tan as he sat up, so that she thought he was going to be sick.

"Oh, Brandon, you look pale. Are you sure that big breakfast was wise?"

Without a reply he buried his head in the paper and disappeared from her view. Oh, well. He was on holiday, he was entitled to the occasional big meal if he wanted it. Astonished, but not greatly upset by the news in the paper, Marianne pulled her sunglasses back down and stretched out on her sun lounger to digest it. How very extraordinary!

The print blurred slightly before Brandon, but Kerry's photograph was unmistakable, the first time he had seen her face for eight months. It brought a ghastly curl to his stomach, and he knew instantly that it would be better not to read the story at all. His marriage was healing now, slowly, but better every day; he should not present it with even this slight risk after all that had been accomplished. But he could no more resist reading the story than the sun could alter its course high in the blazing cobalt sky.

His vision cleared, and there it all was, almost a quarter of a page devoted to the strange tale. Kerry Laraghy, the eighteen-year-old heiress to trainer Eamonn Laraghy, had met a busker in the métro of Paris and married him four months later, in the mairie of Kremlin-Bicêtre. The civil ceremony had been attended only by her brother Brian, his fiancée Lucienne de Veurlay, and one other friend. Neither parent had attended, and it was understood that Eamonn Laraghy had severed all ties with his only daughter, who had originally been expected to join him in training some of the world's greatest racehorses. The couple were now preparing for departure to Senegal on Africa's west coast, where they would take up third-world voluntary work after the wedding of Brian and Lucienne, scheduled for September 10 and also, seemingly, a source of extreme vexation to Eamonn Laraghy who was not expected to attend this ceremony either.

Brandon's heart contracted as he let the newspaper fall to the deck. A busker! A girl like Kerry, so bright, so beautiful, so promising in every way . . . it was heartbreaking. What a terrible, terrible waste. Vividly he remembered her as she waltzed into his arms, falling, laughing, dizzy, incarnating the brand-new year in her own tantalising young body that night in the ballroom of Ashamber when he had, he thought, fallen head over heels in love with her.

It had been no such thing, of course. It had been the indulgent self-deception of a man weighted prematurely down by overwhelming business concerns and a stagnant, burdensome marriage. Now he could see it in perspective, quite clearly since the dreadful day he hit Marianne and all his troubles came pouring out, he knew it had been nothing but midnight madness. A flash in the pan, a ship in the night, whatever; just one of those things.

Now, with Marianne eagerly, happily reciprocating his own efforts to mend the marriage, he felt no further need of Kerry Laraghy. Certainly not the acute, aching need he had felt that night, and for so many nights afterwards. Sure, her photograph still made something tighten a fraction in his chest, but that was just the normal reaction of any healthy young man to a gorgeous young girl – very young indeed, almost thirteen years younger than himself. How absurd ever to have thought she could mean anything more than that! Brandon grimaced as he thought what a fool he had made of himself.

But a busker—? What kind of stupid, wilful thing to do was that? And now she was ostracised by her family, penniless, and on her way to darkest Africa? Had she taken leave of her senses? After such a comfortable, cosseted life as she had led, one day of this volunteer nonsense would kill her!

Who was he, this man who would permit it, take her with him? A gold-digger, whose plans had backfired? Or just a thoughtless adventurer, footloose and carefree as once he had so ached to be, himself? A young man, of course. No ties. No children.

Brandon could see his own from where he sat, leaning over the side trying to catch some fish on makeshift lines. Two happy kiddies on a summer cruise with their parents, immensely privileged kiddies who would one day be faced with the choice of accepting their own destiny, or rejecting it.

He had elected to accept his own, make the best of it, and his efforts were rewarded. For the first time in his life he was almost happy in the rash marriage contracted, under so much pressure, while he was still little more than a youth. Alone, he could not have done it, but he had to admit that Marianne was meeting him more than halfway.

He turned to her and smiled as she stretched languidly in the hot rays of the sun, as contented as a tabby cat before a glowing fire. Indeed there was something almost feline about her, she was so sleek, so purringly pleased with life as she lay there supine and indolent. But she deserved this holiday, after five months of painful work on their marriage. It had been very hard, but they were doing their best, and their best seemed to be working. After banishing her mother to a flat of her own, Mari even spoke now of having another baby, without any apparent concern what pregnancy might do to her figure at thirty.

Slowly some of the old vigour had seeped back into Brandon, his taste for life revived, and he was grateful for the weight eased off his shoulders. Standing up, he padded over to Marianne in his bare feet, lean, tanned and fitter than he had felt for a long time, his hair and eyebrows bleached a startling blond by the sun, so that he looked Nordic, a Viking.

"Drink, darling?"

She raised her sunglasses to squint up at him against the light.

"Mmm . . . lime juice, please. I'll just go and check on the children while you're getting it."

There were no nannies on this voyage, no staff at all. Greg, Louis and Brandon were sailing the yacht themselves, their wives were cooking and minding the children, and everyone was having great fun. It was the perfect way to spend the month of August, with everything dead on the business scene anyway.

Mari hitched up the straps of her polka-dot swimsuit to attend to the kiddies, but before she could get up her husband's lips were on hers, his tongue seeking its way into her mouth, his hands pulling the straps back down again.

"The children are fine, Marianne. Greg can see them from

the wheel and Susie can see them from the galley. Why don't you and I have a little quickie before they miss us, h'mm?"

His fingers began to find their way inside the swimsuit and she felt herself liquefy under their touch. Urgently she stood up, took him by the hand and almost ran with him down to their cabin.

Part Two

6

Kerry sat sprawled on the sand, her right foot idly tracing patterns in it, her left hand slapping absently at the flies and mosquitoes, a beer bottle grasped in her right, her eyes narrowed against the incessant glare of the sun. Even now, after two years, she couldn't get used to it; it left her drained, her energy sapped long before noon each day. Which was just as well, she sometimes thought, since there was nothing to channel it into. Nothing at all.

"Congratulations, Kerry! I'm so pleased for you!"

Cameron McKinnock was beaming at her, raising his own beer bottle in salute.

"Thanks, Cameron. I'm glad somebody is."

Her tone was fairly weary, ironic. Not at all, Cameron thought, the jubilant exuberance of a young mother-to-be; rather the same tired tone he often caught in the voices of the other young women in the village and in Dakar too, girls no older than she but already worn out by their fourth, fifth, sixth pregnancies. They had their problems, and he understood their exhausted indifference. But in Kerry Laraghy it was inexcusable.

"Oh, come on, Kerry, snap out of it! You should be thrilled. I'm sure Darragh will be."

"Cameron, I'll wager you my last bottle of beer that Darragh will be very far from thrilled. *Au contraire.*"

She took another swig of the warm beer and scratched the blister on her thigh. Why she persisted in wearing these totally unsuitable shorts and T-shirts, instead of covering up like the locals, he could never fathom. Her fair skin would never accept the ravages of this climate, and yet she stubbornly refused to adapt. For such a bright girl, she could be incredibly stupid.

"But of course he will! Why on earth not?" Cameron felt uneasy in the knowledge to which he, as a doctor, was the first to be privy. He had thought he was bringing good news, but evidently he was mistaken.

"Why not? I'll tell you why not, Cameron. Because Darragh de Bruin is a pig-headed, self-centred bastard who's far too busy saving the world to give a tuppenny damn about his own wife, much less any child who might take the spotlight off him for three seconds." Vaguely she waved her free hand up and down the beach, and beyond into the dusty nothingness, to indicate "the world" of Darragh de Bruin.

"Don't be so hard on him, Kerry. He has achieved a great deal, you know, given enormously of himself. He deserves credit – particularly from his own wife."

"From me? Why would he need it from me, Cameron, when he gets it from everybody else? He doesn't need anything from me – certainly not a baby, to tie him up and tie him down, put a crimp in his style."

Cameron smiled a little despite the bitter twist to Kerry's mouth. There *was* something swaggering, swashbuckling about Darragh, something that precluded the vision of him rocking any small babies to sleep. You had to laugh at Darragh, because if you took him as seriously as he took himself, he would suffocate you. But then Cameron was older than Kerry, more experienced in treating people as they deserved to be treated. Quietly he stretched over to her and laid his hand on her forearm.

"Every man is pleased and proud to hear he's going to be a father, Kerry. Darragh will be delighted to hear he's going to have a little replica of himself, just you wait and see."

"Yeah, well, I'll grant you that, Cameron. The idea of another wonderful little warrior marching into the world to save it probably will flatter his pride, right enough."

Irritated with her and yet sorry for her, Cameron drained the last of his beer and stood up.

"I have to get back to the hospital, Kerry. Look, why don't

you go indoors and get some rest? You'll roast alive out here, it's almost midday."

"Sure, Cameron. I'll do that. Take a nap in that big fluffy bed of mine, turn up the air-conditioning and take a nice cool bubble bath, maybe call up a few girlfriends for a chat about matinée jackets."

Cameron wrestled an urge to shake her. What the hell had she expected, coming out here? If she hadn't been prepared for the filth and the squalor and the poverty, the heat and the insects and the lack of sanitation, then why had she agreed to come? But he knew why. She had come because she was a teenaged girl who knew no better, madly in love with her new young husband, dying to see the world. Well, now she was seeing it.

"But Kerry, how can you call him self-centred and accuse him of being a *salvator mundi* all in the one breath? He can hardly be both."

It was the first time that she had openly admitted the marriage was in trouble, and the admission made Cameron most uncomfortable. He thought of his own wife, Fiona, nursing their new baby back at the bungalow; even if they had any personal difficulties, which they had not, they would never air them publicly like this.

"Because he's not doing it for them, Cameron!" She opened her eyes wide enough to stare at him as if he were a backward child. "He's doing it for himself! For the personal honour and glory of Darragh de Bruin!"

There was a grain of truth in that, Cameron knew, a messianic zeal in Darragh that basked in the reflected lustre of Dakar's new prison rehabilitation unit. Every time a convicted murderer or felon was released back into society, waving a chair or a table or some such object carved with the aid of his talented teacher, Darragh's picture appeared in the local newspaper. Not that too many people could read the details of what he had done, but they made the association.

Everybody for miles around knew what a wonder-worker Darragh de Bruin was, how he had come here to give Senegal the benefit of his immense talents, free gratis, for a period of two years minimum. From day one he had launched into his mission with gusto, taking up his remedial work with the prisoners of Dakar's overflowing jail, teaching them crafts, English, music, anything and everything that might permit them to carve new lives for themselves upon release. Simultaneously, they were saved from themselves and society was saved from them, and they were equipped to earn a living into the bargain.

The programme was working perfectly. Working because Darragh worked so hard at it, with such steely determination, such single-minded dedication. And now, if his marriage was working less well as a consequence, Cameron was not entirely surprised. There was a price for everything, particularly success. That was tough for Kerry, since she seemed to be the price in question, but somehow Kerry had failed to fit in from the start. Cameron got the feeling that this expedition had started out for her as a lark, an adventure that had gradually gone beyond a joke. She was very young, very wilful and impetuous, a most attractive and likeable girl but one who had seen little of life.

To her, Senegal was simply an exotic, alluring destination; the reality of it had never crossed her mind, Cameron was sure, for an instant. Even now, she could not pinpoint it exactly on a map, could not gut fish or skin chickens without the most theatrical show of distaste, could not bargain in the markets without getting into a fight. It was a whim, a romantic impulse that had gone wrong – badly wrong, possibly. But there was nothing Cameron could do about that. He had his own work and his own wife to think about.

He climbed onto his bike and blew her a kiss.

"Take care of yourself, kid. And cheer up – he *will* be pleased, I'm sure of it. Oh – and you shouldn't be drinking, you know, in your interesting condition."

With a wave over his shoulder he pedalled off in a cloud of dust.

"Och, aye, Dr Cameron" she called after him, and cracked open another bottle of beer on the cement step of the hovel that was home. "Cheers. Here's to a bonnie wee baby."

* * *

Cycling the six flat, arid miles that separated the fishing village of Yoff from the steaming, stinking humidity of Dakar, Cameron kaleidoscoped the thing in his mind. It was none of his business, but he had thought Kerry was on the pill. Indeed he had seen her himself at the hospital's family clinic, one of the few women both eager and interested in the powers of the magic pill. So how come this, now?

The last thing Kerry needed was a child. She was still just one herself. What she needed was what she'd had when she first arrived in Senegal; a thirst not for beer but for life. Then, she'd been perky as a sparrow, lively, curious, adventurous, all that a healthy young woman should be. It was quickly obvious that she could not live in Dakar, where the heat was simply too much for all of them, but she'd settled soon enough into Yoff, out on the coast with its godsent cooling breezes. Within weeks, she'd even found a job, teaching English to a group of Dakar businessmen while Darragh taught carpentry to the prisoners and worked on the building site of a new medical facility too, during his allegedly free time.

They'd seemed happy, then, making easy friends with himself and Fiona and the rest of the small ex-pat community, returning to the bungalow in Yoff each evening on their bikes or in some rattling car in which they'd hitched a ride. At nights they would all eat in each other's houses, companionably swigging beer out on the verandah or the beach, swimming naked in the moonlight, smoking pot from communal joints as they set the world, and Senegal in particular, to rights.

Kerry had cropped her hair shorter and shorter until she could almost be mistaken for a boy, freckles multiplying like amoebae all over her face and body, smelling faintly and permanently of aloe vera, joining animatedly and intelligently in their ongoing arguments about the Senegalese economy, politics, society, infrastructure, future . . . anything and everything. Barely ten years released from the shackles of colonialism, the country's history reminded her of Ireland's, she said, even if it was the French and not the British who were the villains of this particular piece. The legacy of oppression was much the same: a deep pessimism riding on the heels of the initial euphoria of independence, a chronic cash shortage, an utter lack of confidence in the people to run their own affairs.

As a doctor, Cameron did not strictly approve of marijuana, but sat there smoking it nonetheless, night after night, unable to tear himself away from the whirlpool of talk. Kerry had opinions, ideas, but he could see that they were only recently formulated, not fully thought through, still embryonic but often worthwhile, usually sensitive and always original. But ultimately it was Darragh who called the shots, who made them all distinguish between theory and reality, put their money where their mouths were. If helping the people of Senegal meant slaving away in foul conditions for no money and even less thanks, then that was what they must do. And that was what he, Darragh, most certainly did.

But after a time the strain began to show on Kerry. Not immediately, maybe only after a year or even more. She never talked about her home in Ireland or her family, and Cameron sensed some mystery there, some life that had precious little to do with volunteer work, or Senegal, or Darragh de Bruin. Once, Fiona had got it out of her in a moment of girl talk that there'd been a row, she'd been cut off, but that was all. Cameron, often homesick himself for the rich deep valleys of Scotland, for the wild heather and snow-capped peaks, detected a growing loneliness in Kerry, but did not probe too deep. It was, after all, her husband's concern.

That Darragh loved his wife, Cameron did not doubt. But he was a strong, vigorous man, utterly resolved to make his mark on Senegal by rescuing the poor of Dakar, the downtrodden, the defenceless. That his wife might need help too never seemed to cross his mind; he expected her to fit into this new life with the same iron will he exerted himself. Now, after two years, Darragh had certainly come, seen and conquered.

But Kerry had not. Slowly she wilted like a rose in the desert, parching, the vitality leaching out of her until she blended with the white sand. She grew impatient with the businessmen, who would not apply themselves to their studies with anything like the professionalism of Europeans, and she grew impatient with the thankless, feckless natives who lolled lethargically indifferent to anything she did for them. That they had never invited any of the volunteers did not occur to her, but it did to Cameron. Would Europeans have thanked any Africans who tried to impose their laid-back attitudes on stressed, materialistic Europe? It was simply a culture clash.

They did not attend the basic hygiene classes she set up for them, on Darragh's suggestion, nor the three-R classes she set up on the beach for the children of the fishermen. The spoken language was French, but most children were semi-illiterate, and their resolve to remain so began to grind her down. Cameron could not say she hadn't tried, but he could not say she'd succeeded either. Sadly, he cycled on into Dakar.

It was late when Darragh got home to the tin-roofed bungalow on the beach, hot, tired and looking as always for sex and food, in that order. Even now, with the first rush of passion gone out of their marriage, and some of the bloom of love too, it never ceased to amaze Kerry how his sexual appetite remained undiminished. After a long day's hard work in crushing heat, he still could and usually did demand sex as soon as he saw her, and again later after they'd eaten, and sometimes in the middle of the night as well, and yet again before they got up next morning.

She knew it was all part of his fierce assertiveness, his need to dominate, his rough raw urges that he had never bothered to refine or control. It became ritualistic, wearing, but in the early days it was often softened by genuine tenderness, by long post-coital talks way into the starry nights. They still talked about art and philosophy and music, all the things that captivated her imagination when they first met, but eventually they began to get hemmed in for lack of stimulus. Dakar offered little in the way of theatres, galleries, museums or concert halls: Yoff was so completely culturally impoverished that people would flock round in droves just to hear Darragh play his guitar for half an hour.

But at least there were the other ex-pats to talk to. Mostly volunteers like themselves, they were an educated, articulate bunch – far better, Darragh maintained, than Kerry's idiotic society friends in Paris, the abrasive little New Yorker who'd taken such an instant dislike to him, the gay poofter with his flamboyant clothes and vapid chatter, the romantic fool of a brother and his bossy, chilly girlfriend. Of the lot, it was Lu he detested the most, with her papa's precious château and her model's preening vanity, and only Zoe had ever seen how much the pair had in common. They were the movers and the shakers, the ones who ran every show, other people's lives included.

He threw his bike up now against the stilts of the verandah, sniffing the air hungrily. A fish stew, he thought: good. He was ravenous. At least that cookery course in Paris had made a housewife, of sorts, out of Kerry, she could tell a swordfish from a halibut.

"Kerry! I'm home! Is that your bouillabaisse I smell?"

The cooking area of the all-purpose room was lit only by candles and a paraffin lamp. At first he couldn't see her in the shadows, but then she materialised, silently, wraith-like. As always, he only had to see her to know that he wanted her.

"Hi there. And how's my little Irish colleen this fine evening?"

Usually she liked it when he adopted a jokey Irish brogue. It made her laugh and smoothed his way into her shorts. His hand slid inside the thin cotton of her T-shirt, and he felt the nipple harden on her small, silky breast. But she drew back from him.

"She's fine, Darragh. She's pregnant."

The shock was such that he did not immediately absorb it. Several seconds elapsed before he gaped at her, open-mouthed.

"What?"

"Pregnant. You know, with child. *Enceinte*. A lady-in-waiting."

"But – but *how*?"

"The usual route, I believe. No immaculate conception or anything, despite the godlike status of the father."

"But Kerry! What about your pills? You haven't forgotten to take them, for crying out loud?"

"No. Food poisoning, actually. You remember, when I threw up that pork a couple of weeks ago?"

He did. She'd been out on the beach half the night, retching into the sea, doubled over with pain until finally he'd had to go over to the McKinnock shack and wake Cameron, get her something from his first-aid box. She'd been pale for a day or two afterwards, quiet, shying away from sex, but the thing had passed. Or so he'd thought.

A baby! But they couldn't have a baby, out here in these conditions! It was impossible. It would howl day and night, drive them crazy with its incessant demands. It would interfere with his work, just as baby Sophie did with Cameron's. Oh, no. No way. He wasn't having this on his plate as well. Not now, with so much to be done . . . a shaft of irony pierced his mind as he thought of the construction in progress in Dakar. When it was all finished, the city would have a most serviceable new maternity unit.

But it was for native babies, not his own! He thought quickly and came to a swift conclusion.

"That's terrible, honey. But don't worry about it. It was just an accident. We'll get Cameron to take care of it. Or – or recommend somebody, at any rate."

"Take care of it?"

"Well, you know – fix you up. After all, we didn't plan it, it wasn't your fault you were sick. We'll make a baby some other time, Kerry, when we're back in Europe and in a proper position to be parents."

Through the grey dusk, her eyes stabbed at him like two sharp green icicles.

"Have an abortion, is that what you mean?"

"Yes. Yes, that's exactly what I mean, Kerry. There's no question of having a baby out here. We just can't afford it, in any sense."

"We? Aren't I the one who's having it?"

"Don't play games with me, Kerry! You're my wife and you'll do as I tell you!"

His voice filled with such menace, suddenly, that she retreated backwards, clutching at the cooker behind her, stumbling over the gas tank on which it ran. But she would not let him frighten her like this.

"You can't tell me to murder somebody, Darragh."

"It's not a somebody yet, Kerry, it's just a blob of jelly! Look, how pregnant are you, exactly?"

"Two months, almost."

"Right then, there you are. It doesn't even have a brain yet, its limbs aren't formed, it can't see or hear or think . . ."

"It's a person, Darragh. It's our son, or daughter. It has a soul, a being. Which is more, sometimes, than I think I can say for you."

He heard the sob rising in her throat and knew that, any minute now, there would be tears. Dear God, but he could not abide weeping women!

"Oh, listen, let's not fight about it now, huh? It's late and I'm tired. Let's eat our stew, have a beer and go to bed, there's a good girl."

They did as he suggested, in silence. In bed, that night, she refused him for the first time. Unable to charm, cajole or reason with her in any way, he could not get her to yield, and had to prise her legs apart. Next morning, husband and wife alike were covered in cuts, bites and bruises.

"Stoppit, Zoe."

"Stop what, Dad?"

"That infernal tapping on your teeth with that pencil. It's making me nuts."

"Oh. Sorry."

Agreeably Zoe put down her pencil, picked it up again and began to tap on her glass-topped desk instead, malevolently gazing at the open pages of an atlas. It was nearly six, time to call it a day, and still she hadn't found the right place.

At this rate, it would be too late and they would miss the whole shooting match. There would be a big blank space in the middle of *Cosmo*, where Zoe Zimner's swimwear for summer '72 should have been, and a line in bold type stating that "this space is brought to you by Richard and Zoe Zimner, who missed their deadline on the shoot." The prospect froze the blood in her veins, made her so desperate she couldn't think straight.

The atlas began to swim before her eyes. Get a grip here, Zoe, go have yourself a cup of coffee.

She went to the perker by the window and poured them both a cup, forcing herself to think of something else. Her mother's new hairstyle came first to mind, a shocking business unveiled just this very morning to her speechless daughter and husband. Carla was a scream, really, going bright red like that at forty-six years of age – not just a discreet auburn or burgundy, but straight from blonde to orange, overnight. Zoe wasn't sure if she liked it, but it was undeniably eye-catching, it reminded her of Kerry Laraghy, sitting with the sun behind her in the Café Cluny.

"Dad! That's it!"

"What's what?"

"Senegal, Dad! It's perfect! It will be cooling off there now, it's got palm trees and a coastline, buckets of native colour, straw huts and exotic flowers and weird animals, dense jungle – it's ideal for a shoot! And" – what a great idea – "we'll ask Kerry to be one of our models!"

Unusually for him, Richard agreed with very little argument. He had other projects in hand, and the *Cosmo* shoot was not quite so uppermost in his mind as in his daughter's. He wanted it over and done with, he had to be in Venezuela by the end of the month. And besides, he liked to humour his only daughter whenever he could. If going to Senegal meant she got to see her friend, fine. But what made her think Kerry would be so great – or any use at all?

"Oh, we were always trying to talk her into it in Paris, Dad. She's really tall and slim, with this terrific long red hair and huge green eyes – a fresh outdoor look, something totally new. She'd never do it then, but I bet she would now – there can't be much excitement for her out there in the boonies, with that unspeakable man of hers. Oh, come on Dad, say you'll give her a try?"

"I'll give her a try, Zoe." He grinned affectionately at her. "But no way will I depend on her. We're taking Sarah, Willow, Lee P'ai and Gold Brown with us too, and anyone else the agency can talk into going to your desert outpost."

"Whee!" Zoe did a little jig. "Thanks, Dad. Leave it all to me. I'll call the airline and the agency and we'll go right away, next Monday say if we can round everyone up by then."

"OK, honeybunch, you do that. It'll be good experience for you to organise an entire shoot, get you out of your sketchbook for a change. Now, what are we going to take home to your crazed mother for dinner? Pizza? Chinese? A shrink?"

Zoe wished she could've called Kerry before they came. But apparently the de Bruins were not on the telephone, there was no way to warn them or get directions. She would just have to suss the village and ask around.

That was easy enough. A tall boy in the first ramshackle hut she came to pointed out the similar structure in which she might find Kerry. Zoe trotted over to the hut and stood slack-jawed with horror. Jesus H Christ. This couldn't be it. Could it?

She climbed the steps and knocked on the door. No answer. Another knock, harder. No answer.

What now? Just wait, Zoe supposed, hang out here till she comes back. Which could be a long time. What the hell. She would take a stroll down the beach, see what locations might catch her eye. Those brightly painted fishing boats might be good, for a start.

Hands in pockets, she wandered over to inspect them, her sunglasses deflecting the ultraviolet, a scarf draped over her tiny nose to ward off the dust and the terrible smell of rotting fish. Phew. It was worse than the Bowery.

And then, out of nowhere, she saw Kerry. Even from a distance she knew the tall redhead immediately, standing so utterly apart from the other long graceful figures on the beach. The Senegalese were a handsome race, seemingly friendly and cheerful despite their poverty, but Kerry just looked so totally different, not only because she was white, but because she was a stranger amongst them.

Shrieking with excitement, Zoe set off at a sprint and soon caught up with Kerry, who was ambling along the water's edge at a snail's pace. She carried something on her back, a rucksack of some kind. It was a – sweet, suffering Satchmo – it was a *baby*. A real, live, pink-faced, blue-eyed baby. Zoe skidded to a stop just as Kerry heard her name called and whirled round.

Impossible to tell which was the more shocked: Kerry as she saw her old friend appear out of a clear blue sky, or Zoe as she took in the skinny, pregnant waif with the swollen belly, bitten limbs and huge grey circles under the eyes.

This can't be her, Zoe thought for a frantic split second. This is some kind of sick joke. This isn't Kerry Laraghy.

But then she was in Kerry's arms and they were hugging, so tight Zoe thought she would asphyxiate, laughing and crying, clutching feverishly at each other.

"Zoe! Oh, Zoe! How – what – when—"

"Just this morning, to do a shoot! Oh, Kerry, I'm so happy to see you!"

"And I you, you little leprechaun!" Kerry laughed and Zoe had her first brief glimpse of the girl she once knew. "Come on, we'll go home and get rid of this child, crack a beer and you can tell me all about it."

Hesitantly, Zoe glanced at the baby slung native-style on her friend's thin back. It seemed a lot sturdier than its mother. But then its mother had another to carry as well, already grown big and heavy inside her.

"Congratulations, Kerry! I didn't know you'd had a baby. Why ever didn't you write and tell me?" She tried to muster pleasure.

"Oh, no, Zoe, this one's not mine. This is Sophie. She belongs to my friends Fiona and Cameron McKinnock – that's their bungalow up yonder. I'm just minding her while they're at work. He's a doctor and she's a nurse, at the hospital in Dakar. My own isn't due for nearly three months yet."

"Oh." Zoe expelled a sigh of relief. One wasn't quite as ghastly as two. But Kerry looked as if she'd had ten. Zoe took a deep breath and decided to shoot, as usual, from the hip.

"Kerry, I have to tell you – you look bloody awful. What's the matter? Are you ill?"

No answer. Kerry stared down into the sea, then out to the horizon, then looked back down at her perky little pal in the trendy trousers and the uptown shades.

"No, I'm not ill, Zoe. Just a little tired, that's all. It's been a very difficult pregnancy."

There was a fenced-off note in her voice that sounded a warning to Zoe. Don't ask.

OK. For once she would be diplomatic and not ask. Not now. She'd wait till they got settled together, take Kerry out for a nice lunch somewhere and then get it all out of her. She looked like she could actually use a square meal, Zoe thought, shuddering. She knew Kerry's father had cut her off, of course, but where was this husband of hers? This was too ludicrous for words.

Mentally, glumly, Zoe scrapped her from the list of models for the shoot. Even had she not been pregnant, they couldn't have used her. Her hair was gone, her skin was a mess, her eyes looked like two dredged pools of mud, she was more starved than slender. Zoe's warm heart went out to her, ached for her. Clearly there had been some kind of disaster or crisis, to bring her to this. At twenty, she looked older than Carla.

She braced herself as they neared the hut. It was going to be grim. But with painful delicacy Kerry did not ask her in, bringing two chairs out on to the verandah instead. Removing the infant from her back she deposited it in Zoe's lap, who received it as if it were a ticking time bomb. She knew as much about babies as she did about astrophysics.

"Here. It's too hot to go inside. I'll bring us some beer out here."

The chair was rickety and Zoe could not settle herself in it; but there was a big shady palm tree only yards away. Moving to that she sank down in the sand and looked gingerly at Sophie. Emerging with the beer, Kerry screeched in fright.

"No! No, Zoe, get up, get up!"

In six strides she was standing over them, dragging Zoe to her feet, pulling them away.

"Sorry if I scared you. But the coconuts can fall at any minute, and kill a small child like Sophie. Kill anyone, for that matter. You can't sit under the palms when the fruit is ripe."

Zoe didn't argue. She hadn't come all the way out here to get brained by a coconut. What an awful country, she thought, returning to the strip of bleached raw timber that Kerry called a verandah.

"Now, Zoe, tell me all! Everything. How are you? Have you heard from Yves – or Brian, or Lu?"

Zoe winced at the pathetic little question, so eager, so tentative. Brian and Lu were still furious, she knew, refusing to accept Kerry's outrageous African Queen act; Yves was hurt that Kerry never replied to the postcards he continually sent. But no wonder. Stanley Livingstone would be hard pressed to find her out here, never mind a postman.

"Yes, I have. Brian was in New York on business last month. You know that he and Yves have gone into partnership? Lu's father loaned them the money and they've got a salon and an atelier in the seventh arrondissement. They're calling their label TLC – T for Tiberti, L for Laraghy, C for Clothes. Yves is doing all the day stuff, and Brian's doing his big night numbers."

She glanced sidelong at Kerry. If anyone could use some TLC, it was this lady, by the look of things. But Kerry nodded, approvingly.

"That's great. I always knew Yves would do well, and Brian too after I saw the wedding dress he did for Lu. What a stunner! And what about you, Zoe? How's Daniel?"

"Oh . . . dear old Danny Boy! We broke up after we got back to the States. He decided that fashion wasn't his thing and went off to UCLA to study art history. But we keep in touch, are still pals."

"And your sportswear, that was so urgent you missed my wedding?"

Zoe grinned from ear to ear.

"Flying. Absolutely flying. I even do flying suits! I love it, Kerry, and it's going just great. I've got orders from Saks and Bloomingdales already, Neiman-Marcus, all sorts of places. I guess it didn't hurt to be Richard Zimner's daughter at first, but now I'm known for myself."

Hastily, Zoe checked her glowing success story.

"Uh – Dad's here with me, in fact. I left him at the hotel with a bunch of beautiful women. He's going to photograph my swimwear for next season, for *Cosmo*, wouldja believe? I've moved into his loft in the Village and we work together – father and daughter, the invincible Zimners!"

Oh, shit. From bad to worse. Ten minutes, and already she'd said the wrong thing, twice. The pain vanished from Kerry's eyes as fast as it came, a barely perceptible flinch, but Zoe saw that happy parental partnership was precisely what Kerry did not need to hear about. With rising desperation, she changed tack.

"Where's Darragh? He must be pretty thrilled about this baby of yours, huh?"

"He's at work."

That was all. Subject closed. Zoe groaned inwardly and abandoned the conversation. Later, when jet lag was no longer making a jelly of her brain, she would draw the whole story out of Kerry. She was here for a week, they would have plenty of time.

Sure enough, it all came spilling out, first in a trickle and then in a torrent. Horrified, Zoe listened without a word, realising that the confession was therapeutic for Kerry; despite her sociable acquaintance with the McKinnocks and with many of the fishermen's families, she was clearly, desperately lonely.

At first, it had been the homesickness, the purgatory of being banished by Eamonn. That alone had been heartbreaking. She had been so sure he would relent, as Maeve had, after meeting Darragh. But where Maeve had detected fine intelligence and potential in the driven young altruist, Eamonn had seen only an impudent brat. In vain both mother and daughter had wheedled and pleaded, until finally Eamonn threw a monumental scene, and both Kerry and Darragh out of Ashamber.

Next, it was the hot muggy hopelessness of Senegal. Unable to keep pace with Darragh, aware of being judged and found wanting, Kerry had wilted as Darragh flourished. Nothing seemed to work, everything she tried floundered and failed, even the people she was supposed to be helping were better able to manage their lives than she was. They were not starving, after all, this was not Biafra or Bangladesh, merely an immature and slightly confused country that would get on its feet with or without her.

Then, it was the marriage. Darragh's interests widened

way beyond domestic affairs, he was in Dakar from dawn to dusk, leaving Kerry to look out for herself. Only at night, she admitted, stammering, her lip trembling, did he start taking any interest in her. Their sex life had turned from a voluptuous feast into a disgusting orgy, another trophy in her husband's rampant ego, a horrible nightmare that extended, now, even to marital rape.

. And finally, it was the baby. The tiny creature brought into being by no will or act of its own, that Darragh had wanted to kill purely for his own convenience. After she defied him on that, he became increasingly belligerent and threatening, never quite violent but rough, callous, frighteningly moody. He pushed and shoved her about, he used his tongue on her like a whip, abusing her physically and verbally even in front of other people.

Zoe was aghast. Remind me never to get married, she muttered darkly to herself, if this is what love does for you. But meanwhile, what was to be done? Kerry was so shaky, she was heading for a nervous breakdown, and physically she was a wreck. Nothing in Senegal agreed with her – not the sun, which darker-complexioned people like Zoe loved – nor the people, who were likable, feckless and impossible – nor the food, which after a week Zoe could heartily understand.

Never had she envisaged conditions such as those in which Kerry lived, without electricity, running water, telecommunications of any kind. Nothing. Even if any of it could be got, Darragh did not believe in drawing distinction between themselves and the local peasants; they could and would live as the natives did. When Zoe tried to talk to him about it, he told her sharply to mind her own business, and after many wasted words her antipathy to the man began to turn into a positive allergy.

By Friday, she had made up her mind. She got into the jeep rented for the shoot, drove out to Yoff and took Kerry back to her hotel in Dakar for dinner, making not even a polite pretence of inviting Darragh. That he cordially returned her frosty sentiments was abundantly clear; they had hated each other from the first moment they met in Paris, and no longer bothered to disguise it.

Kerry was looking better tonight, her cheeks stained with a little faint colour, wearing an olive silk sundress that Zoe had hijacked from Gold Brown. The models had lots of clothes, Gold didn't mind, whereas all Kerry's own lovely clothes lay abandoned in France and Ireland. There hadn't been room for trunks of such frippery on the way out – and she wouldn't need them, Darragh had said, using up their full luggage allowance for his books and carpentry tools. Zoe had yet to see Kerry in anything other than tatty shorts, colourless shirts and a hideous maternity smock borrowed from Fiona.

Zoe called the waiter and ordered for them both without consulting Kerry, and then reached down into her tote bag.

"Here."

Kerry took the envelope and slit it open with her breadknife. Photographs, undoubtedly; Richard had taken dozens, and she was curious to see the results.

It was a one-way ticket, first class, to New York.

"What – Zoe, what's this?"

"What does it look like, Kerry? It's a heist. We're airlifting you out of here."

Slowly Kerry put the ticket down on the table, saying nothing, touched to the quick by her friend's concern and generosity. How could she explain to her why she could not accept it?

Anticipating argument, Zoe held up her hand like a policeman diverting traffic.

"Don't say anything, Kerry. Let me say my piece first."

Kerry frittered at the napkin on her lap.

"Say it."

"Item one. I know you're going to give me that Irish Catholic spiel about marriage being for ever. Fine. Then you don't have to divorce him. But you don't have to live with him, either!

"Two. Your equally pigheaded Irish pride is going to say you can't call it quits. Let me tell *you*, where I come from we don't call that pride, we call it stupidity. You own up to your early mistakes, learn from them and go on from there. You don't pour your whole life down the tubes over something you did at eighteen!

"Three. Money. You think you haven't enough to go live in the States. But what have you got here? Nothing, that I can see. We'll find you a job in New York . . . and what about that trust fund when you turn twenty-one? Will your dad have closed that off too, do you think?"

Zoe paused for breath. "And four, think of the baby, Kerry! This country has cholera, typhoid, malaria, polio, yellow fever . . . the works. Political problems, economic problems, social problems. What kind of education or future can you hold out to a child here?"

Piqued, fretful, Kerry twisted the napkin into knots of agitation.

"OK, Zoe, enough, enough! Look, let me answer your questions. I do worry about the baby's future. Of course I do. And about money – I'd be very surprised to receive a red cent from that trust fund in December. As far as I understand it, Dad wrote me out of the whole script.

"As for my marriage . . . yes, it *is* a permanent commitment. I can't just run away from it."

"Kerry, you *must*! You have no choice! Darragh has proved that he doesn't deserve your love or loyalty at all. He's just beating his chest and playing the caveman, not behaving like a proper husband, not even earning your respect."

"But Zoe . . . maybe this sounds crazy, but in some strange way I do still love him."

"It's not love, Kerry, it's infatuation! And even if that's enough for you, it's not enough for your baby. You have a duty to the child as well as to yourself, and it doesn't lie here with the king of the jungle! Does it?"

Kerry sighed, not meeting her eyes.

"Oh, I . . . I just don't know, Zoe. I thought I was breaking free of my future, and now I'm trapped in the present. Where would I go, what could I do?"

"You'd move in with me. I'm twenty-two now, and that's far too old to be living at home with Mom and Dad. I'm going to find a place of my own and you're going to share it with me."

"But I – Zoe, I haven't any money. Not one cent of my own. I couldn't afford a night in New York, much less to live there."

"You can stay at my parents' place with me until I find an apartment and you find some means of support. It'll be like old times back on the rue St Antoine."

"Oh, Zoe, I just don't know . . . look, let me think about it, OK?"

"OK. Sleep on it, and then decide fast, 'cos we're outta here tomorrow night. Come with us, Kerry, make the break and pull your life back together, while there's something left to pull!"

"All right. I will sleep on it, and let you know tomorrow."

Zoe nodded and called for the bill, concealing her surprise. She would have expected a lot more resistance from Kerry Laraghy. In Paris the feisty redhead could be positively incandescent when she got into argument; here, she was barely lukewarm.

Kerry awoke early next morning. It was only just after six, but Darragh's side of the bed was empty. A vision of him out in the other room, preparing breakfast for her, made her stifle a dry laugh; never in a million years would it occur to him to bring breakfast in bed to his pregnant wife. Getting up, she threw on a shirt and padded out on to the verandah to inspect the new day.

It was a beautiful morning, the clear sky glazed a pale, limpid green as the sun edged up over the horizon, faintly streaking it with pink, gold and sapphire. As yet the beach was deserted, nobody moving except for a few distant fishermen already loading their nets into their longboats. Not the slightest breeze ruffled the palm leaves; only a couple of iguanas leaping up the bark of the trees betrayed any sign of life. The sand, at this hour, was fresh and pure, washed clean overnight by the tide, and at its fringes little wavelets lapped gently, shushing among the shells. Later, the sun would rise high and fierce, the water glinting under its relentless power, but for the moment all was silent, tranquil, serene.

Kerry inhaled deep lungfuls of the tangy, salty air, marvelling at the glassy quiet of this sometimes turbulent stretch of the Atlantic. They were well into September, though, soon there would be storms for sure . . . Was that music she heard?

It was. Down by the water's edge she spotted Darragh, cross-legged in the sand, wearing only shorts, peacefully playing his guitar. She recognised the song: it was "Galway Bay".

Her heart clenched. Ireland! So far away, so far beyond her reach. She could never go back there now, ashamed, defeated, admitting her failure to the father who might not even have her back. Yet she ached to see him, see her country, with its own Atlantic dawns, all down the length of its own west coast, so very beautiful . . .

No. This was not the time for nostalgia. This, as Zoe said, was a moment for reason, and decisiveness. Steeling herself, she stepped off the verandah and walked purposefully down to where her husband sat.

"Morning."

"Morning."

He played on, conjuring a picture in her mind of all Galway's little fishing villages, so strangely like this one four thousand miles away, only they had drystone walls, trawlers instead of skiffs, wild wind-torn trees instead of palms, neat whitewashed cottages instead of concrete shacks . . . but the sea salt on the air was the same . . .

"Darragh. I want to talk to you."

"If it's about the baby, I'm not interested."

The finality of the words hit her like a brick. Right. If he wanted to play rough, he would get it rough.

"Darragh. Put that thing down and listen to me. I'm leaving you."

The flash of shock that scorched his features afforded her a brief, bitter pleasure. So he did care, did he?

He hit a wrong note, and stopped. But his recovery was fast.

"I beg your pardon?"

"I said, I'm leaving you. I'm going to New York, tonight, with Zoe and her father. I'm not coming back."

"I see." He paused, considered. "May I remind you, Kerry, that you're my wife? At your own insistence, I might add."

That was true. He had merely wanted her to live with him, it was she who had demanded marriage or nothing, competing with Brian, as furious with her father as she had been humiliated by him. Wives were not welcomed by Voluntary Service Overseas, but she had got her way, even without the skills that Fiona McKinnock could offer.

"Yes, Darragh. I know that. That's why I will continue to be your wife, although we could divorce under French law. I took you for better or worse, for richer or poorer, in sickness and in health. But look at it, Darragh! It has been for worse, hasn't it? And certainly for poorer. As for sickness – well, that's all you seem to think my pregnancy is. A nuisance bout of the baby blues. We can't go on like this."

His next words rocked her back on her heels.

"But, Kerry, I do love you. You know that."

The words she had waited for, so long; but now they were in a foreign language, flung at her, incomprehensible.

"*Love* me? Is that what you call it, when you're raping me?"

"*What?!*"

"That's what it's called, Darragh, when you force a woman to have sex against her will. Whether you happen to be married to her or not is irrelevant. I don't call it love, I call it bestial, and unworthy of you. Of us both."

She could see he was genuinely taken aback, an army of arguments marching across his face. But abruptly he picked up his guitar and began to play it again, softly, some snatches from Edith Piaf, as if he hadn't heard her. "La Vie En Rose", "Je Ne Regrette Rien" . . . Was he actually mocking her? Again? *Now?*

Despite herself the music wafted her back to Paris, to those dusty-blue days by the Seine, those bright green mornings in the Luxembourg Gardens, those nights afloat on wine and talk and love in the studio at Ivry . . . at least, it had seemed like love, then.

He smiled up at her as she squatted back on her heels.

"So. My wife is leaving me, is she?"

He seemed so unperturbed she was flummoxed. But then he added the rider that clinched it.

"And it's that American cow who's done her thinking for her, is it?"

Cow?! How dare he speak like that of Zoe, her dear friend, who cared so much more about her than he did himself? Zoe, who had understood her misery when he had not even noticed it.

"Yes. Yes, it is. She's worried about me, and about the baby."

She knew he caught her drift. He put down the guitar once more and looked at her – almost, she thought, with a glimmer of amusement.

"Kerry. Even when people are married, they're still two independent individuals. They can't force attitudes or emotions or lifestyles on each other. If you need, or want, to go, then go."

That was it? That was all? No scene, no fight, tears, pleas? Nothing?

"Yes. I'm going to pack now, which shouldn't take long. Zoe is coming by at noon to pick me up."

They stared at each other like sphinxes.

"Fine. But I'll tell you something, Kerry. Our marriage isn't over. You'll come back to me one day."

"Don't be ridiculous, Darragh."

"I told you that before, remember? I knew you'd come back to find me in the métro, and you did. And you'll come back for me again."

"You egocentric fool! There's only one condition under which I'll ever speak to you again, Darragh, and that's if and when you acknowledge the existence of our child and come to me prepared to be its father. A real, proper father and husband, who cares as much for his own flesh and blood as he does for the shambling millions of Africa! Until then, I will never even tell the child that it has a father, much less who or where he is, that he rejected it before it was even born."

Suddenly furious, she stood up. "Goodbye, Darragh."

He didn't answer. As she strode away from him she heard him pick up his guitar and begin to play once more.

It was "When Irish Eyes Are Smiling". She burst into tears.

* * *

Fiona McKinnock was waving from the bungalow, signalling with her hands and mouth that he should come up and have breakfast with them. Oh, well. They might as well know sooner or later. As much as they needed to know.

He turned to them conversationally.

"I've decided to send Kerry home for a rest. She's been having a tough time with this pregnancy."

Cameron frowned. Kerry was planning to fly at six months? Should he not have been consulted? And where exactly *was* home, anyway?

"I mean, home with her friend Zoe, to the States. She could use a break, poor thing."

Puzzled, Fiona and Cameron eyed each other across the table. This was very sudden, to say the least. But Kerry had been so distant lately.

"Well then, we'd better go and wish her bon voyage."

"Oh, I wouldn't disturb her. She's having a lie-in. Such a long flight ahead of her."

Kerry was sleeping late? But they had seen her down on the beach not ten minutes ago. There was something distinctly fishy about all this. But the cut of Darragh's jaw precluded questions: a steel shutter had clanged down over his countenance.

"So – will you be coming into Dakar today, then?"

"No. I'll wait to see her off, give her a farewell kiss."

Going to work was out of the question. As were farewell kisses. He knew he would be unable to cope with either. With an airy wave he saw the McKinnocks on their way and wandered back down to the beach, dying a sudden death inside himself, savagely distressed.

How could things have come to this? Was she really so miserable? She hadn't always been, only since that damn baby was conceived, making her so withdrawn and mopey. It was her hormones; they must be out of kilter. The thought cheered him somewhat.

As for this business of having "raped" her – it was absurd. She liked their sex play a little rough and tumbled, it gave her a kick. She was imagining that he had taken things any further than that, embroidering and exaggerating them in her mind the way women did. Rubbish.

But as for her rebuttal when he insisted he loved her – that did hurt, badly. Couldn't she see it? She knew he wasn't the type who made flowery speeches, but his love and need of her were obvious, as obvious as Senegal's love and need of him.

Which was another thing. Why couldn't she settle down here? Why must she be so impatient, expecting miracles of people whose initiative had been systematically stolen for centuries? Drive and enterprise were simply new concepts to them, that was all. Rome was not built in a day.

As for poverty . . . well, maybe that was hard to take, but that was the idea, to see how the other half lived! In Paris she had yearned to turn every stone, plumb every depth. Then, she had looked up to him as her teacher and mentor, with eyes full of adulation and admiration, so impressed by all he showed and told her. Other girls preferred bars and dances to museums and galleries, but not her, and admittedly it had been very convenient, unable as he was to afford conventional means of impression. He thought of the day he took her to see Rodin's *Kiss*: how thrilled she had been, how perceptive in her response! The female, she claimed, was more in love than the male, you could tell from the way she leaned into him, grasped him more firmly than he did her.

And he would have battled a thousand armies sooner than confess that he loved her just that tiny bit more than she did him – enough to marry her, even, when he had no need or want of a wife. And now, here she was claiming that he didn't love her at all! But that was ridiculous. Yes. Her hormones had clearly run wild. When she had the baby she would return to normal, wake up to herself and start missing him, come running back.

Only this time his certainty did not border quite so firmly on the cosmic. It took him the rest of the day, two swims and several miles of walking on the sand, to kick Kerry out of his mind.

Killian Laraghy was yanked, kicking and bawling, into the world on the icy Christmas Eve of 1971. Such was his resistance to the idea of being born that Kerry began to think he would not come at all, that he was going to struggle with all his might to stay inside her for the rest of his days. Trust Darragh to stick her with such a bloody little prizefighter.

The nurse placed the messy bundle in her arms and she peered down at it, dubiously, resentfully. How dare such a puny scrap of a thing give her such a hard time? Her insides felt like a punchbag. Whatever it was she was supposed to feel, she didn't. No bonding, no swell of emotion, just pain, resentment and doubt, in that order. What was she supposed to do now? The manufacturer's instructions weren't very clear. Thankfully, she handed it back to the nurse and slid down into merciful sleep.

"But Kerry, you can't register him as Killian Laraghy! His parents were – are – married. Darragh is his legal father."

"Zoe, I bore him and I'll name him. His father's name can go on the birth certificate, if it must, but he'll be known as Laraghy. Who knows? That might even please my own father. Anyway, you can be godmother, if you like."

Zoe did like. That baby urgently needed somebody around him with a head more firmly fixed on her shoulders than Kerry Laraghy's, and the discovery of this latent maternal instinct astonished Zoe as much as it mortified her. Paying Kerry's hospital bill, which was colossal, she gingerly drove the two home to Riverside Drive and made a pot of tea while they considered what to do next.

Shamefaced, Kerry nursed the baby reluctantly. She hated having Zoe pay for everything like this, and she hated the screeching wretched baby. Why hadn't she done as Darragh wished and got rid of it? Stubborn pride, that was all. She'd wanted it just because he didn't. And yet pride had not prevented her accepting Zoe's unlimited help since last September.

"Look, Zoe, now that he's born, I'm not taking another penny from you. He can go to a crêche and I'll get a job, repay you as fast as I can."

But Zoe was not concerned about the money. She was concerned about the likelihood of Kerry ever getting a job.

Already she had helped her find five, before the birth, but every interview had ended in failure. People were put off, Kerry said, by her pregnant state: nobody wanted to grant maternity leave or wait until after the child was born. Zoe hoped that this was so. But the plain truth of the matter was that Kerry hadn't tried very hard, languishing in African lethargy that was very provoking. Furthermore, her qualifications were nil, and her breezy attitude to that was beginning to rankle. Two years ago, Kerry had left perfectly good career prospects in Ireland to flit off on a whim to France, where she had married on another whim and floated away to Senegal on yet another.

Naturally patient as a rule, Zoe suddenly felt the exasperated need to knock sense into her friend.

"Good, Kerry, I'm glad to hear it, because tomorrow starts now."

"Just give me a day or two, Zoe, that's all . . . well, it might take a week or two, I suppose."

Maddened, Zoe did not return the winsome smile. A day, a week, a month . . . she should have left the silly slob in Africa after all, to stew in her own damn juice. Abruptly, she rounded on the lazily nursing madonna.

"No, Kerry! Your time's up! I gave you a birthday present the other day, and another one for Killian, and now it's time you gave me something to celebrate! There's always some kind of work to be got in a big city like this. Try the bars, the pizza parlours, the nightclubs, the big houses over on Fifth Avenue. And get a job by January 1, because otherwise I'm kicking you out on the street."

Stunned, appalled, Kerry gazed at her in consternation.

"But Zoe, that's only three days away!"

"Exactly. Let's start the new year as we mean to go on."

Kerry's eyes filled with tears. She'd just had a baby, for God's sake! She was worn out. Why was everybody being so mean to her? First Daddy, then Darragh, now even Zoe? Not to mention that horrid child who clawed at her incessantly, sucking and biting at her as if she were a milch cow, just like his father.

It wasn't fair. It just wasn't fair.

Guiltily, Zoe subsided. Perhaps she was being too harsh, too soon. But now she had issued her ultimatum, she would stick to it. She had supported Kerry for three months already. Even a part-time job would be evidence of firm intent.

"I don't care if it's only answering somebody's telephone for a few hours a day, Kerry, and I don't care if it pays peanuts. The point is that you're taking a hike to the nearest employment exchange tomorrow morning. Your salad days are over."

7

Eamonn poured himself a second whiskey and Maeve judged that the moment was right.

"Look at this, dear. A letter from Kerry. She's had a baby boy."

Eamonn grunted. She could have a bloody soccer team of them for all he cared. He whooshed a shower of soda into the tumbler and returned to his armchair by the fire, not answering.

"We're grandparents, Eamonn! Isn't it marvellous? I'd so like to see the little fellow . . . shall we send her some flowers?"

Maeve's tone was wistful.

"Ye can send her anything ye like, Maeve. Just leave me out of it."

He got up again and went to the window, pulling back the heavy velvet curtain to peer out into the night. Would those damn dogs never stop barking? The lambs always had this effect on them, driving them to yowl night and day, driving him to distraction. If they didn't shut up soon he would go down there to that barn and give them what for, by God.

"Oh, Eamonn. Be reasonable. It's been over two years. Don't you think she's been punished enough? Haven't you punished yourself enough, for that matter? The both of us?"

He had. Christmas had been a wretched affair, and New Year, and the ones before that. The hole in his heart where Kerry had been gaped wide and deep as a moon crater. He knew what those looked like, now that he had witnessed the first landing on that planet, via television here in his own sitting room. He had never thought to see such a thing in his lifetime.

But that wasn't the point. The point was that Kerry had betrayed him, welshed on her promise to him, left him for some bewhiskered bloody busker. He would never forgive her. She would pay for her marriage for the rest of her days, just as he had paid for his. Not that revenge was sweet. It was sour as dandelions. But there it was.

"Look, Maeve, ye know ye're perfectly free to do whatever ye want yerself. Send her all the flowers ye like, go and see her if that's what ye want. But I'll not have anything to do with any of it."

Maeve considered. She knew how he ached for Kerry, piling up the pain inside him until it was palpable, poisoning his whole life, his mind and even his body. He was a heart attack waiting to happen. But she also knew that, like his horses, he responded far better to carrots than to sticks. Deliberately she let the letter lie visible in her hand, with Kerry's large script flowing alluringly across it.

"I tell you what, dear. Why don't we both go to America? I'll visit Kerry and the child, and you can go down to Kentucky to meet this Schuster man? You know you're going to have to do that soon in any event."

He was. Bill Schuster, a former lumberjack from Oregon, had made a fortune out of forestry, bought himself a Kentucky ranch complete with two dozen horses of varying quality, and now wanted to meet Eamonn Laraghy with a view to his training them. If he got the commission, it would be Ashamber's biggest overseas deal to date.

Among the animals, Bill had genially assured Eamonn over the phone, were several very promising colts, fillies and geldings. Eamonn was champing at the bit to see them already.

Would he take the carrot? Maeve got up and poured herself a rare drink, not letting him see how her hands were shaking, how she was holding her breath. Not that Kentucky was anywhere near New York, but it was in the same country, it was half the battle. Once there, she would figure out what to do next, how to get the stupid, stubborn pair of them together. It was time for at least a little forgiving and forgetting – with effort on Kerry's part, too.

Eamonn exhaled a spiral of smoke from his pipe. He knew from experience that what Maeve wanted, Maeve usually got. And he did need to meet Schuster, right away before the man called up Vincent O'Brien instead. If he could kill both birds with one stone, get into Maeve's good books and Schuster on to his, simultaneously – well, why not? Just so long as he didn't appear too eager.

"All right. Have it yer own way. I'll go down to Kentucky and do a bit of business, ye can stay in New York and do a bit of shopping, see the wretched child if ye must."

Maeve didn't know whether that referred to their daughter or to their daughter's son, but she didn't care. He would have to fly to New York first; there were no direct flights to Kentucky out of Ireland. Eureka! On the plane she would ply him with whiskey, pamper him, butter him up in every way humanly possible, and by the time they got there . . .

Neither of them ever saw the Uzi as it splintered the window and spattered the room in a storm of bullets, showering glass, whiskey, soda and blood in all directions, fountains of the liquids mingling and spurting high up into the air, soaking the lovely carpet, walls, furniture, everything.

Kerry Laraghy had told a lie, Amos Finkelstein reckoned. She had told him, amidst myriad other gifts and fruits of the gab, that he would not regret hiring her. Now here he was, barely a month later, regretting it sorely already.

First, it became quickly apparent that she didn't know nearly so much about literature as she claimed. All that waffle she had blinded him with during the interview, about Proust and Camus and the rest of it, had been precisely that – waffle. Oh, she could charm the customers all right, charm the pants off them, but she couldn't deal with the serious ones, the ones in search of specific references and information. Already he'd had to move her from the modern literature section to the romances and thrillers section, and if she continued as she was going it would soon be the children's section.

Then she had come in late, three times already, breathlessly claiming some fresh crisis with her baby. As a rule Amos steered clear of hiring mothers for this very reason, and in omitting to mention her son at the interview she had, Amos maintained, told him another lie.

And now, there was a personal call on the line for her, some agitated long-distance voice jabbering and squawking, demanding that he produce her. Amos did not approve of staff receiving personal calls at work, it cluttered up his lines and distracted attention from the customers. Since it sounded so urgent, he would let her take it, but just as soon as she was through he was going to have it out with her.

Grimly he handed her the receiver but stood his ground, ungraciously refusing to budge six inches out of earshot. But, when she spoke, everyone in the shop heard her plangent cry.

Wide-eyed, her face taut and aching from crying, Kerry stared out of the tiny window, tears streaming down her cheeks long after she thought there could be no more left to weep. Three thousand miles, from America to Ireland, but still she wept, desolate, desperate.

Not knowing. That was the worst, this frozen suspense in which she was held, just as the plane held her aloft, locked in, poised over the grey infinite ocean.

Maeve, she knew, was dead. That was final, unarguable, a stark fact. But her father, Eamonn—! At this very moment he might be breathing his last, dying all alone in some hospital bed, without her.

Was he in pain? Was he conscious? Asking for her? Or already just a cold dead body, like her mother? Frantically Kerry urged the pilot on, faster, faster, *faster*! Oh dear God, let it hurry, let it get there soon, in time. But flying at over five hundred miles an hour, the plane felt like an elderly mare, plodding along some country road, taking an eternity to reach its destination.

Oh, Daddy, Daddy! No! It was all a mistake, some terrible mistake, Eileen had got it all wrong, she must have . . .

Unseeing, she gazed down on her first view of her homeland as it slid at last into sight, languid in the early morning. Here and there herds of cows trooped in orderly file to their feeding troughs, fat and sleek in the pristine sunshine, the dewdropped green hills and valleys unrolling behind the cleft of the Shannon estuary with its clear sparkling waters, tumbling dawn-bright down into the white Atlantic rollers. Flying low, the plane circled and lost altitude, descending at last – but only into Shannon, to drop off passengers and drive her into a ferment of tortured anguish.

Then up, and on again, over the peaty brown midlands with their bogs and castles and copses, until Kildare lay below, mauve in the morning mist, lush and peaceful . . . home. She craned her neck for Ashamber, but could not see it. Minutes later, the aircraft arced in a wide semicircle out over Dublin bay, its emerald islands standing sentry in the twinkling azure waters, and banked steeply for its final approach into – into what?

The hospital, or the – the morgue? Despite the drowsy warmth of the cabin, Kerry's teeth began to chatter violently, her hands icy as her mother's on her cold marble slab. Scarcely had the plane touched down than she was running, running into the arrivals hall where Eileen's husband Paddy stood waiting for her.

Stifling his horror at first sight of the girl, her face like a puff adder's, Paddy led her out to where Maeve's Bentley stood ready for the short journey to the Mater hospital.

From Paris it was little more than an hour back to Ireland. Brian sat upright and composed, his face paper-white, throughout the entire flight. He did not weep, he did not speak, he hardly moved a muscle, not even to comfort Lu when she began to dab at her eyes with a small linen handkerchief. When she reached for his hand, he moved it away, recoiling into himself like a wounded deer. But she understood, and left him alone. Later, she knew, his need of her would be very great.

Neville McCormack was waiting to meet them, and at first Brian did not recognise his mother's friendly neighbour. Silent and shrunken with shock, Neville stared in turn at the two statues standing before him, the woman protecting her privacy in dark glasses, before helping them into his car and heading for the hospital.

*   *   *

Brian made it. Kerry did not.

Eamonn Laraghy died, far more peacefully than he had lived, moments before Kerry struggled free of the phalanx of journalists on the steps of the hospital. Hustled inside by two strong young doctors, she broke free and set off at a run through the maze of corridors, following the signs for Casualty. But not in time.

She knew it immediately she flung open the door and looked into Brian's brown eyes, as glassily blank as Eamonn's.

"He's gone, Kerry. He's gone."

Brian's voice was raw as sandpaper as he clenched himself against the lacerating grief that rose up in his gut. He stretched out his arms to her, but she did not even see him, only her father.

"No! Daddy! No, NO!"

It was the wail of a banshee, so shrill it froze the blood in Brian's veins. In one move Kerry flung herself headlong on Eamonn's dead body, stretching the full length of him, entangling her hair and clothes in the tubes and cables still attached to his face and limbs. Her shrieks and sobs were heartbreaking, but dazed, overcome, Brian made no move to restrain her. For fully ten minutes she lay prostrate, holding Eamonn's dead body, crooning into his ear, brushing back the little wisps of hair from his temple, hugging him as if to will him back to life. A doctor came to reason with her and she swore at him; another tried to prise her off and she struggled in his arms, kicking and scratching until a nurse was called, and sedation administered.

But even through its calming stupor she stood up, racked, and turned to Brian as if it were still a matter of life and death.

"Did – did he suffer, Brian? Did he speak? Say – anything—?"

He knew what she meant.

"No, Kerry, he didn't suffer. He was drugged, most of his nerves were destroyed anyway. He didn't even know I was here."

"He didn't – didn't – ask for me?"

"Kerry, he couldn't."

"Oh!"

She sank suddenly onto a chair, and Brian went to her then, gripping her to him as she folded and shuddered in a feeble way that was alarming.

Never, amidst all the tangled leaves of her life to come, would Kerry discover how happy her father had been at the moment he was shot. How delighted Maeve had been by the way she had found for him to go to her at last, without losing face, without pretending he'd been brought to America under anything other than the most urgent pressure of business and the most reluctant protest.

The funeral was a vast affair, but afterwards Kerry was unable to remember anything about it: who was there, who conducted the service, what Bible reading had been chosen. Numbly she blanked the whole thing out of her mind, refusing to believe it was happening, had happened.

Hundreds of mourners thronged Ashamber all that day, sympathising, speculating, profoundly shocked. Sometimes, if the deceased were very old and had died peacefully, an Irish wake could take on an almost festive air, with irreverent laughter, banter, food and drink. Dutifully Eileen provided the latter, but the hush of stunned bewilderment lay on the house like a pall, and if anyone needed any reminder of the sombreness of the occasion, Kerry's face furnished it.

Many of their closest friends were unable to attend: Zoe, minding baby Killian in America; Yves, in Australia on a first promotional visit for TLC; Lu's parents Claire and Lionel, away on business in Singapore. But other, older friends clustered round, warm and close, buoying the devastated family on a wave of stricken solidarity.

Desperate to rouse Kerry from her sleepwalker's trance, they enquired curiously about the baby, hoping the subject might stir her.

"Where is he? He'd be such a comfort to have here with you, Kerry."

"He's only two months old. I was afraid the altitude in the plane might damage his ears."

Indifferent, Kerry let the conversation drift off around her.

She didn't want to talk to anyone, she wished they would all go away. Eventually they did, and finally the day came when she was alone in the huge, empty house with Brian and Lu. But tomorrow, after the will was read, they too would leave for France, and the prospect panicked her. No love was lost between herself and Lu, but Lu was the one who was coping with everything, holding all the fragile threads together. In the two years or more since her defection to Senegal, neither Brian nor Lu had ever contacted her, and yet she found she needed them now. What would she do, when they went? Stay here, alone, or go back to that child, that chafing job, that expensive apartment she couldn't properly afford? For a year, or two, or ten? Run away, again?

What would she *do*?

In her heart she knew it was Lu who had caused Brian's chill antipathy, Lu who blamed her for declining all advice and choosing Senegal over the charms of France, the waiting duties of Ireland. Brian had sided with her, cutting his sister off, and at a stroke their childhood bond was gone. In its place lay a vacuum, a brittle politeness that irked Kerry more than any outright showdown, and she could not help the bitterness she felt.

Had she not accepted their marriage, against her instincts? Had she not tried to win Eamonn round, for them? So why could Brian not do as much for her? Oh, he'd attended the ceremony admittedly, but half-heartedly, in the shadow of his wife's blatant disgust. Whereas she, Kerry, had danced all day at their big wedding in the Loire, loyally celebrating a union she did not sanction. Now grief was the only thing left in common. Grief and guilt, on both sides. Or just on hers? She looked at her brother, and saw only a man mourning the mother he worshipped, turning for comfort not to his twin but to his wife.

For now, Brian held his tongue, did not say "I told you so", did not mention the failed marriage at all. Instead he enquired about his new nephew, and agonised endlessly over the unfathomable reasons for the murder. They could come to no logical explanation. But the police could, and did.

On Thursday evening, Detective Inspector Kevin Barry sat

the three of them down in Eamonn's study and presented them with his theory.

"Sectarian, we believe. The bullets came from a gun of the type used by the IRA, a Uzi sub-machine gun recently smuggled, we suspect, from Libya."

"But why? *Why?*"

Brian was baffled; this kind of thing happened up North, not down here in the Republic.

"Your mother was a native of Lisburn, sir, and a Protestant by birth. Is that right?"

"Yes."

"Well, there you have it. This was intended to be a lesson to everyone, North and South, not to enter into marriages of mixed religion. Your mother's Unionist background made her a 'legitimate' target, while your father's wealth – ah – if I may be so crude, I'm afraid this was also a fund-raising expedition."

That much was already obvious. The killers, in hooded masks, had tied up the night staff and blitzed the house from attics to cellars, ripping paintings off the walls, scooping artefacts and jewellery into sacks, denuding it of everything they could find. It was a well planned, singularly successful raid, carried out in cold blood; even Fionn had been shot dead. Kerry was glad of that, thinking dully how the dog would have pined to death without Eamonn, just as she would do herself.

The police were right. That same evening, the IRA claimed responsibility for the shooting, right out on RTE's nine o'clock news bulletin. It put the fear of God into Protestants everywhere, married to Catholics whose only crime was to love them without reserve, without prejudice.

"Signed by me, Eamonn Laraghy, being of good health and sound mind, this thirtieth day of August, 1969 . . ."

Xavier Markey, the family's solicitor of more than twenty years, removed his glasses and looked around him apprehensively. But thirty-one people sat assembled before him, and all but three were smiling in incredulity, in gratitude. A difficult employer but a fair one, Eamonn had made a bequest to each member of his staff, ranging from the merely decent to the very substantial indeed. If nobody had a job any more, everyone had something to be glad of, particularly Eileen and Paddy Casey, head groom Jerry Flynn, and Mary Sexton the elderly cook, who had catered so long and so literally to the Laraghys' every whim.

In all, almost half a million pounds had gone to the workforce. Another half million had gone to a woman whose name meant nothing to any of them, but about whom they swiftly reached a unanimous private conclusion: Helen Craigie. So, Eamonn had had a mistress. Well, now, but wasn't he the boyo! Not wishing to think ill of the dead, the staff could none the less understand, even sympathise, with this. Maeve Laraghy had been an exemplary woman in many ways, but a very cold fish with it. If Eamonn had found solace elsewhere, well, good luck to him. The state of his marriage had never been a very well-kept secret.

Xavier turned to the children, as he still thought of them, as guiltily as if he personally had wielded the pen that wrote the will. In fact quite the contrary was the case; he had pleaded with Eamonn for days to reconsider. But to no avail whatsoever. Bull-headed to the bitter end, Eamonn had drawn up the document five days after Kerry's marriage in Paris to Darragh de Bruin, his eyes like two rocks on a beach at ebb tide.

With Brian's marriage just ten days away, and pressing inexorably ahead, Eamonn had been as powerfully angry as Xavier had ever seen him. Two documents had been drawn up in less than an hour, one in the event of his predeceasing his wife, the other the one Xavier now held in his hand. Neither was a pretty sight.

Brian, eventually, would get some money. But the trust fund intended for his twenty-first birthday had been scrapped and everything redirected into a new trust, to be inherited on his thirtieth birthday instead. Nine years away! Until then, he would have a very modest annual allowance, unable to touch a penny of the three million pounds which would, by the time he got hold of it, be considerably more. In 1980, he would be a very rich man, and he would also,

Eamonn hoped aloud in his will, be mature enough to handle it. Now, demonstrably, he was not.

Seated on Xavier's left, Brian was impassive, his face betraying as little emotion as his wife's betrayed transparent shock. Xavier shrugged and suppressed a tiny smile despite himself. The young Mrs Laraghy was every bit as cold, he thought, as her previous incarnation, and also every bit as clever, as manipulative and as calculating. Well, let her calculate her way out of this one. She would hardly starve: her own family in France was, from what Xavier gathered, an impressively well-heeled outfit in its own right. And who knew? – maybe some day the boy would even make some kind of profit from his clothing venture.

But Kerry – ah, now there was a different matter. Xavier shuddered inwardly as he looked over at her pale, drawn face. What Eamonn had done to her bordered, really, on cruelty.

Not a penny. Not one single penny. Admittedly, she had been left the contents of the house, but how could Eamonn have foreseen that virtually everything of value would be stolen by the same savage thugs who had taken his own life? Even her mother's jewellery, and some lovely pieces that had belonged to her paternal grandmother – all gone before she'd even had a chance to try them on.

She'd been left the house itself, too, and the estate, and a very valuable horse called Blue Moon, worth nearly three-quarters of a million pounds. But only on condition that she undertook, legally and in writing, to run the estate as it always had been run, showing an annual profit in keeping with its current growth. If she were not prepared to do this, or failed in the attempt, then the entire estate was to be donated to the Sisters of Charity, for the foundation of a school, hospice, old folks' home or whatever purpose they might deem suitable. Her progress, if any, would be reviewed annually by a nominated firm of accountants.

Xavier caught her eye and sent her what he hoped was a sympathetic smile. It was terrible. How could a girl of twenty-one be expected to take over a place like this, train all the horses, oversee the finances, do all the promotion, administration, everything, and show a profit without one penny to start her off? What cash was in hand at the bank would just about cover the expense of the funeral, repair the damage done in the attack and pay this month's salaries. After that, she was on her own.

Such a frail, forlorn little thing. She couldn't possibly do it. Privately, Xavier knew that the Sisters of Charity would have their magnificent premises within the month. Indicating that the business was complete, dismissing the gathered staff, he made his way over to where Kerry sat with her brother and sister-in-law.

"I'm so sorry," he began, respectfully, apologetically. "I did everything in my power to try to dissuade him – but he wouldn't have a word of it, insisted on doing things this way. His way."

Young Mrs Laraghy looked as if she were about to spit on the offending document, but Brian raised a half-hearted smile.

"Yes. Well, that's good old Dad for you. Never would listen to anyone! We knew he didn't approve of our marriage, and I guess we got what was coming to us. But at least we have enough to live on, and a lot to look forward to."

Lucienne chimed in. "To contest in court, you mean."

Xavier shook his head sadly. "I'm afraid not, Mrs Laraghy. There is a codicil, to the effect that anyone attempting to challenge this will automatically forfeits their right to any share in it."

He hadn't thought it possible for her to get much whiter, but she did.

"*Mon Dieu. Quel salaud. Quel salaud déguelasse.*"

Brian winced. No matter what his father had done, nobody had a right to call him a "filthy bastard". With an injured look, he leaned across to restrain his wife, and Xavier thought it diplomatic to turn his attention to Kerry. The girl had not yet uttered a single word.

"Kerry. My dear child. If only there were some way to rectify things, something I could do . . ."

She raised her face to him. "Do, Mr Markey? About what?"

Good God. Was she still in shock? Denying it all? Evidently she was. She hadn't heard a word he'd said. His kindly heart went out to her.

"Dear me. About this whole dreadful mess. I begged your father, implored him, to make proper provision . . ."

She looked at him blankly.

"But he has, Mr Markey. He's given me a chance. A chance to make something of my life, which I needed, and a chance to make amends to him, which I needed even more. And he's given me what I needed most of all – a good, cracking slap in the face."

Xavier blinked, bewildered. Admittedly the girl was wild, spoilt, headstrong, and over the years he had often thought that he would like to give her a good hard slap or several himself. But not like this. What did she mean, she had been given a chance? If she thought for one moment she could take over Ashamber, and achieve an iota of the success her parents had, she was very much mistaken. Very much indeed. The notion was preposterous.

Brian looked uncertainly at his sister, taken aback by her matter-of-factness, and Lu produced a smile like a gin and tonic, full of ice and lemon.

"Oh, Kerry! Don't tell us you think you can take the thing on! You haven't a hope, *chérie*, you are simply not cut out for it . . . We have all seen how you start things and never finish them, how you dodge all responsibility. It would be madness! You must hand everything over to those nuns, now, sell that horse and run away to play. Otherwise you will simply get into debt, and make a fool of yourself again."

Suddenly animated, Kerry sprang at her like a coiled snake.

"Shut up, Lu! You've got your money, the easy way, but by the time you inherit it I'll have mine too, the hard way. You forget that Ashamber is my birthright, dowry, heritage, everything – and that that chair your elegant ass is seated on now belongs to me."

"This chair will have to be sold, Kerry, to pay the debts you incur! You can't afford the risk."

"No, Lu, *you* can't afford it! That's what you mean, isn't it? You think you and Brian will have to bail me out after I've screwed up as usual. Well let me tell you—"

Xavier and Brian saw a row brewing. Peaceable men both, they intervened hastily.

"Well, now, girls, I think we could all use a drink before lunch, after that nasty shock? Sherry, everyone?"

Brian poured it without waiting for an answer. But it was Kerry who proposed the toast.

"Here's to Dad. And Mother too. Here's to what they left us – the opportunity, and the ability, to make as much of our lives as they did of theirs."

Noting the feverish sparkle in her eyes, everyone raised their glass and drank obediently. In silence.

There was no way out of it. Before returning to Paris, Lu informed Brian, he would have to sit Kerry down and knock sense into her. Reluctantly, he asked her to join him in the library.

"Look, sis, we've all had a series of horrible shocks. I think the best thing for you to do now is nothing at all. Take time to consider your options. You don't realise the magnitude of what's involved here, Kerry. It would be insanity to try to set up as a trainer, without Dad, and it would be just as crazy to try to run this place the way Mother did. Mother was a businesswoman, with a natural aptitude for figures, just as talented in her field as Dad was in his. They were exceptional."

"And I'm a nobody, isn't that so? A dummy, a basket case with no aptitude for anything."

Brian shifted uncomfortably in Eamonn's leather armchair. Why did she always have to be so prickly, so contrary?

"No. Of course you're not. It's just that – it's too much for you, Kerry! You haven't got . . . well, you haven't exactly made a go of anything else, have you? Marriage, or Senegal, or even that job in the bookshop? Motherhood either, it seems."

He knew it was hard for her to hear this, but it was hard for him to say it too, and for her own good she had to hear it from someone. A busker, a baby, a disaster from start to finish. Her track record was zero, hopeless.

She had the grace to look ashamed.

"A dead loss. All right, I admit it. But Zoe told me something once, Brian, that I've never forgotten. She said you had to overcome your early mistakes, learn from them and move on. That's exactly what I'm going to do, with your permission or without it. I'm a mother now, as you say, and I have a son to consider. One day he'll grow up and hear all about his grandparents, about their wealth and their estate, and he'll want to know where the hell it all is. Do you expect me to say that I gave it away, quite calmly and casually, to the Sisters of blasted Charity? Because if that's the case, then you can do the explaining. I'll refer him to Uncle Brian when he comes looking for his money and his land."

Brian swallowed.

"So, what are you saying to me, Kerry? That you know enough about horses and estate management to take over Ashamber? That you can convince the owners to leave their horses here because Kerry Laraghy is as outstanding a trainer as her father? For God's sake! Those horses out there in the paddocks are worth millions! Millions! Nobody will trust them to you for one minute, much less this coming season, you're just a girl who used to ride well to hounds!"

What was it Lu had said? That men shop for success, and you must serve it up to them on a silver salver, or they will look elsewhere? Well, she, Kerry, would get hold of a silver salver right away.

"The owners are my first priority, Brian. Obviously, not all of them will stick with me, but I'll get some of them to give me a try, with their less valuable animals at any rate. And don't forget, I own Blue Moon too. His sire won the Derby and he's in training for this year's. He may not win it, but by Christ he won't come last either."

"Kerry, the flat season doesn't peak till June! How can you live till then? Feed the horses, run the house, pay the staff, vet, farrier? Hire jockeys, organise transport, tax returns, racing tack . . . you're out of your mind."

"No. I may know nothing about all that stuff, but I know about horses. I grew up here and I learned a lot more than you might think, while you were sketching your little skirts. Jerry Flynn has just inherited a bundle of money from my father and he owes it to me to stay on, teach me everything Daddy taught him. I'm sure Eileen and Paddy will stay too, if I ask them, and some of the lads . . ."

He could see he might as well talk to the wall. In his chest, frustration began to tie itself into an angry knot.

"Fine, Kerry. Have it your own way, just like Dad always had to. Consult with the owners, the bank manager, anyone nuts enough to listen. But don't ever say that nobody tried to warn you, tried to save you from yourself. We did that before, Lu and I."

Sweetly, she smiled at him.

"You're always right and I'm always wrong, of course. What I should do now is sell Blue Moon and go back to America with enough to live on, if I'm careful, for the rest of my insignificant life. Well, I'm not going to, Brian. I'm going to keep him and race him and that's that. Zoe will design my colours for me, straight away."

He didn't know whether to laugh or cry.

"You can't keep him, Kerry! You can't race a horse of your own if you're training other people's . . . you don't even know that much. Please, Kerry. Forget this whole thing and concentrate on your child instead. You have no business leaving him with Zoe."

"She's bringing him home here next week. She can bring my things too, because I'm not going back there."

Kerry didn't add that she owed Zoe a lot of money, right down to the airfare which had flown her home. But Brian guessed.

"You owe Zoe a lot, sis. She's been a good friend to you."

"I know." Jesus, what a patronising bastard he had become! Her voice shook with fury. "I do have some very good friends, Brian."

Pointedly, she glared at him. How dare he! Was this really her brother talking, or his wife?

His duty both finished and failed, Brian stood up, took her by the arm and marched her into the dining room for dinner. This sorry business had only one benefit that he could see; it had shaken her out of the tortured lethargy which, all week, had threatened to engulf her.

Studiously he avoided further debate over the meal, raising instead the curious matter of Mrs Helen Craigie. Clearly, the woman was their father's lover. Nobody could think what to make of it.

"So what are we going to do? Do we want to meet her?"

No. They decided they did not. Much better to let sleeping dogs lie. She had been Eamonn's secret; let her remain so. Lu envied the woman her sudden good fortune, but Brian and Kerry were inclined to pity her, knowing what it was to be bereaved. She must have endured a lot, over the years, and Eamonn must have been very fond of her that she should inherit so much money. But the subject made them feel disloyal to their mother, and they dropped it.

That night, Kerry lay in bed with her arms under her head, thinking. For the first time since the dreadful day of the murder, she was not crying herself to sleep; rather, she almost glowed in the dark.

Daddy gave me a second chance, she exulted, and now I can make it all up to him! I can, and I will. Even Mother would be proud of me – for a change. Tomorrow I'll ride right round the whole estate, go through the books, make an appointment to see the bank manager. I'll sweet-talk him into lending me a year's money if I have to sleep with him.

She grinned to herself. Old Mr Connaughton would throw himself under the wheels of Maeve's Bentley sooner than countenance such a proposal – which was another thing. She would sell the Bentley, it was a collector's item by now, and probably quite valuable. There was no end to the things she could do – and would do, regardless of anybody's futile prognosis.

Next morning, Brian awoke with a similar sense of resolve. He had only to ask his in-laws, he knew, and they would lend, or give, him whatever funds he required.

But he was not going to ask. They had done enough already, financing TLC, handing over the deeds of the apartment as a wedding gift. He would not impose on them any further, and he would not indulge Kerry in her imbecilic scheme. That would be irresponsible, as Lu said. Kerry had to learn to accept the consequences of her actions, and if she persisted with this nonsense she would learn with a vengeance, be cured once and for all. Then, Lu would authorise some small allowance for her, and for the child who should be her priority to begin with. Or so he hoped. Lu, he had to admit, could be a very tough cookie when people displeased her.

A difficult business, being equally tough himself. Despite everything he felt some irrational affinity with his sister, some covert admiration for her perverse determination. But it *was* perverse, and emotion must not outstrip logic. That was what had muddled Kerry's life all along, and brought it to this ridiculous pass. It was time the girl grew up. Meanwhile, he had his own career to get back to, and his wife was waiting for him.

8

At Hollyvaun, forty miles distant, Brandon Lawrence also awoke with a sudden sense of direction.

Nearly a week had elapsed since the day of the Laraghy funeral. Every day since then, he had striven valiantly to wipe the memory of Kerry from his mind, but he could not. Although it was her parents who had died, it was she who haunted him, in her long black coat, her black leather gloves, her veiled black hat over green eyes dimmed, almost extinguished, by shock and grief. In his dreams she continued to stand there, under the dripping trees, bowed and motionless as the priest intoned the prayers for the dead. Helpless, she could not come to him; he must go to her.

Go now, today, because tomorrow he would return to London and it would be too late. He had made a promise once, and in the Lawrence code a promise made was a promise kept. There was no more to it than that.

He and Marianne were perfectly contented these days. It was just a sense of duty, that was all, an offer of the help on which he had once told her she could count. Knowing Kerry, she would in all probability send him packing for his pains.

A thick white blanket of snow lay under his bedroom window, and he cursed as he dressed. Damn these country roads, they would be treacherous in such weather. But that was what powerful expensive cars were for; he would borrow his father's massive Mercedes and get there somehow. Zipping a leather jacket over a warm cashmere sweater and thick corduroys, he dropped a kiss on the brow of his sleeping wife and quietly let himself out.

The morning was sabre-sharp, and it took three hours to negotiate the forty miles, but despite several unnerving skids the idea of turning back never entered his mind. His hands were clamped to the steering wheel by the time he reached Ashamber, pulled open the heavy gates and let himself in. First and foremost, he thought, he must make Kerry install security on those gates. On everything. The whole place would have to be fortified, electrified, protected by all manner of alarms and remote controls.

Sad, that such things should be necessary. This was not the Ireland he knew and loved, where people rarely bothered to lock a door or a bicycle. But after one murder, who could say what might not follow? The death of Eamonn and Maeve was proof, if proof were needed, that yelping dogs were no defence against this new, insidious evil.

The teeth of terrorism had been sunk into the body of the nation it claimed to defend, and with savage wrath Brandon prayed that its perpetrators would be caught, and consider themselves fortunate that the same death penalty did not exist in Irish statutes as in their own. Again he recalled Kerry's ashen, shattered features, her young body rigid with disbelief as she bent over the open grave of her parents. Who did these pigs think they were, to so dispose of human life – Jesus Christ? Nobody had ever been hanged in Ireland since Michael Manning back in 1954, for the murder of Nurse Catherine Cooper, but if ever he got near these thugs he would knot the rope himself, tighten it round their thick godforsaken necks until they knew the meaning of death. Fulminating, he stopped the car in front of the house and got out, frowning. Ashamber was a house he had always seen at its best, filled with light and music and people, but today it looked bare and bereft, and although he knocked loudly he heard the sound reverberate into a silent vacuum.

After a long pause, and many more hefty bangs on the door, he heard bolts being undone, and it swung open just far enough to reveal the anxious face of a woman he remembered from previous visits. Relieved to see a friendly face, Eileen ushered him in, and as Brandon followed her to the library he was conscious of his own footsteps echoing on the flagstoned floor. No fire was burning, Eileen apologised, since Mr Brian had left for the airport and Miss Kerry was out on her horse conducting an inspection of the estate. But it was so good of him to have battled all the way here in these dreadful conditions, he would make himself comfortable and she would bring tea . . . Brandon smiled warmly at the woman, evidently promoted from maid to housekeeper, and gratefully accepted her offer. He would like a reviving cup of tea, yes please, and he would like her also to tell Kerry's husband that he had a visitor. The two had not met, but in the circumstances it was appropriate that they should.

But Mr de Bruin was not here. Eileen withdrew without further explanation, leaving Brandon perplexed. This husband of Kerry's had not been visible at the funeral either, and in charity he could only assume that the man had been detained by some very urgent matter – discussions with the police, perhaps, unsuited to his wife's distressed condition? There must be some such explanation. Gratefully Brandon drank his hot tea and found himself unable to await Kerry's return. He would go out, now, and meet her as she returned from her ride.

He did. He heard her before he saw her, or rather he heard Zephyr, cantering across the home paddocks in a muffled flurry of snow. The mare's stride was rhythmic and even, but suddenly Brandon's heartbeat was not.

Despite not having ridden for three years, Kerry sat the mare as easily as if she were a rocking horse, tall and supple in the saddle, slim and unexpectedly striking in polished boots, black hacking jacket, gloves, jodhpurs and a bowler that had graced Maeve on many a winter's hunt. Its fine veil obscured her face, but immediately Brandon sensed a new and definite beauty in the distant figure. Poise, too, altogether unlike that tentative charade of New Year's night so long ago . . . but then, she must have matured a good deal. As she rode closer into view, he almost did not want to look.

But he did look. Her red hair, shorter now than he remembered it, was tucked thick and glossy into a net under the black bowler, her skin radiant in the freezing air, her eyes alight with renewed vitality. As she urged the horse on, still unaware of his presence, he clenched his fists and drew his breath in sharply.

It was as if Zephyr had kicked him in the stomach. With one glimpse of her his immunity was pierced, dissolved like a fallen snowflake. Until this moment, he'd thought his brief passion for Kerry extinguished, snuffed out like a shooting star. But it wasn't. She torched it and it flared up again instantly, as bright and searing as before, so painful he involuntarily recoiled from the flame.

He must *go*! Go now, immediately, before she saw him, spoke, touched and destroyed all that he had built up since last they met. Stumbling on the lethal ice, he reached backwards, groping for the car, for escape – and in that second, she spotted him. Narrowing her eyes, shading them with her palm against the glare of the winter sun, she checked Zephyr, wheeled the mare round and came bounding over to him at a gallop, plundering clear across the snow-filled flowerbeds.

"Brandon! Brandon Lawrence! Oh, my God! It is!"

In a flash she was swinging down out of the saddle and he was reaching up to catch her, pull her down into his arms and enfold her in a kiss hard as a padlock. Christ, what a fool he'd been! How had he ever persuaded himself he could live without her, when she was life itself?

Tenderly, he touched her face with his hand.

"Oh, Kerry! At last . . . but this husband of yours . . . where is he?"

"He's not here, Brandon. And your wife – where is she?"

Kerry raised a somewhat accusing eyebrow. It was not proper for a man, she was sure, to make a condolence call on a single woman alone. But of course he had expected to find Darragh here, and Lu, Brian – all the people who were not here. And he wasn't just a man, he was a businessman, exactly the person she needed! He would not get away from her until she had picked his brain clean as a vulture's skeleton. Brandon was extremely pleased to see her instantly tether Zephyr to a fence and lead him inside, a wide and clearly welcoming smile on her face.

"Eileen! Mr Lawrence will be staying to lunch, tell Mary."

Eileen nodded and trotted away to the kitchen. Where the money for guests and lunches was to come from any more, she had no idea, but for the moment the pantries and fridges were fully stocked. Later . . . well, things would work out somehow, God would provide.

Kerry hauled Brandon into the library and swivelled an even bigger smile on him, bright as the beam of a lighthouse. It lit up his whole world and buckled his legs at the knees – God, but she was beautiful! Different, of course, her hair short and her being faintly shadowed with sorrow, but looking infinitely better than he had expected. Where was the devastated wraith of the graveside?

"Apéritif?"

"Thank you."

Her apparent assurance amused him, but his own assurance dried up like a stream in summer. What to say, now that he was here? Politely he embarked on small talk, his nervous caution making her stilted in turn, but by the time they finished their drinks the stiffness was relaxing, the recent course of their lives unravelling like wool in the claws of a kitten.

So much packed into her story, so little into his! He did not bore her with his business concerns, but told her of his Aegean cruise instead, and the sailing he had done. Interested, she lingered over the lunch table, pouring coffee while he lit a small cigar, inhaling its mellow aroma with pleasure. But if there were things he was not saying, there were things she was not saying either, he sensed.

"France sounds wonderful, Kerry. But tell me more about Senegal."

She glanced at him, and then down into her coffee.

"You're sure you want to hear?"

"Yes. Please."

In a gush, it all came pouring out. The marriage, the baby, the poverty, the rescue, every doleful detail. She did not shed a tear, did not blame anyone bar herself, but Brandon heard the pain, and the relief, in every blurted word.

"So, the marriage is over, then? You'll divorce him, in France?"

Brandon hoped that Shakespeare was right about there being no art to read the mind's construction in the face as

he moulded his tone into mere fatherly concern. But she
turned away from him, her look abruptly remote as she
propped her chin on her elbow, contemplating the fat, falling
snowflakes.

"Such a lovely view, after the sand, the cities . . . no, I
won't divorce him, Brandon. Marriage is for life – you're
Irish, you know that. But nor will I live with him, after
the way he treated me, so cold, so arrogant, so wrapped
up in himself . . ." As she spoke Kerry could see Darragh
clearly, sitting on the beach as she walked away from him,
calm, cross-legged, playing his guitar.

"But why on earth did you marry him, in the first place?"

To his horror, her face lit up.

"Oh, because he was so exciting! At first, anyway, when
we were in Paris. He was so interesting, Brandon, so lively,
so – so *different*. He knew so much about so many things,
he could talk the hind legs off a donkey, it was all so new
to me, so romantic . . . He'd play that guitar of his and my
whole body would just *melt* . . . our sex life, I have to tell
you, was positively incandescent. He may have turned out
badly in the end, just as everyone said he would, but there
certainly wasn't a dull moment anywhere in those two and a
half years, not even when he – when he was really wicked
to me, after I got pregnant. After all, that was what I went
to France *for*, for fun and adventure, and that was exactly
what I got from Darragh de Bruin. Mummy was the only
one who ever took his side, though I'm still not entirely
sure why. Daddy said he was a long-haired layabout, but
she seemed to think he had a future."

"But now, Kerry – what of your own future?"

"Now, oddly enough, I sort of wish Darragh were here.
He was so good at taking things in hand, deciding what to
do . . ."

Brandon saw his chance, and seized it.

"Kerry, that's exactly why I'm here. I reckoned you must
need some help and advice about – about all this." He waved
an expansive arm to encompass the estate outside.

"You know I've been disinherited, Brandon?"

"*What!*"

"The will was read yesterday. I got no money, only this place, and unless I make a go of it I lose it as well. It goes to the Sisters of Charity if I can't turn a profit right from the start. Brian got all Daddy's money, in trust."

"But Kerry, your father can't have done that to you."

"He can and he has. The punishment fits the crime, I guess. But he's done me a favour with it. Two years ago, I was a spoilt brat. Two weeks ago, I was a shop assistant in Manhattan. Now, I have the chance to make something more of myself – a great deal more. Not to mention make up for having disappointed him, and avenge him on those bastards who killed him. He also left me a horse called Blue Moon, whose sire he'd hoped I would train. Everyone says I should sell it, but I want to train it, show them all what I can do. Then I'll get more commissions – lots and lots!"

Her eyes sparkled and he saw that she was serious, very determined and possibly a little high, riding on the euphoria that often follows shock. Reacting, too, against so many things: against an exile that had naturally deepened her yearning for home, against her bereavement, her collapsed marriage, her venomous contempt for the men who had killed her parents. All of these factors added up, probably, to a welter of conflict inside her, but if she did not fight them, they would overpower her, eclipse her for ever. And besides, what was the alternative? The idea that she should languish all the rest of her life in Manhattan, settling for mere survival, horrified him. Her talents might be amorphous as yet, but surely she had some – her father's with the horses, if not her mother's with the money. What she needed now was a firm hand to guide her. His hand.

"So, how are you going to go about it?"

"Well, already I've set up an appointment with Mr Connaughton, the bank manager, and then I'm going to call the staff together, throw myself on their mercy and try to establish some sort of a co-op situation, the kind of thing Darragh advocated in Senegal. Then I'll talk to the owners and explain everything to them as well, and then . . ."

He smiled, rather sadly.

"Whoa, Kerry! Let's be realistic right from the start. First and foremost, Mr Connaughton isn't going to give you a penny."

"What? But why not?"

"Because you have no collateral. If you fail, he can't sequester the property – it goes, you've just told me, to the Sisters of Charity. He might be a nice old man, Kerry, but he's not the manager of that bank for nothing, believe me. He'll be terribly sorry, but his answer will be no."

"Oh." Her face fell, deeply disconcerted.

"Next, the staff and this co-op business. Have you any idea, dear girl, of the extent of the corruption in the horse industry? Unless some very knowledgeable person keeps everything under constant tight surveillance, there will be widespread racketeering, horses doped, lookalikes substituted in races, weights doctored . . . so much fiddling that you'll soon lose the licence you haven't even got yet. Your father had his employees terrified of him, and unless you can bully and terrorise them too, they'll turn round and do it to *you*. Oh, not all of them, I'm sure some are honest, but enough to ruin you."

"Oh." The face fell yet further.

"And as for the owners, Kerry – they're businessmen, not angels of mercy! Not one of them will leave one horse with you for one day."

She was almost in tears.

"Oh, Brandon, you're so negative! I thought you'd come here to help me." Miserably she bit her lip, undermined, uncertain.

"I will help you. Tell you what, let's take a walk outside and talk it over, h'mm?" He wanted to check the place out, assess its condition.

"All right."

Ashamber, for all its stately beauty, had never been a house that stood on ceremony. Homey clutter vied with dilapidated elegance, fishing rods and shooting sticks tumbling into corners crammed, before the raid, with Ormolu clocks, Meissen china, paintings by Lavery, Yeats and Turner, picnic baskets and dogs' leads flung anyhow under the majestic staircase.

Brandon was taken aback to notice, now, all the blank spaces and broken debris, but carelessly Kerry yanked a warm overcoat out of a closet, and they set off into an icy afternoon so stinging it made their eyes water.

It was breathtakingly cold, a silver filigree of frost scratching and clawing at their faces, making their blood tingle and their breath rise in static puffs before them, airy and disembodied. Plunging their hands deep into their pockets they kicked through the curling drifts of snow that reminded Brandon, with a fleeting stab of guilt, of the icing on Christopher's birthday cake. The boy had recently turned eight, but despite their hopes for a daughter no new child had yet materialised. He pushed his family out of his mind: he must have this one day without them. One day, to call his own.

What he saw pleased him. The stables were in good order, neat and organised, the paddocks properly fenced, the paths freshly tarmacadamed, the barns filled with hay, everything bespeaking prosperity and the thriving enterprise it was.

"But there are tough times ahead for all of us," he warned her as they strode on and out over the fields, white and peaceful as a picture postcard. "The sixties' boom is over, Kerry, and there'll be a recession in the seventies. Soon. It's touching us in London already. You're going to have to look outside these islands for your owners and investors – to the Middle East, particularly. That's where the big money is going to come from next. Oil money."

She nodded.

"Yes. I think Daddy saw that coming too. There's been a Mr Schuster on the phone, from America, terribly upset to hear what happened. He was going to send several horses here for Daddy to train; it would have been quite a coup to get so many from abroad."

"Well, maybe Mr Schuster isn't lost to us yet, Kerry. I have a lot of friends in America, and in other places too. In fact I was thinking of buying a few horses myself."

She stopped short and looked up at him. What was he saying? That he could, and would, put business her way?

"What would you say, Kerry, to an offer for Blue Moon? If I were to buy the horse from you, and then give it back to you to train? That way, you'd have the capital *and* the horse. You could finance the venture and advertise it simultaneously."

She was speechless.

"Let's think it over, Kerry. Did I tell you I've been thinking of getting out of London? I want to bring the business back home here, where it belongs. London's no place to live any more, it's so noisy and dirty, and there's such hostility to the Irish since all those bombs started to go off. The IRA is doing far worse damage to its own compatriots than it is to the British."

Mother of God. He was going to move back here – for her? She opened her mouth to say something, and closed it. For Marianne, for the children, for any number of reasons, not for her!

"What do you say we go into partnership, Kerry?"

He stopped, put a hand on her shoulder, and looked down into her face. She saw that he was perfectly serious. He actually thought that she could do it. Her first vote of confidence – and from what a source!

But. But what? There had to be a catch to it. There always was.

"Brandon. I don't know how to thank you. Do *you*?"

He caught her meaning.

"Just let me see you occasionally, Kerry. That's all I ask. To see you prosper, and see you for yourself."

"For myself? Brandon, let's get this clear from the start. Are you just being an even better friend to me than Zoe, or are you saying you want to get involved with me – personally, as well as professionally?"

He hesitated. She was in mourning. It was the wrong time to assail her with new emotional onslaughts. But he had lost her once before. He wasn't going to lose her now. His voice fell on the waning light.

"Yes, Kerry. I'm afraid I do want to get involved with you, as you put it. I'm in love with you. I always have been. I just refused to accept it before."

He took her hand in his and held it there, dumbly, humbled by this young girl, the one thing in life he desperately wanted, the one thing he couldn't have.

It was a long time before she replied, her voice lower than his own, her eyes fixed on the ground.

"Brandon. In the past few years I've thought I had the love of the three men in the world who meant everything to me – my father, my husband and my brother. And now I've lost it all, them all. I'm sorry, Brandon. There is no possibility of my ever getting involved with any other man ever again. I just can't take any more."

Oh, no, no. Why had he not considered all this? Why had he rushed in and frightened her off? She was perfectly right. Of course she would learn to love again, some day, but it would not be soon. She had a lot of healing to do first, so much of it that his heart sagged with pity for her.

"They all betrayed me, Brandon, in their various ways. And now I have a son, you have two sons, and a wife. How can you possibly stand there and talk to me of – of involvement? You hardly even know me!"

He didn't know what to say, beyond that he wanted her so badly he could not articulate it. Didn't she feel anything for him – anything at all? But there was no reason why she should, and looking into her eyes, tilting her face up to his, he saw only pain, loneliness and emptiness.

"I'm sorry, Kerry. I had no right. I just wanted you to know, this time, that I won't abandon you the way I did before. But I won't press it, don't worry, or try to force your feelings, or even speak of it again. If friendship is all you want, then that's what I'm offering you. Is that – all right?"

"That's wonderful, Brandon, and I'm very grateful for it. But don't misunderstand. It won't turn into anything more, now or ever."

How could it? She had invested her every emotion in those three men, and in return she had watched their love for her crumble in the face of the first adversity. She had nothing left to give. She would rather starve, lose everything, than trust any man again.

She scuffed the ground with the toe of her boot.

"So, have we been at cross purposes, then? Is our deal off?"

Off? He would as soon cut off his right hand.

"No, Kerry, of course it isn't! This is my first chance to prove how much I love you – by doing what you ask of me, confining myself to friendship when that's what you need."

"Even though friendship is all you'll get in return, Brandon?"

Was it? He wondered. And despite her resolve, he hoped. Maybe he would wait a long time. Maybe he would wait all his life, for nothing. But he would take the risk. She was worth it.

"It's best for the moment in any case, Kerry. You've been badly hurt, and I'm still married, the father of small boys who won't be grown up and away for years yet. I won't give up hope on you, on us being free and eager for each other whenever circumstances change. But for now, you've got a deal."

And I, he thought, have hope. That, and something to aim for.

She looked at him steadily, reassured by his acceptance. She could not afford any more mistakes, but she needed help, and by the time it got her to her goal, he would have forgotten this silly infatuation. Meanwhile, he seemed to see the scars, understand her predicament – how different from Darragh, whose fierce proud will always had to triumph!

Ironically, his stoicism was endearing. But then he was so much older than Darragh, wiser, able to see things in perspective.

"Well, then, if we have a deal, can we put it in writing? I know that sounds terrible, Brandon, but I don't want to have to trust anyone – not even you. If it's too much to ask, I'll understand."

Just as independent as before! More so, even. His heart clenched with love for her, with years of ephemeral emotion suddenly clarified, solidified.

"No, Kerry. It's not too much. We'll put it on paper, and I'll only ever come here by invitation. How's that?"

She threw her arms around him.

"That's perfect! Oh, Brandon, I can't tell you how much this means to me, it's such a help, just when I most need it. Thank you so much!"

He did not attempt to capitalise on the moment, but wrapped his arm about her waist and resumed their walk, moving on to the subject of Ashamber's strengths and weaknesses.

"Obviously, you're its worst weakness right now, Kerry. You have no experience, not even a trainer's licence, no knowledge of book-keeping. But you have so many other qualities, it'll balance out, you'll see a return on your energy and enthusiasm, honesty, dedication. And you're your father's daughter. Horses are in your blood. But you won't set it all in motion overnight. What you're going to need above everything is patience."

Patience. She hadn't a shred of it. But she would have to cultivate it somehow, so frightening was the alternative, if she should lose the house, the horses, the estate and all the money Brandon evidently planned to invest in her. Maybe he would lend her someone to help with the books, or she could do some kind of crash course? Anything. Whatever it took. Failure was a possibility she wouldn't even allow herself to contemplate, whereas success . . . her eyes lit up and shone with anticipation.

As they walked, dusk began to fall, and Brandon knew he would have to leave before the roads iced over again. Taking her face in his hands, he kissed her on the forehead, and forced himself to turn for home. But when she saw his car, she uttered a sudden wild whoop of delight.

"Oh! How could I forget! I bet it's still there – come on!"

Running round with him to the outhouses, she pulled open the doors of a garage, panting with exertion and apprehension until, there before his astonished gaze, stood a gleaming Mercedes convertible, white like the snow, intact, perfect.

"Oh, Brandon, look! Isn't it smashing? It's still here . . . my parents gave it to me when I was eighteen, and it represented such freedom to me, such independence. And now I can use it, sell the old Jag as well as the Bentley! How much would I get for them, do you think? What would it cost to tax and insure this?"

He laughed, but his tone was sombre as he surveyed her face.

"I'll send someone to help with the money side of things, Kerry, till you get on your feet at least. I don't want you turning into a little calculator. You just concentrate on the horses."

"With pleasure. Figures bore me brainless."

Oh, if only she could jump into the Mercedes, right now, and zoom off into the blue in it! It might be days before the ice thawed, before she could put her foot to the floor and feel the wind whipping her hair. Still, it was there, and it was hers, another insurance policy from Eamonn after all.

Pleased for her, Brandon got into his own car and drove off slowly down the long avenue, aching to ask when he could see her again. But, as promised, he did not specify a date, and she did not volunteer one. It was just as well; he needed all his powers of concentration for the unpredictable road ahead of him, and to master the chaotic emotions which, for the first time in his life, had overpowered him body and soul.

Sitting on the steps of the shack, Darragh thoughtfully regarded the pile of wood shavings at his feet, curling and drying already in the hot February sun.

He should be in Dakar today. But not even he was impervious to the painful injuries inflicted on him, most unexpectedly, by a prisoner who had interrupted their routine carpentry class to swing at him with sudden malevolence and a claw hammer. The result had needed twenty stitches, and Darragh was smarting as much in spirit as in body. Administering ointment, but not much sympathy, Cameron had advised a break from work, with plenty of rest and vitamins.

Vitamins. Well, he could only hope he was getting those, from the tins from which he ate these days, now that Kerry was not around to cook for him. Still not around, damn her!

Forced to rest, Darragh was forced, also, to take stock. According to his calculations, Kerry would have had her baby by now, six or seven weeks ago at least. Here in Senegal, women returned to work the day after they had their babies, but needless to say Kerry Laraghy was making a mountain out of a molehill. Lounging on a bed somewhere, he supposed, twittering with that Zoe woman while they fussed over the child, dressed it up like a guy and invited their girlfriends round to bill and coo at it.

It. A him, or a her? She might have written to tell him that much – not that it mattered, but just as a point of information. After all, she would be back to normal by now, there was no further excuse for her peculiar attitude. Any day now, she would tire of New York, pack her bags and her baby and return to him, return to her senses.

What else could she do? She certainly couldn't go back to Ireland after that gruesome row with her father, and she certainly wasn't equipped to get very far in New York, a far stickier jungle than anything Senegal could provide. Zoe would be keeping her, probably, but even Zoe's funds couldn't last a lifetime. A letter would come soon, and Kerry would follow.

She must. Because, now that he had time to think about it, things were not the same here at all, without her. Things were hot and difficult, dirty, disorganised and – and appallingly quiet.

Once a mecca for communal meals and long fascinating conversations, the bungalow was empty now, nobody ever seemed to come and visit any more – or issue invitations to theirs, for that matter. Not even Cameron and Fiona, whose contract was about to expire, leaving them free to resume their medical careers in Scotland with two years of experience in tropical medicine under their belts.

The prospect troubled Darragh. Not just because life would become still quieter, but because he, unlike them, was not building up anything that could be put to use elsewhere. With his own contract recently renewed for another two years, he was helping the people he had come here to help, but he was not helping himself, at all.

Well, that was not the purpose of this undertaking. But he could not do it forever. The physical demands were punishing, and his mind was atrophying. He read books, but he rarely finished them, because what was the point, when there was nobody to discuss them with? He carved toys for the children, played his guitar for them, but as soon as they got what they wanted they ran away. Ran away, just as Kerry had done, as

Cameron and Fiona were doing, leaving him high and dry.

Occasionally he brought a girl back from Dakar, hoping she might cook a meal for him, or clean the hovel up a bit, but he had not slept with anyone, since Kerry. Too risky, what with infectious diseases, girls who got pregnant at the drop of a hat, and tribal fathers who did not take kindly to white men meddling with their daughters. Besides which, they were virtually illiterate, these girls; trying to converse with them was an exercise in frustration.

God, that much he would say for Ireland! Everyone got a decent basic education, everyone kept up with the news and had opinions on it; you could walk into any pub and get into well-informed argument. In retrospect, there was a lot to be said for it.

How old was he now? Twenty-four, going on twenty-five? A quarter of a century, a turning point. Decision time.

Plenty of time, yet, with eighteen months or more stretching ahead. If Kerry came back – but even if she did, she would have this baby to consider, and certain conditions would, undoubtedly, be demanded. She would want to know what his plans were, for her and for it. Much as he hated plans, he could not tell her he had none. And much as he hated babies, this one was his own. It was entitled to something – a home, and an education, at any rate.

If she came, things would have to change. And if she did not . . . ? Darragh felt the stitches in his shoulder twinge painfully, and put down his penknife to gaze, bleakly, out to sea. It was a beautiful day, but unreasonably he wished it would rain, rain buckets, the way it did in Ireland. Clean, cold, fresh buckets: he thought of an Irish rainstorm, and saw the gloss fade off Senegal even as he looked at it.

He would stick it out, of course. But where was she? Where *was* she? Surely she knew he would never come looking for her – finances forbade that, as much as pride. But if she came to him, he was prepared to make a few concessions, now, barter with her the way the natives bartered, and include the child in the deal. At the end of his tenure, they would return to Europe, and he would find some way to support them. He was a graduate after all, with a college degree.

My God, he thought in surprise, I have a degree. From a university. There must be something I can do with that, something that would feed a family and still give me some scope, some challenge.

If only I can figure out what it is.

9

Nobody knew that Eamonn Laraghy had a widow, Helen Craigie thought wryly, but he had. She had been his widow for almost three months, from the first moment she heard the news on television, through the rending days of the hospital and funeral, when decorum and sensitivity restrained her from going to the dying, the dead man she loved, right up to this moment of rising from yet another sleepless night.

The few friends who knew of the liaison warned her that the nights would be worst, and they were right. But they referred only to the silence, the absence of distraction that night brings, and felt that Helen would survive. She was a survivor, by nature. She was used to spending nights without her man, used to solitude. Of course she would survive.

She was, and she did. Whenever she felt low enough that she might hit bottom, she would call one of them up, or Paul or Antoinette, to talk. It helped immensely; but what nobody could imagine, much less discuss, was how much she missed Eamonn physically. Not just the warmth of his hug or his smile, not just his booming laugh on the telephone, his schoolboy grin as he smuggled her off on a weekend adventure abroad, but his body, their sex life together.

Infrequent as it had been, it was an exceptional thing, deeply satisfying to them both, as perfect a union as when they first consummated it, over ten years before. Helen thought she would go mad without it, but could confide her loss to nobody. People did not expect a woman like her, a suburban mother in her forties, to have such feelings. It was neither right nor proper; they would be horrified. All she could do was soldier on – but to where, to what? Helen was not at all sure, at this stage of her life, that there was anything ahead of her worth aiming for.

There was, of course, the money. But what could it buy? It couldn't buy Eamonn back, it couldn't buy a fraction of the happiness she'd known with him, it could only ever enable her to be miserable in comfort. Helen didn't want to be miserable in comfort; she wanted to be with Eamonn, hold him, kiss him, talk to him softly late through the night in the warm balm of sated love.

Paul and Antoinette tried to comfort her, to talk consolingly of the holidays she could have now, the new car, clothes, jewellery, even that beach cottage at Brittas she'd long dreamt of . . . except that Helen no longer dreamt of it, or of anything, except Eamonn. All she wanted was to be with him. But first, there was something she must do.

She must talk to this poor child who'd been left so little by her father, explain his thinking of the time, tell her how much he had loved her in spite of his unreasonable rage, how very much she meant to him. And then she must give her the half million pounds that Eamonn had, wrongly and irresponsibly, left to her. She didn't want it, but from what she heard Kerry needed it badly. So, she would simply go to her and return what was rightfully hers.

Helen picked up the phone, this bright budding morning in April, and dialled Ashamber. It was the first time she had ever done so, although Eamonn had given her the number, trustingly, years ago. He knew she would never abuse it, and she never had. But now, as the phone began to ring at the other end, she felt a frisson of trepidation. There was no way of telling how Kerry would react.

The housekeeper answered and put her through to Kerry, who sat at her mother's desk grappling with a pile of ledgers that might have been writ in Sanskrit. Helen found herself trembling as she heard the girl's voice on the line.

"Hello? Mrs Craigie?"

Taken unawares, Kerry was also shaking. Daddy's other woman! The woman he'd kept secret from her, loved more than his wife – more than even her, his own daughter? Resentment and curiosity ripped her in two.

"Kerry . . . I'm sorry to bother you, dear. Do you know who I am?"

"Yes, Mrs Craigie, I believe I do. You're the woman who seems to have made my father a very happy man."

Caustic, or genuine? Helen couldn't tell which.

"Kerry, I don't know whether you know the extent of the whole thing, but your father and I were very deeply involved for more than ten years. During that time he talked about you a great deal, and said many things I think you should now hear. If you'd like to, I thought we might meet?"

Meet? Kerry drew back from the telephone as if from an obscene caller. *How* could Eamonn have done this to her? But then, she had failed him. Mrs Craigie had not. Who was she, this woman? A fortune-hunter, a usurper, a ghoul? Or only somebody warmer than Maeve, more constant than herself?

For Daddy's sake, she would have to find out. Give the benefit of the doubt, at any rate. But only on her own turf.

"Yes. I would like to hear them, Mrs Craigie. Shall we make an appointment? Have you ever seen Ashamber? Perhaps you'd care to come here some time?"

Tears stung in Helen's throat, making her pause for a moment while she fought for control.

"Yes, dear, I would. I'd love to. I never have seen it. What about Saturday? Would that suit?"

Kerry couldn't see the desk diary amongst the clutter, but didn't need to.

"I'm afraid I have to go to a race meet on Saturday. What about Sunday? Shall I send someone to come and fetch you?"

"No. I'd like to drive down there myself, Kerry, thank you for offering. Sunday would be fine."

"Good. Well, then, come for lunch, Mrs Craigie. I'll expect you at about one o'clock?"

Still trembling, Helen confirmed the arrangement and hung up. What a surprisingly nice girl. Eamonn had made her sound so difficult and flighty, even though he adored her, that Helen had expected a far more volatile greeting. But now here she was, actually invited to come and see the house where he had lived. How very sweet of the girl.

For the first time in ten weeks, a tiny smile rose to Helen's lips, and carried on up to her eyes.

"What an absolutely magnificent day, darling. Just perfect for your dive, wouldn't you say?"

Lucienne turned to bestow a smile on her husband, a smile bright and airy as the breeze that rushed through her hair, blowing the scarf off her curls to ruffle them out like the wandering hand of a lover. A nuisance, this breeze, but a comb and some spray would fix everything when they arrived, and if in the meantime she could cheer Brian up by letting him drive at 120 kilometres an hour with the top down, well, it was a reasonable exchange.

"Yes."

Another monosyllable, another smile wasted. This was becoming rather trying. It was a long drive to Royan, with over two hours still to go. By the time they got there he might well be running out of even monosyllables. Suppressing considerable impatience, Lu turned to him again.

"Just think, *chéri*, when TLC is as big a name as YSL and Dior, we'll be able to buy a summer place down on the coast, and you will be able to do lots and lots of diving."

"Yes. When. If."

If! What did he mean, *if*?

"But darling, of course it will. Look at last season! A triumph, a sensation, order books full to bursting . . . we are way ahead of plan already!" She made a little moue. "So why so pessimistic, *mon amour*? On this lovely spring morning, with a whole day on the beach to look forward to?"

No reply. She racked her brains for something that would surely make him smile.

"Maybe we will find a little cove all to ourselves, yes? It's too early for tourists – a tiny cove where we can stretch out and make love on the sand?"

"Lu, you can do all the sunbathing you want. But I'm going down there to dive. Don't expect me to babysit you all day."

For Brian, this constituted a very sharp retort, and left her foundering. What on earth was wrong with him? Was he perhaps still a bit mopey over his parents? Well, then, she would try harder to distract him, as was a wife's duty.

"So tell me, darling, what's it to be for next season, h'mm? What are you and Yves cooking up this time?"

Last summer's collection, based on the paintings of Monet and Paul Klee, had indeed rocked Paris. Brian had taken the romantic Impressionist as his theme for evening, while Yves had used the whimsical Surrealist to stunning effect in a daywear collection so clever, one critic sardonically accused, that it bordered on the intellectual, a joke at the expense of those who would wear it. Princess Grace had been in the audience, applauding with her fourteen-year-old daughter Caroline as the two wedding-day models came down the ramp to the blazing music of Bizet, the first marching boldly ahead in a geometric collage of white and yellow inspired by Paul Klee, the other trailing shyly behind in a cloud of white tulle edged with ivy green. It had taken the audience a couple of seconds to see that she was in fact wearing one of Monet's water lilies.

Viewers and buyers alike had gone wild, there had been all but riots as they clamoured and jostled to place orders. Even Princess Grace had been on the receiving end of a dig in the ribs as she led Caroline backstage to meet the two designers – and had returned it, Lu noted, with an equally firm elbow.

Rescuing her fell to Lu, who did it with speedy tact and aplomb. Now, the winter unveiling of the TLC collection for summer 1973 was barely five months away, and here was Brian full of ifs and buts. Really, it was too bad of him. Already, it was the end of April, three months since the death of his parents, time he started pulling himself together a bit.

"Well, *chéri*? So what's it to be? Shouldn't the wife be the first to know?"

He slammed on the brakes with such force that she was flung forward, grabbing at the dashboard as the Mercedes rocked from 120 kph to a standstill.

"Lu, the answer to your question is that I don't know. Just don't know, OK? I haven't got one single idea in my head for next summer. Not one. That answer your question? Can we drive on now, and talk about something else?"

Too shocked to answer, she nodded dumbly, and he slid

the car back into gear, his profile as stony as the Berlin Wall. They did not exchange another word for the remainder of the journey.

At Royan, a scattering of early visitors were already sauntering through the streets in shirt sleeves, although the weather was as yet merely warm, not hot. But just a mile or two up the coast, near La Tremblade, they found a small stretch of virtually deserted sand, and Lu set up her parasol over the picnic paraphernalia while Brian inspected and adjusted his scuba equipment. Diving was a sport he had grown very fond of since coming to France, but he had never previously explored this section of the coast, preferring long weekends in the warmer waters of the Mediterranean to this Atlantic excursion. But today they had only one day to spare, and the Riviera was too far away.

As he watched Lu change into a peach-toned swimsuit, and felt the gentle kiss of the sun on his own body, Brian began to uncoil from his tight knot of tension. After all, she had only asked a perfectly logical question. It was his own bottled-up feelings that were the source of the problem, not her concern about the collection. Wordlessly, she handed him a tube of sun cream to smear on her back, and he smiled as he took it from her.

"Sorry, darling. I didn't mean to bite your head off back there. Am I forgiven?"

She looked at him thoughtfully.

"Yes, Brian. Of course you are. But wouldn't you like to tell me perhaps what is the matter? Is it your parents? Is that it?"

Was it? Naturally it was. Well, partly. The memory of his father's final moments, that grisly last touch, still disturbed him dreadfully, bringing his body out in cold sweats night after night, driving his mind to distraction during the day, leaving him listless, unable to concentrate, uninterested in his work, even his marriage, anything.

But it was more than what had happened to Maeve and Eamonn, awful as that was. It was Kerry.

How could he have left her there, so cold-bloodedly, all alone at Ashamber, with no money and huge responsibilities?

After three years away from Ireland, her old friendships were outgrown, there was hardly anyone for her to turn to. She was mourning her dead marriage, quite apart from her parents, and she had a new baby to bring up all by herself. While here was her twin, her only brother, off on a jaunt to the beach on a sunny spring day, with not a care in the world beyond the glossy pages of the fashion magazines.

Thinking this over, now, Brian knew why he had vented such rage on Lu in the car. Because it was she, his wife, who had brought about the rift between himself and his sister. She who had been furious when Kerry slipped out of her grasp, after Maeve had entrusted her into it, in Paris in 1969. She whose snobbery had been outraged when Kerry brought home her busker; she who could not accept the idea of her sister-in-law going to help the people of Senegal out of the distress in which France had left them. She, the woman he loved, who would not allow him freely to love his own sister.

But yet, as his wife, he knew that she wanted only what was best for him. Ah. That was it, precisely. He was never to be allowed a say in what that might be. Lu knew best, leave it all to Lu. But she was only twenty-one, the same as himself, and didn't know better than he did at all. She only thought she did.

He began to work the cream into her shoulders, glad of having her back to him while he thought this out a bit. Did she love him, really? Or did she love Brian Laraghy, the million-aire's son, the gifted designer, the handsome man to show off at parties? It embarrassed Brian to think of himself as hand-some, but women confirmed the fact to him as well as any mirror, swarming all over him as soon as they saw him. Well, now was Lu's chance to prove it went more than skin deep.

"Yes, *chérie*. It is my parents. You don't get over it, just like that, in a week or a month, when your parents are brutally slaughtered, to no purpose whatever, by total strangers. But it's more than that, Lu. It's Kerry. Frankly, it's your attitude to Kerry."

He felt her shoulders stiffen.

"You've never really liked her, have you, Lu? Oh, at school maybe, when you were two giggly girls together, but not in recent years. Not since she started to go her own way."

A memory came to him, a memory of Kerry in her brand new Mercedes and scandalous scarlet gloves, giving cheek to Sergeant Mulligan. Another memory, of Kerry on the plane to Paris, tossing back champagne, laughing and defiant, a naughty child. How much of that spirit, that verve, had already been beaten out of her, beaten back down inside her? It would be beaten out of him, too, if he let it, although he knew he had less of it to begin with. He was their mother's son, more conformist, agreeable, preferring to skim surfaces than plumb the depths Kerry did. But if he continued like this, he saw, his ability as a designer would never truly develop, never blossom into full and unique originality, never be anything more than a pretty façade. It was time to make a stand.

"Lu, she and I are twins. Not identical, but opposite sides of the same coin. I've known her far longer than I have you. And I want her back, Lu. Our parents have died, but in many ways she's the one I miss most. I've treated her very badly these past few years, and I want to make it up to her. Intend to make it up. Whether you like it or not, I'm going to call her when we get home tonight, find out how she is, and my nephew, and Ashamber. See to it that she starts accepting some money from me."

Brian had already sent money to Kerry, small amounts agreed and controlled by Lu, but they had been returned without comment. Henceforth, he would allot her a regular percentage of his income, small as it was, and make her take it. Lu could like that or lump it.

He put down the tube of cream and she turned round to him.

"So that's what's wrong. Kerry. Your other woman."

"Yes."

To his surprise, she did not raise her voice, did not seem terribly ruffled by his decision.

"If that's what you think best, Brian, then that is what you must do. Now, why don't you go for that dive of yours, and leave me here in peace to get my tan. When you come back, we will have a nice lunch together."

Undermined by this, not sure whether she agreed with him or was humouring him, Brian picked up his scuba gear, kissed the air near her face and set off for the distant rocks from which he could plunge into the Atlantic. Lu watched him go, and then lay down full length, luxuriously, on her towel in the sand. The shifting sand, she thought ruefully; but if it were indeed shifting, then she would shift with it.

So, Brian wanted to re-establish his links with home, did he? That was natural enough, after such a trauma as had happened, and maybe it was for the best. Kerry would see his success, and be thrown into competition with it. Personally, Lu did not think she would ever equal it, but she would be forced to come to grips with reality, account for herself to the one remaining member of her family. Brian's revived fraternalism was perfectly predictable in the circumstances, and would wear off in time. Much better to indulge it than to thwart it; it was not so very important.

But as the sun reached its zenith and she turned over on to her stomach, Lu realised what was important. Brian's attitude, that was what. It was the first time he had ever challenged her – or anyone, apart from his extraordinary resistance to his father when he married at eighteen.

So, he was capable of taking a hard line when he chose? No matter. She, Lucienne, would take one step backward to achieve two steps forward. If she permitted him to relate to Kerry, he would permit himself to relate to everything else again too, shake off this oppressive weight he was carrying. If a wife gave in gracefully on minor matters such as this, she could keep her powder dry for much more important ones. A simple case of *réculer pour mieux sauter*.

Lu wriggled contentedly into a more comfortable position under her parasol and began to doze gently. It seemed like hours later when she heard Brian's voice again, calling excitedly from quite a distance away.

"Lu! Lu! Jellyfish!"

Jellyfish? Oh, no. He had been stung. The sting of a jellyfish could be extremely painful, and worse, highly poisonous. Devoutly Lu prayed that it was not his hand that had been stung, the hand that drew the designs for TLC. Jumping to her feet, she ran towards him with a bottle of antiseptic she had packed for just such emergencies.

But he was smiling broadly, dripping wet, flippers still on his feet, his mask pushed back on his head, the hairs on his chest streaming salt water.

"I've got it, Lu! I've seen it, found it! Jellyfish!"

She didn't understand. Was he hurt, or not?

"You should see them! Thousands of them, so beautiful, in every colour you could imagine, wafting along on the currents, drifting, translucent . . . oh, you should see them, Lu."

See them? She'd already seen a few dead ones, beached, and could imagine nothing more hideous.

"That's our summer '73, Lu! Jellyfish! All kinds of fish, in fact, I can't wait to get them on to paper, do all those tendrils, the coral, the seaweed, the mother-of-pearl, the lovely watery flow . . . it's going to be even better than the paintings, Lu, it's going to be an underwater world, an Atlantic experience . . ."

Oh. She began to catch his drift. Interesting. Maybe he had something here – and for Yves, too, if Yves could be enticed down on a dive. He could do the stronger, sharper fish, the sharks and sea urchins and other strange creatures, while Brian worked with the softer, more delicate varieties. Yes. That might work very well indeed. Smiling back, she blew a kiss to her husband as he lumbered closer, and placed another on his lips when he came within range.

He threw his arms round her, his earlier angst forgotten, and they walked back to their place in the sun, discussing the fish, all the seething marine life that he would bring to life on his sketch pad, on his ramps, a year hence. He had found his theme, and was happy as a sandboy. Lifting the lid of the picnic basket, Lu removed a range of tempting delicacies: baguettes, radishes, anchovy pâté, grapes, galettes, a bottle of Muscadet packed in melting ice.

"What will it be, *chéri*? You must be so hungry."

He peeled off the last of his gear, his swimsuit and hers, all before she had time to realise what he was hungry for.

"You bet I am. I'm starving. What was that you said earlier about making love in the sand?" As he spoke, he pushed her down onto it.

"Cheeky boy."

"Cheeky girl."

His hands slid under her and lifted her body up to his, his mouth on first one nipple and then the other, licking, sucking, taking each breast in turn deep into his mouth, savouring it, leaving it glistening with saliva and sea water. She began to twist and turn, half away from him, half to him, her eyes closing under the shimmering sun, her lips swelling and parting.

His tongue moved down over her midriff, her flat smooth stomach, down into the cleft between her legs, licking it open, flicking hither and thither till she thought she would scream. Then, raising her higher to him so that her head fell back, still gripping her from underneath, he balanced himself on his knees, looking beyond her into the rolling dunes, and entered her at an angle that dissolved her into one of the aquatic creatures he had just seen, rubbery, spineless, defenceless. The pleasure was so acute, she was washed away on immediate orgasm, moaning, her hair trailing in the sand, her arms flung out behind her. Then, pulling back, he waited a moment, plunged in again and went to work on his wife with memorable new power.

Dressed in cool, simple cotton, Kerry stood before her bedroom mirror, grimacing as she clipped on a pair of fake pearl earrings, longing for the lovely diamond ones she had been given on her seventeenth birthday. But they were gone, for good. No point in crying over spilt milk. She would merely improvise as best she could.

If only this dress didn't make her look so young! But it was years old, the only one she could find suited to such a hot day, and like the earrings would have to do. Some lipstick—? That might help. As she slicked some on, licking her lips so nervously it was almost instantly obliterated, she could hear Lir racing around down in the hall below. Still only a pup, Fionn's son was a handful these days, licking people's faces, slobbering all over their clothes, his paws already able to reach the shoulders of the shorter ones.

Kerry hoped he wouldn't do it to Mrs Craigie, but could hold out no guarantees.

Eileen knocked on the door. "Your visitor, ma'am."

"Eileen! Stop calling me that! I'm not the Queen of England!"

"Yes, ma'am."

She went away and Kerry glowered belligerently at her own reflection. Now that Mrs Craigie was actually here, she wasn't sure about this meeting at all. Daddy had a hell of a nerve, starting such a thing, and now look at the trouble it was causing . . . Flustered, smoothing her pageboy bob, she walked out on to the landing and gazed down into the hall, where music had once played and guests celebrated the New Year, aeons ago. Now, only one guest stood there, intently inspecting a Lavery painting with a bullet hole through it. The cheek! Did she want to take that too, as well as the money? The woman had another thing coming. Kerry ran down the stairs and extended her arm like a bayonet.

"Mrs Craigie? Kerry Laraghy."

Helen jumped. Where had the girl appeared from? She didn't sound nearly so friendly as she had on the telephone, barking her name like that. Was this going to be a mistake, after all? Kerry was dressed like a gypsy, but looked ready for armed combat, and Helen felt herself under militant surveillance.

So, this was Helen Craigie, was it? Kerry didn't even pretend to conceal her inspection. But, try as she might, she could see no sign of the tarty trollop she had half decided to dismiss.

Instead, she saw a pretty, compact woman in her forties, impeccably dressed in a dove grey suit as befitted a woman in mourning, not for a relative but for a close friend. Her chestnut curls were partly covered by a darker grey little hat, the rest of her accessories unadorned black leather, the sobriety of the ensemble relieved only by the heightened tinge of colour in the woman's apple-round cheeks. No cheap glitz, no rollicking barmaid; just a pink-and-white little matron with rather sad blue eyes.

Damnation! Kerry groped for ammunition, but couldn't

lay her hand on any. Despite her discomfort, Helen smiled warmly, encouragingly. This wasn't easy for either of them, and in Eamonn's tall, slender daughter she sensed unease, a hostility that masked, probably, mere defensiveness. The girl's cheekbones were hollowed out with traces of pain and exhaustion, the eyes were wary, hurting – but still, somehow, there was a trace of humour behind those eyes, and an emerald glimmer of determination. Her father's daughter, for sure.

"Come in, Mrs Craigie. I've been looking forward to meeting you."

Kerry made it sound as if she'd been looking forward to meeting Adolf Hitler, and didn't even begin to fool Helen.

"Have you really, Kerry? Or would you rather I'd stayed in the shadows, as is customary in these awkward situations?"

Leading the way through to the dining room for the lunch she'd like to pepper with arsenic, Kerry stopped in her tracks.

"Since you so frankly ask, Mrs Craigie, no. No, I haven't. My father used to say you should let sleeping dogs lie, and he might have been right at that."

Helen flinched. What was Kerry saying to her? Implying that she was a bitch? That the skeletons of old mistresses were better left in their closets? Painfully wounded, she also stopped, unable to conceal her hurt.

"Then I'll go, Kerry. It's not too late. We'll cancel this meeting and just pretend I never came here. That would be better, wouldn't it?"

Disconcerted, Kerry saw the damage already done, and swore inwardly. For her father's sake, she must hear this woman out. She attempted a redeeming smile.

"Why – why no, Mrs Craigie. Not at all. On the contrary. You were obviously important to my father, and that makes you important to me."

"And you to me, Kerry, as his daughter. I can't tell you how sorry I am for your loss. And for your father's extraordinary treatment of you in his will, which is why I'm here."

"You – it is?"

"He only told me about that will, Kerry, long after he'd written it, and by then he was sorry about what he'd done. At the time, he wanted to teach you a lesson, was very disappointed that you'd chosen not to work with him as agreed. But after we talked it over and he began to see that children must be allowed to live their own lives, he regretted it. So much so that he promised me, only a month before he died, to change the will. But he never got – got round to it."

"Did he really? Was he really?" Kerry gazed at her intently. "You mean to say, Mrs Craigie, that my father had forgiven me? That he'd accepted my marriage, my going to Senegal, the way I turned my back on him?"

Disturbed by the girl's anxious, almost desperate tone, Helen hesitated. Clearly Kerry needed to hear something more comforting than the strict truth, which was that Eamonn had been a long way from absolving her. Something that would soothe her obvious pain, her visibly consuming guilt.

"Yes. I believe he had. Not forgotten, perhaps, but forgiven – yes. He had no business to leave me so much money, nor make your brother wait so long for his inheritance either. It was very wrong of him, and I think he'd seen that."

"Mrs Craigie, the money doesn't matter. What matters is that you say my father forgave me. I can't tell you how much that means to me."

"And can you forgive him, do you think, for what he did? Leaving you here like this, with no word of reconciliation, no way of surviving without massive borrowing?"

Kerry didn't reply immediately, conscious only of the huge weight she felt lifted from her as Eileen ushered them to table, uncorked a bottle of wine and made them comfortable. Looking at it objectively, perhaps Eamonn's behaviour did sound callous; but then he'd presumed her happily married to Darragh, and maybe even engineered the situation to test him as well. There was any number of extenuating possibilities. Radiant with relief, she turned back to Helen.

"Yes. Of course I forgive him. I loved him, and I know I disappointed him, failed to keep a major promise. But I was so young then, Mrs Craigie. I don't think he realised how much he was asking of me. He was fifty-seven when he died, and probably didn't even remember what it's like to be young. It was the only time I ever let him down, but now I have a chance to make it up to him, and for having given me that, I can forgive him all the rest."

It was Helen's turn to say nothing. What a generous nature this girl had, apparently devoid of any resentment even in the face of her profoundly unfair punishment. Which brought Helen to the purpose of her visit.

"Kerry, I want you to have the money your father left me. You need it, I don't."

So taken aback she almost choked on her soup, Kerry leaned back in her chair, astonished.

"But Mrs Craigie, that's your money! He wanted you to have it, and so do I. There is absolutely no way I would take a penny of it."

"Please, Kerry. I wish you would. I have no use for it. Really."

"Of course you have, Mrs Craigie! Everybody has use for half a million pounds."

No, Helen thought firmly, I haven't. Because tonight, after I've seen this house properly, and given this girl her rightful money, I'm going home to take every one of those sleeping pills the doctor gave me, and a bottle of whiskey with them, and I'm never waking up again. So no, I won't be needing the money.

"Mrs Craigie?"

"Oh – what? I'm sorry. Please call me Helen."

"Helen. I was wondering . . . how did you meet Daddy? How did you manage your relationship? Did my mother know? Please tell me all about it."

"All? Are you sure you want to know?"

"Yes. Please."

"Very well."

From her handbag Helen took out a wallet of photographs and handed it across the table.

"The first one was taken the day we met, at the races at the Curragh in 1960. He had just had a winner in a big race and was all excited, buying drinks for everyone in the bar. I had been brought there by a friend who'd backed the horse he'd trained, and that was how we met. He was so ebullient, so outgoing, as thrilled as a child, very popular – I was drawn to him immediately. But it was such a surprise when he followed me out of the bar later and asked me to meet him for dinner that same night. If I'd known then that he was married, I doubt that I'd ever have done it."

"And did you – did you regret it?"

"No. Not for a single moment."

"How did you feel when you found out?"

"Shocked, of course, but probably not surprised. He was at the age when most men are. I'd just been hoping he might be widowed, like myself, but not really believing it in my heart. But by the time he told me, we were already so involved, it was far too late even to consider breaking up. We loved each other so much, Kerry, it was never just a fling, never anything sordid or underhand. Oh, we had to keep it a secret, obviously, but only because neither of us wanted to hurt your mother, or you two children."

"But didn't you want to be together all the time?"

"Yes, of course! But life isn't that easy, that simple, is it?" No. Kerry knew now that it wasn't. "So my mother never knew?"

"No, I don't think so, although most women do tend to sense such things. Maybe she – she chose to ignore it, for her own reasons. Once, after they'd had a dreadful row, Eamonn said he wanted to tell her, get a foreign divorce and marry me. But I knew he didn't mean it. We were always agreed that breaking up your family was out of the question, and even if he'd persisted I'd never have allowed it."

Good God. Daddy had considered leaving home, even if only for one heated moment? And now she, Kerry, had this woman to thank for having baulked him? Oh, he never would have done it. Never. But still she must be grateful that Helen had never encouraged him to, never exploited his anger. Mortified, she avoided Eileen's eye as the housekeeper brought in the main course and hovered over it, agog with curiosity, dying to complete a full inspection of Eamonn Laraghy's lover.

"Thank you Eileen, I'll ring when we're ready for dessert."

Reluctantly, Eileen left the room with what snippets she could bring back to her few remaining colleagues.

Her look, as she shut the door loudly behind her, spoke

volumes and made Kerry's face crack into a grin that showed Helen, suddenly, how very attractive the girl was. How very like her father.

"I'm sorry, Helen, but I suppose you can see you've caused a stir! Will you have another glass of wine?"

Kerry stretched to pour it and Helen found, most unexpectedly, that she was enjoying this lunch. It was the first food she'd really tasted since Eamonn died, the first conversation that interested her.

Resuming it, she went into all the details, amazing Kerry with how much she knew, tiny incidents and anecdotes that Kerry had herself long forgotten, little snippets of family folklore buried in the debris of time. No wonder Eamonn had been so fond of her – what a warm, lively woman! Practical, too, by the sound of it, and singularly unselfish. How many people would offer to return half a million pounds? How many would forgo the chance to marry the man they loved, for the sake of his family?

When Eileen opened the door yet again, Kerry's impatience was instant and obvious.

"What is it now, Eileen? I said I'd ring."

The housekeeper looked wounded. "It's baby Killian, ma'am, I thought you should know, he's crying his head off in the nursery and nobody can get him to stop."

"Oh, all right. Bring him down here."

With a sigh, Kerry helped Helen to another hot floury potato. She didn't eat much herself, Helen noticed, probably dieting like all the girls these days, even when she didn't need to. What she needed was her mother, to make her eat properly.

"This baby of yours, Kerry . . . a friend of your father's told me about him recently, and I'm so pleased I'm going to see him! But may I ask . . . doesn't his father . . . where is . . . ?"

Helen's voice trailed off. It was none of her business. She had put her foot in it. But Kerry answered her question.

"His father and I are separated. He's no fit man to be let near the child. As a matter of fact I'm not fit to be his mother. I see Darragh in him every time I look at him, and to be perfectly honest the sight repels me. Killian reminds me of a terrible marriage, a terrible failure and a whole episode of my life I'd much rather forget."

Helen was horrified. How could anybody not love a baby? It was unthinkable. As soon as the small blue bundle was carried in, howling, she had it in her arms, rocking, crooning, soothing the child until, magically, the tears stopped. Kerry showed no more interest in the whole affair than she might have in a passing raincloud.

"Frankly I prefer the horses. Far more interesting, far more tractable, far more beautiful for that matter."

"Kerry! You can't mean that?"

"I do mean it. I know it sounds awful, but that baby is nothing more than a burden and a nuisance to me."

Aghast, Helen peered down into the little face, the eyes still screwed up, threateningly, as if he might cry again, the tiny fists pummelling the air. Poor, unloved little thing.

"How old is he?"

"Four months – five? Not old enough, unfortunately, to be packed off to school – or better yet, go out and earn a crust."

Lord above. If this young lady needed a mother to look after her, then her infant son needed one even more. Feeling a somehow grandmotherly affinity with him, Helen replaced him carefully in his basket and continued her meal, less enthusiastically than before.

"Would you like to see the rest of the house, and the estate, Helen? It's such a beautiful day, I thought you might like to take a look round."

Would she? This was the moment she had been waiting for, the moment she got to see every inch of Eamonn's home at last. Pushing away the last of her cheese and coffee, Helen was on her feet immediately.

"And – maybe we could take young Killian here with us? I'm sure the air would do him good too."

"Certainly, if you like." Offhandedly, Kerry sent Eileen in search of the pram, and the trio went out on to the terrace, where the fountain was tinkling gently in the early summer sun, and thence on down onto the gravelled walk.

It *was* a lovely day. Contentedly, Helen pushed the pram while Kerry showed her all over the stables and paddocks and rippling, pale green meadows full of mares and stallions, colts and fillies and geldings, loping across the fields, munching the grass, swishing their tails.

"And this is Blue Moon, the boy who's going to save my bacon when he runs in the Derby in June."

Animatedly, Kerry launched into the horse's history, even confiding how a friend had bought him from her and then given him back for training, leaving her with enough cash in hand to run the place for the rest of the year, and inspiring several owners to leave one or two of their lesser animals with her too.

"So you see, I really can manage without your very kind offer, Helen. But thank you for it anyway. I do appreciate it, very much."

Helen exhibited no sign of the alarm Kerry's premature confidence detonated in her, even as she saw clearly why Eamonn had loved both daughter and estate so very much. What a wonderful place to live! So full of life, and yet so peaceful. There was something strong here, something comforting that made her feel very much at home as they wended their way back to the house.

"And in here . . . this is Daddy's study . . . the library . . . my mother's drawing room where – where—"

Kerry could not bring herself to say it, but Helen guessed. Anxious to divert tears, she went over to Maeve's desk and fingered its gilt inlay.

"What a beautiful piece. Your mother must have enjoyed working at such a desk."

"Yes. I wish I had her head for figures, but I haven't. Fortunately the friend who bought Blue Moon also loaned me his accountant, one morning a week, to sort out the first and worst of it. But it's a hellish job."

"I can imagine. I used to do my late husband's books for him when he had his own business. I was very glad when he took a proper job and I could devote myself to the children instead. It must be a nightmare for you."

"It's as if my parents had died over the controls of a jumbo jet, Helen. I've got to fly the thing and land it safely, without the remotest . . . what did you say?"

"I said it must be difficult for you."

"Yes, but what did you say about yourself? That you used to do your husband's books? That you had children?"

"Yes. They're grown up now, and Antoinette has gone to live in Texas. My son Paul is only in Dublin, so I see a lot of him, but naturally a mother misses her daughter."

"Helen! That's it! You're perfect!"

"I'm sorry?"

"Perfect! For the books, the baby, everything! Would you do it? Would you like to come and live here, at Ashamber, be my – my minder, my girl Friday, whatever? Do the bloody books for me, look after Killian, play secretary to all these people I'm trying to deal with? It would leave me so much more time for the horses . . . oh, it would be wonderful! Please say yes, Helen – unless you have a job already, of course, or something else you're planning to do?"

Kerry's eyes widened appealingly.

"I couldn't pay you, hardly anything this year at any rate, but then you've got the money from Daddy – please, Helen, think it over at least?"

"What a persuasive girl you are Kerry, no wonder you had your father twisted round your little finger! Well, until you did such an impulsive thing, anyway, just as you're doing now."

"Oh – does that mean no?"

It didn't. Helen was thrilled by Kerry's proposal. But she was afraid to rush in, afraid to contemplate the implications. And, as Kerry said, she did have something else planned. Something that would put her out of pain for good, like a mare with a broken back. A broken heart. The last thing Kerry needed was another one of those. Sadly, but firmly, she declined the offer.

"But Helen, if you miss Daddy, this is the ideal place for you! I'm in bits, Killian cries non stop, Mary and Eileen are like Macbeth's witches, the bank manager is in blackest mourning, Jerry Flynn's look would curdle milk . . . one more miserable person won't matter at all!"

Kerry beamed, well pleased with her logic, and Helen was amazed to discover that the laugh she heard was her own.

"Oh, look, then . . . let me think about it."

"OK. Give that baby his bottle, if you like, and I'll get Eileen to bring us some tea. Tell me, Helen, what was it you loved most about my father? What do you miss most?"

Was Kerry manipulating her? Steering the conversation back to Eamonn so she'd consider the link and take the job? No. Hardly. The girl didn't have that kind of guile, although she would need some if she were to run this business.

"I think what I loved most was his generosity of spirit, the way he always thought big. But what I miss most, if you must know – well, you're old enough to be told – I miss cuddling up to him in bed, Kerry. He was a most wonderful lover."

Astonished, Kerry gaped at her. Daddy, a wonderful lover? Ludicrous! Maeve had conveyed that he was a clod, that sex was a monstrous thing long gone from their lives . . . and now here was this middle-aged woman saying she missed it above all else? It was absurd. Kerry exploded into fits of laughter.

"What's so funny?"

"Oh, the idea of Daddy being good in bed! And that that should be something you miss. I thought I was the only deprived woman in this family. My husband wasn't much else use to me, but he was hot stuff in the sack, let me tell you."

Why *was* she telling her? When had this woman turned from an enemy into a friend? Helen was laughing too, chuckling so that she wobbled slightly, like a little jelly on a plate.

"What a disgraceful way to talk of our men! We're going to have to curb that, if we're to be deemed respectable in the world of big business, and give this young lad a proper upbringing."

"Oh, Helen . . . you'll take the job, then?"

Take the job? Or those pills, and the easy way out? In silence Helen wrestled with herself, thinking out her options, thinking how terribly tired she was, how bereft. But then she thought of her children, and Paul's new baby, and she thought of Eamonn, the way he had always relied on her. She thought of Maeve, the woman she had wronged, and she looked at Kerry, their daughter, Killian, their grandson.

"Yes, Kerry. Yes, I will."

No more than her father before her could Kerry pinpoint the exact moment at which she fell in love with Helen Craigie. All she knew was that she too now needed this woman in her life, quite literally, for good.

Brandon was in Tokyo, on business. But his mind was in Ireland, on Kerry.

He had telephoned her this morning, and she sounded so perky his heart plummeted. Had this husband of hers been in touch? Had she – he could hardly bring himself to ask – had she met some new friend, perhaps?

Yes, she replied, she had. She'd found a secretary who was going to tackle the books and the baby. A middle-aged lady, an old friend of her father's, a wonderful woman altogether.

That reassured him. But it made him realise, too, how life was going on without him. Who else might she find? And how could he possibly stop her, stop them? Ever since, he had been worrying the problem like a terrier, but no matter which way he shook it out he could come up with no answer.

His own fault, obviously, for having gone to see her. As a rule Brandon was a highly disciplined man, conditioned to resisting all the things that were potentially bad for him, detrimental to the achievement of a long, full life. Except that now, without her, it wasn't full at all, it was sere and colourless, stretching into dreary infinity like a desert road. But he was glad he had done it, because at least now he knew he was alive, he could feel the cold sharp stab of it in his chest. Before, he hadn't even known he was unhappy, mistaking routine content for what he supposed must be happiness, his nice life with Marianne and the boys.

A nice life. What a vapid phrase, meaningless! In ignorance he had lived it for the last three years, resigned to his duty, comfortable in his patched-up old marriage. Dermot was happy. Marianne was happy, the children were happy. Everyone was happy, at his expense. But now there was Kerry, and he had no more left to give to anyone else.

At thirty-three, he was emotionally bankrupt. He had rescued his dependants, and now it was his own turn to seek help. I've done my best, he told himself, I've earned a pardon! I can't expect a woman like her to stagnate forever, or to become my mistress. I want to marry her. But then, what of my little boys . . . ?

I could move corporate headquarters back to Ireland. Marianne would hate that, but it makes sense financially. Overheads would be cheaper and there are lots of tax incentives. I could convince Dermot, and I'd be closer to Kerry. How much would Marianne hate it? Enough to leave me, and stay in London? Because Kerry would never consider me if I were the one to desert, to leave my family fatherless the way Darragh left his.

But Marianne is being co-operative lately. If she came to Ireland with me, I'd be in an even worse fix, I'd never get to see Kerry at all. Not that she lets me near her now. But some day, she might.

Might consider divorcing Darragh. Might have me. Or might not. Leaning his head on the hotel window, Brandon wanted to throw up the sash, lean out and implore the entire city of Tokyo to help him figure it all out.

10

"Don't you shout at me, Eamonn Laraghy. It's my money now and I'll do as I please with it."

Crossly, Helen got into her car and drove off, rather stealthily, down the drive. Really she must get out of the habit of talking to Eamonn like this; conversations with non-existent people were the province of infants, not women of her years. Nonetheless, Eamonn was strongly opposed, she felt sure, to the idea of betting ten thousand pounds of his hard-earned money on a horse trained by his amateur fool of a daughter. It was a lot of money. But, if by any miracle Blue Moon pulled off the Derby, think what it could do! Kerry wouldn't take back a penny of Eamonn's misdirected legacy, but she could hardly oppose the installation of a new computer system bought with the profit on the bet. The horse was at long odds, thanks to the change of trainer, and this investment would constitute a public vote of confidence in it.

Helen wasn't at all sure how one went about placing a bet, but no doubt the clerk in the bookie's shop would explain quick enough when she produced her ten thousand pounds. It was only two miles into the village, and as she drove she slowed down here and there to wave to a neighbour, to allow a herd of cattle across the road, to admire the new bungalow being constructed on a site where, formerly, a tumbledown ruin of a stone cottage had borne witness to the horrors of the Famine. Over a hundred and twenty years ago, but only now were people getting rid of the evidence, the shame of what the British had done to their colonised people.

Never mind. Maybe Irish eyes would have cause to smile at Epsom next month. Only a few weeks to go, now, and

Blue Moon was in fine fettle. Kerry was doing a great job on him, the lads said – for a girl, that was. In recent weeks everyone had seen the progress in both horse and trainer as they attuned to one another, visibly hitting their stride. Often, she would ride the animal herself, out on the gallops of the Curragh plain at first light, urging him on faster and faster, grabbing the stopwatch the instant she dismounted, yelling blue murder if the time were a fraction out on the previous day's.

But it rarely was. Over this past week, the horse had gained a full second and a half on anything formerly achieved over the distance. But still she stamped and bawled, levitating with impatience, a fury who had half the lads gagging with fright, and the other half laughing.

Then, after breakfast, she would corner Jerry and huddle into conference with him, fussing over the most fiddly details of diet, temperature, even the bedding in the creature's stable. Patiently Jerry would go into it all with her, and Helen was pleased to hear her ask interminable questions, admitting to ignorance and mistakes whenever she was guilty of either. There was a world of difference between assisting Eamonn as a teenager and actually doing his job herself, Kerry conceded, but she would get there; like Blue Moon, she had the genetic advantage.

They had only qualified for the race by the skin of their teeth, but to Helen's surprise Kerry entered a second Derby contender as well, a colt called Wandering Star. Its owner, Bob Cummins of Belfast, was one of the very few who had kept their horses on at the Laraghy yard, and for that Helen saluted him. Not all Northerners were evil, by any means, and this one almost seemed to be trying to atone for the sins of his compatriots.

Bob was a nice man, quiet and shy, but doggedly determined to see his horse compete in the Derby. He didn't expect a win, he reassured Kerry: owning the horse and seeing it qualify was satisfaction enough. If Wandering Star came anywhere in the top half of the field, he would continue to train the horse with her thereafter, and his other colt and filly as well.

Musing on his touching optimism, Helen drew in outside Kilbally's one and only bookie's shop, sailed in and handed the clerk her bulging envelope. His eyes flew open in fright, but the transaction was speedily completed, and minutes later Helen was on her way once more, well pleased with her clandestine morning's work.

It was a pleasant drive back to Ashamber, and Helen was within half a mile of home when suddenly, out of nowhere, a large black car came screeching round the bend on the wrong side of the road, almost putting her into the ditch. Swerving out of its path, she shut her eyes and commended her soul to the Lord, and by the time she opened them again it was gone. Belatedly blaring her horn in its wake, she continued on in a state of rare but considerable outrage.

"Yves! I don't believe it! Oh, *mon ami*!"

Squealing, Kerry shot out of the stables round to the back of the house where, directed by Eileen, Yves had been told he would find her. He only had to call her name once; she knew his Breton accent instantly, so strong it was almost a parody of itself.

"Kerry!"

His face lit up with delight as she ran into his arms, and they pranced round in a ridiculous circle, laughing, hugging, shrieking as each absorbed the sudden appearance of the other.

"You've cut your hair!"

"You've – you've grown a moustache!"

In the three years since Kerry had last seen him, Yves had developed from a youth into a man, grown more robust, adult, sophisticated in his dress and stance. But his smile was as endearing as ever, mischievous as a marauding schoolboy's.

"Oh, Yves, it's so good to see you! How are you – how's TLC – how did you get here – are you going to stay for ages and ages?"

He grinned as she dragged him to a seat on the terrace and straddled another, looking rough but healthy in jeans and a white T-shirt, browned by a sun which he had been informed, mistakenly, never shone in Ireland. He too wore jeans and

T-shirt, but unlike hers they were not damp with sweat, nor tagged with wisps of hay.

"I drove over on the ferry – my 2CV fell apart, so Brian loaned me his car – TLC is great – and yes, I am going to stay for a few days, if you'll be so kind as to accommodate me?"

She laughed at his cavalier tone.

"Oh, yes. We'll put you in our most sumptuous stable. Why didn't you warn me to expect you, *mon chou*?"

"Decided to surprise you. Your dear brother has granted me leave, and I've long wanted to see this island of yours, which I'm told is so very like Brittany."

"Yes, bits of it are, I believe, especially Connemara . . . How is my dear brother, anyway?"

He heard the note of irony, quite metallic, in her voice, and braced himself against it. He hadn't come prepared for quite such immediate combat.

"Brian and Lu are very well, *chérie*, and send you their love. Also, a cheque."

She snorted. "Oh, yeah? Do they, now?"

He sat back and looked at her with eyes of disarming, lazy Caribbean blue.

"Yes. Brian is a little upset, Kerry, that you keep refusing to take any money from him. He hoped that maybe I could persuade you. I hope I can – and from me, too."

She had to laugh. Offers of loans were pouring in from everyone – except Mr Connaughton.

"Yves, I've already refused money from my friend Helen Craigie, because I can't guarantee repayment. From another friend, a businessman, because it might compromise me. From Brian, because he's a sod, just salving his guilty conscience. Now I'm going to refuse it from you too, because I know you're in debt to Mr de Veurlay, and probably still paying off your student days besides."

"But, Kerry, it's not a loan, it's—"

"*No*, Yves! It's very kind of you, but I won't do it. As for Brian, you can roll up his cheque and have yourself a smoke."

"Kerry, would you give the guy a break, would you? He knows that he behaved badly, and this is his way of saying sorry."

"Yves, I'm sick and tired of being regarded as a problem. Daddy, Darragh and Brian all washed their hands of me just because I wouldn't live my life the way they wanted. It's my life and I'll live it any way I damn well want, and there'll be nobody to apologise to at the end of it."

He turned his palms up with a helpless shrug, rolling his eyes theatrically, renewing the bond of deep affection forged in the cafés and *allées* of Paris. What a tonic he was! The only one who never judged her, who knew how it felt to be out of step.

"Well, if madame should ever change her mind . . ."

"Madame would sooner throw herself off the Eiffel Tower."

"Or throw her brother off, better still?"

"Yes. You may not know it, Yves, but Brian never wrote to me once all the time I was in Africa. Never sent congratulations when Killian was born, never said a word of encouragement when I opted to take on Ashamber. Not to mention that prize bitch he's married to . . ."

Kerry's attitude to Lu, always ambivalent, had hardened like quick-setting cement on that day the will was read, the day Lu had called her father *un salaud déguelasse*.

"Lu's our manager now, Kerry. I have to tell you that she's very good for the salon. Knows everyone, organises everything, has taken all the logistics off our hands. That's how I've been able to finish my half of our next collection so quickly – it's an underwater theme and if I say so myself, it's terrific. Lots of scope for puns on sharks and piranhas!"

"Oh, Yves. You sailed very close to the wind last time, too. You'll end up in terrible trouble."

"Look who's talking. However, since you won't take the money, I have something else for you. Follow me, *ma belle*."

Taking her hand, he led her round to where Brian's car stood, opened the boot and hauled out the first of several cardboard boxes.

"My God, Yves, what have you got in these? Hold on, I'll get someone to help you."

She waved to a man getting out of a jeep, a fortyish individual with a cap on his head and a cigarette on his lip.

"Jerry! Would you come over here and give Mr Tiberti a

hand with this stuff, please? Oh, and Jerry, put that cigarette out before you go near the stables, there's a dear?"

She smiled winningly and the man came over, touching his cap to her but glowering darkly at Yves. So, this was the foreign fool who'd nearly killed Mrs Craigie, was it? Chequered history notwithstanding, Jerry and the rest of the staff had greatly taken to the woman with her motherly, efficient, no-nonsense manner and ways. Grudgingly, without a word, he helped Yves pull the other cartons out, muttered something unintelligible and stalked away, squishing out his cigarette with the heel of his boot.

"What a charming man!"

Kerry grinned. "Oh, don't mind him, that's just his way, a bit gruff at times. He's a godsend, really. Let's get these boxes inside; I'm dying to see, and then we'll find you something to eat. *Haute cuisine* for you I suppose, proper French food?"

"Oh, no, Kerry, I hear that Irish food is so subtle, so exquisite, the toast of all Europe."

"Oh, very droll. Zip your lip or it'll be bread and water!"

Together they lugged the cartons up the steps, panting, and stacked them in the ballroom where space was plentiful. Yves whistled.

"*Chérie*, what a wonderful room! You could have some splendid parties here."

"Yes, we did, once. But the fairytale is over, Yves."

"Oh, no, Kerry, don't sound so sad. Soon you will get up on your feet, there will be lots more parties, someone to play this grand piano – have faith, *ma petite!*"

He hugged her to him, fondly, and she returned the embrace with a wistful smile. Why couldn't Brian behave like this?

"I thought Darragh might play it, if we had ever . . . he was quite a musician, you may recall?"

"So he was. Great guitarist, lousy husband. Have you got over him, yet?"

Had she? Yes. Certainly. No. Never. She hung her head.

"I'm so mad at him, Yves. He really was a total bastard. But I miss him, too, in many ways. Does that sound contrary? *Tant pis.*"

Seeing she didn't want to discuss it, he changed the subject lightly.

"Fetch a knife, and open your boxes."

She went away, leaving him admiring the mirrored, beautiful old ballroom with its columns and architraves, where once so many people had indeed danced the night away, orchestras had played and joy had been tangible. How bittersweet it must be for her, now! Alone in such a house, except for a small baby, some middle-aged staff, and this demented dog running in to yap at his heels. But she would restore it all, one day, give wonderful parties of her own, dress from head to foot in TLC . . . Remembering his mission, Yves began to rip at the first of the boxes.

By the time she returned, with a knife in one hand and a plate of sandwiches in the other, the room was festooned in clothes: suits draped over a chaise-longue, day dresses hung on the backs of chairs, trousers, blouses and gossamer mohair woollens ranged around the other furniture. Flummoxed, she stopped dead.

"Suffering Moses! What is all this?"

"It's my good luck gift to you. I presume you do occasionally need to look presentable? These are all from the Painter's Box collection. I had to estimate your size, but will make any adjustments necessary. The critics loved everything you see here, but don't let that put you off."

She was staggered. She had seen some of these clothes just recently, in a magazine Helen had bought . . . Flinging the sandwiches at him, she knelt on the floor to slash the remaining cartons open. In the last one lay a very delicate chiffon affair, in shades of coral and seaweed, trailing languidly on the air as she lifted it aloft.

"Jesus Christ."

"That's from Brian. A sample from the new collection. He had it made up specially for you, but I bet him a thousand francs that it will clash with your hair."

"You mean to say, all this is for me? For me?"

Yves was no less touched by her tone of childlike surprise than he was by the gifts.

"Yes, of course it is, *chérie*. We thought that if you are to lead your winner into the enclosure in style at Epsom, why then it had better be in TLC style."

"Oh, Yves!" Remembering his sexual orientation, she burst out laughing. "You really are my fairy godmother!"

The slang bypassed him completely, and he smiled in satisfied approval as she touched one thing after another, lifting it up to her in the mirrors, exclaiming, pirouetting, coquetting with her reflection. What a pity, he thought, that she had always refused all entreaties to model. He would hire her on the spot.

Only the chiffon evening dress, finally, was deemed a failure. As predicted, the pink was disastrous on Kerry, making her leer triumphantly.

"Hah. I told you, Yves, my brother doesn't know me nearly so well as he thinks he does. But if he shortened it – a lot – it might look well on Lu. Or is it too romantic for her, do you think?"

"Oh, Kerry! You are savage!"

"Yeah. And she's the epitome of civilisation."

Yves was inclined to side with Kerry; he did not find his partner's wife a particularly appealing woman. But her father was his financier, and so he loyally held his tongue. As Kerry flitted amidst the fabrics, a neat little woman came bustling into the room, all business.

"Kerry, would you mind telling me who owns that black car outside?"

"Brian does, but my friend here drove it over from France. Helen, this is Yves Tiberti – Yves, Helen Craigie."

Helen drew herself up to her full height, such as it was, and puffed out her chest like an irate pigeon.

"How do you do, Mr Tiberti? I'm so glad to meet you, because I thought I was going to meet my Maker. Your driving is a thundering disgrace."

Kerry laughed. "In trouble already, is he? Don't worry, Helen, I'll have Sergeant Mulligan clap him in irons for you. But look, Helen, he's brought me all these amazing clothes, the owners will be knocked out when I wear them to meetings, and the races!"

Helen's lips pursed primly.

"Very nice. And high time, if I may say so, that you got something to wear. Did Brian design them? They'll be a wonderful advertisement for him – at Epsom especially, with so many fashionable people and television cameras there."

Oh. Was that why Brian had sent the evening gown? For the society parties during Derby week? Kerry bit her lip and looked at Yves, who intervened with a firm handshake.

"I apologise if I frightened you, madame. And you must blame me for these garments, also. With the exception of the ballgown, I designed them all. They are merely a small gift to a dear friend."

"I see. Well, Mr Tiberti, I'm glad your talent at the easel so greatly exceeds your talent at the wheel."

Archly, but indulgently, Helen smiled at him, but Yves saw the seed of doubt take root in Kerry's mind, and was disconcerted. These clothes were purely for her personal pleasure; the possibility of publicity at Epsom was not their *raison d'être* at all.

Abruptly, Kerry excused herself. She had work to do.

"I'll leave you in Helen's hands, Yves. She'll show you round and entertain you to lunch – Helen, will you ask Eileen to make up a room for him, that nice big one overlooking the lake? If I can finish work early enough, Yves, I'll take you for a drive this afternoon, show you the countryside."

Realising her faux pas, and regretting it, Helen set her mind to the task of amusing Yves as graciously as possible. It did not prove onerous; he was a most likeable, charming young man. Over an informal lunch out in the sunshine, he volunteered a great deal of information, and Helen discovered that Brian was engrossed in the final stages of his second, crucial collection. Lu knew he must not be distracted with other worries, and that was why she had permitted the clothes for Kerry. Brian, Yves asserted, would never think of using his sister for publicity – but perhaps the thought had struck Lucienne, yes.

"And you, Mrs Craigie? Kerry is a lucky girl, to have found such a secretary."

"I'm – I'm more than that, Yves. There is a family relationship, of sorts. Kerry needs looking after, and so does her son. She puts all her attention into her horses, and it falls to me to see that the boy is properly cared for. It's not his fault he's his father's son . . . Tell me, what do you know of the man? Is he ever likely to come here looking for his wife and child, do you think?"

"I doubt it, madame. He is an intransigent man, and a very egocentric one. Kerry is better off without him."

"H'mm. There's another man too, Yves. I can't make head nor tail of it. He has given Kerry a great deal of help and advice in recent weeks, and his firm has bought a horse called Blue Moon for purposes of corporate publicity, hospitality at the races, and tax deductibility. He's never been here, but he rings her up all the time . . . She seems to listen to him, and rely on him quite a lot."

"Kerry listens? He must be very persuasive! Unfortunately, Darragh was the only person she ever listened to before. Why did this man buy the horse – is it an exceptional animal?"

"Yes, and she's training it for him. Eamonn, her father, bred it, and it's entered in the Derby. But frankly I don't understand why the man didn't engage Vincent O'Brien if he wants a winner. That's where all the other owners took their horses, and you can't blame them."

"No. But Kerry is cheaper, I suppose! Maybe the man is taking a chance in the hope of getting a bargain."

"Maybe. I only hope he gets it."

It was a long, wild, wonderful drive out through Kildare's lush pastures and on down into the mountainy recesses of Wicklow, with their deep folds and dark lakes, hair-raising turns and torrential waterfalls. Kerry knew every inch of it and kept up a running commentary for Yves, pointing out landmarks of interest until they came to an austere mansion brooding far below on the edge of a lake.

"And that? What is it, Kerry, a prison?"

"It's called Hollyvaun. Ugly old thing. But the same people have owned it for centuries, an odd clan who made their first money out of crystal, then linen or something – all sorts of things over the years. Only the father lives there now, a nasty piece of work by all accounts. But the son is quite – uh – civilised."

She kept her eyes on the road as she sped on, and Yves looked at her with sudden intuition.

"Does he own any horses?"

"Oh! Who told you that?"

"Mrs Craigie." Yves smirked to himself. He had thought it would take longer.

"Then Mrs Craigie has yet to learn the first rule of her new job – namely, discretion."

"Aha! Come on, Kerry, spit it out! You have a beau!"

"I have a business, and you have a big mouth. As does Helen."

He grinned, but did not press her further. She would tell him if and when she wanted to.

"Let's stop for a drink, Kerry? These bends are making me dizzy."

A few miles further on, they found a small pub near the monastic settlement at Glendalough, where prehistoric bee-hive cells and a triumphantly phallic tower drew busloads of tourists at weekends. Today, a Monday, there was hardly any-one about. Installing themselves on a bench outside, shaded by a yellow parasol, they ordered beer and poured it in studious silence.

"So. Tell me about TLC, Yves? I hear you have some very glitzy clients already?"

He paused to brush a hovering bumble bee from her sun-burned arm, and smiled modestly.

"Yes, we have. We're amazed. Jane Fonda, Raquel Welch, Candice Bergen . . . Lu says we must try for Isabella Rosellini next, Paloma Picasso, Princess Caroline when she's older, Caroline Kennedy . . . she's drawn up a whole list of targets, as she calls them. Though frankly I haven't the faintest interest in the marketing side of things, especially not on paper. It's so clinical – how can Lu tell what tastes, what personalities these women might have?"

"Still, you must think ahead. We all must. It's hard work starting out, isn't it? But great fun too."

"You're happy, then, at Ashamber?"

"Oh, yes. I'd never have forgiven myself if I hadn't taken the chance. Besides, Zoe insisted, even though it meant having to find a new flatmate. Wanted to lend me money as well, though I wouldn't take hers either. Owe her enough already."

"Zoe's a pal, Kerry, and a businesswoman. She doesn't expect anyone to pay up immediately."

"Thank God for that. She *is* such a good friend – and so are you, Yves. It was adorable of you to bring me all those clothes."

She paused for a moment, reflecting, and then looked up at him.

"Tell you what. Fair's fair. Tonight, we'll raid what's left of Daddy's cellar, have a really nice dinner, I'll try on the clothes for you to see, and then, if you're a very good boy, I'll tell you about the mystery Mr Lawrence."

Conspiratorially, he raised his glass to her, and winked.

"Lawrence. So that's his name. How convenient. You won't even have to embroider new initials on your towels."

He started to laugh, but was quelled by her look.

"Yves Tiberti, you are a romantic fool. That's what I used to be too. Now, thankfully, one of us has grown up."

Loftily, she finished her drink and returned to the car with frosty dignity.

Briskly, Kerry stripped off her filthy denim duds, pinned up her hair and showered away the day's dust. Mucking in with the stable lads wasn't just an economic necessity, it was a point of honour as well, to gain their respect; literally, she mucked out too. The work was back-breaking, so hard there were days when she felt like crying. But not today. As she towelled off she was conscious of a new sensation, something she hadn't felt for longer than she could remember.

Happiness. Plain, pure, simple happiness. It had been a lovely day, flaming with sun, the wild mountain flowers nodding and bouncing in riots of colour as she sped along with Yves, hugely enjoying his company, the exhilarating speed, the breeze that tore through her hair, the faint whiff of gorse and hay and turf on the open air. Delightful, delicious, the whole day, now carrying the smell of clematis, wisteria and freshly mown grass, seeping through the open window; the old, enduring, reassuring fragrances of childhood summers. The scent made her sleepy, but joyfully she thought of the no less pleasant evening stretching ahead, and contemplated with interest the topaz velvet dress waiting to be worn for the first time, its tawny folds almost umber in the evening shadows.

Although the day had been hot, and the sun was still blood-red as it dipped down to the west, the night would be just cool enough to justify the velvet. It was her favourite of the three cocktail dresses Yves had brought, cut on the bias, criss-crossed over the bust so that it made her look as if she *had* one, a proper, womanly affair that made her feel something else she hadn't felt for ages – feminine. It was very short, and she chose dark bronze tights to go with it, a pair of chocolate-toned shoes and, ambitiously, some bronze nail polish. Her hands were raw as a washerwoman's, but working on Lu's principles she would, as of now, start caring for them. Nobody should see, at Epsom, that these hands hauled bales of straw, wielded pitchforks, currycombed a dozen horses every morning. Lu might have turned out a millstone and a nuisance in many ways, but perhaps her advice had not been all bad.

Her toilette complete, Kerry went down to the dining room where Yves was already ensconced with Helen, affably sharing a gin and tonic. He too had dressed for dinner, in a burgundy wool sweater and cream linen pintucked trousers, bottle green leather loafers and a matching belt; the effect was such that Kerry felt a pang. What a pity, she thought, what a waste of such a beautiful man. But that's not how he sees it, and it certainly simplifies things between us.

Gallantly, he jumped up as she entered the room, his eyes widening with pleasure as he took in her transformation. Helen, too, stifled a little gasp of surprise. She had never seen Kerry looking like this, her hair offsetting her dress so perfectly, her skin so coppery, like one of Titian's women. And on just the right night, with this gorgeous Frenchman here to see and admire her! Helen felt a surge of satisfaction. This was more like it! A lovely young girl and a chivalrous, handsome man . . . what could be more right?

Simultaneously, they saw what she was thinking, linked eyes and nearly suffocated in the attempt to pretend they didn't. Oh, dear! Oh, well. There was nothing they could do. A frank explanation of Yves's sexuality was hardly the most appetising of hors d'oeuvres. Helen would have a choking fit.

Eileen came in, ceremonially bearing platters of poached salmon and clusters of watercress from the river, with zingy twists of lemon. Like Helen, she too had had an eyeful of Yves and thought him a fine catch, a very fine catch, for Miss Kerry. With Mary, she had spent the afternoon devising a deeply thoughtful menu, atavistically convinced that the way to a man's heart, especially a Frenchman's, was via his stomach.

Yves tilted his head as a low shaft of sunlight caught Kerry's neck and throat.

"*Dieu – comme tu es superbe ce soir!* But Kerry, a finishing touch of gold, perhaps, with that dress? Just one piece of jewellery?"

Kerry blushed, but smiled at him quite matter-of-factly. There was no need to pretend, to play any games with this old friend.

"Haven't got any, Yves. The gunmen took the lot."

He felt a surge of anger rise from his stomach clear up to his ears. Did they, by God? He would go shopping, tomorrow.

"But let's talk about more pleasant things. Tell Helen about our drive today, what you think of Ireland so far?"

Enthusiastically, he obliged, and they all relaxed as Paddy brought in the wine for the salmon, a perfectly cold, dry Sancerre that made their tastebuds tingle. From the terrace, the scent of summer roses wafted to join those huge ones already overflowing in great bowls around the room, and all three of them were conscious of a great sense of contentment, of mellow, pervasive peace.

The salmon was followed by a chilled soup of asparagus fresh from the garden, and hot brown bread straight out of the oven, wrapped in linen napkins. At least we have that much left to us, Kerry thought, and enough silverware to set the table; the raiders had simply not been able to grab everything in their brutal urgency. And so many of the staff had stayed on, nearly half. Things could be so much worse.

By the time they got to the saddle of lamb with buttered new potatoes and peas not an hour out of their pods, and Paddy had poured a bottle of well-warmed Château Palmer 1961 with a bouquet as richly expansive as the roses', Yves's face was such a study of surprise that Kerry laughed.

"Only simple peasant fare, *mon vieux*, but not too bad, h'mm?"

He held up his hands in surrender.

"I take it back. Everything the French ever claimed to gastronomic superiority . . . but then I am not French anyway, I am a Celt like yourselves."

"Ah. Defecting already, eh?"

Helen listened to their easy banter and almost purred with pleasure. Yes, indeed. What a smashing couple they made. She would marry them off before the year was out. They were mad about each other already, she could see it. What on earth had kept them so long apart? Why had Kerry never mentioned this gem before? She was so secretive, where men were concerned.

Cheeses followed, without biscuits or crackers, but with more of the Château Palmer. Eamonn had won four cases of it in a bet, years ago when it was still a very young, unpredictable wine. It had been a worthwhile wager. There was a side salad too, of tossed spinach leaves from the eternally providential garden, and then came a misty black-currant mousse, coffee, and a square old decanter of Armagnac. Helen waited to quaff one cup of coffee before decamping, lighting a side lamp in the gathering dusk as she went. That, with the gently glowing fire, was all the illumination they would be needing. With an excuse about checking on Killian, she tiptoed away, leaving the pair to what she hoped, and fully expected, would be a most romantic night.

The moment she was out of earshot, they collapsed in laughter.

"Oh, Kerry, *chérie*, I am terribly sorry!" Yves didn't look in the least sorry, or anything other than suffused with hilarity. "I am afraid she thinks I am the man for you! Did you hear all those questions, about my family, my background, everything?"

"Yes . . . I heard a lot more questions than answers, Yves. I could have told Helen she'd never get much out of you in that department. But I'm glad she asked, even if her motive was mistaken. She's so good to me, and for me, takes such an interest in all my activities – and such good care of the baby, too. You might have told her just a little – about how you learned to speak English, even."

Yves evaded her accusing look, and latched on to Killian.

"I barely saw the baby, only for a minute. Tell me about him."

"Oh, he's a bright little thing, perfectly healthy, alert, putting on weight, playing with his toys. Pretty much as per schedule for babies."

Idly, she twirled the decanter stopper in her fingers. End of conversation.

"Tell me something else, then. What about the insurance, on your jewellery and everything? Didn't you claim it?"

"Of course I did. But I didn't replace any luxuries. It all went into my main priorities, which are the house, staff and horses. Besides, the premiums are astronomical now."

"I see. And this man you promised to tell me about?"

Again she twirled the faceted top of the decanter, looking up, looking away, looking back at him again.

"Brandon Lawrence runs, as you've discovered, the Lawrence corporation, which over two hundred years or so has grown from a little Irish firm into a big international one. Officially, his father still owns it, but he's retired and Brandon is chief executive. We first met about three years ago, and I guess you could say it was a *coup de foudre*. But he was married, I was on my way to Paris, it was just a near miss – didn't last, couldn't last.

"Then, after my parents died, he showed up here one day out of the blue, all sympathy, offering help and perfectly nonsensical declarations of undying love. I was glad to see him, naturally, and not in a position to see off anyone who might be able to help me get on my feet.

"But I made it perfectly clear to him that I didn't reciprocate his feelings, that I would only accept help on a businesslike basis, a risky investment admittedly but one I think he'll profit from yet. I also told him I was married, and a mother, so he could forget any romantic notions he might still be harbouring. He refused to do that, but he did accept something I didn't expect him to – that our terms be in writing, and that he never come here without permission.

"He's stuck to that, I must say, and I respect him for it. But he thinks I'll change my mind – only I won't, Yves. Not now, not ever."

"But Kerry, if you fell for him the first time you met, how could that evaporate so completely?"

"Because I was only eighteen then! In the meantime, I'd been married, and I can tell you I'm vaccinated after that experience."

Yves digested this before replying.

"Brian said you were opposed to divorcing Darragh on religious grounds, Kerry. But it sounds to me as if you are using your married status as a shield."

"What? How can you say that? My family has always been Catholic, and divorce forbidden to us."

The indignation in her tone steered Yves swiftly off the vexed subject of religion and back on to the one that interested him.

"But don't you find this man attractive? If you don't want him, I'll have him."

"Oh, Yves! Yes, he is attractive – and *married*, I'm telling you, like myself. Oh, sure, he's adult and assured where Darragh was just a buccaneering boy. This guy doesn't have to prove a thing. But I don't want him, or anyone, messing my life up. It's a new life now, and it's mine. Mine alone."

"What if he tires of waiting, withdraws his help?"

"He's committed, on paper, to five years' investment minimum. Tax deductible and all. Suits him, suits us both."

Yves saw that Kerry's mind was closed tighter than an oyster on the subject of Brandon Lawrence's personal merits. But instinctively he was sure she was using her marriage as a defence. People of their generation didn't see divorce as immoral or impossible, and he had never known her to mention her religion before. Clearly Darragh de Bruin had done great damage to the girl who had once been so open to everything and everyone.

"Look, Kerry, it's not my business to tell you what to do. I can only say what I think as a friend, which is that you might be facing a tricky situation here, with maybe a lot of pain involved. But life is short, and for the living. At whatever cost."

She wrinkled her forehead. She'd had enough pain, thanks. But her parents' death had forced her to realise that life could indeed be short, and should be sweet. If Eamonn had ever regretted not claiming Helen – well, now it was too bad, too late. His chance was gone and, sadly, Helen's with it. But they had deemed the cost too high. Yves's radical philosophy was not for everyone. Anyway, it was time he pontificated less about her, and talked more about himself.

"What about you, Yves? Any romance? Work without play isn't your style at all, as I recall."

He smiled, rather oddly.

"Oh, yes. In Australia, in January. An investment analyst, of all the unlikely people. We met on a television show. I was talking about creativity in business and he was talking about the commercial side. Afterwards, we got chatting in the hospitality room."

"And?"

"And we found we were both gay, and we had a *coup de foudre*, just like yours. It was wonderful – except that I had to return to France two weeks later, and leave him in Sydney."

"Why? I mean, I know you're all tied up with Brian, and being in fashion means being in Paris, but couldn't he come to you?"

"No. He has a seven-year contract with his firm. They'll sue if he breaks it. Besides, he doesn't speak French, and the financial language is so difficult, nobody in Paris would hire him."

"Oh, Yves, how sad for you. Does it still hurt, *mon ami*?"

"Yes. It seems to get worse, not better. He was so – I thought – oh, Kerry. The distance is just too great. We did try."

Seeing the walled-up sorrow in his normally bright eyes, she felt a terrible stab of pity for him. His need of love was something he had never been able to camouflage, and she felt he would cherish even the tiniest morsel anyone should throw him. Platonic love was not nearly enough, but it was the best she could offer, and it was unconditional. Maybe it would help. Wordlessly, she reached her hand across the table to him, and he grasped it gratefully, with a tight little smile.

At length he raised his gaze from the dying embers of the fire and spoke, quietly, with a faint crack in his voice.

"Don't worry, *chérie. C'est la vie.* I'm fine – or will be, soon."

But he looked so lost, she was filled with sympathy for him, and sat massaging his hand slowly, tenderly, until night fell. Then, extinguishing the lamp, they wandered out of the room and up the stairs, hand in hand, into his bedroom. Undressing in the dark in silence, he gave her a T-shirt and donned another, and they climbed into the high, soft bed, snuggling down together into the warm fresh cotton, cuddling close like children in a forest, innocent, weary, baffled by their misfortunes. He held her until sleep overtook him, and she drifted away on dreams of her own, her face nuzzling his shoulder. It was a night of great comfort and healing for them both.

Yves remained at Ashamber for almost a week, and Kerry bloomed visibly in the warmth of his company. Despite her busy schedule she found time to walk and talk with him every day, she accepted with delight a gold pin he bought for her, and in return she taught him to ride. A natural athlete and skier of already competitive standard, he learned quickly, fearlessly, loving all the attention, bonding easily with the tractable horse she furnished.

"You're doing so well, Yves. When will you come back for more?"

Helen hoped that it would be soon. Here was a man who did wonders for Kerry, who clearly adored her and was everything that she, Helen, could wish: caring, giving, cultured, kind and thoughtful in every way. Despite her puzzlement

concerning his family, or lack of it, Helen took to him so
much she was almost inclined to tears on the eve of his
departure, and wondered whether there might be some kind
of announcement in the morning.

But there was none, and it was only then, as she watched
Yves throw his bags into the car with streamlined grace,
that Helen had a sudden, belated flash of insight. Everything about Yves was so stylish, so full of panache and
yet so gentle . . . so that was it!

Helen had never met a homosexual man in her life, and
never expected to, but now the truth dawned on her as
inexorably as the sunrise, and she began to understand why
Kerry related so freely to this man. Safety! Of course. Feeling
that she had been somehow duped, Helen had a strong desire
to go to Kerry and wring her brass neck for her.

But when she tackled her, Kerry informed her that she did
not understand at all. At *all*. Her friendship with Yves Tiberti
was very special and precious, not to be questioned in any
way. It was fluid, it was private, and it was quite different
to what any third party might infer. Greatly distressed by
Yves's departure, she slammed away to her room on the brink
of tears, and did not appear for any meal that day.

Worried, Helen was tempted to pursue the matter, but
wisely she did not. The strange, apparently symbiotic relationship was something both parties seemed to need, and neither
would thank her for interfering. Furthermore, whatever the
irregularity of it, the fact was that Helen liked Yves Tiberti
immensely.

It was some party, Zoe had to admit, a rumbustious bash
crammed with New York's most interesting, influential faces.
In the far corner she could see Andy Warhol holding court,
emaciated and intense, dispensing pearls of wry perception
from his pale lips. Nearby, Steve McQueen was dancing with
Ali McGraw, her Indian complexion accentuated by a lot of
fringing and beading, drawing every male eye like a magnet.
People came and went, milling noisily around before heading
off to other parties, nightclubs, wherever; it was a hot, loose
night, that kind of pace. Far too hot for Manhattan, where

the heat would be intolerable, but perfect for Long Island with its cool shore air. Not that there was much air in this house, but what little there was the fans whipped into action, refreshing the bronzed bodies of Bianca Jagger, Yoko Ono and the legendary Halston.

Zoe lifted another Bellini from a passing tray, speared several cocktail snacks from another and downed the lot with an uneasy mixture of pleasure and guilt. Whenever she looked in a mirror, there was no denying the weight she had put on – but there were no mirrors here, were there? This was a party and she was supposed to enjoy it. She swallowed the last salami puff and looked around for another waiter.

"Hey, Zoe, congratulations! I hear you're doing big business with Christina Onassis?"

"Yeah. Yeah, I am, Chloe."

And soon, Zoe thought, they'll all be calling me what they call her. Thunderthighs. Why can't I stop eating? Or drinking, either? It's all Kerry's fault, and that baby she stuck me with last winter.

At first, the child had been a terrifying responsibility. But then it had got to be kind of fun. By the end of the week, Zoe was crazy about baby Killian, wishing there was some way to keep the boy, flabbergasted by her own reactions. And then he was gone, back in Ireland where, she grudgingly conceded, he belonged. Not that anyone would have thought so from the way Kerry received him, dumping him on a sofa as if he were a sack of potatoes. Ever since, that baby had been on Zoe's mind, and she had been eating, eating, eating.

It couldn't go on. Forcing her eyes off yet another tray of savouries, she pushed her way into the centre of the room. She wouldn't meet anybody tonight if she didn't make an effort, start mingling. To her surprise, it worked.

"Hi. Like to dance?"

She nodded over the blaring music and they began to bop, vaguely, looking like the two total strangers that convention currently demanded that dancers be, and which they were, anyway. He was an attractive enough guy, thin, tallish, with angular features quite different from her own increasingly blurred, rounded ones. His hair was sandy, longish, unkempt around his collar, his eyes half-closed, his clothing the ubiquitous denim that could have been anyone's.

"Drink?"

"Mmm."

He got them one apiece and she gulped hers thirstily – gin, not a Bellini, but what the hell. He seemed an OK guy, she would try to stick with him. After three more dances, one indistinguishable from the other, he propelled her out of the throng, his hand on her shoulder, over to a spot near the door.

"Here."

"What?" He was holding something out to her.

"You wanta score?"

What was it? Cannabis? Coke? LSD? Zoe had never done drugs, and didn't know the difference. It must, she supposed, be whatever was fashionable this year, the sweet smell of it filling the room like incense. She hesitated. This she didn't need. But him – yes, she did need.

"Sure."

Forcing herself not to gag, she chewed the sickly stuff, feeling her nostrils water and sting, her head begin to swim, the room lurch slightly. Urrgh. She shouldn't have had so much booze, already.

"What's your name?"

"Joe."

Joe was not very inclined for conversation, not even asking her name in return. Smiling feebly, she tried a few times more, but made negligible progress. She was surprised when she felt his arm slide around her back, and then his mouth on hers, the music washing louder and louder in her head, drumming, pounding, as strong as his arms around her, pulling at her . . .

"C'mon, lady, unwind! Here, go again."

It must be LSD, she reckoned; a small quantity of cannabis wouldn't affect anyone this hard or this fast. But maybe it would relax her, like he said. A first time for everything, I guess . . . maybe for this guy, tonight. He was stroking her face rhythmically, his clear grey eyes seeming to get lighter, clearer, lighter and lighter . . .

She didn't know how long it was before he led her outside, the night air throwing all her senses into confusion, and then they were in somebody's car – his? hers? – roaring away from the party, down the dirt road that led to the ocean which seemed to be ebbing and swishing in her head. They rounded a corner and she almost threw up. But no, she couldn't do that, he'd think her a total berk, drive off and maybe even dump her here in the middle of the night, the middle of nowhere. She'd never see him again, and that would be all wrong, she thought fuzzily; he was to be the father of her baby, she couldn't let him go off like that.

She was thankful when, eventually, they slowed down into a side road, little more than a track, and bumped down on to the beach. He slewed the car in close to the dunes and turned to her.

Why, she wondered, were there so many octopuses – octopi? – strewn over the sand? Why did the sun seem to be shining, at night? Why could she still hear the music from the party, so far away?

His hand went to her face and up into her hair, riffling her black curls and then, suddenly, pulling them tight back off her face, so tight it hurt.

"So, where is it, hey? Where is it?"

Down in her stomach something convulsed. Up in her head, something connected. Behind her eyes, a red light began to flash.

"What? Where's what?"

She tried to keep the panic out of her voice. But he yanked her head up so high, so hard, she felt her jawbone slam into itself.

"Jesus, don't give me any crap! The money, the purse, the jewellery, all the stuff you society girls bring to your fancy parties— C'mon, get it off, gimme, gimme!"

Oh, Christ. Oh, no.

"I – I – I think I left my purse at the party— I'm not wearing anything valuable, I—"

"Yeah, sure, that's what they all say. Come on, now! Everything!"

It was a knife. It was. A knife, on her throat, razor sharp.

"But I haven't – really – honest—"

In one movement his free hand ripped her dress down to her waist and the long valueless chain from around her neck.

"No jewellery, huh? OK, your choice, let's do this the hard way."

The menace in his voice made her sick with fear, the tiny part of her that was still sober unable to overpower the gooey mess of stimulants in her system. She screamed as he ripped the earrings out of her ears, the rings off her fingers, the pain so searing she thought she would pass out, wished she would.

"Right. Now get the rest of that dress off, or do I have to do that too?"

He did. Her fingers were trembling so violently she couldn't grasp the fabric, the zipper, anything.

"No – no – please, no!"

She was so hoarse he didn't even hear her as he clenched his fist around the hilt of the knife and brought it down into her face, connecting with her cheekbone and sending a dull crunching pain all the way up to her skull, down into her teeth.

In seconds he had her clothing off and was tearing at his own, the edge of the knife still wedged at her jugular. Frantic, sick with panic, she made one last effort.

"Joe – don't – uhh, no—"

His left fist thudded down into her solar plexus, the right slashing with the knife until she saw her own blood spurt up over her eye, heard her own earsplitting screams coming from far, far away, like the howl of a distant dog on the briny air.

Back at the party house, Chloe felt the heat rising, muggy and clammy as a sauna. She needed some air. Picking up her Bellini, she sauntered out on the deck, her wrapover dress clinging like Tutankhamun's bandages to every contour as she took alternate sips of drink and air. Leaning on the white wooden rail, she looked out, indifferently, over the wave-washed shore.

What was that? Distinctly, she could hear something. A cry, high-pitched, piercing as a whistling kettle. But it was a human cry. Wow. Somebody must be making out down there on the beach. It sounded as if things were getting a little wild.

Were they? Well, that was their business, not hers. People in this city should be well able to look out for themselves. Sagely, calmly, Chloe downed the last of her Bellini and strolled back indoors.

11

Epsom. Kerry looked at it and her nerves jumped like fat on a hot skillet. Many places of childhood memory had shrunk when she returned to them as an adult, but this one had expanded to awesome proportions. She felt like a Lilliputian confronting Gulliver.

But many of her father's old cronies were here, friendly and paternal, teasing her, inspecting her, passing her round with jocular words of encouragement. Behind some of the smiles she sensed reserve, chauvinism, even derision, but that was the least of her worries. This might be their turf, but there was plenty of it to go round. For now, she was the only woman on it, but some day there would be others, and the men would simply have to learn to share it.

Fear of the unknown. Oh, well, that was their problem. She turned her attention to the horses, glad to find them recovering from the journey in the care of their new girl groom, Cara Jordan. Cara, only sixteen, was a great find, and Kerry was glad of some female company. The girl had come up to Ashamber from the village one day, begging to be allowed work with the horses, for nothing, over the summer holidays, and dubiously Kerry had agreed. She was totally inexperienced, but any extra pair of hands was very welcome, particularly a free pair, and Cara's had turned out to be worth half a dozen.

The night before the race, taut with nerves, Kerry fussed over the animals like a mother hen until finally Cara persuaded her to join Jerry, Frank and herself in the local pub for dinner and a drink. Hardly had they walked in the door when they heard a booming American accent, and instinctively

Kerry knew it was the voice she had heard over the phone from Kentucky: Bill Schuster. He was a big man, bigger even than Eamonn, and although she was tall she felt almost invisible as she shook his hand, introducing herself with what she hoped was calm, confident poise.

He looked down at her and his mouth twitched.

"So this is little Kerry Laraghy, eh! I'd imagined you different, somehow, but you sure do have a good Irish mop of hair there! C'mon, sit down, join our table."

She liked the look of him right away. He had a frank open smile, freckles just like her own, a neck like a side of corned beef and hands that no amount of manicuring could ever refine into anything other than two ham sandwiches. Obediently, she sat, and while drinks were ordered he appraised her candidly.

"So who's it gonna be, Kerry – you or me?"

She knew what he meant. Was his entry, trained by Vincent O'Brien, going to win the Derby, or was Brandon Lawrence's, trained by her? Impishly, she grinned at him.

"Why, me, of course, Mr Schuster. But yours will win next year, after you've given it to me to train."

He slapped the table and roared with laughter.

"Ha! That's what I like to see! Girl with a bit of go in her! So you're going to train my string for me next year, are you now?"

"Yes."

He saw she was serious.

"H'mm. Well, I'll tell you what, little lady. Howzabout we talk after the race? I know your dad was a grand old man, I was mighty keen for him to take my string, and after he died I had a word in my ear from one of your Mr Lawrence's pals that I should go with you. Mighty sorry about what happened to your dad, ma'am – but after all, business is business now, is it not?"

"It most certainly is, Mr Schuster. I wouldn't entrust any valuable horse to any unknown person either. But now that we've met, I do hope you'll reconsider – after the race, as you say."

"Well, I'll say no more for now. Let's see how things go tomorrow. I'm prepared to give you the benefit of the doubt, *if* you put up a decent show."

"That's all I ask, sir. I'll see you then – in the winner's enclosure, if you can manage to join me there."

With as much dignity as she could muster, Kerry stood up, feeling his eyes on her as she did so. Men! All the same, the lot of them. Well, she would exploit their weakness. Deliberately, she winked at him.

"Best of luck, Bill. I may call you Bill, mayn't I?"

He leapt up to pull her chair out of her way.

"You sure may, ma'am, and I hope I may call you Kerry?"

"Indeed you may."

With a little smile, she was gone, leaving Bill Schuster feeling ten years younger and ten years older, all in one last wave of her hand. He mopped his brow with a large handkerchief. What a very hot night it was. These damnblasted pubs should have better ventilation, the way bars did back home in the States.

Kerry had economised by travelling to Epsom by ferry, and been horribly seasick on the rough crossing for which her skeletal staff accusingly held her responsible. But cheerfully she rejoined them now, ordered a hearty helping of shepherd's pie and tucked into it, her appetite quite restored.

Hotel accommodation was another expense that could be saved. Despatching Frank and Jerry to a local inn, Kerry shared the horsebox's perfectly comfortable two bunks with Cara. Waking early next morning, she arose to find a sky pregnant with rain, and muttered in disgust as low metallic clouds stacked heavily over the racecourse. Soft going wouldn't suit Blue Moon at all, although it might favour Negril, the filly owned by Marianne Lawrence.

Brandon had bought the horse for his wife and presented it to Kerry for training. Today, it would run in a novice race for maidens after the Derby, for fun and for experience. Marianne had never even been to see the horse at Ashamber, but no doubt she would show up today, with so many photographers about. Kerry sensed that the woman had no interest in racing, but correctly guessed that the cachet of owning a horse – from a safe distance – appealed to her. Bob Cummins, the owner of Wandering Star, would also be here, and Kerry's heart sank at the prospect: the poor man was wasting his time.

Arriving at the stables, she found Wandering Star in fact the liveliest of her three charges, skittering nervously on his straw, rolling his eyes in a lather of agitation while Cara brushed him down. But Blue Moon stood placidly licking a salt block with no trace of star temperament, while Negril was so daintily composed that Kerry had to smile. Like her owner, the filly evidently expected to carry the day on points.

The morning was so busy that Kerry had no time for nerves until, at noon, she changed into one of Yves's fortuitous suits and headed for the Lawrence corporate marquee, its company colours of gold and crimson flying on a pennant overhead. Taken aback to be quizzed by a security man on the door, she entered with trepidation, and was engulfed by over a hundred people, milling about tables of food and drink so that she could see no sign of Brandon.

But then she spotted him, her heart contracting as she realised how very little her presence mattered. Surrounded by people much older and more polished than herself, he looked alien, almost intimidating in a grey morning suit, white cravat and striped grey waistcoat, no longer a friend but suddenly an impressive executive. She faltered; and at that moment he saw her, jumped up and personally came to claim her.

Steering her to his table, he held up a hand for silence, and got it.

"OK, everyone, hold it! I want you all to meet my trainer – our trainer – Kerry Laraghy from Kildare. Some day you'll all be asking her to train for you, if she has any vacancies left!"

Politely, his guests welcomed her, and she felt the strong comfort of his hand on the small of her back as he introduced everyone until, last of all, he brought her to a dark, pretty woman with huge violet eyes, wearing a raspberry pink suit, an enormous cream hat and a studied smile.

"Kerry, this is my wife, Marianne – Marianne, Kerry Laraghy. I know you've met before, at Ashamber, but I don't believe you've ever actually been introduced, have you?"

It was the moment Kerry had rehearsed in her head, over and over, though she hardly knew why. After all, the woman had known her mother for years.

"How do you do, Mrs Lawrence? I hope I'm going to be able to provide you with a winner this afternoon, right after your husband's."

Marianne nodded in rather a queenly fashion and patted the seat beside her, indicating that Kerry should sit there and not on the one Brandon held ready. She sat beside Marianne.

"What a lovely suit, Mrs Lawrence! I do wish I could wear that gorgeous colour, but with my hair, I'm afraid . . ."

Her sigh tailed off tragically, just as Maeve's used to do, despairingly, whenever the question of Kerry's colouring arose.

"Yes, it is rather sweet, isn't it? I'm so glad you like it. Will you have a glass of champagne?"

Kerry declined, needing to keep a clear head for final conference with the jockeys, and Marianne twirled her engagement ring, a sapphire and diamond circle so large it bordered on the criminal, as she surveyed Kerry without much effort to conceal the fact.

"So, you really think Blue Moon is going to win, then, and Negril as well?"

"There's no such thing as a racing certainty, Mrs Lawrence. But I can honestly say that both your horses are in tip-top condition. Blue had a tendon problem, but it healed nicely."

No point in blinding the woman with science, with details of weights and handicaps and starting positions. They smiled and chatted desultorily, and on her other side Kerry was aware of Brandon turning away, back to his guests, leaving the ladies to their small talk.

But his attention did not turn away. It continued to focus on Kerry like a rivet, so intensely he thought it must surely be visible through the back of his neck as he nodded and gestured to his colleagues and their wives, itching to speak only to Kerry but not daring to betray the slightest sign of unusual interest in her.

She looked good enough to eat, he thought in anguish, a far cry from the dizzy dancer of the night, a far cry from the glowing horsewoman of the snowstorm, but just what this occasion demanded: polished, ladylike, in command of herself and the situation. He knew she would say nothing remotely to compromise him – if only there were something she *could* say! But still there was nothing, apart from that kiss of years ago. Five whole months now since they had been reunited, and still she held him at a distance, as if she were lunging a horse at the end of a rope in a paddock.

His body cried out for her, his mind and heart cried out for her, there were times when he thought he would explode with frustration. And this, now, was one of them. But only after another ten minutes did he turn back to her and to his wife.

"Well, are we ready, then, for the big moment? We are going to win, aren't we, Kerry?"

"Negril is still a very young, untried horse, Mr Lawrence. But Blue Moon – well, the competition is stiff, but winning this race is in his blood." She turned to Marianne. "My father bred him from a previous winner, Blue Heaven. I'd love him to win, for Daddy's sake."

"What about his tendon? Is it completely healed?" Where, Brandon wondered, did she get that suit? It must have cost an arm and a leg – oh, the brother the designer, probably.

"The vet says it is, and he's been running like the wind."

"Let's go and take a look at him, then, shall we, and Negril as well? You coming, Marianne?"

No, he howled inside, don't come. Let me be alone with her, let me have just five minutes on my own with her, please, please.

"Yes, I think so, darling. It's time I saw my own horse, isn't it?"

Marianne smiled like an angel and he thought he would strangle her. Damn, damn, dammit to hell!

In the stables, both horses were being given a final pep talk by Cara. The girl had that affinity with them, Kerry saw, that no amount of lecturing could teach, exactly the right mixture of respect and affection, indulgence and authority. Brandon laughed.

"This young lady seems to think she's addressing the board of directors!"

"Well, in a way she is, you know. Psyching them up, making them understand exactly what's required of them. The human element is indefinable, but very important, where thoroughbred horses are concerned."

"Really?" Marianne's drawl indicated that already she was bored. "So which one's mine? Which is Negril?"

Politely Kerry showed her, but Marianne did not approach either animal, terrified of the creatures and even more terrified of having her clothing ruined. Brandon patted them fondly.

"Do we have a lump of sugar I can give them?"

"Good God, no!" Kerry flashed him a furious look. "They're about to *race*, their diet has been calculated to the last gram. Don't you dare give them *anything!*"

Startled, Marianne drew back, gasping nervously at Brandon, and immediately Kerry regretted the outburst. She shouldn't ever shout at an owner like that, showing his ignorance up in front of his wife . . . but he just looked at her quizzically, and nodded.

"Sorry. You're perfectly right, of course."

"Shall we go, darling? I promised Caroline I'd bring her to watch the race in our box. You'll join us later, in the parade ring, Kerry?"

"Yes, if I can. But I promised Bob Cummins I'd watch the race with him. He's come from Belfast to see it – he owns Wandering Star, and some other horses I'm also training for him."

There now, let her see she wasn't the only fish in the pond. It wouldn't do Brandon any harm, either.

Brandon's face fell almost to his chest, Marianne's brightened immediately.

"Oh, well, never mind. Perhaps we'll meet up afterwards."

Airily, Marianne drifted off, leaving her husband to follow. But not before he had turned to blow a kiss to Kerry, which she pretended not to see.

"We've won, Kerry! We've won, we've won!"

Bob Cummins was lifting her off her feet, bellowing, his face beetroot with excitement, and Kerry stared at him bewildered.

Won? What was he talking about? Was he drunk? She certainly hadn't won. Blue Moon was only now limping past the finishing post, a miserable fifth, his quartered colours of gold and crimson a blur amongst the many other also-rans. He'd broken too soon, peaked too early, thrown the whole thing away like a wet Kleenex, and now she was going to go down there to his jockey and roast the stupid man alive.

It was unforgivable. From the start, she had felt the steady thrum of Blue's hooves as he strained for his head, just as he did out on his training runs in the breathy, translucent mornings, every muscle interlocking, moving like pistons, a powerful, perfectly tuned machine thundering over the dusty turf. The rain had held off, he'd had everything going for him – and then that cretin of a jockey had given him his head, at only five furlongs, and ruined everything. She would thrash the disobedient fool to a jelly.

The crowd, seething with anguished tension, hushed abruptly as the loudspeaker crackled.

"A photograph for first, number three and number eleven . . ."

Eleven? *Eleven?* Dimly, the number registered in her mind. Wandering Star was numbered eleven. She hadn't even seen him run, her eyes fixed on Blue Moon from splendid start to dismal finish. Hadn't noticed him creeping up, his sudden burst into the straight . . . Mother of God, he had *won*?!

Clutching at her, Bob babbled on, beside himself, unrecognisable as the stoic Belfast widower who normally looked, and was, quiet reserve incarnate.

"It's a photo, Kerry, but he did it, I know he did!"

Was it actually possible? She fought to hide the fact that she didn't know, hadn't seen, hadn't cared, hadn't even credited the horse with a fighting chance. But she couldn't hide the reality from herself: the fact that, no matter how she might rationalise Blue's poor performance, blame the jockey, blame the tendon, the sea journey, the condition of the track, anything and everything, she was ultimately responsible. She had trained a potential winner, and it had lost.

And so, it turned out, had Wandering Star. After several more minutes, the result was announced: an unknown Arab owner had won with Shiraz Rose, Wandering Star was second and Bill Schuster's contender was third. Kerry turned to console Bob, but couldn't get a word in edgeways as his torrent of words flowed on. He was ecstatic, dazed with delight as they made their way down to the winner's enclosure.

Jerry was there, triumphantly holding Wandering Star for Bob to lead in, his face creased into the first full, real smile she had ever seen on it, and immediately Kerry smelt a rat. Betting. Strictly against all her rules, the little bastard had had a bet.

"How much, Jerry?"

"Ah, miss – just a few quid."

"How *much*?"

"Ah, well – ten thousand, or thereabouts."

Ten thousand! She was appalled. His next words horrified her even more.

"I only backed him to place. But Mrs Craigie's lost her shirt on Blue."

Helen had been betting too? They had some sort of partnership going? She would disembowel the pair of them, along with that jockey, just as soon as she'd abjectly apologised to Brandon Lawrence. But through the mist of rage she felt Bob's thrill too, buoying her up as the runner-up's rosette was pinned on Wandering Star. As she went to pat the horse, still disbelieving, a dapper, anonymous man made his way up to her.

"Miss Laraghy?"

"Yes?"

He bowed and presented her with an embossed, gilded card.

"The compliments of Sheik Feirah Zul Mahrat, with his congratulations on giving him such a very close run. His Majesty wishes to meet with you, madame, if you would be so kind as to visit his box."

Bowing again, he was gone, leaving Kerry holding the card blankly, accepting the congratulations of people she hardly knew, or didn't know at all. Hadn't they ever heard that to be second was to lose?

Leaving Bob to his delirious friends, she made her way

out of the enclosure and up to the VIP boxes in the grandstand, knowing by the time she got there that she looked flustered and dishevelled. In the Lawrence box, Marianne greeted her coolly, but Brandon congratulated her sportingly and enthusiastically.

"Thank you, Brandon. I'm just so sorry about Blue, it's all my fault, I just hadn't the experience, you never should have trusted me . . ."

"Silly girl. Don't worry, we'll live to fight another day. And there's still Negril in the 4.30. Here, have a drink?"

"No, thank you, I have to find some Arab's box, the man who owns Shiraz Rose, he wants to see me . . ."

Instantly, Brandon was alert, sizing up the situation.

"Let me come with you, Kerry. He's going to talk business to you. You'll need somebody to handle things for you, you know you're hopeless about money."

"Is he? Would you? But what about Marianne?"

"We'll bring her with us. She'll love meeting royalty. Come on."

Five minutes later, all three of them were making their introductions in the Arab sheik's box, first to bodyguards, then minders and finally to the sheik himself, a short, heavy man in a dark grey suit who seemed to have no neck and a ponderous line in conversation. Kerry was exploding with impatient curiosity, but Brandon encouraged what seemed like hours of irrelevant pleasantries before, at last, they got down to business.

"I am much impressed, Miss Laraghy. You almost stole the race from me, and at very long odds."

She opened her mouth to confess to the fluke, and Brandon kicked her hard under the table.

"You may not know very much about my country. It is a small sovereign state on the Persian Gulf, with much oil but no water. Therefore, no grass. Nowhere to train my many excellent horses. I must send them all to America, or to England, or to France. Most tedious."

He paused, apparently for sympathy, and everyone duly clucked and tutted. Get to the point, Kerry thought, get to the bloody point! We have a runner in the 4.30!

"Thus far, I have never thought to send any animals to Ireland. Such a small country, so remote, although of course it does have the celebrated Vincent O'Brien."

Kerry fumed. If he was going to hire Vincent O'Brien, why the hell was he wasting her time?

"However, Mr O'Brien is, ah, getting on, I believe. Still an outstanding trainer, but now nearing his sixties. What I have in mind is somebody younger, for one or two of my younger horses . . . I had thought of an excellent new man in France, but after today's performance, Miss Laraghy, I am inclined to take a chance on you. Purely on a trial basis, but if you would be interested . . . ?"

She thought of Blue Moon, plodding feebly into fifth position, and swallowed. If she blew another shot like that, she would take the humane killer and blow her brains out – if this sheik didn't beat her to it. He looked formidable, and something told her his horses were worth a packet.

Brandon leaned forward.

"The thing is, Your Majesty, Miss Laraghy has already agreed to train exclusively for me."

Dumbfounded, Kerry choked down a strangled gasp. Brandon had two horses on her books!

"I see. Well, in that case, Mr Lawrence, perhaps we might negotiate . . ."

Twenty minutes later, Kerry had verbally agreed to take on four of Sheik Feirah's horses, novices, for a sum fixed by Brandon at £20,000 apiece, for a year. If any of them won, there would be a ten per cent bonus. If none of them won, the contract would be terminated next year after the flat season. It was, in any event, subject to her seeing the horses and assessing their quality. At her convenience, His Majesty's private plane would fly her out to inspect them, papers would be drawn up, dotted lines signed and half the fee paid in advance.

The man was a fat little teddybear, but Kerry could have hugged him – and Brandon as well. Left to her own devices, she would have talked her chances down a drain. Not by a flicker of her eyelashes did she reveal her soaring excitement, but Brandon caught it as if by osmosis, and once out of the box they jumped into each other's arms, shrieking, laughing like kids who had pulled a successful heist on a candy store.

Bored, Marianne had long since gone back to the Lawrence corporate gathering, but from down the corridor she heard their whoops of glee, and frowned in irritation. Her husband's place was by her side today, not with that bony little twiglet who was, nowadays, just one of the many people who worked for him.

However, half an hour later, her good humour was restored. Negril won the novices' race by two lengths, and neither woman could wipe the smile off her face as the flashbulbs went off for all the sports and gossip pages.

It was a hectic dash up to London, for the Owners & Trainers Ball that had once been one of Maeve Laraghy's favourite social events. Kerry wouldn't have dared attend had all her runners lost, but in the circumstances she hummed happily in the horsebox where, incongruously and uncomfortably, she was obliged to dress for it. Out came the navy star-spangled gown of three Christmases ago, up went the hair, on went perfume, make-up and an eager grin. An expensive hour's taxi ride later, she stood in the foyer of the Grosvenor House Hotel, absurdly wishing Darragh were with her.

It was nerve-racking to have to walk into the ballroom all by herself, without an escort, even though she knew that Darragh, had he been there, would have been more trouble than he was worth. He would have made supercilious and possibly offensive comments about the silly charade of it all, the wasteful expense, the indecent luxury, the capitalist brashness of such a vulgar display. But he wasn't, and so she missed him, idiotically and pointlessly, feeling vulnerable until Bob Cummins came almost running up to dance with her.

She was amused by his pleased, shy blushes, thinking what a nice man he was, deriving far more pleasure from his near win than, probably, anybody else would have. Amicably, they chatted as they danced, and she discovered to her horror how Bob's wife had died in a bomb blast as she shopped to buy him a birthday present in Belfast. The bomb had gone off outside the shop, but a shard of splintered glass, nearly a foot long, had come flying in and pierced her temple, killing her instantly. Kerry felt a wave of nausea.

"Oh, Bob, how horrible . . . how can you even bear to talk about it?"

"I never do, as a rule. Don't know why I'm telling you now. Sorry."

He mumbled contritely, bending his face over her shoulder, and she found herself patting his back, soothingly. She knew what it was to lose someone in such a sickening fashion.

"That's why I stuck with you, Kerry. Felt so sorry to hear you'd lost your own parents to mindless violence."

She was touched, and smiled down at him; he was just a little shorter than her.

"I'm very glad you did, Bob. Most of the other owners took away their horses straight off, without even giving me a chance."

"Ha – I'll bet they're sorry now!"

They both laughed, and he confided to her that he had won even more on his bet than he had from his winnings.

"I'm going to buy another horse with the money, Kerry. A really good one this time. I know Wandering Star just got lucky. I want you to train this one, too. Will you help me pick it out?"

"Of course I will. I'm only sorry I haven't had time yet to get into the breeding side of things myself. Some day, I will."

On and on they danced, enjoying themselves, blithely unaware of the other men around the room, watching them. Bill Schuster sat waiting his turn, anxious now to firm up the deal he had offered Kerry earlier. If an Arab sheik wanted her to train for him, as rumour had it, then so did he. As soon as possible, he would have her fly to Louisville and pick out those horses best suited to her methods.

Further away, at a table occupied exclusively by men, Sheik Feirah also watched Kerry dance, noting how the light of the chandeliers picked up on the sheen of her dress, her hair, her lipstick, his eyes drilling into her as if for his precious oil. She had given him to understand that she had been

altogether indispensable to her late father, a tale he suspected
of having been liberally embroidered, but no matter. Anyone
who could get an indifferent animal like Wandering Star into
the winner's enclosure was worth taking a chance on ... how
old was she, anyway? Twenty, twenty-two? His eyebrows
beetled as he looked at her. What exceptional talent. What
exceptional red hair. Sheik Feirah knew very few red-headed
women, but adored their exotic, smouldering look. Smoothing
down his ceremonial robes, he signalled to a minder to engage
Kerry to dance as soon as she was free.

But, in his corner, Brandon Lawrence had exactly the
same idea, drumming his fingers impatiently as Bob waltzed
on, and on, exasperatingly. Would the bloody oaf never let
her go? No. Apparently not. He would just have to cut in,
then, American style. Explaining to Marianne that etiquette
demanded a dance with her winning trainer, he went over
and tapped Bob on the shoulder.

"Excuse me."

Reluctantly, Bob relinquished Kerry and Brandon took her
into his arms, firmly, proprietorially.

"You had no business to do that, Brandon! Bob is a very
nice man, and we were talking business besides."

"Business, my ass."

"Brandon!" She was half annoyed, half amused. But how
could she scold him? He'd been so good for her, to her, today.
Sociably, she danced two dances with him, and then he
fetched them both some champagne. She sipped it demurely,
but drained the glass; she'd forgotten how good the stuff
tasted, and was astonished when he started to laugh.

"No hiccups tonight, no? Got a grip on the booze, have
we?"

Mortified, she blushed as the music changed tempo and
he led her on to the floor again, holding her closer, whirling
her round, dancing with an easy, casual grace that gave
confidence to her own rhythm.

"You're wearing that dress on purpose, Kerry, aren't you?
Trying to tell me something?"

She looked so lovely, he thought, felt and smelled so
delectable, he wanted to throw her over his shoulder, carry

her out, take her upstairs to a bedroom and stay there with her for the rest of his life. And that must be what she wanted, too; otherwise, why this so-special dress, the one she had worn that first night?

"Brandon, if you must know, this is the only evening gown I possess. Brian sent me a new one, but it was pink, all wrong with my hair."

He buried his face in her neck, breathing hard.

"I'll see to that first thing tomorrow, Kerry, buy you a thousand new dresses."

"You'll do no such thing! I'm your partner, not your kept woman!"

He felt like crying. Would she never relent, never melt, never give in? Dear Christ, couldn't she feel how he wanted her, feel *anything*? She was wounded but she was not dead . . . Softly, he raised his hand to brush back a tendril of hair that fell over her eye.

"Kerry. I know you don't want to hear this, but I have to say it. I'm in love with you, Kerry. I fell in love with you the first moment I saw you, and I fell in love with you all over again the next time. I'm still in love with you now, tonight, and I will be in love with you for the rest of my life. What's *wrong* with me, Kerry? Why can't you give me a chance?"

"You know perfectly well why."

Suddenly, Brandon felt a desperation bordering on insanity. If he didn't make her understand, make her care, right now, Bill Schuster would take her away to America, the Arab would take her away to the Middle East, her horses would take her away all over the world. For years he had suppressed his own self, but he could do it no longer. It was now or never.

Reckless impulse went entirely against his grain, but gut instinct urged him on. In full view of anyone who cared to watch, he pulled her to him, kissed her face, her hair, her ear, and flicked his tongue over her skin so sensuously she shuddered.

"Marry me, Kerry."

Aghast, she leapt back from him, her wide green eyes reflecting her shock back at her in his intent, very serious grey ones.

"I mean it, Kerry. If you'll divorce Darragh, I'll divorce Marianne, and marry you. It can be done, in Haiti or somewhere. I want to spend the rest of my life with you."

A welter of conflicting emotions showered down on her like hailstones. He loved her, that much? He would put her above and before all else in his life, protect and care for her all the rest of their two lives? She was as deeply moved as she was distraught.

"Oh, Brandon." He could hardly hear her whisper over the music.

"Kerry, darling, say yes. Please say yes."

Yes! Her heart said it, and to her terror her body said it too. Her soul said it. But her lips did not say it.

"No, Brandon. I'm sorry, I can't, and you know all the reasons why. I had no idea that you – I – things – had got so out of hand. Please don't ask me again."

But he saw her eyes glisten, and was greatly gladdened.

"You care. You do, Kerry, don't you?"

Yes. Yes, she did care. She couldn't deny it, hide it, ignore it any longer. How could she not care, for a man so caring himself? He was so strong for her, so supportive, so generous . . . and now, so loving as well, so tender and so passionate. Her insides fluttered from his kiss, a little trail blazed its way to her heart.

"Yes. I do care, Brandon."

"Do you love me?"

Even if she said no, he would find a way to make her change her mind. But she laid her head on his shoulder, slipped her arms around him inside his jacket, and pressed her cheek to his, her voice almost inaudible as she admitted it.

"Oh, God . . . yes, Brandon . . . I think I do."

Yes! She did! She loved him! His heart soared like an eagle.

"Oh, Kerry!"

He couldn't remember when he had last wept, but he thought he would then. Tilting her face up, he kissed her mouth, yearning, aching for her, rapturous as he felt her face flaming against his own, her fists clenching as she fought against what could not be fought.

"So – you will get a divorce, then? And I'll tell Marianne? Now? Tonight?"

Marianne. They had completely forgotten her. Where was she? Had she seen? Frantically Kerry scanned the room, but could see no sign of her.

"Will I? Will you?" His tone was urgent, insistent.

"I – I – Brandon, let me get my breath! I don't know how this can have happened – there's so much to consider, so many people . . . please, don't rush me. Give me time, let me think."

"Sleep on it, and then say you'll do it! Kerry, I can't tell you how much I love you. I was so proud of you today, you can't imagine. I never knew it was possible to feel this much for any woman."

The orchestra was playing the theme from *Casablanca*, and they clung together, the ivy and the tree, not dancing any more, just moving, slowly, oblivious of everyone and everything. Vaguely, distantly, Kerry heard the words of the song creep up from her memory, something about a kiss being just a kiss . . .

A kiss. That certainly was a kiss. She still tasted him on her tongue, salty, masculine, hot in the summer night. If only they could just vanish into it. But rash emotion had been her downfall before. This time, she mustn't let it, she must think things through.

"I'll tell you tomorrow, Brandon, before I go home. I promise. Just give me this one night and then you'll have your answer."

He knew it would be a mistake to force her hand, this headstrong, wonderful girl masquerading tonight as a perfect lady. What would she be like if ever, when ever, he got her to bed? A starburst, he suspected.

"All right, darling. Think it all out tonight, and in the morning, say yes."

"I can't promise, Brandon."

But he knew that she was his. She loved him, she had said so. She would say yes. And he would end his marriage, tonight, because it was over anyway.

* * *

Cara had gone out partying, and Kerry lay alone in her bunk, twisting and turning, tortured in body and soul, drenched in perspiration as she wrestled with her feelings and her conscience. Brandon was not the problem. The clarity of her need and love of him stared her in the face, making her wonder how she had ever denied it for so long. In her mind's eye she could see him in every detail, the blond hair above the strong, calm face, the slate blue eyes with their tiny lines, full of love and concern, pain and desire, warmth and comfort and anguish all etched into his grave countenance. He was older than her, but that was not the problem either; she could feel his lean body as if he were still beside her, hear the vibrant timbre of his voice, sense the strength in his bearing, the intensity under the control, the life force that fought and flowed out of him . . . how he looked at her, as if she were the only woman in the world!

But she was not the only woman in the world, and that was the problem. Marianne was his wife, as she was Darragh's wife, blameless now as she had been, last September, in Senegal. If Brandon could leave Marianne, then he was not the man she thought he was, or the man she wanted.

A man who could renege on one woman could renege on another. And his was already a marriage of many years, with two sons who did not deserve to be robbed, as Killian had been robbed, of their father.

Helen could not do it, she thought wretchedly, and neither can I! My father's impulse was to marry her, and now Brandon's is to marry me. But he'll come to his senses in the morning, as Daddy did, remember his responsibilities and his commitments. He has so many . . . and a long established lifestyle that would suffer terribly, cause untold heartbreak in its destruction. Eamonn couldn't do it, Helen couldn't do it, and I can't do it.

But what am I to do, now that I see everything I tried to ignore? He's not just kind, and constant, all the things that are as wonderful as they are suddenly obvious; he's more than meets the eye. I thought he was a good friend, a good man, but tonight I saw a new Brandon, prepared to change direction as I have myself, take a huge chance when life offers it. I took one, and now I have another – but what am I going to do with it? I don't know Marianne at all, but I know how a broken marriage feels. I don't love my son, but I wouldn't wish his fate on her sons. Helen never did it, to me or to Brian . . . but how lonely she must have been, while Daddy was at home with us! And his marriage never did get any better, because his heart was never in it.

How can such misery have passed from one generation to the next? If I say yes, I'll cause more. If I say no, I'll ruin my own life, and Brandon's. Dear Jesus, how has this happened to us all? How would Zoe solve this nightmare? Some problems *are* insurmountable, whatever she says. Look at Yves, moping his life away for that man in Australia. He can't live with him, he can't live without him, and neither can I live from this day on without Brandon Lawrence.

I promised him I'd tell him tomorrow. Tell him what? Something got loose tonight, something got out of him that won't ever go back in, I think. He won't take no for an answer, he'll make my life a hell, and his own with it. I love him, and that love will lie a loss till the end of our days.

Maybe Marianne would get over it. Maybe the boys would survive. Maybe . . .

"Kerry! Kerry, wake up, get up, come quickly!"

In one leap Kerry was out of the bunk, flinging open the horsebox door as Cara pounded on it. The horses. An accident. A fire.

"Cara, what is it? Tell me, *tell* me!"

"It's Helen. She phoned the inn where Frank and Jerry are staying. There's been – something has happened – your friend in New York—"

Zoe. Oh Zoe, oh God, oh *no*.

Sitting in an easy chair, still dressed in her white organdie ballgown, Marianne idly began to file her nails, back and forth, as she admired the recently redecorated room around her. It had been done just before Brandon dropped his bombshell about wanting to move back to Ireland, about relocating the company from London to Dublin. She didn't want to go. She had her friends here, her social position, the boys' schooling to consider. London suited her so much better than that horrid provincial little city, and she was not going to go.

These days, she humoured her husband as much as she could, and although like most men he didn't even notice, the net result was a period of unprecedented tranquillity. It seemed a pity, now, to have to rock the boat, but on the matter of Ireland she would stand firm. In everything else, she had made the necessary sacrifices, giving up so much of her social life for those awful sailing weekends, doing everything a woman possibly could to be a loyal, loving, dutiful wife. Brandon would not be pleased to find her so totally opposed to moving, but he would acquiesce when he heard what she had to say to him.

Leaving the party so early, tonight, had been a shame. But she was terribly tired, and where was the point in spoiling his fun? Let him enjoy it, and when he eventually came home they would have a cup of hot chocolate together, discuss the pros and cons of this new racing investment. Owning her own horse, she had to admit, gave her quite a kick. How kind of him to think of it, and how pleased he would be with the little surprise she was planning for him! One good turn deserved another.

It was quite a while later, when she was almost on the point of giving up and going to bed, that she heard his key in the hall door, his footsteps on the tiles. His eyes were bright as he came into the room, elated, but somehow, slightly wary.

"Marianne? My God, where have you been? It's not like you to leave a party so early. Why didn't you tell me?"

"Oh, I was exhausted, darling, but you seemed to be having a good time, so I just rang for the car and came home."

He eyed her as he sat down on the sofa opposite her, removed his bow tie and steeled himself. He must do it now, right away, gently but decisively. There was no question of sharing the same bed for even one more night.

"Marianne. There's something I want – have – to talk to you about."

She smiled, so eagerly his insides churned with self-recrimination.

"Oh, yes, darling, and there's something I want to talk to you about, too. The most marvellous news, Brandon. I've been saving it up until I was absolutely sure . . . We're going to have a new baby, at last! A little girl, I hope. Every father should have a little girl to spoil, don't you think?"

A little girl. A baby daughter, just when he had the most wonderful girl in the world, almost within his grasp! He was unable to speak.

"Brandon? Aren't you pleased, after all these years? After all we've . . . been through?"

After all these years. All these years. He felt his bones turn to lead.

"Yes. Of course I'm pleased, Marianne. It's just the shock, after – after so long."

"Well then, come here and give your wife a kiss!"

Somehow he managed to stand up, negotiate the acreage of carpet that lay between them, bend down and plant a kiss on her head.

"Congratulations, darling."

12

Zoe opened her eyes and tried, feebly, to focus. There seemed to be faces floating around her, but she could not make them out. Three faces. Whose were they? Where was she? Exhausted by the effort, she closed them again and drifted back to sleep.

Kerry grabbed at her shoulder, desperately, unwilling to let the brief sign of life flicker out. But to no avail. Richard Zimner sighed, wearily.

"Please, Kerry. Don't tire her. She'll come back to us in her own time."

Behind her, Kerry heard Carla Zimner start to sob, quietly, as she had been doing on and off for the past three days as each fresh hope filtered away.

"Oh, Richard, will she ever, really? Will she?"

"She will, Carla. Zoe's a fighter. She'll make it."

Richard swallowed, and looked down at his daughter, white and inanimate as the sheets on which she lay. He was beginning to doubt it himself, bracing himself to accept reality. The likelihood of Zoe ever returning to her easel and sketchbook in the loft receded further and further with every slowly passing minute. But for his wife's sake he forced a confident smile to his face.

"You stay here, Kerry, while I take Carla to the canteen and make her eat something."

Kerry nodded as the door closed quietly behind them, and laced her fingers into Zoe's, massaging her hand gently, playing with each finger in turn, willing some life back into the cold limb.

"Come on, Zoe. Come *on*."

No response. Nothing. Just as the doctors had said. It could be an hour, or a day, or a month, or a year. If ever. How long, she wondered, could she stay here like this? Already, everything was in chaos, the meetings with Bill Schuster and Sheik Feirah postponed, Ashamber in turmoil without her, Helen holding the fort as best she could, fielding all the calls into a vacuum with no idea how long Kerry might remain captive at a bedside in Mount Sinai hospital.

But Kerry didn't care. If it took for ever, so be it. She had failed her father in his last hour, she would not fail Zoe. Zoe, her saviour who had rescued her from lonely exile in Africa, brought her back to civilisation, loaned her money, housed her, minded her child while she dealt with her own traumas. She would never desert Zoe. No way. If she had to sit here till kingdom come, then that was all about it.

Smiling down at the little face, with its bluish shadows and damp black curls, translucent pallor and swollen lips, it came to Kerry that theirs was a blood bond, the closeness of sisters. From this friend she'd had more loyalty, more support than from her own brother. What on earth had Zoe been thinking of, to get in that car and go off with a total stranger, in a place like New York above all? Even now, nobody knew who he was, the police were still drawing a blank, concluding he must have been a gatecrasher. Not by nature vindictive, Kerry mentally etched the man – the pig – on to the same list with the terrorists who had murdered her parents. Some day, they would pay. They would all pay.

How could anyone do it to such a sweet little thing? Zoe was just a half-pint, an open, innocent little fairy who wouldn't hurt a fly. She'd have been altogether unable to defend herself against a boisterous pup like Lir, much less a murderous thug, a knife-wielding rapist, alone on that night-black beach. Kerry wanted to make a fist of her hand and slam it between the bastard's eyes, slam it again and again until she heard the bones crunch, knock him down and kick his insides out, leave him in exactly the same gruesome state as he had left Zoe.

But she just went on holding Zoe's hand in her own, kneading the fingers, the palm, the small, bitten nails . . . a twitch. She felt a twitch.

"Zoe?"

A sigh. Another faint brushing of the eyelashes. And then, a word, a sound, something. The eyes began to open, very slowly, as if each lid were weighted with concrete. Another sound, or groan, until, miraculously, they were fully open.

Kerry held her breath, not daring to move.

"Zoe? Wake up . . . come on, it's me, Kerry, do it for me!"

"Kerry?"

She had spoken her name. Definitely, recognisably. Tears welled in Kerry's eyes and spilled down her cheeks as she reached across Zoe to ring for a doctor.

A doctor came, and a nurse with him, to examine Zoe, flash a light in her eyes, take her pulse, readings from monitors. They said little, but Kerry sensed their satisfaction.

"She's coming round, all right. Would you mind leaving her with us, Miss Laraghy? We'll call you soon."

Kerry protested, but was ushered outside, where she stood waiting in spirals of uncertainty until she thought of Richard and Carla, and raced away to the canteen.

It was nearly an hour before they were readmitted.

"She's out of it. She's OK. You can see her now."

Zoe lay motionless, still white, still bruised and battered, but awake. As they tiptoed in, nervously, she smiled the wan ghost of a smile, and the doctor turned to them encouragingly.

"It's all right. You can speak to her."

But now that they could, nobody could find any words to say. Kerry simply stood there, limp with relief, seeing what she had prayed to see – animation. Recognition. A miracle. But Richard and Carla drew up their chairs and she realised it was time to leave, give them some private time alone with their daughter. She followed the doctor out of the room.

"Doctor. Just a minute."

Over the past three days Kerry had become acquainted with this doctor, a capable, genial man in his early thirties, his black skin and deceptively nonchalant manner reminding her vaguely of the people of Senegal.

"I want you to tell me the position, exactly."

"All right. I will. Sit down."

They seated themselves on two plastic chairs in the corridor and he looked at her frankly.

"The nervous system is OK. No brain damage, despite the massive loss of blood. She'll be walkie-talkie in a week or so, and should have a complete change of scene straight away. A vacation about a million miles out of New York, not alone, not near a beach under any circumstances."

Kerry exhaled a slow breath of gratitude. She could arrange that.

"But as for the internal damage – irreparable, I'm very sorry to have to tell you. She's going to need further surgery, but even then her chances of reproduction are gone for good. She'll never have children, maybe never even a normal sex life."

Kerry stared at him.

"Your friend is extremely lucky to be alive, Miss Laraghy. Right now, I wouldn't ask for any more than that."

"But she will recover? You're sure?"

"Yes – apart, as I say, from the damage to her uterus and ovaries. Ironically, it's so bad that there's no chance of pregnancy resulting from the rape."

"But there must be something—"

"No. There isn't. I'm sorry. I only wish there were."

His bleep went off and he stood up. Belatedly, she thought to thank him. It was not his fault, individually, even if collectively he belonged to a species that had begun truly to sicken her.

Back at the Carlyle Hotel, Kerry peeled off her clothes, wrapped herself in the hotel's dressing gown and sat down on the bed. Now that Zoe was conscious, she was whacked; but there were two calls she must make before indulging in the luxury of sleep.

First, Helen. The phone rang on the double, buzz-buzz, Irish style.

"Kerry! At last! How is she?"

"Alive. Awake. Not great, but over the worst."

"Oh, that's wonderful . . . Yves phoned from Paris, wanting news, and he put Brian on the line too. I must say it was nice to make your brother's acquaintance, even in such worrying circumstances."

"Yes, well, you can call them back and put them out of their misery. Now, what's happening, Helen?"

"I've rescheduled your meetings with Mr Schuster and the sheik. You're to go to Louisville direct from New York. Mr Schuster will have you met at the airport if you let him know your flight time. Then you're to contact His Majesty when you want his plane to take you on to him. And Bob Cummins is looking for you, and a man from the Turf Club, and Jerry says to tell you . . ."

Kerry scribbled it all down, suddenly daunted and drained as she jotted names and numbers, remembered a dozen things to tell Helen.

"OK, then, Helen. I'll go straight to Louisville from here, and then to see the sheik. Unless you hear to the contrary, you can take it I'll be away for about another ten days, but I'll keep in touch. Now, tell Jerry I want that tendon X-rayed again, and remind Frank about those new girths . . ."

Three thousand miles away, Helen pursed her lips as she noted the long list of instructions grimly. Sooner or later, she supposed, Kerry would remember to ask for her son.

"Right, that's all for now, Helen."

"I'll see to everything, Kerry, don't worry. Oh – and little Killian has cut another tooth. He's starting to crawl, too."

"Really? That's good. Give him a kiss from me. 'Bye, Helen."

Ignoring the deeply accusatory tone in Helen's voice, she hung up, her head spinning with details. OK. So she was a bad mother. It was as simple as that. Like mother, like daughter. She had caught the allergy, whatever it was, from Maeve. Once the child was safe, fed and watered, she couldn't care less if it cut a hundred teeth.

But her pulse quickened as she sat contemplating the telephone, calculating the cost of the next call. It was going to be astronomical. Brandon said he was prepared to pay it, as he was paying for everything since her precipitate departure from England. He had begged to be allowed to do it – so. Why couldn't she dial the number?

She could see it on the pad beside her, but couldn't register it. Couldn't, now that the moment was at hand, do something that everything in her background, her culture, told her was wrong. Wrong, in the short term, even if it might be right for the rest of her life . . . Her eye fell on the mass of yellow roses on the writing table, fresh from Interflora today as every day since she arrived in New York. What a thoughtful man! The only man, apart from Yves, who had given her any reason to trust in him.

She took a deep breath and picked up the phone with a clammy hand.

In London, it was late afternoon. Louise answered on the second ring.

"One moment, madam."

And then she heard his voice, with its deep Irish intonation, calm, but resonant with concern.

"Kerry! My love – how is she? How are you?"

As she told him, she could see him in her mind's eye, drawn by his voice into the office she had never seen: a serious, masculine place in which he sat, soberly suited, with the obligatory portrait of the founder on the wall behind him, his desk neat and organised as he worked his way through another long day. A very different man from the one who had pounded into her heart, less than a week before. But the same, under all those trappings of office.

"Thank you so much for the flowers, Brandon, and for being so patient. Now that Zoe is out of danger, I didn't think it fair to keep you in suspense . . . I've come to a decision."

There was a pause, in which she felt a little giddy, hearing her own heart thumping loudly down the line.

"Brandon – I—"

But even as she took the plunge, he caught her, and held her back.

"Kerry. Oh, my dearest. Don't say it. Don't say anything."

"What? But you've been waiting – what do you mean, Brandon?"

What *did* he mean? This was the moment he had thought would never come! But intuitively she knew. Knew as surely as if he'd already said it. Something was wrong. All wrong.

"Kerry, before you tell me your decision, there's something I have to tell you."

No. *No!* Don't, Brandon, whatever it is, don't do it to me, to us! I won't listen, I don't want to hear it, *don't*—

"Marianne is pregnant."

For a very long time, fully a minute, she did not grasp his meaning. Only then, very slowly, did it sink like a stone to the pit of her stomach.

"Pregnant?"

"Yes. Oh, Kerry, my darling girl, I'm so sorry. Sorrier than I can ever tell you. But you must see what it means. I won't tell you any lies. I can't leave her, Kerry. Not now."

No. Of course he couldn't. He wasn't that kind of man. On the receiver, her knuckles whitened, and when she spoke again, she did not recognise her own voice, so hollow, so distant did it sound.

"It's all right, Brandon. I was going to tell you I can't marry you."

It was his turn to be silent.

"So I'm very pleased for her, Brandon. For you both. It's for the best, and will take your mind off me."

No tears. No argument, no pleas, no protests. What would be the point? Had it made any difference, with Darragh? With Eamonn? Did it ever, with any of them? She felt an arctic ice freeze in her veins.

"Kerry, my mind will never be off you. Not for one moment. Never."

If she didn't hang up, when he said that, she knew she would be undone. She drew on a strength that seemed to belong to somebody else.

"Well, mine will be off you, Brandon."

"Kerry! It's only a temporary setback! After the baby is born, I – I—"

"You'll abandon it? Is that what you mean? I think not, Brandon. I think not. You won't, and I wouldn't want you to. I told you, I can't marry you anyway."

There was some sort of noise at the other end. Static, or what?

"Kerry, look, when you get home, will you – will you let me see you? Talk about this? Please?"

"No, Brandon. It wouldn't change anything. I hope we can

still be partners, in business, but in future Helen will keep you informed about your investment. I – I don't want to see or hear from you. Goodbye."

Immediately, expressionless, she put down the phone. Then, her eyes fixed on the wall, she took it off the hook.

It was almost nightfall, four days later, when the small sleek jet touched down in Kutari, its royal pennant unfurling above the cockpit as soon as the wheels touched the runway. Whisper-quiet, it taxied to a stop, and two gold-braided attendants sprang to open its door, lower the blue-carpeted stairway and help their sole passenger out into the flaming sunset, scorching low across the purpling sky.

The heat hit Kerry as she unbuckled her crested seat belt, curling into the cabin, wrapping itself around her like a hot, damp towel. Gathering her things, she murmured polite thanks to the attendants, to the stewardess in her lovely blue robes, and descended the steps to where a long, white limousine stood waiting silently, eerily, in the dusk. It had been a long flight despite its opulent comfort, and she was very tired.

From the tinted windows of the car, she saw nothing as she was driven away, nothing but the blessed obscurity of rapid darkness. Disorientated, she sat dissecting the details of the deal she had finalised with Bill Schuster, her mind clinging to anything, anything, that might keep Brandon out of it.

But, dazed as she was on finally alighting from the car, she stopped in awe to behold her first view of the building that Sheik Feirah Zul Mahrat called home. In the twilight it was a vision, unearthly, its pale pink walls washed in early, glimmering starlight, its golden minarets glowing softly under the first caress of a crescent moon, its scalloped domes receding into infinity. On every side, palm trees soughed in the faint breeze, invisible insects whirred and chirped, there was the hiss of sprinklers in the sparse, precious grass. In the distance, from some tower in the city she guessed, a mullah began to call the faithful to prayer, keening, chanting, his rhythmic incantations echoing disembodied and compelling, a foreign sound in a foreign land. So lost, so alone did she feel, Kerry could hardly recall her own name.

Brandon! Oh, Brandon, Brandon, Brandon. Her heart was breaking as she was led inside this wedding cake of a palace, thinking of him at home now, sleeping in the arms of his pregnant wife. While here she was, alone in this unknown country, surrounded by smiling strangers. It was unreal, unreal.

Several turbaned young men took her into their care, removing her luggage, leading her down a warren of corridors until they came to a suite, settled her into it, and left her.

Once, she would have laughed aloud on beholding it. Once, only a week ago, she would have run to inspect every corner, to gaze amazed at the mirrored walls, the mosaic marble floors, the tented ceiling, the silken pillows, the sculpted drapes, as she inhaled the mingled fragrance of mimosa, bougainvillea and eucalyptus. In Ireland, wealth was traditionally low-key, vague and concealed; here, it was blatant, flaunted, stunning all the senses. How impressed Mummy would have been, how Daddy would have bungled around this room, like a bull in a china shop! But tears stood in her own eyes as she sank on to an ottoman, and dully wondered what she was supposed to do next.

In due course, a maid arrived to attend to her, turn down covers, ignite incense and unpack bags. Desultorily, Kerry bathed and changed, put on a fresh face, polished her nails and waited to be summoned by her host.

Feirah prided himself on being an excellent host. As soon as he saw Kerry he stood up, beaming, welcoming her, introducing her to the many people in his presence. A servant stood waiting to take her shoes, and as she looked around the long, high white room, she was glad of the excuse to steady herself.

There were no chairs, no table. Everyone sat on the floor, on cushions, greeting her indolently, the women shy and curious behind black leather masks, the men stroking falcons, hooded like the women, which perched arrogantly on their shoulders and wrists. Beneath cotton robes, all were barefoot, and in her charcoal dress of raw silk Kerry felt absurdly overdressed. It was a strange scene, so alien and so unexpected that she could only smile and murmur mechanically as she sat amongst them, wondering who, if anyone, spoke English. Some of the men did, after a fashion, and she struggled to penetrate their thick accents, responding politely to their enquiries about her trip, her state of health, her visit to America. Never, ever, had she felt more alone.

It was very quiet at the Château de Veurlay, Lucienne thought. Far too quiet, even by the standards of such a peaceful haven. Putting down her book, a history of modern French art, she sat back on her padded sun lounger, and listened.

Not a sound.

Despite the sultry, oppressive heat, she shivered slightly in her fine muslin blouse and loose, drifting pink skirt. The skirt had surprised Brian, pleasantly, as she had known it would when she selected it that morning; he found it a change from her usual trim, fitted style, blending prettily with the château's pastoral setting. But now, there seemed to be something very faintly wrong with the tranquil summer tableau, something just a fraction out of kilter. Lu could not put her finger on what it was. Nothing she could name; rather an absence of something, a stillness which seemed to have no centre.

The fringe of trees around the paved terrace was deathly quiet. Not a leaf quivered, not a bird sang, not a ripple crossed the silvery surface of the small man-made pond. For five, perhaps ten minutes Lu continued to listen intently, but nothing happened.

Even the cows in the meadows seemed suspended in time, like props in a painting, not a French one such as she had been reading about, but an English one, Turner perhaps, or Constable. The haymakers had gone in for their lunch and would not return, she knew, for two hours at least, longer if the sullen heat did not lift.

Well, never mind. It was nearly time for their own lunch. In a few minutes, Yves would come down from the attic where he was closeted, at work on winter sketches which, he said, were giving him trouble. Brian would appear from wherever he had hidden himself and her parents would return from their walk in the woods to partake of the midday meal, which on this hot day would be eaten outdoors, under parasols. But Lu wanted a few minutes to talk with Yves first, alone, and was thankful when she heard his footsteps breaking the ominous silence.

Yves had been pale lately, for a Breton who normally took the sun so well, and considerably quieter than his naturally effervescent self. She hoped he wasn't sickening on her, moping or pining for something in the terribly moody way his race was prone to. But feminine instinct told her that he was. Arranging a smile on her face, she turned to him, motioning him languidly to sit down; really this heat was so enervating. She hardly found the strength to raise her hand. But he was a guest, she must be considerate of him.

"Campari, Yves?"

"Merci, ma belle."

That, or Pernod, was his preferred apéritif, but he sounded so indifferent, today, that she might equally have offered him tap water. The heat, she supposed. Hoped.

"Any progress?"

He sighed, taking the glass from her, gazing out on to the fields and vines beyond, his eyes throwing off the flat blue of the sky, extraordinarily bleak.

"No. Worse, if anything."

In her stomach, Lu felt a small, sick twist. The more success they had at TLC, the more they were obliged to have, and already she was beginning to live in terror that the two partners had peaked too soon, that like fireworks they would fall apart just as they reached their spectacular zenith. Of the two, Brian was the more steady, the more secure despite his occasional troughs, and she knew she could handle him. But Yves was so mercurial, nightmarishly inconsistent, an enigma that drove her to disguised despair.

The winter collection on which he was now working was based on ancient Egypt, on Cleopatra, the Pharaohs, the Nile, the Pyramids, the sphinxes, the fatal asp. At first, he had been very fired up by the challenge to his imagination, the geometric puzzles of construction, the poisonous decadence of such a strong, paradoxical era. With Brian, he predicted a dazzling collection, full of fire and ice, flaming reds and blazing golds, intricate patterns and subtle drama. But now, he was stuck; hopelessly stuck. Not just with the technical problem of translating the ancient court into contemporary images, but with something that Lu saw running much deeper. His imagination, flaring initially, had waned, his creative flow seized up.

Frustrated and exhausted, he had been wilting visibly in the Paris salon, working unmerciful hours in inverse proportion to the results. He went at everything with such fervent dedication, bursting to get it all out on paper while the mood lasted, but then he collapsed like a pricked balloon. Lu thought he needed a break before he made himself ill, and that was why she had invited him here for this weekend; his brief sojourn in Ireland had not been sufficient. But now, this didn't seem to be either, and she didn't know what to suggest next.

For a quarter of an hour or so they sat sipping their drinks quietly, fanning themselves with newspapers, contemplating the problem in their different ways. But Lu could not help, she knew, until Yves first helped himself. He would have to unburden, express whatever it was that troubled him.

"Should we call in a shrink? A mystic? A faith healer?"

He laughed, but it was a brittle, warning-off laugh, and Lu did not pursue the levity. You couldn't handle these volatile, creative people in the usual way – especially not Celts. Yves could be every bit as mulish as Brian or Kerry when he chose, and she knew she would have to try to lead him blinkered past this oblique stumbling block.

It was a heavy responsibility, pressing on her with this muggy day, inhibiting her greeting as she saw Brian emerging from the house. But her husband looked much brighter than his partner. Smiling tentatively as he approached his wife, he kissed her on both cheeks, poured himself an apéritif and turned to address them both.

"I've been talking to Zoe on the phone. She says she expects to be out of hospital by the end of August. So I've asked her whether she might like to join us."

His tone was so carefully casual that at first Lu thought he meant for a holiday, and wondered at his obtuseness. Brian had already accepted Kerry's proposal, via Yves, that Zoe come to convalesce in France. But then she saw Yves rouse himself, with such a look of interested anticipation that she realised there was more to it. The pair had been hatching something.

"She's said yes, she would. She'd love to leave New York altogether, to come and work with us."

It was a *fait accompli*. Brian had calmly engaged a new partner, without consulting her. Lu was unable to mask her shock as Yves was unable to conceal his delight.

By the end of day one, Kerry knew she had the sheik's respect. By the end of day two, she knew she had his confidence. By the end of day three, she found to her consternation that she had his son as well.

Prince Nabdul Zul Mahrat was twenty-five years old, an honours graduate in ophthalmology who, like Brian Laraghy, was determined to pursue his chosen career. Against his father's wishes he was to return to Cambridge in September, for post-graduate studies which, Feirah predicted, would be an utter waste of time. One day Feirah would die and Nabdul would be a monarch, not an eye surgeon. But with luck that day would not dawn for some time, and in the interim Nabdul had no intention of squandering his talents on the idle life of a playboy.

But for now, it was summer, he was on holiday, and he was sitting, this sweltering night, in front of a woman like none he had ever seen before. Her unfeigned indifference startled him, he into whose royal clutches other women fell as inevitably as grouse on a winter's shoot. She was distant, almost remote, and behind the defensive barrier Nabdul sensed uncertainty. Here was a woman quite different from those he met on London's hectic social circuit, and he found it almost a relief to be ignored by her, a cooling shower after months of desert heat. Intrigued, he watched her closely.

Kerry felt the crackle of electricity run like forked lightning across the room, and averted her eyes. She had no more interest in him than in the man in the moon.

Piqued, Nabdul selected a damson from a Georgian silver épergne and removed its skin with his very white teeth, studying her, noting how his father's eyes lit up whenever he addressed her. He knew his father of old, and knew his intent. But he would not have this one. This one would be for him. His tawny eyes flickered with pleasure as he scrutinised her, his nostrils flaring in his slightly hooked nose, his dark skin prickling under his blindingly white robes. He would not even share her, this one.

Without appetite, Kerry tried to eat, knowing a refusal would be an insult, feeling that she was the focus of attention and hating it. But Feirah sensed her unease, and in a kindly, paternal way he began to draw her into the conversation, questioning her about Ireland. Nabdul listened intently as she began to speak, diffidently at first, but with increasing animation as she described her country.

Attuning to the company around her, she became quite entrancing as she talked about her home, her horses, her life as a child with her father, so much simpler an affair than Nabdul's own weighty youth. But what was wrong with her, that she was so impersonal, so unaware of him? It wasn't very flattering. But it was certainly a change. Tomorrow, he would take her out riding, show her what a horseman he was, show her all the colourful sights and customs of Kutari, bring it to life for her – and her to life, for him.

But next morning Feirah spent a long time in conference with Kerry, and it was noon before Nabdul was permitted to join them, fermenting with impatience, to ride out into the desert on three of the proposed horses for training. Once there, he set himself single-mindedly to showing off, executing all sorts of daring feats that did, finally, make her smile. But it was a wan smile, as if she had tuned into a television channel that did not really capture her attention. Baffled, Nabdul redoubled his efforts, but might as well have been trying to impress one of the peacocks that stalked the palace gardens.

Feirah surveyed his son's antics with faint displeasure. This was a working expedition, not a circus! Besides, he had first claim on this woman, even if it was refreshing to see his son's mind off his infernal studies for once. Perhaps, after all, he should relinquish his own designs on Kerry Laraghy, and let his son have a little fun? At forty-seven, Feirah's taste for the chase was no longer what it once had been, which was legendary. Very well, then. If Nabdul could get her, he could have her. Provided it didn't interfere with business.

As the days went by, it became clear that Kerry didn't want anything to interfere with business either, and Feirah was amused to see his son increasingly miffed, increasingly desperate, as he took her out falconing, camel racing, shopping for exotic fripperies in the souks and bazaars of Kutari's single city. She acquiesced to each outing only after finalising negotiations with vets, lawyers, accountants, and after she politely sought permission from her host. Feirah gave it with resignation. It was time Nabdul did something about his bachelor status, and a Western woman was no longer anathema: in the years ahead Arab countries would rise to much greater importance than heretofore, there would be an unprecedented amount of trade as the West consumed more and more oil. Arab influence would be a powerful new check on Western dominance, relations would shift significantly. A pity, though, that this woman did not have more status, or come from some more powerful country! America would be ideal, or Britain, Germany, Japan. But to throw obstacles in Nabdul's path would be to incite him all the more, Feirah knew, and so he left matters to take their own course. Nabdul was getting nowhere, in any event, and even if he did, the woman would hardly leave her home, her work, her country for him. Never had either man encountered such puzzling indifference to such an eligible prize.

Business dealings progressed with maddening slowness, and Kerry could have wept for Brandon to help her. With Bill Schuster in Kentucky it had been just the reverse, all signed and sealed in four days flat, whereas here it seemed impossible to pin anything down, and she found herself obliged to extend her stay several days beyond its original limit. But after a week, it was concluded at last, albeit rather more to Feirah's benefit than to hers, and wearily she acceded to Nabdul's request to take her for a picnic and a swim before her departure.

In the relative cool of the morning, he intended to take her to see the mosque at Kiroual, which as a woman she would be allowed to explore only from the outside, and then in the afternoon's heat on to the tiny, lovely stretch of coast that led Kutari on to the Persian Gulf, with its tangy breezes that would surely revitalise her. Furnished with swimming things, she climbed into Nabdul's jeep and they set off, long gauze scarves deflecting the ubiquitous sand out of their mouths and eyes as the jeep gathered speed.

As he drove he began to question her, cautiously, about her personal life, and was surprised to discover that she was married. But what matter? If the man were still on the scene, which did not appear to be the case, he would be simply paid off, persuaded to divorce and disappear. There were few things, in Nabdul's experience, that money could not buy.

A son, though? Here was news that did dismay him. A child was worse than a husband, a legal nuisance when it came to the question of precedent. If ever a relationship could be established, the boy would have to be taken into account – or more precisely, written out of it. However, things were a long way from that stage yet, and for now Nabdul was content that the girl simply seemed to be talking to him.

Her coolness melted as they flew along, her curiosity aroused when they came to Kiroual by the splendid mosque with its imperious magnificence and its bloodcurdling history. Here, he informed her proudly, there had been a memorable massacre, of which he could recount every detail – and he did, until he saw her pale and flinch, and had to add that it had been over four hundred years ago, which softened it marginally, blunted the barbed spikes of the gruesome story.

After this, they went on to the coast, the jeep jerking and jolting in giddy lurches as he steered it up into the forty-foot dunes, laughing when she gasped in fright, taking her hand protectively as they crested each one and lunged at the next. It was a wild and wonderful experience, but Kerry was relieved nonetheless when they levelled out on to the flat sand of the beach, amazed to see huge breakers where she had expected a dutifully tractable millpond.

"Come on, Kerry, let's swim!"

In seconds he had stripped off and was running into the waves, leaving her to fumble with the buttons of her cotton

dress, uncomfortable in the knowledge that, from a distant
second jeep, a squad of servants and bodyguards was watching through binoculars. But the water did look tempting, and
eventually she edged her way into its shallows, uncertainly,
conscious of her pale skin contrasting with Nabdul's copper
sheen, of being a foreigner who knew these waters not at all.

"Come on! Come in! It's great!"

And so it was, when finally she took the plunge, the salt
stinging her eyes, the spray lashing her face as the ocean
rushed up over her body. Then, with growing confidence,
she struck out; it was easy to swim in this clear buoyant
water, surging with energy. Once, she had swum like this
in Senegal, and now she found she could do it still, and
smiled as Nabdul swam up to her. Taking her by the waist,
he steered her out to where it was deeper, so that the big
waves carried her back in as if on a roller-coaster, and after
the first apprehensive ride she relaxed, started to enjoy it,
letting herself go with the flow.

Again and again the mountains of water engulfed her,
swallowed her up and carried her off on their magic carpet
until she was deposited, laughing and spluttering, back on the
beach with the eddy swirling all around her, and suddenly,
surprisingly, she found that she was having fun. Great fun.

Freedom, she thought. This is freedom! I'm not worrying
about Ashamber at this minute, I'm not mourning anyone, not
fretting about anything. I'm just a girl here on a hot sunny
beach with a new friend, having a ball! How that can be, I
don't know, but it's impossible to be miserable here, with the
sun shining, the water washing me clean and fresh and free,
free of the pain, free as a newborn baby.

Nabdul swam up again, and boldly kissed her neck, but
she was too elated to resist, playful, laughing and shrieking
with wild invigoration. Encouraged, he kissed it again, but
another wave crashed down and carried them apart, leaving
her waving mockingly, leaving him on fire with frustration.
After that one brief touch, he wanted her so badly he thought
his body would combust with the intensity of it, and had to
swim way out into the biggest breakers to compose himself.

But, much as he wished to, he would not risk everything

now. She was loosening up, and he would let her continue
to do so, in peace. Already she was obviously in a much
more positive frame of mind than before. He would wait
until tonight to tackle her, with all the romance he could
muster, with all the tricks he had learnt from that practised old lecher, his own father – the most important of
which was patience. For now, she appeared to be happy,
and that was conquest enough.

That night, after another bizarre dinner, Kerry sat back on
her cushion and toyed with a bowl of pickled rambutans,
preparing to make conversation once more with her host
and his family. A hospitable, congenial man, Feirah loved
to hear her recount the ancient myths and legends of her
homeland, and it pleased her to indulge him in this small
whim. Upon request, she began to conjure up the ghosts
and fairies, furseys and ghouls, kings and combatants so
vividly that everyone could clearly visualise the ephemeral
creatures in their ditches and hedges, and she was amused
to see the interpreter frown as he struggled to keep the
gathering informed. How it had got started she didn't know,
but it had, on that first night when, shy and lost for words,
she had fallen back on these familiar tales of childhood:
Cuchulainn and Conchubar, Queen Maedbh, Fionn, Gráinne,
Deirdre of the Sorrows and the Children of Lir, all the fabled
creatures and characters after whom the Laraghy family
named its dogs to this very day.

Then, there had been many people present, diplomats and
courtiers as well as the Mahrat family, and she had been
fascinated to see them fall gradually under the spell like
children, transported in spirit to the faraway Ireland they
had never seen, growing quieter and quieter as she spoke,
until they were completely silent, hypnotised under the aura
she had unwittingly woven.

But now, there were only nine of them, Feirah and Nabdul,
Nabdul's two sisters and their husbands, his younger brother
Rahzat, who had a girlfriend, and Shanjzah, who was only
twelve and didn't. They all wanted more of the stories, clamoured for them, but unexpectedly Feirah raised his hand.

"No. It is late. Tomorrow our guest leaves us. We must not exhaust her before her long journey home."

Imperiously he clapped his hands, and in a flash they were all gone – all, except Nabdul. Bowing low, the sheik took his leave of them, and with horror Kerry realised she was being deliberately left alone with his son. Before she could think what to do, Nabdul turned to her with a liquid smile.

"Shall we take a turn in the gardens, Kerry?"

The fountains played in the celebrated gardens, tonight, on Nabdul's express instructions. The people of Kutari resented the water they spewed, more precious than oil, high into the sky, and benevolently Feirah restricted their play to special occasions. But this, he had been persuaded, was such an occasion, and the significance of it dawned on Kerry. If she refused, she risked giving offence. If she accepted, Nabdul would think she was giving him licence to – to what? She didn't know what, exactly, and didn't want to.

Through the week of her visit, she had felt his interest and mounting ardour, but stupidly had not thought out its implications. And now, here she was, with a huge slice of business resting on her ability to humour him, to keep the son as happy as the father. One word from him, she knew, and the deal could be cancelled. Dismayed, she returned him the sweetest, most apologetic smile she could summon, with a genuine excuse.

"Thank you, Nabdul, but you've given me such a wonderful day, you've worn me out! I must get some sleep. But in the morning before I leave, I would be very happy to walk with you in the gardens."

He inclined his head, his eyes hooded, before looking back at her unperturbed, formal in his acceptance of her wishes.

"In the morning, it will be my pleasure."

"Good night, then, Nabdul, and thank you again for today. I'll never forget it."

"Nor will I, Kerry. Good night."

He got up as she took her leave of him, with no attempt to delay or restrain her. Reassured, she followed the waiting servant, back to her suite, longing to wash the day's lingering traces of sun and sand away in a warm, soporific bath. But, exhausted as she was physically, mentally she was wide awake. Awake, belatedly, from the stunned state in which Brandon had left her, absorbing the romantic beauty of the palace, congratulating herself on a mission accomplished.

The scented bath was already waiting, filled by an unseen hand, making her skin tingle as she stepped into it, scorching from the day's sun. What a lovely custom, to bathe by candlelight! Eileen would mutter, and Helen would laugh, but she would do it this way at home, in future.

Sleepily, languidly, she sank down into the water and thought of Nabdul's invitation into the gardens. Should she have accepted? Probably. He might well be annoyed, under his gracious exterior. But that was too bad, if he was; there was nothing she could do about it, no way she could handle his overtures.

What was it, this bad karma? This negative fate that seemed to ruin all her relationships? Why did it always go wrong, so swiftly and surely, always? Already, at only twenty-one, she could not think of the past without sorrow, and dared not think of the future at all, so desolate did it loom.

Where would she be, ten, twenty years from now? At Ashamber, she felt she would succeed. Knew it. Eamonn had been right, from the first day he brought her to the sales at Goff's, a little girl of seven or eight, to sit on his knee on her best behaviour. Obediently she had watched one horse after another paraded round the ring, until suddenly she had jumped up, pointing and exclaiming, telling him to buy one particular animal. Not asking, but telling. It was the very horse he had been waiting for himself, and as soon as he heard the decision, the certainty, in her voice, Eamonn had known where Kerry's future lay.

But now, if she achieved the success he had always expected of her, what would she do with it? Would it be enough, without anyone to share in it? She might make a great deal of money, but she would be alone. Alone in a big house with only a son who meant little to her, an estranged brother abroad, a staff considerably older, with their own lives to lead. Not much to look forward to.

If only she could get beyond the pride and the pain, and forgive Brian! If only Zoe were not so far away. If only Yves were not gay. If only Brandon . . .

No. It was late. Far too late for fuzzy, fruitless speculation in this tired state. She would get out of the bath and go to bed. Lazily, she stretched out her hand for the towel she had left ready . . . where was it? It was not there. But it must be.

Nabdul was holding it. Holding it out and open for her, waiting for her to stand up and step out of the sunken bath. Her intake of breath as she saw him was somewhere between a shriek and a sob, swallowed up in the darkness with the shadowy contours of his sinewy muscles. He was wearing nothing.

Softly, he spoke.

"Come here, Kerry, and let me wrap you in it. Stand up."

Her hands flew to her body, protected as it was by the white hills of foam. How had he got in?

"The door was open, Kerry, this door and the bedroom door too. If you did not want me to come, I knew you would have locked them."

Locked them? But she never locked doors. Nobody ever did or ever had at Ashamber. And that, for the second time, was the undoing of the Laraghy family.

What, she floundered in rising panic, was she going to do now? How dare he do this! Still he stood in the shadows, his arms stretched out to her, waiting, while she cowered in the water. Several seconds elapsed before he spoke again.

"Kerry, don't be frightened. I am not here to hurt you, or rape you, or cause you any pain. I want only to give you pleasure. These are not the Middle Ages, even in Kutari. I do not impose droit du seigneur on my father's guests."

Don't you, she thought furiously? Well, you're giving a damn good imitation of it.

"Come, Kerry. You will catch cold. You can't stay there all night."

Oh yes I can, she fumed. Oh yes I can. Just watch me, buster. And wipe that smile off your bigshot macho face!

Mutinous, outraged, she did not move.

"Well, I must say, this is the first time I have ever encountered such resistance! What is it, Kerry? Don't you like to make love? Don't you enjoy sleeping with a man?"

Love? A man? She had slept with nobody since leaving Darragh, almost a year before. And, as soon as he said it, and she thought of it, she realised the need of it. The need of a balm for her body, if not her soul . . . one that would put her at a remove from Darragh, and from Brandon. This man was all but a stranger, she could sleep with him indifferent, and wake up uncaring. She could be the one to do the loving and leaving for a change. Especially the leaving, she thought with sudden detachment, surveying Nabdul's form clinically, bitterly. How young and alive he was! And he had made her feel that way too, earlier today. Could he do it again, now?

Right, then. Let him try.

Slowly, deliberately, she stood up. Patiently, he waited; she caught the gleam of his eyes and teeth in the flickering candlelight. But he said nothing, and she knew he would not cajole her further, not reduce himself to pleas or entreaties. The water dripped down her back and arms and legs, evenly, like the ticking of a clock.

Do it. Go on. Do it. Get laid. Get even.

And then she was out of the bath, on the slippery marble, standing in front of him, waiting for him to envelop her in the towel. But he didn't. Instead, he dropped it on the floor, hunkered down a little and scooped her up, soaking wet, into his arms. Carrying her through to the bedroom, he put her down on the bed and motioned her not to move while he returned, briefly, to the bathroom.

Nabdul was not the man she wanted. But he was the man who was here. Where were the others? A million miles away, getting on with their lives, busily obliterating her from their minds. They had pushed her away from them; but this one wanted her to come to him. Tomorrow, she would leave him, empty-handed, taking nothing of him with her but his father's business.

He returned holding something, a small item she couldn't see. Then she smelt sulphur, heard a tiny spurting, hissing noise as he lit a match and put it to a candle so that this room too was dimly illuminated. He picked up the small object again as he climbed on to the bed and knelt over her.

"Turn over."

Curiously, she turned, glad to hide the small insistent something that was beginning to clamour inside her, and heard a clink as some cold hard thing was put down on the bedside table, a lid of a jar or bottle perhaps. What on earth was he doing? It was a good thing it was such a warm, mellow night or she would catch her death lying here waiting for him, wet and unclothed.

His hands began to move across her back and neck and shoulders, and she knew what it must be that she had heard: the lid of the onyx jar of body oil, one of dozens of such jars with which the bathroom was thoughtfully provided.

"A bath isn't a bath without a massage afterwards, Kerry."

You could be right about that, she thought as he kneaded his fingers into her skin, stroking the oil on gently and then leaning harder as he massaged it in. Slowly, taking his time, he worked downwards, slicking more oil into the small of her back, on to her sides, tapering down to her waist, pausing occasionally to kiss each new section with a butterfly touch, a fleeting flick of his tongue.

Oh, but this was delicious! Darragh had never given her a massage, nobody ever had. Now that he had started, she silently implored him to continue, thinking how wonderful this would be at the end of a killer day in the stables, how blissfully unwinding.

"Do you like it, Kerry?"

"Mmmm . . ." One by one, her bones were dissolving.

He grinned to himself, rather grimly, in the obscurity. If she liked this, she would like the rest a lot more. Applying more oil liberally to his fingers and palms, he carried on, anointing every hollow, every crevice, moving down over her hips and buttocks, marvelling at the promise of their pink creamy contours, letting the oil roll freely down inside her thighs, arousing her so that she shuddered, and he smiled.

"Oh . . . my God . . . oh!"

"Sssh."

Firmly he kneaded the oil in until she was gleaming,

moving on down over her legs, the backs of her knees, her
calves and ankles, the soles of her feet, lifting each foot
to lick its individual toes, so that she curled them back,
instinctively, and groaned again.

"Sssh . . . quietly, quietly. Turn over again, Kerry."

She turned and lay on her back, perfectly still, regarding
him solemnly as he surveyed her in turn. The moment he
saw her breasts, he wanted to clamp his mouth on to them,
to lick and suck the nipples and sink little bites into them.
But not yet, not yet.

As soon as she saw the dark hair on his chest, she wanted
to bury her face in it, to pull him to her and hold him tight,
close, admit the effect he was having on her. But she wouldn't
give him the satisfaction . . . wrenching her eyes away, she
shut them, and he laughed outright.

"Why don't you just give in gracefully, Kerry?"

No answer.

No matter. He leaned forward and kissed her lips, so that
she felt his flat, hard stomach on hers, felt him pressing and
swelling against her, and swore to herself. She couldn't resist
this, nobody could! But she did, for several more seconds,
until finally her lips parted of their own accord, her eyes
dilating as she opened them again, her thighs quivering as
he slid a finger between them, and she knew she would have
to respond. With a trembling hand, she grasped him, and
indicated what she wanted next.

"Oh, no, Kerry. Not for a long time yet."

Not yet, he said? But she would die, she would die!

"Now, Nabdul, now." She heard her own hoarseness.

He neither answered nor complied. Instead he picked up the
onyx jar and poured some more oil into his cupped hands, and
as soon as she felt it gliding on to her throat, her collarbone,
her breasts, she felt the orgasm rise inside her, rise as surely
as the sea had risen, earlier, to carry her away on its crest.
His tongue touched her right nipple.

She tugged at his arm.

"Nabdul . . . I can't . . . I'm going to . . ."

"Oh, Kerry, what nonsense! You European women are
all the same, no control at all, it's like putting a torch to

petrol. Think of something else, Kerry, restrain yourself!"

There was a hard note in his voice, quite imperious, and she gritted her teeth. Well, if he could do it, then so could she. Would have to, or she would be useless long before he got anywhere near her. With a long sigh, she clenched her fists and allowed him to lubricate the front of her body with stoic calm. As yet, he had not even touched her where she so urgently wanted to be touched.

He was massaging her stomach now, serenely, much enjoying her discomfiture, thinking how she would not be offhand with him in future, how she would jump at the chance of a return match. Delicately, he stroked her lower ribs, tickling under them, and bent to kiss her stomach before moving his hands down, at last, lower and nearer to their objective. Sharply, she gasped and drew her knees up, clutching at him with both hands.

"No, Kerry. I told you, later. Lie back, now."

Gently, but with some determination, he pushed her back down on to the bed, and her arms up over her head to where they could not reach him. Then, putting his index finger to his tongue and licking it, he drew a lazy circle on the very base of her stomach, and slipped it down further, and further, until it was between her parted legs and then, in one smooth motion, inside her. Just an inch, but enough to make her cry out and cause him to clamp his other hand over her mouth.

"If you do not stop moving, Kerry, and making such a fuss, I will beat you. Arab men do beat their women, you know."

She stopped, staring at him transfixed. He couldn't be serious!

"Now, where were we? Ah. Yes."

More oil, more glossy massage. Spreading the insides of her thighs with the palms of his hands, he worked it in, then on to the fronts of her legs, her knees, her shinbones, and finally her feet. Thank God. At last it was over, at last now he would take her. But he placed his hands, moist and warm, on his own penis to soak up the remainder of the oil.

"Now, flip over – not on your stomach – but upside down."

Dear God. It would never end. But she knew what he wanted, that she should take him in her mouth, and give him a fraction of the pleasure he had already given her. Darragh had wanted that too, sometimes, and she had done it, but never with much enjoyment. With Nabdul it was different; he had earned it, and she could hardly wait to do it. Inverting herself, she took hold of him, placing on his penis first a kiss and then her tongue, and as she did so she felt his own tongue find its way to her, and her whole body surrender, pulsating. So this was what sex was! Altogether different from what it had been when she was married, all that harsh rasping wham-bam, all that biting and kicking and bruising . . . this was something else entirely. This was paradise.

For some time they rocked back and forth, giving each other the greatest pleasure, until finally she heard him moan and knew he was ready. Disengaging himself, he lifted her back up to her original position, perfectly conventional, smiling at her through half-closed eyes as he leaned over her, steadied himself and entered her, as hard and deep as he could go.

Once secure, he set up their rhythm, pushing in and out, up and down, evidently resolved to make this, too, last for ever. But she felt the orgasm rise again, and knew that a moment would come, soon, when there would be no more holding back.

When it came, there wasn't.

Kerry woke next morning to find Nabdul's arms around her, holding her loosely to him as he slept, quietly, innocently, his long black eyelashes fringed on the pillow, bearing no resemblance at all to the demon of the night before. She experienced a small, tentative twinge of tenderness; but then she thought of Brandon, and Darragh, and pulled away.

The door opened softly, and a maid came in with a breakfast tray. Kerry cringed, good old Irish Catholic guilt to the fore, as the woman's gaze fell upon her, albeit without surprise.

"Oh – I will bring another tray, for His Highness."

What? Were the maids accustomed to finding him like this, in a guest's bed? Apparently they were. He stirred as she looked down at him speculatively, drawing her closer to him. But then, how else could he have got all that practice? If Olympic medals were to be awarded in a sexual marathon category, Nabdul Zul Mahrat would have a whole chestful.

Sleepily, he stretched and opened his eyes, grinning up at her.

"Good morning."

" 'Morning. The maid is bringing another breakfast, for you."

"Great."

Contentedly, he lay on his back, watching bemused as she clutched the sheet to her bosom with one hand, trying to lift a glass of mango juice with the other.

"Oh, here, for heaven's sake, get comfortable!"

He sat up and lifted the tray while she arranged the pillows, letting the sheet fall without further concern for the maid. If the staff were accustomed to finding their employer in women's beds, then no doubt they were accustomed to finding those women naked too.

He stretched over to kiss her, and she smiled vaguely, but did not return the gesture.

"No kiss for me, no?"

"No, Nabdul."

What a very strange girl! She would give him her body, but not a kiss? Usually it was the other way round. Sitting up, he began to eat his breakfast silently, contemplating what best to do now. There must be some way to make better contact with her than this, some way of getting under her leathery hide. Not that it looked leathery. Not at all. In the pale light of dawn it looked exceptionally fragile, vulnerable even, bespeaking none of the rejection he did not propose to savour. He ran his eyes down over what was visible of it and felt lust mount up in him as she spooned some chilled yogurt into her mouth.

"Good?"

"Uh huh."

Taking her tray, he put it down on the floor with his own, and eased the pillows out from under her back.

"Lie down."

She looked at him quizzically, and lay down.

Removing the spoon from the bowl, he swung himself over, knelt between her knees and, without any warning, inserted it, yogurt and all, inside her. She yelped in shock, and he waited a moment to watch with satisfaction the succession of diffused emotions on her face. Then, leaving it there, he scooped a handful of yogurt up from the dish, smeared it on to her left breast and lowered his lips to suck it off, rolling over on to her so that she felt his full weight, pressing down on the spoon so that she was acutely conscious of its presence.

Long before the yogurt was all licked away, she was writhing under him, conveying by every twist and turn how much she wanted him to finish what he had started.

"Give me a kiss, Kerry?"

"No!"

So be it. He wasn't going to insist: pointless. Anyway, he wouldn't have to. Sliding down her body, he applied his mouth to the inside of each parted thigh, removed the spoon and replaced it with his tongue. He didn't have to look at her for the result of this operation; he could feel every nerve leaping, igniting inside her.

"Kiss me?"

In one movement she sat up, kissed the top of his head and collapsed back onto the bed. He would pay for that.

"I don't call that much of a kiss, Kerry. I want a real one."

He raised his face and looked at her enquiringly, trying not to laugh as she nodded almost imperceptibly, allowing him to embrace her with tangible reluctance. His heavy lips met her lighter, finer ones, and as he got what he wanted his whole being filled up not just with pleasure, but with joy. It was a long, very fulfilling kiss. She was not, he thought, a girl to renege on a bargain.

"And now, your turn to get what you want."

Damn him! He wanted it too! But he held all the cards, he was the one with the self-control, an art she had never yet acquired. Still sitting upright, he entered her as soon as he spoke, and the pleasure of it drove everything else from her mind. She nearly howled as he pulled back out again, all the way out.

"Another kiss, perhaps?"

Oh! It was blackmail! Forcing herself to concentrate, she kissed him again, and only when he was sure that she was not suddenly going to retaliate with a bite or scratch did he relent, and plunge back inside her. It was more difficult sitting up, but more pleasurable for the novelty of it, the new angle, and somehow she managed to hold back, knowing he would make it worth her while.

He did, very close to his own climax before she reached hers, holding her gently while she shuddered and whimpered until he could no longer stand it either, and exploded into her.

Afterwards, as she lay in his arms, he saw how drained she was, and felt contrite, sorry for her. She had yielded only under pressure and was dazed now, he thought, probably somewhat confused amidst the tangle of sheets and pillows. What was she thinking, or feeling? Something, surely. Now was the moment to reinforce his position.

He stroked her hair, thoughtfully.

"Kerry – about your journey home today. You have a lot on your plate, with those horses to manage, all their equipment, everything. I don't think it's fair just to send a groom with you. I'll come myself."

She opened her eyes and looked at him coldly.

"That won't be necessary, thank you. Your grooms are perfectly competent."

He suppressed an urge to shake her. Why must she be so difficult? Was the prospect of a few more days of his company so intolerable? A small anger began to burn in him.

"Kerry, my father is handing several extremely temperamental, extremely valuable horses into your care. If I choose to see that they are properly settled into it, then I shall do so."

Her eyes blazed instantly with resentment, and they both opened their mouths to shout at each other. But then, abruptly, she fell away from him and smiled with the most casual nonchalance.

"Whatever you wish. They are, as you say, your horses."

He was taking advantage of his position, and she was furious. But for a change she wasn't going to let her feelings

show. At worst, she would humour him until he got bored.
But, at best, she saw what this opportunity might offer. A
visiting Arab royal would do Ashamber's reputation no harm
at all – and, if Helen could help her to handle things the right
way, what further investments might not be encouraged?

After Nabdul had left her, Kerry went into the bathroom
and looked, appraisingly, at her reflection in the mirror. She
did not altogether like everything she saw in it, but she
recognised everyone who lay behind it. Brandon. Darragh.
Brian. And, further back again, her own parents.

She might be her father's daughter, in the heat of the night,
but in the clear light of day she must aspire to be her mother's
too.

13

Mutinously, Yves pulled on the last half inch of his Gauloise before stubbing it into the ashtray. Lu didn't like anyone to smoke in the salon, precisely why he was enjoying it so much. If she had told him herself that she wished to see him, if she had *asked* him to drop in for a chat, that would have been acceptable. But she had not. She had summoned him, via their joint secretary Estelle, and that was not acceptable at all. Sending back word that he was busy, he had kept her waiting for almost an hour.

But now, he might as well get it over with. This encounter had been coming for some time, and could be evaded no longer. Automatically he found himself buttoning the high collar of the double-fronted shirt he currently favoured, and had to force himself to stop in mid-preen. *Merde!* Lu had this effect on everyone, he knew, but that only made it worse. He was not an office junior, and he was in no mood to be treated as such.

Deliberately he did not knock on the door of her office, but strode straight in. Unable as yet to afford the plush furnishings she wanted, and realising that they might clash anyway with TLC's bright young image, Lu had done the room in a spare, stark style which, he had to concede, was very striking, exactly right for what they were trying to convey. But then, Lu always did get it right, didn't she? Working with her was like working at the Vatican, infallibility so automatic it was practically computerised.

Now that Zoe was to join them, Lu made it seem as if she had not only participated in the decision, but instigated it, authorising the acquisition of this new asset as if she were, somehow, the only one with real authority. But, from Yves's point of view, Zoe was a far greater asset than young Mme Laraghy herself. He didn't bother to suppress a smile as he marched into the room.

Painted plain white, the walls were relieved only by two Chinese posters, framed in black, and a black and white clock in the shape of a daisy, one petal for each hour. On the windows, thin Venetian blinds, also black and a far cry from the lace curtains so dear to every Frenchwoman's heart, kept the summer heat at bay. The desk was a glass sheet on a perspex trestle, and the seat onto which Yves now lowered himself without invitation was a director's chair in black Spanish leather, its mate in white at the other end of the table.

Dressed in TLC as always, Lu was a very fine advertisement for his own creativity as she sat before him, jotting in her diary, not looking up until several seconds after his graceless arrival. She looked every inch the young executive, he had to grudgingly admit, one of the few women who could really wear that Klee-inspired suit. In just a few more years, she would be a formidable individual, but as yet her methods of intimidation were still obvious and contrived.

Yves, not in the least intimidated, crossed his long legs and reclined with an air of urchin insolence.

She put down her pencil, picked it up again and pointed its sharp end at him. He had kept her waiting, so she would waste no more time.

"*Alors*, Yves. The Cleopatra collection."

"Nothing, Lu. *Rien du tout.*"

"Nothing? Still?"

"Still."

She said nothing, waiting.

"That's the way it goes, Lu. I can't find inspiration all day, every day, round the clock to order. Sometimes, like any other man, I get tired, I get distracted."

"Are you distracted now?"

Yes. He was. But he wasn't going to tell her that. Wasn't going to have her hold an inquisition into his personal affairs.

"I am – how shall I put it – a trifle off centre. Nothing to concern yourself about. We are ahead of schedule."

"And will we end up on time, even?"

On time! As if he could just churn it out with a snap of his fingers, as if he were manufacturing sausages or tripes!

"I hope so. But I cannot guarantee."

Ah. Now he was beginning to get difficult, flaunt the creativity thing, ignore the business side of it all. She wrestled down a flash of impatience.

"Do you want to tell me why not?"

"No. I will do my best. That is all I *can* do."

Push him, she reminded herself, and he'll walk out, slam the door, sulk for a week. She summoned a smile.

"Of course it is. That's all anyone asks of you, Yves. I am only a little worried because it is I who have to deal with the suppliers and the buyers, I need to know what fabrics to order, how much, which models to book, what angle to take on the show. What music will we need? What kind of flowers? Accessories?"

"Lu, this show is months away! It's the one after next!"

"Yes, but we must plan it, prepare everything so that we get the best. What can I do to get the best of *you*, Yves? Do you need another holiday? More money? What?"

I need Keith, he howled far down inside himself; I need Keith! I can't live like this for another minute, I can't fill up this empty space with anything or anyone else. I'll go crazy if I don't get back to him. Completely, certifiably mad.

It was pointless, without Keith. Absolutely pointless. For months he had tried to pretend otherwise, tried to convince himself he would get over Keith Charles. Every morning he jogged in the Bois, every evening he wore himself out, at nightclubs, restaurants, theatres, suppers and soirées all over the city. He had gone to Ireland, he had gone to the château, he had skied, he had played tennis . . . and not for five minutes had he assuaged the tearing need for Keith.

He changed tack.

"Lu, I did not care for the way you invited me to meet with you this morning. *Summoned* me. You are not my boss, you know."

That stung her. Lu was smart enough never to make the claim, but she simply assumed it, and that everyone else did too.

"Perhaps not. But I am your manager. If something is wrong, I must know what it is, Yves."

"If something is wrong, it is my personal affair. And my personal choice, whether to tell you, or Brian, or nobody at all. We are partners, we must rely on trust and friendship. Brian may be married to you, but I am not. I do not require your management skills in my private life."

Exasperated, she cracked.

"Yves, may I remind you who is financing this business? My father, that's who! And I am answerable to him, even if you feel you are not!"

She saw the cold snap in his eyes when she said it, and subsided, momentarily uncertain. He hated to be reminded of the debt.

Abruptly, he stood up and went over to the window, where he stood contemplating the traffic below, the *tabacs* and the *brasseries*, the *ouvriers* sluicing the gutters, the *boulangeries*, fruit and vegetable stalls, fishmongers, draperies, *pâtisseries*. He loved Paris so much . . . but he loved Keith more.

"I want to leave, Lu."

Leave? *Leave?* Oh, *mon Dieu.*

"Yves, what do you mean? You *can't* mean that! You're a wonderful designer. This is just a temporary crisis. It will pass."

"I want to go to Australia."

Australia? She couldn't have been more flummoxed if he'd said Mars, Jupiter or Pluto. Australia – that chunk of macho rock and sand twenty thousand kilometres away? But he was insane!

"We have Zoe now, Lu. Her sportswear is a ready-to-wear line. If it will help, I will continue to contribute on a consultancy basis, and nominate her to supervise my couture designs. I think she would enjoy that, perhaps. She's very capable, and it would stretch her."

"But Yves, it's not the same thing! Zoe is very busy already, and she's a different person – it's you the clients come to."

He swung back from the window, and looked at her with a kind of desolate irony.

"Nobody is indispensable, Lu. I'll return twice a year for the shows, and the clients will be satisfied. I'll keep in touch with the really important ones, and the rest will be happy enough once they have the quality, and the label. That's the best I can do. I'm sorry if it isn't enough."

Oh, no. This was terrible. Terrible. There was just no way they could afford to lose him. The company was still only three years old, flourishing but a long way from financial independence. Yves was a crucial part of it, and the clients adored him. They would be ruined if he left, ruined overnight. Lu felt a slam of the sheerest panic.

"May I ask why you want to go there, Yves?"

"No."

But she had a right to know! He couldn't just up and go without any reason, any explanation. It was totally unbusinesslike, and would be disastrous. Didn't he care about that, couldn't he see the damage this would do? She would make him see it. She would say nothing, herself, but she would make Brian take him out, get him drunk, prise the whole story out of him while she marshalled her forces. Brian was better at this kind of personal thing — although Brian, she thought, was going to be very angry when he heard about this. No formal documentation had ever been drawn up, but each partner had tacitly accepted a permanent commitment. To defect was nothing short of treason. Icily, she looked at the traitor.

"As you wish. I will not pry into your affairs. All I can say is that I am most upset, and disappointed in you. I find it inconceivable that you should betray us like this."

She chose the verb intentionally, and saw it hit its mark, saw the colour heighten on his cheekbones as he returned his attention, ostensibly, to the window behind her.

Oh, of course he didn't want to opt out, let them down! But what could he do? If he stayed, he would be betraying himself, and that in turn would wear him down, drain his vitality, extinguish that sparkle which was essential to his personal life if his professional endeavours were to flourish. He *had* to go to Australia, to Keith. He couldn't survive another week, another hour, in this spiritual tundra.

Miserably, he turned back to her.
"I am sorry, Lu. But I am as I am."

With Kerry on the plane from Kutari went four horses for
training, a magnificent pure-bred Arab stallion for her personal
use, the optimistic good wishes of Sheik Feirah, and Nabdul.

Besotted with Kerry despite her hostility, or perhaps because of it, Nabdul had received his father's blessing to
pursue his case. For the first time in his life, he was in
love, and he was a very bad loser.

Kerry knew what she was doing without consulting anyone.
She was cultivating Nabdul, as a gardener might cultivate a
new hybrid. A year from now, five years, she would have
many more rich Arabs' custom, if she made Ireland and
Ashamber irresistible to this one. He could forget any notions
he might have about seriously romancing her, but that didn't
mean writing off his friendship. It was a simple matter of
managing him, of making sure he had a good time without
letting it go too far. And that was the great thing about
Ireland – doing business there was always fun, an enjoyable
experience that drew people back even when it drove them
mad. She would make sure Nabdul had lots of fun – and that
Brandon Lawrence heard about it, too. With luck, and a few
of the judiciously planted rumours she knew she could rely
on to spread like wildfire, he would come to know that she
could survive perfectly well without him. In every sense.

Already, she knew she was doing the right thing. Nabdul
was good company, he was the right age, he was sensational
in bed and he had even more money than the Lawrence
corporation. He would be a distraction and a challenge, and
far from feeling guilty about sleeping with someone other
than the man she loved, she welcomed the opportunity with
savage relish. After all, had Brandon not done exactly the
same thing?

How could he have? Oh, how could he have?

With all the illogical pride of a woman wounded in love,
Kerry quite forgot that she had given Brandon to understand
that his was a hopeless cause, propelling him back to his wife
while she got on with her work and her life. Only that one

night, after the Derby, had she ever told him she loved him, and the many other things she had been going to say had got lost in the confusion afterwards. Now, it was too late. He had a baby on the way, and she had Nabdul. This time, she would be a lot more careful.

It was raining when they arrived, heavily, and Nabdul was mystified to see her eyes light up as she beheld the surly overcast sky, the sodden fields and dripping hedgerows. To him, it was a glum scenario: but to her, it was home. Home at its most elemental, home in its natural, everyday incarnation, and she almost ran into the arms of Frank, waiting to meet them at the airport. There was no Bentley now, no Jaguar, and so Nabdul's first Irish odyssey was a fifty-mile bump and clatter over tortuous roads in the back of the jeep, left to amuse himself there while Kerry embarked on a long inquisition with Frank about the horses. Knowing little about her work, and caring less, Nabdul sighed sulkily as they bounced along, not at all used to taking a back seat.

Frank knew that Nabdul was a member of the ruling family of some godforsaken distant desert, and was not in the slightest degree impressed by the fact. The Irish had had their fill of royalty, years ago, and been left with little reason to retain any fondness, or even respect, for it. But, so long as this Nabdul person didn't get in the way or start throwing his weight about, Frank was prepared to put up with him; like Kerry, he saw a good investment here.

But Kerry, nonetheless, had better watch herself or she would soon get quite a reputation. This was her second male guest at Ashamber in only a month, right on the heels of that French fellow . . . was she planning to build up a whole string of them, or what? It didn't seem entirely kosher. She was a married woman, and a mother, there would be talk in the village. But then, when had there ever not been talk there, about the Laraghys? Not that Kerry cared, he suspected, unlike her father who had at least been discreet about it. But that didn't make it right. No. It really wasn't right.

Eileen was waiting for them at Ashamber, out on the steps, eager to inspect Kerry's latest conquest. A prince! How Maeve would have loved that – even if the man was foreign, and very dark. But then Kerry had never spared a second glance for any of the suitable young men Maeve had manoeuvred into her path. Contrariness was second nature to her, had already led her into trouble, and would doubtless get her into a lot more. But this man was a guest, and accordingly Eileen sent Paddy scurrying out to take the luggage, before a royal prince of wherever-it-was should have to haul his own bags into the house. With Paddy went Lir, barking dementedly as he rushed to examine the newcomer, leaping and clawing at him with frantic affection and huge, muddy paws. Nabdul recoiled, aghast and unnerved, as Kerry sailed past him into the hall.

"Eileen! It's so good to be home! But where's Helen?"

Eileen mumbled something to the effect that Helen was out, so evasively that Kerry demanded the truth, which was that Helen had gone off somewhere with Bob Cummins.

"Bob Cummins? Where? Why?"

"I don't know where, or why. He called out of the blue a few hours ago to see his horses, and then he took Mrs Craigie away with him in his car . . . I must say, those Northern registration plates give me the shivers, even when it is only him. Anyway, they said they'd be back in time for dinner. Mrs Craigie invited him to stay and eat with us."

Did she, now? Kerry was intrigued and rather miffed all at once. It was a bit cavalier of Helen to issue invitations like that . . . Where had she gone, anyway? To see some horse Bob proposed to buy? But Helen didn't know the first thing about judging a thoroughbred. Maybe Bob had just wanted company on some business excursion or other. Chewing over the various possibilities, Kerry went up to her room, expecting to find Nabdul already in it. But he was not, and it took her a few seconds to work out that Eileen must, prudishly, have put him somewhere else. But then, she could not be expected to know on what intimate terms they already were. Going in search of him, she found him gloomily ensconced in the room formerly occupied by Yves, and it crossed her mind to wonder whether Eileen was being sarcastic. There did seem to be rather a lot of men in her life . . . But this one was going to earn his keep.

"So, Nabdul, what do you make of Ashamber?"

Not much, was Nabdul's candid response, but he bit it back. He was tired after the long journey. No doubt things would look better tomorrow, when the rain stopped and the mad dog was brought under control, when he adjusted to the scale of things. Not that the house was cramped or uncomfortable in any way – on the contrary, it was a very big, substantial place. But it was so cluttered, so casual and disorganised! Why were the staff not in uniform? Why were things scattered everywhere? Why was that damn dog allowed to run wild? Why was no servant assigned to him personally, and why was he in this room, with Kerry in another? Was he supposed to creep down the corridors like a thief in the night?

"Very nice, Kerry. Very nice."

She saw that his mood was dark, thick and black like the clouds.

"Oh, come on Nabdul, cheer up! You can't expect everyone to live in a palace and be danced attendance on! Things are relaxed here, we don't stand on ceremony. That's what makes it home. But don't worry, I'll take you to lots of interesting places, introduce you to all sorts of nice people, there's no need to fret."

With a confident smile she vanished, leaving him to mull over his chosen holiday destination. Where, he wondered, was the nearest beach? The nearest nightclub? What was he going to do all day while Kerry was busy with her wretched horses? Would the sun ever come out? This country might be an astonishingly green place, but already he was feeling distinctly blue. If things didn't improve, he would leave his father's horses to their fate and go straight home.

Contrary to expectation, Nabdul did not stamp away in a day or two, finding instead that he was cheering up as per orders. Why that should be, he couldn't think, but he was. Several times already, he had been soaked to the skin, caught out in thunderous deluges of rain; he had never seen so much water in his life. The roads ran with it, the gutters spluttered and gurgled with it, the horses steamed and snorted in it, the grass squelched and squished with it, it was everywhere, *everywhere*. But then, disconcertingly, it would stop as suddenly as it began and a pale watery sun would peep apologetically out, the branches twinkling and sparkling as the birds began to twitter nonchalantly, and the most spectacular rainbows would arc triumphantly across the sky, hazy, luminous, dazzling in their gorgeous colours.

There was no more hope of getting to a beach than of getting to Tibet, but as the days passed he began to find that he no longer cared and that, stranger still, he was actually looking forward to his morning tramps across the verdant pastures, with their briary hedges and ditches, their fairy forts and petrified trees which, Kerry assured him, were haunted by all manner of nocturnal creatures. It was like walking through an infant's book of fairytales, and, although he did not publicly admit it, Nabdul gradually came to be quite bewitched.

Despite the eternal rain to which they seemed condemned, the local people were cheerful, saluting him with their black-thorn sticks as they met him on their walks and rambles, so casually he might have been the village postman. They must know who he was, he was sure, since the police had had to be informed of his presence, but if they did know they didn't seem to care. At first, his pride took a fall, but then he began to revel in the new freedom, the anonymity of being an ordinary mortal left to his own devices. This didn't happen in London or Cambridge, where almost everyone was conscious of his status, and from being a shock he came to find it a pleasure.

Warmly waterproofed in boots and Burberry, sweaters and scarves and an incongruous tweed cap purchased from the local drapery, the Prince of Kutari explored everything with increasing eagerness, sometimes riding Zephyr, sometimes with a camera when the light looked like permitting photography. In the evenings, Kerry assiduously arranged trips to concerts, parties and theatres in Dublin, or hosted small dinners at home, introducing him to everyone she thought appropriate. Invitations were returned, of which two in particular appealed to him: fishing with the nearby club, and temporary membership of the pub's darts club.

Nabdul had never held either a dart or a fishing rod in his life, but now he took up both, with such deadly aim in the one and such patience in the other that soon his days were full to overflowing. Sometimes he was too worn out even to creep into Kerry's room at night, but she grinned archly as his flying visit extended into a week, a month and beyond. Every weekend, she took him racing, turning each meet into a contest of such heroic and valorous proportions that, in due course, ego compelled him to buy a horse of his own, and then another. Thrilled, Kerry ran to inform Helen of her success, and between them they made sure the news found its way to every other owner and trainer in the country. It was a small country, with a most efficient grapevine.

But, enjoying himself as he was, Nabdul found Kerry's attitude disconcerting. Try as he might, he could get no word of affection out of her, while his body seemed to be a mere instrument for her physical pleasure. With other women, he had behaved just the same way, but now the situation was infuriatingly reversed, making him feel both used and patronised.

And there were other reasons, too, why she might be unsuitable after all, lovely and lovable as she was. First and foremost, she did not pay him nearly enough attention; brusque when she was busy, flippant when she was not, treating him like – like a pet! She strode ahead of him when it should be quite the other way round, played with him when she had time, but never connected with him in any tangible way. At best, she seemed to regard him as an equal, reserving the royal treatment for her precious horses.

Slowly, inevitably, Nabdul resigned himself to the fact that his passion for Kerry was doomed, a summer bloom that would fade. Difficulties multiplied by the day – her child, her religion, her rootedness in a life he saw she would never leave. One day, he presented her with a beautiful diamond brooch, and although she thanked him effusively she did not pin it on. The thought came to him that she actually intended to sell it, as soon as he was safely out of sight, and although the suspicion saddened him greatly, he could not dispel it.

He was on the point of giving up. But one more week

remained of his visit, and he resolved to give it his best
shot. Anything worth having was worth fighting for.

"Kerry, I have seen little of your country, small as it is.
If you could make some free time, perhaps we will drive to
the west, or the south? Just for a few days? I would like to
take some more photographs."

She bit her lip. There were a number of important races
coming up . . . but on the other hand, Nabdul's happiness was
vital, and soon he would be gone.

"OK. I suppose a quick break wouldn't hurt. Pour me a
drink, there's a dear, and I'll get out the map."

Awkward and embarrassed, he fumbled at the drinks cabi-
net while she went to search the library. Fixing drinks was
the work of a servant in Kutari, but here, incredibly, it
often seemed to fall to him. Where the hell was Paddy, her
alleged manservant? Never anywhere to be found, when he
was needed. It was no way to run a home.

Helen watched them set off for Donegal with a mixture of
apprehension and relief. Getting there meant cutting briefly
through the North, if they took the shortest route out of the
colourless, featureless midlands, and the idea gave her cause
for concern. The last thing Kerry needed was to scare this
man off with the sight of soldiers, machine guns, barbed wire,
all the border security that made foreign investors swiftly
rethink their plans. And, apart from being an important new
contact, Nabdul was such a nice chap; how unthinkable, if
he should come to any harm! Without much conviction, she
hoped that Kerry would have the patience and the discretion
to take the longer road, through Sligo.

But maybe, just maybe, she should give Kerry credit for
a glimmer of sense. The girl had changed in recent weeks,
Helen thought. There was a new decisiveness about her,
increasing evidence of maturity, ability to see further than
the end of her nose. She was dealing with this man very
well, nursing him along without any emotional involvement,
any of the hectic intensity previously characteristic of her
relationships. Nabdul, clearly, was badly infatuated with her,
but who did the man think he was?

If he aspired to get involved with Kerry, he was surely mistaken. Helen could envisage no way by which she would leave Ashamber now, volunteer to go off and stifle in his Muslim society, risk being merely the first of four wives, relegate her son to a status inferior to that of any subsequent children. Senegal had taught her a hard lesson, and the value of her own country, language, people; she could no more relinquish that heritage than Nabdul would dream of abandoning his. There appeared to be a newly rugged strength about her – as well as a perspicacity that had its drawbacks.

The night before Kerry left with Nabdul for the west coast, Helen found herself the subject of an altercation. Confronted by Kerry, she was forced to confess that yes, a friendship had indeed sprung up between herself and Bob Cummins. A cheery, comforting friendship between a widow and a widower: where was the harm in that? But Kerry read deeper into it.

"It's a bloody disgrace, Helen! You're not just Jack Craigie's widow, you're practically my father's too! How can you live here in his home, with his daughter, and then start seeing somebody else? It's not even a year since his death, it's not – it's not on!"

Helen found herself ill-prepared and ill-equipped to fight back. The friendship was purely platonic, but unarguably its timing was bad, it did look ungrateful and a little insensitive.

"Things happen as and when they happen, Kerry. I didn't plan this, and I don't propose to send Bob packing just to humour your delicate sensibilities. He lives in Belfast, for goodness' sake, he only comes here once or twice a month. I knew your father very well, and I know he'd be happy to see me making new friends."

Ah, but that was just it. Kerry said no more, but was palpably jealous on Eamonn's behalf, decamping with some muttered remark about "decency and consideration" that left Helen rattled. It was the only disagreement they had thus far had, and it was fortuitous that Donegal now beckoned. By the time she returned, she would have forgotten her reservations, or dealt with them. The short holiday would do everyone good.

Kerry found that it did do her good. Like Yoff, the villages
of Donegal depended on fishing, and in their salt air she smelt
sturdy, weatherbeaten resilience, a territory of character, and
energy, and great good humour despite the hardship of the
maritime life.

Sometimes chatting amicably, sometimes arguing politics
or religion, ethics or economics, whatever might enlighten
them both for future reference, they drove on down the
Atlantic coast under fleecy white clouds that seemed to keep
pace with them amidst the harbours and haystacks, piled turf
and trawling nets, tarred currachs and lobster pots. Every day
they swam in the freezing sea, from powdery beaches and
rocky ones, exclaiming over the odd things they found: crabs
and shells and washed-up logs, curious rock formations and
mysterious footprints. One day, they met a man in a pub over
a lunch of oysters and beer, and Kerry persuaded him to take
them out in his boat, a Galway hooker with a black hull and
a flapping red sail. In this ancient vessel they had the most
wonderful time, sighting dolphins, sharks and seals, even a
hidden cave in which, the man told them, guns, bullets and
dynamite had once been stored for purposes of rebellion.

Nabdul was fascinated by this, recalling his own country's
chequered past as they sailed right up to the concealed
entrance at the base of a cliff, and Kerry tried to explain
hers in turn, simplifying its myriad convolutions as best
she could, laughing with their host over some of the more
outrageous exploits. There had been a man called Parnell, she
told Nabdul, who had once been known as "the uncrowned
king of Ireland", but he had lost his crown, and how? Over
a woman, that was how, over a foreign, married woman with
whom he had fallen in love to the fury of his fanatically
conservative supporters. Nabdul digested this in silence, and
shuddered.

But as the days passed, he gradually came to see the futility
of his own aspirations with irrefutable clarity. Torn in half, he
grew closer to Kerry with every breath she drew, but saw that
he could no more entice her away from her homeland than he
could transplant a succulent flower to the desert. He would
have to explain that to her, he supposed, and looked forward

with little joy to their last night together. His comportment
had been that of a man intent on proposal, and even if she
did not encourage it she must anticipate it.

He didn't want to lose her, but couldn't think how to keep
her. Unless, perhaps, through the horses . . . ? He had already
bought two, which would provide an excuse to keep in touch,
visit from Cambridge whenever time permitted. And, if he
referred other owners to her, she might be grateful to him,
allow their physical relationship to continue. Overnight, he
discovered that he was very interested in racing indeed, and
that Ireland would become the base of extensive equestrian
exploits.

On the final night before they returned to Kildare, they
drank several pints of the alcohol that he was not, officially,
supposed to touch, joining haphazardly in a musical session
in a crowded pub. Not knowing the words of any of the
songs, his mind drifted out onto the pearly, tranquil night,
lit by a half-moon and many clusters of shimmering stars.
Somewhere a donkey brayed in a field, and he thought what
an eclectic country this was, the whole island so elusive and
contradictory, redolent now of all the night smells of summer,
heather and fuschia and cow dung wafting pungently together
in a mixture that was somehow poignant.

Everything seemed to change with the light, which was to
say every twenty minutes, but it was an inconsistency that
tantalised and intrigued him. Abruptly he reached for Kerry's
hand and squeezed it, pleased to find her reciprocating until,
disconcerted, he saw a film of tears in her eyes.

"What is it, Kerry? What's wrong?"

She sniffled, and wiped the back of her hand inelegantly
on the sleeve of her shirt.

"Nothing."

She wouldn't tell him, but he thought he saw the same thing
she did: an ephemeral ghost of some sort, interposing itself
between them. He had intuited its haunting influence before,
and supposed it must be the husband she had lost.

"Come on. I'll take you home to bed."

Home, for the night, was a rented cottage, so simple an
abode that Nabdul thought his father would have a heart

attack if he could see it. But hotels were sparse out in this wilderness, and the tiny cottage had the advantage of total privacy. They walked the short distance back to it, hand in hand down a sandy by-road in the pale warm night, each struggling in silence with unspoken, stifled emotions.

He felt the strongest desire to take her straight to bed, to release the tension in the sexual way that seemed to work so well, and about which he had taught her such a lot. But instead they sat down in the cramped kitchen with a pot of tea, and he looked at her frankly.

"Kerry, we must talk."

Expectantly, she waited.

"Kerry, I think you must know by now how much you have come to mean to me. You are the first woman who ever has, and I wish with all my heart it were possible for us to be together. But it isn't. Shall I tell you why?"

Her lips parted as if she were about to say something, but she bent her head so that a curtain of hair swung down over her face, hiding a brief battle that had, Nabdul guessed, something to do with pride.

"No, Nabdul. There's no need. The reasons you want to give me are the same ones I have to give you."

So, he wasn't going to ask her for anything, then? It was a relief to her, but something of a shock too, as if one of the horses had suddenly bitten her. Her feelings were not hurt, but her ego was.

"You would have said no, Kerry, had I asked?"

She eyed him warily.

"I would have had to, Nabdul. It's not a matter of what I want or you want. It's a matter of circumstance."

Yes. That was it, exactly. He kissed the tip of her nose.

"I'm glad you see it for yourself, beloved. I did not want to cause you any pain."

No. Nobody ever did want to, did they? They just went ahead and did it. How right she had been, to keep her defences up this time! How could he call her beloved, when love played no part in things at all? The soul that had once given so freely fled to take refuge.

"No, of course you didn't, and you haven't. Not at all."

Now he was the one to tread warily.

"Good. We can be friends, then? I want us to be, Kerry. I've come to like you, and your country, very much, to feel great affinity between us."

It was exactly what she had been aiming for, and she could isolate no reason whereby the victory should feel so Pyrrhic. Glumly, she plucked at the oiled tablecloth, and he looked at her keenly as she sighed vacantly.

"There's somebody else, isn't there?"

How he knew, she couldn't imagine. Had she let him get a little closer than she realised? Or was he just guessing, stabbing in the dark? Whatever. An outright lie was simply not in her nature.

"Yes. I'm afraid there is, Nabdul – or was. It's over now, but I'm not over it. Not enough time has passed, it's too recent, that's all."

Her tone was raw and wistful and he wished he could help her. Wished he could help them both. Then, remembering something, he got up and disappeared into the bedroom, searching his suitcase until he found a matt grey velvet box.

"Kerry, I brought this with me to give to you if – if – well, anyway, it's for you, and I still want you to have it."

He put the box into her hands and stood back as she opened it, wide-eyed, curious in spite of herself. Inside, on pale green satin so worn it was almost frayed, lay an emerald ring, necklace, bracelet and small, square earrings, all set in white platinum. Stunned, she stared speechless at the lovely antique set, realising it had belonged to someone else.

"It was my mother's. She died last year. My sisters inherited all her other jewellery, but I kept this for – for whoever else might one day matter to me. I didn't expect it to be so soon. But a woman with eyes like yours should have stones like these, Kerry."

Anxiously she searched his face for the irony she thought must be implicit in his words, but found no trace of it. Then, wordlessly, softly, she reached up and kissed his cheek, and he returned the kiss with a lightened heart. These stones, he thought, she would wear.

*   *   *

Before leaving for London, refreshed in body if ambivalent in spirit, Nabdul bought three more horses, bringing the total number of Zul Mahrat animals at Ashamber to nine. Thrilled, Kerry requested one last favour of him, brazenly disguised as an honour. Would he escort her to the races at the Curragh on Saturday, a big meet at which she had three horses running? It would be an opportunity, she said, for him to meet other owners and compare notes on the quality of their assets. Not that anyone's could compete with his.

He laughed, no longer under the slightest illusion about her, and acquiesced chivalrously. He had been to this track once before, and liked the easy rural atmosphere of the place. Helen and Bob came with them, and Bob had a winner in the very first race, largely thanks to its favourable draw at the off and a dry week which had hardened the ground to its liking. Once again he was delirious with joy as he led it into the winner's enclosure, but in the other two races Kerry managed only a sixth and a second.

"Always a bridesmaid, never a bride" she commented drily and unjustifiably, making Bob, Helen and Nabdul all scoff teasingly. Nabdul turned to her with a cheeky leer.

"Never mind, beloved, we will make a bride of Helen here instead!"

Helen flushed furiously, but Bob joined in their mocking laughter until they were all laughing mercilessly – and, at that moment, a photographer's flash went off.

Next day, the photo was on the front page of one of the Sunday newspapers, with a directive to "the full story" in the social column inside. The columnist, obviously working from an informed source, had done his research thoroughly, and chronicled Nabdul's six weeks in Ireland fully, speculating overtly on his new interest in the indigenous racing scene and, particularly, in Kerry Laraghy.

In another, smaller photo, Bob and Helen were cropped out, leaving just Nabdul smiling at Kerry, who was wearing what looked like some of the most superb jewellery this side of the equator. The editorial homed in on the emerald ring "not yet being worn on the third finger of the left hand", and left Kerry levitating with anger as she flung

the paper on the library floor in disgust. Now that she had
the publicity she had sought, she was at pains to inform
Nabdul she'd had nothing to do with it. But, used to such
reports, he was indifferent, and she was mollified by his
composure.

At least the columnist had had the sense to add news of
her contract with the Zul Mahrats, and its rapidly expanding
parameters. That would make her father's former clients sit
up, and a few new ones start reaching for the phone.

But, nearer to home, the village was rocked with consternation. Touting for business was one thing, permissible in
Kerry's straitened circumstances, but this was overstepping
the mark. Demonstrably, the girl had become personally involved with this Arab. A nice enough Arab, who had been
welcomed into their darts and fishing clubs, even lent a cachet
of sorts to the golf course – but only on a temporary, honorary
basis! The man was perfectly free to visit, to socialise and
spend as much money as he liked, but that was a very
different thing from this brash infiltration of their society.

As for Kerry, was it not enough that she had left her
husband, moved Eamonn's mistress into her house, accom-
modated a very questionable Frenchman and flirted with
Brandon Lawrence, all in the space of a few months? And
now, to accept such conspicuous, compromising jewellery
from this person, so swarthy he was almost black – it was
going too far. Throughout the village heads were shaken and
newspapers crumpled as the community collectively wondered how it could possibly be that Maeve Laraghy, a lady
to the tips of her manicured fingernails, had produced such
a calculating, promiscuous slut.

And, weekending down in Wicklow, Brandon Lawrence
was also filled with bitter dismay. Vacant with shock, his
eyes darkened to pewter as he perused the story, confronted
the undeniable photographic evidence.

Christ, he thought wretchedly, she might have waited. She
could at least have done that. I feared I might have ruined
her life, left her to pine for what might have been, and it's
some consolation to see she's not doing that. But this man? So
soon? Her personal guest at Ashamber, all summer – and

now, this jewellery? She'd never have accepted it, if the relationship were wholly business.

His business *is* a great coup, of course, and I'm glad I got her started, with his father. But she has established herself. She's got what she wanted, and I admire her for it, more than ever. Even if it does include marriage, to this man she brought into her life the day she shut me out of it.

Oh, Kerry. I hope he'll make you happy. But I can't endure it, if he does. You know I love you, and you can't love him.

But the newspaper conveyed that she could. Consumed with chagrin, aching with anger, he pitched it into the fire.

Part Three

14

Seven years later, on a blustery day in the late spring of 1980, Marianne Lawrence stood in a bay window of her Richmond home, watching the wind batter the cypress trees outside. It was a chill, charmless scene, but she turned away from it with reluctance, because in the room around her the temperature was still lower.

At the opposite window, her husband sat in a leather swivel chair, blocking the view and blocking her plans in a dogged way that irked her greatly. Tenacious by nature, he had come to border on the obdurate in recent times, and Marianne found it increasingly tedious to engage him in debate. Every year, she widened her circle of friends, spent more time with them and less at home, so that if there was little harmony there was no outright antagonism either. Those who knew the couple saw only the acceptable façade of a marriage behind whose preservation lay neither succour nor substance. But with the children away at school, the redbrick Victorian house rang more hollow every day, and sometimes Marianne felt dangerously close to the end of her tether.

"We're not going, and that's that." Brandon's tone was the one she recognised as unarguable. But she argued anyway. Once, long ago, she had agreed to everything for the sake of peace, but in the end it had availed her nothing. Now, she got her own way as much as she could, if only to assert herself, to remind him of her existence.

"But Brandon, I've already accepted, and bought the sweetest new dress. We *will* go. I want to."

She wanted to go? Actively, actually wanted to? Brandon was incredulous. Even had they been asked to be godparents, he would have refused; but they were only guests, two among dozens, and Caroline Somerville-Norton would understand their refusal even if Marianne herself, unbelievably, did not.

"No, Marianne."

"But it's the very last one! All our friends are past the baby stage by now . . . it's a wonder Caroline was able to have Jamie at all, she must be nearly forty."

Marianne's plea was more in the nature of a petulant whine, with a jagged edge to it that shredded Brandon's nerves. He slammed his folder of paperwork shut with such force that Marianne jumped.

"No!"

It was out of the question. For one thing, they wouldn't be in London at all on the date in question, they would be in America at this damnblasted fund-raiser for Matthew Breffni. But for another thing – the real thing – what about Julie? Didn't she care at all? Didn't she remember the pain, still feel it as keenly as if it were only yesterday?

All right. So it was seven years ago. But that made no difference. He would never forget, *never*, the day of Julie's christening, and her death that same night.

Even now, medical science was unable to explain it. One minute, the tiny infant was sleeping peacefully in her cot, breathing rhythmically, her minute fists balled into the duvet with its elves and fairies snuggled protectively round her, her downy skin faintly exuding that delicious, unmistakable baby smell. The next, she was dead.

He had been the one to find her, when he crept back into the nursery for one last look at his beautiful new baby girl, this last little scrap of love in his life. She had cost him one future, but she was the start of another, and he simply adored her on sight, long before she was even able to return his smiles. Night after night he raced home to be with her, to cradle her in his arms, murmur to her as she drowsed innocently into sleep.

The joy she gave to him, the fulfilment, was overwhelming. His devotion verged on the besotted, drawing from him every emotion he had thought extinguished. And then, she was gone. Ripped from his arms, carried to the chapel at

Hollyvaun in a white coffin twenty inches long, a rigid porcelain doll in her christening dress, lowered into a small deep trench to turn to dust.

Brandon turned to dust with her.

And now, Marianne wanted to attend the baptism of Jamie Somerville-Norton, because she had a new outfit and all her friends would be there? His eyes were murderous as he stared at his wife. But she met them calmly.

"Well, then, I shall simply go alone, and say you're away on business."

"No, Marianne, you will not. You will come to America with me, as agreed."

She threw him a contemptuous glance, but dropped the discussion, recognising its futility. For all his racehorses, Brandon was more like a carthorse himself under pressure: you could shout at him, cajole him, take various whips to him and beat him with them, all to no avail. His intransigence made her want to scream, frequently to walk out and leave him, but she never had. Too many factors bound them together, manacled them like prisoners sharing a cell. There were the boys, there was money, society, convention, and there was the intangible bond of time. Eighteen years of marriage counted for something, even if neither of them could define what that was exactly . . . like the bottomless lake at Hollyvaun, it had simply always been there.

But in the daily run of things, their lives rarely crossed. Agreed that they could not bear to have another child, they slept apart, and often Brandon went to Ireland alone, or with Chris, who at sixteen was having a tortuously difficult adolescence. What they did there she neither knew nor cared; she still hated the place, and was very glad that Brandon's plans to relocate in Dublin had been spiked by a barrage of economic difficulties.

First a crippling bank strike, then the oil shortage of 1973, then another paralysing strike in 1976. The country had teetered and wobbled its way through the seventies, forcing Brandon to accept reality, granting her a reprieve, provoking Chris into a sudden and inexplicable obsession with the island's politics. From Harrow, the boy's headmaster complained regularly of insubordination, intractability, seditious activities that were as disruptive as they were inexcusable. Marianne was rapidly running out of patience with her elder son, but derived comfort from Harry, a dear, docile boy of fifteen who gravitated naturally to his mother.

She looked back at Brandon to see whether his ire had waned. Apparently it had, in the knowledge that he had won this round. So. She would turn defeat into victory, be a credit to him in America, perform her wifely duties with poise and tact – and go shopping for a whole new wardrobe before setting foot amidst the senators' spouses.

"All right, Brandon. I said I'd go, and I will."

He did not reply, swivelling his chair so that he faced the window, the argument closed, his mind a million miles away from her, at Hollyvaun with Julie.

Absently, Zoe stirred three cubes of sugar into her *café crème* and debated whether to have another pastry from the trolley.

The hell with it. She summoned the waiter.

She felt his glance, and the old battle begin again inside her. The battle that went on and on, fruitlessly, round in circles, reducing her life to a farce of self-loathing, a conflict that seethed and fermented perpetually inside her like a geyser. But still she sipped her coffee, still she bit into the latticed apple tart, hating every mouthful, hating herself.

It's all Brian's fault, she consoled herself, for being so late.

No, it isn't. It's your own, for being so weak. This isn't food. It's slow suicide.

But I can't help it!

Yes, you can.

I can't, I can't!

It was an exhausting battle, but she knew who was winning. Not Zoe the victor, but Zoe the victim, Zoe the screaming girl on the deserted beach, Zoe the ashen heap in the hospital bed, Zoe the infertile woman walled up alive inside a fortress of food. To this day they all still tried to get through to her, every friend she'd ever had, but nobody ever did. Lu made her attend a clinic; Brian reasoned, wheedled, bribed and finally threatened; her parents wrote from New York, Daniel from California, Kerry from Ireland and Yves from Australia, wasting miles of paper on a fruitless campaign. Day in and day out, she continued to stuff her face.

Now, she couldn't even take a bow at the end of a show, couldn't cash in on the celebrity of success, couldn't afford to be seen by the media whose cameras scanned constantly for sight of the mystery "Z" whose input had turned TLC into TLZ.

Tiberti, Laraghy and Zimner, the toast of *le tout Paris*. But where was Tiberti? On their letterhead, in the magazines, down in Australia, trying to maintain by post and the magic new fax machine an erratic association satisfactory to neither him nor them. And where was Zimner? Cowering in the Café Cluny, that happy haunt of her youth, cramming herself full of calories.

Zoe didn't live in the city of Paris. She hid in it. Often, she longed for home, yearned for her family and friends, for the noisy zip and zing of New York, for the skyscrapers and taxi drivers, the skaters at Rockefeller Plaza, the hooting horns of the ships in the harbour, the Statue of Liberty and the Twin Towers. Paris had the Louvre, but it didn't have the Frick or the Guggenheim, its sandy parks were not the scuffed yellow grass of Central Park. It had no skateboarders or squirrels, it had elegance and intellect but it didn't have any brash, wisecracking wit. It was a refuge, a sanctuary she dared not leave.

And where was Laraghy? Perplexed, Zoe consulted her watch. It was unlike Brian to be late. Had she mistaken the time, the place?

But then she saw him coming, at last, rumpled and flustered, his face creasing into a frown as he noted the plate in front of her.

"Sorry I'm late. Got held up."

"That's OK. I wasn't in any hurry."

She never was, these days. Other than work, her life held no demands. In the mornings, she went to the salon, and in the evenings she went home again, or out to eat somewhere. Then she worked on her designs, in the apartment taken over from Yves on the rue St Antoine. It was refurbished, now, and he stayed there whenever he condescended to visit, cheering her with his gossip and outrageous exploits, camp humour and unflagging kindness. He was the only man who ever slept there.

Brian ordered a Suze and swallowed it in one gulp.

"Hard day, huh?"

"Yeah. Hard day."

Working in their separate studios, they had not seen each other since morning. Brian had been tense then, as he evidently still was now, and Zoe knew why: Lu. The perfect marriage had begun to show signs of stress in this last year or more, visible to everyone as Brian chipped away at his wife, trying to wear down her resistance to bearing the child he so desperately desired. The irony of it grieved Zoe, as did the abrasive effect it was having on Brian's once gentle character.

Lu was twenty-nine, on top of her career, able to afford a baby so easily in every sense. She was married to a man who loved her, with the money to give a child everything it could need or want, even if Brian were not due to inherit seventeen million Irish pounds at the end of this year. But she held out, he persisted, and they fought constantly. Screaming matches were not their style, but the stiff silences were infinitely worse.

"So what did you want to talk to me about, Brian?"

"Did I? Oh, yes . . . it's about Yves, Zoe."

"What about him?"

"He called this morning. Says he can't make our Easter show. Some administrative hassle, paperwork he says can't wait."

Zoe smiled. Yves hated paperwork, bureaucracy of any description.

"Well, he'd hardly volunteer for that if it weren't essential."

"Not the point, Zoe. The point is that he's letting us down again. He knows how important it is to put in an appearance, keep the women happy. Frankly, I'm fed up with this whole situation. He's neither here nor there. Before, it was all those long lunches, his social life, outside interests . . . then it was Australia, leaving us with all the marketing, budgeting, shipping, everything, while he does his own thing. I'm sick to death of it."

"But Brian, he's the one who wanted to make a clean break! We asked him to retain the link, make a contribution, and he's done his best. What more do you want?"

"I want to lose him. Cut the connection."

"But you're the one who made him keep it! You and Lu, both."

She couldn't believe her ears. Yves had done them a great favour by agreeing to this troublesome, logistically difficult arrangement – and this was to be his thanks? That Brian could be so coldly ruthless appalled her. What had happened to the dreamy, romantic spirit of old? Nowadays, all his romance was channelled into his evening wear. And where was the loyalty he valued so highly in others, had demanded so righteously from Yves in the first place?

He called for another Suze, and Zoe, wondering how he could drink the bitter stuff, requested another *café crème* for herself, catching his disapproving eye as she did so. Probably, she thought, he'd like to shake me, but at this moment I could shake him too. He's been getting so hard lately, so demanding of everyone, blind to all personal considerations bar his own. It started a long time ago, that day Kerry threw his money back in his face . . . But what a face it is, still.

I don't want to fall out with him. But I don't want to oust Yves, either, there'll be nothing left of our little family, nobody to sustain me.

The barren prospect panicked her.

"Brian, there must be some other way to sort ourselves out. People need daywear more than they need ballgowns or yachting sweaters. Yves is the apex of our triangle."

"The pink triangle," he muttered dourly, and unwillingly she flared up at him.

"That's contemptible! Yves is our friend, Brian, and he has a big heart, at least he'd never be petty like that!"

He glared at her.

"OK. You tell me what we should do then, Miss America."

The tag needled, as he intended. Never for a moment did he let her forget the bright, pert, pretty woman who owned this seventy-kilo bulging body. But it was a form of tough love, and she knew that underneath the hostility they were very fond of each other.

Putting down her cup, she looked at him sagely.

"If it were up to me, I'd ask him to come back, lock stock and barrel. He may be doing well, but Kerry says he isn't happy, Brian. His lover rules his whole life, and he can't seem to please him no matter what he does. He's homesick, too. Australia doesn't suit his temperament at all, it's too – too easy for someone with such a complex palate."

"He's made his bed there, and he can damn well lie in it."

"No matter what the cost, to us or to him? Look, why don't I call him, see if I can make him an offer he can't refuse?"

His hand reached across the table and grabbed her forearm, hard.

"You'll do no such thing. I won't stand for it. Won't have him back."

"Take your hands off me! You men are all the same, with your ridiculous pride! You never care who suffers, do you?"

He released her, got up, paid the bill and walked out. Sadly, Zoe watched him go, thinking that it wasn't just Yves Brian needed to bring back. It was Kerry, too. Kerry, who kept in touch with everyone except her own brother . . . someone should take both twins and knock their thick skulls together.

Neither had ever admitted it, but it was obvious to Zoe that they missed each other acutely, perpetually . . . and what about Killian? Did nobody ever consider the child? He had a right to his uncle, just as Brian had a right, and a duty, to him. With no male guidance, the boy was a handful at only eight years of age, a wild child on the seat of whose pants nobody dared plant the boot he so urgently needed. Kerry ignored him, Helen pampered him and Zoe, living in France, did not see nearly enough of him. He was a catastrophe under construction; but trying to get his family to see that was like trying to square the wheel.

Gathering up her bag and jacket, Zoe made her way to the métro and thence to the large empty apartment on the rue St Antoine, wondering how best to fill in the void of the evening. But as she let herself in the phone was ringing, and she was surprised to hear Helen's voice.

"Zoe, I'm sorry to disturb you, but glad to get you . . . it's about Kerry. There's a problem."

But there had been a problem for years. Divorced without warning by Darragh in 1977, Kerry had been building a shell around herself ever since. Hurt and humiliated, she saw the legal dissolution of her marriage as a final rejection, a public proof of misjudgment, the document that had changed her from an extroverted girl into a deeply introverted woman.

Deaf to Helen and Zoe's cries of joy, going trance-like through the dealings with French solicitors, she had disappeared thereafter for a short holiday alone, and come back a changed woman. Now, she had toughened up to the point where her staff called her Boots, and lived in fear of her tyrannical outbursts. Stamping and swearing, raging and bawling, she exercised complete dominance over them, livid and fearsome as ever Eamonn had been, a demon who subsided only to sleep.

But simultaneously she had built Ashamber up into a robust, remarkable success, surviving one crisis after another by whatever means came to hand. In 1978, a coughing virus struck every horse in her yard, as in yards nationwide, but shamelessly she staved off creditors, tax inspectors, everyone who forecast doom or might precipitate the collapse that was wiping out so many of her competitors. Exhorting Helen to cook the books, she fended off every demand, fought like a fury, and survived.

Since then, winners already legendary had sprung from her nine hundred fecund acres, winners of Arcs, Derbies and Breeder's Cups, classics across first one continent and then another. Among the colts, fillies and geldings now in her care cantered many million pounds' worth of horseflesh, owned chiefly by Arabs, and with eyes dark as ivy leaves

she watched each animal hawkishly, relentlessly, to such an
extent that she knew no other life.

No wonder Helen was worried. Zoe sighed.

"What's the matter with her, Helen?"

"She's had some very nasty news. From her solicitor,
Xavier Markey. He was in court today, up in Dublin, and
he heard some talk on the legal circuit, about a brilliant new
barrister . . . Zoe, it's Darragh."

"*Darragh?* But he's in Africa!"

"Not any more. Xavier says he's been back here for quite
a while actually, but it's only lately his name has come to
anyone's notice. Anyway, she's in a terrible state, and frankly
so am I. Since you know the man, Zoe, do you think you could
come over here and tell me about him – and talk to Kerry, too?
She's gone very silent, I can't get a word out of her."

Instantly, Zoe wrote off the holiday she had been planning,
at Club Med in Morocco, after the Easter show.

"Yes, Helen. We're up to our eyes at the moment, but I'll
be there as soon as I can."

Gratefully, Helen located her diary on the large desk in
the blue room that had once been Maeve's nerve centre, now
filled with screens and keyboards, computers keeping track
of every detail of Ashamber's extensive operation.

"Tell me exactly when, and I'll make sure Kerry is free."

A date was agreed, and in her apartment Zoe hung up
to set about cooking dinner, speculating on the implications
of Helen's horrendous news. Why had Darragh returned to
Ireland? For his own reasons? For Kerry? Or for Killian?
Granted, Kerry was a far from perfect mother, yet Zoe foresaw
bloodshed if he should attempt to muscle in on her son. The
boy needed a father, but he did not need Darragh de Bruin.
After eight years, the man's case was altogether hopeless. She
must reassure Kerry about that.

As for his chances of getting Kerry back – Zoe almost
laughed. Since Nabdul had married in London two years ago,
Kerry had lived like a hermit, all but hostile to men, dating
nobody, going nowhere. Darragh would never even get inside
Ashamber's gates, much less into her house. Besides, he had
divorced her, and he was not the kind of man to change his

mind. If it was Killian he wanted, he would have come for him by now.

Clinging to that thought, Zoe faced an uneasy, restless evening. In Ireland, Helen accepted the same prospect, filing away her day's work with a mixture of panic and resolve.

Despite her marriage to Bob, and the crevasse it had initially caused between herself and Kerry, Helen had not forgotten Eamonn. Far from it. Eamonn would have steered Kerry through this crisis, with Maeve's help, and so should she. Under no circumstances would she ever allow Darragh de Bruin near their daughter, or their grandson. He had thrown away his wife and son, and he was never getting them back. Never.

Perhaps he did not want them. Thus far, he had made no appearance, no attempt at communication. But, whether he did or not, Kerry was going to have to be prepared for the possibility – and so was Killian. His mother never mentioned his father, but the child himself occasionally asked, and it was time his questions were answered. Without alarming him, Kerry must speak to him, brace him against the seduction, or even abduction, that Darragh might stage at any moment.

It was Helen's worst nightmare, a vision that had always haunted her. Anxiously, she returned to her house, built on the ten acres that were Kerry's wedding present to them, and sought out Bob for an urgent consultation.

Claire de Veurlay glanced up at the clock on the blue-tiled wall of the kitchen, cradling a bowl of hot chocolate in her hands. Nine o'clock. It was late, by any standards: the morning was well advanced, Lionel had long since departed to his vines and his growers' meeting. The château hummed with hoovering and dishwashing, all the activity necessary to the upkeep of such a large house, and she herself had been up since seven. Usually, she met Lu for breakfast at about that time, but this morning her daughter had neither appeared nor announced her intention of sleeping late.

Claire didn't begrudge Lu a rest. The spring show was always a frantic business, and although it had gone well it had taken a lot out of Lu. This weekend at the peaceful château was just the breather she needed, even if Brian had not been able to accompany her. Claire was very fond of her son-in-law, but wished he wouldn't drive himself with such relentless determination. Couldn't this business of finding a new daywear designer wait a few days? Brian said he wanted it all settled before their annual Easter excursion to the Riviera, but Claire was at a loss to see what the hurry was.

Dear Brian! He was such a devoted husband, normally; both she and Lionel felt greatly vindicated in their decision to finance him, and permit their daughter's marriage at such a young age. It was a pity there had been such unfortunate repercussions in his own family; for their part they were very proud of him, and of Lu, who managed his interests so adroitly.

Where *was* Lu? Claire finished her chocolate and decided to go upstairs and take a peep at her, make sure everything was all right. But, even as her hand descended on the brass handle of the bedroom door, two minutes later, she knew that it was not. She sensed it with a mother's intuitive sixth sense, and confirmed it with her own eyes as soon as they fell upon the milk-white young woman sitting up in the bed. Lu's gamine blonde hairstyle was tousled and damp, her hazel eyes were huge, her forehead beading in perspiration on this clear, fresh spring morning.

"Darling! What is it? Are you ill? Let me look at you – is it something you've eaten?"

Lu shook her head, offering no explanation, not even raising her cheek for the customary kiss of greeting.

"Oh, Lu, *chérie*! Don't worry, I'll call Dr Michel right away. Where's my diary?"

Claire began to bustle off in search of the doctor's number, but before she reached the door Lu's sepulchral tone stopped her.

"No. Don't bother, *maman*. I've already seen a doctor. I'm not ill. I'm pregnant."

"Pregnant? Oh, Lucienne! How wonderful!"

Thrilled, Claire ran to embrace her. It was what she and Lionel had been hoping for years, not that they had ever been so indiscreet as to broach the subject. Lu never mentioned it either, so that it had gradually become somehow taboo – but now, at last! Claire felt an urge to rush to the windows and throw them open, call the news out to Lionel there and then in the midst of his budding vines.

"No, *maman*. It's not wonderful at all. It's dreadful."

"Dreadful!? What? But why . . . what . . . is the baby . . . not right? Is there some problem? My God, Lu, tell me!"

"Oh, no, *maman*, nothing like that. It's perfectly healthy. It's just that – that I don't want it, that's all."

For a moment Claire could not grasp what she meant, so foreign did it sound. Not want it? What was she talking about? But of course she wanted it! They all did. Didn't they?

"Wh-at? You don't mean to say that Brian – that Brian – isn't pleased?"

"Brian doesn't know. And, *maman*, he isn't going to. I'm going to have an abortion, and I'm not going to tell him. Neither are you, or papa, or anyone."

Claire's mouth opened and closed, idiotically, like a fairground doll's. This was beyond her. She just couldn't absorb it.

"An a-abortion? You're going to kill your child? Lu, tell me I've got this all wrong, I've misunderstood you, haven't heard you properly."

"You heard me."

Claire didn't so much sit down on her daughter's bed as sink onto it, feeling her legs about to give way. For several minutes she was incapable of speech. The last time she felt like this, the Germans had been marching into Paris.

She could not say her sang-froid returned, but gradually her wits did.

"Lu. Darling. I think you'd better explain this whole thing to me. All of it, slowly and carefully."

"Well, the thing is, *maman*, I've never really wanted a child. I'm an only child myself, and I don't find children attractive. I have a good husband and a satisfying career, and that's enough for me. A child would be a nuisance. So messy, so noisy, so time-consuming. Plus, it would ruin my figure, and you know how important my appearance is – not just to me, but to TLZ – and to Brian."

"But Lu, of course he won't mind you getting big with his child! He's its father!"

As she said this, a thought too horrible to contemplate crossed Claire's mind. But on that at least, Lu reassured her.

"Yes, he is. But still, you should see how he looks at Zoe Zimner, how disgusted he is by her weight . . . anyway, the main thing is that *I* don't want it, and I've made up my mind on that, so please don't argue with me. I've already made the appointment, for next week. It's a simple matter of a single day in the clinic. Brian won't know anything about it – and I want you to give me your word you won't tell him. There's no point in upsetting him, or papa either."

"By which I presume you mean you're too ashamed to tell them?"

"No, *maman*. I am not! I'm a modern working girl, it's the 1980s, I have a right to such decisions and facilities if I choose to avail myself of them – and I do."

"But Brian is your husband! He has a right to know! And speaking of – of facilities, if you didn't want to get pregnant, then why did you? Isn't *that* supposed to be the modern woman's first choice in such circumstances?"

Lu nodded impatiently. "Oh, yes, of course it is. I've been on the pill for years. But that's just it. The doctor thought it was time to take a break now that I'm about to turn thirty, started going on about chemical build-up and all the rest of it. He suggested I move onto a lighter brand, but that I take six months off it altogether first."

"But there are – other things."

"So there are. We've been using condoms for the past four months. And that is how I come to be pregnant. One of them must have slipped, or burst, or something."

Had it? Claire didn't tell Lu that she and Lionel had used condoms for years at one stage of their marriage, and that nothing had ever gone wrong for them. Could it possibly be that Brian had been . . . well, maybe deliberately careless?

"Tell me, Lu, is Brian keen to have a baby?"

"Well, yes, as a matter of fact he is. I'm fed up hearing about it, if you must know. But that doesn't make any difference. I'm not having this one, now, or any others in the future."

"But Lu, I promise you you'll come to love it! And I'd so love it myself, as would your father, and you tell me Brian would too . . . darling, please reconsider. I really think you must, for the sake of your marriage, for all our sakes. Please."

"*Maman*, I can assure you that I would not come to love it. Look at Brian's sister. She never came to love hers, did she?"

Lu smiled drily. That much, at least, she had in common with Kerry. That fool of a sister-in-law, who had thrown away the chance of marrying Arab royalty and opted instead to become an eccentric recluse in that ridiculous rural backwater of hers. Her eight-year-old was a perfect savage, like its mother, unwanted and unloved.

Claire couldn't think what to say next. She needed time to reflect, plan some strategy.

"Very well, Lu. I know that sometimes girls can get a bit silly and hysterical in your condition. Why don't we both think it over for a little while, and talk about it again later?"

"Because, *maman*, there is nothing to talk about."

Before leaving for America, Marianne had a wonderful time, shopping with a vengeance, spending as much of Brandon's money as humanly possible, even though it was like baling out the Thames with a sandbucket. In a single week she spent over nine thousand pounds on suits, shoes, dresses, hats, accessories that would see her through any and every eventuality. April in Washington would be wonderful, Caro assured her, especially if they happened to catch the cherry trees in full blossom; it was an unforgettable sight if you timed it exactly right. Mari smiled; timing had always been her strong point.

However, the indoor activities held far more allure, all the functions that were lined up for them in Georgetown, the Kennedy Centre and the White House. Mari intended to look the part, impress the American women who thought they had it all – but they didn't have a husband like hers, for a start, did they? They had to break in a new one every few years, but she had held onto Brandon, in body if not in spirit. Distant as he might be, he was still quite a trophy, handsome, hard-working, generous and very astute.

But so preoccupied with it, so *absent*, in that dreadfully silent, mutinous manner she could not ignore. He never hit out at her, physically or verbally, but nowadays his gradually coagulating obstinacy extended even to his father. Dermot's health had been poor of late, making him cranky and exceptionally difficult, and Brandon knew all the risks of arguing with him. Yet he had done so, on the contentious subject of America.

The trip was all settled now, and the boys were even to come with them, but Brandon had almost come to blows with his father over it. For months he had refused to discuss the issue, evaded his father's orders to do so, before finally engaging in a hideous confrontation that had left everyone shaken.

The last thing he wanted, he insisted, was to get involved in politics, particularly Irish-American politics which, he maintained, were a sure recipe for friction and disaster. But then Matthew Breffni's supporters had contacted Dermot, and there had been a scene at Hollyvaun, in the course of which it was forcefully pointed out to Brandon how much the Irish in Ireland depended on the Irish in America. Not just for money, but for less tangible things: referred tourism, the restoration of Georgian houses, networking on behalf of illegal immigrants and visa lobbying. Things that Brandon had no business to endanger, Dermot shouted apoplectically, until finally Brandon had agreed to go, grumbling and muttering about the loathsome Mr Breffni to whose campaign fund he would hand over a cheque for five million dollars.

Accordingly, on Saturday, they would fly from London to Washington by Concorde, on one of the first ever supersonic flights between the two cities. The more she thought about it, and the more she shopped for it, the more Marianne began to look forward to the whole thing. She would miss Caro's christening party, but she would attend lots of bigger, much better parties.

Seated on the fence of a precisely square, eight-acre paddock, Kerry threw an unwitting splash of colour against a panorama of gleaming, rain-polished grass. In an apricot mohair sweater and blue denims, black leather boots and gloves, she sat with her feet wedged behind the lower slats, gripping the upper rail for balance. Thus had she been sitting for twenty minutes, which was to say, twenty times longer than she could normally be found in any one place.

Overhead, the vivid sky was a mile high, briskly blue on this no-nonsense, let's-get-on-with-it morning. Cheeky puffs of wind teased her hair loose from its habitual French plait, so persistently that she left the wisps to blow where they would, focusing on nothing in particular. Years of intensive physical work had tautened her into a lean, muscular woman, strong and supple, with eyes that rolled perpetually over her domain like two green, glass marbles. As domains went, she reckoned, it was one of the finest in the country, and Eamonn would have been most impressed.

Everybody was impressed. She was impressed herself. She had achieved everything she set out to achieve: not just financial success, but the far more important independence that went with it. Autonomy, even power, the glowing satisfaction of a job well done.

Sure, it was still hard work. Dealing with horses meant getting kicked, bitten and crushed, wet, dirty and worn to the bone. Meant having constantly to motivate everyone, and take the blame when things went wrong. But it was the life she had chosen; she controlled it and she reaped its rewards. In real terms, she had little to complain of, and she knew her mother would be hugely irritated if she could see her here now, lost, lethargic, moping for a moon that had long ago disappeared behind the clouds.

She couldn't even put a face on the moon. Was it Brandon's? Brian's? Nabdul's? Darragh's, even? Or her parents' whom she silently, hopelessly missed? Was it the simple fact of being single in a world that was loved and partnered? Brian had Lu,

Helen had Bob, Yves had Keith, Nabdul had Shairi, everyone had someone – except her, and Zoe who seemed similarly to exude some kind of aura which warned people away.

There were the horses, of course. Some of them were so willing, so smart or so gentle that she related to them almost as if they were human, talking to them late into the long, slow evenings. But when was the first success that had fallen flat, the first win that failed to thrill? When had she begun to sense that she was urging them on, not just to victory, but away from something too?

She could not say, any more than she could justify these twenty introspective, wasted minutes, and she knew her mother would not approve of her ingratitude.

"Get on with it, my girl" Maeve would say, brusque but perfectly right. "You've got your career, your money, your status and your fine home. You've made it, and you just count your blessings."

Regularly, Kerry did count them, and foresaw more to come. With the training side of things so well in hand, now was the time to start into breeding. The making and shaping of winners was hugely satisfying, but it was no more than the moulding of raw materials given to her by other people. What she wanted next was to create the raw material itself. Should she ever have a bad season, the owners could take all their horses away to a new trainer overnight; but nobody could ever take her own blood line away.

Except Darragh. Tomorrow, next week or next month, he could try to take her son away. He could *try*! But already Kerry was rallying after the fright Xavier had given her, assessing the odds and finding them heavily stacked in her favour. She could not honestly say she loved Killian, in the doting way that other mothers loved their sons, but he was her responsibility, her flesh and blood. She might raise him badly, but with Helen's help she *would* raise him. If Darragh tried to set foot next or near the boy, she would set the dogs on him, take her father's hunting gun and blow his head off.

Meanwhile, she glumly supposed, she would have to do as Helen said, and speak to the child. Forewarned was forearmed. But what to say? Fretfully she sat on the fence, watching the horses canter in their fields, until she heard the scrunch of car tyres on the gravel. Helen, bringing Killian back from school for lunch.

The two got out of the car, the boy making straight for the house with his usual lunging stride, his anorak a bright red flag blowing in the breeze, his dark fringe falling into his eyes. But Helen called out to him, and he stopped enquiringly, his gaze following her pointing finger until it rested on his mother. Desultorily, Kerry waved, and he waved back as he came running over to her.

"Hi, Mum!"

Affectionately he hurled himself at the knees of the jeans that were level with his eyes, all eager smiles. No matter how coldly or how indifferently Kerry treated him, he never seemed to retaliate; on the contrary, he tried all the harder. But in vain.

"Hi. How was school?"

"Great. We have football after lunch, I'm in a hurry – Helen says you want to see me. What's it about? Can I have a tuna sandwich? Barry Cronin nicked my ruler this morning, so I took it back and hit him with it – uh – I think Mrs Cronin might be going to call you later, Mum . . ."

Frequently, Kerry argued the case for sending Killian to boarding school. Fine, Helen responded; when he leaves I leave too. Then you can do all the apologising to the other parents, you can explain his behaviour to everyone, you can run your estate and your family yourself.

Killian remained, therefore, at day school. And Helen could defuse Mrs Cronin this afternoon. Kerry jumped down off the fence, shoved her hands in her pockets and set off at a trot, leaving her son to follow.

"Where are we going? I'll be late for footer!"

"Never mind about football. Let's go for a little walk."

"Why?"

"Because I say so. I want to talk to you. About your father."

Behind her, the child stumbled in surprise, his dark brown eyes oval with astonishment, his small mouth open.

"Who?"

"You heard me. You've often asked, and I've decided to tell you."

Confused, he reddened. Before, she had always brushed him off, told him to stop pestering her. What had changed her mind? Was she angry with him? Was she going to – to give him away, to the shadowy stranger he knew she didn't like? Frightened, but defiant, he looked up at her.

"It was only because some of the other kids – said – how come – they all have fathers! I don't want to know! I don't care!"

Hitching up his dungarees, he took a belligerent stance, ready for battle; but Kerry kept on walking.

"Never mind who said what. The point is that you do have a father, Killian, just like all the other boys at school. He does exist, and we were married when you were born. But now we're divorced. Do you know what that is?"

"No."

"It's when two people go their separate ways, for good. After that, they're free to marry other people, and your father may even have a new wife now, for all I know."

"But – but you're my mum!"

"Yes, I am. That won't change. I'm only telling you because . . . well, your father used to live a very long way away. In Africa. But he's not there any more. He's moved back to Dublin."

Dublin? Blankly, Killian gazed at her, struggling to understand the difference. Everybody knew Africa was miles away, but so was Dublin. He'd only ever been there once, when Helen took him to see Santa last Christmas, in a department store. It had been an awfully long drive.

But maybe, to grown-ups, it wasn't so far?

"Is he going to come here, to see me? Am I going to see him?"

Braced as she was, Kerry felt a twinge of pity, and held off. How could anyone, even an adult, cope with the truth? Your father probably doesn't want you at all. Doesn't know he has a son, and doesn't care.

"Well, you're certainly not going to see him. He's not a very nice man, Killian. If you don't believe me, ask Zoe when she gets here this afternoon. She used to know him, and she didn't like him one little bit."

Pausing, she watched him make the connection. If Zoe, his favourite person next to Helen, didn't like this man, then he had no cause to either. But what if – if the man came here, to get him? To take him away?

"Mum?"

"Yes?"

"He's not going to – to take me, is he?"

"No. But he might try, Killian. That's what you need to know. But don't worry. I won't let him. Unless you want me to?"

"No! I want to stay here! With you, and Helen!"

"Then that's what you're going to do. I'm only warning you so you wouldn't be scared if he did show up. But it's very unlikely. Put it out of your head, now, and forget about it."

But he couldn't just do that. For several minutes he was silent, walking along beside her, thinking, wondering. For all her careless treatment of him, he sensed that he could trust his mother. She would not let anything bad happen. But his mind filled with questions.

"What does he look like, Mum? What's his name? What does he work at? Is he very old?"

"Hah! He's absolutely ancient, Killian, four years older than me. He looks like you, though. And he works at something very important – to him."

"What?"

But on this, Kerry had made up her mind. To tell Killian his father's name, or occupation, to put any kind of face on the man could well backfire. In his teens, he might use the information to go running off and find Darragh – which, in a place like Dublin, would not be a Herculean task.

"Look, let's just say he's like Uncle Brian. You've never seen him and you probably never will. He lives a long way off and he's a very busy man. Much too busy to bother with us."

"Do we not matter?"

"No. To your uncle and your father, we don't."

"But we do to Helen? And Zoe?"

"Yes. That's why Zoe is coming today. To see us."

"But Mum . . . if Zoe doesn't like my – my dad – then why does she like Uncle Brian?"

"She has to. She works with him."

"Yeah. I s'pose. But she likes him . . . you know . . . the way grown-ups do. All smushy."

"What?"

"You know – like on telly. Romantic stuff. Any time she comes here, she's always talking about him and ringing him up and everything."

Sideswiped, Kerry stopped in her tracks. Out of the mouths of babes . . . never once had she noticed that herself. But as soon as she thought about it, she realised that Killian was right. Zoe did refer often to Brian, and indeed usually defer to him on matters of opinion. Egocentrically, she had assumed guile on Zoe's part, an unrelenting effort to reconcile brother and sister by keeping each up to date on the other. But could it possibly be anything more . . . Zoe, in love with her brother? A married man?

She had better find out, right away. Not that it could be possible.

"Yes, Kerry. I'm afraid it is. That child of yours has eyes in the back of his head."

Nervously, guiltily, Zoe perched on the edge of an armchair in the rose sitting room, still wearing the grey wool suit in which she had travelled from Paris. Kerry had waited exactly five polite minutes before confronting her, and she was completely unprepared for such a raw reception. Her small hand trembled as she accepted the drink which, she thought for one terrified second, her friend was going to throw over her.

"I'm sorry, Kerry. Believe me, it's not something to which I'd subject myself voluntarily. I've been fighting it from the start."

"And when, may I ask, was that?"

"In Paris, when we were just kids. I fell for him the moment we met. But he had Lu and I had Daniel then. I thought it would wear off once I went home. How could I know I'd go back there, and work with him? Kerry, I can't help it!"

"You'd better bloody help it. Do I need to draw the pain for you with a crayon? Married men are lethal, Zoe, and my brother is as married as they come. He's *addicted* to that wife of his."

"Yes. I know that."

"Well, then! For God's sakes, Zoe!"

Kerry flung herself down on the sofa and sighed in a way that sounded, Zoe thought, like one of the horses snorting.

"Learn from my mistake, before it's too late! Don't you remember what happened to me? Have you forgotten what a fool I was?"

"No. I haven't forgotten what you went through when Brandon went back to whatshername. But at least then he was out of sight, you didn't have to go on seeing him every day."

Abruptly, Zoe's voice shook, on the verge of tears, and Kerry softened her own marginally.

"Well, yes, I suppose that did make it easier in the long run. But now you're going to have to do something similar, Zoe, for your own sake and for Brian's too. Would you consider leaving TLZ?"

For Brian's too . . . ? So, Kerry did care about Brian? Zoe stored that nugget away for future reference, and focused on the matter in hand.

"Actually, we've been having a few problems at TLZ anyway, Kerry. We can't go on as we are, with Yves I mean. This consultancy arrangement has got too complicated. I want to ask him back, full time, but Brian won't hear of it. There's been a bit of a coolness over it."

Kerry didn't need to reflect on that.

"You won't win, Zoe. Once Brian makes his mind up either for or against something, you might as well argue with that chair you're sitting on. He's the only person I know who ever defeated my father, outright, by sheer force of willpower."

Zoe smiled a little, so fondly and idiotically that Kerry could have slapped her.

"You'd never think it, would you? He looks so vague, so dreamy, as if he lived on some other planet . . . but even Lu is finding him tough going these days."

"Is she? How so?"

"Oh – Brian wants a baby, she doesn't. They row a lot."

"Good." Kerry grinned, pleased, but her smile faded as the corollary of that information sank in. If Lu's grip was loosening, did Zoe think hers was tightening?

"Zoe, Lu is just as hard and determined as Brian. She's got a hold on him like a vice. I wouldn't hold my breath till she lets him go if I were you."

"No, of course not, I didn't mean that – I just mean that things are pretty fraught at the salon between one thing and another."

"Well, there you are then. Now is the time for you to get out and leave them all to sort themselves out. You were a big success in your own right in New York, Zoe, and you can do it again, anywhere else you choose."

No answer. Intently, Kerry scrutinised Zoe's face under its little cap of black curls, but found no clues as to her intent.

"I'm telling you, Zoe, Brian won't have Yves back if he doesn't want him. He probably intends to punish him for desertion for the rest of eternity. But quite honestly, I very much doubt that Yves would come anyway. He's making a lot of money in Australia, and he's besotted with that boyfriend of his."

Unexpectedly, Zoe changed direction.

"And what about you, Kerry? Do you intend to punish Brian for evermore too?"

"Me? I'm not punishing him for anything. I simply don't find his company congenial, that's all."

"When did you last try it?"

Kerry banged down her glass on the coffee table and leaned forward so aggressively that Zoe cringed.

"After my father's funeral! And I didn't like it!"

"But that was years ago! And he's regretted it ever since!"

"Bullshit. You've just told me he's the same self-centred sod he always was. And his wife is another. They left me to sink or swim in Africa, they told me I'd never make a go of Ashamber, they've never once asked for Killian, sent him a present or a birthday card, anything . . . Brian even tried to use Yves as a go-between once, when he hadn't the guts to come to me himself. They can go to hell, the two of them."

Zoe sat back and twirled her drink in her glass, sadly.

"Oh, look, Kerry, I've only just arrived. I didn't come to fight. I came because Helen said – felt – you were upset about Darragh. Are you? Is there any way you can find out what he's planning? Why he's back?"

It dawned on Kerry that she was being less than gracious.

"Sorry, Zoe. Perhaps I am a little wound up. I've had to have a chat with Killian about his father, and it wasn't easy. All I know is that Darragh has decided to use his BL after all, and has been called to the bar in Dublin. God knows why."

"Couldn't Xavier find out?"

"Yes. He's been making enquiries. Nobody seems to know what brought Darragh back to Ireland, but everyone finds his future more interesting than his past. He's specialising in political criminology, Zoe – defending people who claim a political motive for murder, theft or whatever charge they're up on. You know – the well-meaning sort who quite justifiably killed my parents by way of making their excellent point."

"You mean – if they were ever caught – he could – he might—?"

"Exactly."

Kerry's look was such that Zoe found herself in the wholly incongruous position of attempting to defend Darragh de Bruin.

"I can only assume, Kerry, that he doesn't know what happened to your parents. He couldn't possibly undertake such a career if he did."

"Zoe, in a city the size of Dublin, he must know. Someone will have taken delight in telling him. Fortunately for his esteemed clients, he's never been one to let personal considerations interfere with business."

Registering the pain in her words as much as the truth of them, Zoe struggled to master her feelings.

"What will you do if he comes here?"

"Have him arrested for trespassing. Then he'll have a criminal record of his own, he'll be disbarred and his career will be a dead duck."

"Good. You have plenty of other ammunition at your

disposal as well, Kerry, and if he ever comes near you, you just let fly with both barrels. There's Killian to think of, as well as yourself. Helen will tell you the same thing. How is she, anyway?"

"Oh, blooming, apart from this little hiccup. Love's young dream, herself and Bob. I was a bit jealous at first, as you know, but things have worked out very well. They're revoltingly happy."

"And what about you?"

"Me? I'm – I'm contented, Zoe. I get on with my work and it doesn't leave much time for thinking about anything that once was, or might have been. You can have the martyr roster all to yourself for a change. But if you have a lick of sense, you'll forget about Brian Laraghy."

Zoe stared at the floor, and did not reply.

Dismissing the subject, Kerry went to fetch her son, who leapt into Zoe's arms with whoops of enthusiasm. Leaving the pair to rough-house together, she returned to her stables, pondering Zoe's hopeless predicament. Even if Lu were not in the way, Brian wanted children, and Zoe could never have any. Then there was her weight, an obstacle to catching any man's eye. It was sad, and unfair, but it was true. Kerry thought her way through the problem, round it and back over it as she attended to her horses, but could see no way out of it.

In the days that followed they discussed it in comforting detail, and while they found no solution they found renewed pleasure in their friendship as they went walking, riding and – unusually for Kerry – shopping. At an auction in Dublin she bought several small sculptures for the collection which, when Ashamber was refurbished, would be properly lit and displayed. Lir and his hoodlum offspring had vandalised the house until there was no longer any denying Helen's pleas for redecoration, and the search was on for an interior decorator who would incorporate fresh ideas into the old character of the place. It simply wasn't possible to entertain clients in such ragged rooms any longer, apart from the aesthetic aspect of things, and since Maeve had always maintained that, so would her daughter.

But bigger schemes also assaulted Kerry's sense of family

duty, and accordingly she left Zoe to go fishing one windy day with Killian, while she drove discreetly away in the white Mercedes that was still perfectly serviceable. Helen asked where she was going, but evasively Kerry replied only that she would be back in an hour or two should anyone call.

It wasn't far to the town where the Sisters of Charity had their convent, just over ten miles, and for once Kerry drove slowly, demurely dressed in a mocha check suit reserved for respectable occasions. On arrival, she was greeted by Sister Benildus, a businesslike nun in her forties, and offered tea; in exchange for which she handed over a cheque for a quarter of a million pounds. It wasn't as much as the success of her enterprise had cost the Order, but it was received with alacrity. Sister Ben announced her intention of using the money to build a home for abandoned, abused or orphaned children, and Kerry smiled grimly.

"That sounds fine. I can even offer you a small boy to start it off."

Sister Ben laughed, privately thinking that Eamonn Laraghy's daughter was not quite so appalling a disaster as gossip had given her to understand. The gift was generous and unsolicited, came with no strings attached, no request for thanks or credit. Airily Kerry assured her of a completely free hand, and the meeting concluded to their mutual satisfaction in less than half an hour.

On the assumption that Killian would have fallen into the river while she was away, and drowned Zoe with him, Kerry drove home rather more quickly, and met Helen as soon as she walked into the hall.

"Oh, good, you're just in time, Kerry. Yves is on the phone."

Yves rang frequently, running up monolithic bills while he chatted from Australia, but this was an unscheduled and unexpected pleasure. Kerry ran into the blue drawing room and picked up the phone with a wide smile.

"Again, so soon? I thought it was my turn to call you!"

"You wouldn't have got me, *chérie*. I'm not at home."

"Oh. Where, then?"

"In London."

London? Even now, to this ridiculous day, Kerry could not
think of that city without thinking of Brandon Lawrence. But
what was Yves doing there? Normally he notified her of any
trip to Europe, and they met on those rare occasions when
timetables dovetailed.

"But that's only an hour's flight, Yves! You can't come that
far and not continue on to Ireland! I want to see you . . . why
don't you come over, even for tonight? Are you in a hurry?"

His drawl was so deep it made her laugh. After more than
six years in Australia, he had the oddest mongrel accent.

"No hurry at all, *ma belle*, I shall be delighted to accept
your kind invitation."

"Great. We'll wait dinner for you. Zoe is here too."

"*Encore mieux.* Would she pick me up at the airport, if I
asked nicely? It's been rather a long haul from Sydney. Tell
her I'll try to get there around six."

He was just off a plane from Sydney? Kerry was bemused.
But Zoe and Helen, when they heard he was coming, were
ecstatic. For Zoe, it was a chance to sound her old friend out
about returning to TLZ, to restructure the partnership that
nature had always intended. For Helen, word of Yves meant
what it always did: renewed sparkle in Kerry's eyes. The man
invariably affected her like a crate of champagne, and Helen
only wished she could bottle that elusive effervescence.

15

The moment she heard Lir barking, Kerry flew out into the hall to accost Yves, smothering him in kisses before he could even put down what appeared to be enough luggage for a year. Behind him, Zoe stood rolling her eyes in a comical way, bending her elbow and cupping her hand to her mouth, trying to signal what Kerry instantly realised for herself.

Unshaven, dishevelled in a leather jacket and battered denims more befitting a rock musician than a fashion designer, Yves was drunk. Not dead drunk, but blurred, disorientated and very unsteady.

"You're bloody plastered!"

He grinned complacently, staggered against a suitcase and surveyed her truculently, his eyes so dilated she wondered whether there was anyone at home behind their navy façade.

"What a warm welcome, *chérie*. Enchanting as always."

He ran an affectionate hand through her hair and she saw that his own was radically altered, the thick shag exchanged for a short, shingled cut that made him look oddly vulnerable, much younger than thirty. He was thinner, too, almost gaunt under a beguiling tan.

"Get upstairs and take a cold shower this minute."

"Yes 'm." He spun vaguely round and stumbled in the direction of the staircase, staring at it as if it were Mount Kilimanjaro.

"Oh, for chrissakes . . . Paddy! Come here!"

Paddy shambled out from some distant lair and was instructed to take Mr Tiberti away, unpack his bags and render him presentable. Kerry didn't know whether to laugh or cry; as a rule, Yves confined his excesses to nightclubs and festive occasions.

"What in hell's the matter with him, Zoe?"

"Search me. He was like this when I met him, and I've hardly understood a word since. He just keeps prattling on in franglais."

Zoe dimpled in amusement, but Kerry frowned. It was as if only a body had arrived, and Yves had yet to join it. There was a vacancy about his face, a remoteness quite removed from reality, and he looked like a derelict. Zoe intuited her concern, but misinterpreted it.

"Don't be mad at him, Kerry. He's exhausted."

"No. But you can play cryptic crosswords with him, Zoe. I want an explanation."

Bob and Helen appeared, tutting as they were informed of their guest's lamentable state, but Yves's reappearance was an improvement. Shaved and somewhat shamefaced, changed into black cords and a yellow sweater, he kissed Helen, sat down in the dining room and poured a glass of water, spilling as much again.

"Sorry. Bit jetlagged."

Kerry eyed him narrowly, but could not connect with him as he plucked evasively at the scarf knotted round his neck, rambling and slurring in response to Bob's cordial greetings.

Dinner was served, and proceeded at a ponderous pace. Yves fiddled with a salad, managed a mouthful of fish and blenched at the sight of dessert. Helen mustered a kindly smile.

"Never mind. A good night's sleep is what you need."

He smiled at her with a kind of pathetic gratitude and embarked on the first of four cups of black coffee. Radiating disapproval, Bob floundered as question after question fell into a vacuum: how was Australia, how was business, how was his – um – partner?

"Fine. Fine. Fine."

After an hour that felt like five, Helen stood up.

"I think we could all use an early night. Kerry, you're not to keep this poor chap up late talking, after that long flight." She bent to embrace the guilty party. "Sleep well, Yves. You'll feel much better in the morning."

He rose to hug her as warmly as if she were his own

mother, causing Kerry to reflect dourly, though not for the first time, on that lady's whereabouts. And where, for that matter, was Keith? Over the years Yves had produced one or two photographs of a solid, rather formal man in a suit, but never the man himself. Tomorrow, when he was capable of rational speech, she would ferret to the bottom of this curious visit. Incoherent as he was, she could clearly hear a cry for help.

Up next day with the sun, Kerry put in two intensive hours of training on the green gallops of the Curragh plain before returning home for breakfast. The horses had run well, and her mood was cheerful as she took a tray from Eileen and carried it up to Yves's room herself, humming. Yves had many friends, she knew, all over the place, but he had come to her. Knocking peremptorily, she strode straight in.

"Morning, sunshine."

He rolled over and struggled slowly awake, hauling himself upright as if by invisible winch, gazing at her blankly for a moment. But then, like a visiting child eager to please, he flashed her a louche smile.

"Hi. May I preface my day with an abject apology."

"You may, but not to me. How's the head?"

"Nothing a guillotine wouldn't cure. Wire me up to the juice."

She gave him the tray and sat down on the end of the bed.

"So. Row with lover boy? Cancelled orders? Car reduced to crushed dinky? Nasty taxman? What?"

He ran a hand diffidently through his shorn, tangled hair, gulped some juice and grimaced as though swallowing nettles.

"Yeah. Something like that. Thought I'd take a break."

"A long break, if that luggage is any indication."

"Oh, just a year or two."

"What?" The indifference in his voice gave her a terrible falling, premonitory feeling, so blasé and glassy it sent a shiver across the back of her knuckles.

"Yves, wake up and sit up and tell me why you're here."

He regarded her frankly, laughed, and shrugged.

"Frocks, Kerry. That's all it is. Just a bunch of bloody frocks. Who wants to spend a lifetime dressing a lot of Barbie dolls? If I'm such a great designer, there must be other things it's time to try, for other people in other places. Graphics, artwork, books, albums, who knows . . . buildings, maybe? Think I'd make a good architect? Get a mature student's grant?"

"Yves, if you think you're going skiving off *again*, you can forget it. You love your work, and if you'd only concentrate on it you'd be even better than Dior, Lagerfeld, YSL, the whole lot of them. This lack of stamina is a positive disease. But you're going to stick with your salon this time, if I have to parcel you back to Sydney myself. You're going so well there . . . I don't understand you."

"Actually, you're the only one who does, usually. But it's not my fault this time, Kerry. Not entirely, anyway."

"What isn't?"

He turned away from her, into the rays of morning light, so that she saw the tension tighten in his collarbone, in the veins on his neck.

"Kerry, my work in Australia is over. My life there is over. I've left Keith, closed my salon and taken whatever I could carry away with me. The rest will shortly be in the hands of liquidators and creditors."

His voice was husky as he turned back to her, his eyes smudged with fatigue, weariness, the lashes lowered over disillusion, fragility, and bewilderment. She searched for words, but they dissolved on her tongue, erased by incredulity.

"What you say is true, Kerry. I do love my work, and was doing well, enjoying life immensely – until my beloved investment analyst overinvested a mite. I left all the financial stuff to him. It bored me so much I never once checked on where my money was or what it was doing. Careless and stupid, as usual."

"Yves, you can't mean to say – to tell me . . ."

"Every penny, apart from my current account, and a few paintings I managed to salvage."

"Oh, Yves, you're not – *bank*rupt?"

Chilled, only partly comprehending, she reached for his hand, delved with her eyes into his, and found them full of devastation. God, could it really happen? Could someone you loved do to you what, if she understood aright, Keith had done to him? They had been lovers for years, there must have been trust, and respect – and now, this?

"But Yves, surely Keith didn't deliberately – use your funds—?"

"Yes. He intended to replace them, of course. With interest. He just didn't want to confuse me with things I didn't understand."

She strove to believe that. But the taste of betrayal rose sharp and bitter in her gorge.

"Oh, don't look at me that way, Kerry! It's only money. I still have all the things that matter – health, and talent, and friends. I'm only thirty. I'll survive. Start over again, somehow. In a way, it's liberating. A challenge, stimulating, full of new potential."

She saw that he meant it. But how could he do it? Starting anew was, as he said, exciting, charged with adrenalin. But he had done it twice already. Under this veneer of optimism, there must lie layers of anguish, shame, uncertainty and throbbing hurt.

"Yves, you can't just walk away from this. From Keith, I mean. You must make him face up to what he's done, and help you to put things right."

"No. I prefer not to see him again, Kerry. One learns from one's mistakes."

The hard part. The part she could see he didn't want to talk about. The emotional numbness, nothingness that Darragh had once explained so didactically to her, quoting Sartre and Camus the length of all those late nights at Ivry. When it hit her, she had succumbed to it, been sucked into its vortex – whereas here was Yves, trying to look on the bright side, cope, get up and fight the next round. And he had no one to lean on, not even a Helen or a Brandon, no family. Nobody, only herself. Her heart contracted with pity, and empathy.

"Oh, Yves. I'm so sorry. I don't know how it is that some malevolent fate always seems to get in on everyone's act and screw it up somehow, sooner or later. But we'll beat it this

time, between us. To begin with, I'll give you all the money
you need . . ."

He smiled, put his finger to his lips and then to hers.

"No, *chérie*. I got into this and I'll get myself out. For one
thing, your brother owes me quite a lot, and I'll be invoicing
TLZ *tout de suite*. Then there's the few thousand that wasn't
in our joint account, and – well, I'm sure someone will offer
me a job. I'd rather take a salary for a while than start over
on anyone else's money, even yours. I couldn't guarantee the
repayments."

"Don't be ridiculous."

"I mean it. All I ask of you is moral support."

"You've got that. Consider Ashamber your home for as long
as you need one. But where is home, Yves? Where do you
want to go?"

It was one question to which the answer was easy. But
for years, pride had prevented the admission of how badly
he missed France. La belle France, with its museums and
galleries, its food and its flair, its lovely language and chic
assurance. The stunning panache of the rue de Rivoli, the
guttural growl of old men playing boules in the sun, the big
noisy brasseries and chugging bateaux mouches, all down
the Seine – wide airy boulevards, pungent markets, sleazy
pugnacious Pigalle, harlequin nights at the Opéra. There
had been days when he could have died for the blue musty
charm of Paris, days when his body fought for the freedom
of cold Alpine air, that biting cold as he launched himself off a pine-spiked peak onto a wild glassy piste, his
mouth filling with flying snow as he pushed down on the
poles and skied to Chamonix or Tignes, every bone taut and
tingling as he shot across the slopes.

His silence was enough. Kerry gripped his bare shoulder
so hard he winced.

"France. That's where you belong, Yves, isn't it? *Isn't* it?"

"Yes. But I've burnt my bridges there. Brian informed me
only weeks ago that my services are no longer required, and
I will not beg to be let back into my own salon."

"Brian's a fool. I'll sort him out."

"Kerry, you haven't spoken to Brian for nearly a decade.

Don't meddle now, and make things worse. Please. I'll sort myself out."

Some hope, she thought dismally, of that. Yves didn't have the organisational powers of a hamster at the best of times, never mind now, when behind the bravado he was reeling with shock. In one terrifying flash flood, his whole life had been swept away. His home, his lover, his career, his credibility. Everything.

She was almost swamped herself, by the sheer scale of such a disaster. But obstinately she fixed her thoughts on Brian, the only lifeline she could throw to the friend she adored. Brian was her brother, goddamit! It didn't matter now what either of them wanted, or didn't want: the point was that Yves needed them both.

Bending to kiss him, feeling every raw nerve under his skin, she made up her mind that he would get them. Both of them, at any cost, any price.

Zoe was aghast.

"Dear Jesus. This is going to be all over Paris in no time, Kerry. Yves will be the laughing stock of the whole city. And there are bound to be legal repercussions, too."

"Yes. But he can only be accused of contributory negligence, at worst. I'm going to consult Xavier about it, and about Keith's position. The blame for this is going to go where it belongs. Tell me, Zoe, where is Brian at this minute?"

"At work. But he's going to Fréjus tomorrow, with Lu and her parents. They go there every Easter."

"Good. If he's out of town, he may not hear immediately . . . that gives us a little time to think."

"About what?"

"About how to make him ask Yves back, obviously! There must be a way."

"I've been trying to find one for so long my brain hurts. This just makes things worse. He'll say Yves is not only a liability, but an idiot as well. He'll never have him back, much less ask him."

Impotently, furiously, Kerry thought of her first distant days in Paris, those days in which she had been so happy, as they all had, thanks to Yves Tiberti. Yves, who had made life so exuberant and vibrant, engaging and exciting, working so hard at the business of living and giving, a court jester nobody had ever once thought to thank.

They were going to thank him now.

She eyed the phone.

"Zoe, what's the number at the salon?"

"Oh, Kerry – don't do anything rash, please."

"I have no intention of doing anything rash. I merely think it's time my brother started taking an interest in his nephew, that's all."

With visible apprehension, Zoe recited the number, and she wrote it down, thought for a moment, and dialled it. Estelle, the salon secretary, answered so swiftly she was taken aback, but steeling herself, she switched to French and asked to speak to M Laraghy.

"May I say who's calling?"

"It's" – oh, God – "it's his sister."

There was a pause, in which she waited to hear that M Laraghy was not available. But after no more than twenty seconds, Brian was at the other end, his voice at once indelibly familiar and contorted by panic.

"Kerry, what's wrong – Killian? Is he ill? Injured?"

She had the sensation of walking off the end of a pier. But she took a deep breath, and kept going.

"No, Brian. Nothing is wrong. It's just that – that I've been talking to him recently. Explaining that his uncle lives too far away ever to come and see him. He's a little upset about it. He says he wants to meet you. And, well, I feel it's wrong to deprive him of that when he has no other family. So I was wondering – whether you might – come and speak to him?"

Incredulous, he looked immediately for the catch.

"Kerry, this isn't some kind of joke, is it? I can't believe you'd suddenly invite me to Ashamber, after eight years, out of the blue."

"Brian, the child wasn't old enough to ask before, that's all. But you could have come any time you wanted."

"Do you want me to, now?"

"Yes. Yes, I do. I think it would be very good for him – and who knows? Maybe for us, too. Zoe has made me see that perhaps I've been a little, well, unreasonable."

Zoe, she thought, might as well have the credit for this mouthful of gall. But it had better be worth it.

"She has? Don't tell me you're actually *listening* to someone, at last?"

Go to hell, she wanted to say then, you patronising goddamn prig. But she didn't.

"How are you fixed for next weekend? Killian is off school till Monday."

"We'll be in Fréjus, didn't Zoe say? But we could leave a little early, I suppose, fly from Nice to Dublin on Friday, maybe. But I don't know how Lu would feel about that."

"Oh, do try to persuade her, Brian. Nabdul and Shairi are coming then too – you know, Sheik Feirah's son? We could have a lovely little house party."

Nabdul and Shairi, for all she knew, might be in Kutari, or anywhere. But they would be at Ashamber on Friday, if it meant Lu would too, with her husband.

"Hold on. I'll check with her."

Putting Kerry on hold, he left her drumming her fingers for several minutes, gnawing her lip impatiently.

"OK, Kerry. We'll come. Lu says she'd very much like to meet your Arab friends. She's seen Princess Shairi in some magazines, and reckons the woman could dress better! So I'll book a flight for Friday, and let you know its arrival time."

She wanted to throw up, but purred instead.

"That's perfect, Brian. I'll send someone to meet you on Friday. Killian will be thrilled. Au revoir till then."

Quickly, she put down the phone before he could think of any ifs or buts. When she looked up, Zoe was regarding her with a look that spoke volumes.

"Cut it out, Zoe! It's what you wanted, isn't it? And it's the only way. Once he's here, I'll think how to manage the rest of it. Lu has earmarked Shairi for business already, she'll see the advantages of having Yves back. And if Brian takes Yves, he gets his nephew. I think I'm offering a more than fair deal."

Uneasily, Zoe conceded that she was. Everyone stood to

benefit, and she could articulate no valid reason for her nervousness.

"How are you going to get Nabdul and Shairi here at such short notice?"

Kerry smiled, unconcerned.

"Nabdul never turns down an invitation to Ashamber, Zoe."

Brandon was right, Marianne conceded as she circulated graciously amongst the four hundred guests in the Virginia home of Senator David Wheatstone. America *was* just her cup of tea. She'd loved it from the moment the long black limousine met them at Dulles, even if Brandon did have to start in on his eternal phone calls the instant they got to the hotel. He was always like that, for ever scything his way through sheafs of messages, huddling into urgent little conferences with his associates like a priest saying daily Mass.

Marianne didn't mind that. It reminded her how important, how indispensable her husband was. Even now, as she talked with the women at this party, and danced with the men, he sat at a table on the other side of the vast ballroom, conversing with Matthew Breffni. Today was his birthday: forty-two, and she had to admit he looked every day of it. But how handsome he was, nonetheless! He still had that leonine blond hair, those autocratic eyebrows, the slightly hooded grey-blue eyes that never missed anything, observing most when they seemed to be observing least.

They'd observed the women here tonight, she knew, but only in the way that all men's did, as a matter of course, and he had actually commented on how very thin the American ladies were – too thin for his taste. He preferred her own, slightly more rounded, fuller European look. Not that Marianne carried a spare ounce, but she filled out her clothes in a most feminine way, she had a discernible bosom and a wasp waist, curving hips and legs that could get a grip on a man. Not that they ever did, these days.

But she had her compensations, and this party was one of them. Laced with the cream of Washington society, it was virtually free of Irish influence for a change; instead there seemed to be a lot of Southern politicians from Georgia, Louisiana, Florida and Texas, oil barons, property tycoons, ranchers and landowners, financiers and surgeons, computer people and television hosts. Some of the Texans, she heard, owned estates the size of Wales. Network your way round them all, Brandon had told her, and she found it agreeable, a pleasant easy assignment for the evening. Introductions were less starched than in London, and she was conscious of looking particularly well in her new magnolia satin gown.

"Ah, Mrs Lawrence, isn't it? My compliments, ma'am. Your host, David Wheatstone."

She had met Senator Wheatstone only briefly in the reception line. But he undoubtedly knew how to throw her kind of party. Marianne picked out a pretty smile from her repertoire and dropped it like an orchid into his lap.

"How do you do, Senator? Congratulations on such a lovely party."

"Oh, please call me David, and allow me to congratulate you on such a very fetching ensemble. Would you care to dance, Mrs Lawrence?"

Yes. Yes, she would. She'd love to get this ballgown twirling and show it off to everyone.

"By all means. But you must call me Marianne."

He took her hand in his, put the other round her waist and led her into the centre of the floor where they could both see and be seen.

"What do you think of our country so far, Marianne?"

"Oh, I think it's wonderful! So lively, so big . . . I've never been to this part of it before."

"Well then, we must make sure you enjoy it. I hope your husband hasn't been working you too hard?"

"Oh, no, he's the one who's working hard, with Mr Breffni."

"And what do you think of our candidate?"

Matthew Breffni? Marianne hesitated.

She didn't like the man. At first, she hadn't known why, but then Brandon had put his finger on it. Breffni was vulgar, he said, nouveau riche, pretentious. He radiated such rampant ambition you could feel it clear across a room, a newly successful, second-generation immigrant who had traded in his father's railway shovel and his mother's lace curtains for a set of perfectly capped teeth. His material success was admirable, but his politics were abhorrent, forever harking back to an "old country" that no longer existed. The phrase set Brandon's teeth on edge, and he doubted that the man had ever set foot in Ireland, much less knew anything about its European context or its newly contemporary attitudes; to him it was a rustic farmyard, full of pigs and potatoes, crocks of gold under romantic, ridiculous rainbows. His politics were pure Tammany Hall, and furthermore Brandon was concerned about the aspiring politician's influence on Chris. Marianne couldn't see that there was any, but then Brandon pointed out how Breffni had taken Chris under his wing from the day they arrived, seeing in the youth fertile new terrain in which to plant his reactionary old ideas.

But Chris is interested in politics anyway, Marianne had reasoned.

Yes, Brandon replied, but he's young and malleable, and Breffni is trying to mould him. He's a buffoon, but he's dangerous, and the sooner we get Chris out of his range the better. I hope his campaign ends in failure, and I told Dermot we never should have got involved. I don't care how much crystal his supporters buy in gratitude, or linen or salmon or anything else; this is wrong for me and wrong for our son.

Marianne looked at David Wheatstone with her big bluebell eyes and beamed.

"Oh, we think he's perfect for the job. Just perfect."

"Do you really? Why so?"

Why? Couldn't he see she was merely being polite, doing her duty? She wasn't expected to have any real opinions, and certainly wasn't about to expose Brandon's. She knew nothing about politics – which, she suddenly realised, was her salvation. Nobody required her to.

"Why, David, I think he's perfectly handsome and charming, and my husband thinks he's qualified in all sorts of other ways, that are much too complicated for me to discuss!"

He eyed her shrewdly.

"It's all right, Marianne. You can level with me. I know why your husband is supporting Matthew, or appearing to."

"You do?"

"Uh huh."

"And – and why are you supporting him, David?"

"I'm supporting him tonight by hosting this party for him at one thousand dollars a head because he's a Democrat and so am I; it's expected of me. Furthermore, he may win the nomination, and exercise considerable influence in the future. That's all."

A man with an eye to the main chance. A man who evidently didn't allow his personal feelings to interfere with his control of things. She approved of that, and smiled up at him again, noting his healthy tan, his abundant white hair, his strong grip on her waist.

"How sensible you are, David."

"And how lovely you are, Marianne."

Serenely, they danced on. From the flower-decked table where he sat with Matthew Breffni, Brandon watched them covertly but intently, approvingly, which was not Breffni's appraisal of him. To Matthew, Brandon was about as exciting as Oregon, and he was bored rigid. The wife was pretty as a picture, though. What could she see in such a dullard of a husband? Money, presumably. There was nothing else that Matthew could see. Suddenly, he felt the urgent need of a whiskey.

"Excuse me, Brandon, I see someone over there I must speak with. Be right back."

Brandon rejoiced, and prayed that he wasn't going to be stuck with the jerk for the rest of the night. Now was his chance to escape; he would get up and dance with one of these women, lose himself in the crowd.

"Mr Lawrence? Telephone for you, sir."

"Oh. Thank you." He took the portable phone and spoke into it tersely, as was his habit even when he hadn't had a bellyful of anyone as ghastly as Matthew Breffni.

"Brandon Lawrence."

"Oh, Mr Lawrence! Thank goodness. I've been trying to find you all night."

Louise? At this hour? But it must be after midnight in London.

Well after it. Instantly Brandon braced himself.

"What's the matter, Louise?"

"It's your father, sir. He's unwell. He's had – had a stroke."

The information made its way down into Brandon's gut like a shot of some illegal substance; raw, jolting, mesmeric.

"How serious is it?"

"Very, sir. I'm afraid he's – the chances are . . ."

"OK, Louise. I'm on my way."

Putting down the phone, Brandon went in search of his wife, still dancing with Wheatstone at the other end of the room. Interrupting them with no hint of urgency, he excused himself politely.

"Marianne, I'm sorry to break up your evening. But I have to go back to Ireland. My father's had a stroke."

Horrified, they both gazed at him, and automatically the senator tightened his grip on Marianne, steadying her against the shock. When she spoke, her voice was tremulous.

"A stroke? Brandon, you can't be serious? Oh, we must all go! I'll call the boys and tell them to pack."

But Brandon looked at her, and at David Wheatstone, and firmly shook his head.

"No, Marianne. I'll take Chris with me, but I want you to stay here, with Mr Breffni's entourage. Dermot won't thank us for abandoning the project he sent us here to support. If I leave Harry with you, can you carry on without me, do you think? Perhaps the senator would help?"

Smoothly, graciously, the senator assured him that it would be an honour. Of course he would look after Mrs Lawrence and her younger son, while Mr Lawrence went straight to his father, as naturally he must.

"Thank you. I'll be in touch."

Shaking the man's hand, Brandon propelled his wife almost into his chest, kissed her goodbye, and left her.

People were starting to flock to the Riviera. It was the start of the long hot season that extended through from April to the end of October, and everywhere the shops, hotels, restaurants and chic boutiques were opening their doors on the emerging sun. Setting out their wares, proprietors lovingly hand-wrote price tags and watched the leggy blondes stroll down to the marina, parading impossible tans, hair uniformly bleached the colours of sand and straw, their men's bank accounts poised equally lithe and fit against the coming onslaughts.

It was just the way she liked it, Lu reflected as she made her way to the beach, her crisp black-and-white tote bag slung over her shoulder, her matching visor deflecting the rays of the sun. Lots of people, lots of buzz, a sybaritic anticipation of the day's many pleasures stretching ahead of everyone. If only Claire and Lionel wouldn't fuss so, with their icebox and parasol, towels and swimsuits, cameras and multitudinous paraphernalia. Had he been here, Brian would naturally have helped them with it, but he had gone on ahead, anxious to catch the tide before it turned, vanishing in a flurry of flippers and masks to a rendezvous with some boatman.

Lu knew he was running away, avoiding further recriminations concerning the coming weekend that he had sacrificed, out of a clear blue sky, to his sister. Ireland, instead of Fréjus. It was altogether reprehensible of him, but she was not going to let it ruin this lovely day. Arriving in due course at their chosen spot, she helped her parents set up their equipment on the sand and stretched out on her own lilo. Bikinis were in fashion this year, and she was pleased with the one she had chosen today, a silvery affair which, with her plain black sunglasses, made her look quite as young and attractive as the starlets orbiting around her. Lazily, she smoothed on some sunblock and reached for her reading material, a thick brochure she had brought from a car showroom in Paris. If she had to go to Ireland, she would bargain for something in return: that old black Mercedes was a disgrace. Brian could keep it, since he was so attached to it, but she would have a new one.

Dieu, but Brian was so trying lately! As crochety as a cat, for ever fretting about finding his replacement daywear designer, for ever whining about children, nagging about every little thing. As for this sudden decision to see Kerry – there must be a catch in it somewhere. The woman hadn't extended the invitation for the good of her health, if Lu knew

Kerry. Eight years of silence, and now this? Were it not for
the Arab couple, she would never have agreed to go.

Brian's inheritance. That was the ulterior motive. Kerry
saw that money looming on the horizon and was about to
stake her claim. The original three million had mushroomed
into seventeen, and she must know that, more or less. But
it wasn't due for another eight months. There would be
plenty of time to circumvent her.

Propping the heavy brochure on her flat stomach, Lu flicked
through the pages with interest, feeling much better than
in recent days. The pain had subsided now, the bleeding
stopped, the cramps disappeared just as the doctor predicted.
A relatively easy solution to a most inconvenient problem,
and nobody knew anything about it, apart from Claire. The
only pangs Lu felt now were hunger pangs; she hadn't eaten
much of a breakfast. Reaching into the icebox for an apple,
she munched it contentedly, read some more, and went for a
swim. When she came back, Brian had returned from his dive
and was telling his in-laws all about it, animatedly describing
the marine underworld as he lifted lunch things out of the box,
setting out their picnic in an endearingly helpful fashion. Lu
smiled: he was still her old Brian in so many ways. Some
day, she might make him just one baby. But not now. She
bent and kissed the back of his neck, and he smiled up at
her in return, pleasantly surprised.

Companionably, they shared the food and a bottle of wine
from Lionel's vines as the noon sun gathered strength overhead, slowing the pace as people retreated into the shade of
parasols. Languor descended with the torpid heat, and Lu
stretched out, with Lionel, to do a little sunworshipping. But
Brian knew his mother-in-law to be averse to the sun, and
solicitously offered to accompany her on a quiet walk along
the water's edge.

Protected by wide hats, they set off across the sand,
murmuring rather than talking, comfortable in their easy
affinity. Claire was a good listener, whose company Brian
always found agreeable, and the two lost track of time as
they meandered ankle-deep in the warm water, idly picking
over matters of mutual interest, stopping here and there to

inspect a shell or stone sculpted by the elements, a piece of wood or flotsam.

Almost an hour, perhaps, elapsed before they turned back on their footprints, detouring to buy ice cream from a vendor, throw a ball back to a little boy, step over a laughing father buried in sand by his children. As they skirted the wriggling body, one of the tiny toddlers made a break for freedom, squealing and splashing gleefully as it ran into the sea, to be chased and scooped up by its mother, whose even younger infant lay dormant on a rug. It was no more than five or six months, and Brian admired it wistfully; such a cute little thing in its sunbonnet, burping at him as he passed by.

With a sad smile, he turned to Claire.

"You know, *belle-mère*, someday Lu and I . . . well, I still hope . . ."

Claire didn't answer. Brian peered at her, his vision obscured by the brim of her hat and his own. And then, horrified, he saw a tear roll down Claire's cheek, falling off her chin onto her loose white shirt.

At first, he thought he must be imagining it, or that it was a spray of salt water. But another one fell, and another, so that he stood appalled as Claire raised her hand to her face, unable to stem the flow, her shoulders shuddering with uncontrollable sobs.

"*Belle-mère*? What is it? Don't you feel well? The heat?"

He put his arm around her, and her face sank onto his chest, transfixing him with anxiety as she wept without explanation. Over her shoulder he could see Lu, rising from the lilo from which she had witnessed the distant spectacle, running across the beach to her mother. As she came closer, he saw the fear in her face.

And then, suddenly, something clicked in his brain. The toddler in the water. The baby on the rug. Those recent stomach cramps of Lu's, the pallor she had put down to fatigue, that unprecedented day she had taken off work. Claire's tears, and the look on Lu's face. More than anything, it was the look that told him.

Without a word, handing Claire into her daughter's frantic arms, Brian left them both and walked away.

*   *   *

"Please, Brian, please! We must discuss it! Why won't you at least do that, like a sensible adult?"

"Because, Lu, there is nothing to discuss."

Looking into his face was like looking down an empty well. A black, infinite void. Lu felt that it was consuming her, sucking her into oblivion. For the first time in her life, she was afraid of her husband. His father's volcanic furies had been legendary, but the silence of the son was immeasurably more terrifying.

"*Please*, Brian!"

"Lu, would you mind leaving me alone? I have rather a headache."

"Brian, I'm not leaving. Not until we sort this out. I'll have another baby, Brian! I'll get pregnant immediately, do whatever you want . . ."

"Do as I ask, then. Leave me."

Desperately, Lu tried to think of another tack. But every word seemed to drive him further away, leave her flailing and floundering to no avail whatever. But he must understand, he must listen, he *must*!

"Brian, I'll give up work. I'll stay at home and have a baby and care for it night and day, if that's what you want. No nurse, no crèche, just you and me and our child – children, as many as you want."

He shrugged, and continued to pull clothes from the wardrobe, throwing them into a suitcase like rags, sweeping possessions off the dressing table, the bedside table, the bathroom shelf. Lu watched as if it were happening on television, to other people in another place, unable to absorb the reality of it. But she was his wife! He couldn't leave her. He couldn't.

Wife. That was it. Brian was Irish. Marriage was for ever.

"Brian, we've been together for ten years. Every marriage has its difficult moments. We'll get over this one, you'll see. We'll work at it, repair it – everyone is entitled to one mistake, Brian!"

He smiled at her a fraction, a smile like a Swiss knife.

"I'll say one thing for marrying a Frenchwoman, Lu. You can divorce her. What a very civilised country this is."

Divorce? No. Oh, no. He didn't mean that. He couldn't contemplate such a thing, he was distraught, just as she was herself, he needed time to think. Time to recover, and put this behind him.

"Brian, you mustn't say that! It's not worth it, you're dramatising everything, forgetting what a good wife I've been to you, the way I've built up your career . . ."

Her voice was starting to rise and quiver, and she had to make an enormous effort to keep the panic out of it. But he would never manage without her. He needed her now as much as ever, and he would see that when he came to himself.

He closed the suitcase, took out his chequebook, scribbled on a page, tore it off and handed it to her.

"This covers, I think, everything the company owes you. Your full settlement will be a matter for the solicitors, settled out of court I hope, and forwarded to you in due course."

She dropped the piece of paper as if it were on fire. He was *sacking* her? Wiping out ten years, in a single day? Dismissing her, as if she were an employee? But it was unthinkable.

"I won't take it. I won't leave."

"Lu, I am the one who is leaving. Naturally you may keep the Paris apartment, since it was a gift from your parents. I will find other accommodation, and you will find other employment. Don't ever set foot in my salon again."

He picked up his bag, took his jacket and went out to the lounge of their rented holiday home, already vacated by her tearful parents. She ran after him, prepared to plead, beg, physically restrain him. But even as she caught up with him, something stopped her.

The realisation that she was wasting her time. As long as he was in this frame of mind, it would be fruitless, a possibly exacerbating assault on his resolute intransigence. Time was the only thing she could bargain with . . . she sank down on the pink leather sofa, and waited.

He riffled briefly through a handful of papers, amidst which she could see his passport, and looked her in the face.

"I'm going home, Lu. To Ireland, as arranged. I suggest that you return to Paris, clear your desk and engage a lawyer. The paperwork will be set in train as soon as I get back – Monday, probably, or Tuesday. Please don't attempt to contact me in the meantime. Your contract is terminated. Just like my baby."

With a habitual gesture he flicked his hair out of his eyes, walked to the door and went out, closing it softly behind him.

She forced herself to remain seated, say nothing, do nothing. Later, in a day or two, a week or two, he would be his normal loving self again, and she would go to him then, reason and beguile him into seeing sense.

It struck her with great force that Brian mattered more to her than anything else on earth.

Kerry was sorry to say goodbye to Zoe, but glad to have a few days alone with Yves. He followed her everywhere, helping with the horses, running errands, anything and everything to make himself useful. The outdoor exercise agreed with him, distracting and energising him, and she made no mention of Brian's impending arrival.

In the evenings, they did not go out, but sat talking on the terrace in the stretching twilights, or in the rose sitting room by the fire. His attitude was positive as he tossed ideas back and forth, devoid of bitterness, self-pity or any of the despair to which he might have understandably succumbed. In jeans and sweaters, boots and scarves, he was a different man from the flamboyant public persona, but his natural charisma was unaltered, his grace and wit so constant that, rather than cheering him up, she found it the other way round. Far from being oppressive, his cares gave her a sense of purpose, resoldering their friendship as she nailed her attention to the question of how to help him. Helen was consulted, and lively debate ensued; he was adamant that he would not take a penny from her either, or from anyone, just as Kerry had once turned down his offer of finance. He made the whole thing into a huge joke, but Kerry watched him carefully, sensing the conflict in him at unguarded moments.

Then, there were all the desolate signs of loneliness, deception and pain in his cobalt eyes, the hurt puzzled look of betrayal; for all that Keith had done to him, accepting the truth was very hard. Kerry probed among the shattered pieces of the relationship, but he deflected her.

"What about you, Kerry? Where are your smitten swains, your suicidal Romeos? We all need love, even if it does come expensive."

"Love, my eye. If I had a pound note for every bore, every drunkard, every gold-digger I've booted out of my sight, I could wallpaper the Bank of Ireland."

Yves frowned. Surely, in seven years, they couldn't all have been so bad? Granted, women were demanding these days, setting standards so high few men could match them, and Kerry was not a woman he expected ever to settle for second best. But it wasn't that, he thought; it was that Kerry had shut herself off at the emotional mains. Brandon had failed her, Darragh had failed her, and Killian was a constant reminder of all the anguish. Yves deplored the way she clouted the child around the place, and lamented the narrowness of the life she had built around herself. But her face brightened as she told him of Nabdul's intention to visit over the weekend.

"Why's he coming? More horses, or more sex?"

"Yves, I told you we had to put a stop to that two years ago, when he married Shairi. He's coming to look at some stud farms, and I'd advise you to be nice to him."

The farm was the bait with which she had lured Nabdul, promising a list of places for his inspection on arrival. And he had risen to it, after she explained all the advantages of owning his own stud, putting down roots in the unique ground that produced such magnificent horses, starting the long line of winners that nobody in the world could rival. He would love it, and she would help him with it, if he took up the opportunity now before Bill Schuster thought to muscle in. Yes, Nabdul had agreed, so easily hooked that she would have smiled had not a more sobering event diverted her.

On television, the news carried a report of Dermot Lawrence's illness, with an attempted interview with Brandon as he and his elder son returned from America. Brandon made no comment, but Kerry sat riveted, catching her first sight of him in many years, so hypnotised that Yves saw straight through the fine defensive veil of her isolation, and felt profoundly sorry for her. One picture, he thought, really was worth a thousand words.

Next day she was all nerves, clamping herself onto Nabdul when he strode into the house, not at all the regal figure Yves had expected. In his experience, wealthy titled clients demanded to be humoured and flattered like spoilt children, and indeed Nabdul's arrogance was obvious as he left his wife to follow several steps behind him. But otherwise the man seemed quite normal. Bearded and bulky in a tweed sports jacket, cords and sensible brogues, he tussled with Lir as he embraced Helen and looked around hopefully for a drink.

"He seems quite human, Kerry."

"I've house-trained him, Yves. He never dares pull rank here."

She turned to Nabdul and Shairi to inform them that they were in luck: her good friend Yves Tiberti was in residence, who with a little cajoling might be persuaded to design a maternity wardrobe for the pregnant princess. Catching the ball, Yves promised to consider it when time permitted, struggling to keep a straight face as Kerry winked at him. But as the hour of Brian's arrival approached her nervousness returned, and abruptly she left her guests to get acquainted over cocktails poured, with a resigned sigh, by Nabdul.

Taking refuge in her bedroom, she changed into five different dresses, went back to the one she had been wearing originally and sentried herself by the window in a ferment of agitation. She shouldn't have done it. Brian would quarrel with Yves, Lu would antagonise everyone, Killian would drive them all to distraction. Unlike her mother, she was no good at this social engineering, couldn't hold all the threads together, would say the wrong thing . . . What *was* she going to say to Brian, anyway? Feverishly, she rehearsed assorted greetings, but knew they sounded false and insincere. Antipathetic at first, then ambivalent, she was finally seized with panic. Brian was her brother. But he was a total stranger.

One by one, the minutes ticked away, stretching her nerves like frayed elastic. But at length there was the sound of a car on the driveway and she heard the thud of doors opening and closing, voices down in the hall, dogs barking, Killian running across the flagstones excited and bewildered.

She must go down. Would go, after she brushed her hair, applied some lipstick, perfume . . . The knock on the door was soft and muffled, but when it came she all but ricocheted across the room in fright.

"All right, Eileen! I'm coming!"

The door opened, and in the mirror she saw a figure enter. Not Eileen, but Brian.

He did not speak, standing alone in the shadows with his hands in the pockets of a crumpled linen jacket, his dark fringe falling across his forehead, looking at her with an expression as apprehensive as her own.

"Brian?"

He nodded as though confirming his identity to himself. Every word she had rehearsed evaporated from her mind, leaving her feeling a perfect fool, staring at him as if he were a waxwork dummy. He waited for some response; but getting none, walked as if in slow motion into the room, a much older man than had set out for France eleven years before.

Where had her brother gone? What other person inhabited this empty shell? And where was his wife? Kerry's mouth was dry with shock as the solitary figure approached her, her body rigid as his arms reached out to her. His fingers touched hers, and he drew her into an embrace that was light as chalk, seeming to crumble on contact. Silently, Kerry held the ethereal creature to her, unable to decipher any of the rasping sounds he made.

16

Small shards of sunlight splintered out from between the rolling cotton clouds as Kerry mounted the white stallion that had been Feirah's first gift to her, and waited for her brother to hoist himself into Zephyr's saddle. The mare was old now, more of a wheeze than a breeze as Jerry cruelly put it, and stood placidly while Brian gathered up her reins, caught hold of the saddle and stiffly seated himself. He had not ridden for years, and would be aching by noon to judge from this beginning, but then he was aching anyway.

Kerry watched him with a mixture of pity and impatience, wondering whether this sad, sullen man could really be her twin, the brother she had adored all the days of her childhood. In his brittle beauty she saw no appeal, no remnant of his young, magnetic self; but they would talk as they rode, and maybe find some common ground here on the estate that had once been his home. Leaving him to adjust his girths and stirrups, she kicked Ali Baba into a trot and clattered off across the cobblestones.

Now that he was here, she would strive to be patient with him and understand his despondency, natural in the face of so serious a disagreement with his wife – Lu, the woman who always won. The woman, he said, who had killed his child.

But Kerry could not help thinking how hard Lu had worked for him too, giving her all to build up his career from small, flimsy foundations, pushing and driving him to the top with ferocious determination. Selflessly and unremittingly she had slaved her way to thriving success, and Brian should be prostrate with gratitude, not grief.

What right had he to force motherhood upon her? What law decreed that she must have children? But then again, why had she not consulted Brian, told him of her pregnancy and her plans? Sadly Kerry thought of the son or daughter lost to him, the baby niece or nephew she would never know; Killian's cousin, Maeve and Eamonn's grandchild.

Yet look at Killian! A precarious project, frequently regretted by *his* mother. At best she felt ambiguous about the boy, did not love him as Helen did, saw no hope in his future, or in Ashamber's. Why did he drive her to despair? Why had his father rejected him? Why had her parents never had another child? Was this whole family determined to destroy itself?

If ever Killian got his hands on Ashamber, he would reduce it to a shambles. He had no knowledge of the horses, no interest, no sense of heritage . . . but then, he had no cause to. She could not discourage that in one way and expect it in another. Just as Brian could not expect sympathy, now, from a sister he had consciously alienated, without first attempting to rebuild their frayed relationship.

As she rode out to the edges of the estate he came up at a lumbering canter behind her, weaving between the trees in the dappled intermittent sunlight, a passive cargo on his mare's indifferent back, sagging into the saddle in a way that provoked her. No flexibility, she thought; no agility, no suppleness at all. Summoning sympathy, she turned to him.

"It'll blow over, Brian. Don't let it get you down."

"No, Kerry, it won't blow over. It *is* over."

"Such melodrama! It's a rough patch in an otherwise happy marriage, that's all. Don't tell me your wife has no say in your life or in her own fertility?"

"She's had her say."

She saw that she might as well talk to the Rock of Cashel. "What are you going to do, so?"

"I don't know. Stay at the Crillon, I suppose, until I can find somewhere to live."

She had an idea. Brian was very vulnerable on two counts. "Why not share Zoe's apartment till then? Yves will be there too, while he house-hunts. You heard he's going back to Paris?"

He looked at her sharply, his brown eyes filling with suspicion.

"Why didn't you tell me Yves was staying with you, Kerry? I wouldn't have come if I'd known . . . Am I to understand he's the reason why you invited me? Has Zoe been working on you, is that it? And now she wants you to work on me? If so, you're wasting your time, both of you."

In those few words, Kerry saw her plans and hopes evaporate in the shifting spring sunshine, and saw too that Zoe was right. Even without Lu, there was something unyielding in Brian, some tone that proclaimed him impervious to argument. What prompted her to smile, against all the odds, she never knew. But she did, innocently.

"Work on you? To reinstate Yves, do you mean? Oh, Brian. I should have told you . . . Yves is back in Europe because he's had a row with Keith, and decided to leave Australia. He's had an offer from Emmanuel Ungaro."

He looked so stunned, so stricken, she had to turn her face away.

"Ungaro? But he's our main rival! Yves would never work for him."

"He doesn't want to, obviously. His first choice would have been to go back to TLZ. But since that's out of the question, and he has to eat, he's accepted Ungaro's offer – a very good one, he says."

"The bastard."

"I beg your pardon?"

"I said, he's a bastard. How could he do such a thing to me?"

"But Brian, you made it clear you don't want him! Do be consistent, if you're not going to be reasonable. Ungaro has assured him of a completely free hand, if he brings his clients with him – Princess Shairi has commissioned a maternity wardrobe already."

Now that she had begun to spin the yarn, she found she could not stop, and was gratified to see him swallow the disinformation as if it were hemlock. With naked distaste, he worked out its implications for several silent seconds, and she left him to digest the unpalatable prospect without remorse. He had this medicine coming.

"And he came to tell you, and Zoe, without informing me?"

"Yes. He preferred to speak to Zoe, who's very concerned, naturally. She tried to talk him out of it, but since you have final authority, there wasn't much she could do. He's going to Ungaro and there's an end to it."

He considered his position as though on a chessboard, slowing his mare to a walk alongside her stallion.

"Has he actually signed a contract?"

"Not yet . . . next week, I believe. But he's given his word, closed his salon in Australia and set everything in motion. Actually, I think it was all those trips home that did the damage. He'd have settled down so much better in Sydney if it weren't for having to go back to your shows in Paris every year."

Brian's face went first blank with dismay, then crimson with anger, and in it Kerry clearly saw him wish for Lu, who would know how to handle this so cleverly, so diplomatically. Casually, she pressed her horse on and changed the subject.

"Bob is breeding wolfhounds, did you know? I gave him one of Lir's pups and he's bred a first litter from her. Lots of demand, lots of money to be made. Wish I had time for it myself."

He didn't answer, absorbed in his thoughts, and Kerry glanced at him with something close to contempt, wondering when and whether he would ever take an interest in anyone's affairs bar his own. He hadn't asked a single question about Yves's row with Keith, never enquired about Helen or her marriage, Zoe's visit or her own activities.

Only Killian struck a chord in him, but the boy had shied away, unnerved by the sudden appearance of the uncle he had been told would never materialise. Kerry could, and possibly should, have intervened, but decided not to. Let nature take its course.

They rode on under the lowering sky that was pregnant with scent of imminent rain, the air moist and redolent of early summer, the indefinable tincture of grass and leaf and bramble, fertile and weighted with bud. In the springy earth Kerry could feel life renewing itself, the season turning on its axis, beckoning warmth in the spreading mantle of gentle tentative sunshine. But Ali Baba kept her mind on the here and now, prancing and powerful as he fought for his head, and she had to rein him in tightly for fear that Zephyr, too, might think to bolt.

After considerable time and cogitation, Brian turned to her once more.

"Kerry?"

"Yes?"

"It's – it's difficult for me to say this. But I have to – to apologise. I know I should have been more supportive, when you decided to keep Ashamber. But I did try. I did offer you some money."

"There were other things I needed more than money at that point in my life, Brian."

"Yes. Well. It's just that – the thing is, I wonder, would you speak to Yves, Kerry? Sound him out for me? If he were agreeable, I'd be prepared to negotiate with him."

Her disgust must be palpable, she thought. But for Yves's sake she wrenched her mouth into a smile.

"Outbid Ungaro, do you mean? Has TLZ got that much to offer? I know it's profitable now, but still – could you really compete?"

"Not today, admittedly. But I'm due to inherit Dad's money in December, and meanwhile I can borrow against it."

"I'm not only talking money, Brian. Yves might be happier elsewhere, after everything you've said against him."

He smiled back at her, so charmingly that she was reminded of the youth he had been at eighteen, open, eager, disarming.

"Oh, all creative people have their clashes, Kerry! Yves is a sensational designer. I've never denied that. It's only his lack of discipline that annoys me, lack of commitment. He'd have to sign something if he came back, a legal contract he couldn't duck out of this time."

But Kerry saw in her mind's eye the sketches that Yves, from force of habit, had been doodling all week, and realised that he did in fact possess discipline. He merely channelled it all into his crisp, structured creations, leaving nothing over for himself. Whereas Brian was just the opposite, indulging his emotions in his work, exacting conformity in his personal affairs. Still, a legal contract could benefit Yves, satisfy Brian, and please Zoe.

"All right. I'll try. But what am I to say to him? And even if he did agree to it, what would Lu's opinion be? Would she want him back?"

"Lu's wishes no longer concern me, Kerry. She doesn't manage my salon any more."

"Oh, rubbish. You'll make up this quarrel and she'll be back bright as a button."

"She will not. I never want to see the woman again."

A likely story. Brian simply couldn't function without her. And yet he looked so resolute, as if he had somehow absorbed her own power of pertinacity. What on earth did Zoe see in him? He was so selfish, like a little boy who wouldn't smile till he got his own way, even if the smile were very winning when it came.

For now, she had him where she wanted him. But she was glad for Yves, more than for herself, and felt only cool appraisal where once there might have been rushing relief. She had missed Brian painfully, these many lonely years, but the break had been of his making. If he genuinely wanted to repair it, then she would permit him to try, because he was the only family left to her – as it appeared she was, now, to him. But he would earn his pardon. Pulling Ali Baba to a halt, she turned round in the saddle and stipulated her conditions.

"Brian, I want Yves back with you, and I want you back with me. If you can get him, then you'll get full access to me, to Ashamber and to Killian. I'm very sorry about what Lu did to your child – but Killian is a child too, and much as it grieves me to admit it, he needs you. Furthermore, he is Eamonn's grandson, and I think he has more right to a share in Dad's money than Lu has. She'll fight you for it, I'm sure, but she is not Eamonn's daughter. I am. I don't need anything, personally, but there are certain gestures you might make if you really want to prove your worth."

He did not reply, but merely inclined his head as he listened to her, hearing not his sister but his mother speaking. Poised and calm, it was Maeve who seemed to sit the skittering horse, manipulating the reins, controlling, dictating, detached.

In a lather of urgency, Kerry raced into the house, ascertained Yves's whereabouts and dashed out again. Beyond the gardens and the lake, way out in the woodlands, she spotted him strolling with Nabdul, following the riverbank at a lazy pace, and called out as she ran.

Arrested by the urgency in her voice, the two men pulled up short, and stood waiting enquiringly.

"Nabdul, take a hike."

"What?"

"I'm sorry, but I must speak to Yves right away. Alone."

Miffed, Nabdul retreated, and she grabbed the sleeve of Yves's sweater, dragging him away under a tree whose branches tore at his face, making him splutter in expletive French.

"Now, Yves, listen up. Brian wants you back at TLZ, and so do I. You started that business with him and I want you to go on with it, whatever your differences."

"But Kerry, he gave me my marching orders not a month ago."

"He's seen his mistake. He's very sorry, now that he realises your worth – not just to him, but maybe to someone else. He's going to make a bid before they do, and you're to take it."

She stood panting with exertion, and he laughed at the spectacle she presented, hair flying and face flaming, the freckles seeming to dance on her skin, eyes glittering with determination.

"So. My interfering little friend has told her brother some tissue of lies, and now has to make sure I corroborate them, eh? What did you say to him, Kerry?"

"Nothing. Well – except that I mentioned Ungaro, because Zoe reckons he would – will – be the first to approach you. But Brian begged me to persuade you not to go to him, or anyone, until you hear him out. He's absolutely desperate. Will agree to anything."

"But he must know I'd never enter into direct competition with TLZ!"

"He thinks you're so angry with him that that's exactly what you want to do. I didn't tell him about the – uh – financial situation."

"Oh, Kerry. You shouldn't have done this. I told you I'd manage by myself. What will happen when he finds out?"

"It'll be too late by then. And do him no harm either, to discover we can be just as tough as he can."

"But what about Lu? I never want to work with her again."

"He says she won't be back – though personally I doubt that, and advise you to get a guarantee of absolute freedom from her influence. He's in just the mood to give you one. And think of the clients, Yves, and Zoe! They'll be thrilled. As for me – well, you must know how I hated your being so far away. I don't want you going off to Bill Blass in America, or anywhere else."

Ambivalence clouded his face. On the one hand he would love, so dearly, to reclaim his old place in the company he had founded, and Paris as his home. To work with someone as sweet and steadying as Zoe Zimner would be a joy; but Brian was so difficult, a moody partner, prone to bouts of pique and treachery – which was Brian's own view of *him*.

But such a mercurial combination could be productive, if you used the vibes the right way, it could even be fun. And he needed some such framework: setting up solo would be unbearably lonely, even if he could ever afford it. There would be no group adrenalin, no mutual support – and, if he went to any of the established classic houses, how much freedom would they permit him, how many risks?

"Kerry, you haven't any ulterior motive for this, have you? I'm not your ammunition in some kind of battle with Brian?"

"No. Killian was my ammunition. Brian has lost his own child, but he's getting mine. But this has nothing to do with Laraghy relationships really, Yves. The point is your professional value. Haven't you any estimate of your own worth?"

He hadn't, much, at this minute. But he could see that he must distinguish between his past and his future.

"Kerry, what brought Brian here? Was he upset about Lu, or did you invite him for this express purpose?"

She was tempted to fib again, to save his feelings. But she knew she'd end up totally muddled, unable to recall what had been said to which.

"Yes I asked him, with Zoe's collusion, because we wanted to help you and help TLZ. I thought it would be uphill, but it wasn't. I only had to mention Ungaro and he was frantic."

Not charity, then. A solid, definite offer, based on common sense. Yves felt immense relief, coupled with gratitude. What a very precious friend she was – so special that he wished he could do more than smile tenderly, and hug her to him.

"*Chérie*, I don't know what to say."

"Say yes, and sign a ten-year contract."

"Yes. I'll sign it, I'll work at it and I'll stick to it."

"That's my boy."

Fondly they hugged each other in mutual delight, until Kerry's smile turned into a laugh.

"I'd better go and find Nabdul, before there's an international incident! I'm sure he's sulking dreadfully. You go back to the house, and when Brian comes to you, give him a hard time. Hold out for everything you want and I guarantee you'll get it."

He could not believe that he would. But for once, Yves Tiberti was not going to be a pushover for anyone. Brian had been an ungrateful, disagreeable fool, and he would have to repair the results just as Keith Charles would have to untangle the chaos he had created in Australia. Yves didn't like the idea of toughening up, but since everyone else seemed to have, he had better make a stab at it.

Kerry watched him walk slowly, thoughtfully, back to the house, realising how much she had achieved in this one day. Honourable salvage for Yves, an uncle for Killian, a nephew for Brian and a tentative rapprochement between brother and sister. How pleased Helen would be, and Zoe.

Yet she did not hasten to tell them, standing instead under the tree, pulling forlornly at its bark until she thought of Nabdul, and went to find him.

Disconsolate and reportedly aggrieved, Nabdul had collected some fishing gear and returned to the river, taking a sandwich lunch with him. He would not, Eileen said, be back for the remainder of the day. In the blue drawing room, Helen was on the phone interrogating some hapless interior decorator, while Killian had taken Shairi over to see Bob's pups, and in the library Brian was already haggling over a fresh agreement with Yves. Kerry was left with no choice but to return to work, although for once her mind was not on it.

It ran instead back over her encounter with Brian, and the question of Eamonn's legacy. Kerry did not need or even want any part of it, but neither did she want it to leave the family, or the country. Brian had neither agreed nor refused her suggestion to that effect, but she hoped it would make him think, put a value on someone other than himself or his wife. Now that he was here, and so distressed, she couldn't find it in herself to keep up a show of animosity; she knew all too well what a painful thing was marital conflict, and even felt some shred of sympathy for Lu. Was she experiencing, at this moment, the same anguish that had accompanied her own break with Darragh, the same loss that Brandon's change of plan had carried with it? Nobody deserved that kind of pain – even if it was self-inflicted, Lu had been a very good wife to Brian, loyal and far more supportive than ever her sister-in-law had been to Darragh de Bruin.

The abortion was very unfortunate, something Kerry had not been able to do herself when faced with the same option. But she opposed it on humanitarian grounds, not moral; over the years Cara had told her many sad stories, of local girls trapped in anguish no matter what choice they made. Now, Lu would have another difficult choice, either to fight Brian in court for half of his legacy, or sacrifice it in an effort to heal the rift. Kerry had no doubt that Lu could be vindictive, devious as the day was long, but for both their sakes she hoped reason might prevail. Brian, as she knew to her cost, could be a very determined enemy.

As for Yves – another tricky time ahead. Any moment now the scandal would break and he would have to return to Australia, disown Keith, tackle a financial nightmare and salvage whatever tatters remained. The press would say he had fled, if only for a week, but Kerry much preferred the

French expression, *"se sauver"* – literally, to save oneself. Yves badly needed a breathing space, tense and gaunt as he was, stripped beneath the buoyant surface. Since coming to Ashamber he had clung to her friendship as if it were a log in a heaving ocean, reaching out to Helen too, and even Killian of whom he was inexplicably fond and protective. For the thousandth time she wondered where his own family was, or what had happened to it. But never once had he budged on the subject, and probably now he never would.

Meanwhile, Nabdul was about to start his family with Shairi, a wife far more suited to him than ever she would have been herself. How wise Feirah had been to indulge their romance, all those years ago, instead of forbidding it and thereby spurring it on – even if Kerry did wonder how on earth Shairi coped with Nabdul's earthy, energetic sexuality.

None of her business. Reverting her attention to the horses, she lectured a groom who had had the stupidity to get bitten, marched him off for a tetanus shot and prayed he wouldn't make some wildly exaggerated claim on her insurance. But all in all the staff were efficient, careful and considerate, dominated by Jerry and Cara, who at twenty-four was newly engaged to Frank. Visibly happy in her work, Cara was a marvel, worth every penny of her substantial salary, and through her friendly rivalry with Neville McCormack Kerry learned much about what was happening in the village, over on Cushla and in other yards too.

Was it true what Neville had confided to Cara, about Cushla's owner wanting to sell? It would be the ideal property for Nabdul, if it were.

She had never had any contact with the man, an elderly old gentleman called Murray Raymond, and Cushla was not on the list of available estates the local agent had given her. But maybe it would do no harm to take a look . . . Neville would let them in, and with any luck Mr Raymond would be away on business as he so often was. She could have a good snoop.

Where was Nabdul? Gone fishing, Eileen had said. She would go and get him, bring him there now while she thought of it. It was beginning to rain, and she threw on an old trenchcoat before setting off to find him. It took about twenty minutes, but eventually she saw him, standing knee-deep in the river in his waders, shrouded in oilskins he had had the foresight to take with him.

"Hi."

"Hi."

He didn't turn round, brooding she supposed over having been so summarily dismissed.

"Sorry I interrupted your walk. Thought you might like to take another one now."

"Where to?"

"A training yard near here. Smallish, only two hundred acres or so. Could have the makings of a nice little stud farm."

"Oh. OK."

He reeled in his line and she waited while he stored his equipment away in the boathouse, an eerie cobwebbed edifice in which she and Brian had loved to terrify themselves as children. Mollified by her interest in his potential acquisition, he thawed, and they chatted companionably as they embarked on the mile-long walk over to Cushla. By road, it was further, but across the fields it was less than half an hour away, and Nabdul rather wished he'd brought his camera to photograph the place. Feirah would want to see it before any purchase was authorised.

Just as the dividing line between Ashamber and Cushla came within sight, they cut through a small thick copse, and Kerry swore as she stumbled over a protruding rock. But, looking down, she saw that it wasn't a rock at all. It was the headstone of a long-forgotten grave, overgrown and neglected, and as soon as she saw it she remembered it. Several times, Eamonn had taken her here to see this grave, wherein lay the body of Timothy Laraghy, his – his what? She wasn't sure. Great-grandfather, or great-great-grandfather? Interested, she knelt down and brushed away the wet grass and lichen until she could see the date; but time had eroded the inscription. 1838? 1858? 1853? Peer and squint as she might, there was no way to be sure.

"I must look it up in the records."

"What records?"

"Logs, diaries, various notebooks Helen found up in the attic in 1973. Ashamber has had six owners and they all kept these records, you should see them, in the most beautiful copperplate handwriting, up to 1945 when my father inherited. Helen put all the information on disc, but kept the books for historical interest. The other five owners, including Daddy, are buried down in the churchyard, but trust the Laraghys to be one short of the full deck! I don't know how Timothy came to be buried here instead."

Maeve's family, she thought, would never have been so remiss. They'd have had their six neat little stones all in a row, shiny and polished, perfectly legible . . . seven, some day, after her own death. Would she too lie gone and forgotten like Timothy, just a worn inscription on a crumbling chunk of granite? Every few days, she either put flowers on her parents' grave or sent somebody to do so, but somehow she couldn't imagine Killian doing that, for her. He would sell Ashamber, or let it fall into decay, and her memory with it.

But she had brought that fate upon herself. She straightened up and shook off her useless melancholy.

"I don't know what's wrong with me lately, Nabdul. I seem to have developed the most macabre sense of mortality. I used to worry more about the present than the future, but now it's the other way round."

"Perfectly normal. You've got a sense of perspective now, you can see that Ashamber is more than just a business, it's the work of generations and deserves to be nurtured from one to the next. I'd be concerned too, if Killian were my son. He's not a Laraghy, Kerry, is he?"

"Not the least little bit. I'm afraid he's his father. Trouble."

"Why don't you send him to Kutari for the summer? Shairi and I could take him falconing, camel racing, swimming . . . I know it's your busiest time of year."

"Would you really? He'd love to go, I can assure you, and frankly I would be glad to have him off my hands for a few weeks."

"Then we'll take him. It'll be a pleasure. I'll knock some sense into him for you."

"You have my full permission to try! And maybe I could send him to Brian for a bit too, assuming Brian is housed by then, or back with Lu."

"Yes. He needs some male influence. Attention, too, and a bit of fun."

They continued on to Cushla, talked to Neville and were permitted to take a quick look round. Nabdul was impressed: he didn't want to start with anything too big, and this looked ideal. He asked Neville to make an appointment on his behalf with Mr Raymond, but even as Neville jotted down possible dates there was the sound of a car returning, and he dropped the pen with alacrity.

"Look, don't say you've seen the place or he'll kill me. Just tell him you're interested and came over to arrange a meeting."

They nodded, and waited rather guiltily for Murray Raymond to come into the reception room where they stood in their muddy boots. The old man was nearing eighty, and walked with a stick, shuffling and grumbling as he entered. Years of heavy drinking had made his face florid, and his hair was snow-white, his hands knotted and arthritic. But the watery blue eyes flew open as if sighting burglars.

"What do you want?"

"Mr Raymond, it's me, Kerry Laraghy. This is my friend, his High—"

"I know damn well who you are, missy. What are you doing on my property?"

"We just came to talk to you. We heard that you might be interested in selling Cushla. If you are, my friend here would like to make you an offer. I'm sure you know that I train for him, and now he wants to breed . . ."

Raymond inspected Nabdul slowly, from head to foot, as if he were some unusually large and repulsive insect. Belligerence gathered on his countenance as suddenly as a summer storm, and when he spoke his bellow belied his apparent frailty.

"An Arab! I'd sooner sell to a band of marauding pirates! And as for any friend of yours, Miss Laraghy – get out of my house this minute, the pair of you. Cushla's not for sale, not to anyone at any price, and most definitely not to either of you."

Astonished, Kerry stared at him speechless. Even if they had invited themselves, how could he thus receive a guest in his home, and a guest in his country? Glancing at Nabdul, she saw him pale, recoil as if the man had actually raised his stick.

"Mr Raymond, I'm very sorry we didn't telephone first. But if you don't wish to discuss the matter, you have only to say so. Why are you insulting my friend like this? And what have I ever done to you?"

"Out! Neville, show them the door."

Hastily, Neville did as he was bidden, muttering apologies under his breath, and all but pushed them out into the driveway as he shut the door behind them. Nabdul stood there irresolute, trying to fathom what had happened until Kerry yanked him away by the wrist and marched off, livid, in the direction whence they had come.

"The goddamn old goat! Who the hell does he think he is?"

Nabdul considered the episode in silence as they strode along, forced to accept what he had never wanted to acknowledge. His money was very welcome here, but he was not. Never had it been so overtly stated before, but under the ostensible friendliness lay permanent reserve, resistance to him and all he represented. Not outright hostility, until now, but a guarded distance that told him he would always be an outsider, peripheral, allowed only into the edges of this society.

It was a pity. In the course of his many visits he had come to know the country well, thought the scenery marvellous, become quite addicted to racing. If he could buy a stud, he would spend his summers here, away from Kutari's infernal heat . . . but if not, he would simply buy one in Britain instead, or perhaps America. He said as much to Kerry, and she pulled up short.

"No, Nabdul. That's a defeatist attitude and you mustn't take it. Some day, when you succeed your father, there will be people who will resent you then too. You must rise above them or you will never be respected. Look on Murray Raymond as a practice run."

He hadn't thought of it like that, and was very appreciative of her insight. He had no desire to succeed his father, but since it was his inevitable destiny, he would make a good job of it. Embracing her as they walked along, he peered enquiringly into her face.

"Do people resent you too, Kerry?"

"Some. Murray Raymond does, because Ashamber is doing so much better than the yards his friends own, and I'm only a woman. Others say I'm a bad mother because I'm not at home with my child all day, and then there are those who say I go after business in an unladylike way. I hear all the gossip. But I ignore it, just as we are now going to ignore Raymond's insults, and find you a farm whether he likes it or not."

"It must be hard for you, all on your own here."

"I'm well able for it. I have my friends. And you're one of them."

The rain was getting heavier, and they huddled inside their raincoats, pushing on through the long wet grass into the foggy gloom, making for the boathouse. On all sides the flat damp land stretched away to the dark demarcating hedges, murky in the low cloud, the silence unbroken by any sound other than their trudging footsteps.

The veil of rain became a sheet, then a thudding canopy, and they hastened into the musty wooden building, grateful for its shelter as they picked the wet tendrils of hair out of their eyes and off their faces.

"Drink?"

"Oh, great."

He produced a silver hip flask and she slugged back a mouthful of whiskey, feeling its peppery warmth snake down into her stomach as she peeled off her trenchcoat and cowled her sweater round her neck and chin. She was sodden, but Nabdul was relatively drier, protected by the green oilskins that flapped like batwings around him. In the obscurity she could hardly make out his features, only the gleam of his teeth and eyes, the dark edge of his beard.

"I see your day hasn't been entirely wasted."

On the floor, two salmon lay neatly gaffed, and he smiled.

"I find fishing so relaxing. There are so many good things about this country, Kerry."

"Yeah. Nice place, shame about the people."

"They'll get used to me some day, I hope. I'm not prepared to accept their insults, but I am prepared to earn their acceptance, if only they'll meet me halfway."

She shivered, gazing down at the puddles forming on the floor from their dripping clothing, augmented by a hole in the roof.

"I'm bloody frozen, Nabdul, and starving too. Where are your sandwiches?"

"Ate the lot. Sorry. Here."

He passed her the whiskey again and she gulped another mouthful.

"Are you looking forward to being a father?"

"Yes. It's my duty, of course, but I think I may enjoy it just the same. Shairi is taking it seriously enough for both of us."

"How so?"

He didn't answer, busying himself with removing his oil-skin and turning it inside out, spreading it on the floor so that there was somewhere dry to sit. Simultaneously they sank down on it, and he put his arm round her shoulder.

"Warm enough?"

"Relatively."

His touch warmed her as he spoke, and fleetingly she wished it could be more. If only he still wanted her! Cared a little, just enough to take the chill away, some tiny particle of the eternal solitude.

He held her hand and began to chafe it, then the other, and she leaned into him gratefully, pushing a slick of wet hair back off his forehead, smelling the wet wool of his sweater, smiling sadly as she thought of the time when he would have kissed her.

And then he was kissing her, eliciting no protest as he stretched her gently down on the floorboards. His hands slid under her back, tentatively, anticipating a rebuff that did not come.

"Say no, Kerry. Tell me not to." His voice was hoarse, but she shook her head, tightening her arms around him, pulling him closer until the old flame was ignited, their bodies torching as they tore their clothes off, feeling only intense heat where cold should be. He was kissing her so hard it hurt. She could not get enough of it, of him.

"Oh, my Kerry, it's been so long – tell me where – there? Here? Here?"

At first he couldn't remember all the old places, where she liked best to be stroked and caressed, but in minutes it all came back, and she was undulating under him, biting her lip and his own, gripping him like a fury.

"Now, Nabdul. Now. Don't make me wait. I want you *now*."

For once, he couldn't wait himself. He entered her straight away and she was filled with the greatest pleasure, the greatest relief she had known in months, in years. Oh, that was better! Wonderful! Together they found a rhythm and rose into it, torrents of frustration releasing into cascades of intense fulfilment. He knew he couldn't keep up such a pace for very long, but he didn't have to; she came just as he did himself, her face clenched, her lower legs coiled around his back, gasping violently.

The pools of rainwater swelled and spread as they were augmented by the sweat pouring off the two writhing, conjoined bodies. Untold time elapsed before first one and then the other ceased to move, lying exhausted as the flame banked down to glowing embers, leaping bright and alive in the rainwashed April dusk.

Later, Kerry supposed she should be sorry. But she wasn't. Far from it. She snuggled into Nabdul and let him continue to caress her soothingly, murmur into her ear until cold overtook them both and they began to shudder. He got up and brought her coat to her, laughing as she huddled into its folds like a distracted Indian.

"It wasn't bad, Nabdul, was it? Not really?"

"Bad? Kerry, it was wonderful! You can't imagine how much I've missed you . . . Don't misunderstand, I do love Shairi, of course I do. It's just that she can be a little – a little shy, in bed, and now that she's pregnant she feels it's better not to – not to hurt the baby, in the early stages."

"I should feel guilty about her. So should you. We're pagan savages, both of us. But somehow I just can't. Is that terribly immoral?"

"Amoral, maybe. Shairi is my responsibility, not yours, and I promise you she won't be hurt. I may be wicked, but I'm not evil."

Evil? She could imagine few things less evil, more glorious than what they had done, finding only comfort, intense physical pleasure and immense spiritual balm in it. Through chattering teeth, she told him so, and he pressed the flask once more to her lips.

"Medicinal."

So it was. As the slow fire sank down inside her Kerry felt everything else melt magically away. She would not do this again, but neither would she ever regret it. Guilt was such a useless, destructive emotion! It ate into a person until they were devoured, destroyed by it, and all to no avail. It was a waste of time. She hugged Nabdul like a child, and he responded in kind, their joint form a bizarre silhouette in the lonely boathouse, their bodies sated and at peace.

One look at Kerry's face, as she came damp, dripping and radiant into the house with Nabdul, told Yves what had happened. He caught her eye, and she returned his gaze with just the slightest hint of defiance, an almost imperceptible lift of her chin. She knew that he knew; they were so attuned no words were necessary.

So what? Let him think what he liked. His own track record, in the early days before he met Keith, hadn't been exactly virginal. She wouldn't apologise to him or to anyone, even if she would not let the event occur again; she had needed Nabdul, for all sorts of reasons.

Yves knew what those reasons were, and disapproved of some more than others. But the episode crystallised something in his mind, and although he was as sociable and extrovert as usual over dinner, he kept one eye closely on her, thinking, until such time as he reached a decision. Before leaving, he must speak with Helen.

Brian remained quiet, and somewhat wary of Yves after a hard day's bargaining. His former partner was looking for rather higher terms and wider scope than he had expected, with Kerry's encouragement he suspected, and he was uncertain of his ground.

Kerry was in a good frame of mind tonight, he saw, animated and relaxed, very attractive in a dark green blouse and trousers that showed off her long slim legs. From time to time, he had seen photographs of her in French newspapers, attending races or related events, and often she wore designs by TLZ. But only in the daytime, when the suit or coat had been designed by Yves; not once, at a party or soirée, had he ever known her to wear one of his own ensembles. It might be politic, when he got back to Paris, to have Estelle assemble and send her a new range of evening wear. Attentively he listened to her conversation, making a point of demonstrating his goodwill, and was pleased to find himself enjoying the evening, even forgetting Lu as the old atmosphere of home overtook him. Killian, allowed to eat with the adults by special dispensation, was a source of great information, and although he spilt things and broke a glass, Brian warmed to the child as he poured out all the village gossip, all the little details of school and family life.

Nabdul was on his best behaviour, solicitous of Shairi, glossing over his insult at the hands of Murray Raymond although Kerry remained indignant to the point of outrage. Bob offered to send Raymond a wolfhound as a gift, if that would help his disposition, but she turned the suggestion down point blank.

"Not unless you have one with six-inch fangs, Bob."

Helen smiled, and advocated patience, wishing Kerry wouldn't always take the hard line. She made life so difficult for herself, jousting instead of compromising, duelling over every little thing. But that was Kerry, and at least there had been some evidence of diplomacy earlier today. Tactfully changing the subject, Helen announced her discovery of a designer, at last, whom she deemed capable of refurbishing the house. But impatiently Kerry waved his name away, having heard from Cara of somebody much more "interesting".

"Andrew Austin? But Kerry, he's – he's far too radical! I've seen his work in magazines, it's practically subversive! He raids old churches for wood, he uses so much glass, he'd wreck the house!"

"Not at all. I'm going to invite him down here so you can discuss it with him, Helen. I'm sure once you hear his ideas you'll see how exciting they are."

Helen, proprietorially, didn't want "excitement". She wanted Eamonn's house restored with dignity and beauty, no more. But Kerry rabbited on, backed up by Yves and politically encouraged by Brian. Outnumbered, Helen decided to keep her powder dry; Yves and Brian would soon be gone. They didn't have to live or work here.

Next day, Yves came into Helen's drawing room, shut the door and sat down in a way that put Helen on her guard.

"If it's about this decorator, Yves . . ."

"No. You can have the pleasure of that argument all to yourself. I want to talk to you about Kerry, Helen."

She took off her glasses and listened intently, not interrupting once until he had finished. Not only was Yves one of her favourite people, he knew Kerry inside out, and it did not come as any surprise to find his forthright views coinciding with her own. After he had outlined his interpretation of the situation, tactfully but emphatically, she asked Eileen to bring them some coffee and entered into a long, thoughtful appraisal of his unorthodox strategy.

From her office, Lu had a wonderful view. She never allowed it to distract her, but visitors were always impressed as they looked down on the bustling street scene from one window, and out over Paris from the other. In the distance stood the hill of Montmartre, with Sacré Coeur shining white on top of it even on the dullest day, even in the bluest of those hazes which so often enveloped the city. En route to the Basilica, the eye encountered much other beautiful architecture, the Gare St Lazare with its *fin-de-siècle* dome and eccentric clock sculpture, the churches of Trinité Est d'Orves and St Augustin, Notre Dame de Lorette and, nearer, the Madeleine and the Place Vendôme with its gilded column. People would exclaim as they entered the room, looking out over Lu's head and forgetting whatever business they were there on, but Lu didn't object to that. It gave her a chance to size them up, get a fix on them before they got one on her.

Their compliments were as effusive as if she had personally created this fine view, fine building, fine day. She had that effect on all of them, sitting there with her svelte figure and sleek suits, her cropped clustering curls and light golden skin, the very incarnation of *jeunesse dorée*. But today, there was nobody to compliment her or admire anything, and she sat at her desk unoccupied, alone.

It was a Sunday, with no staff about, nobody to help her file her paperwork neatly away, pack personal possessions into a series of boxes and cartons. In the morning, the room would be quite simply empty, and when he came back Brian could explain why. Lu didn't want any goodbyes, any attempt at awkward excuses. A clean break was the best thing.

Her packing done, she thought of leaving Brian a note, but decided against it. Now that her parents were coming round, getting over the shock and remembering that she was, after all, their only daughter, she would persuade them to intercede for her instead. They adored Brian, and would probably achieve much more than she could herself. He would listen to them, and come to realise the futility of trying to do without her.

Oh, if only he would! He *must*. That she should really lose him now, just when everything was otherwise so perfect, was unthinkable. He was a major name now, created and honed by her own hand, an asset in every way just as she was to him. And he was about to inherit all that money . . . *Dieu*, how could he be so short-sighted, so intransigent? Just like his father, who'd never budged on the question of their marriage, never even accepted Kerry's, never given an inch on anything.

It would be a long, uphill battle, and she did not relish the prospect of it. But she would win it. Looking back over the years of their marriage, she could remember very few disagreements with Brian, certainly nothing that had given her reason to suspect the steel inside that soft exterior, and the discovery was a revelation. But now that she knew what she was dealing with, she would do some lateral thinking, and bear in mind that time was on her side. Time would demonstrate his stupidity, bring him to see beyond that baby.

At the moment, he saw it in an emotional light, saw probably an actual person, some seductive little boy or girl lisping up at him. But it wasn't. It was just a blob of jelly, at seven weeks, it hadn't been fully formed, it had no awareness of itself whatsoever. Several of her girlfriends had had discreet abortions, and all confirmed the insignificance of the event; you got on with your life and soon forgot all about it.

Eyeing the phone, she toyed with the idea of calling one or two of them. It might help to talk to Inès or Véronique . . . they would, for a start, take her out to lunch and cheer her up, extend invitations to amusing dinner parties or *vernissages*. But how odd it would feel to attend those things, without Brian on her arm! Without anyone.

Would he actually allow that, make public their disagreement? Surely not. Their social life was well established, their circle was tight and secure; he couldn't throw that away too. Somehow there must be a way to keep him by her side, socially at least. He was her husband, he had a duty to her, there would never be any proclamation of a rift that would only embarrass them when it was mended.

Where was he planning to live, in the meantime? Who would look after him? With sudden horror the thought struck Lu that Paris was full of very lovely women, women who would see in him all the qualities and attributes she did herself. No. She would never permit any of them to get near him, any more than she would allow anyone to steal her jewellery, any of the assets she had acquired over the years. He wore a wedding ring, a ring that meant much more than any fit of pique – a ring that should be damn well welded into his finger.

He's my husband, she thought fiercely, and that's all there is to it. *Mine.*

17

Mme Lucienne Laraghy was not the only one who had recently attended a gynaecologist. Zoe Zimner had also consulted one, and come away in an even greater state of turmoil.

Avidly following every new development in medical science, Zoe had convinced herself that there must, after all this time, be something that could be done for her, some magic recipe which would restore her fertility.

But there wasn't. Dr Prévost was apologetic as he spread his hands helplessly, soothing as he spelled out the alternatives in his large, deceptively old-fashioned rooms on the rue Duvivier.

"Surrogate parenthood, madame. Should your partner be willing, and a suitable host mother available . . ."

But, according to herself, Mme Zimner did not even have a partner. The dear lady was trying to put the cart before the horse. And, as long as she hid away behind this defensive barrier of excess weight, her chances of finding a partner remained remote. The whole project was an exercise in futility.

She paled as he pronounced his prognosis, and for a moment he thought she was going to faint. Women so often did, here in this coffee-and-ivory room of studied tranquility, and he was a little weary of opening windows, running glasses of water, patting clammy hands paternally. But she didn't. She recovered herself, stood up and thanked him, shaking hands in the French manner as she bade him goodbye. On the way out, she stopped to write a cheque for his receptionist − a large one, but Dr Prévost felt no guilt. His two daughters had been known to purchase swimwear and tennis dresses bearing the TLZ label on occasion, and he merely thought it a crazy world that paid as much for such fripperies as for expertise like his. Sadly he wished her au revoir, and sadly she made her way out, with the desolate look of a little girl forbidden to go on the school picnic.

Down on the street, Zoe felt marginally revived as the fresh air fanned her prickling skin, and walked slowly away from the oppressive seventh arrondissement into the looser, livelier sixth, looking for a café in which to compose herself. On the rue de Grenelle, she selected a corner bistro, ordered a *café crème* and resolutely braced herself against the glass-domed pastry trolley with its viscous array of temptation. With enormous difficulty she had lost four kilos since returning from Ireland; one lapse just wasn't worth it – not now, with Brian looking at her the way he increasingly did, his brown eyes so accusing, so critically disapproving.

He never said anything any more, but in her mind's eye she could hear his soft voice, trace every line of his face, see that dreamy remote look of his, sharpening whenever it fell on her. Even if she could never have him, she could have her self-respect back. Kerry was right: she would feel much better if she lost ten kilos, infinitely better if she lost twenty. Not if. When.

The waiter brought her coffee and she stared absently into it, wondering how Kerry was getting on with Brian. Eight years lost, between brother and sister . . . it was criminal, and so unfair to Killian. Brian should have stepped in at the start, taken Darragh's place as a father before demanding a child of his own. How ironic, that Lu should refuse him one! Refuse everything she would so love to have herself, alienating the husband in whom she was so lucky, taking for granted everything that she, Zoe, knew to be so rare and precious.

But of course she would keep going, fill all the barren days somehow, get through to a brighter, better future. There must be one, out there somewhere. Perhaps Yves would come back to Paris, for a start; that was worth looking forward to. She wouldn't let Dr Prévost's prognosis get her down. It was a nice spring day. What about walking home, doing a little window-shopping in the Marais?

The district was being done up lately, old houses renovated, plaques appearing on the buildings in which famous people had lived, writers, composers, scientists, heroes of the Resistance. Always an atmospheric place to live, now it was interesting as well, and Zoe loved to wander in it, often stopping for a chat with Mme Cadanet who liked to practise her English, or M Pauvert who sold smoked gefilte fish in his dark, wonderfully aromatic old delicatessen. But one particular development disturbed her.

On the wall of the Jewish school, a list had been mounted of fifteen children's names. Fifteen children who had been taken out and shot, or away to concentration camps, during the war. As a human being, as a woman and as a half-Jew, Zoe never failed to feel a frisson of terror, a surge of nauseous horror, whenever she passed by. To do such things, to innocent children! It didn't bear thinking about. But she did think about it, and although she made regular donations to UNICEF as a tiny gesture of reparation to children everywhere, she could not dispel the lingering sorrow the plaque had brought with it. Having no children of her own, all she could do was try to help other people's, caught up in today's wars around the world.

And it was certain, finally, that she would never have her own. As clearly as if she had been amongst them, Zoe knew the caged despair of those fifteen infants as they were dragged out to their deaths.

Brian was relieved. After a weekend of walking on eggshells, firm terrain had miraculously materialised under his feet. Yves was not going to Ungaro; he was going back to TLZ. A fresh contract, and a fresh start – with him, and therefore with Kerry. The visit had been painful, but productive, and Brian hugged Killian rather euphorically as he prepared to depart.

"I showed your mother all over Paris, Killian, when she and I were young. Now I want to show it to you, too. Promise you'll visit me soon?"

Dubiously, Killian nodded. He hadn't quite digested Uncle Brian.

"And Kerry – you'll come as well?"

His tone was anxious. But his sister's was casual.

"Sure. Whenever I get the time."

"Oh, you can afford it now, Kerry. You've got this place well under control. Dad would be delighted with you."

She lit up. Nothing else he might have said meant as much to her as that. Not that he was to know it.

"Where's Yves? Aren't you going to say goodbye to him, Brian?"

"No need. He's driving me to the airport before his meeting."

"What meeting?"

"I don't know exactly, just some guy he's seeing somewhere. I don't know why he won't just come back to Paris with me now, but he won't."

Because, Kerry thought grimly, he's going to have to go back to Australia first and sort out that bloody awful mess that you don't even know about. But where's he going today?

He was outside in her old Mercedes, waiting for Brian, looking remarkably purposeful. She pinned him with similar purpose.

"I suppose Helen gave you the keys, so you could go off to meet your new Romeo? It is a lover, I presume?"

He waved a vague hand. "Could be, *ma belle.*"

"Yves! You tramp! You silly, stupid—"

"Kerry, I will be back tonight. It's nothing. In the meantime, may I suggest you make a little experiment?"

"Such as?"

"Such as shutting up."

The car was halfway down the avenue before she found her voice, and called after it.

"Brian! Don't let him do anything rash! Don't let him . . . !"

Brian didn't catch the last of her sentence, but found himself laughing as he left Ashamber. So rashness was still to be her exclusive monopoly, was it? In many ways, his sister had changed a great deal. But under the skin, she hadn't changed one whit.

Highly insulted, Kerry stalked back indoors, thought for a moment, and then dashed to the phone.

"Zoe? Zoe, I've done it! I fooled Brian into thinking Yves was going to work for Ungaro and he nearly died. Offered a new contract, all sorts of promises and incentives. Yves pretended to decline for the whole weekend till he was sure, and then accepted. Everything went beautifully."

"Kerry, that's great. Absolutely marvellous. But the strangest thing has happened here. Lu's office is empty. All her stuff is gone and the staff don't know anything about it. Did she say anything to you?"

"She wasn't here, Zoe. She and Brian have had a massive row. He left her in Fréjus."

"Really? What happened?"

"Well, don't tell him I told you, but she's had an abortion. He's furious. Says she's an evil bitch and never wants to set eyes on her again."

"She what? Oh, Kerry . . . how could she? Oh, surely not?"

"Yes. I gather he was putting her under ferocious pressure to have a baby, but she simply didn't want one. Didn't even tell him she was pregnant. He blew about fifty fuses, and sacked her amongst other things. That's why her stuff is gone."

"Sacked his *wife*? But Kerry, she's our manager. He had no right to do that without consulting me."

"He's done it. The whole thing is bitter as a barrel of limes. Anyway, you've got your daywear designer back, but if I know Lu, she'll be back too."

Outraged, Zoe hung up, leaving Kerry to see belatedly the advantage her friend had gained, if she chose to use it. But Zoe wasn't capable of such cold exploitation, she was sure, even if Brian were not impervious to her femininity. To him, she was a colleague, no more. Besides, Lu would make any woman pay for looking twice at her husband.

Kerry wished she could help Zoe. But perhaps it was enough, for now, that she had helped everyone else, even Brian who would round on them both when he discovered Yves's plight in Australia, and the deception which had led to his reinstatement. Even Nabdul had benefited, not getting his stud farm admittedly, but something he savoured even more.

Shairi, Kerry foresaw, would have a lifetime of infidelity to contend with in Nabdul. But henceforth she would have no hand in that infidelity. One lapse was forgivable, but two would be collusion, and greedy.

With many of the staff away on Easter holiday, it was quiet in the stableyard, and Kerry snapped on the radio normally used to keep track of racing results. The midday news was in progress, and she listened with cursory interest until a familiar name arrested her.

Dermot Lawrence was dead. Kerry had never met the man, but the whole country knew who he was. A difficult, irascible character, he had succumbed to the stroke which, she assumed, was the end product of his choleric temperament. But where did his death leave his son?

In a position of great power, the radio said. But for the first time in many years, Kerry thought of Brandon without automatically checking herself, without the exhaustion or low spirits which could sometimes conjure up his memory unbidden. How would he cope, with the loss of the iron-willed figure who had so extensively influenced the course of his life? For one insane moment, she thought of sending him a message of sympathy, but rejected the idea even more swiftly. They were strangers now, linked only by the horses whose interests were handled by an intermediary. He had never again come to see them, never discussed their progress or made any personal contact. But reluctantly she continued to visualise him, at Hollyvaun on its many-hued mountain moors, mauve and grey amidst the heather, dotted with yellow sheep, sentried by that cold indigo lake.

A parent dead, an era ended.

The house had its own small chapel and graveyard in which, the report went on, Dermot would be buried. Only forty miles away, but Brandon might as well be forty thousand. Once she had almost hated him, consumed by anger and by grief, but now she pitied him . . . longed, if she were honest, to see him, to look into those blue eyes that must be so bleak, today. She knew what it was to lose a father.

What a godsend Brandon had been, when Eamonn died! Might have been to this day were it not for Marianne. Lucky, clever Marianne, whose timing had been so very accurate.

Had her pregnancy been deliberate? Almost certainly; but Kerry no longer blamed her if it was. Desperate situations demanded desperate remedies. Was she happy now, with Brandon, and he with her? Did his sober face still become boyish, by turns? And what of the boys? Chris and Harry. Funny how she could still remember their names. The elder one had been wayward, contrary like his grandfather, the younger one quiet and devoted to his mother. And then there had been the baby, whose birth had cost them both so much. Was she a joy to him, a comfort after all? Julie Susannah. Kerry had seen the announcement in *The Times*, and estimated the little girl to be about seven by now. A terrible sacrifice, for her, but surely a worthwhile one, for Brandon at least. Fatherhood had always been such a serious thing to him, and because she loved him, she had let him go.

Now he had another loss to bear. But his pain was no longer hers. She must not let herself think about it, let it infiltrate the defences that had become so solid. It was not her concern.

With an effort she diverted her mind back to Nabdul, who valiantly insisted on seeing two more stud farms before departing. After a quick lunch she took him to inspect them, and was careful to invite Shairi also. But neither establishment was deemed suitable, and in the early evening the couple flew empty-handed back to London. An hour later, Yves returned to Ashamber, looking harassed.

"How was your little tryst?"

"It was interrupted. But not before I got what I wanted."

"Dare I ask what you did want?"

He wouldn't tell her, and she was amazed by his unprecedented ability to keep a secret. But after they had eaten, he began to pack, and her indignation turned to dismay.

"Must you go, so soon? Don't you want to see this man again?"

"No, *chérie*. I've had my pause for thought and now I must face facts in Australia, clear up everything before I rejoin TLZ."

She knew he was right. But next day, she found it very hard to say goodbye to him, and he clung to her equally disconsolate, reluctant to leave the sanctuary of her friendship and her home.

"I hate it when we're apart, Kerry. You know I'm always with you in spirit, don't you? Sometimes I even think – I wish—"

He could not finish his sentence, but knew she understood, and touched his lips to hers.

All the rest of that day she felt the kiss soft and sweet on her mouth, and some strength in it as she forced herself to concentrate on other matters, other people. Brian, who needed her help even if he did not deserve it: the anguish of a broken marriage was something she understood and could maybe assuage. Killian, who had exploded with joy on hearing that he was to spend the summer in Kutari, blissfully unaware that he was being farmed out: Helen would go mad when that news reached her ears. Nabdul, who must be kept happy and at arm's length, all at once: and Brandon, so near tonight at Hollyvaun, so far away.

Brandon! The others occupied her mind, but from nowhere she felt him creeping up on her, threatening to invade her soul. With a skill honed over the years, she took it away to where he could not reach it.

As the season rose from spring to high summer, Kerry found her mood rising with it. The chill dark days gave way to light and warmth, lifting her loneliness, putting a new colour on things. Suddenly solitude looked more like independence, and she was conscious of everything it had permitted her to achieve. Never again would she know the soaring optimism of youth, she thought, but instead she knew her own self. There was no longer any question that she could survive; she had survived. She would enter her thirties healthy and solvent and free, unburdened by any of the various problems that beset her friends and her brother, and the achievement was satisfying to her.

Andrew Austin arrived with his workmen, turning Ashamber into chaos and Helen into a termagant, but Kerry enjoyed the novelty of eating al fresco as the dining room was demolished, camping in a different bedroom while her own was done over.

Austin's innovations were radical, as Helen had darkly predicted, but she gave him his head, laughing as she speculated what her mother would have made of his handiwork. Much of Maeve's furniture was given away and Kerry's stamp put in its place, whereupon Helen pointedly went off on holiday with Bob. But not before she had issued exact instructions for the refurbishment of her own blue drawing room, and beaten Andrew Austin down to three-quarters of his quoted price.

Delirious with anticipation, Killian departed for the deserts of Kutari, where Nabdul's promised agenda sounded exciting in the extreme. But in France, Brian remained homeless, ensconced at the Crillon, endeavouring without much success to cope with the loss of his wife and unborn infant. Without Lu the salon was a rudderless ship, but he stuck to his guns, and finally engaged a new manager. A lawyer was also hired, and a divorce sought, which to his surprise Lu said she would not contest. But she expressed a wish that he might reconsider – a futile wish, he retorted via the lawyer.

Lu responded by taking a new job at Dior, and he was furious. But Kerry thought the woman perfectly sensible. What else could she do, but utilise her experience and her talents? Nonetheless, the move demarcated battle lines, and both Kerry and Zoe foresaw a bitter struggle ahead. Vividly Kerry recalled the day, nearly nine years before, when Lu had called her father "a filthy bastard", and could not forgive the insult even now. But she advised Brian to be generous with what assets Lu had helped him to acquire, while safeguarding his inheritance from her undoubtedly predatory claim, and surprisingly he agreed.

The court hearing was fixed for several months hence, and in the meantime Brian had the more immediate question of Yves to address. At Kerry's request, Yves sent her newspaper cuttings describing developments in Australia, and Kerry all but wept for him as she realised the extent of his financial ruin, and the hellish humiliation of its very public exposure. Over three months elapsed before he returned to Paris and plunged into rebuilding his life, with such earnestness that Brian forgave the duplicity that had led to his reinstatement.

But despite the pall of shame and anxiety, the old Yves struggled through somehow, and as the summer wore on Zoe, amused and exasperated, began to report on his new friends and activities. Keith Charles's name was never mentioned again, but in July Yves moved into his old apartment with Zoe, joined a gay rights movement and gathered to his bosom a motley assortment of new friends, poets, painters, philosophers and all the bohemians whose nocturnal procession afforded Zoe many a sleepless night. A dissolute lot, Brian accused, but she found them fun, if exhausting, and during working hours Yves's behaviour was impeccable. Arriving each morning for work at eight, he laboured all day without so much as a lunch break, and did nothing that could be held against him.

Privately, he confided to Zoe that his philosophy of design no longer coincided with Brian's; to him it was a fascinating art form, while to Brian it had become almost exclusively commercial. Sensibly Zoe took no sides, supposing that the two would eventually work out a modus operandi, bonded perhaps by their common losses, if Yves had the wit not to provoke fresh friction.

Killian's sojourn in Kutari was punctuated by a series of illegible postcards, and extended to a second month. Kerry marvelled at Nabdul's patience, guiltily aware that she did not miss the boy at all. But when Helen returned, she tried conscientiously to pretend that she did.

"Don't lie to me, Kerry. It's bad enough without that."

"But he's having a ball, Helen! Why shouldn't he stay on?"

Helen picked up the phone and dialled Paris. If Killian's mother didn't want him, as was clearly the case, then the boy should go to his uncle. She would sooner see him taken into welfare custody than start looking to Nabdul Zul Mahrat for a role model.

But, when Killian finally wended his way home, Nabdul's influence was all too sadly apparent. Within minutes he was demanding that Kerry buy him a falcon, and threw a spectacular tantrum when his request was thrown out of court. Shortly thereafter, he announced his intention of running away from home, and was found attempting to start the jeep. Kerry yanked him out of it by the scruff of the neck and spanked him, hard; in return he bit her.

"He's turned into a perfect monster, Helen! That's what comes of spoiling him."

"No, Kerry. That's what comes of neglecting him."

Kerry cursed Nabdul under her breath, cut off Killian's pocket money and packed him back to school with relief. Three weeks later, he came home with a note of thanks from the headmaster: it had been a joy to have the boy, but now that pleasure might profitably be shared with another, more resilient, establishment. Autumn was well advanced before she found one.

In November, Cara married her colleague Frank, and Kerry summoned Yves to escort her to the wedding. He arrived with a suitcase full of presents for everyone, and Helen watched ambivalently as he danced with Kerry, holding her close, nurturing their strange deep friendship. At this rate, she would never get Kerry off her hands – and maybe, like Maeve before her, didn't want to. But things couldn't go on like this for ever!

"I think you should throw a Christmas party, Kerry. Eamonn used to so enjoy them, with all his friends, he'd talk about them for weeks afterwards . . ."

It struck Kerry that Helen had never been able to attend a single one. Also that she had much to celebrate – health, prosperity, and a fine new house to show off. It was time to revive the annual festivity. Overnight, she drew up a plan.

Fireworks, champagne, music, guests . . . Kerry's mind was on all these things as she made her last round of the stables one frosty night in early December. Helen would help her with all of it, and not for the first time she thought what a blessing the woman was. Often, in moments of irritability, Kerry knew she snapped at her, but Helen never took umbrage, never harboured rancour or let her calm equanimity be ruffled in any way. Often, when she went to place flowers on her parents' grave, she found Helen's already there, and was touched: despite Bob, Eamonn had never been forgotten. Like herself, Bob adored Helen, and for that Kerry had come to love him, her jealousy a thing of the past.

But now, if she didn't get her mind off parties and onto horses, tomorrow would be a double day's work. Zipping up her anorak against the chilly night, she went first to the tack rooms and feed bins, noting equipment to be repaired or replaced, blankets and bedding to be adjusted, supplies to be replenished and fences, as ever, to be mended. Making a list in her head as she went, she stored it all up until every horse had been checked, and let herself into Cara's office when she had finished. Switching on the light and the heater, she sat down at Cara's desk and compiled the list, to which Cara would attend first thing in the morning.

Absorbed in her work, she didn't hear the footsteps on the cobbled yard outside, and was startled by a soft, sudden knock on the door.

She didn't have to guess very hard who it was. Jerry had a way of coming to her last thing like this, when everyone else had gone home, with bundles of queries that could delay her till all hours once he started in on them. But she was lucky, she supposed, to have such conscientious staff, and sighed resignedly.

"Come in, Jerry."

The wooden door opened, and in the night outside she saw a taller, heavier figure than Jerry's, muffled and unidentifiable in a thick scarf and a leather blouson with the collar turned up. Instinctively, she froze, gripping the pen tightly in her hand as her mind flew to her father's hunting gun, up in the house and out of reach.

"Who is it? What do you want?" Somehow she forced steadiness into her voice, and a challenge, but she thought of that other winter's night long ago, and was terrified.

"Kerry? I didn't mean to scare you – it's me. Brandon."

No answer.

"Brandon Lawrence, Kerry, don't you even remember me? Please, don't be frightened. Helen told me I'd find you here."

She gasped as he came into the tiny room, relief and shock turning her bones to water, leaving her speechless.

In the light, she could see that it really was Brandon

Lawrence. But her apprehension was unabated, her tension as great as if it had been a stranger come to kill her. The face was the same, ascetic and almost forbidding, more deeply lined than she remembered it, the eyes grey and sombre, the shape square and strong; and the voice was the same, calm and deep, assured but very far from reassuring. She recoiled as if from a live cable, her fright translated into fury.

"What in hell – how – what do you think you're *doing*, sneaking in here like this? If I'd had a gun I might have killed you! How dare you scare me like that!"

What *was* he doing, bursting in out of the blue with no warning? After seven years, he was to all intents and purposes a perfect stranger, and all her senses were thrown on guard.

"If you've come about your horses, you should have made an appointment. I don't see anyone at this hour – and neither do they, for that matter. Go back to the house and Helen will arrange whatever it is you want."

"She already has, Kerry. I want to see you."

"Me?"

She stared at him as he lowered himself onto the rickety chair on the other side of the small table, and he had the temerity to smile at her icy belligerence.

"Yes, you. Calm down. I haven't got a poker under my jacket. I just want to talk to you, that's all."

Nothing stirred in her, no emotion of any kind. She sat rigid, eyes stony as jade.

"What could possibly be urgent enough for you to turn up like this, I cannot imagine. If your manager is good enough to deal with your horses for seven years, he's good enough to do it now. In office hours."

He looked across the table at her, frankly, for a long moment that made her feel under surveillance. Implacably, she returned the stare, thinking how he hadn't changed, and how he had. The blond hair was faded to ash, the body had set slightly, thickened, solidified, and there was some new aura about him. Of what? Weariness, she thought. Exhaustion. And yet, determination.

"I told you, Kerry, it isn't the horses. I've always left you to train them as you see fit, and I'm very happy with the results. It's you I'm not happy about."

Neither his appearance nor his words made any sense. What did he mean, he wasn't happy about her? He knew nothing at all about her. And even if he did, he had no reason to care. She sat back on the chair exuding animosity, trying to repel him by sheer force of will.

"My wellbeing is of absolutely no concern to you, Brandon Lawrence. But as it happens, I am very happy about myself, so there's no call for your touching intervention. You can leave now."

He leaned forward and placed his forearms on the table with the implacable look of a man not about to be shifted.

"Kerry, I want you to hear me out. We can do it here if you like, but it's been a long and quite dangerous drive over that mountain, and I would very much appreciate it if you would ask me into the house, give me a cup of tea and listen to me. That's all. Then I'll go, if you still want me to."

His tone was reasonable, and did something to soothe her fright if not her anger. What the man wanted, she could not imagine, but if she were to find out, she supposed – well. She glanced at her watch.

"Dinner is at eight o'clock. You have until then."

Abruptly, she stood up, tidied the makeshift desk and walked out, leaving him to follow as he chose. Outside, it was dark and chillingly cold, and her footsteps reverberated loudly all the way up to the house where, she noticed, the light in Helen's office was extinguished. No matter; she would have several choice words to say to Helen tomorrow about condoning nocturnal visits from marauding ghosts.

In the library, the fire was lit and burning ready for her, her customary gin and tonic standing on a silver tray. Ungraciously, she picked it up and downed half of it in a single gulp, indicating the bottles that lined the mahogany sideboard with her other hand.

"Help yourself."

If you must, her tone implied, but he did, to a brandy.

Raising his glass when he had filled it, he stood looking at her soberly for a moment before he spoke.

"Here's to you, Kerry. My congratulations on making an outstanding success of this place. I'm very proud of you."

"What else would I make of it? You hardly thought it'd fall apart without you, did you?"

"No, of course not. Must you be so touchy, Kerry?"

She flung herself down on the leather sofa, turned to a side table and extracted a cigarette from a box normally kept for guests. On average, she smoked perhaps ten cigarettes a year. Crossing her legs, she lit it from a heavy table lighter of Connemara marble and exhaled a cloud of smoke as she sat back, regarding him with a kind of stoic expectancy.

"We agreed many years ago that you'd never come here without permission, Brandon. Now that you've flouted that agreement, get to the point."

He sat down and hunched himself around the brandy balloon.

"It's not entirely without permission, Kerry. I checked with Helen, after your French friend suggested it."

Flummoxed, she gaped at him, unable to think for a moment who her "French friend" might be.

"Yves, do you mean? Yves Tiberti? But you don't even know him!"

"No. But we have met. Helen made an appointment for him to come to Hollyvaun, on the same day my father died. I had to cut the conversation short, when I heard, but not before he'd told me quite a lot about you. It was an impulsive thing for him to do, admittedly, but since Helen arranged it, I knew it must be important. He was only trying to help."

"Help what? I don't follow a word of this."

"Help you. He was concerned for you – seemed to think you were lonely, and leaning rather too heavily on – ah – people who were not really dependable. On one person, in particular."

Her anger was eclipsed only by her bewilderment. Was she overtired, hallucinating? But then she remembered the odd excursion Yves had made, one day last April, to see some unidentified man. But he had been to Brandon – to tell him about Nabdul? It was preposterous. A flush of mortified confusion suffused her face.

"Brandon, if Yves Tiberti really did such a thing, which I find incredible and outrageous, let me tell you he was very wrong, both in what he thought and what he did. He is a man of the most vivid imagination, totally unreliable and in no way to be taken seriously. He's – he's eccentric. And I'm going to kill him. Had you nothing better to do than entertain such nonsense?"

"He didn't think it was nonsense, and actually neither did I. He merely said he knew I was an old friend of yours, and that it might do you good to see me. I can't tell you how surprised I was. In fact, I'd assumed you were married to – uh – to the unsuitable party he spoke of."

She spluttered into her gin.

"Nabdul? Nabdul Zul Mahrat? Brandon, he's married to someone else, has been for over two years! What on earth gave you that idea?"

"But Kerry, there was a report in a newspaper, and a photograph. You were wearing an emerald ring and a lot of other serious jewellery he'd given you. I was upset, naturally, but only for my own sake. For your sake, I tried to be happy. Everything Yves said in April was a complete revelation to me. But I wasn't in a position to act on it then."

Act on it? Nonplussed, she pulled deeply on her cigarette, pondering what direction to take as if lost at a crossroads. The door opened, and she was profoundly glad to see Eileen, announcing that dinner was ready. Brandon eyed her curiously, with some concern.

"Do you normally dine alone, Kerry?"

"No I do not. Helen joins me, when she isn't scuttling away from the consequences of her meddling. Normally she'd be here, with her husband, or I'd go over to them. And at weekends Killian is allowed to stay up, or I have friends in – not that it's any of your business."

"Who are your friends, these days?"

"They're mainly in Dublin, or scattered around – nobody you'd know."

"What about the local people? Don't you have friends here, nearby?"

"Some. I'd have a lot more if my son would refrain from trampling their crops on his pony and shut their gates once in a while."

"How is your son?"

"Perfectly well, thank you."

There was an impasse. In silence, she drained her drink, hostility masking uncertainty, and Brandon nursed the last of his, wondering what to do. But he had come this far, and wasn't going to leave now.

"May I stay and eat with you, Kerry?"

She stood up. "Please yourself. But won't your wife be wondering where you are?"

"No. She won't."

"Very well. I'll ask Mary to cook another chop, or something. It won't be much at this short notice."

He didn't care if it were only bread and water. His eyes followed her out of the room, absorbing the confidence in her bearing, the authority of a woman very much in command of her domain. The lovely girl was gone, but in her place was a beautiful woman. And, when she returned, he was encouraged to find her attitude slightly softened. Or was she merely remembering her manners?

"I forgot that you've had a bereavement, Brandon. My condolences."

He looked at her, sardonically.

"Shall I tell you something, Kerry? My father is no loss whatsoever. What's more, I helped to kill him."

She froze to the floor.

"Oh, not literally. I didn't stab him or strangle him, much as I would have liked to. But I fought with him when I knew it wasn't medically advisable. He had appropriated my whole life, dictated my marriage, my career, everything, and I'd had enough. Now, he's gone and it's my turn to call the shots."

She saw the sudden steel in his face, and did not know what to think. Dermot had, indeed, been a notorious dictator, but so had her own father in his way, yet that had never stopped her from loving him. Even now, she felt a pang at the memory of his rending death.

"Brandon, when you came here, I thought – I thought you were one of the people who murdered my parents, or somebody similarly dangerous. I apologise if I was rude to you. But it's your own fault."

"I know. But if I'd asked first, would you have agreed to see me?"

"No. Most definitely not. I have my own life now, and I don't want it disrupted. It's only very recently that I've learned to appreciate the value of what I do have, and to stop wasting time worrying over what I don't. But since you are here, you may as well tell me why."

They went through to the dining room, where Eileen served avocados, but Brandon showed little inclination to eat, and it dawned on Kerry that he was nervous. A strange state, in a man who had always seemed to her the very epitome of assertiveness.

"So, your father is dead, Brandon, and you're planning to make some changes? Might I ask what this has to do with me, or with Yves's extraordinary interference?"

"Well, for a start, I'm coming back to live in Ireland. Company headquarters will be moved to Dublin, and I'm going to live in Wicklow."

"Wicklow? That'll mean a lot of commuting to Dublin."

"No. It won't. I'm setting up new management structures, appointing a chief executive to whom my current role will be delegated, and starting a new enterprise of my own."

"What kind of enterprise?"

"A hotel. I'm going to move into the dower house at Hollyvaun and gut the main house. It's the most horrible mausoleum, but when I've finished with it it'll be unrecognisable."

"Horrible – mausoleum?! But I thought you loved it!"

"I love Ireland, and Wicklow. Not that dump. I'm going to turn it inside out, make it a place people will enjoy coming to for a change. It already has facilities for fishing, sailing, riding, shooting, and I'm going to install a golf course, pool, gym, restaurant – everything that Dermot would hate."

"But Brandon, a member of the Lawrence family has always run the corporation!"

"Not any more. I'll still own and control it, with fifty-one per cent of the shares, and that's enough for me."

"You can walk away from it, just like that? But what about your wife and children? Aren't the boys at school in England? Doesn't Marianne love London?"

"My children will stay at school in England – at least, Harry will, for now. Chris says he wants to move here, so he can go to Glenstal or Rockwell or whatever Irish school will take him. He's very unsettled. But I didn't come to tell you about him, Kerry. I came to tell you about Marianne. She's left me."

Tentatively, he paused, letting the implication of his words sink in. But what he saw on Kerry's face could not have been further from the reaction he so desperately desired. Not an eyelash flickered as she looked down into her plate, mute with horror.

Oh, no. Not now. Not when I least need him, least want him. For the first time in my life I'm able to cope alone, I'm emotionally whole again, I'm well and strong. Dear God, don't let this be true. Not now.

Dismayed, he waited for her to say something, but she didn't. At length the silence became so unbearable he was forced to continue.

"When Dermot had his stroke, we were in America. Attending a political function in Washington. Marianne was dancing with a man called David Wheatstone. I left her there, with him."

"But you just told me she left you!"

"Yes. In the long run, she did. When I saw the attraction between her and David, I saw my chance, and I facilitated them. Our marriage had been finished for years. Now, as soon as our divorce is final, she's going to marry him. It worked out exactly as I intended."

Once, his words would have caused Kerry to jump up exclaiming for joy, run to him and riot with happiness. But too late. Too late. She lifted her face to him, and he was distraught to see it filled with sadness.

"Oh, Brandon. So many divorces, so much unhappiness . . . what's wrong with us all? Why can't we make a go of things, any of us? Didn't you try, after – when – the baby was born? Hasn't she brought you back together, baby Julie?"

Putting down his fork, he reached across the table for her hand. But she did not give it. It was not her place to comfort him, wretched as he looked.

"Kerry, Julie died. On the day of her christening, when she was six weeks old."

"Oh, my God. Oh, Brandon . . . I've heard it said that the loss of a child is the worst agony imaginable."

"It is. I thought I'd lose my mind. How did you know her name, Kerry?"

"I saw it in *The Times* . . . Oh, this is terrible. I'm so sorry."

He could see that she genuinely was. In her face was something almost as stricken as what he'd seen there on the day of her father's funeral. But whatever he wanted from her, it wasn't pity. With an effort, he got a grip on himself.

"So – after that, what was left of the relationship just disintegrated. But I found I still couldn't desert Marianne, Kerry. It wasn't her fault any more than it was mine. We married far too young, with Dermot's encouragement, long before we had any idea what we wanted out of life, or love. We did try, and we did stick it out for more than enough time to save it, if there was anything to save. But there wasn't. It's over now."

Aghast, Kerry began to grasp what he was trying to say to her, and fumbled for words that jerked out unpremeditated.

"But Brandon, this has nothing to do with me! You're not talking to the same person as before – Brandon, I just don't need you now!"

It was blurted out before she could help it, and she was horrified to see him turn his face away as though she had struck him, the pain as loud and clear as if he had cried out. Impotently, she sat looking anywhere and everywhere but at him, until he turned back again, with an attempt at recovery.

"No. Of course you don't, Kerry. I can see that. It was stupid and selfish of me to think . . . hope . . . otherwise. But I had to try, especially when Yves said . . . thought . . ."

His voice cracked, and it looked as if his composure would crumble, if she did not assume some herself.

"As you said earlier, Brandon, he meant well, and maybe he was even right at the time. I can't honestly say why I feel different now. But I do. This has been a difficult year for everyone except me, and it's made me realise that there's more to life than I used to think. My brother's marriage is in tatters, Yves himself has been badly burnt, while poor Zoe is breaking her heart over Brian . . . The price of love is just far too high. I've already paid it myself, and I'm not going to pay it again."

And why, he admitted, should she? Darragh had cost her enough already, and so had he. She had no reason to trust him, after all the bleak years she must have endured, so hard for a young woman alone, so different from all he had hoped to give her. Now, they were both free, but for her that very freedom had become precious. More precious than love? Without much hope, he met her eye questioningly, sadly.

"Do you really intend to stay single all your life, Kerry?"

"Yes. I'm afraid I do, Brandon. I cherish my friends and my work – in a funny way, I actually love the horses. They, and Ashamber, mean everything to me, and I'll never jeopardise them for anyone. Not even you. Frankly, you were one of my more expensive mistakes."

In a bittersweet way, he was glad she'd said that. Even if it worked against him now, it confirmed that once she had cared. Cared enough to be hurt. What right had he to expect any more vulnerability? But the thought of letting her go, after this first renewed sight of her, was excruciating. She was so beautiful as she sat there, quiet and sad, unconscious of the dust on her shirt, the wisp of hay in her hair, the freckles he'd always loved and she'd hated. Even her hands, rough and callused, told him so much about the life she'd endured in his absence. A life that had, as she said, changed her.

"You look much stronger, Kerry, than I remember you."

"I am stronger. More focused, as befits a grown woman of nearly thirty. I'm not the girl you remember at all."

"You've always been my girl, Kerry. Not a day has gone by that I haven't thought of you, wondered how you were."

"Really? You disguised your curiosity very well."

"I did as I was told, Kerry. Stayed away from you, at your own request. You can't imagine how hard that was. Is it really what you still want me to do?"

She didn't waver, didn't even hesitate.

"Yes, Brandon. I'm afraid it is."

If ever she had had the capacity for bitterness, she might have had it then. Seven years gone, stolen, wasted, and all for nothing. The child had died, the marriage had failed, their sacrifice had been squandered. Such appalling waste. How Maeve had always hated waste.

But it was a long time since Kerry had shed any tears over what could not be changed.

"There's nothing to be done, Brandon. I have my life and you'll just have to make the best of yours. Tell me, how can you get a divorce anyway, since you were married in Ireland?"

"We were resident in London long enough to get one there. It's quite straightforward, actually. Marianne and I will share custody of the boys, and she can keep the house in Richmond, have as much money as she wants. There's no animosity. In fact I'm glad one of us has found happiness."

"That's generous of you. And now you're going to live at Hollyvaun, you say? All by yourself?"

"Yes. There are a lot of things still to be sorted out in London, and I'll have to keep an eye on the new set-up in Dublin. That, and renovating Hollyvaun, are my two priorities."

She smiled. "I can let you have the name of an excellent designer, if you like what you see here."

Absorbed in his purpose, he had not even noticed the new décor, but now that she mentioned it he realised that the look of heroic dilapidation was gone. Ashamber was transformed, as Kerry was herself, and he clutched at the tiny straw she unconsciously held out to him.

"I'd be very glad of the name of whoever did this. And when work starts on my place, maybe you'd come and take a look at it? Even if we can't turn back the clock, Kerry, I'd still like us to be friends."

"I would too, Brandon. But it wouldn't work."

He was tempted to throw caution to the winds. If it would avail him anything, he would plead, beg, implore her for a second chance. But he resisted. This was not going to be achieved in a night, or a week or a month. The only thing he had on his side was time.

"If you say so, then I won't argue. But now that I'm going to be living at Hollyvaun, would you do just one tiny thing for me?"

"What?"

"Let me see my horses in training once in a while?"

She looked at him warily, with some annoyance.

"Well, obviously I can't forbid that. But I'm telling you now, the horses are all you'll see."

Quitting while he was ahead, he stood up.

"I won't ask for more. I won't even stay now. Will you excuse me? My apologies for having upset your evening. It won't happen again."

Before she could think what to say, he was gone.

Neither Yves nor Helen was repentant, and several days elapsed before Kerry's anger waned. But eventually it did, and she pushed the unsettling episode out of her mind. Christmas came, and the New Year to which she was looking forward. On December 31, she strode into Helen's blue room, now an impressive abode of glass and leather, and demanded to see the finalised guest list for that night's party. Wordlessly, she ran her eye down the hundred and fifty names, nodded, and handed it back. Helen smiled: she wasn't quite senile yet. She had indeed invited Brandon, but without writing down the fact in black and white. If he came, fine; if he didn't, no harm was done.

He did not. But everyone else did, even Brian with all his woes, and Kerry was thrilled with the success of the event. Lights shone in the trees, music played and champagne flowed, some of it down the throats of people who had only come to ogle, or preen or network. But she didn't care, thinking how pleased her parents would be, and when Brian expressed his admiration she felt an unprecedented sense of oneness with him. It was the week of their thirtieth birthday, and they danced together with mutual goodwill, careful not to refer to the past. Zoe never took her eyes off him all night, but Kerry made sure all the men danced with her so that she had no time to mope, and Yves was instructed to keep an eye on her, even if the other was on an attractive waiter from the catering firm.

Nabdul was precluded from attending by the recent birth of a son, who had been brought to Feirah for inspection. Kerry was glad; it made the night less complicated, and she enjoyed her own party immensely. But its preparations had cost her valuable time, and in January she resolved to work extra hours in lieu.

When Brandon finally arrived, at the end of the month and by appointment, she was ready for him. Greeting him casually, she assigned Cara to show him to his horses' stables and drive him to the Curragh thereafter to watch them run.

Freezing, he stood with his hands in the pockets of a sheepskin jacket, watching at first impassively and then with interest. In a way, the training gallops were more exciting than a race, more real, and Kerry's enthusiasm was contagious as she urged them on, brandishing a stopwatch, berating jockeys, jumping up and down with cold and agitation. He was impressed, and thanked her with genuine pleasure. And left it at that.

A month went by before he came again. This time, tea was offered afterwards in the tack room from a chipped mug, and he accepted it as if it were the elixir of life. Eight other people were there, and he hardly got a chance to speak to Kerry, but didn't push his luck. It was enough that he was learning something of her life, and that his peripheral presence was tolerated.

In March, he brought sketches of Andrew Austin's proposals for Hollyvaun, on which work had already begun. She showed cursory interest, which he chose to interpret as encouraging rather than merely polite, and after she left him he stayed to chat with Helen. Helen was on his side, he knew, but she was realistic.

"Don't hold your breath, Brandon."

"If I did that, Helen, I'd have expired long since. But it took me years to get rid of Dermot, and Marianne, and now, if it takes years to nail Kerry Laraghy, then so be it."

But as spring came and went with no sign of a thaw, he began to grow desperate. He couldn't even flatter himself that she was punishing him, rejecting him as once he had rejected her. She simply wasn't interested. So near, and yet so far: he thought he would go crazy.

The pleasure of seeing her became a torture. But at least he knew he was alive, that Marianne had not numbed his senses for ever. It was agony, but it was better than nothing. Masochistically, he began to visit Ashamber every week, so that Kerry looked at him askance.

"Haven't you more important things to be doing?"

"No," he answered honestly, "I haven't."

He had a company to relocate and reorganise, a hotel to build, a leisure centre to market and two sons to look after. None of it mattered. At the end of May, in desperation, he bought a new horse.

"Come and see what you think of it, Kerry."

"You should have consulted me before you spent your money. Helen has all the major pedigrees on disc for reference."

But she agreed to go to Hollyvaun to see it, and the renovated house besides. Fighting down the desire to escort her there on the spot, he left her to name a date and make her own way down to Wicklow.

On a hot day in June, she set out on the long hazardous drive, across the treacherous mountain road with its blind turns and sharp precipices strewn with boulders that had rolled down over the centuries. The ancient Mercedes rebelled, giving trouble with the clutch and gears, and by the time she arrived her nerves were on edge.

"Jesus, Brandon, I could use a drink."

Solicitously he sat her down, outdoors in a deckchair, with a soothing view of the lake. Tall cold minty drinks were brought, and a wide straw hat to protect her from the sun. She laughed.

"It's no use, Brandon."

His stomach clenched. "What isn't?"

"This hat. My freckles are out and will stay out till winter, no matter if I wear a hundred hats."

Weak with relief, he subsided beside her, and said little more while she relaxed. It was the first time he had seen her in a dress, the customary jeans discarded for a loose floating business in pale mauve voile, sprigged with tiny white flowers. He ached to tell her how pretty she looked, but didn't dare. She was talking about the car.

"I think it's on its last legs. Letting Yves Tiberti drive it was the *coup de grâce*. It's never been right since."

"Mercedes are built to last, Kerry. I know a chap who specialises in restoring vintage cars. He might be able to do something with it."

She lit up.

"Oh, do you really? Would you ask him, for me?"

"With pleasure."

The ice broken, they went to see the horse, a bay gelding over one of whose hooves she peered intently, lifting the foreleg gently, running her hand several times the length of the fetlock.

"You've been sold a pup. There's a touch of nevicular in this hoof. Get rid of him."

Surprised by her detached assessment, he nodded obediently, and led her out of the field up to the house, which was encircled by scaffolding, piles of bricks and lengths of timber. But inside, the ambience was warm and welcoming in shades of cream and peach, lit by sunshine streaming through the mullioned windows. Proudly, he showed her round.

"You never saw it before, Kerry, but it was a tomb. A cathedral. Suits of armour, the works. I can't thank you enough for recommending Andrew Austin."

Looking out of a window, she turned to smile at him.

"You can, actually. Send that man to see about my car."

"I wish I could do more than that."

She grinned mischievously. "All right. Take me out in that little boat on the lake, and we'll call it quits."

It was a much larger lake than the one at Ashamber, wide and deep, with a rough stone jetty to which he eagerly led her, helping her into the wooden craft, rigging the sheets and sails with such consummate ease she thought he must surely be able to do it blindfold. Her eyes widened in exhilaration as they shot away, out over the brown peaty water at invigorating speed, propelled by an offshore breeze that felt stronger on water than on land.

She was reminded of something, some memory too faint to distinguish, but idly let it slip from her grasp as they glided out into the middle of the lake. Looking at Brandon in his red T-shirt and light cotton trousers, she thought how confident he looked, how much younger than forty – forty what? Two or three, at least. Already the early summer sun had bleached his hair and tanned his face, accentuating his eyes, more blue today than grey. A handsome man, for whom she felt vaguely sorry.

Saying little, they sailed on, up to the furthest reaches of the lake, where fish jumped in a daredevil way that made her laugh.

"Nabdul would love this! You'd swear they were offering themselves up."

Nabdul was not Brandon's preferred subject, and he took another tack.

"I could take Killian out some day, if you think he'd enjoy it."

"Oh, he would."

Was that a yes, or a no? He couldn't tell. But he pressed on, asking many questions about Killian, introducing his own sons into the conversation.

"Harry has gone to America to spend the summer with his mother. Chris is here with me at the moment, but he's going cycling in Spain next month. Madness, of course, in July, but if that's what he wants I won't interfere."

So. He really was determined to shed Dermot's mantle. Was that possible? Her own experience told her that genetic inheritance was a powerful force, something you couldn't repudiate because you couldn't even see it. All she knew was that her own father was alive and well, somewhere inside her soul, roistering and prospering. There were even moments when Maeve seemed to join him, out on the perimeter.

Seeing her shiver slightly, he turned the boat round,

confronting her with a magnificent view of the distant house, so panoramic it took her breath away. Trailing one hand in the cold water, she bit her lip, and fell silent.

Back at the jetty, they moored the boat, and Kerry looked pointedly at her watch. But he took her by the arm and steered her away from her car, round behind the house where dense shrubbery had not yet been cleared away.

"Where are you taking me?"

"There's something I'd like to show you before you leave."

They battled uphill for a short distance, through the thick greenery until suddenly there was a low stone wall, encircling other white, smooth stones. The cemetery.

As many as thirty Lawrences lay buried in it, old men and women who had died of natural causes, younger ones who had perished in a variety of accidents, duels, hunting falls, early aviation mishaps and, in two cases, suicide.

He showed and narrated them all to her, even Alex of whom he had been so fond as a boy, Dermot whom he had so detested as a man.

"And this is Julie."

The grave was so small Kerry was standing over it before she even saw it, not at all sure that she wanted to. But Brandon knelt down, and moved a bouquet of simple summer flowers away so that she could read the inscription.

"Julie Susannah. February 27, 1973 – April 11, 1973. Dearly beloved baby daughter of Marianne and Brandon Lawrence."

That was all. No verse, no biblical quotation, no photograph despite the fashion for them. Almost, she thought, as if nobody could bear to say anything.

What could she say, herself? She turned to him, and saw a faint moist film over his eyes, felt the devastation inside him. But no tear fell, and his voice was steady when he spoke.

"This is the little girl who cost us so much, Kerry. But I loved her as much as I loved you, every bit as much. She was so innocent, so perfect. The memory of those six weeks has kept me alive for the last seven years."

"Were they very hard for you, Brandon?"

"Yes. As they must have been for you. I only wish I could make them up to you . . ."

He turned to her with such intensity as she had only ever once known in him before, that night in London after Blue Moon lost the Derby, and he had asked her to marry him.

"Is it too late, Kerry? Is it?"

Everything in his face, in his voice, pleaded with her that it wasn't. Zoe, she knew, would agree; it was never too late for anything. But life had gone on without him, taken other directions, led her into a blind alley from which escape seemed impossible. It was as if she were enclosed in the Bermuda Triangle, knowing where she was but unable to let anyone else know. Nobody could find her, nobody could reach her. Sadly, she squeezed his hand.

"Oh, Brandon . . . I don't blame you, or Julie, or anyone, for those lost years. But I've had to rearrange my whole life around them, choose other priorities. Ashamber is what matters most to me now."

"Of course it is. But remember what happened before, Kerry, when Darragh's obsession with his work cost you, and him, a marriage. Do you want to do that to yourself, this time?"

She was shaken. She'd never thought of such a parallel.

"That was different, Brandon. Darragh had a choice. I don't see that I have any."

"You haven't had, perhaps, until now. Trust was a luxury you couldn't afford. But I promise you, Kerry, you can trust me now. Maybe I won't ever come to mean more to you than Ashamber, but if I thought I could come to mean as much . . . it breaks my heart to see you stagnating, fencing yourself off this way. Will you think about it, at least? Give me permission to try?"

Looking at him, she could not doubt his sincerity. He wanted to reach out for her, find her, claim her, purpose written into every line on his face. Taking her other hand as well as the first, he smiled as if out of an old photograph.

"I still love you, Kerry. I've never stopped. Even if I can't bring you back, I'll never stop. But I won't crowd you, either, won't rush or pressurise you. All I ask is an open mind. Is that fair?"

It was fair. But Ashamber was her baby, and it had not

died. It was alive and well, healthy and lusty, and it needed her. Would always need her . . . or someone, some Laraghy whose roots were in its soil.

"My mind is open, Brandon. I'm just not sure that my heart is."

He encircled her loosely in his arms, and, thinking that he was going to kiss her, she tensed away. But he merely looked at her gravely, and released her.

"Don't say anything more for now, Kerry. Just promise me you'll think about it."

She did think about it, all the way back to Ashamber in the shuddering car, and for many days and nights thereafter.

18

Never had Helen seen Kerry bloom as she did in that hot wet summer of 1981. Day by day, she opened out, her mood slowly expanding from benign to vivacious, until a time came when she was unashamedly, unprecedentedly happy, golden and glowing in the volatile fruitful sunshine.

At first, her renewed acquaintance with Brandon was random and cautious, insubstantial as the washed clean air. Days went by, weeks on end, punctuated by nothing more than short calls and visits, small gifts which, as often as not, she gave away. Protectively Helen monitored every step she took on the long path back to the man who adored her, finding his patience reassuring, his word reliable, his love almost overwhelming. Sometimes, when he came too close, Kerry shied away from him, but again and again he coaxed her back, acknowledging her trepidation, leaving her to set her own pace, no matter how hesitant it might be.

The long days of June succeeded each other like pearls on an endless necklace, shimmering on down through July, changing hue so subtly that Helen could not discern the moment at which the friendship began to deepen, weave into a pattern of long walks and quiet talks, languid river picnics in the warm twilit evenings. During the dry hushed days of August there were many barbecues on the lands of Ashamber and Hollyvaun, and in their flames Kerry's face was radiant, but still she said nothing, quiet and contemplative, turning things over in her mind, thinking, tasting, assessing.

If she were falling in love with Brandon all over again, she divulged nothing of what she was feeling, and Helen could only surmise that it was so as she discussed every small nuance with Bob, worrying now about the danger to which she had exposed Eamonn's fragile daughter. Calmly Bob replied that Kerry was a grown woman, capable of judging things for herself, but Helen continued to fret even as she wondered how best to prepare the ground with Killian.

Over the latter part of the summer she brought him together several times with Brandon's sons, to go fishing or riding, play tennis or chess, anything that might ease the situation without appearing calculated.

But Killian was suspicious, surly and tearful by turn as he deliberately antagonised the two older boys, interrupting their stories of Spain and America, picking fights, defining status and territory of which he was visibly uncertain. Equally confused themselves, the brothers retreated with a mixture of disdain and sarcasm, leaving Helen to wish fervently she had not been so precipitate. Clearly, their parents were in no such hurry.

As summer ceded to September, all three boys departed for their various schools, leaving Kerry and Brandon to wander the harvest fields for many weeks more until, one day when the autumn leaves were crunching underfoot, Brandon was taken to that most private of sanctuaries, the grave in which Maeve and Eamonn lay buried. Helen did not comment, but she sensed the significance of the event, and that a turning point had been reached.

Late one moonlit night shortly thereafter, when the fragrance of Hallowe'en bonfires lay on the air, there was a knock on her door, and she opened it to find the couple trembling with cold and excitement, Kerry's eyes as luminous and lovely as the ring on her finger. Helen burst into tears.

She continued to weep as Bob came down in his dressing gown to open champagne, whereupon Kerry wept too, so that absurdly Brandon had to comfort her. Helen watched him put his arm around her shoulder as she nestled into him, half laughing at her own idiocy, and was deeply satisfied in the midst of her tears.

But next day, she interrogated Kerry searchingly. Was she sure, this time? Was she really happy? Doggedly she drew forth every nugget of information, stacking them up until she had enough to make something of. Where once Kerry would have babbled like a schoolgirl, now there were tiny dams, and it was hard work. But Helen deemed it no more than her duty.

"Have you considered, Kerry, that now you'll be responsible for three children? Are you prepared to invest the time and effort this new family will need?"

Kerry beamed.

"Oh, yes. I know all the boys are a bit muddled at the moment. Brandon and I are going to devote some time to them, and then I'm going to give them a joint present. A baby sister. That should bond everyone nicely."

"Kerry, please be serious."

"I'm perfectly serious. Getting pregnant is one of the many reasons why I've decided to marry Brandon. Having a child with him will put me on an equal footing with Marianne, make up in some tiny measure for Julie, and be a second chance besides. I know I've failed with Killian, but now I can try again, and make a better job of it this time. I so want to hand this place on to someone who might really love it – *understand* it, Helen."

"There's no guarantee of that. You fought shy of it yourself, when it was what Eamonn wanted. And Brandon is breaking with his family traditions now as well."

"I suppose you're right. It's just a hope. Oh, Helen, everything will work out, won't it? I've always made such a mess of things before, with men. Do you think I'm really mature enough to be any better in the future? To have what you have, with Bob?"

"I think you are, Kerry, if you set your mind to it. You and I are two exceptionally lucky women. We want to be married, to men who love us, but we don't need to be. We're economically independent. That gives us the luxury of choice. So just be sure you make the right one. You know I'll always be here to help, but ultimately you must make your own happiness."

The marriage was fixed for the following Easter, to allow time for the boys to acquiesce. During the early winter Brandon buttered up Killian shamelessly, taking him on trips and plying him with treats, and a collective skiing holiday was proposed for Christmas. Kerry laughed.

"It's blatant bribery and corruption, Brandon."

"Maybe. But it's more too. We need to get comfortable as a unit. The children are disrupted and unsure of themselves – unsure of us, too. Mine have already had to accept David Wheatstone and now yours is going to have to accept me. It's important for everyone to spend some time together."

It seemed to work. They went to Austria, where Killian's yells and whoops echoed all over the slopes of St Johann, and although he did not take to skiing, Harry enjoyed the Tyrolean snowscape in his own quiet way. Chris, cool and laconic, allowed his formal acquaintance with Kerry to thaw into acceptance, but made it clear he expected to be treated as an adult. They saw little of him, but if he was not enthusiastic he was not overly difficult either.

"He's so remote, Brandon. I can't get a fix on him at all."

"Don't worry. Nobody ever has."

They sat late one night in the bar of their hotel, drinking glühwein, discussing Marianne's obscene divorce settlement and Brian's struggle with Lu, who ten months after his decree absolute was still contesting its terms.

"Breaking up is a bloody business, Brandon. Let's really try to make sure it never happens to us. I'm going to give this marriage my very best shot."

He curled a finger through her hair, and smiled.

"It's about time somebody's marriage worked, Kerry! We're mature adults, we know what we're doing and we've worked very hard to get this far. I love you so much . . . there's absolutely nothing I won't do to justify your faith in me. I can't tell you how happy, how alive you make me feel."

She traced the outline of his lower lip with her index finger.

"You can thank yourself for that. You're a new man since you moved back to Ireland and sloughed off all those terrible pressures. Do you ever miss that big busy life you used to lead, in London?"

"Not in the least. It was no life at all. Playing the country squire suits me much better. But that would be meaningless too, without you. What would I be? Just one more middle-aged man, that's all."

Middle-aged? That jolted her, but she supposed it was true. On and off, they had known each other for thirteen years. But now, she knew herself as well, and was certain of him.

"Are you nervous, Brandon? I am, in a way, but in another I can hardly wait."

"I'd marry you tomorrow morning if it weren't for the boys . . . and I'd take you to bed tonight, if you'd let me."

It was difficult to resist, but she did. Physically close and attuned as they had become, something in her wanted to wait for marriage, this time. Why that should be, she didn't know, but as his hand slid under her sweater she pushed it away, laughing and reproving.

"Stop that!"

"It's not fair. You get all your little treats. I get none."

Laughing back, he let her go, wondering what it was about this woman that so made his blood tingle. Beautiful as she was, it wasn't just that – Marianne had been beautiful, a million women out there were equally beautiful.

Was it something in the composition of that beauty, the tilt of the chin, the line of the neck, the angle of the arm, the hollow of the throat? Yes. But more. The total exceeded the sum of the parts. It was her – her what? Her vigour, her careless grace, her fey humour? Yes. It was all of those things too. More than anything, perhaps, it was her attitude to life that captivated him, that earthy determination and elusive charisma, stamped with something unique, and very special.

No wonder her father had loved her so dearly. But he could not define it any further, and was glad. To define the indefinable would be to destroy it.

One Sunday in February, the putative new family met for lunch at Hollyvaun, a traditional collation of roast beef, floury potatoes and homegrown vegetables. The old house, now a hotel, was hearteningly filled with guests intent on golf and shooting, but the dower house stood apart and well screened on its twenty acres. The boys devoured their food, and Brandon reached for his newspaper, but Kerry laid her hand on his so that he could not open it.

"I'm told the best time to ask a man for a favour is after a good meal."

"That must be so, because I'm saying yes already."

She smiled winningly.

"I have to go to Paris next weekend, so Brian can fit the dress. Will you come with me?"

He groaned. "Oh, God. Is this going to be one of those awful women's fashion jaunts?"

"No. I promise you. The fitting will only take an hour, and then we can relax. It's just that I'd like you to get to know Brian a bit better, that's all, and Yves and Zoe as well."

Brandon had seen little of his future brother-in-law, whom he remembered as a callow youth at that cataclysmic party, and as a harrowed young man of twenty-one, standing in the rain over his parents' open grave, tightly holding his sister's hand. It was, he conceded, time to establish some sort of relationship.

"OK. Provided I don't have to offer an opinion on this creation."

"You won't even be let see it. It's a state secret."

The sketches Brian had sent were wonderful, but when Kerry arrived at Roissy airport six days later, her heart sank. Waiting in the arrivals lounge, her brother had aged ten years. Limp and forlorn, he stood with his hands in his pockets, subdued and lacklustre. If the dress was shaping up anything like he was himself, it would be a disaster. Appalled, Kerry went to embrace him, unaware of her own new vitality, and the contrast they made. Temporarily forgotten, Brandon turned to the little woman jigging excitedly at his side. She looked all right, at any rate. A pretty scrap of a thing. He extended his hand.

"Zoe? I'm Brandon Lawrence."

Zoe stared as she took the hand, noticing immediately how much older than Kerry this man was, and how assured. It wasn't a quality any of the rest of them had ever possessed. But he was attractive, for his age, and if he made Kerry happy that was good enough for her. As she smiled up at him, Kerry seized her from behind.

"Zoe Zimner! Where have you gone to? You've been tampered with, Zoe!"

"Yeah, isn't it great? Only five kilos to go."

"Oh, Zoe, I'm so pleased. Congratulations. You look absolutely marvellous – much better than this poor soul."

Brian barely looked able to carry the luggage, but he did, and minutes later was swinging his car out onto the Periphérique. As ever, Kerry's heart soared to see the signs in French, to inhale that peculiarly French smell of France, redolent of warm dough and chestnut leaves, garlic and Gauloises, ripe cheese and expensive perfume. No matter how much she travelled, it was her favourite city.

They drove straight to the salon, where Zoe was deputed to entertain Brandon while the fitting was in progress. She led him away to the Beaubourg Centre, and Brian took Kerry on a tour of the premises, recently expanded with a staff to match.

"It's amazing! You really have moved into the big league, Brian."

They had. Yves's return to full partnership had resulted in a flock of new clients and business had never been better.

"But where is Yves?"

"In his studio, slaving over the desk to which I chain him."

Immediately, Kerry guessed which one it was – the one from which the voice of Jacques Brel was wafting. She pushed it open and stood nonplussed for a moment, unable to locate Yves amidst a kaleidoscope of colours. Fabrics, papers, record albums, swatches and clip files lay strewn everywhere, and Yves sat with his back to her, sketching at his easel, resplendent in silk waistcoat, pin-tucked Oxfords and a baseball cap. She laid a hand on his shoulder and he whirled round, his face detonating in pleasure.

"Enfin, ma belle!"

She was engulfed in kisses, clasped to his chest so that he did not see her dismay: he was haggard, with a kind of hunted defensiveness emanating from somewhere under his beguiling bravado. Playfully, she tickled his moustache.

"I see my brother is starving you, as well as himself. But it's Saturday, and I'm taking the two of you out for a long lunch."

Yves stood back, and wagged his finger.

"*Au contraire.* You and Brandon will lunch with Brian alone, *en famille.* Then, tonight, it is I who will take you out, to Maxim's. Our table is already booked."

Maxim's. How like him to remember. He'd probably ordered the Billybi soup, too. Brian tugged at her sleeve, anxious to get started, and she blew him a kiss as she was dragged away. Solemnly, he sat down at his easel and made a great show of resuming work.

"Are you pushing him too hard, Brian? He looks dreadful."

"He's pushing himself. Become a positive workaholic. That's fine by me."

But Brian didn't want to talk about Yves, for now. His mind was solely on his sister as he produced the dress and began the fitting. For some time he worked in silence, while Kerry's mind drifted back to Yves; but then, as he knelt at her feet with a mouthful of pins and a handful of bunched fabric, the silence suddenly caved in. He made some strange sound, and when Kerry looked down she saw that his eyes were full of tears, the abject look of an errant spaniel expecting to be beaten for its crimes.

"Brian! Dear God, what's the matter?"

He straightened up, dropped the pins and the fabric and folded her into his arms with fierce, clumsy possessiveness.

"Kerry, it's still not right between us, is it? We talk now, but we still don't communicate. I miss you terribly, constantly. Can't we make it up, properly this time? Can you forgive me?"

He looked so starved, so pitiful, so humble, her heart ached for him, and she gripped him with equal fierceness.

"I can and I do, Brian, of course I do, you're my brother, my twin. I miss you too . . . but it wasn't your fault we got lost, Brian, was it? It was Lu's."

"Yes. She started it. But I should have fought back. Fought harder."

"So should I. Should have got down off my high horse and made the bloody effort."

Saying no more, he clung to her, and she held him tight in turn, her wedding dress lying crumpled on the floor, her lower lip working furiously as she felt his ribs through his shirt.

"Brian, this can't go on. You must promise me to put on some weight, and find a proper home."

"I'll try, Kerry, if it'll make you happy. It's just that it's all been so – very – fraught."

He was in bits. She could almost touch the suppressed pain clenched inside him, taste the salt of his checked tears. Embarrassed in the way men were when emotionally exposed, he looked away, but she did not let him go.

"How long have you been at the Crillon? A year, now? It's ridiculous, Brian! Besides, it must be costing you a fortune."

"I neither know nor care what it costs. Which reminds me, what have you been doing with the cheques I send? Not that you have to account to me or anything, I just wondered . . ."

"They're being put to good use. We don't need them at Ashamber, but there are other people who do. Let's say they're being invested in the future. Now, what I want you to do next is buy an apartment, move in and pull yourself together. Paris is full of other women, Brian, and you're a young, attractive man. I'm sure there's someone waiting out there for you somewhere. Maybe right under your nose, if you'd only look down."

Evading her eyes, he knelt and resumed his adjustments.

"Don't talk about anyone else, Kerry, please. It's too soon, I really couldn't cope."

She sighed. He would just have to cope, sooner or later, the same way they all did in this difficult world. Whatever his problems, he had a lot going for him – Zoe included, if only he would see that. And, if he didn't see it, to whom might he fall prey? Some other incarnation of Lucienne de Veurlay, manipulative, beautiful on the outside, ruthless behind an exotic façade?

But it was the wrong moment for a row, and for mention of Zoe. She weighed her words before speaking again.

"Is Lu still after your money, Brian?"

"Yes. But she's had all she's getting. Not one penny of Dad's legacy will go to her, now or ever."

"For sure?"

"For very sure."

She had heard that tone before, years ago when he was fighting Eamonn for his future. It had a stony, final ring to it, and she felt the victory hollow.

"So. Happy with the dress?"

He stood up to adjust a fold on her hip, and she looked down in delight. This dress was going to be sensational.

It was part of his overall theme for 1982, a very detailed, difficult creation that relied on light and shade for its axis and effect. Light, that most fleeting, intangible, volatile of substances, was what fascinated him now; lamplight, firelight, sunlight, shade, reflection, translucence, a new dimension every day. Claude Monet could not have been more obsessed, Zoe said, in his studio at Giverny. Just as Kerry had been obsessed with her horses, her brother was at his best with his back to the wall, feeling his way through a period in his life that she had already weathered. She knew what he was going through.

"You must regard your difficulties as productive, Brian. Look at Yves, who lost so much more than the person he loved. He may not be happy, but he's trying. Can't you try, too? Think of the end of your marriage as the beginning of the next phase. It gives you new freedom."

He grimaced through a fresh mouthful of pins.

"What's that Kristofferson song, Kerry? Freedom's just another word for nothing left to lose . . ."

"Brian! It's like this dress. Everything depends on what light you see it in."

They had a marvellous time at Maxim's, despite Brian's relentless interrogation of Brandon, so paternalistic a business that Kerry was at first amused. It was as if Brian were forty-four and Brandon the supplicant of thirty-one, rather than the other way round. But then, bored, she got up to dance with Yves, whose boundless physical energy belied his jittery mental state.

After half an hour she relinquished him to Zoe, and prodded Brian into asking a young woman from a neighbouring table. It was Brandon's cue to claim her, but instead he looked at Yves, speculatively.

"I have a lot to thank that fellow for, Kerry. What he did was impetuous and foolhardy, but it was just the encouragement I needed. What I can't understand is why he didn't want you for himself. It's so obvious he adores you, I should be jealous."

"Jealousy is a stifling thing, Brandon, and quite superfluous in this instance. Yves is homosexual."

Of course. He should have guessed. Grateful to the man on the one hand, he felt faint revulsion on the other. For Kerry's sake he quelled it, but the disclosure went against the grain. Yves, granted, was gracious, charming and beguiling . . . but what if he had had a lover, and brought him along tonight? Would they have had to suffer a blatant display of such unnatural proclivities?

Worse, what if Yves came to stay at Ashamber, as he was bound to do? What would they tell the staff? Could Helen possibly know already, and condone such a thing? Surely not.

"Brandon?"

"Mm?"

"Are you shocked?"

He didn't want to ruin her evening.

"Oh – let's just say I need time to adjust."

"He's my dearest friend, Brandon, and always will be. You're going to have to take him as you find him. Nabdul, too. Marrying you doesn't mean dropping any of the people who have given me reason to love them."

He saw it would be a bone of contention, if he let it. But they were in Paris, and should have romance, not a row.

"We'll discuss it some other time. Come on. Let's dance."

They danced, and drank a lot of champagne, and dropped the subject. Next morning, Kerry awoke late and bleary-eyed at the Crillon, but after a brisk shower she was ready to ransack the flea markets of Clignancourt. Brandon had never been to a flea market in his life, and demurred.

"Oh, but you must come! It's full of fascinating stuff – you might even find some of those old books you're so keen on. If you don't, I'll make Brian take you to see the sewers instead."

"The sewers?"

"Yes. They're one of the sights of Paris. Most educational. Tours on the hour. Would you prefer that?"

He went to the flea market, and was surprised to find it indeed fascinating. Encouraged to haggle over prices, he did, wondering at his own enjoyment; Marianne, he was sure, would never have permitted such a thing, had she even known it existed. Lunch, which he had mentally pencilled in for the Tour d'Argent, consisted of hot dogs dripping with mustard, and when he suggested the Tour d'Argent for that night instead, Zoe triumphantly produced tickets for Rod Stewart's concert at Parc des Princes.

Brandon had never been to a rock concert in his life, or any concert for which black tie was not required, and his reluctance elicited incredulous laughter. Feeling a fool, he went along, wondering where and how he had ever lived – existed – until now. The sheer energy of the spectacle was a revelation, at the end of which he turned to Kerry and clasped her hand in high spirits.

"I'm so glad you made me come here, Kerry – to Paris, I mean, the whole thing. I've never seen anything of the city before except offices and restaurants. Are you enjoying it too?"

"Yep. Always do. Paris is a most enchanting sorceress."

"As are you! But it doesn't remind you too much of Darragh?"

"I never think of him at all. That chapter of my life is long closed."

"And ours is opening. I can't *wait* to marry you, Kerry Laraghy!"

"Well, you'll just have to wait. Patience is a very important thing, as Nabdul Zul Mahrat once taught me."

He didn't see what was so funny, when she roared with laughter. Nor did he find it funny when he drew a blank, for the second time, at the door of her hotel bedroom. Invigorated by their energetic evening, he was left to mull frustrated over her sexual reticence. But he saw that it had something to do with the trust and confidence she was building up in him, as well as the new value she set on her own self. Roundly he cursed the delay, but he respected her wishes, and had to admire her resolve. When he had earned her, he would get her.

"Mum! You're back, you're back! Did you miss me, did you bring me a pres—?"

Anxiously Killian arrested his leap into his mother's arms. They were not outstretched. But Helen came behind him, and under her scrutiny Kerry bent to kiss the boy.

"Yes, of course we did, Brandon got you a kite."

He dived on her suitcase, and, leaving him to rummage in it, Kerry turned to embrace Helen, espying over her shoulder a stack of parcels and crates on the floor.

"Been shopping, Helen?"

"No. I've been playing golf. These are for you. Wedding presents."

With cursory interest Kerry glanced through the cards on top, all duly catalogued by Helen, who with Eileen had spent a most enjoyable weekend speculating as to their contents.

"How nice."

"Yes. And speaking of gifts, Kerry, Bob would like you to have the first pup from Oisin's next litter."

"Pipped at the post, eh? I had thought that maybe Brandon and I would have some offspring to show you, first."

Helen stared over her glasses. "What?"

"But I've decided to do things the right way round for a change. No sex in future, without love and commitment. Body *and* soul. Lovers are out, husbands are in."

"I should think so. You rushed in far too fast, with Nabdul, it was an utter disgrace."

"Helen Craigie Cummins, you old Jezebel! That comes well from my father's demon lover."

Helen blushed like a schoolgirl. "Well, circumstances were different then, I mean to say . . ."

But what could she say, when she abhorred the casual way people partook of sex these days, as if it were a drink or a cigarette? For herself and Eamonn it had never been just a physical indulgence, but a deep spiritual bond; exactly what she wanted Kerry to forge now with Brandon.

Kerry grinned as she flipped through the list of wellwishers, mostly business associates of Brandon's.

"Sauce for the goose, eh, but not for the gander? Well, a new baby will be just the thing to rejuvenate you, and Brandon too. I intend to devote my honeymoon to the single-minded pursuit of pregnancy."

Not at all sure she liked the turn the conversation was taking, Helen diverted it to the boxes, and made a note of all the secretaries to be thanked. They would be appalled, she was sure, to know that Brandon Lawrence's role in life nowadays appeared to be chiefly that of a sire out to stud.

But as the last months before the wedding elapsed, signs of change in the man were visible to everyone. Shedding his suits for jeans and sweaters, he seemed to undergo a spiritual metamorphosis, and Kerry revelled in a *joie-de-vivre* that was contagious. Early one April morning, he turned up to wake her at six o'clock, demanding that she get up to watch the sunrise with him. But she was already dressed, and suggested they ride right out into it. Setting off at full gallop across the glittering grass, they disappeared over the lush lands of Ashamber, jumping fences and hedges, clambering up and down ditches, laughing as the dew flew off low branches into their faces, tasting the new day and finding it sweet.

Gradually the low pale light spread up and out until the sky was the colour of a freshly peeled grapefruit, and they reined in to admire it, marvelling as if it were a miracle. And it was theirs, all theirs, to make of what they wished! They made the most of it, and of every day thereafter.

Only in the final week did Kerry show signs of nervousness, when the first guests began to arrive from overseas. Most were housed at Hollyvaun, which closed for business to accommodate them, but some had to be put up at Ashamber: David and Marianne, Nabdul and Shairi, Bill Schuster and his wife Candy, Sheik Feirah and his retinue of minders. The diplomatic allocation of rooms was a nightmare from which she recoiled.

"Brandon, get me out of here. Let's go sailing?"

They drove to Hollyvaun and took all three boys out on the lake with them. It was their first sail together, and she never forgot it: the blinding glint of the water, the high clear sky, the whoops and shouts of the boys as their boats scudded out over the lake before a warm wind that tore their clothing loose.

Brandon, in his element, took Kerry and Harry with him in one craft while Chris took Killian in the other, with much yelling and waving between the two, their voices carrying over the water, Killian dangling almost into it until such time as he managed to catch a fish on his makeshift line. Brandon made a great fuss of this fish, guessing its weight admiringly, insisting that it be cooked for lunch, so that the child's small windburnt face lit up eagerly, and even Chris was heard to congratulate him. Pleased, Brandon turned to Kerry.

"You were right, darling. This is much better than agonising over who's going to sleep where and sit where. Helen will sort everything out twice as fast without us."

It was Helen, finally, who had found the Justice of the Peace who was to marry them. Precluded from a church wedding by their divorces, they had sought a priest to officiate privately in the chapel at Hollyvaun, but could not find one. Infuriated, Kerry had driven down to Father Mulcahy in the village, announced her intention of quitting his "intolerant, unchristian and patriarchal" faith, and written a letter to the bishop thereafter, outlining her reasons for her resignation.

The sorrowful reply that was received in return was torn up, flung on the fire and consigned to the flames of eternal damnation.

"We'll marry right here at Ashamber, Brandon, and the hell with their church."

Brandon didn't care where they married so long as it was

legal and it was soon. Helen, voicing her disapproval but not seeing what else was to be done, applied her attention to the problem, and came up with Mr Morton by way of a solution. An affable man who owned a chain of supermarkets, Mr Morton was rarely called upon in his capacity as a JP, but replied that he would be delighted. Grimly, Kerry had instructed the florists to bedeck the ballroom accordingly, while a marquee was set up on the lawn for dancing out there instead. Now, she was glad.

"It will be lovely to be married at Ashamber, Brandon. And I hope we'll be very happy living there too."

He knew what she meant by that. But the dower house at Hollyvaun was not large enough, apart from being too far away from her work. Moving into her home with his boys would require adjustments all round, but he was willing and eager to make them. Helen, he was sure, would meet him halfway, and the boys adapt in time to what was, after all, a house just as large and beautiful as either of their previous homes.

He squeezed her hand and kissed her in full view of their three sons, who reddened and grimaced, mortified.

"We will be happy, all of us. You'll see."

The day's sailing was a welcome break, and they returned to Ashamber elated, to find Nabdul arriving with his wife and father amidst considerable fuss. Feirah swept up the steps in full regalia, accompanied by two bodyguards, but Nabdul stopped dead when he saw Kerry, with a smile that all but stripped the paint off the hall door.

"My dear Kerry! How good it is to see you! May I?"

He brushed the back of her hand with his lips, and she thought her knuckles would combust. Christ, she thought, you haven't lost it, you old lecher. She smiled at him, and saw the ironic amusement in his tawny, gold-flecked eyes as he took in her tousled hair, the sweater knotted askew across her shoulders, the damp trousers in which she had sailed all day. Oh, well: if he thought she was going to stand on ceremony for his benefit, tough luck.

But the next day, when all their guests had arrived, she dressed with great care for Marianne's benefit. Gritting her teeth, screwing a smile into place, she put on a short, almond-coloured silk dress and went downstairs, deliberately late, to welcome the woman.

Marianne, escorted into the rose sitting room by Harry, sat waiting beside David, while Brandon stood over by the fire with Chris, admiring his fiancée as she came into the room. Rejoicing at the length of leg she was able to boast over Marianne, Kerry smiled brightly, noting a faintly territorial atmosphere.

What a charming family tableau, she thought, may the bitch's teeth fall out.

"Why, hello, Marianne! David, how nice to meet you!"

Proprietorially she turned to Brandon, and put her hand on his arm. "Darling, have we poured our guests a drink?"

"Paddy's on his way with some champagne."

There was a tiny warning bell in his voice: screw up, Kerry, and I'll smack you from here to Skibbereen. Good relations were important for the sake of his sons. Marianne, she had to concede, looked a million dollars – as well she might, having relieved her former husband of several. Her suit, in grey and grape folds of velvet, draped her figure in a way that emphasised it, but it was her enormous violet eyes that made the main impact.

Beside her, David sat adoring as a hypnotised puppy, and Kerry felt like shaking him, telling the man to get a grip and retrieve his wits; his wife was not Shirley Temple, no matter how long she affected those ridiculous curls. But his infatuation was her salvation, and so she smiled instead.

The champagne was produced, and a wedding gift in return, to which Kerry dutifully responded with thanks and kisses, noting Chris's amusement out of the corner of her eye. God, but he made her nervous! No matter how she tried she could not build a relationship with him; always he seemed to be watching and weighing things, from a distance, polite but somehow judgmental. With relief, she heard Eileen announce Brian's arrival, and all but sprinted out of the room, flinging excuses over her shoulder as she silently saluted her brother's timing.

His car reached the steps outside just as she did herself,

and they all tumbled out of it, Brian, Yves and Zoe, crumpled after their long ferry trip. Lu, on Brian's strict insistence, had not been invited.

Zoe, she thought, looked wonderful, many kilos lighter now, glowing in a red bolero jacket and navy drainpipe trousers, proudly pirouetting for inspection. Yves was a sight, in some kind of vaguely military ensemble, but Brian looked much better, his frame adequately padded at last, his dark eyes quite animated, minus their shipwrecked look. He had developed a number of new mannerisms, she noted as he spoke, a tendency to let his sentences trail off, to pluck at imaginary fluff on his clothing and gaze into the distance – or was it just his eye roving, quite naturally, over Ashamber?

Oh, if only it would rove over Zoe! Effusively she exclaimed over her friend, but he took no notice, asking instead for Killian as he went up into the house.

Killian came bowling out, and to Kerry's delight made a beeline for Zoe, who gathered him into an equally enthusiastic embrace.

"Doesn't she look fabulous, Brian?"

"Yes, I suppose so. More presentable, anyway."

Presentable? Brian Laraghy, she thought, you don't *deserve* Zoe Zimner. If you're not careful, you'll end up all alone, as I nearly did, with only yourself to blame.

That night, on the eve of their wedding, Brandon and Kerry hosted a formal dinner for their guests, and towards the end of it Brian redeemed himself by handing his sister a large manila envelope.

"I've done what you wanted, Kerry, and bought an apartment."

"About time too! Are these photographs of it?"

"Yes. Take a look."

She opened the envelope and drew out half a dozen pictures. The first two showed the exterior of an old sandstone building which appeared to have been restored, with geraniums spilling down from window boxes and a tall wrought-iron gate, unmistakably French, enclosing a tiny but very pretty courtyard.

The other four were of the interior; a black-and-white-tiled kitchen full of copper pans and dried flowers, a long, low bedroom with a beamed ceiling, a lounge with a sloping glass roof and another room with a pale oak desk, shelves and worktop space.

"There are other rooms, too, but you get the general idea. It's in the Marais, near the Place des Vosges, just round the corner from Zoe. What do you think?"

"It's gorgeous. And a great weight off my mind."

He smiled. "There's only one small problem about it."

"What's that?"

"Where am I going to find another one, just as nice, for myself?"

"For yourself? But isn't this – what do you mean?"

"Look in the envelope again, Kerry. You'll find the deeds in it. They're in your name, and Brandon's. This apartment is for you both."

"F-for me? For us?"

"Yes."

Silently, Kerry laid the envelope down on the table, took her brother's face between her two hands and held it there, her eyes locking with his as she absorbed the implications of his gesture. He wanted her back, near him, beside him?

Yes. He really did. Henceforth, a part of her would always be in Paris, the city in which he lived, in which their happiest days had been spent together. For once, she was lost for words.

But Yves had brought a gift too, a small square package which she accepted with a smile, hoping he hadn't taken out a mortgage on whatever it contained.

Inside layers of tissue lay an early charcoal sketch by Odilon Redon, executed long before Redon had discovered the joys of oil or colour, but already imbued with his characteristic ambiguity. Was it a portrait of a girl – or a boy? Kerry could not be sure which, but she found its hermaphroditic obscurity compelling. In a week or a month, it would reveal far more than now met the eye, an enigma which, like Yves himself, would repay constant study. She regarded him thoughtfully.

"Beautiful isn't the word, is it, Yves? Too obvious. Provocative, maybe? It'll take me a while to get to know this person . . . Where on earth did you get it?"

"Oh, it's only charcoal, *chérie*. One acquires these things, browsing on the quais . . ."

She was right. It had cost him a fortune. Some instinct held her back from showing it to Brandon until after he had drifted away.

As she expected, he hated it.

"My God, what a hideous thing! I thought Yves had better taste."

"Brandon, don't make up your mind just like that. It's fascinating, if you just look more closely, for longer, think about it . . ."

"You think about it. But for God's sake don't hang it anywhere I have to see it."

No. She would keep it to herself, then, as she was sure Yves had intended. Brandon's reaction was Brandon's loss, but he would thank Yves anyway, because she could not bear her friend's feelings to be hurt, even if he was used to it.

Tradition decreed that bride and groom should not see each other on the morning of their marriage, and so Kerry spent it with Zoe instead, confident, optimistic and visibly happy. Today was her day, a day she had never thought to see, and now that it was hers she would savour every minute. If anyone was nervous, it was Zoe. Arriving in Kerry's bedroom in a Chinese dressing gown, smelling exotically of some fragrant bath oil, she fiddled with her damp black curls and expressed the fervent hope that, this time, the right decision had been made.

"It has, Zoe, don't worry. I'm not going to the gallows today."

Touched by her friend's concern, but not disturbed, Kerry sat on her bed indulging in the luxury of painting her nails. On the dado rail, her wedding dress hung shimmering in the Easter sunlight, surrounded by cards and flowers from wellwishers unable to be there in person. Outside, the first buds of cherry blossom caressed the window, birds carolling in its branches under a clear, bright blue sky, and she was gratified to see nature complying so expressly with her wishes. Happily she chatted with Zoe, giggling like any bride on the subject of her future husband, until she thought she saw some slight hesitancy creep into Zoe's face.

"Your turn will come too, Zoe."

Kerry had arranged for Brian and Zoe to help Helen with Killian at Ashamber while she was on honeymoon. Yves would return to the salon, the other guests would depart, and they would be alone together. But Zoe couldn't see any point in it.

"Brian's just as keen on children as ever, Kerry, and the doctor says there's no way. We're even too old to adopt, and of mixed religion besides."

"Don't worry about that. Just concentrate on him."

Not wanting to dampen Kerry's high hopes, Zoe turned to smooth the folds of Brian's handiwork with a professional touch. Her own bridesmaid's dress hung beside it, its fitting a heartbreaking affair; Brian might as well have been working on his tailor's dummy. But then, Kerry's case with Brandon had once been hopeless too. She brightened as Killian was propelled into the room for inspection, crammed into his page-boy outfit by Brian, who steered him with an avuncular air.

"My nephew wants to give his mother a kiss for luck."

Killian scowled over his lace cravat, but Kerry proffered her cheek, on which he solemnly placed his kiss, and smiled. It was not every day that Mummy accepted his favours so readily.

"Now, Killian, I want you to be very good today, and every day while I'm away. You're to look after Brian and Zoe and make sure they behave themselves, OK?"

He nodded eagerly. It would be fun to have Zoe around, and maybe she'd even cheer Uncle Brian up a bit. But at this moment, Brian's attention was on his sister.

"No nerves, Kerry?"

"Not any more. Everything is ready, and I'm perfectly relaxed."

Satisfied, he took Killian away. But when Helen appeared, elegant beyond recognition in dark blue and burnt orange,

Zoe took one look at her face and edged tactfully out of the room. Normally so placid, Helen had clearly worked herself up into a state of some emotion. Close to tears, she went to Kerry, but then stopped, fumbling for a Kleenex to dab at her eyes, hardly able to speak.

"Oh, Kerry, I promised myself I wouldn't do this, on your big day . . . but I – I just can't help it."

Equally tearful and distressed, Kerry stood up in her camisole, thinking suddenly of her mother and father, who should have been there for her, with her, on this bittersweet, very special day. But then, there would have been no Helen.

"Please don't cry, Helen, I can't bear it. Please?"

But Helen sank down on the bed, sobbing and forlorn, choking out the words between floods of tears.

"I know I can't replace them, Kerry, but I've loved you every bit as much as ever they did . . . tried to do everything they would have done . . ."

Gently, Kerry put her arm around her.

"I know, Helen. I know. Where would I ever have been without you, all these years? Daddy never could have left a better person to mind me, I only wish he could know how much you mean to me . . . don't upset yourself. He wouldn't want you to."

But tears streamed down her own face as she brushed them off Helen's, and neither woman could regain her composure until, finally, they had a good cry, and smiled wanly.

"This is absurd, on such a happy day . . . let's cheer up now, Helen, and enjoy it? I'll be back here at home with you in three weeks, and nothing will change between us, I promise you."

Sniffing into her hanky, Helen nodded, and went away before she should ruin Kerry's day entirely. Only then, when she was left alone to dress, did Kerry's thoughts turn to Brandon, and the commitment that was less than an hour away.

What she felt for him now was not, she knew, the yearning love of old. It was strong, and ardent, but it was not the passionate flame that had once consumed her every waking moment, at a time when she had needed him far more than he needed her. Now, the reverse was true, but in that knowledge she sensed strength, and maturity, freedom from all the desperate intensity of youth. Then, she had sought to take everything he could give her; today, she brought to the relationship attributes of her own. It would be an equal partnership, this time, and she felt equipped to deal with whatever demands it might make on her. Not, she supposed, that anyone could ever see into the future, but she was serenely disposed to it, and very happy in her choice of husband. She had grown up a good deal, while he had loosened up, and despite the differences of age and outlook they now had much in common. Much, she realised, of what really mattered. She was not afraid.

Quietly, she dressed her hair, fluffing it out into pre-Raphaelite clouds over her shoulders, weaving in the tiny silk flowers that she preferred to a veil, and put on the dress that needed no adornment. Shortly before noon, as she was finishing her make-up, Brian knocked on the door.

"It's almost twelve, Kerry. Do you want to be late, or not?"

"No, Brian. I want to marry Brandon Lawrence now, this very minute."

He helped her with the little final details, and crooked his arm for her to take, leading her out onto the landing where Zoe and Killian were waiting. Down in the hall, the musicians were playing Pachelbel's *Canon*, and as she descended the staircase with its banisters rolled in flowers, Kerry was suddenly very glad she was marrying here in her own home. Overhead, the great chandelier glittered, every prism polished and winking in the sunlight that poured through the windows; but, bedecked as it was, Ashamber was simply the old, familiar house in which she belonged.

They reached the ballroom, and two hundred heads turned simultaneously: friends from the racing world, the Arab contingent, Brandon's old cronies Louis and Greg, David and Marianne, Frank and Cara, Eileen and Paddy, Helen and Bob, Bill Schuster, Jerry Flynn . . . so many people who had supported her in difficult days. And Brandon.

Turning to her, his face came alive with pleasure and

pride as he caught sight of her, and she was conscious that he found her beautiful. Even now it was not a word she could apply to herself, but in Brian's dress she felt as close to it as ever she would come.

Eschewing bridal white as he had been instructed, her brother had created a dress for Ashamber instead, blending with the hues and shades of the land, its rich variegations and seasonal tones. Knotted on one shoulder, it fell to handkerchief points in every permutation of leaf and tree, glowing coppers and mellow bronzes, blazing russets and softest old golds, sage and sepia, ochre and tawny olive. Knotted again on one hip, it wove through the rays of sunlight as Kerry walked, and she wore only ballet slippers with it, carrying a simple sheaf of dried harvest flowers in colours of pastoral rose and corn, bound with a pale cream ribbon.

Brandon, expecting a traditional bride, was astonished. More astonished still when Kerry handed her bouquet to Zoe, touched his arm and winked at him. It was a big, bold wink, lazy and deliberate, so full of innuendo he thought his knees would turn to water as he reached, with indecent eagerness, to take her hand.

It was a short ceremony, and soon Chris was stepping forward to give his father the ring to slide onto Kerry's finger. It was secured with a kiss, and a murmur of love, and they were married.

Outside in the gardens, there was applause as Kerry and Brandon emerged from the house for photographs, and she threw her bouquet with fine markmanship into Zoe's outstretched hands. But then, positioned on the terrace ready to pose, Kerry suddenly tugged at Brandon's sleeve, distractedly gazing into the distance.

"Brandon – those horses – they're not any of mine. How did they get into that field? Christ, they must have got loose from Cushla."

He laughed, pleased that the secret had been kept.

"They are yours. My gift to you, of mares and stallions from which, some day, you'll breed winners of your own."

In a flash she had gathered up her skirts and run down

the steps, across the grass to where the animals cantered, wedding party forgotten.

"Oh, my God! Look at them! How many are there – five? No, six! Such beauties! Wherever did you find them?"

"Here and there. Two in Italy, one in America, the others here in Ireland. Helen has all their backgrounds on disc."

She was strongly inclined to hike up her skirts and clamber over the fence, there and then, to inspect them at close quarters. But Brian's lovely dress would be ruined, and impatiently she restrained herself. Later, when nobody would notice, she would change and sneak back out to them. For the moment, she reached instead up to her husband of five minutes, entwined her arms around his neck and kissed him with a fervour he found infectious.

They returned to be photographed, laughing and informal, before everyone drifted into the billowing marquee where the musicians had assembled. Champagne circulated, and as she accepted a glass Kerry caught Brandon's eye and spluttered into it, no more ladylike now than on that first mortifying, memorable night. Brian and Zoe came to kiss her, all smiles, and Chris offered the handshake that was as much, she thought, as anyone would ever get from him. But Harry hung back, and although Feirah and Shairi were effusive, Nabdul's congratulations were cool. She laughed at him.

"I do believe your nose is out of joint, Nabdul!"

He huddled into his ceremonial robes like a vulture baulked of its prey, eyed her nostalgically and glided away. From a corner, she felt Yves watching her, and sensed emotion no less mixed. Anxiously, she went to reassure him.

"Don't tell me you're sulking too? Oh, Yves. You know perfectly well that things will never change between us. Don't be silly, now, and spoil my day."

He smiled, with an effort, and raised his glass to her.

"You look stunning, Kerry. That Laraghy fellow might make a name for himself yet."

His tone disturbed her, but she let it pass, thinking how stunning he looked himself, in a terracotta suit and saffron Cossack shirt, oblivious of the women ogling him from every table. Did they know he was gay? They must, she supposed, after all the publicity of two years before; every social event must be an ordeal for him, thin-skinned as he was.

Later, she would make sure to dance with him. But first she had her duties as hostess, at the table where Brandon was waiting for her. There were cheers and witticisms as she joined him, and then food was served, a delectable banquet of lobster and prawns on beds of starfruit, followed by sorbet, fresh river salmon and glazed crispy duck, with Chablis and aged claret to drink. With the cheese and port came an expectant pause, in which Brian stood up. Chris had declined to make a speech.

Happy as she was to have fraternal relations restored in time for this milestone family day, Kerry was nervous for him, wondering whether he would mumble inaudibly, or fluff the whole thing. But Yves picked up the telegrams and fed them to him with such lewdly witty comment that everyone laughed, and eventually Brian got through his short speech, faltering only when Maeve and Eamonn were mentioned, but getting creditably through to the end. With Brandon, Kerry stood up to cut the cake, toasts were drunk and the formalities were over.

Relieved, she let herself be led onto the dance floor, motioning to Brian to ask Zoe to come too, but he waited until, first, she and Brandon completed a full circuit on their own. They moved off to the music of Andrew Lloyd Webber, and as soon as she felt his arms strong and supportive around her, Kerry forgot their audience, and was in heaven. Dancing had always been one of the things Brandon did best.

He smiled at her, his hand gripping the small of her back as they found their stride.

"Have I told my wife yet that I love her?"

"No. Feel free."

He kissed her, his eyes alight with love and admiration, and she snuggled against his shoulder, suddenly suffused with reciprocal emotions. Neither of them saw Brian and Zoe come to join them, then Helen and Bob, until the floor was thronged.

Irish style, the celebrations would go on all day, Kerry knew, but she was determined to take another look at those horses before evening fell. Relinquishing Brandon to Helen after several dances, she wondered how she might discreetly escape; but then she recalled Yves, and made her way to him instead, feeling a little guilty.

He had been dancing with a series of women, many of whom flatteringly wore his own handiwork, and showed every appearance of enjoying himself, but as Kerry approached him she thought his face a little too flushed, his china-blue eyes alarmingly bright, his smile unusually fixed and brittle. Taking his arm, she steered him out of the crowd to a side table, and he immediately took refuge in his native language as though in a fortress. Taking his hand, she found it was shaking slightly.

"Relax, Yves. You can stop pretending now."

"I don't know what you mean, *chérie.*"

"I mean just that. I know this is a difficult day for you. Everyone speculating about your personal affairs. Everyone partnered, except you. Not much fun, not easy at all."

He shrugged, and dredged up a smile.

"There's one thing worse than having people talk about you, and that's when they don't. I flatter myself that it is my work in which they are interested."

"Speaking of your work, Yves, Zoe says you're wearing yourself to the bone, hardly sleeping four or five hours a night. I want you to take a breather, as soon as possible. Will you spend part of the summer here, with us?"

She saw that the invitation pleased him. But he shook his head.

"I don't think Brandon would want that, Kerry. He distrusts me, I feel, and despises my sexual status."

Candidly, she nodded.

"Yes. He does mistrust you a little, I think, because you were my friend all the time he wasn't, and platonic friendship is an unknown concept to him. He comes from a different world, Yves, and unfortunately it's one in which homosexuality has never been acceptable. But he's married to me now, and going to have to make an effort – after all, you brought us back together! Please be patient, and he'll have come round by summer, I promise you."

He looked at her with a shyness so rare she was amused, and dropped his eyes.

"I wouldn't want to play gooseberry, *chérie*, while the lovers disport themselves. This summer will be special, for you two alone."

"Oh, Yves, don't look at me like that. I want everyone to share in our happiness. Besides, maybe you'll have someone too by then."

But instinct made her doubt it. He had many new friends, but nobody special. Safety in numbers, she thought sadly; it was a shame, a waste of a loving, tactile, generous nature. Having survived one assassination attempt, he was not about to put himself in the firing line again. But the alternative was hardly palatable either.

"Kerry?"

"*Oui, mon vieux?*"

"Are you happy this time? Will it work?"

"Yes, Yves. I think it will. I won't pretend to you that I love Brandon in the same way I did before – I mean, of course I love him, but I'm not so insanely *in* love with him, if you see what I mean. But all these years alone have taught me a lot. I know who I am now."

"It's not that you just can't resist a challenge?"

"No. But I did realise that I was being cowardly. If I didn't open up to him, I never would to anyone. It's still a risk, but a calculated one . . . you can't keep your head in the sand for ever, Yves, you have to come up for air sometime."

And some day, her tone conveyed, you'll have to do it too. Maybe you'll get hurt again, then. But life doesn't come with a guarantee. It's dangerous, but it's meant to be shared. And the scars do heal, even if they never disappear.

For some minutes, they sat in silence. Then, abruptly, he stood up and propelled her onto the dance floor, clasping her hand until they were back in the midst of the festivities, rocking to a Beach Boys number with such verve that people turned to watch. What a mercurial man! His eyes flashed as the music pulsated, igniting with a sudden change of emotional pace, and Kerry looked at him keenly, not at all deceived.

Had things been different, she knew in her heart, Yves was the man she would have married. To this day, she felt everything for him she ever had, and more. But things were as they were, and she was happy with them, hoping protectively that he was too. He gave so much, for so little in return, and his friendship was one of her most cherished possessions. Would remain so all of their lives. Whatever helping hand she could give him in the future, he must know that he didn't even need to ask.

She became aware of Nabdul watching them dance, and blew him a kiss. He glared, but then relented, and blew one back with an arch gesture that reminded her how he too had somehow got under her skin, recharging and revitalising her at a time when new blood had been badly needed. Now, his was a friendship that would have to be redefined. But she would keep it; like Yves he was a part of her life, just as Marianne was part of Brandon's.

Brandon located her at that moment with his eyes, and came towards her so purposefully she felt a little frisson. Surely he wasn't going to cut in on Yves?

It appeared that he was. Possessively, she wondered how to deflect him gracefully, not wanting a discordant note on their wedding day, above all. But Yves sensed him coming, and relinquished her chivalrously, with a last little clutch of her hand.

Sweeping her away so that Yves was lost to her view, Brandon smiled at her so tenderly that she abandoned herself to him, wholly and without regret.

19

It was raining when Kerry and Brandon arrived in Dingle, and it was still raining a week later, the icy Atlantic wind hurling sharp spears against the windows of their rented cottage, obscuring the great purple cliffs and surging seas that crashed against the ancient stone below.

Brandon sighed loudly. "Looks like we'll have to stay in bed again today."

Kerry giggled. "It's frightful. A whole week in bed, all by ourselves . . . what kind of honeymoon do you call this?"

He leered lecherously. "The best kind. The only kind."

They snuggled back down into bed, hugging, cuddling, unable to get enough of each other, not caring if the sun never shone again.

But today, at last, it did. Struggling free of the waterlogged clouds, it prised them reluctantly out of their drowsy burrow, and Kerry sat up wide-eyed, looking round her like a child in its new nursery.

It was a small, simple bedroom, as was the house itself, a beach cottage close to the edge of the cliff on which the wind hammered mercilessly. But they were falling in love with it as they were falling in love with each other, shrieking as their bare feet touched the cold stone floors, racing to light fires in the huge open fireplace, shivering, half-naked, elementally joyful.

There was no doubt about it. The sun was coming out. Kerry looked down and prodded her new, just slightly used husband in the ribs.

"Get up, you lazy lump, and make me my breakfast."

If he was a lousy cook, she was worse, altogether unable to apply rusty French skills to the rudimentary kitchen and restricted local supplies. But they muddled along, glad of having chosen this wild secluded venue over some oasis of Caribbean luxury. Travelling widely as they did, it was wonderfully welcome not to have to venture beyond their own island for a change, and in this westerly outpost they felt purely, profoundly savage.

With a grin, Brandon suddenly leapt up, threw on trousers and a sweater and decamped to the kitchen. She watched him go, and lay back on her pillows with a contented sigh.

The first night had almost been a disaster. Exhausted and apprehensive, disorientated and not a little cold, their attempt to consummate their marriage had fizzled towards fiasco until, incredibly, Brandon had laughed.

"We're out of practice! We need a beginners' manual!"

And suddenly the laughter was relaxing them both, releasing years of denial into hours of passion, affirmed over and over again in the days that followed, and Kerry was astonished to discover the utter difference love made. She had known other men, but she had never known this, every facet of her self interlocking with his, exulting in his arms. For what felt like eternity they scarcely left their bed, forgetting the whole world, intently learning to know each other, finding in their glorious intimacy the wordless sanctity of sex. How much they had been missing, all this time! More than once they wept over it, but it had been worth waiting for.

He brought her brunch, and she smiled lazily up at him.

"Scrambled eggs again? I'll have you know I'm used to finer things."

"I'll have you know I am too. But they never tasted as good. My palate has been magically cleansed."

So, she thought had hers; she had never felt so hungry in her life. Devouring the eggs, they decided on a long walk afterwards, if only so that they could say they had seen something of the Dingle peninsula in the course of three whole weeks.

They muffled up and set off into the teeth of a strong, invigorating wind. Brandon worried that Kerry would be blown clear off the cliff, so fragile did she look even in her thick sweater and knotted scarf, clumping valiantly through the bedraggled grass in brown leather boots. It was how he liked her best, with her hair blowing free of its plait, her hands gloved, her face bright and happy in the crystal-cold air.

"Have I told you lately how much I love you, Kerry?"

"Not for an hour or more. I was getting worried."

"I really do, Kerry. More and more every minute. If I were to die today, I would die a very happy man."

"Brandon! Don't say such things! You and I are going to live to be old and ancient together, as old as Gallarus oratory."

The medieval monks' cell was a captivating sight when they reached it, after a long brisk march across the heathery fields and narrow by-roads. Like thousands of others over the centuries, they marvelled at how such poor, simple monks could build an edifice of such perfect symmetry, twelve hundred years before, with their bare hands. Each stone interlinked with the next, imbued with the patina of the land around it, so that although the tiny cell looked grey from a distance, it was on closer sight speckled with the fuschia of the hedges, the blues and greens of the ocean, the bright orange of early montbretia, the mauve of the hillsides and the cream of the clouds.

They sat down on a wide flat stone, and looked at it for a long time.

"It's a cell, Kerry. But look, it has a window, and a door. People could come and go as they pleased. The men who lived here were freer than I've ever been in my whole life, up to now."

She was curious.

"Didn't you ever try to break free? After the baby died, I mean?"

"No. Not then. I was frozen with the pain, walled up in it. I could barely get through from one end of a day to the other. The only way to deal with losing Julie, and losing you, was to shut myself up where nobody else could reach me. Not even Marianne."

"Oh, Brandon . . . isn't it strange, how little happiness our children have brought any of us? Your daughter, my son, Brian's unborn . . . they all cost us our marriages. And yet we risked another marriage, and now I want another child. Is that very perverse?"

He considered.

"Yes. Perhaps. But that's human nature. I want another child too, Kerry. Only this time let's promise each other that our children will bring their parents together, not drive them apart?"

"Yes. I think the timing is better now, Brandon. If you'll talk more, I'll listen more. I know I was defensive before, and abrasive, dealing with my own pain. But I'm a nicer person now, really I am!"

Laughing, he grabbed at her.

"You're delicious. And I'm crazy about you."

"You must be altogether insane to have married me . . . but since you have, I've decided to be a wonderful wife. My mother always regarded my father as the key to the safe, but you're the key to the prison I was locked into. I feel so – so liberated!"

Even as she said it, Kerry felt the difference between her former life and the flood of release she was experiencing now. Tightly, she gripped Brandon's arm and looked into his face, searching his eyes between the flying strands of windblown hair.

"Marriage won't just change the course of our lives, will it, Brandon? It'll change the texture of them too. The whole feel of everything is different, already. I think we were only half alive before."

"And didn't even realise it. We have a lot of living to catch up on."

For a moment, she hesitated, but then plunged on.

"You know, Brandon, I – well, there were several reasons why I decided to marry you. I can't say love was the only one. But I can honestly say that I do love you, and will give it every chance to take precedence in the future. It'll take time, but it will grow – is growing, even now."

He freed his arm from hers and put it round her shoulder, pulling her face into his sweater, burying his other hand in her hair.

"I know that, Kerry. I'm well aware of all the things you

expect from me, and that some of them have very little to do with romance. But I won't disappoint you in any of them. There's nothing you need be frightened of. You can trust me this time, and rely on me."

She nuzzled closer into him, feeling like the survivor of a shipwreck. So many people *had* been shipwrecked around this treacherous coast! It was where the Spanish Armada had foundered, and the *Lusitania*, scattering bodies up on the bleak salty beaches, and some living people too, who had never expected to sight shore again.

"I will try to trust you, Brandon. But you must trust me, too. I've lived alone for many years, and built up a very close circle of friends – people I want you to like now, for all our sakes."

He knew what she meant, and grimaced stoically.

"Yes. I will work at it. Whatever it takes to make a success of this marriage, you have my word I'll try everything. You have no idea how much you mean to me, Kerry."

She lifted her head, and looked up at him in a way he found irresistible.

"Do I, Brandon? Really?"

It amazed him that she was not sure of it, even now.

"You must believe me, darling. Isn't there any way I can make you?"

Suddenly, she sparkled up at him.

"Yes, there is. You can get me pregnant. I'd like a daughter, this time."

Her mind flew after the word as she uttered it, but could not retrieve it. Oh, Julie! Was he hurt? But he didn't flinch.

"It will be an honour and a pleasure! I'll do it right now, if you like. Any particular size, shape or colour?"

They both laughed, and Brandon was very glad he could give his wife what she wanted at last, without counting the cost.

The simple honeymoon meandered into infinity as they walked and talked, explored and sailed whenever the lurching seas permitted. A small yacht was acquired, in which they were pursued by friendly dolphins, as dark and exuberant as the ocean itself, and once or twice they almost capsized in heavy squalls. But the terror was a thrill, honing every nerve as they made love afterwards with blazing abandon. Late every night they lay by the fire when all their senses were satisfied, wrapped in blankets, sipping red wine, utterly united in mind and heart. The solitude was complete, unbroken by any intrusion, slipping through their fingers until, one day, it was all gone.

"We haven't even taken a photograph, Brandon. We'll have nothing to remind us of our honeymoon."

"We'll have a baby, if any credit is given for effort."

"I hope it's a friendlier specimen than your previous creations."

"Don't let the boys bother you, Kerry. I'm sorry they haven't made more progress, after you've tried so hard. But Harry is genuinely shy, and Chris is as much of a mystery to me as he is to you."

Reluctantly, they slung their possessions into suitcases and prepared to depart in the old, restored Mercedes. But when Kerry went outside, it was gone.

"Jesus, someone's stolen my car!"

"No they haven't. I sent it back to Kildare last night with the guy who loaned us the boat. He's coming back by train."

"What? You gave him my Mercedes? But why? How are we going to get home?"

"Come with me."

He picked up the bags and led her round to the back of the cottage, over a stone wall and into a field where she gasped: a helicopter stood on the grass, a pilot waiting at its controls.

"I thought this would be a quicker way for you to get to race meets, Kerry, and for me to get to Hollyvaun across that bloody mountain."

"This is yours? Ours?"

"Yes. In you get."

She was thrilled. Other trainers did use this form of transport now, quite commonly, but something in her had always quailed from such a large expenditure. Ecstatically, she kissed Brandon as it took off.

"Could we do a little detour?"

"Sure. Where do you want to go?"

"To my grandmother's farm, in Tipperary. Other people own it now, but I'd love to see it. Daddy used to take me there in the summers, when I was a child . . . he'd want to know it was being properly maintained."

They reached it in twenty minutes, hovering low over herds of fat cows and placidly grazing sheep, red barns and serried rows of crops.

"Oh, look – I can even see the water trough I used to push Brian into! God, Daddy would be delighted. Everything looks so prosperous."

And even more delighted, Brandon thought, if he could see Ashamber. They lifted up and flew on to Kildare, where Kerry's thoughts were already turning to the horses from which she would start her own, new blood lines.

Under the soughing ash trees, they cantered free in the fields with several others, but she pressed her nose to the window and was able to tell immediately which was which.

"I can't wait to get at them!"

"Don't you mean you can't wait to get at me?"

Tickled with the success of both his gifts to her, he hugged her to him, and she responded eagerly, her heart impaling itself on him as if on barbed wire. To unhook it now, she thought, would be more painful than could ever be worthwhile.

And then a curiosity distracted her.

"Have they done it, do you think? Brian and Zoe? Has she got him interested? Into bed, yet?"

Brandon grinned as he thought of Zoe, a determined little pixie in pursuit of her quarry.

"Like a lamb to the slaughter, I should imagine."

Moments later Kerry was swooping on Helen and Bob, levitating with impatience to see her friend, her brother and her new horses. Cara would have the vet's report on them by now, and his prognosis for breeding strategy.

"Where is Cara, Helen? And where's Brian, Zoe?"

Helen hesitated. To spoil this happy homecoming would be a shame. But Kerry would pummel all the news out of her anyway. She took a deep breath, and instantly Kerry felt a clench in her gut, a prickle of apprehension as if someone were creeping up on her.

"What is it? What's wrong?"

"They've gone, Kerry. Brian and Zoe, I mean. To New York."

"New *York*? But Zoe never goes there. Is it her parents? What?"

"It's the police. They've caught the man who – who."

"But that's wonderful! After all this time? Incredible."

"Yes. But they want her to attend the trial and give evidence. She was terribly upset when they told her she'd have to do that. The man is an habitual offender, and it seems the trial could be most unpleasant."

"Oh. I see. So that's why Brian went too?"

"Yes. But she was in tears before he finally volunteered. To be frank, Kerry, they didn't hit it off too well in your absence."

"Why not? What happened?"

"I don't honestly know. At first everything seemed fine. But then there was a chill, they started avoiding each other . . . I didn't like to pry. Anyway, she left her parents' number for you to call her at."

"Dammit. I should have been here when she needed me."

"It's just as well you weren't. Murray Raymond sold Cushla last week."

"What – after he said it wasn't for sale, to anyone, at any price! I'll have his brains for breakfast, the fucking bastard."

Helen winced. Matrimony, clearly, wasn't quite the mellowing influence she had hoped. Kerry stormed off, Lir at her heels, and both Brandon and Helen jumped as they heard the front door slam behind her. In the hallway, Killian stared open-mouthed, wondering what he had done that his mother hadn't even said hello to him.

"I don't care what age he is, Brandon. He asked for it and by Christ he got it. I'm not taking that kind of crap from anyone."

"Calm down, Kerry. Here, let me soap your shoulders."

Kerry snatched up the soap from the water in which she

was bathing and flung it vehemently at Andrew Austin's
rag-rolled wall.

"Nabdul needed that fucking farm, Brandon! It was perfect
for him. If Raymond wouldn't sell it to him, then he should at
least have had the decency not to sell it to anyone else. It was
a deliberate insult, just because Nabdul's an Arab."

"Kerry, there could be a million reasons why he changed
his mind."

"He couldn't give me even one."

"Well, why would he, when you went for him head-on like
that? He's an old man, Kerry, who presumably has his pride
like all that generation. They don't respond well to being
browbeaten by a woman. You should have let me go."

Brandon sighed as he got up off the side of the bath,
removed his robe and joined her in the foaming water. Used
as she was to doing everything for herself, Kerry had never
even thought to consult him, and now she had made an
enemy for life. Maybe several. Sympathy would be on the
old man's side.

Already, he could see that life with this woman would
never be easy. Always, he would have to compete for her
attention. But he had to admit it beat the dinner-party circuit
any day, even now when she was prickling like a hedgehog.
Thoughtfully, he began to massage the back of her neck.

"Promise me something, Kerry?"

"That I'll apologise? Hah. If anyone's doing any apologising, it'll be that old toad, to Nabdul."

"No. Never mind that, the damage is done. I just want you
to promise that in future we won't ever talk business up here,
in the bathroom or bedroom?"

She pouted sulkily.

"Oh, all right. But first thing in the morning, I'm going
to get on to the estate agent and find somewhere else for
Nabdul."

Damnation, Brandon thought with sudden fury, is this
wretched Nabdul never going to go away and leave me
alone with her? He's a lecher and a menace, and already
he's ruining our first night at home together. Under his
hands, her muscles were tense.

"Brandon, why do you suppose Brian and Zoe didn't get on?"

"Oh, he's a slow burner, that's all. Maybe Zoe rushed him. Or maybe he's a bit thrown by me. Thinks I'll take Killian away from him, usurp the child's affections."

"And will you?"

"To some extent, I'm afraid I will. I intend to be a proper, full-time father to that boy."

Kerry was glad to hear it. Now Helen could stop nagging, the burden would be shared . . . but then, Brandon would share every burden. What a change, to have someone who cared, undertook responsibility and dealt with things! Of course, Helen always had . . . but Helen couldn't soap her back like this, couldn't massage her preoccupations away. Sliding down into the water, closing her eyes, she left Brandon to do whatever he judged best.

Next day, it was common knowledge that Kerry Laraghy had given Murray Raymond an almighty roasting, and all over the village hearts hardened against such monstrous cruelty. The elderly man might have had a seizure, a heart attack, anything. And all because he had sold the land he was no longer able to manage. Kerry had left him for dead, rumour went, beside herself with rage on behalf of her foreign friend, seething that her acquisitive plans had been thwarted.

But why should Murray sell to her, so that she could install this Arab in their midst? He was a blow-in, and an arrogant one at that, who thought money could buy everything. Well, it hadn't bought Cushla, and now they would see to it that it didn't buy anywhere else in the locality either.

Kerry heard the gossip, and was disconcerted.

"Now they'll all clam up, Brandon, and Nabdul will never find a place. Can't they see what business he'd bring, what employment? Why must they be so pigheaded?"

He smiled wryly.

"It must be something in the water, dear. Tell you what. Why don't you take those emeralds Nabdul once gave you and sell them, donate the proceeds to some local charity? I'm sure that would help."

"I'll do no such thing. That jewellery belonged to Nabdul's mother. You just don't want me to wear it, do you? I'm beginning to think even *you* are jealous of him."

There was a grain of truth in what she said, but Brandon had his pride too, and did not acknowledge it. Instead, he spent the evening conscientiously helping Killian with his homework, and Kerry shut herself into the library for a long chat with Zoe. On the other end of the line, three thousand miles away, Zoe sounded desperate.

"It's going to go on for weeks and weeks, Kerry. There's any amount of evidence to be called before mine. Yves will be left on his own at the salon and God only knows what mess he'll make of it. Our new collection will be late, I have reporters chasing me everywhere, Brian is like a bag of cats, I haven't even got a lawyer . . ."

"Zoe, get a grip. Now, first, why is Brian a bag of cats?"

"Because he should be in Paris, of course, it's a terrible delay, I can't possibly ask him to stay here till I'm called."

"You tell him I said he's to stay. Will I come over, too?"

"No, you have enough on your hands where you are. Richard and Carla will look after me, and I'll send Brian back to Paris."

"Zoe, it's not just the salon, is it? What's the real reason you want to get rid of Brian?"

"It's – that – oh, God, Kerry, I've made the most terrible mistake. The most appalling fool of myself."

"Why? How?"

"I told him how I feel about him. Told him how long I've been in love with him. We were getting on so well together at Ashamber, we drank a lot of wine one night and somehow everything just came pouring out . . . but he looked at me like a zombie, Kerry. It meant nothing to him, nothing at all. I was so humiliated, and now I've got this public humiliation coming too, the whole thing is horrible."

"Listen, Zoe. Forget Brian for now. Just concentrate on getting through this trial first, and we'll worry about him later. Think how great you're going to feel when that guy is sentenced – and how much safer you'll have made your native city for every other woman in it. As for lawyers, ask your dad's advice, and take it."

Despite her distress, Zoe had to smile wanly at her friend's prim tone. Since when had Kerry been so hot about taking anyone's advice?

"Has marriage made a new woman of you already, Mrs Lawrence?"

"Hmph. Hardly a new one, Zoe, but maybe a slightly better one."

"The honeymoon went well, then?"

"You could put it that way, yes."

From Singapore to Paris, it was a very long flight. Lucienne de Veurlay-Laraghy sat listlessly in her first-class seat, uninterested in the film, in the food, in any of the airline's numerous diversions. Over and over again, she riffled through the sheaf of photographs in her hand: Mathieu at the Batu caves, Mathieu on Clifford Pier, Mathieu and herself beside the statue of Sir Stamford Raffles. Mathieu in Change Alley, sweating in the gelatinous heat. Fair-haired, good humoured, a stocky successful man who had so considerately taken her on this perfect holiday.

A perfect man. A perfect holiday. A perfect waste of time.

Now that her divorce was final, Lu was a free woman, and a relatively wealthy one. Not as wealthy as she should have been, and would have been if any justice had prevailed. But it had not, and there was no use in crying over spilt milk. How much more productive to go on this holiday instead, with a man whose bachelor days were certainly over, at forty years of age. She was thirty-two herself, and in something of a hurry; much older, and it would be too late. To marry Mathieu would be to accept defeat, in one way, an acknowledgement that Brian was gone for ever. But in another, it would be a triumph, and one that Brian would get to hear about.

But now, the chance was gone, and Mathieu with it. Not only turning down her proposal, he had actually laughed at it. Next time, he said, he would like to be the one to do the asking. But there would be no next time. Pride permitted no such second chance, no prolongation of a humiliating test of endurance, and Lu regretted losing him as bitterly as she regretted having so precipitately asked him. Within hours of the ignominious event, she had boarded this flight, alone.

He was right, perhaps, when he said it was too much, too soon. They had known each other only three months. But they were well suited, agreed on the priority of their careers, agreed on not wanting children – and what a coup it would have been, the capture of Mathieu Clérand! Far and away the most highly regarded commodities trader on the Paris Bourse, Mathieu was not a man to leave on ice for very long, and why should a woman not, in 1982, take the initiative? Lu had thought he would admire her decisiveness. But it had repelled him and left her baffled, undermined.

Not normally given to introspection, she found herself forced to study her behaviour as the plane flew on, and see a certain pattern. A certain tendency to take control of things – control them, and destroy them?

But such important matters could not be left to chance, and marriage was so important. A woman needed its status, its social cachet, its protection. Bad enough to lose her first husband, and his inheritance – but to lose Mathieu as well, already . . . ! It was unendurable. And now, there was no way to get him back. He was gone, as surely as Brian was gone. Like the Singapore river, flowing inexorably out into the Great China Sea in the photographs, they swept away from her and left her stranded.

Mathieu she regretted, and badly. But at least she had not been in love with him. Fond, yes, but in a way that bore no resemblance to what she had known with Brian . . . Brian! Where was he now? What was he doing? She was consumed with curiosity, impotent and imprisoned as the jet sailed silently, efficiently, on its course through the ice-blue sky. Oh, Brian. *Brian.*

Two years now, and not one single word, after all she had done for him, all they had built up and shared together. That he could be cold did not surprise her, but such perfect callousness left her hollow with horror. Like the blue void outside, it was breathtaking, terrifying, awesome in its remote nothingness.

As soon as she landed she took a taxi home to her new apartment, that was not home at all. A handsome building, elegantly furnished, she felt eerily alien in it, oddly lost. Tired and unprecedentedly dishevelled, she lay down in her bedroom and tried to sleep, but couldn't. Outside, it was broad daylight, the traffic was noisy, the city teeming with tourists and shoppers all perfectly, blithely oblivious of her existence. Getting up again, she summoned Tui, the Vietnamese maid, to unpack her bags and make some tea.

Tui glided away to do as she was bidden, and in due course Lu sat cupping the comforting clear green liquid in its china bowl, inhaling its aromatic steam. Wrapped in a new satin kimono from Singapore, she sat staring vacantly out at the Eiffel Tower, noticing for the first time the ugliness of its girders. The kimono was pale lemon, and suited her blonde complexion very well, but inside it Lu was a shivering bundle of nerves.

Fighting a losing battle with mounting panic, she felt it invade all her senses, disarming them one by one until she succumbed to a force greater than any she had ever known, and no longer even beat her gilded wings against the bars of her beautiful cage. It was some time before Tui returned, to find her employer lying limp on the floor, the tea spilling unheeded into the carpet, not an eyelash fluttering in the glazed porcelain face.

Richard and Carla Zimner were ecstatic to have their daughter back in New York, regardless of the gruesome ordeal she faced, and a final verdict that was by no means a *fait accompli*. The quiet, clean-shaven, accused man was the nephew of an archbishop who had engaged the most devious lawyers money could buy, and already their loquaciousness was tearing Zoe's working year to tatters. But her parents were determined it would not tear her testimony to shreds, and meanwhile rejoiced that she looked so well, resilient and reasonably optimistic.

"Pity the same can't be said for that guy with her."

Richard glowered into his whiskey as he waited for his daughter and her companion to dress for dinner, and even Carla could not summon enthusiasm.

"Who'd ever imagine Kerry Laraghy would have such a brother? She was a wild, headstrong girl, but I liked her . . . often happens with twins, I'm told. Opposite sides of the one coin. Try to be civil to him, Richard. Maybe still waters run deep – Zoe must think so, anyway."

The older couple did what they could to cheer up the younger as the trial progressed, but in the moist, mounting summer heat even Zoe began to wilt under the strain. Initially, she was not required to speak at all, but it was agonising enough to have to sit listening to the evidence of other young women who had suffered similar injuries to her own; seven of them, in the years since the night on the beach on Long Island.

Her anger ran riot.

"Nobody ever helped! That's the worst of it! You've heard all those people testify, Dad, about how they heard screams and scuffles, you'll hear Chloe admit to the same thing when she's called. How can people do it? Just stand there and do nothing when somebody is being attacked, maybe murdered? What kind of hellish city is this anyway?"

"It's not just this one, Zoe. All big cities are like that now. People are afraid to interfere."

"Huh. I wouldn't let a dog suffer like that, if I heard somebody kicking it."

"No. You wouldn't and I wouldn't. But most people would, and do. That's the way the world is going, Zoe. It's only if and when people are attacked themselves that they change their tune."

"It's disgusting. I'm more horrified to know that Chloe ignored the whole thing than I am to know who did it, or how often he did it."

It was the second week in June before she was called, externally composed and trembling inwardly, to relate the events of the night she met Joe Sumner. She knew how hard it would be, her lawyer had schooled her for weeks in every detail, but as she mounted the witness stand in the packed courtroom she was dazed by the wave of palpable antipathy that hit her from all directions at once.

Near the front, the archbishop sat frostily surveying her, daring her to convince anyone that his nephew had touched her, daring the jury to believe it, believe a hysterical woman like her. And she *was* almost overcome with hysteria as she looked at the strangers to whom she was expected to reveal the most explicit and intimate details of her life, at a time when even she, herself, had not found it salubrious.

But then she saw her parents, radiating support across the room, and Daniel who had come all the way from Carmel to be with her, and Brian who had stayed on all these weeks. In her right hand, she clutched a tiny teddy bear, thrown to her by one of the hundreds of women on the street outside, rape victims themselves whose own assailants, she supposed, had never been brought to trial. Hers finally had; and for their sakes as well as her own she was going to nail him, make him pay as she, and they, had all paid.

But ultimately she was alone. Only she could achieve anything now, it was up to her to overpower the expressionless man who sat with his defence lawyers, aloof and apparently indifferent. Zoe had never seen him clearly before and was staggered by his ordinariness, his air of perfect normality, as if he were a salesman who'd sold her a Hoover or a lawnmower that had not performed satisfactorily.

She swore on the Bible, answered the first preliminary questions and began to recount her experience in a low, calm tone, remembering everything her lawyer had advised, everything that had been chiselled out of her memory since first they had begun to work the blurred jumble of events into logical, watertight sequence. It took fully twenty minutes to get back to that night on the beach, and another twenty to get through it, but by the time she finished she was no longer aware of anything except her own reborn pain, fear, and fury.

There was a silence. The Sumner lawyer approached her for cross-questioning.

"We are to understand then, Miss Zimner, that you had been drinking on the night in question?"

"Yes. Two Bellinis, and then something else given me by this – this person. I think it may have been gin."

"So you had accepted quite a lot to drink, a mixture of alcohol?"

"Yes."

It all came out; first the booze, then the drugs, the voracious appetite for food, every terrible detail that the reporters scribbled busily into their ruled notebooks.

"And prior to this, ah, alleged seduction, Miss Zimner, do you claim to have been a virgin?"

"I make no claims to anything."

"Were you, then, a virgin?"

"No." Soon, she thought, this law must change. He has no right to ask.

"Ah. But you were not a married woman either?"

"No. I was not married."

"Ah."

And so it went on, until an impartial onlooker might have thought Zoe a sex-crazed manic alcoholic, depraved and deranged, driven from childhood into a web of determined dissolution. But Zoe didn't waver, outwardly. Sumner's other victims had done enough crying: he wasn't worth one more tear, from anyone. She caught Daniel's eye, and held onto it tightly.

Dear Daniel, who was so much changed since their teenage days as callow sweethearts together in Paris. He had matured beyond recognition, into a bespectacled professor with an air of considerable authority, no longer shy at all. His rumpled suit and receding hairline were, she thought, somehow endearing, and she felt his whole being full of strength for her. She continued to gravitate to him as the archbishop's money began to talk, loudly and at length.

"Your parents did not marry, then, until you were eight years old?"

"No. They were of mixed religion, and . . ."

Her lawyer objected, and she got no further, frustrated that she could not tell the court, and particularly the archbishop, that her parents were the kind of people money couldn't buy. Gripping the teddy tightly, she forced her attention onto the next question, and the next, until it felt as if she had been interrogated for hours, days, weeks. But finally it was over, and she was permitted to step down, exhausted.

"Court is adjourned for lunch. Reconvention is at two o'clock."

Instantly Richard gathered his party and led them away to a pizza joint where, he hoped, the press would not think to follow them. Apart from Zoe and her parents, there was Brian, Daniel, and her lawyer Carol Silverstein, all full of praise for her performance.

"You were wonderful! Good girl! With luck, it's all over now. We should have a verdict this afternoon."

Awkwardly, conversation lapsed, everyone still shocked and recoiling from the dreadful details she had revealed, aspects of the physical and psychological pain previously unknown even to her parents.

Their sympathy was immense, Daniel so outraged that he promised retribution even if the man were acquitted, and had to be restrained by Carol from outlining its precise and irreparable nature. Only Brian said nothing, his head bent over a slice of pepperoni pizza, and Zoe was conscious as she looked at him of sudden irritation. Normally, it was this very quietness in him she loved, this quality of detached dreaminess, but right now she wanted to take the slice of pizza and slap his face with it. Everyone else was so horrified, so traumatised by her account of events: didn't he care, at all? Hadn't he even been listening?

He gave no indication that he had, and briefly she wished Yves were there instead, to cheer and cajole her out of her misery with his irreverent comments and caring nature. But when they returned to the courthouse, the crowd of women was still there, and she was buoyed by their cries of encouragement as she went in. Total strangers, all of them, but so much on her side. Maybe New York was not so heartless, so anonymous, after all.

As expected, the case was concluded within minutes, and after summation the jury retired to consider its verdict. Fingering his ruby ring, the archbishop smiled reassuringly at his nephew, who also had his supporters on the street outside, men and women who believed that nobody from such a family could be guilty of such a crime – or if he were, then Zoe and her sex had seduced him into it.

The jury's deliberations went on for over two hours. Perspiring and claustrophobic, Zoe had to go outside several times for air, but there was nowhere she could be alone. When finally Richard came to fetch her, her legs were so shaky she could barely walk.

"Come on, Zoe. You want to see him sentenced, don't you?"

She was no longer sure what she wanted, other than escape. But, when she returned, she was glad she had.

"To be detained in a place of penal correction for seven years, on the first count; for five years, on the second count . . ."

Thirty years, in all. She looked at the face of the man who had ruined her life and saw no change in it; no regret, no remorse, no trace of any emotion. Standing, he listened impassively to the judge; but she felt the ground fade from under her own feet.

"Brian, we went out to dinner last night, and tomorrow we have a plane to catch. I'd really rather have an early night if you don't mind."

"It will be early, if you like. But I want to talk to you, Zoe, just the two of us without your parents. I've already booked a table at the Four Seasons. Do come, please."

Once, Zoe would have exulted at the prospect. But not now. Drained by the rigours of the trial and by the celebrations that attended its outcome, she could only gaze wearily at Brian and wonder what it was he might, belatedly, have to say for himself. But he had stuck around for six weeks, she supposed: it would be churlish to refuse, apathetic as she felt.

But Brian had discovered that apathy too, and was excruciatingly uncomfortable in it. Faint and chill, he had sensed it from the moment they left Ireland, three days after Zoe's embarrassing outpourings. Kerry's wedding had gone to her head, she had said some extraordinary things, and now she was as obviously constrained as he was himself. If he let it go on, they would no longer be able to work together.

He left her to shower and change, and was taken aback when she reappeared, refreshed and marginally revived. Wearing an ensemble chosen by Carla, he had never seen the dark, dimpled little thing look so appealing, in a tiny fitted dress of cerise silk with a black leather belt, long dangling earrings and several silver bracelets that tinkled as she walked. She misunderstood his surprise.

"Too much? Should I lose the bracelets?"

"No, no. They're lovely."

"I got them in Senegal, donkey's years ago. I'm still fond of them."

The whole look was novel and eye-catching; but Brian couldn't catch her eye at all as they sat down at the Four Seasons and waded through their gazpacho as if it were a moat. Loosening his tie, fiddling with his cutlery, clearing his throat, he dived suddenly, desperately, straight to the point.

"Zoe, we're old friends, and we have to talk."

"About what?"

"About us."

Her heart lurched until she realised he meant "us" in the business sense.

"Yes. We've lost a lot of time. We're going to have to work round the clock when we get back."

Relieved, he swallowed hard.

"You – you are coming back, then? I was afraid you might – not."

She regarded him evenly.

"Look, Brian. I'm sorry about what happened, and at first I was embarrassed about it. But it's over and done with now, and quite frankly that may well be for the best. It's not that I don't appreciate your having stayed here with me all this time, but – well, you didn't seem nearly so concerned as everyone else. Even Daniel was more supportive, and I haven't seen him for years. I've come to the conclusion that you may not be quite the person I used to think you were. But TLZ is my work and my life just as much as it is yours, and I have no intention of quitting just because of a – a temporary misunderstanding."

"No. Of course not. I'm glad you see it in that light. I don't want you to feel bad, Zoe. I may not be able to reciprocate your feelings, but I do value you as a partner, and as a friend."

Why her patience snapped at that precise moment, she never knew. But it did.

"A friend? Brian, you don't know the meaning of the word."

He flushed furiously, waited till the waiter served his steak and her Caesar salad, and tried to speak again.

"What?"

"Oh, don't croak at me pathetically like that. I meant exactly what I said. I know you only came here because of the way Helen was looking at you, and only stayed because Kerry insisted. But you were no more use than a rag doll, all the time the trial was going on – just as you were no use to your sister when she was in difficulty in Senegal. You treated Yves badly and you treated Lu badly. You set such high standards for everyone else, Brian, it's a great pity you never follow them yourself."

"But I – I gave Lu a lot of money, and Yves too, and I offered it to Kerry, only she wouldn't take it."

"Correction. The judge gave Lu what money was rightfully hers. You paid Yves what he was worth. And you tried to buy Kerry back because you wanted Killian."

"Zoe, that's not true—"

"Yes it is true. I don't know where you get it from, Brian, but you seem to think money is far more important than people. When did you last call Lu, for instance, and ask her how she is? She could be ill, for all you know, or have God knows what problems . . . but heaven forbid your pride should ever permit you to pick up a phone, even to your own wife."

"Ex-wife . . . Zoe, she aborted our baby!"

"So, you don't have a baby – or now a wife either, or anyone. I don't have a baby either, Brian, much as I'd like one, but I just have to get on with my life and make the

best of it. We all have our crosses, but you're the only one
who keeps dragging yours round with you, up hill and down
dale, and I for one am sick of it."

Astonished, he fell silent, burning with a slow sense of
shame. Over the years since Zoe first came to France, he had
never really thought of her as a woman at all, and certainly
not that her lack of fertility was a source of sorrow to her.

But of course it must be. And now, even with Lu flaunting
and spurning maternity in her face, she could feel concern for
the woman – while he, as she said, had never once spoken to
Lu, punishing her as he punished everyone. He *had* done it to
Kerry, too, and Yves, and even harboured negative thoughts
of Brandon. What on earth was wrong with him?

Now that he was forced to think about it, there was
hardly anyone he hadn't alienated – and hardly anyone he
hadn't had to make amends to either, at considerable cost.
Would Zoe be next? Dear God.

The waiter came with a dessert menu, and he was on the
point of ordering some consoling delicacy, until he saw her
shake her head. The diet, of course. She never discussed
it, but it must be hell. Abruptly, he gave the menu back
and ordered black coffee for them both, so wrenched with
shock and guilt his voice shook. Across the table, he edged
his hand tentatively towards hers.

"I – Zoe, I hardly know what to say, except that you're
right. I can't help the way I behave. It's just my nature."

"Bullshit. You can help it. You could give Yves a break
once in a while, you could take Lu out to lunch once in a
while, you could even ask me how I feel."

"How do you feel, then? I never knew you wanted a baby."

"No. Because you never asked. If you ever had, you'd
know that I feel bloody miserable more often than not. My
twenties are over, Brian, and I'll never get that time back
– the time in which women are supposed to have fun, and
dates, and babies. All I ever had was nightmares about being
raped, and a lot of horrible surgery, and people making
jokes about the way I looked."

"Well, you look great now."

"Yes – and still, the first man I approach turns me down

flat. You didn't have to accept, Brian, but you didn't have to be quite so insensitive either."

Oh, God. He'd never even thought of that aspect. Of the courage it must have taken, nor of the blow to her fragile self-esteem. Only of himself.

"It wasn't that I didn't want you, Zoe. It was that I didn't want anyone."

"Well, then, that's that. You don't want anyone and I can't have anyone."

Her face puckered, and he thought, cringing, that she was going to cry. But instead, she was laughing, giggling like a little girl.

"Who's going to push our wheelchairs when we're old, do you think? Will Yves push mine, or you push his, or will we take turns on Tuesdays?"

Old. *Old?*

"But we're only in our thirties, we have years ahead of us . . ."

Sharply, she sobered up.

"Right. So let's make the most of them. I plan to, anyhow. You can do whatever you goddamn like."

It dawned on him that he had no idea what he would do, no plan of any kind. Nobody even close enough to discuss it with. No home in which to think it over.

"Zoe, when is Yves moving out of your apartment?"

"I don't know – whenever he clears the last of his debts, I guess. Why?"

"Well, I was just thinking . . . how nice it would be . . . to have some company."

She pierced him with a very pointed look.

"Oh, no, Brian. No way. Your company we can do without. *I* can do without, even after Yves goes, if he ever does. I plan to look forward, not back."

He deserved that, he supposed.

"Well then – would you maybe just let me come round to dinner, now and then?"

His brown eyes were so bleak, she almost felt sorry for him. Might have, if she didn't know who he was still chiefly thinking of.

"Tell you what. I'll supply the food, but you can cook it. Better still, you can take me out to a few more decent restaurants like this one – and Yves too, by way of proper chaperone."

He had to smile.

"You drive a hard bargain, Zoe."

"Yeah. I have this great role model. Also Lu's new address."

New? He didn't even know she'd moved.

Far out to the west of the mackerel sky, the sinking sun flung the last of the late light up the fields, rimming each cloud with rose and gold and green as it dipped down under the silent amber horizon. It was late July, and warm even after nine in the evening. Whistling up the dogs, Kerry threw a sweater round her shoulders and set off in no particular direction, as pleased as not to be alone. In the library window, Chris and Killian sat silhouetted over a low table, playing chess. The little boy would win, as he usually did; since the start of the summer holidays Chris had developed a surprisingly fraternal affinity with him, taking him riding and fishing, sailing and cycling, filling up his days so busily that Kerry rarely saw her son at all.

A week hence, Chris was going once more to Spain, to the Basque region this time, and since June Harry had been in Virginia with his mother. Killian would be bereft, she supposed, but meanwhile he was permitted to beat Chris at chess as often as he liked, so that even Brandon wondered at his son's magnanimity, which extended thus far and no further. He had spoken to his son about his indifferent treatment of his wife, but Chris remained as politely aloof as if they were two strangers waiting for different trains at a railway station.

She didn't want to think about Chris. She wanted to savour this still, beautiful evening, and think about the stud farm that had finally been found for Nabdul. Two miles from Ashamber, it was small and picturesque, with stabling for only twenty horses, and acres of potential. Unfit for human habitation by Nabdul's standards, the dilapidated farmhouse was being done over by yet another of Andrew Austin's teams of workmen. That was not a problem, but she foresaw that staffing it thereafter would be. Nabdul had outbid four local buyers at auction, and already graffiti had been daubed on its boundary walls, minor vandalism been perpetrated on the gates and fencing.

Nobody had been caught in the act, and nobody ever would. In time, a hostile truce would settle, but anyone taking a job there would find himself drinking alone in the pubs at night, and even Feargal Corrigan the vet expressed reservations about the consequences of visiting there. Nabdul would have to import his own personnel, from Britain or Kutari or wherever else he could find them: not for nothing had the word "boycott" been invented in Ireland. But Kerry saw the impact new Arab stock would have on the Irish racing scene, and her mind was made up that Nabdul should, in spite of everything, enjoy himself. In a year or two – or three or four – they would clear this hurdle, and meanwhile she was heartened by her friend's dogged investment.

Skirting round the southern edges of her estate, she found herself making for the dark coppery thicket where Timothy Laraghy lay buried, thinking contentedly that Brandon would probably be home by the time she got back. After three months, she had not yet conceived, but in a way that was not a disappointment. Adjusting to marriage was a pleasure she had not expected, bringing as it did new discoveries every day. Much of the time, Brandon was away in London or Hollyvaun, but she was touched to find that he invariably brought her back some small gift, maybe only a book or a cassette or some jokey item that made her laugh, and always an armful of flowers.

He thought of her constantly, and she found herself doing the same thing, often at the most inconvenient moments so that she lost the thread of conferences with Helen or Cara, and was teased for a romantic idiot. But she was happy in her idiocy, and didn't care who made fun of her. In turn, she teased her brother, who had rented a house near Zoe's in the Marais, and for some inexplicable reason was learning to cook.

"Get a housekeeper," she advised, convulsed at the thought of Brian in an apron, juggling a lot of burning pots and pans. He retorted that men were liberated creatures these days, expected to shift for themselves, and she left him to it, confident that the experiment would soon come to a sticky end.

Timothy's grave, when she came to it, was a peaceful oasis, cleared now of the weeds and brambles that proliferated in the damp undergrowth. What it was that drew her here she hardly knew, but for nearly twenty minutes she stood quietly communing with the man, updating him on events, promising him a new descendant for 1983, wishing she had some way of putting a face to his name. Then, feeling both chilly and faintly ridiculous, she pulled on her sweater, rounded up the dogs that had gone snuffling for rabbits in the ditch, and headed for home. In gratitude for finding his farm, Nabdul had commissioned a painting of the grave, and she contemplated it with pleasure as she walked.

If it turned out well, she would ask the painter to execute a series of them, depicting the house and stables, fields and horses – maybe even Helen and Cara and Jerry at work at their various outposts, although she shrank from similarly immortalising herself. Oils might be old-fashioned, but she much preferred them to photographs or, worse, a video.

But that was another day's work. Suddenly keen to get back to the house, and Brandon, she quickened her pace, throwing sticks for the dogs, jogging intermittently until the lake and gardens came in sight, misty in the dusk. Beyond them, lights burned in several of the windows, welcoming and cheerful, and from the open French windows on the terrace the sound of a piano drifted out. At first, she thought one of the boys must have put a record on, but as she climbed the steps she heard first one discordant note and then another.

Who, or what, was it? The sound led her inside, to the ballroom; and there, seated at the grand piano that had not been touched for years, was Killian. Alone, he thumped lustily and cacophonously, but gradually the mangled sound became recognisable. He was playing "The Rose of Tralee".

Rooted, Kerry stood arrested on the parquet behind him, watching, listening, incredulous.

After ten or twenty seconds, he sensed her presence, and spun round on the piano stool. He had never had a music lesson in his life.

"Killian. How – when – where did you learn that song? Did somebody teach you at school?"

"No. I just picked it up. Maybe it was on the radio or something. Was I good, Mum? Did you like it?"

Delighted with himself, he beamed up at her. But she did not see his child's face, nor the ruddy beloved face of his grandfather. She saw Darragh, standing in the métro in an Aran sweater, his brown eyes full of irony, laughing at her.

The Louvre, according to Yves, was a stuffy old museum, far too pompous to inspire anything more radical than a raging thirst. But its basement was full of Greek and Roman statues, and so, muttering to himself, he spent an entire afternoon in it with Brian, executing small swift sketches. Antiquity was the theme for their next collection, although how he had been talked into it he could not imagine.

"Enough. I'm exhausted. Time for a Pernod."

Two Pernods, Brian thought: you're not going to like what I have to say to you. Nodding agreeably, he closed his pad and followed Yves up and out onto the street, where they sat down at the first pavement brasserie that came to hand. Lighting a Gauloise, Yves pulled on it with a martyred air.

"Nobody will wear it, I'm telling you."

Brian sighed. Even now, with more clients besieging him than he could cope with, Yves still had not got it through his head that women would wear *anything* he designed. Bedevilled by insecurity, his neurotic perfectionism threw up frequent scenes at the salon, with sobbing models and irate tailors left to be placated in his wake. But the wearing trauma was worthwhile, and everyone other than Yves himself saw that he had passed a turning point.

Long regarded as a pioneer, he was very close now to claiming his place among the classics of his century, no longer merely a witty innovator but one of the greats whose influence would be global, powerful and permanent. But the slightest hitch could yet trip him up, and it was with trepidation that Brian broached his contentious subject after they ordered their drinks.

"Yves, there's something I have to ask you."

Brian was more in the habit of telling people things than asking them, and Yves looked at him with eyes abruptly blue and cold as sapphires.

"Go ahead."

"It's about Lu."

"*Oh, non! Pas ça!*"

"Yes. I'm afraid so. I can't win – either you'll be angry, or Zoe will. She wants me to see Lu, Yves. Forgive and forget, sort of thing."

"Brian, take my advice and let sleeping dogs lie. You don't see me sending any bouquets to Keith Charles, do you?"

"No, but he's at the other end of the world. Lu is at Dior, and – uh – that means Dior has a much better manager than we have. If she were agreeable, I thought I might – ask her back."

"To work for us? Fine. She comes, I go."

"Would you just listen for a minute, would you? Look, I know I gave you my word I never would. But you wouldn't have to see much of her, and she wouldn't be allowed to hassle you in any way."

"I've been a fool, as usual. I should have made you put it in writing, as Kerry told me."

"If you're really upset, then I won't do it. But I thought you might give it a try, at least. I could offer her a short-term contract, and if you weren't happy after six months, say, I'd just pay her off with some kind of golden handshake. It's a conciliatory gesture, that's all."

"You say it's Zoe's idea?"

"Yes. She says my previous behaviour was too – uh – high-handed."

Yves threw back his Pernod and sat staring down the street, thinking. It was the last thing he wanted. But if Zoe wanted it, and Brian did too, then he was outnumbered.

"Very well. Zoe is a sensible woman, and I trust her judgment. But only on an experimental basis, Brian, and on condition that Lu never – *ever* – comes into my studio, or interferes with my work."

"Thanks, Yves. She won't. She'll just organise all the marketing and paperwork and you won't hear a cheep out of her."

No, Yves assured himself, I won't. Not if I have to wear my Walkman for the rest of my life. Throwing down a handful of coins on the table, he gathered up his sketching equipment and pushed back his chair.

"I have a meeting at six. Excuse me."

Brian watched him go, feeling guilty, and somehow abandoned. But back at his new abode he dialled the number that Zoe had given him, and forced himself to wait for an answer.

"*Allo?*"

"Lu? Lu, it's Brian. I know this may be something of a shock, but I – I was wondering if we might talk. There's something I want to discuss with you."

Discuss? Was it possible, after all this time? Transfixed, Lu dug her nails into her palm, biting back her first words until she could choose them carefully.

"I have a rendezvous at eight, Brian. Is your business urgent?"

"No, but – but the sooner it's settled, the better. I could meet you now, if you have just an hour to spare."

"I have half an hour. You'd better come straight here. Do you have my address?"

He hesitated. An impartial venue would be better. But he didn't want to start off by instantly quibbling.

"Yes. Zoe gave it to me. I can walk there from here."

Fifteen minutes later, he stood in the lobby of an apartment as large as Zoe's, but infinitely more manicured and, he thought, more anonymous. A Vietnamese girl showed him into the salon, and suddenly he felt a desperate desire to run. But there sat Lu, waiting for him, impeccably dressed and made up, cool and composed in one black armchair as she graciously indicated another.

But she was not Lu. She was a china doll. Glassy, brittle, her hazel eyes were so empty that Brian was horrified, and had to suppress a sharp gasp. Once so slim, slender but supple, Lu was now achingly thin, her legs like matchsticks, her fingers bony as the claws of a bird as she took a cigarette from a box beside her and waited, silently, for Brian to light it.

He picked up the table lighter and held it for her, aghast. Lu, smoking? Her fingers were steady, but his own trembled as the flame ignited the white paper and dull yellow tobacco, throwing light on a face devoid of any human, recognisable emotion. What on earth, he wondered, had brought her to such a state? Was it actually possible that *he* had?

She looked up at him as he drew back, and saw in him what she had always seen: a tall, dark, gentle creature whose physical beauty was untarnished. That same straight clear profile, those same mahogany eyes, the same seductive sweep of eyelash, black against his soft sandalwood skin. She saw her husband, her creation.

She inclined her head and smiled at him. A ghastly smile, he thought.

"I knew it, Brian. I always knew you'd come back, one day."

"Yes. I should have done, before. Long ago. But I wasn't able to. It's only now, from the perspective of time, that I can see how cold I was, how unforgiving. That's why I'm here. To apologise, and try to make reparation."

He looked down at the floor and she smiled again, unseen by him, with satisfaction.

"I accept your apology, Brian. I, too, am sorry. We've both done things we were bound to regret."

He looked up. "Do you, Lu? Regret it?"

"Yes. Very much. I should like now to let bygones be bygones."

It irked him that she should sound as if she were the one dispensing largesse. But he sat down in the armchair, linked his fingers and tried to look humble. Briefly, he enquired solicitously about her health, her work, her friends, but she did not reciprocate, and so he was forced to the point.

"I have come, Lu, with what you might call a modest proposal."

Ah. She was right. He had come to his senses. He wanted her back.

"I was wondering – we, all of us – were wondering whether you might consider returning to the salon. You're the best manager we ever had. I know you don't need the money, but we would pay you more than whatever Dior does, and you could work whatever hours you chose."

So! He had come at last, for this? To re-employ her? To remind her how much money he was making and throw a few pennies to her, not because she was his wife but because she was the best salon manager in Paris. He did not need her in his life: only in his office.

Every bone in her body contracted as she stood up, her eyes shrivelling like walnuts, and walked over to him. Leaning down, she slapped his face, and spat in it.

He was so shocked, he could not even recoil. For a silent eternity, he just sat there, staring at her, stunned. Then, with a look of the most profound sadness, he took out his handkerchief and wiped his face.

Why? Why? What had he done? Did she really hate him, as much as that? But he saw from the look on her face that she did. Curdled with contempt, it was livid with bitterness.

He tried to go to her. But she jumped back with the wild vicious look of a cornered rat, all teeth and claws.

"Don't! Don't touch me! Don't speak to me!"

Something in the pitch, the timbre of her shriek frightened Brian. It was a primal wail, that made his scalp prickle and needles dart through his knuckles. He saw, then, all the coiled anger inside her, all the searing pain, the bottomless loneliness. But, if she had created him in her image, then he had created her in his too. He had created this violently unhappy woman.

"Lu – please, I – I—"

"Get out! Get *out!*"

He reached his hand to her, but she pounced backwards, shrieking, badly, urgently wanting to bite it. To sink her claws into him and tear bloody tracks down his beautiful face, to grip his neck in her teeth and rip the veins out of it. She could not contain herself, she *would* do it.

"Ouuut! Ouuut!"

Horrified, deeply shocked, he went. As he edged away he collided with the maid, running in at the sound of the screams, and watched Lu crouch down on the floor, her fists clenched, her shoulders heaving.

My God, he thought. Oh, my God.

Part Four

20

A wet, wretched winter's day, early in December 1986. The residue of autumn leaves lay clumped in dark, damp ruts along the sides of the roads, their copper colour darkened to bog-brown, dank after recent incessant rain. Stripped of their foliage the trees stood stark and wiry, infested with crows, ravens and the plague of magpies that besieged the whole island, cawing and carking as they scavenged fields and hedges, carrying dirt and pestilence on malevolent black wings.

But in Ashamber's big dining room everyone was cosy and comfortable, seated around the debris of a long late lunch, warmed by the crackling log fire as they talked and smoked on into the lost afternoon. Seated at one end of the table, Kerry stretched her legs under it, unwinding in the aftermath of an event that had gone surprisingly well. The gathering was an unlikely assortment of friends and family, people she had not expected to mix, but somehow they had come together.

Brandon sat at the far end of the table, and between him and her were Nabdul and Shairi, Chris and his Spanish girlfriend Ana, their student friends Diana Kiely and her Dutch boyfriend Andrej van Loos, Bob, Helen and Killian. Kerry had expected Chris to come alone, and been mildly perturbed that he should choose the same weekend to visit as Nabdul, one of the many figures he generally treated with restrained contempt. But, without asking, he had brought his three friends. A lively bunch, they had somehow diffused things so that there had been none of the friction she feared.

Nabdul, with a cigar in one hand and a glass of port in the other, was talking about his stud farm. After many early problems it was now up and running, producing some fine progeny, a joint venture with Kerry whose mares and stallions had been mated with his own. Satisfied after a good season and a good meal, Nabdul was a little flushed and, Kerry thought, just a tiny bit smug.

He gestured down the table at her.

"So often, Kerry has told me of her father's wish to breed and train a Derby winner. He never achieved it, but his daughter is going to. We have a young colt, Deoch an Doras, which has the makings of spectacular success. It will win the Derby the year after next, without a doubt – is that not so, Kerry?"

"It is, Nabdul. I've never seen an animal like it."

She smiled at his certainty, and at his perfect pronunciation of the Irish name she had chosen. For many years Nabdul had worked at a London hospital, but he spent so much of his free time in Ireland that he had become part of the furniture. The people who had once disliked him had come to admit his fairness as an employer and his generosity as the benefactor of their numerous local charities. There was no more vandalism, no more graffiti.

But unintentionally he was hogging the limelight today, in the manner of a man accustomed to captive audiences; he never flaunted his royal status, but he never quite forgot it either. Brandon turned to Chris.

"So, tell us about Trinity, Chris. We see so little of you, your studies must be very interesting."

Sipping from his glass of rather good Médoc, Chris turned to address the whole table with every bit as much confidence as Nabdul. At twenty-two, he looked older, and was very sure of himself. A charmless, cocky bantam whom Kerry could not abide.

"Yes, Father. My studies are extremely interesting. We're reading the early twentieth century this term. Ireland, India, Africa – it was a time of rampant imperialism."

Kerry winced. Why had Brandon got Chris onto politics? She shot him a look, but too late: Chris was off the leash. Leaning forward across the table, he faced Nabdul with sudden, withering scorn.

"We're reading about people like *you*, Nabdul. Greedy nobodies who thought the world was their personal treasure chest because their fathers had seized it for them, and their fathers before that. Guys with egos the size of their armies. Guys who grabbed land and money and power like spoilt brats in a toyshop, bashing and booting their way around till they got everything they wanted, or smashed what they couldn't get. Guys who raped, raided, looted and—"

In the silence, Kerry's voice thundered like a cannon.

"*Chris!* How *dare* you! Apologise to Nabdul or get out of my house!"

He looked at her.

"Your house? It's my house too, Kerry. I live here now, remember? My father is your husband, and we're all one big happy family, aren't we?"

Brandon stood up.

"Chris. Apologise, and then leave."

For a long moment Chris looked at his father, a moment so taut it snapped like ice. Throwing back his chair, he rose and turned to his friends.

"Come on. Let's all get out of here. Ana, Diana – don't forget to curtsey to His Royal Highness."

They were out of the room, and out of the house, before anyone found their voice. As she went to Nabdul, Kerry's was trembling.

"Nabdul – I—"

With regal composure, he took her hand.

"My dear, please don't distress yourself. The boy is young. He had had some wine, I think. Let us finish our meal, and think no more of it."

Kerry was distantly aware of Helen taking Killian out of the room, of Bob stuttering at Shairi, of Brandon rushing to her side. But she saw none of it. All she saw was the work of a lifetime, the sixty horses out in her fields and stables, owned by Arabs who, tomorrow, would take them all away.

She could find no words. Brandon could; his tone of low fury rumbled in her ears like thunder. He was speaking to Nabdul, and incredibly Nabdul was speaking to him.

" . . . of no consequence, I assure you. My father's régime is benevolent, but there was a time . . . your son was referring to history . . ."

It seemed like hours before he left, with Shairi. But it was only minutes.

"Kerry, he's not going to take his horses away from you. He's not going to shut down his stud farm, and he's not going to say a word to his father, his friends or any of the other owners. He told me himself, it'll take a lot more than one hot-headed, bitter young man to drive him away. You must believe me. Believe him, if you'd rather."

Eight hours had elapsed, eight hours in which Brandon had said and done everything humanly possible to calm Kerry. But while he undressed for bed, she still paced the room, up and down, up and down, up and down.

Brandon felt sick to his stomach. Just ten days, since her miscarriage, and now this. Never had he known her to be anything less than resilient, but tonight she was very close to the edge. He drew her to him.

"Darling, *stop* it! You're torturing yourself for nothing. Nabdul has accepted our apologies, and put the thing in context. It'll all blow over, if only you'll let it."

"Let it? Until the next time, you mean? Brandon, we have no idea why he did it, and we have no idea when he'll do it again."

"He won't do it again. You have my word. He will write a letter of complete and unreserved apology to the Zul Mahrats, because otherwise I'm taking him out of college, cancelling his bank account and leaving him to fend for himself. He will also apologise to you."

"I don't want his apologies. They're meaningless. I want him . . ." But even as she drew breath to say it, Kerry stopped herself with the most enormous effort. After four years of Christopher Lawrence's endless polemic, taunts and innuendoes, she wanted him out of their home, their family and their entire life. But he was Brandon's son.

"I want him kept out of my sight, Brandon. I know he doesn't come here very often, and if it were up to me he would never come here again. But he's your son, so I will permit him to. On condition he never enters the same room as any of my clients, never sits down to table with any of our friends, and never, ever mentions another word about politics."

He was very relieved.

"Yes. I'll see to all that. He will grow out of it eventually, Kerry. All youngsters go through this anarchic phase."

"Not at my expense! If Nabdul had chosen to take offence, I'd be ruined, Brandon! Ruined!"

He had to admit that she might well be. Every day, Arab influence in racing and bloodstock grew stronger, wider, and Kerry had long ago put most of her eggs in that one basket. With the exception of Bill Schuster, who was now very elderly, nearly all her commissions came from the contacts she had forged over the years with Nabdul.

"I'm not trying to diminish what Chris did, Kerry. I know it could have been fatal. He is my son, as you say, and it's up to me to keep him under control. I'll do that. Now, simmer down, please."

Suddenly exhausted, she sank down on the bed.

"All right."

Taking her in his arms, he held her quietly until her breathing slowed, her heartbeat quietened against his chest and she was almost limp with fatigue. The loss of the baby she was carrying had taken far more out of her than she would admit, and Brandon cursed Chris for his stupidity.

"That's better. Tomorrow this will all be ancient history. Get some sleep, now."

Her body overtaking her mind, she did as she was bidden. But he lay awake beside her into the night, thinking about ancient history, and his son's preoccupation with it.

If only Chris had been the one to go to America, and Harry the one to stay here! But quiet, easy-going Harry had left school in England, joined his mother in Virginia and enrolled for physics studies at Princeton. He missed his younger son much more than he ever told Kerry – and he must do something, after today's incomprehensible outburst, with his elder.

But what?

He did not want to lose, or alienate, the only child left to him. Troublesome as Chris was, he was intelligent too, a youth with a bright future if only he would see it, and invest in it.

His behaviour was out of order, provocative and exasperating, but it was the behaviour of youth. If he could be got through this difficult time, intellectually harnessed somehow, he would be all right. And it fell to his father to ensure that he was.

Was it the divorce that had unsettled him? No. He had been spiky long before that – but then, so had the home in which he grew up. Perhaps he had absorbed something of its atmosphere, was expressing hostilities and breaking constraints kept hidden by his father? Was articulating, even, his father's long camouflaged resentment of Nabdul Zul Mahrat, whose great crime it was to have been Kerry's lover?

And all because Brandon had not been around then himself, busy with the sons whose welfare had been paramount. Sorely aware of the irony, Brandon folded his arms around her possessively and fell asleep in the bedroom where Nabdul was never supposed to encroach.

Three weeks later, just before Christmas, Brandon was not surprised to find himself having a row with Kerry. Physically recovering from her miscarriage, and mentally recovering from Chris's onslaught, she had almost found her equilibrium, but not quite. She knew she was being unreasonable, he thought, but she was in a state of emotional flux, accusing him of wrapping her in a cocoon of loving concern that was too tight.

"The New Year party is a tradition, Brandon! It meant a lot to my parents and it means a lot to me. I'm going ahead with it and there's an end to it."

"Kerry, you're upset and you're very tired. You don't know what you're saying. There's no question of organising such a big event this year. If you like, we'll invite Brian for the holidays, Zoe, anyone you wish. But we'll have a quiet family gathering, no more."

"But it's my birthday, as well!"

"Yes. I'd like to see you live to celebrate many more. You won't if you go on like this."

She caught the finality in his tone. But, even as she limbered up to go another round with him, she espied a chink in his armour.

"Anyone, you say? We'll invite anyone you like?"

Too late, he saw the trap he had set for himself.

"If it will make you happy, yes. You can even invite Nabdul, assuming he'll accept. With Shairi and the children, of course."

The humouring of Nabdul, he supposed, would have to go on to the end of the century.

"I wasn't thinking of him. I was thinking of Yves."

"You're being deliberately difficult, aren't you, Kerry?"

"Brandon, if it weren't for Yves, you wouldn't be here. I've never understood your attitude to him, and I don't understand it now."

"I don't have an 'attitude', as you put it. If you wish to ask him, then go ahead. I'll be the perfect host, you needn't worry."

"And Robbie?"

"Who's Robbie?"

"His new boyfriend, Zoe says he's—"

"Kerry, let's get this straight, if that's the word for it. I am prepared to entertain your friend, since that's what he is, but if you think I'm having a pair of poofters sleeping under my roof, you're going to have to think again. It's out of the question! What about the staff? What about Killian? It would be scandalous!"

His roof? *His* roof, he said? Well, he had a right to. Naturally. But she had her rights too.

"Brandon, you're talking rubbish. The staff will do as they're told, and anyway they've always liked Yves. As for Killian – well, I can only hope he'll grow up to be a lot more broad-minded than you are. I'm his mother and I'll decide what's good for him."

Brandon bit down on the sarcasm that sprang to his lips. If she was going to tolerate Chris over Christmas, then he would have to tolerate Yves. But the example couldn't be good for Killian.

"Can't you put them in separate rooms, then? Compromise?"

"No! This is the first decent relationship Yves has formed in years, and I want it to go right for him. I want him to feel at ease and at home. This is Ashamber, not a reformatory."

Not until Chris arrives, it isn't, he thought. He'll have to toe the line, while Yves – oh, dammit, if he does get his game together with this other guy, maybe we'll see less of him in future. And I don't want her getting excited. She's overwrought.

"OK, Kerry. There's no need to fly off the handle. I don't like it, but I'll do it."

Quixotically, maddeningly, she smiled sunnily.

"Good. We'll forget the party then, just this once, and have a nice restful break instead."

Three days later, the group arrived from France. Zoe was in high spirits, Brian trotted amiably at her heels, but Kerry felt a frisson as Yves presented his new lover, with a shyness as pathetic as it was unusual. He had had a wonderful year, and achieved much to be proud of, but he edged forward as if committing some unforgivable sin.

"Kerry, this is my – my friend, Robbie Richler."

In cleated hiking boots, thick olive cords and a sweater of mustard wool, Robbie looked more like a mountaineer than an assistant professor of English literature. But behind his John Lennon glasses Kerry noted considerable powers of observation in his tea-coloured eyes. He sized her up frankly, but with a humorous twinkle that disarmed her. Six years younger than Yves, and two inches shorter, his rugged outdoor look belied his academic status, and she saw he was far more in command of the situation than was Yves himself. Shaking her hand confidently, he spoke in a Canadian accent.

"Thank you for inviting me to your beautiful estate, Kerry."

"Thank you for the compliment. Have you been to Ireland before?"

"No, never. I live in Montreal, but my university sent me on an exchange to the Sorbonne for a year. That's how Yves and I met – at a jazz club my students took me to one night. Ever since, life has been like a Fellini movie!"

Behind her, Brandon nodded as if some irrefutable fact had

been confirmed. But then he introduced himself cordially, and embraced Brian with fraternal warmth. It was established now that, where Killian was concerned, a stepfather must take precedence over an uncle.

The group dispersed to shower and change, and afterwards Kerry sought Zoe out.

"Let's go for a walk, Zoe. I want to hear all the news."

Zoe grinned as she threw on a coat and scarf.

"The news is excellent, Kerry. We've had a great year – especially Yves. The critics went absolutely crazy for his collection, as you know, and the reviews went to his head like rockets to the moon. It was exactly what he needed, and then he met Robbie as well. Robbie is one of the nicest guys I've ever met. Much more mature than Yves, very sensible, very stabilising. The only problem is, he's due to go back to Canada in June, so I think Yves is trying not to get too involved."

"He looks quite enamoured already, to me."

"He is, poor thing. I hope they can work something out. I'd hate to see him get hurt again. After his last disaster, I think he's scared stiff. It's taken a lot of courage to let Robbie into his life. Until now, nobody has lasted longer than a month."

Mentally, Kerry scribbled herself a note, but then eyed Zoe nonchalantly.

"And what about you? Is Brian still boring holes in your heart?"

"That's the thing, Kerry. He's not boring, any more. He's making a real effort. We've become very close. Yves has been talking about moving into his own apartment after Christmas, and I'm almost of a mind to let Brian move into mine."

"Oh, Zoe! Surely you don't need to live together, after all this time? Why don't you marry him, and have done with it?"

"Because he hasn't asked me, for one thing, though I think he might soon. But you don't ever really know someone until you live with them. I want to make sure I'm not just a substitute for Lu. Besides, it would be unfair to marry him if he still wants kids as much as I think he does."

"I told you before, don't worry about that. If you two

marry, which I hope you will, I'll see to that side of things."

"Kerry, what are you talking about?"

"I'll give you a child, for a wedding present."

"Kerry! They don't grow in cabbage patches! Or do you think you buy them in Sex, Fifth Avenue?"

"Oh ye of little faith. Trust me, Zoe."

For an insane moment Zoe thought Kerry meant to turn Killian formally over to her, and laughed rather hysterically.

"You're crazy. But how is Killian, anyway?"

"He's fourteen, Zoe. Need I say more? He's short, dark and handsome, and bloody difficult. Someday I'm going to take some scissors and chop his damn ponytail off. He's a mess."

"He's your son, Kerry. I hope you did what you were told, about his music lessons?"

Kerry scowled as they rounded the last bend in the avenue and let themselves out onto the narrow country road. Bowing to pressure not only from Zoe, but Helen and Brandon too, she had accepted that Killian must be treated like one of her racehorses, in need of a top trainer, and enrolled him at a music academy of whose fat fees she begrudged every penny.

"Yeah. I did. Now he plays the piano morning noon and night, and a guitar, his tutors are even talking about concerts. I hope you're satisfied."

"Yes. You've done the right thing. I'm sure Brandon is pleased?"

"He is. He takes the business of being a parent to Killian so seriously – much more than I do! But then his own sons have turned out so badly, I think he's compensating."

"Badly?"

"Badly, Zoe. Harry has defected to his mother, and Chris is a little bastard. You wouldn't believe what he said to Nabdul, I'd never forgive it except that I have to. I feel so torn, and guilty! Marrying me has cost Brandon Harry, and now he's having to keep Chris at arm's length too. That's why I so want us to have another child, Zoe. To make it up to him."

A reason, perhaps, Zoe thought. But not the only one.

"You've had three miscarriages in four years, Kerry. Are you sure it's wise to keep trying? What does the doctor say?"

"She says give up hunting, drinking, heavy work and late nights. So I have. I live like a nun. I'll get there yet, if it kills me."

"Kerry, it will kill you, if you don't ease up. It often happens when you're least expecting it. Stop thinking about it, and pay more attention to Killian instead."

"Zoe, Killian's father was a ghastly mistake. The next baby's isn't. He's a wonderful husband, and we're going to have a child between us, and that's that."

"Perhaps nature is punishing you, Kerry, for neglecting Killian. Waiting till you prove you're fit to be a mother."

"Oh, why does everyone always harp on about Killian? He's Brandon's baby now. Brandon and Helen's. I want one of my own."

She's my friend, Zoe thought. But right now, I could smack her in the teeth. She hasn't a clue how lucky she is.

It was not until Christmas Eve that Kerry got her chance. While Yves helped Helen decorate the tree, Chris was sent to chop logs for his sins, and everyone else went riding across country, she cornered Robbie in the library. Curled in an armchair with a book, he did not hear her come in, and she studied him for a moment, thinking how self-contained he looked, and how ordinary. Everything that Yves was not.

"Robbie?"

He laid down his book politely, with a barely perceptible flicker of amusement. He had been wondering when she would get on his case.

"Come on in, Kerry. You're much prettier than Sam Beckett."

She sat down on the floor on a cushion, crossed her legs under her, and regarded him frankly.

"I want to talk to you. About Yves. I don't know whether you know this, but—"

"But you and he have been friends all your lives, right? You're blood-bonded, and if my intentions are not honourable I'll have you to answer to?"

She smiled with her mouth, but not with her eyes. "Precisely."

He sat up straight and considered her soberly.

"I've only known Yves three months, Kerry. But I know the kind of people who usually gravitate to him. He's far too open and vulnerable for his own good, and he attracts abuse. He wears his heart on his sleeve and people take pot shots at it. He has as much street savvy as a child of six; and I don't want to change him one iota. But I don't want to exploit him, either."

"You'd better not. He's been badly burnt before. I know he lets people rip him off. But I won't let anyone, again."

"I know. More than you think, in fact."

"What do you mean?"

"I mean that Yves has told me certain things about himself . . . things he's never told anyone. He needs love as a matter of life and death."

Always, she had sensed that need in Yves, heard the muffled plea he strove to stifle, and done her best to answer it. Now she heard something else; a rare whisper of jealousy.

"What did he tell you? The things he's never told me?"

"Yes. In confidence, which I can't share. He didn't volunteer, but I made him. I don't propose to spend the rest of my life with an enigma that might shatter at any minute. It hurt, but I got it all out of him . . . right up to the money he lost, Keith, the other so-called lovers he's had before and since. Everything. Honesty is *my* price, Kerry."

Virtual stranger that he was, she connected with him suddenly, and assumed a right of friendship.

"If he's trusted you, I warn you, you'd better *be* trustworthy. He may seem frivolous, flamboyant, whatever, but he's fragile as glass."

"Again, more than you think. He's exposed himself to terrible risks. But his dancing days are over. If he's going to live with me, then he's going to be living a quiet life from now on. No more nightclubbing, no more booze, parties, one-night stands. Finito, kaput."

"You intend to stay with him, then? For the long haul?"

"Yes. I'm going to resign my post in Montreal, find a new job in Paris, leave my country, my home, my family and my friends, and move halfway across the world for someone

I've known twelve weeks. Does that answer some of your questions, at least?"

Her gaze fell on the blond hairs on his forearms, soft and silky in the firelight, as she thought of such a sacrifice as she had once made herself, as much in love as he.

"Yes. It does. I can't ask for greater commitment than that, and I think you're mature enough to know what you're doing. I was just worried because – well, people have always seemed to love the lifestyle much more than the man."

"I know. He's starting to make serious money again now, Kerry, and he needs protection. I want him to start taking care of himself, instead of everyone else."

Glad of his perceptiveness, she realised how far it might extend.

"I hope you feel comfortable here, Robbie. My husband can – is – has rather traditional views of things, sometimes. But I don't want you to let that constrain you."

"Most people are like that. They fear or disdain what they don't understand. But we are guests in your home, and used to being discreet."

Grateful to him, she found herself warming to him as well, confident that he understood her position along with his own: her kinship with Yves would not be threatened by this man, but enhanced. Half rising, she stretched forward to put her hand on his, but as she did so the door opened, and Yves himself came into the room, ghostly in the early dusk.

"Rob? Why are you hiding away from me in here? Why don't you – oh, hi, Kerry. I didn't see you down on the floor."

Robbie laughed.

"Don't let her position fool you. I'm the supplicant. She doesn't think I'm good enough for you."

Quietly, Yves came up behind Robbie, bent down over his chair and wrapped his arms around him, placing a kiss amidst the sun-streaked flaxen hair.

"You're much too good for me."

Such was the reverence in his voice, Kerry felt as guilty as if she had barged into their bedroom, and excused herself to slip away. But ten minutes later she was back, pressing something into Yves's hand, rattling out words as if from a slot machine.

"It's the key to our apartment in Paris. We only go there for two or three weeks a year. It's disgracefully wasted and neglected and I – we – were wondering whether you two would look after it for us. Live there, I mean. There's lots of room and you can fix it up any way you like. We'd be honoured if you'd regard it as your home."

Nonplussed, Yves clutched the key, unaware that Robbie's decision to stay on had been taken.

"Kerry, we couldn't possibly, we'll find a place of our own, it may be only temporary anyway, Robbie may be going back to Canada . . ."

"I don't think he will, Yves."

Incredulously, he turned to Robbie for confirmation, and got it without a single word being spoken. In the emotional silence Kerry was profoundly moved, and glad of the rash thing she had done.

"Take it, Yves. Please. To be perfectly honest I haven't quite gone into it all with Brandon, but I know he wants what I want."

Belatedly, Yves caught her drift, and pulled her to him without a word, unable to speak in either of his two languages. It would take more than bricks and mortar to cement the new arrangement, but if she would try then so would he.

"But, *chérie*, we must speak with Brandon first."

Anxiously, he frowned at her, his eyes searching for some sign that this gesture had been already ratified. He saw none; but he saw that it would be.

It was. Four years of marriage had taught Kerry that Brandon was an obstinate man, but it had also taught her to trust his love for her, which finally overrode every other consideration. Furious when he heard what she had done, he berated her remorselessly, but she knew she would win, and stood her ground.

"Darling, we won't be using the place this year at all, if I finally manage to have a baby. Let's not worry about it for the moment, h'mm?"

"Baby. That's another thing. When are you going to give up this madness, Kerry? It's affecting your work and your health and your judgment. I'm going to have a vasectomy, and there's an end to it."

"Oh, no! Don't do that! Let me try just once more, Brandon, please. I know you want a baby as much as I do."

"I did. But not any more. You've miscarried three times and you're exhausted. I want my wife to be well far more than I want another child. Let's just be glad of the ones we have."

"But Marianne has taken Harry away from you . . . oh, please, Brandon? If I lose the next one I will stop then, I swear it. Give me one more chance."

She was close to tears, the apartment forgotten. But, although Brandon had seen her almost weep before, he had never been able to let her actually do it.

"Don't, Kerry – you know I only want what's best for you. If you really need to try again, then we will. One last time."

She wiped her face on the back of her sleeve, and lacerated his heart with a look.

"Oh, Brandon, thank you. You're so good to me. And it is better, you know, to have the apartment lived in. They'll take great care of it."

The apartment? But it was the baby he was agreeing to – oh, the hell with it. He never knew where he was with Kerry. But he was with her, and that was enough.

Thereafter, she was docile as a lamb, concentrating on the elusive business of conception, envious of the ease with which mere mares in the field managed it. Refusing all new commissions, she conserved herself physically, channelling all her mental energy into Deoch an Doras, a feisty little foal which had matured into a hardy, rangy colt in a matter of months. Mapping out his début with Nabdul, Kerry's sights rose rapidly: with proper pacing, the colt would be well able for the Dewhurst and National Stakes as a two-year-old. After that, Group One races, and finally Eamonn's magic double, a Derby winner bred and trained by a Laraghy.

Breaking and schooling Deoch was a joy; quick and willing to learn, he responded to touch and to voice as if specifically to please her, and she grew very fond of the big, sweet-natured animal. But what a dilemma, if she should be pregnant by the time next year's Derby came round! No matter what the cost to her, or disappointment to Nabdul, she would have to drop out. Nothing was worth endangering the life of her child for, and for once she must allow nature to dictate her priorities.

But nature did not ask the sacrifice of her. Six weeks after Easter, she found that she was already pregnant. Ecstatically she gave thanks, but very quietly, afraid to celebrate too soon or risk the excitement. All through spring and summer she held her breath, edging gingerly past the point at which the other babies had been lost, until autumn came, and serenity with it. Anxiously, Brandon and Helen fussed over her, but she felt well and strong. This time, she knew she was going to make it.

At the end of November, she went prematurely into labour, and was flown by helicopter to Dublin. From the terminal, an ambulance transferred her to the Rotunda hospital, where Brandon harangued the staff frantically, beside himself with worry. Stoically, a nurse brought him a cup of tea.

"Don't panic, Mr Lawrence. We have delivered babies before. Just relax, now."

He could no more relax than he could speak Urdu. But Kerry, despite the memory of Killian's crucifying birth, smiled up at him from eyes green and huge with happiness, grateful he was there with her, even more grateful for the epidural she needed no encouragement to accept.

It was a short, astonishingly easy birth. After little more than an hour, Brandon sat in his sweat-soaked shirt cradling his new baby son, and with equal wonder Kerry held her tiny daughter to her, tears streaming unheeded down her face.

"See? You didn't think I could manage even one, and now we've got two."

He burst into tears.

"Oh, God, Kerry, I'm sorry, but you – you have no idea how terrified I was. If anything had happened to you, I – I—"

"You'd have been stuck with Killian? No wonder you're upset."

They laughed, and cried some more, and very nearly smothered the indignant twins.

*   *   *

The question of godparents was a vexed one. Out of patience with all the permutations, Kerry informed Helen and Yves that they were to do double duty for both babies.

"This christening business is a lot of nonsense anyway, Helen. But Brandon insists."

"He's perfectly right. It may be the wrong moment to mention Julie, but I wouldn't argue if I were you, Kerry. Now, have you chosen the names?"

"Saoirse and Séamus. What do you think? Saoirse means freedom, and Séamus is just a nice strong, sensible name we both liked."

Massive bouquets of flowers and a crate of champagne preceded Yves's arrival for the christening, and Kerry saw that he was both touched and thrilled. The blue eyes blazed with emotion as he swept the babies into his arms, peering at them fascinated.

"I can't believe you're really entrusting the moral and spiritual welfare of these innocents to me, Kerry."

"Neither can I. I must be losing my marbles."

Yet again, Brandon had taken infinite persuasion. But had Kerry expressed a wish to see the Taj Mahal transplanted to the bottom of her vegetable garden, he would have got it for her, and so, lamenting and decrying the decadence of it all, he finally sanctioned Yves's appointment as godfather. But, as they stood in the chapel at Hollyvaun, he watched Helen undertake her duties in conjunction with Yves, and was conscious of immense reassurance and relief.

After the baptism, everyone crammed into the dower house, and Brandon raised his glass aloft, precariously, a baby in either arm.

"To my beloved wife, Kerry, to our daughter Saoirse, and to our son, Séamus."

On cue, the infants screamed piercingly, and he handed them hastily to Kerry.

"I don't know why you're giving them to me! You're much better at it."

But that, this time, was not altogether true. Kerry felt completely different about these children to her first, and had fallen in love with them the moment she set eyes on them – the moment, perhaps, they were conceived. How adorable, how delicious they were, with their gossamer pink skin, their puny clenched fists, their imperious squalls! They were darlings, perfect darlings, the two of them, instilling in her a joy such as she had never known, bringing out in her every powerful emotion her luckless elder son never had.

But Brandon had warned her of the danger of making Killian feel excluded, and so she called him over now, and bestowed Saoirse on him with an apprehensive smile. At only nine weeks, already the lusty little redhead's eyes were wide and green as her mother's, and eagerly Killian looked down into them, tickling her under the chin as if her dimpled charms might rub off onto him.

Languidly, Chris glanced at the child, and at Séamus with equal brevity. Wishing he did not have to be there at all, Kerry was provoked to sarcasm.

"Well, Chris? Demented with joy, are we?"

"Oh, this country supported a population of eight million once, you know. I daresay it can afford to feed two more mouths now."

Kerry wanted to hit him. But instead she turned to Harry and put Séamus into his arms, glad for Brandon's sake that he had come from America for the christening. It was the first time in a year that father and son had seen each other, and likely to be the last for at least another. Harry had made a point of siding with Marianne, and letting it be known how much he had taken to David Wheatstone. Not cruelly, but hurtfully.

Seeing her unburdened, Brian came up with a glass of champagne, and she accepted it with an apologetic smile.

"I hope you don't mind about not being godfather, Brian. But you'll have a child of your own some day, whereas Yves never will."

"No. That's OK. But why didn't you call them Maeve and Eamonn, Kerry? I was sure you would."

"I did think of it. But Brandon said it was unfair to impose other people's personalities on them. Said he didn't want them to have to live up to anything or anyone."

"Hmph."

Not overly impressed, Brian rejoined Zoe and Robbie, who were teasing Yves and Helen about their solemnity in the chapel. But Kerry knew that both would take their job seriously, and was honoured to make them officially part of the family.

Yves was still nervy and frenetic in the salon, but anchored in his private life, and with Robbie's help she knew he would not lose himself again. Watching the two as they stood together, she felt their consummate bond, deep and indissoluble, and that Yves had got something very right at last.

As she had herself. At thirty-five she stood strong and secure on her own plateau, that moment in life when every wrinkle on the map is smoothed out, but no direction is more enticing than the one already taken. It had been a long gruelling trek, but she had survived it: the theft of her parents, the rigours of Africa, the trauma of a brutal marriage, a long period of frightening penury and single parenthood. It was scary, she thought, but it's behind me. My ship has come safely into harbour.

Who steered it there? Who, or what, gave me the courage to marry Brandon when I was afraid? What made me pick up the phone that day and bring Brian back? How did Helen let herself into my life, when I thought she'd stolen Daddy's love away from me? I don't think there's a God up there, but there must be somebody, or something, holding me in hands I can't even feel.

Later that night, when Ashamber was full of sleeping people, Kerry woke up at about two o'clock. Time for the babies' feed. Her body was so attuned to its new rhythm that she didn't even need to hear the summons to duty. Creeping out of her bedroom, she tiptoed to the nursery, picked up the slumbering mites and put one to either breast. Sleepily, contentedly, they snuggled into her, and she smiled down at them, suffused and overwhelmed with love.

"But I'll bet there can't be many trainers doing this!"

The house was very still, and she sat there for a long time after the sated infants were once again bedded down in their cots, watching them settle in the dark, listening to their precious breathing, utterly at one with them and with herself. It was three before she returned to her own room, but as she slipped back into bed Brandon stirred and rolled over, taking her in his arms with a little spasm as her cold feet touched his, holding her warm and close, murmuring against her face.

"My Kerry. God, I love you so much. So much."

"And I you. Sometimes I still can't believe we really are married."

"We are. Very, very married."

He kissed her gently as she fell back to sleep, her arms entwined about him, thinking himself the luckiest man in creation.

If Killian's birth had been painful, Kerry found that of the twins hurting her just as much, in the pocket. Farmed out to assistants and other trainers for the duration of her pregnancy, many clients did not return, choosing to stay with the men who would not desert them for mere babies. But Nabdul was always there, at the core of her business, and she was as thankful for that as she was worried about it, every time she thought of Chris.

With one word he could destroy everything, at any moment, and despite the lid Brandon kept on him she knew he was still capable of it. Restless and idealistic, he plagued her thoughts, riding shotgun on the perimeter of her life. Unlike Darragh, she could not shake him off, and only when she was with the babies or out on the gallops with Deoch, did she forget him for long enough to know any real peace.

But he stayed away, and in April Kerry was distracted by news she had long waited to hear. After three months of living in blissful sin, Brian and Zoe had decided to marry. The wedding was to be immediately, in May, and when she got to Paris two weeks later Kerry could not but be infected by the couple's contagious happiness.

It was a simple ceremony, conducted at the local mairie, with a festive meal afterwards at La Fermette Marbeuf. For a wedding present she and Brandon gave them a honeymoon in the Seychelles, and as Brian pocketed the envelope full of airline tickets and hotel vouchers, he looked at his sister accusingly.

"So, where is it?"

"Where's what?"

"The real present. The baby you promised us. Why isn't it in this envelope, giftwrapped?"

She was pleased to hear him make light of a subject that was usually so vexed, and giggled, demurring in a way that made Helen cross with her. Taking Brian aside, Helen assured him that proceedings really were in train. When he came back from the Seychelles, he would come with Zoe to meet Sister Benildus.

"Who?"

"The nun who runs the children's home – where all your cheques go – good heavens, Brian, don't say Kerry never told you?"

Instantly he was all ears, and Zoe too, desperate to know how it could be done in view of their age, Brian's divorce and their joint lack of regular religious practice.

"It can be and it will be."

Kerry was furious with Helen for letting the cat out of the bag, thinking that now the honeymoon would be spent in a ferment of impatience, exacerbated by the copious paperwork and long procedure yet to be got through.

But it was done, and so she repaired to the restaurant's powder room to have a good cry over Zoe, the new sister-in-law whose face was a study of hope, joy and apprehension. With the door firmly shut behind them, Zoe also collapsed in tears.

"Oh, Kerry, what news on our wedding day! You're the best friend, the best sister-in-law anyone could ever ask for . . . I'm so h-h-happy . . ."

"Then stop crying! I will if you will. I didn't mean you to know so soon, because it won't be easy. But it will be worth waiting for – as I hope my brother is."

Hiccuping, Zoe dabbed at her running mascara and pulled herself together.

"Oh, yes. He loused up his last marriage but he won't do

it to this one. Now I'm a Laraghy I intend to turn into a bully just like the rest of you."

Kerry was taken aback, but had to laugh as Zoe marched back to her husband with a proprietorial air. Just as Robbie bossed Yves about, Zoe would take no nonsense from Brian, but as a dictator she was far more benevolent than Lu. Everyone departed for the airport, and on the plane home Kerry was touched to see Bob furtively kiss Helen, apparently infected by the romance of Paris and the wedding. Dear Helen. She must be sixty-four by now, Kerry realised with something of a shock, and there's no doubt that lately her rheumatism has got worse. Do I work her too hard? I must have a chat with her about it.

A few days later, she did, but got short shrift for her pains.

"If you're thinking of turning me out to grass, you can forget it. I plan to drop in harness, thirty or forty years from now, and it'll be a sad day for you when I do, madam."

With her mouth set in rather challenging lines, Helen conveyed to Kerry that the conversation was at an end. Physically, she looked as well as ever, but the chestnut curls were iron grey, the soft peachy skin crisscrossed by lines which, Kerry hoped, were not entirely of her making. When she walked long distances, she tended to tire a little, and her stance was not as upright as once it had been.

But still she was at her desk by eight thirty every morning, and rarely left it before six, a doughty warhorse who undoubtedly had indeed many years left in her. It was to Helen everyone came with their problems, especially Killian who would sit at her feet in his slashed jeans and leather bracelets, serenading her for hours on his guitar. Where would they all be, without her? It was a question Kerry would have to face some day, but for the moment she left well enough alone.

But, on the matter of Brian and Zoe's adoption, she got moving. Shortly after their return from honeymoon, they were summoned to Ireland and driven, in a state of extreme apprehension, to the convent in Kildare. Despite her departure from the Catholic Church, Kerry had the greatest time and respect for the nuns to whom her father had willed Ashamber in the event of her failure, and for the nuns throughout the country. Tirelessly they ran the care centres and hospitals, the old people's homes, hospices and schools, all the institutions they had founded long before the State had had the means to do it, undertaking all the work the priests considered infra dig. Oh, no! They had Africa to convert, and South America to set to rights; no dribbling babies, no babbling geriatrics for them. That was women's work, and these women did it with a selfless efficiency Kerry greatly admired. For years her cheques to Sister Ben had been regularly given and gratefully received, along with Brian's unwitting contribution, and she beamed now as she sat down before her mother's old Chippendale desk in Sister Ben's otherwise spartan office.

Sister Ben indicated chairs for Brian and Zoe, linked her fingers as she sat down behind the desk, and surveyed them intently. Already possessed of much of the information she needed from Kerry, what she wanted next was not facts, but a feel for the couple. All the rules were against them, but Sister Ben was a practical woman when it came to rules and when it came, particularly, to the children in her care. Her priority was to find homes for as many as possible, strong loving homes offering a stable environment for their physical and spiritual growth. Over and again, the State placed obstacles in her path, sought to tie her down in red tape, but Sister Ben wielded ruthless scissors when it came to red tape. Like many nuns, she was politically astute, and had no hesitation in shaming government ministers and their officials, on radio or on television, into complying with her demonstrably justifiable wishes.

She knew everyone for miles around, as well as many influential people in Dublin, and on election days candidates right across the board would quail as she drove up to vote in her white minibus with a convoy of her fellow sisters. It was a lot easier to go along with Sister Ben than it was to oppose her, and the bishop was far from alone in his terror of her.

She directed her gaze, now, at Zoe.

"So, Mrs Laraghy, Kerry tells me you are half-Jewish?"

Small and demure in one of Yves's more restrained suits, Zoe was so nervous she could barely whisper.

"Yes."

"And that you have come through a dreadful ordeal in America, with the greatest fortitude?"

"With a lot of help from my friends and my family. But it's over now, and I prefer to forgive and forget it."

"Quite."

A long conversation followed, very long, some of it seemingly irrelevant to the issue. Sister Ben wanted to know all about the clothes they designed, the people they designed for, the salon in Paris and the people who worked there: Brian's interest in scuba diving, Zoe's battle of the bulge, any number of things about which Kerry had, apparently, freely informed her.

It was on the question of Lu that Brian felt himself coming unstuck.

"You have had no contact with your first wife, then, since your divorce?"

"No. I mean, yes. I did try to reinstate her at the salon. But she turned me down."

"I see."

Sister Ben did not pursue the matter, but something in the way she folded her lips told him he was on thin ice. He began to rationalise and flounder, but Kerry shot him such a warning look he shut up in mid-sentence.

The convent bell struck the hours: ten, eleven, noon. As brisk as they were exhausted, Sister Ben signalled after nearly three solid hours that the interview was over, and dismissed them with a mere nod of her head. There was no hint of whether an adoption might be possible, whether any suitable child was available, whether any exception might be made for their irregular application. Neither did she enquire into Brian's enormous inheritance, or even indicate that she would be in touch or wished to see them again. Nothing.

Out on the gravel in front of the convent, Brian and Zoe stood irresolute and downcast. The orphanage was a separate building, some distance away, but there was no sign of any children.

"Oh, Kerry. We blew it."

They were in agonies of disappointment, all too aware that

Sister Ben was their only hope. No official agency would countenance them, here or anywhere; demand far outstripped supply, and many far more conventionally acceptable couples wanted children.

"No, no, you didn't. Wait and see."

Jauntily, Kerry tossed her russet plait as she held open the door of her vintage Mercedes, but Brian and Zoe dragged their feet despondently, convinced that their last hope was gone. This time, Kerry was not going to meet the target she had set herself.

21

Kerry had been to Epsom any number of times. But never had it looked lovelier than today, glimmering in the heat haze, festooned with ribbons, preening in the reflected glory of the flowers and hats and bright jockeys' silks.

It was a long way removed from Fairyhouse or the Curragh, in the grey wet chill of a rainy day. There, the racing was for racing's sake, stripped of all the trimmings, so that it was the horses that counted, not the people orbiting around them. Here, she could not slug whiskey in the owners' and trainers' bar, hold a postmortem in a trenchcoat and muddy boots, smell the steaming horses and wet leather from under a cavernous golf umbrella; it was all style, all society, all controlled by corporate sponsorship.

But it was her goal, and Deoch an Doras was going to reach it for her.

Fingering her wedding ring, she looked around for Brandon, but in vain. Like herself he was networking, drumming up trade for Hollyvaun and for the Lawrence corporation with the practised ease of lifelong experience.

Nabdul could not be seen either, but Kerry knew where he was; up in his box, throwing a lunch party for dozens of guests, bragging about the stupendous horse he had bred with Kerry Laraghy whose equally stupendous training skills were now going to win the Derby for him. It was her father's dream, and she was every bit as good as the legendary Eamonn Laraghy.

In the parade ring, Deoch was primed for combat, circling in Nabdul's chequered colours of blue and silver. Quickly, Kerry ran through tactics one last time with his American rider, and smiled as Brandon slipped into the ring to squeeze her hand encouragingly. The arrested grey in his hair had begun to encroach again, and for that she blamed Chris, whose erratic lifestyle had developed into a worrying mystery. Now in his final year at Trinity, Brandon's son was an honours student, but his interest in politics was more than theoretic, and although he did not discuss his activities Brandon sensed that they existed, as did Kerry.

Such was her certainty that she had braced herself, only a month before, to interrogate him. As more and more Arabs had moved into Irish stud farms, some had bred very valuable stock, and now a stallion called Shergar was missing – kidnapped in a botched attempt, rumour had it, to raise ransom money for the IRA. Like her counterparts all over the country, Kerry was anxious to step up security, find out what had happened to Shergar, and she felt that Chris might somehow have an idea. But he dismissed her so scathingly she was almost persuaded she was mistaken, even as she resolved to keep the tightest possible watch on him, and on Deoch an Doras.

What more could she do? And yet her relationship with his father was such a success, it never ceased to amaze her how the man held sway over her heart, without ever compromising her autonomy. The mood of their marriage changed with the weather, sometimes sunny, sometimes tempestuous, often teasing. When she least expected it, Brandon would whisk her up to dance to a song on the radio, or take her out somewhere silly, crack a joke that doubled her with laughter. She never knew what he would produce next, and for his part he said he loved the way something was always happening in her face. Some marriages might be set in concrete, but this one was full of mobile vitality, and that was how they liked it.

Taking her arm, he led her out of the ring and up to Nabdul's box, where a private sweepstake was being organised amidst good-natured mayhem. She did not draw Deoch, but that didn't bother her as the white flag went up. The horse was going to win, and that was all about it.

As planned, Deoch spurted out in third position from the starting gates, fighting for his head but not getting it, sucked into a blur of speed with several other young colts whose prowess was undisputed worldwide. He held his position throughout the second furlong, and the third, but then began to rev inexorably up the field, passing out the French challenger who held second place, drawing level with the American leader. On the hard dry turf Kerry heard the thrum of the hooves beating up into the straight and gripped Brandon's hand violently, swearing to herself as the American contender lengthened his stride with casual ease. For a sick moment she remembered that other dreadful day at Epsom, when her sure bet had come to nought – but then, she'd had a nerve to enter that Derby at all. Now, she knew what she was doing, and even as she reminded herself of that fact Deoch shot into overdrive with the force of a cruise missile, flying past the seven-furlong marker like a thing possessed.

The whips were out, but Deoch's rider, cautioned for overly enthusiastic use two weeks before, merely pressed on the horse with his hands and legs. It was enough. Deoch cleared the winning post with two lengths to spare, and Kerry's shrieks were swallowed up in the delirious roar of a crowd whose favourite had delivered. Exultantly she yanked Brandon away, down to the winner's enclosure with Nabdul, whose grin was that of the man who broke the bank at Monte Carlo.

Cameras swivelled as they converged around the horse, and with immense pride Brandon stood back to let Kerry be interviewed, shake hands with everyone, and even pose with Nabdul's arm around her shoulder for the clicking photographers.

There was the Cup, there were the kisses – and then, there was the ultimate compliment.

"You're not just as good as your father, Kerry Laraghy. You're better."

They returned home to find the baby twins down with a bad cold, snuffling pathetically as Sophie, their nurse, tried to spoon-feed them in their high chairs. Stricken, Kerry flew to them, snatched them up and cuddled them, crooning, in her arms. But it was Brandon who took the spoon from

Sophie, replaced them in their chairs and began patiently to cajole them into eating, tiny morsels that Saoirse, on principle, promptly spat back at him. Creamed rice dribbled everywhere; but he persisted, gently, firmly, until the bowl was empty.

I've cost him Harry, Kerry thought, but I've given him these beautiful, beautiful babies, and his own youth back. He's nearly fifty, but look at him: a man fulfilled, a man alive. Once, I wanted him for what he could do for me, as Mummy wanted Eamonn, and now I'm thankful for all I've done for him. It's not so very much. But it's my best. We've brought that out, in each other.

She left him to it and went to check the messages left for her by Helen. Mostly routine, until she came to one from Sister Ben, and sat back astonished; after only two months, a child had been found. Not a newborn, as Brian and Zoe had hoped, but a toddler. Would they consider that?

Would they what? Immediately Kerry picked up the phone and punched the Paris number, praying her brother had not gone out for the evening. But he had, and so it was to Zoe she broke the news, and got ten minutes of total incoherence in return.

"*Already?* Oh, Kerry, we thought it would take months, years, if it happened at all . . . how can we ever thank you . . . ? Is it a boy or a girl . . . ? When can we come and get it?"

"I don't know, Zoe, but it sounds as if it will be soon. You'd better buy a lot of clothes and toys and stuff, and brace yourselves for a hectic Christmas."

The very next day, Brian and Zoe flew to Ireland once more, rented a car and drove straight to Kildare. At the convent, they found Xavier Markey waiting with Sister Ben and a mountain of paperwork, and as they signed the forms their hands shook uncontrollably. Only preliminary forms, with a trial period to be supervised by the social authorities in France – but then, a child to keep, to call their own, for ever! Overwhelmed, they followed Sister Ben across the gravel to the orphanage, and were led into a reception room on whose floor a young nun knelt with a chubby, very dark little boy of about two, racing his toy cars up and down the waxed parquet.

Absorbed in his fun, he whizzed the cars back and forth without noticing their arrival, until one glanced off Zoe's foot, and he looked up at her enquiringly, with eyes as big and brown as her own. Quietly, Sister Ben outlined the infant's situation: abandoned at birth by his unknown parents, he had been fostered since, by a family unable to adopt him permanently.

"His name is Marcus, but he can't pronounce it, so we just call him Marc."

Buckling rather than bending, Brian dropped to the floor and smiled tentatively.

"Hello, Marc."

Silently Zoe knelt beside him, trembling with apprehension, and reached out to the boy. He did not run to her, and did not answer Brian, but stood inspecting them gravely. Then, with a proud smile, he placed his miniature car in Zoe's outstretched hand, lifted his dimpled fingers to her face and touched it, the whites of his enormous eyes a bright and happy landscape.

The face felt very wet, and anxiously Marc looked up to inform Sister Ben.

"Lady cwy."

Zoe was still sobbing when she carried Marc into Ashamber half an hour later, and when the new family landed in Paris the following day, and for many weeks thereafter. She wept whenever she looked at Brian holding the baby, and frequently found him in tears himself. But little Marc hardly ever cried, even when his new-found parents did: he just went on smiling cherubically, as if knowing his job in life was simply to be happy.

On a fresh, sunny Saturday morning the following April, Brandon stood at his study window, his hands in his pockets, contemplating the view.

Everywhere there were daffodils, thousands of them, peppering the lawns, ringing the base of every tree, a massive, belated profusion of carnival colour after a long, needle-sharp winter. The breeze caught at the water of the lake, lifting it into tiny curling plumes, filling him, as water always did, with a sense of great freedom and energy. But duty dictated otherwise, and much against his will he turned away from the vernal vista to tackle the matter in hand.

On the other side of the room, Chris stood waiting, wondering why his father had summoned him. It was unlike him to be slow in coming to the point, and he wished he would get on with it. But Brandon remained standing, surveying his son as intently as he had surveyed the scenery, oddly speculative and yet detached. Once, long ago, he had been close to his son, taking him to sail at Hollyvaun when the boy had been a teenager and he had been so very unhappy in London, shackled to Marianne; but now they were polarised.

Both men were similarly dressed, in tweed sports jackets, check shirts, cord trousers and comfortable loafers. But where Brandon looked clean and countrified, Chris looked scruffy. There was no other word for it, Brandon thought: he was quite simply a mess and an insult. His hair had darkened to a dirty strawberry blond, falling in disarray over his forehead; his chin was stubbled, his loafers were dusty, his glasses out of kilter and out of fashion. Brandon wondered why he didn't get contact lenses, and had suggested it years ago, but Chris wouldn't. Worst of all, the grey traces of the black eye with which Chris had arrived at Ashamber were quite distinct, as was a healing scar on the side of his neck. It was these latter, together with his frequent trips to northern Spain and a lot of recent cogitation on Brandon's part, which had precipitated his decision to confront his son. He looked at him directly now, one adult to another.

"Chris. You're in the IRA, aren't you?"

Hoping to provoke a kneejerk denial which would confirm the fact, he got only a raised eyebrow.

"What a very curious question, Father. Of course I'm not."

"Aren't you, Chris? Can you swear it?"

"Most certainly. I swear it on Julie's grave."

Brandon hesitated. He had never known Chris to tell a direct lie, and did not think him capable of actually under-pinning one in such a manner. But the chilling suspicion did not melt in his gut.

"Are you in any illegal organisation, then?"

"No."

Chris had no need to lie. Sinn Féin was not illegal; it was the perfectly legitimate political wing of the IRA, the school for soldiers.

"But you are mixed up in politics?"

"Yes. I have an honours degree in politics, as you know, and will be starting a master's in September."

"Don't play games, Chris! You're active in politics!"

"Yes. Very well. I am. Is that a crime?"

Brandon sighed, and sat down at his desk.

"No. But why the secrecy, Chris? Why dissemble? This is a free country. If you want to make a career of politics, stand for election, I'll be only too pleased to help you. Have you joined a party?"

"No."

This was a lie. Brandon knew it, and Chris saw that he did.

"I don't want your help, Father, or your money, or your interference. People of your wealth are a liability, not an asset."

Whatever Chris might produce, Brandon had made up his mind not to be stung. He paused before speaking again.

"Sit down, Chris, and take that macho look off your face. You're not leaving this room till we sort this out."

He put as much forceful authority into this as he could muster. Chris was an adult, twenty-five, more than capable of standing up and walking out if he wanted to. Trying to get a fix on him at this stage was impossible; for years he had been slowly slipping out of Brandon's grasp, taking advantage of so many other matters that clamoured for attention. If it was not too late already, it was very close to it, and Brandon strove to keep an edge of desperation out of his voice.

"You say you are not in the IRA, Chris, and I take your word for it. I'm very glad you can give it to me, because you do know, Chris, what happens to youngsters who join, grow up and decide they want out?"

"Yes. Juniors are kneecapped, seniors are shot."

How matter-of-fact he sounded! Almost as if he approved. Suddenly, Brandon realised the depth of his concern. He was more than merely worried.

"You think the Ku Klux Klan is bad, Chris, or the Mafia, the drug barons, the K 14 in China? Check out the IRA. You're in your twenties now. Think ahead to the day you're thirty, forty. To the day you have a wife, children."

"Unlikely."

"What?!" Dear Jesus. Was he homosexual, as well? But what about Ana?

"But what about Ana?"

"She and I are friends. Comrades. I have no intention of marrying her."

"Is there something I should know?"

"No. I'm just not interested in acquiring excess baggage. You, of all people, should know how expensive that can be."

Again Brandon paused, checked himself.

"Look, Chris. You know and I know that there is something wrong here somewhere. I can't make you tell me what it is. But I think I have a right to know why, at least. Why don't you want – anything? The normal things?"

"The Lawrence things, you mean? The money, the houses, the wives? They may be normal to you, Father, but to normal people they're anything but."

It took all of Brandon's strength to ignore that. But he did.

"What, or who, got you started on all this, Chris?"

"You did. You moved to England and you sent me to school there. You paid thousands for me to learn how the British treat the Irish. How they regard them, how they despise them and how they raped them."

"Chris, you're living in the past! It's history, it's over! We're Europeans now, and so are they. Maybe old habits die hard, but that's their problem, not ours. If you're as educated and as intelligent as you demonstrably are, you don't let them get to you. You don't even care. You get on with your work and your life and you rise above this outdated racism. Anyone who can get a first-class degree can figure out that much. Besides, if you feel so strongly, why study at Trinity? Shouldn't you be at UCD?"

"Because Trinity was founded by Elizabeth I. It's a British institution. I can achieve far more there than I could at UCD, preaching to the converted."

"Preaching what, exactly?"

But Chris saw his mistake, and closed over.

"Father, when you lived in London, you joined White's and a number of other London clubs. Why? Because there was nothing to be gained by joining the Irish Club on Eaton Square. No point to be made. At White's, there was a point – the same point that I'm making at Trinity."

"Chris, that was twenty years ago. The point has been made. Now, we're in the EC and Britain is just one of our several trade partners. None of it matters any more."

"So why did you relocate your company headquarters in Dublin?"

"Convenience. I was about to marry Kerry."

"You'd decided to do it before that! Wanted to, for years! Don't give me that, Father."

He was right, and Brandon was forced to concede the fact.

"Very well. Let's say my roots were a consideration. But that doesn't change the terrible mistake I think you're making now. What do you suppose would happen, Chris, if you got what you really want? If Britain pulled out of Northern Ireland, and took its money with it?"

"Jesus! The money! Is that all you ever think about?"

"Money is what creates employment, Chris. Don't be so naive. The truth is that the Republic can't afford the North, and the North can't afford to lose its subsidies from London. But even if anyone could afford the luxury of a united Ireland, how could it be made acceptable to the Unionists? They're not going to walk meekly into a State in which divorce is proscribed, contraception is frowned on, any number of social attitudes are completely foreign to them. They'd fight it every step of the way, and there would be civil war, as well as crippling poverty."

"So, the Catholics in the North are to go on as they are, is that it? A bunch of handy hostages to fortune, the price of our comfort and prosperity down here?"

"Their lot will be improved by diplomacy, Chris, not violence."

"And how long is this pussyfooting to go on? Where is it getting them?"

"Where is the violence getting them? Or anyone?"

It was the old story. Better, more specialised minds than theirs had tried to solve it for centuries, and got no further. Brandon leaned forward, trying to be fair, and impersonal. Enough families had been divided on this subject already, North and South.

But he could no longer defer what would have to be done if Chris rejected this last chance he offered.

"It's better to count your blessings than your burdens, Chris. This country has made staggering progress in the seventy years since it became independent. You won't be doing it any favours by plunging it back into the very bloodshed and starvation it's cost so much to get out of. The EC affords unprecedented new opportunities. Don't blow them. Nobody will invest in a war-torn island."

"This country isn't independent, Father. Not all of it. But everyone's got so comfy and complacent, haven't they, in the Republic? Let the good times roll."

"Yes! Let them! Look forward, not back."

"And the hell with the North? Let the Brits boot it around all they like? Let it go away and disappear, come back when it's ready to behave itself?"

"Oh, God almighty. You know perfectly well we're arguing strategy, not philosophy. What I'm trying to tell you is that you're a fool if you're mixed up in anything subversive. You don't realise how few people require your services, or the consequences of giving them."

"I'm sorry. I entirely disagree. And what's more, I think your pragmatism is an acquired taste. When I was a child, my father was a different man."

"That's the point! People grow up – and I hope you will, soon. In the meantime, argue all you like, with anyone you like. But do it openly and do it legally. If your cause is worthwhile, there should be no need for any more secrecy about it."

"The IRA didn't proscribe itself, Father. Its own government did."

"And why do you think that is? Don't join it, Chris, for God's sake don't! You'll never get out! It will take over your whole life, it will destroy you, consume you with fruitless bitterness. Contribute new life to this country, instead of throwing it away."

"I have no intention of throwing it away. Merely of spending it in any manner I deem fit."

"And other people's, too?"

Coldly, Chris looked at him. "I'm not a murderer, if that's what you mean."

No, Brandon thought, you're not. Not directly. You're too clever for that; clever enough to know that the IRA needs brains like yours much more than it needs expendable martyrs. You won't die. You'll send others out to die, but you'll soldier on. You think you can disguise that messianic gleam in your eye, Chris, extinguish the fire for my benefit. But you haven't learned to dissimulate yet. I see the coldness, I see the implacability, I see something far worse than passing young passion.

Panic didn't just creep up on Brandon then. It marched up and arrested him. If he lost this battle, he would lose his son. But he was lost already, and how many other parents might now lose theirs, at his hands?

"Chris, my wife's parents were butchered by the IRA. You know that. Shall we go and find her now, so you can tell her what their death achieved?"

"I would imagine she knows already, Father. It was a lesson to everyone about marrying across the sectarian divide. Her mother's family was Unionist . . ."

"You can actually say that, here in her house? You say it to my face, and you would say it to hers?"

"Yes. Her parents owned far too much land, and money, as she does, Nabdul Zul Mahrat does, and you do yourself."

It was useless. Brandon saw that the ideology which consumed Chris was complete, a brick wall which would come crashing down on him some day, maiming and killing many others in the process. He could not save him, or them. All he could do was save his family: Kerry, who was so alarmed now, Killian who would be tainted by every word from the stepbrother who knew his loneliness, and exploited it. If he did not forestall Chris, Killian would become his young recruit as once he had been Matthew Breffni's.

Brandon had survived many things by switching off his emotions. A stifling marriage, a baby's death, a long period without Kerry. He switched them off now, and faced his son.

"Chris. You are in the IRA. Whether you admit it or not, you are, spiritually if not literally. You belong to a brotherhood of murderers. Therefore you no longer belong to this family."

Disciplined, trained against shock tactics, Chris did not speak.

"You are no longer my son, Chris. You no longer have a home in my home. I will never see you again. When I die, you will inherit nothing, no part of the land or the money you despise, earned by every eldest male Lawrence for nearly two hundred years. You bear my name, but if I could take that away from you too, I would. You are nobody."

The concept of heritage, paradoxically, was axiomatic to Chris. But the concept of family was redundant. Standing up, he turned his back on his father, and walked out.

For the rest of the morning, Brandon sat alone in his study, looking out over the lake.

For Kerry, he told himself, for Killian. For myself, I could not have done it. But for her, and for her son, I have repudiated mine.

Killian is my son now. My eldest son. I have lost Harry, I have sacrificed Chris, but I have Kerry, and the babies, and Killian.

They are my family now. They will get everything I have, every part of me. They are my only family, my real family. They are my blood.

Zoe was exhausted, expected to be exhausted for a long time more, and was blissfully happy. Nowadays, there was no need to diet; she could consume as many calories as she liked, knowing they would all be burned off by the time she fell into bed, a paradise about which she often hallucinated during the course of her busy day. But still she was a glutton – a glutton for punishment, who had begged Sister Ben for a second child. Baby Blair arrived in October, a tiny exquisite doll with the face of an angel, the lungs of a diva and the temperament of Genghis Khan. Barely three months old, she made Zoe feel every day of her thirty-seven years, and there were times when mother and daughter contemplated each other as balefully as wrestlers in the ring.

Unlike Kerry, Zoe simply could not breeze through motherhood. A late starter, she took every fractious moment to heart, as serious about her job as any lawyer or accountant. But Brian assumed his half of it fair and square, and between them they more than managed, growing closer in their own relationship, no longer merely partners but a full family, a complete and profoundly contented unit.

Often, Yves and Robbie volunteered to help, and it amused Zoe to watch the two men earnestly set out for the Bois de Boulogne or the Jardin de Luxembourg, pushing a buggy laden with toys, bottles and nappies, oblivious of the incongruous spectacle they presented. But invariably they returned from these excursions laughing and invigorated, and Zoe was very glad of their reliable, generous input. It eased tension, too, between Yves and Brian, who were perpetually at loggerheads in the salon. Disenchanted with mounting commercial pressures, Yves had begun to seek other outlets for his creativity, and was taking life-drawing classes at an art college. A harmless pursuit, but Brian resented such diversification, fearing it might grow into more than a hobby. Sometimes they rowed spectacularly, but with Robbie Zoe saw to it that their tantrums always ended in lunch at the Cluny, with grudging apologies, a lot of wine and jokes, and finally bonhomie.

Robbie, everyone agreed, was the best thing that had ever happened to Yves. Settling into what he considered a marriage, he assumed full responsibility for his volatile lover, shouldering all the little tasks that Yves found irksome, organising his life into order and harmony. Although their apartment was frequently filled with friends, who slept on sofas and deprecated like locusts, it acquired a homey atmosphere, and even Brian had to salute the sudden stability of his errant partner's lifestyle.

Everyone's bachelor days were over. But nobody regretted them, and on this still evening in early winter, Zoe stood over her pot of *coq-au-vin*, savouring the palpable peace of her domestic scenario.

In their nursery, the children lay in bed asleep, and while Zoe pottered in the kitchen Brian sat in his tapestry rocker by the fireplace in the next room, putting the finishing touches to a series of experimental sketches under the pooled light of an Émile Gallet lamp. Like his mother before him, he loved antiques, and they suited the old apartment perfectly. Since moving in with Zoe he had acquired many worthwhile pieces, despite his inability to bargain for toffee. Unless accompanied by some responsible person, he generally paid far too much for his finds, but derived satisfaction and inspiration nonetheless from his oaks and brasses, leathers and thick old crystals, faded silks and moth-eaten canvases. But this evening, he was solely focused on these sketches, his pencil laid down at intervals as he held his pad at arm's length, considering them thoughtfully, critically.

Elderly and dignified, a grandfather clock ticked sonorously in the corner as he reflected on his work, and on the other things stored up in his mind. Later, he must deal with them, but for now he was preoccupied, and in turn Zoe also lapsed into silence, considerately leaving him in peace.

At length, however, dinner was ready. Wiping her hands on her apron, Zoe came in to summon him to table, but stopped when she saw how absorbed he was; she too hated to be disturbed when the creative juices were flowing. For several minutes she stood in the doorway, leaning against its lopsided oak frame, watching him fondly, appreciatively. Everything in the Marais seemed to lean slightly to one side or the other, and in the early days Yves's apartment had made her seasick – typical of Yves, she had thought, typical! But now she was used to it, and would not trade it for the finest duplex on Fifth Avenue. It felt as if she had lived here all her life, and been married to Brian not for two years but for ever. Theirs was not the passionate, all-consuming union that Kerry and Brandon's had become; it was quite a different relationship, very soft, very gentle, very expansive in its parameters, fitting them like a glove so perfectly tailored they were hardly aware of it. It was simply right, it always should have been, and now it felt as if it always had.

Against expectation, they found themselves able to work and live together, one of the few favoured couples whose sanity could survive constant proximity. Of the two, Brian was the more equable, the slower to be roused, but knowing the steel underneath the silk Zoe resolutely avoided the temptation to chip away at her husband's soft exterior. Thankful for all they had together, she could find no reason to challenge fate, and their joint life bloomed like a flower in watered soil.

But if she did not rouse him now, dinner would be ruined. Padding quietly over to him, she stood looking over his shoulder, fascinated.

"Baby clothes! Brilliant! Why did we never think of that before?"

She bent down and planted a kiss on the nape of his neck, seeing in the raw sketches the tender newness of birth.

"Because we never had babies before, I suppose. D'you think they'll catch on?"

"Are you kidding? All the trendy mamas will go mad for them! We can incorporate them with the sportswear, under the *prêt-à-porter* label."

He was pleased. Her approval mattered to him, personally and professionally, and his smile was gratified as she brushed her hand through the fine hairs on the back of his neck.

"Do you want to wait dinner, then, till you've finished?"

"No, no, I'm starving. I'll give you a hand with the table."

She liked this domesticated streak in him: there was nothing of the celebrity prima donna about Brian. They had a maid, but she did not live in, and on weekends they cooked and cleaned for themselves.

"Thanks, but no need. The wine is breathing, everything's ready."

He followed her through to the dining room and sat down at the circular, dark oak table, lighting the fat beeswax candle as he sniffed the air hungrily. Many candles had burned on this table, and they couldn't get the splashes off, but neither could they bear to cover the solid, glossy wood with a tablecloth. She served up the stew in floral china plates, and he looked at her speculatively across the bowl of winter chrysanthemums.

"Zoe. What am I going to do about Lu?"

In one way, Zoe was flattered that he should consult her, even after her initial advice had so badly backfired. But it bothered her too. She frankly wished that Lu would evaporate into the mists of Paris; but Brian worried the problem like a terrier.

"What do you want to do?"

"I don't know. Make things up to her, somehow. It's my fault she's in hospital. Nervous breakdowns only happen to terribly stressed, unhappy people. People who feel unloved and unsupported."

"Brian, it was in her character. Always. She was tense, brittle, wound up from the start. She had to have everything to order, and had no mechanism for coping when she didn't get it."

"No, but she had other qualities, and I should have made more of them. She did me so much good, and I homed in on the one bad thing. I made her feel less than perfect."

"She *was* less than perfect! If she'd only admitted it, she might have kept her sanity, might have adapted to the new life she never even tried to build."

"She did try. Claire told me. She was seeing someone else, but he wouldn't marry her."

"But then he can't have loved her. If he did, she wouldn't be where she is now. Maybe he found her too overbearing. Or too materialistic. Greedy."

Brian flinched, knowing Zoe would not say such things if they were not true. But Zoe had done her best for Lu, long ago; it was unfair to burden her with the problem which might have been solved if he had only listened then – not just to Zoe, but to the need that Lu was too proud to articulate.

"Would you mind very much, Zoe, if I went to see her?"

Zoe thought she would mind dreadfully. While many ex-husbands and wives were able to maintain friendly relations, Lu would never be able to. She had had a nervous breakdown and she would exploit that, use it as a weapon in a lifelong campaign of emotional blackmail. She would oblige Brian to pity her, and then start making other demands, find ways to keep him in her sights for ever.

Yet she was to be pitied. She had lost everything, while now she, Zoe, had so much.

"Is it important to you, Brian?"

"It's important to Claire, and Lionel. They were so good to me when I came to France, the least I can do now is give their daughter some smidgen of the same support. In a way, Zoe, I'll always be responsible for Lu."

"She's not a child, Brian."

"No. But she's ill, and she needs me."

Zoe found the phrase painful. But who had taught Brian to respond this way, to know when people were hurting and empathise with their pain, even at his own expense?

She had, herself.

"Then go to her."

He looked at her in a way she hoped he would never again look at Lucienne de Veurlay.

"Thank you, Zoe."

She dipped her head down over her plate, hoping he could not read her thoughts.

I must trust him. He married me, he loves me and he loves our children. We are secure, we can take this test. But oh, God, Lu is not the only one reaping as she sowed. I am, too. Kerry will say I'm a fool. Lu is still beautiful, still young and seductive, probably as clever as ever.

Would money appease her, I wonder?

"Brian, why don't you give Lu some of your father's money?"

"How thoughtful of you. I think I will. Speaking of money, Zoe, Estelle said a curious thing today at the salon. I don't think she meant it maliciously, but she wanted to know whether it had cost us a lot to adopt. Seemed to be wondering whether it was sort of possible to buy a baby."

"Oh, how absurd. The money we gave Sister Ben has enabled lots of other couples to take children, people who couldn't have managed otherwise. But if we hadn't had it, I'm certain she'd have helped us just the same. What she wants for her children is what we were chiefly able to offer."

Thoughtfully, Brian nodded. Unable to shake off Lu's legacy entirely, he was acutely aware of monetary considerations at the salon, and it shamed him somewhat to encounter people with other priorities. But like Yves and Kerry, Sister Ben was her own person, scornful of the acquisitive age in which she lived, one of the few people he knew whose lives were not run by accountants. How she survived he could not imagine, but she did, and he admired such independence in a corporate climate. Without a penny to her name, the nun was happier than many of his spoilt, affluent clients.

But Lu was not Sister Ben. He smiled.

"If you promise for chrissakes not to tell Kerry, I'll give Lu ten per cent of Dad's money. *And* I'll bring her an armload of roses."

"That's very nice of you, Brian, and I'm proud to be married to such a kind-hearted man. Just tell the florist to leave the thorns on."

Laughing at her rare acerbity, they finished their meal on a lighter note, returned to the lounge and mulled some more over the intriguing new sketches. The aroma of the food lingered pleasantly in the air while Zoe poured coffee, went to check on the children, and put a disc on their new CD player. Jean Ferrat, singing the poetry of Louis Aragon: Brian loved that, as she did herself.

Settling down into a comfortable evening at home, Brian appeared to forget about Lu. But Zoe knew he had not. At the back of his mind, he was guilty about his once gorgeous young bride, tracing her illness back to its source with chagrin in his heart. He had treated his wife exactly as Darragh de Bruin had treated his sister, and could not exonerate himself.

Lu would always have a hold on him, and the prospect ate into Zoe. Oh, of course she needed help! But what would happen, when she was well again, when she left the clinic, when her parents were not around to chaperone her? Until now, she had always got what she wanted, and she had always wanted Brian.

But after an hour or more, Brian looked up at his wife, almost idly, as an afterthought.

"Zoe, when I go to see Lu, would you do me a favour?"

"Of course. What is it?"

"Would you come with me?"

Oh, the relief. He did not want to be alone with Lu. He wanted his wife with him, to proclaim his marriage loud and clear – maybe, she thought wryly, even to protect him.

"Certainly. But what if she wants to see you again? Later, when she returns to Paris, to her apartment?"

"If she invites me, I'll go. We all will. It's a very nice apartment. The children will love it. And I'm sure Lu will just love having them."

22

"This one's for you, Helen."

Killian grinned at the woman he considered his grandmother, and began to strum the first chords of "Kentucky Woman". Helen laughed, knowing he was teasing her, thinking that the cheeky child was a child no longer. Seventeen next month, he sat on the floor in his ubiquitous frayed denims, his hair tied off his face in the ponytail his mother hated, caressing his guitar like a lover. He sang the song with careless abandon, but then changed his tune, whimsically, and lowered himself into a moody French song, one he had picked up from Brian probably. A sombre piece by Serge Reggiani, it was called "Le Pont Mirabeau", and he put such thought and emotion into it that Helen was transfixed, her mind floating away with his under the bridges of Paris, "*où coule la Seine* . . ." his voice was fully broken, and he sang it like an adult, belying the behaviour that could still be so juvenile and hesitant for his years.

Like Brandon's own son Harry, Killian was growing up slowly, in his own sweet time, but now Helen saw something in him that she had never seen before, and heard it too in his plaintive, masculine tone. With ease he picked up and held the song's sad, thoughtful resignation, seeming to understand something he could not yet possibly have experienced, melting Helen's heart although she understood the lyrics not at all.

My God, she thought, how many hearts is this boy going to break? Where did he learn to sing like this? How bittersweet, to see him here on the verge of manhood . . . but I'm going to have to accept it. He's not a boy any more, my boy. Look at him. Look at those new planes in his face, look at the muscles and sinews in his arms, the hair on his chest, the tautness in his whole body. He's ready to move on; but not away, I hope. Not from us, from me.

But, over December and January, a long separation loomed. To mark his fiftieth year, Brandon had handed over chairmanship of his various enterprises to deputies, and embarked on a sailing expedition with his friends Greg and Louis to Polynesia. Absent for ten weeks already, he was in sight of his goal, and at the end of the week Kerry would fly out to join him in Tahiti with her three children, her brother and his family, Yves and Robbie.

They had all implored Helen and Bob to come with them, but Helen knew the long flights would be far too arduous, and that on arrival there would be a lot of sailing, which wasn't her scene at all, thank you. Kerry argued that some sun would be good for her creeping rheumatism, but Helen retorted that the enforced rest here at home would do it quite as much good. At sixty-seven, there was much to be said for the golf club, the bridge club and company of one's own age.

The others were excited, however, even Kerry who after a busy year badly needed the break. Deoch an Doras had been retired to stud, but Nabdul had other horses ready for training, including a couple of yearlings that had the makings of real flyers. Six weeks was a long time to be away from them, but it was now or never, and in conscience she felt she owed it to Brandon to acknowledge his achievement.

From outposts all down the Atlantic and across the Pacific, he had sent flowers from every port he put into, and telephoned religiously every week. Undemonstrative in public, he was quite the opposite in private, and Helen knew Kerry missed him far more than she admitted. So did Killian, whose glowing future as a guttersnipe had been averted, in Helen's view, entirely thanks to Brandon.

The boy's song died away on a slow, seductive note, and a sad thought struck Helen. She must speak to him, since Kerry would never think to.

"Killian, when you go to Polynesia, you know, you'll be thrown together a lot with Yves and Robbie."

"Yeah. Great. Actually, I've been thinking, Helen – d'you

think they'd let me stay with them in Paris after my exams next summer? I'd love to spend a bit of time there. I could earn my own keep."

"Oh, yes? How so?"

"Busking. In the métro. I bet Mum would be thrilled. You know how she's always going on about making my own way in the world."

Helen couldn't see why not. But that was eight months away; Polynesia was now.

"We'll see. If you get your exams, and your music diploma, I'm sure Brandon – and your mother – will want to reward you. But the thing is, Killian . . . you know Yves and Robbie are homosexual, don't you?"

He stared at her. Surely this elderly lady was not, bizarrely, going to start in on the subject Brandon had also broached before leaving, while teaching him to drive?

"Yeah. So what? Does that mean I can't stay with them? But they stay here all the time!"

"So they do. I just want you to be aware of the situation, that's all, and sensitive to it. Sometimes young lads of your age react in rather a hostile way to – to men like them. I don't want you to do that. Life is difficult enough for them as it is."

"Why?"

"Just because they're different. But they can't help that. They pay a high price for loving each other, and they can't have children. Yves has been your mother's closest friend all of his life and hers, and I want you to remember that. No jibes, no jokes, OK?"

"Sure. OK. But I wouldn't anyway. I like them a lot."

"I know you do. But they deserve respect as well. They're two wonderful men, very good, kind friends to us all. It takes a lot of honesty and courage to live as they do. You don't realise how hard it is for them at times."

Suddenly Killian caught her drift. He was not to treat Yves or Robbie as Brandon did, with bare tolerance. That was the one failing he had ever noticed in his stepfather, but it had never occurred to him to perpetuate it. On the contrary; Robbie was an interesting guy, and Yves was a hoot. He liked them very much.

"Don't fuss, Helen. You can rely on me."

She smiled at his tone, as if he were the adult reassuring a fretful child. Such a conversation did not come easily to her, but the boy had no concept of the sheltered life he lived in this lazy rural environment, far removed from the drug and crime-raddled cultures of Europe or America. She wanted to protect him, but that meant educating him, informing him of the influences he would encounter. If he was to travel, then he must do it with his eyes open.

Really this was Kerry's job, dammit! But Kerry had her precious horses to worry about, and the twins in whose future she invested so much more vision. All his young life Killian had been left to run wild, and then blamed when he did. Nowadays, of course, there was Brandon, but he had not been there for the crucial first years, any more than the boy's natural father had. At odd moments Helen still speculated about that gentleman, and wondered whether his son took after him. But Darragh de Bruin was never mentioned, Kerry did not possess so much as a photograph of him, and had never once been persuaded to describe him. Never, not once, in seventeen years.

It was a long, exhausting flight to Papeete, via London and Miami, and by the time they touched down on Tahiti everyone was weary, fractious, dehydrated and thoroughly muddled. Only Yves was able for the children, and Kerry abandoned hers into his arms, not caring if he fed them on caviar and champagne so long as it kept them quiet.

But then, there was Brandon, waiting to meet them, after three months! She hardly recognised the bronzed, rugged man who came rushing up to her in shorts and a T-shirt, gathering her into his arms with cries of joy. If this was what life at sea had done for him, then she was vindicated in having let him go; his eyes shone with achievement, health and vitality blazed from every pore, his whole mien was so happy and handsome she fell in love with him all over again, there on the airport concourse. Forty-nine when he set out, he was now round the corner into his fifties, but she knew men half his age who looked twice it. Thrilled, she kissed him over and over, until he led her away to where a convoy of rented jeeps stood waiting, leaving the others to follow like a troop of drunken ducklings.

Too tired to talk, or take in the startling scenery, she let herself be driven to the water bungalows, on stilts in the ocean, where they would spend their first acclimatising days. There, she took one look at her low wide bed and threw herself face down on it, almost weeping with gratitude. In that swooning state of disorientation that produces dizziness, she closed her eyes and did not even see the look of mixed amusement and discomfiture on her husband's face.

Having had several days to recover himself, Brandon was now extremely fit and well, and just dying to see Kerry. Idiotically he had envisaged a most romantic reunion, quite forgetting the rigours of long-haul travel, and thought that Kerry's main interest in the bed would be him. But it wasn't. She could barely speak, and if Tahiti should happen to sink to the bottom of the ocean at that moment, well, she was very sorry, but she could not lift her little finger to help it.

He stood looking at her as she slipped into deep sleep, sprawled fully dressed on the bed, her hair illuminating the white cotton pillows, one shoe fallen on the floor. Gently he eased the other one off, lifted her under the duvet, and tucked her in with tender resignation. She was dead beat, and would sleep round the clock; but after that, he would have her all to himself, with not a single horse to compete for her attention.

Over the days that followed, everyone regained their spirits and their equilibrium, adjusting to the new time zone, to the climate, to each other and to the beauty of the island. Tahiti was so French in orientation, they felt singularly comfortable from the start, as well as dazzled by its rich tropical colour.

Flowers grew everywhere in the warm lush air, spreading their lovely scent all over the island, and wide-eyed in wonder the children chased after butterflies and iguanas, trying to climb palm and tamarind trees, browning rapidly in the open air. Kerry freckled furiously, as did Saoirse, but the others turned to the buttery hue of the natives who seemed to smile perpetually, swaying their hips as though issuing invitations to dance. Eager to entice Kerry into the sensuous mood of the place, Brandon took her to see Paul Gauguin's hut, which she loved even more than he had hoped. But in it she experienced a strange sense of déjà-vu, wondering what it could remind her of . . . Monet's house at Giverny, was that it? Or – or Auguste Rodin's house, in Paris? That was it. As Brandon steered her enthusiastically round she remembered that other day, a lifetime ago, when another husband had taken her on just such an excursion, with the very same pride and fascination for so great an artist.

But it didn't distress her. Rather she rejoiced in her good fortune in having found another man who loved her so much more, in a way that was infinitely less possessive, less didactic. Poor Gauguin had had a hard time of it, but she was touched by the ironic way in which his sufferings had enriched Tahiti, and marvelled at so much colour, so much glowing beauty, from the hand of such a lonely man, who had been jeered at and ridiculed throughout his long stay on this languid, lucent island.

Next day, she went back with Yves to see the hut again, leaving Killian saddled with the children, who kept staggering away to inspect flora and fauna with gurgles of gleeful triumph. But if it kept his mother happy, then Killian didn't mind, and in some respects he preferred the kiddies to the adults. After five days, Greg and Louis departed to their waiting families in London, and Brandon was left with the yacht and a new chartered crew. He decided to take everyone out to some of the other, smaller islands, accessible ones like Moorea and Bora-Bora, so near that there was no danger of the infants being seasick.

It was a very large ocean-going yacht, on which they set sail early one blood-red morning for Moorea. Lambent in the scarlet dawn, the sea gradually changed to the clearest, most miraculous shade of emerald green, so that everyone clustered up on deck to admire it in overawed silence. But Kerry had eyes only for Brandon, standing at the helm in his tattered shorts, happy as a sandboy as he handled the hefty yacht with casual ease – the same way, exactly, in which he handled *her* on the dance floor. A light warm breeze filled out the sails as the craft began to scud along under a high azure sky in which minuscule clouds drifted distantly, and as she listened to the soft slash of the water it came to Kerry that this was one of the most memorable moments of her life. Totally at one with herself, with the whole world, she put her arm around Brandon's waist, seeing in him not a businessman but an adventurer. Like all the yachtsmen who sailed these seas, he had the aura of a wanderer, a knife in his belt, a compass round his neck on a long string, a map perpetually at hand as he navigated with a sure, deft hand.

She hadn't the faintest idea which way they were heading, but apparently it was north-west, and in due course Moorea came into view, a tiny blur on the infinite horizon until its jagged, dramatic twin peaks slowly assumed more definite shape. Negotiating the approach was tricky, because of the coral lagoons with their firefinger reefs that could so easily hole the boat. Clearly visible under the crystalline water, some outcrops were as big as the yacht itself, but Brandon and the crew inched safely past them, dropped anchor in the shelter of Opunohu Bay, and lowered the dinghies over the side for access to the long, dusty pink beach.

Drinking in the glorious panorama, Yves came up beside Kerry as she leaned over the rail, and draped his arm fondly around her shoulder.

"Even prettier than one of your brother's gowns," he commented drily, and Kerry nodded, enchanted.

"Isn't it just, Yves. I've never seen anywhere so exotic. Even Senegal wasn't a bit like this."

To her surprise he kissed her lightly on the cheek, and stood sharing her wonder for several minutes, in a silence that was lengthy for him. But espying picnic baskets going down into the little boats with the children, he grinned suddenly.

"Ah. Lunch. Good."

Lean as he was, and disciplined nowadays, Yves remained a true Frenchman, the pleasures of the senses never very far from his mind. Taking her hand, he led her to the swaying rope ladder on whose lower rungs the children clung precariously, trying to touch the armies of vivid fish patrolling their arrival. He helped her down, and they were joined by Robbie who, she noted, never let Yves out of his sight for long. Oh, how glad she was, that they had found each other! Utterly devoted, they were friends as well as lovers, giving enormously and receiving in equal measure, living their joint life to the full. But as he leapt the small distance from the larger craft into the smaller, Yves gasped sharply, twisting on the ankle he had injured while skiing in Canada the winter before. It had never healed properly, and instantly Robbie reached out to catch him, with a look so concerned that Kerry felt a twinge herself.

"If conventional medicine can't fix that, Yves, why don't you try homeopathy?"

Steadying himself, Yves nodded airily, the pain gone as suddenly as it had come.

"Maybe I will. But it's nothing. Everyone who skis has accidents."

Had he been one of her horses, Kerry would have pursued the point. But it didn't seem to bother him, and she turned to watch Brian, already on the beach, donning his scuba gear for a plunge into paradise. With a flick of his flippers he disappeared, and by the time they beached the boat Zoe sat complacently surrounded by her children, who now numbered three, peeling bananas that Marc shovelled into his mouth with savage, sandy fingers. Blair, a beautiful moppet with the voracious appetite of a jumbo jet, snatched hers in turn, while Francesca, the current baby, lolled patiently on a canvas mat. Seeing their cousins thus favoured, Séamus and Saoirse began to fight over an apple that Brandon sat peeling for them with his Swiss knife, three-year-old terrorists with murder on their minds. With a lazy grin, Brandon slapped them away.

"Button it, brats, or you won't get any."

They subsided; Brandon always kept his word, be it a threat or a promise. Leaving him to play with them, Kerry stripped down to her black and green swimsuit, designed by Zoe, and contemplated the alluring idea of a swim. Diffidently, Killian came up to her.

"Are we going to stay here for a few days? Can I sleep on the beach, if we are?"

"With pleasure, if it means we won't have to listen to that infernal guitar of yours all night."

The idea of camping out appealed strongly to Killian, but – but why did his mother always seem to be pushing him away? He looked at her, and saw the affection in her eyes as she passed a tube of sun block to Brandon, the fleeting, but positively adoring way she glanced at the twins.

What about me, Mum? Won't I ever get one of those looks of yours – not even one, ever? He racked his brains for something ingratiating to say.

"That's a great swimsuit, Mum. You don't look old enough to be my mother."

I'm not your mother, she thought. There's the plain truth of it. I'm somebody who's in charge of you till you're old enough to fend for yourself, which, with luck, will be any day now.

"Thanks, Killian. Why don't you get a snorkel, now, and swim out to Uncle Brian?"

"OK. Are you coming too?"

"In a minute. You go ahead."

He decided he might as well. Clearly she wanted him to. Rebuffed, he loped away, and as she watched him wade out into the water Kerry sighed impatiently. Apart from this one thing, her life was so bright and shining now, in every way. Waking every morning with such zest for it, she wanted to exult aloud, hardly daring analyse it too much in case she damaged it. It was a halcyon thing, that she could almost take in her hands, turn it round to admire every new facet, a perfect sphere of profound fulfilment.

Perfect, except for her elder son. As much as she could, she left him to Helen and Brandon, but he was still *there*, existing, irritating. How much longer? Another year, at least, till he came of age . . . Sensing suddenly that she was being watched, she spun round, and found Yves cradling a twin in either arm, regarding her in a way that made her drop her gaze.

Dammit, she thought. Yves Tiberti knows me far too well. But I don't care. I love him, and he loves me, unconditionally. I do wish he'd do something about that ankle or he'll be left with a limp. What a shame if he were! He's such a beautiful man, really quite beautiful.

Drawn by the naked admiration in her eyes, Yves relinquished the twins to Robbie, who took them away to paddle, and came to stretch out beside her. It was very hot, and with Zoe they lay sunning themselves in the murmuring heat, wandering somehow onto the subject of Lu. Lu was relatively well now, Zoe said, back at work with Dior, as competent as ever. But her nights were filled with dates, dances and men, a whole series of them as once Yves had had.

Just for a moment, Kerry saw a flash of Lu, laughing with a waiter in a café on the Champs Elysées one night in Paris – her first night, nearly twenty years before. What a waste, what a waste! If only she hadn't wanted so much, too much, and ended up with nothing.

"And still Brian keeps in touch with her, you say? He's a silly old softie. She'd buy and sell him, if it suited her."

But again, Yves looked at her, rather sharply.

"Brian is hard as nails, and so are you, madame, when you choose."

Sweetly, she made a moue.

"Oh, let's not bicker. It's too hot. Don't be cross with me, Yves."

He never could, for more than five seconds. But Christ, how smug she could get some day, soon, if somebody did not let the air out of her balloon! Provoked as he was by her treatment of Killian, he was almost glad nonetheless that she had that one ongoing difficulty to deal with. Perfection, he thought, would become her very badly.

Sitting up, he brushed the sand off his chest and offered to watch Zoe's children building their sandcastles, so that "les girls" could go for a swim. With only token protest, they took him up on it, and he set about his supervisory duties quite seriously, considering it a privilege to be entrusted with such adorable little people.

That evening, tingling after their hot day in the salt air, they pulled on sweaters, moved further back into the cove and built a barbecue. Silhouetted in the setting sun, the men went in search of wood, and as the sky sank into an incandescent blaze of imperial reds and molten golds, Zoe and Kerry circled dubiously round a bucket of live lobster caught earlier by Brian and Robbie. The creatures wriggled noisily, and Zoe quailed, harrowed by their plight.

"Oooh! This is awful! What are we going to do, Kerry?"

"We're going to let Brian deal with them, that's what. He caught them and he can bung them into their boiling water."

Zoe grinned. Kerry wasn't quite as tough a nut as she liked to make out – not quite. She let other people do her dirty work for her when it suited, although had it been necessary she would surely have despatched the lobsters every bit as ruthlessly as Brian. And yet, she could be so tender too, especially where the twins were concerned. Already they had their first ponies, and in Saoirse Zoe saw her mother reincarnate, bobbing bossily along in front of Séamus, tossing her red curls as she flounced round the estate that would one day be hers.

The girl child had no fear at all, and even out here, so far away from Ashamber, ran headlong into every new adventure. Séamus, chubbier and more blond than his sister, didn't stand a chance – unless, somewhere in his genial nature, there was a streak of Brian, or Brandon. Whatever way it might roll, the die was cast: there would be no more children now, for any of them.

Laden with driftwood, the men came back and they all listened in admiration as Brandon recounted his tale of marine odyssey. In the amethyst sky, the Southern Cross rose twinkling, and a sliver of crescent moon slid shyly into view. It was very quiet, very beautiful, and Yves could not take his eyes off the sweeping horizon, the hushed sea, thinking what a wonderful, intrepid thing Brandon had done. The Breton blood in him was fired by such a risky voyage, and he gave Brandon every credit for breaking free, for embarking on such a singular venture. Unlike Kerry, he did not brag or chortle over his conquests, but there was no doubt about it; she had truly met her match.

Eventually the fire was blazing, showering sparks up into

the purple night, and they sat around it, the lobster bubbling after much cowering, shrieking and sadistic enthusiasm from Marc, Séamus and Saoirse. Never having seen one cooked before, they were transfixed, agog, their mouths as round as their eyes.

Finishing his story, Brandon turned to Killian.

"Why don't you play us something on your guitar, Killian?"

It lay on the sand in its leather case. Pleased to be asked, he took it out, tuned and fiddled with it for a few moments; and then, as Kerry sat riveted in horror, he crossed his legs under him, and began to play "Galway Bay".

She couldn't endure it. She couldn't. She could not help herself.

"*No!* No, no!"

How could he? How could he sit here on this sand, in his denim shorts, with his black hair over his eyes, his *father's* eyes, and play that song? Trembling violently, she ran to him, thrust the instrument out of his hands, and kicked it out of his reach.

Too stunned to react, nobody moved. It was Yves, finally, who got up and went to Killian, picked up the guitar, put it back in his hands, and walked slowly up to Kerry.

She was sobbing, and he put his arms around her.

"Kerry. Come with me. I want to talk to you."

Brandon did too. But he saw that Yves understood this, whatever it was, and wisely decided to let him take first crack at it. But by God she'd better explain herself later, to everyone. For now, he would concentrate on Killian.

"Go on, Killian. Play it, or something else. Whatever you like. Your mother has had too much sun, that's all."

But tears stood in Killian's eyes, tears he struggled not to let fall. He was too old to cry. But he couldn't play. His fingers were shaking. What had he done?

"Come on. We all want to hear you. Don't we, guys?"

Hastily Brian, Zoe and Robbie replied that they did, and encouraged him until he began to pick at it again, and Yves led Kerry away into the dunes.

He sat her down there, and she cried her heart out, stricken by the way he looked at her. That made it worse, and she howled and hiccuped until he pulled her to him, and let her cry on his chest until there were no more tears left.

"Oh, Yves, I'm so sorry, really I am."

"For yourself, or for your son?"

"F-for both of us! It's not his fault, but it's not mine either! His father sat on a beach, just like this one, wearing shorts and his hair in the very same way, with his legs crossed, singing that very same bloody song, the morning I told him I was leaving him. Killian is an exact replica, and I can't stand it."

"Yes, well, that's understandable and very unfortunate. But listen to me, Kerry. Killian can't help who he is or what he is. He tries so hard to earn your love, and you try so hard to pretend he doesn't exist. You abuse him horribly, *ma chérie*, and I am ashamed of you."

"What? Yves, you're exaggerating! I don't abuse him. I've never laid a hand on him in my life – well, hardly ever."

"I don't mean physically. I mean spiritually, emotionally, mentally. You're far more cruel to him than if you beat him."

"But he has Brandon, and Helen. They worship the ground he walks on."

"Kerry, you are his mother!"

So rare was the anger in him, Kerry saw that some nerve in him had been struck, was vibrating in a way that silenced her.

"Shall I tell you about my parents, Kerry? Shall I?"

Now, after twenty years? He was going to tell her? Suddenly, she was afraid of what she had unleashed.

"This ankle of mine, Kerry, that you are so concerned about. It will never mend. It will never mend because it was broken before. By my father, when I was two. Again, when I was six. In the twelve years that I lived with my parents in Brittany, nearly all of my bones were broken, most by my father, some by my mother. They drank, they fought, and I hated them. I wished they were dead. When I was twelve, I ran away. To sea, on a trawler. It was my job to mend the nets, and that's what I did until I was eighteen. I stayed on the boat, I never went to school, I never knew what love was. I had no home, no education,

no family. I could hardly even read. All I knew how to
do was sew. It was a terrible life, but it was no worse
than the life you're giving Killian."

"No worse? Yves, it's much worse! Oh, I had no idea – but
I've never done anything like that to Killian, never . . ."

"Kerry, you have hurt him deeply, and deliberately. My
parents didn't do it deliberately. They were very poor, they
were alcoholic, they were frustrated. Over the years I have
found many reasons to understand what they did, and try to
forgive it. But Killian will never forgive you."

She was silent.

"Violence can take many forms, *ma chérie*. The form you
have chosen is invisible, but it will leave scars, and if it does,
I will not forgive you."

"But Yves, what am I to *do*?"

Over her head, he looked up at the blackening sky, filled
with stars shimmering in their millions. Such a beautiful
world if only people would see it, and accept it, and leave
it alone.

"Let him be, Kerry. That's all. Simply let him be whoever, whatever he is. Stop being a bully like your father,
stop emulating that cold, hard mother of yours. Why can't
you and Brian let go of them?"

Aghast, Kerry stared at him, appalled by his intuition.
Yves had never met her parents, and yet he sensed their
presence, just as she did herself, palpitating in her, and in
Brian. Eamonn's genes were frank and obvious, as the man
himself had been, but how much more subtly Maeve held
sway, now as then . . . they were *stamped* on her, and on
her brother, both of them. Irrefutably stamped, imprisoning
their children in some terrible, powerful, invisible trap.

But Yves could see it with those blue eyes that bored
through into her very being. And what else could he see? See
that, in marrying Darragh, she had married her own father,
as in Lu Brian had married his mother? It was incest, incest!
They hadn't only married their parents, they had married the
people that Maeve and Eamonn aspired to be, if only they
had not been trapped themselves.

That was why she and Brian had not spoken for so

long, each resenting what the other was trying to become. That was why Brian was so vengeful, why she was so domineering and why they were both so forceful in their own ways, opposite sides of the one coin. Sometimes Maeve, sometimes Eamonn, they carried both parents within their separate selves, crosshatched, caught in the web of time, the course of blood.

Panicked, she sought Yves's face frantically in the dark, and was impaled on a look no less anguished.

"Why didn't you tell me, Yves? Why did you never say it before, if you always saw it?"

"Fear, Kerry. I was afraid. Afraid that if it was true for you, it must be true for me, too. Every day of my life, I fight my own parents off, fight against turning into either one of them. I did not consciously choose to be gay, but I think it's no accident. I will never have children, because for me sterility is much safer. Your parents were not evil, but mine – they had lost all control. They were inhuman. If I had not met Robbie, I don't know what form my own misery might have taken."

"But what am I going to do? How am I going to escape them?"

"Fight them. Assert yourself, as you did before. Look at Brandon. He did it."

Yes. Dermot Lawrence had been baulked of Brandon. A tyrant in life, he did not dominate in death – but then, what about Chris? From where had his single-mindedness sprung? And Killian – Killian! From nowhere, Kerry recalled something crucial. Darragh de Bruin was not the only musician she had known. Eamonn had sung all of his songs, long before Darragh did, and had she not heard that once Maeve played the piano, long before she married him?

Not one generation, but two; possessed, possessed.

Terrified, she clung to Yves. "Yves, they've got him too, they've got Killian, they're *alive*."

"Yes, they are, *ma belle*. But in him they are alive and well. His legacy is positive. But yours will be negative, if you do not fight it."

"I will. Now that I know, about you, about me, and about him, I'll . . . I'll try, so hard . . ."

Lamely, she trailed off, immobilised by fear and shame, and he frowned as she hid her face in his chest once more, mumbling incoherently.

"I've punished him for years, Yves, punished the wrong person . . . how am I ever going to make it up to Killian? And how am I going to steer the twins out of it, away from me, away from their grandparents? Sometimes I look at Saoirse, and I see myself, riding Mick round Ashamber . . . Oh, God, Yves, *how?*"

"*Chérie*, calm yourself. Let us start by going back to Killian so that you can apologise and feel better."

"In front of everyone – Robbie, even? He must think me quite crazy. I can't! I'll do it later – tomorrow, first thing."

"Robbie understands a lot more than you might think. He doesn't say much, but he doesn't miss much either. You will do it now, *chérie*, or you and I will no longer be friends."

Jolted, she acquiesced immediately. Not for anything would she risk such a friendship.

"All right. And will you forgive me, then?"

"Don't I always?"

"Yes. You do, insufferable as I am. We understand each other so well, don't we, *mon vieux?*"

Taking his hand, she put her other palm to his sunburnt cheek.

"I've never told you how much I love you, have I, Yves?"

Singularly moved, he slid his arm about her once more, whispering into her hair.

"As I love you, from the first moment we met . . . I thought you would run away, when you found I could not be what you wanted. But you didn't, somehow I was the one person you took as you found . . . Do you still, Kerry? Really?"

"Absolutely. For ever. I'd be lost without you."

"Oh, my dearest. You wouldn't, you know. But thank you for thinking so, and saying so."

He bent his mouth to hers, and she lifted her lips to receive his kiss, soft as the balmy air, holding him tenderly to her in the dark for a long moment, a moment out of time. It was simply one of those things that felt right, and had nothing to do with anyone else in their lives.

"Come on, *chérie*. It's getting chilly. They'll have search parties out for us."

Arm in arm, they made their way back through the dunes to where the fire was burning, and all the children were singing lustily to the sound of Killian's guitar. But the music stopped when they appeared, everyone shrinking back apprehensively, uncertain what she might do next. Leaving Yves, she strode over to Killian, bent down and hugged him to her, saying loudly and clearly how sorry she was. He was cursed with a mad mother, and would he forgive her?

Yes. Of course he would. Even if he still had no idea what he had done. Then a kiss for Brandon too, begging his pardon for being a perfect bitch. Amazed, he assured her that she wasn't – much – that she was pardoned, and the lobster was still hot if she would care for some?

Yes. Please. Thank you, Brandon. Very meek, choking on humble pie.

Brian, who hated scenes, exhaled tangible relief. Robbie, suppressing a smile, thanked the fates for so ordaining it that he could never be married to Kerry Laraghy. Reassured by the released tension, the children resumed their song, the fire illuminating their faces as it cast long shadows down the beach. Warm in the leaping flames, the camaraderie crept back into their midst, and Kerry picked up a bottle of wine, slugging it inelegantly by the neck, wishing it was whiskey.

Slowly the music lulled the little ones to sleep, and she gathered Séamus and Saoirse into her arms, nuzzling the tops of their heads as they nodded off, warmly wrapped in a rug. But then she sought out Killian, and smiled across them to him, too. He was her son, just as Séamus was, and his legacy was not of his own making. She must accept that.

In the shadows, Brian lay kissing Zoe, just as he had done with Lu one night up at Sacré Coeur, so long ago. Did he know, too, who he really was? He was so much older now, but like herself he could be quite infantile at times, worse than their own children. But they were all healthy, and happy, and prosperous. It was a lot. She had no right to disrupt it, to pluck at the fragile flower of happiness as it blossomed in this high summer of their lustrous, lucky lives.

But what was this? Distracted, Kerry blinked, unable to believe what she saw.

Robbie was sitting upright, with Yves leaning against him as he stroked his face lovingly, and then they were kissing too, as deeply and openly as Brian and Zoe, declaring themselves a consummate couple like the others. There was an aura about them that Kerry had never seen before, and she felt Brandon stiffen beside her as he saw it too.

Never once, in all the time they had known each other had Yves done this, or permitted Robbie to. Knowing from the outset that Brandon would bar them from Ashamber if they ever flaunted their homosexuality, they had played by the rules, discreetly and diplomatically. But now this? Brandon turned to Kerry with a look of the sheerest outrage, but she put her hand on his arm, and restrained him. The children were asleep, and did not see; and she felt deeply sorry for the two men besides, who must have some reason for losing their restraint.

"Please, darling, don't say anything?"

"They have a goddamn nerve, Kerry."

"It's all right. They wouldn't do it if the children were awake. I'll talk to them tomorrow."

"You'd better. What about Killian? It's even a shock to *my* system."

Privately, Kerry thought it quite good for Killian. But there had been enough trouble for one night.

"Let's go back to the yacht, Brandon. Yves and Robbie have the right idea. We should be making love too."

With a grunt, he conceded the point, unable to get enough of her after their long separation. Throwing the sleeping babies over their shoulders, they got quietly into one of the dinghies and rowed back, leaving everyone else to make what they would of the tropical night.

For many long, indolent days they remained on Moorea, swimming, fishing, exploring, living for the wonderful sake of living. There was so much to see, all kinds of timorous wildlife, fluttering insects, plants and succulent vegetation, coves and lagoons truly created by the hand of heaven.

On and off, Brandon pressed Kerry to speak to Yves, but she held out, unwilling to shackle him to some senseless convention.

During the day, he and Robbie continued to exercise caution among the children, but at night there was no longer any pretence about it; they were as one, out of the shadows, claiming their place in the sun. Never, Kerry thought, had she seen Yves so full of fun, brimming over with *joie de vivre*, revelling in each day, each new discovery. His wide smile glowed in his tanned face, and she had not the heart to cavil as he cavorted on the sand with his lover, laughing as the silvery powder sheered away from under his weakened ankle.

From Moorea they sailed on to Bora-Bora, by way of Vaitore. The winds were light, so that often the yacht drifted becalmed on the infinite expanse of the South Pacific, its luminous clarity sometimes filtered into mystical hazes, making them lose all sense of time and place; all, except for Brandon, who was navigating, and in his element.

Mostly they slept on board, but occasionally Killian camped out on the beaches, and Yves and Robbie began to do the same. This suited Brandon very well, and took the pressure off Kerry, but eventually there came a morning on which she found herself alone with Yves on a sheer stretch of sparkling sand, soundless apart from the rustling coconut leaves, the faint whir of birds and insects, the lapping of the wavelets.

"I do so love this scent of vanilla, Yves . . . It reminds me of our old cook Mary, baking cakes for us children in that great kitchen of hers. We never knew what vanilla was, never wondered where the pods came from, certainly never thought to see or smell them in their natural environment."

Yves, smarting after a heated discussion with Zoe concerning France's role in the destruction of that environment, changed the subject.

"Did you hate leaving home for boarding school?"

"Yes. It was Mummy's idea, not Daddy's. Sylvermore Convent for young ladies, in Galway, where I met Lu. We were only sixteen."

"Young ladies, eh? I hope they gave your father a refund?"

"Yves Tiberti! I can be perfectly ladylike – which is more

than can be said of your own ungentlemanly conduct of late."

"What? What do you mean?"

"All this kissing and canoodling with Robbie. Oh – I'm just teasing, Yves. I don't mind at all. You have every right. It's just that . . ."

"That Brandon objects? I'm sorry, Kerry. We won't do it any more."

"Oh, Yves. Of course you must. He'll get used to it."

Idly, Yves traced a pattern in the sand under him, lying on his side, pulling intermittently on one of the five cigarettes a day Robbie allowed him. Uncut for weeks, his black curls fell shaggy and untamed over his face, and like the others he was very dark, wearing only shorts, a towelling wristband and an unusually inscrutable expression.

"Life is so short, Kerry. We should all savour it."

"Yes. I think we do, by and large, don't we?"

"I hope so. You have so much, Kerry. Brandon, your children, your brother, your horses, your friends. Can't you spill a little love over onto Killian?"

"But I am trying, Yves. Haven't you seen? He plays his guitar from dawn to dusk, and I applaud – but I have to tell you honestly, I love those twins of mine beyond all reason. Aren't they just the dearest little things you've ever seen?"

"All children are beautiful, Kerry."

"I'm sorry. You're right. That's what Brian says too, he adores Blair even though she's a brat, and Francesca whose deafness makes her so difficult sometimes . . . Oh, Yves, I just can't stop thinking about what you told me, about your childhood. It must have been a hell. I don't know how you ever survived. I'd have helped, years ago, if I'd known – we all would. Isn't there anything I can do for you, even now?"

"You know what. Killian. Let your priorities balance. The horses aren't everything."

"No – but yes, they are, too! Ashamber is a living creature to me. I only wish Daddy – well, anyway, Deoch an Doras is the best horse I've ever trained, even if Nabdul owns him, his dam was mine, and now the line will continue, it's so interesting, you can't imagine."

Yves could well imagine. Really, Kerry was obsessed with her horses quite as much as ever Redon or Gauguin had been by their painting, Rodin by his sculpture. But he felt the same way about drawing and designing, could not live without his work.

"What about your next season, Yves? Another *tour de force?*"

He flinched, and from nowhere she saw some penumbra briefly obscure his face, like a cloud passing over the sun. Twisting to him, she brushed his cheek with her finger.

"Is it, *mon ami?* Is everything all right, between you and Brian?"

Sitting up, he linked his fingers in hers, marvelling at her marching freckles.

"Yes, everything is fine between us. I'm just considering my future a little, in the long term, that's all."

"What – but – *again?* Oh, Yves, no! You can't leave TLZ, Zoe will be so disappointed, Brian will go insane!"

"I may not have to leave. I don't know. I'm just trying to think. But I have a contract which doesn't expire for a long time yet, and I hope to honour it. Want to."

Again he traced shapes in the sand, in silence, until a slight breeze came up, a whispering zephyr that fluffed the wavelets and made them both think of a swim at the same time. Questioningly, he indicated the water, and she nodded.

"Let's! I need to clear my head and think about this. If you have some problem, Yves, then tell me, and we'll talk it over."

"I will, *chérie.* As soon as I know more myself, and have some idea what I'm talking about."

"Hah! If I wanted to hear sense, I'd go to Robbie Richler."

He smiled as she jumped up and ran to the water's edge, diving in ahead of him.

"No head start for a handicapped man, no?"

"No! You can swim perfectly well. Race you!"

They raced, and he won despite the ankle, and she feigned indignation as she splashed out at him.

"You might have let me win, and humoured me!"

"It'll be a cold day in hell I'll humour you, madame. Your

head is quite big enough already. Too bad you can't win everything!"

Ah. That stung, like the salt in her eyes. But it was only fun, the fun Yves brought to her whole life. She swam up to him, the hot sun glinting brilliantly in her wet hair, and they hugged and kissed as they trod water, revelling in their vigour and freedom, the tangy tingle of their touching skin, playful as puppies.

From the deck of the yacht, Brandon saw them in the distance, and felt a hot jealous flash. Always somebody, something else! Had it been Nabdul, he would have dived overboard and swum up to him, livid; but in the platonic context of Yves's relationship, such behaviour would look absurd. Averting his gaze, he dismissed the spectacle, knowing that in spite of everything there was an innocence in Kerry that was always, entirely, reliable.

Nobody wanted to go home. Late into the nights, they sat indulging in the luxury of wild speculation, peering round corners into the new directions their lives, if they so chose, could take. But Brandon's, if Kerry had any influence in the matter, actually was going to undergo a sea change of sorts. She didn't want him working so, hard in future, at so many things, succumbing to a heart attack like all the other frayed, frantic executives. Another five years, and then she would decree semi-retirement, and a lot more sailing. It had taken her a long time to get him, and she didn't want to lose him. But in her own case, it was different: look at Vincent O'Brien, still the maestro on into his seventies! She still hadn't beaten, or even equalled, his record number of winners – but by the time she reached his age, she would.

December came and went, a powerfully hot, sunny month in which Kerry, Brian and Killian celebrated their birthdays with candles stuck into rum-soaked pineapples, ablaze amidst a shower of frangipani petals. Brandon gave her a camera, with which she began to plague everyone as she took shot after shot, toting the thing round her neck like a tommy gun. They were heading back to Tahiti, where the boat would be berthed, and they would fly home at last.

"Let's stop off at Moorea again, darling. I didn't have the camera the first time."

"OK, but only for one night. There's bad weather forecast."

As yet, they had encountered none. Sometimes, black clouds stacked up on the far horizon, but with the children aboard Brandon wasn't taking any chances, and avoided them. For him, the real sailing was over; this was a doddle, a fun run with his family. As they cruised up to Moorea Kerry stood on deck, exclaiming over the magnificent light, training her sights on her quarry.

First Brian, with Francesca on his knee, turning the pages of a picture book. Neither even looked up as she focused the camera, immersed in their story. Then Killian, leaning over the side fishing; Zoe, wrestling Blair into a tiny swimsuit as the tot made the funniest faces; then Yves, sketching on his pad, his back braced against Robbie's legs. Golden and gleaming, Robbie regarded the camera gravely, a distant look in his sepia eyes; and then Brandon, pretending to throw Séamus overboard as the toddler yelled deliriously in his arms. Before she knew it they were dropping anchor off Moorea, the dinghies were lowered once more, and one last lovely day lay ahead of them.

A game of rounders was soon in progress on the beach, played by everyone except Yves, who couldn't run very well, and Kerry, too engrossed in her photography. He began to peel a bucket of prawns for their lunch, and winked at her as she clicked away, not at all camera shy. Laughing and clowning, he was a natural study, making Kerry feel yet again the throb of tenderness that seemed to accompany this whole voyage.

She shot the entire roll, and left off to help him peel the wretched things, which tore their fingers and made them bleed.

"Been fun, Yves, hasn't it?"

"The best. The ultimate trip. How can I thank you for inviting us?"

"But you're part of the family."

That meant much to him, so much he was speechless, and looked down at the ground in silence. Finishing their game eventually, the others returned, starving savages, for a lunch that went on for hours with a lot of wine and laughter. Drowsy, the children nodded off afterwards, and leaving Killian to supervise their nap, the six adults drifted away in pairs, in different directions. Trying not to think where they might be sloping off to, Killian knew perfectly well, and wished he had been allowed to bring Meggie Kavanagh with him. As yet, his mother ruled the roost, and had vetoed that plan; but no matter. Next summer, there would be Paris, and lots of pretty girls.

Hours later, Brian and Zoe returned sheepishly to claim their children, followed by Yves and Robbie who were not sheepish at all. If anything, they had never been more blatant, and came into sight holding hands, grinning from ear to ear, making Brandon want to cleave them apart with an axe. But he took a deep breath, and organised a game of water volleyball instead.

It was a perfect day, and at the end of it a fire was kindled once more, with steaks spitting over it this time, potatoes baking in the embers. Kerry made a huge salad, chatting with Robbie as she worked, trying to elicit some information about whatever was on Yves's mind. But he was not forthcoming, and as they sat down to eat the conversation somehow channelled itself into other things, sports, social gossip, current affairs. Robbie made some reference to Canada, Zoe chimed in about America, Killian piped up with questions, and suddenly they were onto politics, shouting their heads off.

Seeing the look on Brandon's face, Kerry realised he was thinking about Chris, and intervened forcefully.

"No fighting! This is our last night together! We're on a subject that always ends in tears, and I won't have it. Killian, get your guitar and play something – something soothing."

Thrilled to be asked, he obliged, and Kerry had the gratification of approving nods from both Brandon and Yves. In classical vein, Killian did calm the atmosphere, but then switched to a Spanish flamenco that made them clap like the gypsies they effectively were. As the moon rose he slowed down again, and played "Moon River", singing it so well, so beautifully that it made them ache for something intangible, something perhaps they already had. They went on till midnight, joining in dozens of songs, but finally, reluctantly, it was deemed time to return to the boat.

Killian, Yves and Robbie were staying to sleep on the beach, and on this special night the hugs were comprehensive and prolonged. Pointedly, Kerry kissed Killian before turning to Yves.

"Good night, *mon cher ami*. Sweet dreams."

"*Eh oui, chérie*. How could they be otherwise, out here?"

He held her tightly to him, until Brandon called her and she left him, with a last kiss and a wave. It had been a lovely, magical night, and she took some of the credit for it.

"Jesus, Kerry, what's keeping your two chums? Row over and get them, would you, and Killian, before we miss the tide."

"OK, OK. Keep your shirt on, Brandon, there are lots of tides."

By now she could row expertly, and five minutes later she was shipping her oars, beaching the dinghy a little way down from the two sleeping bags, Yves's and Robbie's nearest, Killian's further away amidst the dunes.

She could see that Yves and Robbie were awake, but they made no move to greet her as she strode vigorously up the beach.

"C'mon, you guys! Eight o'clock, and we're ready to sail!"

No response. She scooped up a handful of sand and threw it in their direction.

"Gentlemen, *bonjour*! Get up, and get moving!"

They sat up, but did not show much enthusiasm for moving.

"What's the matter? Hung over, huh? A pair of mutineers today, are we?"

Yves turned to her, with such a wan smile, so forced, that she hastened to his side. Perhaps he really wasn't well. But Robbie looked similarly remote, almost drained. Clearly neither of them had slept much.

"Sit down, Kerry, and stop shouting. We want to talk to you before Killian wakes up."

Yves spoke so quietly that she did as she was told, forgetting the urgency with which Brandon had despatched her. Time seemed to matter so little, out here.

"Isn't it a little early for conversation?"

Normally Yves was a night owl, bleary in the mornings, uncommunicative until after the several coffees he liked to drink alone.

"Perhaps. But it's our only chance, before Brandon, Killian, everyone's around."

Oh. Something personal. Something to do, she thought, with whatever had been going through Yves's mind for the past few days.

"Sorry. I didn't mean to harass you. Go ahead, and take your time."

Robbie looked down at the ground, distressed, while Yves mastered the voice which did not sound at all like his own.

"Kerry. I can't tell everyone, all in a rush, all together. But I have decided I must tell you."

She waited.

"It's about Keith. Keith Charles. Just before leaving France, I heard that he had died."

Was that all? She couldn't say that she was sorry, or even particularly moved. Nor did she see why Yves should be.

"He wasn't much of a friend to you, Yves. Robbie is a much better one. I'm sorry if you are, but really there's no need to be. I know you were with him for years, but . . ."

"That's the point, Kerry. I was. What killed him is going to kill me, and Robbie. Both of us."

It took for ever to sink in, permeating her mind like a slow, certain poison.

"Oh, God. Oh, no. Yves, *no.*"

"Yes, Kerry. I haven't been tested yet, but it is almost sure. Keith, and the life I lived before him . . . There is no point in pretending it can be otherwise."

It *was* otherwise. It must be. She would not allow it. She would deny it, will it away, from her and from her friends. In the rising warmth of the sun, she was very cold.

She took his hand, and Robbie's.

"No. You're wrong. You'll see. We'll get you back to Paris, to a doctor – every doctor . . ."

Yves looked at her, Robbie did not, and in the empty air she heard the answer to all her questions at once. This was why Yves would leave the salon. This was why he was so open now in his love of Robbie, his love of life. They were making the most of whatever was left to them.

And Robbie must have known, or thought of it, from the start. He knew Yves's history, he knew the risk. Yet he had taken it, he had chosen Yves. For his lover, he had committed suicide.

On the deck of the distant yacht, Brandon stood waving and gesturing, a caricature in a grotesque pantomime. Nothing responded in her, nothing at all. Her mind withdrew, her heart stalled.

But Robbie was speaking to her. Speaking quite normally.

"Kerry, we're so sorry. We have caused you terrible pain, and are going to cause more, to everyone. But first we need to be by ourselves, just for a little while. Would it be all right, if we didn't go back with you and the others?"

"You – you want me – us – to leave you here?"

"Yes. We'll hitch a ride on some other boat, later, back to Tahiti, and return to Paris from there. We just need some time."

Time. How much did they have? But she could give it to them. That, and anything else they might need, or want. Anything.

"Of course. I'll arrange things for you, in Papeete. But first, I must tell Brandon, you must tell me – we have to . . ."

She had no idea what she was saying. But Yves's grip on her hand told her that she didn't need to. He knew what was in her mind, and what else was going to come into it, soon.

"Don't tell Brandon just yet, Kerry. Or the others. Take your son, go back to them, and wait until you've sailed, without us."

"But I can't – you need . . ."

"We don't need anything. Really. Only your understanding, and your help. Please, Kerry. Do as we ask."

"Leave you alone?"

"We're not alone. We have each other."

Together they looked at her, and she held their eyes, returning every emotion she saw there. But she saw no tears, and so she did not weep, herself.

Only in her heart did she weep, weep and rail against whatever malignant fate had singled Yves Tiberti out for its victim, singled him out from the start. The fate that had lurked over him all his life, and waited until he came this close to thwarting it to play its final card.

But he had thwarted it. He had what he wanted. He had Robbie, and he had love.

Saoirse was mystified. Why was everyone so quiet? Why had Mummy gone off for so long this morning? Why was she not talking to her now, or playing with her? Where were her uncles, Yves and Robbie?

"Mummy, are Yves and Robbie not coming on the plane with us?"

"No, darling. They're staying on Moorea – the island, you can still see it."

"For how long?"

"I – I don't know, Saoirse. But they send you their kisses. Here."

Kerry kissed the child, and she smiled, satisfied. Uncle Yves would turn up again, sooner or later, as he usually did. A pity, though, that he wouldn't be there to amuse her on the plane.

"Where did you go this morning?"

"I went to say goodbye to Yves and Robbie."

"Oh. Did you have a party?" Uncle Yves was a great one for parties.

"Not exactly. We had a long chat. And other nice things."

"Neato. Why didn't you bring me?"

"You're too little."

"Not fair."

"Sometimes life isn't fair, Saoirse."

Saoirse decided to bow out of the conversation. It was maybe going where she couldn't follow, and she liked people to think she understood everything. But she couldn't go to

Daddy; he was busy sailing the boat. She would find Uncle Brian instead.

Brian was down in the main cabin with Zoe, reading the same letter that Mummy had given him hours ago, from Yves. It was a very soggy letter, she thought; Mummy must have let it fall into the water. She would write him a nice new one, much better, with her crayons. She opened her mouth to tell him so, but then decided not to. Uncle Brian was a dab hand with the crayons, but today he did not seem to be interested. Oh, boy. It looked like being a long trip home. She ran off to find Séamus.

At the helm in the wheelhouse, Brandon stood lost in thought, his eyes automatically scanning the limpid celandine horizon, unseeing.

Had he, by word or look or deed, contributed to Yves's and Robbie's refusal to come home? Had he made them uncomfortable, unwelcome, unwanted? Had he undermined Yves's new-found, hard-won confidence? Had he *not*, perhaps, said or done something he should have? It was possible to sin as much by omission as by act.

But the pair had seemed so content, never in better form . . . how had they concealed what they knew, for so long? How had they endured the worry, the agony of it? Why had he not made more effort, as Kerry had so often told him to, and accepted them? What would they do, now? Did they feel fear? Pain? What?

Oh, for Christ's sake, Brandon. Pull yourself together. This fruitless introspection will get you nowhere, change nothing. They're going to die, and there's nothing you can do about it.

And there was the nub of it. There was nothing he could do. The thing was out of his hands, inevitable, impossible: and "impossible" was a word he had thought exorcised from his vocabulary. It was infuriating, this situation without solution, this sorrow that Kerry must face. Yves, she said, had faced it already, but unlike him, Brandon was not a fatalist. Things were not necessarily as bad as they seemed.

Except that this time, they were. He felt a presence behind him, and sensed Kerry.

"Hi."

"Hi."

Was she blaming herself, too? After all, Yves was her friend, she knew him inside out . . . did she feel she had failed him somehow, for not guessing sooner? Turning, he prepared to find tears in her seagreen eyes. But there were none.

"You're torturing yourself, aren't you, Brandon? I can see it."

"Yes. I suppose I am."

"Don't. This has nothing to do with you. You took them on a marvellous holiday that they enjoyed to the full, as we all did. Our memories of it will last for ever, and they'll be happy ones."

"Oh, Kerry, this is dreadful. Dreadful."

"Brandon, they are not in any kind of pain. Yves was, about Robbie, but we talked it all out. He has come to terms with Robbie's choice, the ultimate proof of just how much Robbie loved him, from the very start. Robbie says he would still choose Yves, even now, and that's a decision he says everyone must accept. As we must leave them to – to work out the logistics of what life they have left."

"They're too young to die, Kerry."

"Are they, Brandon? I wonder. They have everything life can offer, already. They've seen and done it all. Perhaps this is a reasonable alternative for people so full of vitality, to an old age without energy, without challenge. I just hope neither of them lingers, grieving for the other."

He was surprised to hear her rationalise so calmly. Anticipating oceans of tears, he had forgotten this unpredictability in her, and the depths of strength. Life had taught her a few hard lessons.

They continued on course for Tahiti and reached Papeete without incident, making straight for the airport, where, in the waiting lounge, Brian suddenly crumbled, handing his children to Zoe while he wept with his back to them.

Kerry watched him while he buried his face in a handkerchief, refusing all comfort, wrestling once again with the guilt of what he had done and said in years gone by. Poor Brian. Life seemed to set him up, over and over, just so it could knock him down again, like Blair's roly-poly toy.

He could not staunch his tears, drawing heavily on the dry strong resources of his sister as they carried the children to the departure gates, and Kerry knew that later her own pent-up pain would be devastating. But for now, she must get through, get home to Helen who would know what to do – even for Brandon, whose guilt was also so very great.

But he had known that his wife loved another man, platonically, and let her go on loving him even when he did not approve of her choice. She must cherish him now more than ever, Yves had told her, and he was right – for if Brandon had one flaw, how many more had she? She who never asked what she did not want to know.

They boarded the plane, and it roared away up into the sky, making Francesca's ear hurt with the change of cabin pressure. Glad of the distraction, everyone turned to fuss over her, but Kerry looked out the window to watch the islands drop away below, each one a beautiful jewel in the incredible turquoise ocean, frilled with a white collar of frothing waves. The plane banked steeply to turn back on its long flight path, and there was Moorea, just a dot, almost invisible already in the glare of the shattering sun.

She bent her head and blew the boys a kiss. Not au revoir, but adieu.

23

Ashamber clamoured for Kerry's attention when she returned, and she plunged herself into her work, allowing herself to think and talk of Yves only at night, to Brandon and especially to Helen.

Deeply grieved, Helen said nothing of her own state of health, which had been less than perfect in recent weeks, but came straight to the point.

"If Yves is going to die, Kerry, then you must let him go. Let him out of your life, and let Killian into it. That's what he asks of you, and if you love him, you will do it – now, while there's still time."

As always, Kerry listened to Helen's advice and strove to act on it, knowing it was what everyone wanted; not just Yves, but Brandon too. Conscientiously she began to take new interest in her son, follow his progress at school, listen to his news and all the trivia she found tedious, studiously fixing a smile to her face. If her heart was still not in him, her mind was demonstrably on him, and Killian responded eagerly, desperate to prove himself worthy of her sudden attention.

In the middle of April, when the cherry blossoms were billowing and the fields filled with many fine young horses, Kerry sat one day in the kitchen, cupping a mug of tea in her hands, looking at the letter which, now that it had finally arrived, she dared not open. It bore a Polynesian postmark, several weeks old, and Yves's handwriting.

"I can't, Helen."

"Kerry, open it and tell me what it says."

In a rush she put down her tea, snatched it up and sliced it open.

Gripping the cameo brooch at her throat, Helen waited.

"It – it says – oh, Helen, they're all right. They're coming back to Paris to have tests, and Yves is going to take on an apprentice, continue to work for as long as he can. Oh, thank God. I was so afraid that he – they – might . . ."

Weak with relief, she read the letter over again, several times, drinking in every word. Some of what Yves said was so delicate, so moving she did not translate it even for Helen, but there was a lot from Robbie too, about feeling quite well, and maybe even living to be forty, an age at which his first wrinkle would appear, and Yves would dump him anyway.

She laughed and cried all at once. Robbie was thirty-three. Yves was thirty-nine. Their attitude concentrated her mind amazingly.

"Mum, guess what?"

"What?"

"I'm going to give a recital. At the Concert Hall!"

Killian was bursting with pride, and Kerry was astonished. Her son often played in public, won competitions and attracted comment. But the Concert Hall – the National one, did he mean, in Dublin?

"When? With whom?"

"At the end of June. All by myself."

"Solo? My Lord, Killian, I didn't know you were that good. You'd better get a haircut."

She was pleased. He could see it, even if she wouldn't show it. But why wouldn't she? *Why?*

"Will you come, Mum? You and Dad, Helen, everyone?"

"Yes, of course we will. I just hope it doesn't clash with any races – what date is it, exactly?"

"June 30."

"Well then, go and tell Helen to keep that evening free in my diary."

He went, revelling in Helen's delight at the news, and then sought out Brandon.

Brandon was in his study, immersed in paperwork which was failing to distract him from the two things on his mind;

Kerry, and Yves Tiberti. At thirty-eight his wife retained much youth, thanks to her freckles and enquiring eyes, her vivid hair and leggy figure, but there was a tiny new line across the bridge of her nose, for which Yves would laughingly disclaim all responsibility. But he had put it there, and every time Brandon looked at it he was reminded of his own responsibility, the unease which had plagued him all the way back from Polynesia.

Over and over he thought back to that last night on the beach, when Yves was kissing everyone as he always did, two on each cheek, French style. Such had been the atmosphere, Brandon had feared the man was about to kiss him, and hung back, receiving in the event only his customary handshake.

Had Yves sensed his distaste? Seen it, and been hurt by it, as now he would be hurt by the distaste of so many others? In retrospect Brandon could think of no logical reason for his reticence; over the years he had come to like and even admire the droll, spirited Frenchman. But he'd never admitted it, and now he cursed himself savagely, wondering how to redeem the damage.

He looked up with some relief as Killian entered the room, his face filled with some news he was obviously dying to share.

"Hi. You look very pleased with yourself, for a chap who says he's going to fail his exams."

Enthusiastically, Killian told him about the musical début which was so much more important, and was thrilled to find that Brandon thought so too.

"*National* Concert Hall? Killian, congratulations! You must be one of the youngest soloists ever, and you must have worked very hard to get there. I'm so proud of you."

"Thanks, Dad. That's real music to my ears."

And it was music to Brandon's, to hear Killian call him his father. But the boy always did, quite naturally, affirming over and again everything that Brandon had lost in his other sons.

My son, he thought. My son is going to play at the National Concert Hall. All by himself, in front of – how many people does it hold? A thousand? More? Just wait till Kerry hears this!

"Come on, Killian, let's go and tell your mother."

"I told her already, Dad."

"Oh? And what did she say?"

"She said she'd keep that evening free, and that I was to get a haircut."

"A what? Christ, I'll kill her!"

As concerned as he had been about his wife five minutes earlier, Brandon was suddenly enraged. All but vaulting over his desk, he left Killian and raced out of the room, through the house and out into the yards and fields that would yield Kerry Laraghy.

She stood in a distant paddock, lunging a yearling which belonged, no doubt, to Nabdul Zul Mahrat, cracking a long whip which Brandon felt the urge to rip out of her hand and use, with all his strength, on her brazen hide.

"Kerry! Come here!"

She looked up, and turned, but continued with her work, engrossed in the animal which was one of this season's favourites. Such a clever, sensitive creature! His ears were pricked in response to her commands, and she flicked the rein, keeping him going, looking forward to the moment at the end of the session when he would nuzzle into her pockets for carrots, blowing into her ear, licking her face, poking at her impudently with his velvet muzzle.

"Good boy . . . steady, steady. Yes, Brandon, what is it?"

She was surprised to see him stride up to her, his face thunderous.

"What's the matter?"

"You are. You, the mother of a boy who's going to play at national level at seventeen years of age, who can't even congratulate him."

"Huh? What? But I did – Brandon, don't be ridiculous. He knows I'm pleased."

"Then say it!"

His tone beat it out of her, instantly.

"Oh, all right, I will. There's no need to get so steamed up."

But he yanked the lunging rein out of her hand in a way that made her quail, tied the horse to the fence and faced her with unabated fury.

"Why couldn't you do it, Kerry? Tell our son the one little thing he needed to hear. One bloody word. Would it have killed you?"

No. It would not have killed her. But she had not said it, and now she could not say why. She deserved the harsh, blunt question that Brandon asked next, the question he had withheld for years.

"Do you love Killian at all, Kerry? Or do you hate him?"

"Hate him? Oh – how could you say such a thing? How could you even think it?"

"Because you give me reason to think it, and say it. Answer me!"

Biting her lip, she dug her boot into the ground, gazing down at the divot it tore up.

"I don't hate him, Brandon. But I don't love him, either. Something went wrong at the start, and it's still wrong. I know I must fix it, because everybody wants me to, but I can't arrange my feelings to order. Not even for you and Helen, who are running out of patience, or Yves who's running out of time. I am trying, but I just can't seem to get past a certain point."

"Kerry. Yves isn't the only one who's running out of time. Killian is too, and so are you. In another year, or two at most, he'll be a grown man. It will be too late. He will leave Ashamber, and if he doesn't feel you want him, he will never come back. My God, Kerry, I've already lost two sons. Don't cost me this one too. Not the one I love most."

"Most? You love my son, more than your own?"

"Kerry, he is my own. Why do you think I sent Chris away, if not to protect him? Do you think that was easy for me? Any easier than what I ask of you?"

"No, Brandon. I know how much that hurt."

"Well then, repay me! Perhaps love doesn't just fall out of the sky with the rain, but it does come, if you wait long enough. And we've all waited long enough, Kerry."

Abruptly, he turned on his heel and walked away.

Stricken, Kerry watched him plough his way back up through the fields to the house, leaving his words lodged in her heart like bullets.

If she loved him, she must learn to love Killian. It was an ultimatum, and it was immediate. She could not procrastinate any longer, if she wanted to keep her husband, her friends and her family, everything that bound their lives together. She had done many other difficult things, and now she saw that she must do this.

Once Kerry set her mind to it, she found opportunities everywhere, cropping up as naturally and as prolifically as mushrooms in the morning grass. All she had to do was take them, and so she sat one morning in the lower yard, astride a bale of straw, holding a conversation with her son.

It actually was a conversation. Not a monologue, a diatribe or a lecture, but a real conversation. Their first ever.

Working saddle soap into a bridle, she watched him as he crouched with his back to her, changing a punctured tyre on the jeep, his expression hidden as he discussed Meggie Kavanagh.

"She's a smasher, Mum. Really gorgeous. Don't you think so?"

Kerry had to concede that she did. Meggie was only sixteen, very sweet and shy, with a quaint, pretty face that flushed whenever Kerry chanced to see it.

"She's a lovely girl. And she seems to be around quite a lot lately. How did you meet her, Killian?"

"Through our music. She doesn't play anything, but she sings like an angel. Would you like to hear her sometime?"

"I already have. And I've heard a lot of giggling . . . but it isn't anything serious, yet, is it? You're both far too young for love, you know."

"Oh, Mum! I don't know . . . I don't really know what love is, yet."

Guiltily, Kerry recoiled, thinking he was hitting out at her. But his irony was completely unconscious. No matter what she ever said or did to him, he was incapable of holding a grudge.

"Well, let me tell you, it isn't something you should get into lightly. Certainly not in your teens. Romance is just for fun."

"Was my father just for fun?"

"Your – your natural father, you mean? Yes, Killian, he was. But it got out of hand, when I was only a year older than you are now."

"And what did your parents say?"

"Your grandmother kept a cool head. But your grandfather was livid. He detested your father, and the consequences affected my whole life."

She braced herself for the barrage of questions that must surely follow. But after a pause, Killian took up a wrench and began to tighten the nuts on the wheel.

"I know what I want to do with my life, Mum. I want to be a professional musician."

"Yes – well, you'll certainly have my permission to do that, and Brandon's as well, I hope. But you're very young, Killian. Are you sure you know what you're doing?"

"Yes. My tutors say I have what it takes. And it's the only thing I've ever wanted to do. I'm going to really work at it, and not blow my future the way Chris blew his."

"Chris?" Kerry was taken aback. No one had ever told him about Chris.

"Yeah. I know why Dad sent him away. He had to do it, after what happened to my grandparents. To protect us. It must have been awful for him."

His casual tone horrified Kerry. He knew all this? And what else, then?

"Who told you about Chris, Killian? And about what happened to your grandparents?"

"Nobody. I just picked up bits and pieces here and there, and fitted them together. Musicians have an ear for things, I guess."

Straightening up, he wiped his hands on his jeans, smiling at her visible shock.

"I know I'm not great at school, Mum, but I'm not as stupid as you might think, either! Maybe some day you'll tell me the full story. But there's only one thing I want to know right now."

Faintly, she forced herself to ask what it was.

"Paris. When I go there in July, can I stay with Yves and Robbie?"

She was thrown, but grateful for the speed at which his mind moved on.

"Yes, if you like, and they agree. But Brian and Zoe have invited you already."

"I know. But they've got all those kids. I don't want to crowd them. Yves and Rob will be on their own, so I thought, well, maybe they could use some company. I could look after them a bit."

Look after them? Knowing what they were dying of, he could volunteer, so readily?

"Oh, Killian . . . what a very kind thought. But they're not well, they tire easily – it would be a responsibility, for a teenager who's supposed to be having fun in Paris."

"I will have fun. I don't mind if we don't go out boozing or wenching every night, they're such great company even at home. And they'll keep me pure for Meggie!"

His laugh touched her to the quick, as did the other things she saw at that moment in her son. Was this the person she had been missing for seventeen years?

If it was, the loss was hers, far more than his. A loss she had never suspected, unsettling and profoundly revealing.

After a lengthy absence, Sheik Feirah had scheduled a visit to Ireland, to see his son's stud farm and those horses in training with Kerry. Delighted to welcome her old friend and mentor, Kerry arranged a formal dinner party for him early in the week of Killian's concert. Brian and Zoe, Yves and Robbie were all flying over for that, and she was anxious to see how Yves was coping with the diagnosis that was now definite – a year, his doctors said, maybe two, probably longer for Robbie. The pain pierced her like an arrow, but when Feirah arrived she allowed him to see nothing but her most gracious smile.

Loyally, Brandon helped her to entertain her valued, influential client, whisking him away to nearby Moyglare Manor for dinner, where a highly enjoyable night was surprisingly dominated by Helen, who quaffed double her usual ration of sherry and was the life and soul of the party. Warmly, Kerry exchanged smiles and hugs with her, the treasured friend who loved them all, and was so loved in return.

Trustworthy, caring and compassionate, Helen had given nearly two decades of her life to Ashamber, and Kerry was very glad of the joy it had brought her in return.

Next day, Feirah insisted on touring the entire estate, but at nearly seventy years of age, found it rather more exhausting than he had anticipated. Wheezing alarmingly, he mopped his brow.

"Excellent, excellent . . . and now, if we might sit down for a moment?"

Hastily Kerry steered him back to the house, where he sank into a chair on the terrace, accepted tea from Eileen, and recovered himself while Kerry tactfully busied herself with her daughter. Saoirse was making a daisy chain, looking very cute in a smocked pinafore patterned with buttercups, her red tresses glinting just like her mother's, her mouth ringed with pollen from the flowers. A grandfather many times over, Feirah loved to indulge small children, and was calmed by the tranquil scene.

"And your elder son, Kerry – how is he?"

"He is more than meets the eye! Not a great student academically, but much brighter than I used to think. He's also a very gifted musician."

"Indeed? And my own son? I see so little of Nabdul, what with his work in London and his racing interests here."

"He's happy and settled, now. People have accepted him, and he has brought a lot of prosperity. He and I have a great partnership. He breeds from the line we established together, and I train the results."

"I'm glad it's going so well. And I'm glad you didn't marry him, Kerry. Some day soon, he will succeed me, and inherit many onerous duties. As his consort, you would have been stifled."

"As a matter of fact, I'd have gone barking mad."

He laughed.

"And what of your own future? Is this little girl to succeed you?"

"I – I don't know, Your Majesty. I've learned lately that it's wrong to force children into what they don't suit or want. But if Saoirse shows any ability with the horses, I must admit I'll be very pleased. She's only three, but you should see her ride her pony, such a secure seat, much better than Séamus . . ."

Oh, no. Even now, she was doing it! Quickly she finished Saoirse's daisy chain and hung it around the child's neck.

"Off you go and play, sweetheart."

Obediently, the little girl clambered down the steps and trotted away, and they sat watching her in the high, hot summer silence until, thoughtfully, Feirah turned to Kerry.

"She is lucky, Kerry. Unlike my son, she has a choice. I should let her make it, if I were you."

Kerry nodded, and the old man saw that his words were not wasted on the young woman who had matured so much over the long years of their association.

The evening of the dinner party was a warm, mellow one, and Brandon whistled admiringly when Kerry appeared in a light dress of sand-washed yellow silk.

"Beautiful! I hope it's not for Nabdul's benefit?"

"Certainly not. It's exclusively for yours."

He kissed the nape of her neck, and she responded in a way that made him wish their guests would all evaporate. But already their voices were audible downstairs, and together they went to greet them: Nabdul with his wife and father, Helen with Bob, and little Meggie Kavanagh whom Killian had begged to invite.

Drinks were served in the rose sitting room, reminding Kerry of how she had once shared apéritifs with Helen and Yves, on another summer's evening, wearing the topaz velvet he had brought her, almost twenty years before . . . twenty years, already? Oh, Yves! *Yves*.

But she would see him soon, and meanwhile Helen was here, exhorting Brandon to put a bet on a horse that would run at Leopardstown the following week.

"Pay no attention, Brandon. Helen is a very bad tipster. She lost her shirt once before, and should know better."

"My word, Kerry, you have a mind like a steel trap. I'd forgotten that myself."

Helen sat mildly astonished on the sofa, and from his corner Killian looked across at her, intrigued. How long had

Helen been here, exactly, and what had brought her? It was another of the many mysteries to which his mother held the key; but although he had various theories he had never asked, and never been told. Somehow Helen was just a fixture and, he hoped, always would be. If only her rheumatism would improve! The blue dress she wore this evening made her look a little pale, but her expression was serene as she sat beside Bob, whose hand rested, as always, proprietorially on her shoulder.

The French windows stood open to the setting sun, pouring liquid gold into the room, carrying the scent of clematis and wisteria, the drowsy hum of bumblebees hovering on the tangled vines outside, and as he looked fondly at Helen Killian was unaware of Meggie, watching him watching his "grandmother". In time, Meggie hoped, she would get to hear him play the piano, in that seductive way that made her want to run away with him – but first, there was dinner to be got through, his fearsome mother to face, and any amount of cutlery to negotiate.

She jumped when Kerry addressed her as if reading her thoughts.

"Don't worry, Meggie! This is just an informal family gathering, and we're very glad you could join us."

Intimidated by the Arab sheik and his unnervingly exotic son, Meggie smiled gratefully, and Kerry was rewarded with a look of thanks from Killian. A look from Brandon, too, so tender she could hardly bear to meet his eye.

It was a wonderful evening, filled with good food, wine and conversation. For once they did not discuss the horses, but talked instead of local events, international affairs, art and music, Paris and Polynesia. Then, over his dessert of fresh fruit from the garden, Feirah turned to Killian.

"Your mother tells me you are a most talented musician, young man. Will you do an old one a great honour, and play for him?"

Beaming, Killian consulted her. Yes, he might play. Something civilised, nothing rowdy.

Majestically Feirah got up, swept his white robes about him and led the way out to the ballroom where, as he recalled, the grand piano was kept. Slipping a tasty morsel to each of the four dogs out in the hall, Kerry permitted them to accompany her into the enormous, mirrored old room.

"Lie quiet, now."

They settled adoringly at her feet, panting gently as Killian seated himself, threw his long hair back over his shoulders, flexed his wrists and considered what might best please his mother.

Some of those French pieces that she was so fond of? They always made her nostalgic, but she loved them. Without need of sheet music, he began to play a poem by Jacques Prévert, a brief melody called "Ce N'est Pas Moi Qui Chante", put to music by some composer who knew all about the things it expressed . . . love and laughter, joy and tears, friendship and the swift passing of the years.

Clustered around the piano, his audience fell silent, and he moved into a song by Georges Moustaki entitled "Tes Gestes", a piece of such disarming tenderness, such charm and innocence, that they were enraptured without need of translation. In the lamplight, he could not see his mother's face, could not see how still she sat, nor her eyes as they searched under his skin, seeing him as if for the first time. Often, she had heard him play, but never had she listened, and never had he played like this.

Her son. Her own son, so gifted, so prodigiously talented? Awed, she absorbed the full power, the crystal beauty of his young tenor voice, his hands delicate as butterflies on the worn ivory keys.

My God. My boy. From where did he get this, from where did I get him? From Darragh, from Daddy, from Timothy Laraghy down in the old bracken copse? Does it matter, any more? Wherever he may have come from, I can see now where he's going. If only his father knew. Oh, Darragh! Your greatest success, and you don't know, don't hear, don't see it. You fool. You brilliant, crusading, utter fool.

Unaware, the boy played on, until suddenly the silence reached him. Had he lost their attention? Should he have sung in English? Anxiously, he stopped. Nobody moved, nobody spoke, nobody applauded. Looking up, he saw his mother, her hand in Brandon's, two tears standing unshed in her eyes, bright as malachite.

He had done it again. Upset her, ruined her night, ripped open some secret scar. And now, his invincible mother was going to cry, here, in front of all these people. Why, he did not know, but desperately he rushed to the rescue, ransacking his repertoire for the first cheerful thing in it, which seemed to be "Tipperary".

Even Feirah and Nabdul knew that old war song, and astonished Killian heard them join in, lustily, with Bob and then Brandon, Helen and little Meggie in her sweet girlish soprano, the ballroom filling with all their voices, strong, rousing, reassuring. And, at length, he heard Kerry. Kerry, who was not going to weep after all, but sing, and smile at him. Wistful as a madonna, she held him with her eyes, and he took that first loving look from her, locking it away into his empty, hopeful heart.

Flooded with emotion, he released it all into his music, hearing each note as if played by somebody else, somebody he had never met before. Heedless of passing time and falling dark, he held his mother in thrall, held them all in thrall, suspended in spellbound infinity. Slowly the late twilight faded away until the room was dark, and in the light of the single lamp they were singing "Danny Boy", oblivious of all else.

Oblivious, even, of Helen, as she closed her eyes and gently fell asleep, the rhythm of her breathing slowing imperceptibly to a standstill.

It was not a proper rainbow. Not a proper rainbow, at all. Just a dim smudge of wan colour, evanescent, illusory, weaving through the fanned leaves of the dappling trees like a fairy under the weather. When she looked up again, it would be gone.

But the rainbow did not disappear. It did exist, as this voice in her ear existed, belonged to someone near and far all at once.

"Please, Kerry. Please. It's damp out here, you'll make yourself ill. Get up now, and come inside, talk to me?"

"Later."

The voice persisted, reasoning, sighing, fretting to itself. But she did not move, and with the dregs of the daylight it drifted away. It had placed some warm thing about her shoulders, some protective thing into which she huddled as she rocked on the steps, clutching her arms around her knees in the somnolent stillness, looking out lacerated over the fields, the lake, the slowly closing bluebells.

Tomorrow, at dawn, each bell would open up again, sending its soft summer scent out into the dewy acres where the children would run, and the horses would swish their tails, and Helen . . .

Helen would not be here. No Helen, ever again, cutting through the morning meadows with a wave and a smile, making purposefully for her blue room, her desk, her busy day. No cheery banter, no coffee, no conference; only a fresh grave, near Eamonn's, heaped white with summer roses, and an old lady, at peace.

Peace. That was Helen's gift to Ashamber, and only in the memory of it could Kerry find any, for herself. The memory of Helen in her dove grey suit and little hat, cradling baby Killian in her arms, saying how Eamonn had not forgotten, but forgiven . . . Helen, a year later, blushing hand in hand with Bob . . . and many years after that, conspiring with Yves Tiberti to bring Brandon Lawrence back where he belonged. Her joy when he came, and Bob opening champagne in his pyjamas . . . Helen, valiant on the morning of the wedding, a surrogate mother losing a daughter, but gaining a . . .

A son. I have a son, Kerry reminded herself, and he has lost the woman who was his mother, all the years that I was not. He is distraught, and I must go to him.

Since the morning's funeral, she had not seen Killian. Composed but totally silent, he had returned from the graveyard, detached himself from everything and everyone, and disappeared. Where was he? He might not want her, she knew, but she would find him just the same.

Stiffly she roused herself, got up and set off to comb the estate where he could hide, with no effort at all, for hours. Her pain was a violent thing, searing, flaying her alive, but she fought it down, assembled her wits and her thoughts as she knew Helen would want her to. She had lost her own mother, all over again, but she was the adult now, and Killian was her child.

He was not in the fields, not in the stables, not in the woods. As she searched, Kerry became worried, calling out his name, listening to it fall away into the mist. Only the river answered her, and the owls, and the scurrying creatures down in Timothy's copse.

"Where is he, Timothy? Where is he?"

And then she knew. The graveyard. He had gone back to Helen's grave.

She could not see him as she reached it, in the crepuscule, but she felt him, and then she heard him. He was sobbing, on the damp earth, his legs crossed under him, his head in his hands.

"Killian? Killian, it's all right, it's only me. Sshh . . . don't cry. Don't cry."

But she was crying herself, as he reached his arms up to her in the way he had reached as a baby, to be held and comforted, consoled and caressed, by Helen. Tears streamed down his face, mingling with her own as she sank down on the ground beside him, gathering him into her, hushing, soothing, murmuring the words that came, finally, so easily.

"Sshh . . . she's gone, darling, but you have me, I'm here, I'm here."

The sobs tore from his throat, the hot tears falling in torrents as he burrowed into her, gasping for breath, incoherent and tormented. For a long time she let him cry, holding him to her, offering no platitudes but only the sanctuary of her arms. How he fitted into them, how he clung to her!

But at length he raised his face, gulping, rubbing his eyes with his knuckles in one of the last gestures of childhood.

"Oh, Mum . . . I'm sorry, I didn't think anyone would find me here . . . Why did she die? Why did she have to go – now, just when I needed her, more than ever?"

"What did you need her for? Was it Meggie? Something special?"

For everything, he might say, and he would be right. But whatever it was, she would give it to him.

"F— for herself. I just always wanted her to be here. She always understood, always sensed everything . . . I was going to play specially for her, next week. I can't do the concert now, without her."

"Darling, she'll still be there, with you. She's here with us now. She'll always be with us."

"But she was looking forward to it, so much . . . She came to my rehearsal, just the other day, she told me how much it meant to her . . ."

"Then you must do it, for her. The last thing she heard was your music, Killian. When you give your recital, she'd want you to play as you played that night. That's how I want you to play, too."

"Do you?"

"Yes. I should have been at your rehearsal. I should have been there for you, all your life. I wasn't. But I am here now, Killian, and I always will be, in future."

"Why weren't you, before? What did I do wrong, Mum? If I knew what it was, I'd have tried to stop doing it."

"Nothing, Killian. You did nothing at all. My crime is that I did nothing either. I left it all to Helen, and never even gave you the time of day. I can't explain it, or excuse it. All I can do is try to carry on where Helen left off. If you'll let me, or want me?"

Slipping out of her arms, he took her hand, helping her to her feet as he rose to his own.

"No, Mum. I don't want you to replace Helen. I just want you to be my mother. Let's leave her here in peace, and go home."

It would be easy, Kerry thought, so easy. She could give in to her grief for Helen, and nobody would blame her. She could go over to the house where Bob mourned alone with his dogs, and partake of his sorrow, indulge the pain she felt, talk out her terrible sense of loss.

But she did not. She turned only to Brandon for comfort, late in the intimate night, while each day she brought Bob to Ashamber instead, to join in the family as he had always done. In his face she saw everything that was in her own heart, but she said nothing that would not be helpful to him, to Killian, to everyone.

Brian was there, with Zoe, Yves and Robbie. Having flown over for Helen's funeral, they stayed on for Killian's recital, and encouraged him to resume his rehearsals. He was reluctant, but they nudged and pushed until gradually the ballroom began to fill again with the sound of Beethoven, Brahms and Rachmaninov, so haunting it was almost unnerving.

At first there was pain in the music, then anger, then passion; the boy was pouring out his heart, and Kerry listened very carefully. Young and serious, his face was intense as never before, his eyes closed as his fingers flew over the keys, producing a sound so resonant, so compelling it transcended mere beauty, and made a powerful statement.

How had he so honed his talent? When had he gained such confidence, such authority? From a youth he evolved suddenly into a man, posing questions, debating them, answering them with a complexity far beyond the amateur listener. As she watched, Kerry realised she was losing her son, losing him even as she found him, to the millions of people who would hear him play. In those few days the last contours of childhood were erased from his face, leaving it focused and inscrutable as he entered the realm to which he so wholly belonged. Playing at first for short interludes and then for hours on end, he embraced his vocation, the music that would become the greatest love of his life, and life itself. The house seemed to fill with the spirit of those who had written it, the knowledge of those who would hear it, until he had confirmed himself as a conduit for the genius of centuries, belonging no longer to Ashamber, to Kerry or Brandon, but to everyone.

He would turn professional, after this. There was not the slightest doubt about it, and as the day of the concert arrived Kerry found herself fighting a sense of elated confusion. Discussing her agitation with Yves and Brandon, she was reassured to find that they shared it, and that in their concern for the boy her husband and her dearest friend had, at last, discovered common ground.

"Jesus, Zoe, we're all a bag of nerves."

"Kerry, tonight is Killian's night, not yours. All you have to do is look like his mother and behave like his mother. Don't fuss, don't steal the spotlight, just give him the support he needs."

With advice from Yves and Zoe, Kerry dressed in a way designed to exude quiet confidence, and went to Killian's room.

"Killian? Are you nearly ready? Do you need any help?"

"No thanks, Mum. I'm all set."

He looked anything but, cramming dress shoes and sheet music into a holdall with one hand while he shaved with the other. Dismayed, Kerry gazed at the electric razor, unable to recall the chubby fist that must once have clutched a teddybear.

But it was too late for regret, and so she put her arm around him instead, with a kiss as she wished him luck.

"Thanks, Mum. I'll try not to disgrace you."

His smile was so cheeky, so winsome, she wondered how she had ever resisted it before.

"You couldn't do that if you tried. I've already disgraced myself more than adequately over the years. But tonight, I want you to forget all about me. Think of yourself, and your audience, and Helen."

"I will. I'll be playing for her. It's a big night, but she'll get me through it."

In the convoy of cars that ferried everyone to Dublin, excitement ran high. But, wedged between Brandon who was driving, and Yves whose hand she held tightly, Kerry sat quietly, feeling her way into her future.

Brandon has always been a real father to my son, she thought, and tonight his wife is going to be everything she should be. Helen is gone, and her place has become mine, sustaining and nurturing our family, holding it all together. I know I'm far from perfect, still fanatical about Ashamber and the horses, but the people who share my life are more important now than the things that drive it. My priorities are changing, and so am I.

Lost in thought, she was dazzled by the bright lights of the Concert Hall when they reached it, astonished to see Killian's photograph everywhere, proclaiming the programme he would play. Yet his inexperience was such that he did not think to enter by the stage door at the back, bounding up the front steps instead, into the lobby where his tutor was waiting.

"Doesn't he get a dressing room, Brandon?"

"Yes, of course he does. His tutor will take him to it. But why not let him enjoy the buzz out here first, just for a little?"

There was indeed a buzz as his friends and supporters surrounded him, and as Brandon went to order drinks for them all, Kerry found herself swept up into the atmosphere of this most exciting night. Many people began to arrive, some of them seeking her out to congratulate her on her gifted son, and speculate as to which international maestro might now take him under his wing. Vivaciously, she chatted with everyone, while keeping a protective eye on Yves, and little Meggie Kavanagh.

Quite some time elapsed before she was conscious of Killian's tutor trying to get him backstage, and Zoe at her side, trying agitatedly to get her attention.

"What, Zoe? You said not to fuss, and now you—"

"Kerry, turn around – slowly – look – over there, at the door."

Turning, she followed Zoe's frozen stare, and saw a man producing his ticket for an usher as he entered the building. A man in a grey suit, with a short thick beard and dark curly hair, brown eyes and an air of authority.

Darragh. Darragh de Bruin.

Kerry's heart stalled. In the eternity of shock, he loomed into her view like an old schooner out of a fog, a schooner long ago given up for lost, returning to disgorge its hideous cargo and claim fresh victims. Groping to steady herself, she closed her eyes.

But it was not a mirage. It was Darragh. Solid, incarnate, a forty-two-year-old man standing alone and intent, come to proclaim paternity of his son, the concert pianist.

After eighteen years, Kerry had not forgotten Darragh, or his quest for glory. No scruple had ever stood in his way – or, she thought, ever would. Signalling Zoe to say nothing, make no scene, she detached herself from their party, and went to face what she had denied for nearly two decades.

Scanning the lobby, he saw her, and as she came closer she sensed that he had expected to. The brown eyes flickered – almost, she thought, with the mocking irony of old. But his face registered pleasure.

His face! Somehow Kerry braced herself to look at it, feeling as she had felt at the moment of Killian's birth, when some agonising thing was ripped from her core. Fighting for control, she gleaned instant information from the jousting eyes, the teeth still so white and even, the new network of fine lines. A strong face, certain of itself here as on that March morning in the métro of St Michel.

Darragh. Her old love, her first love, her lost love. But all that she had loved was gone: the guitar, the ponytail, the irresistible whiff of rebellion. In their place, the uniform of commerce, the stance of success, and something she least expected – the signs of conformity. At some point in the years since last they met, Darragh de Bruin had been caught, and tamed.

Something fluttered and struggled inside her, like a bird in a clenched fist. Yet the body was the same, compact and muscular as before. And the eyes, challenging and compelling as they inspected her openly, with the old taunting sedition. He had caught her on the raw, and seemed to know it.

"Kerry. Kerry Laraghy. After all this time. How lovely to see you."

His tone was conciliatory, even sincere, as he reached out to her. Swiftly, she evaded the embrace.

"No, Darragh. Not Kerry Laraghy. Kerry Lawrence."

"Yes. Of course. But Kerry just the same."

"You know that I remarried? After you divorced me?"

She could not disguise it, and he heard it; a tiny tremble in her voice, some quiver of hurt that distressed him, and gladdened him. Whatever she felt, it was not apathy.

"Yes, I know. That was why I did it. When you didn't

come back to me, I thought you must want your freedom, for somebody better."

Better? He could conceive of somebody better, than himself? But then, he must have changed, perhaps even matured as she had matured. Conscious of Killian standing only yards away, she grabbed his arm.

"Darragh. Please come outside."

He had no choice as she propelled him forcibly out into the grounds and indicated a bench.

"Sit down, and listen to me. Listen carefully."

He sat. Taut as a bow, she drew breath.

"This is neither the time nor the place, Darragh, for us to meet, much less discuss what we've been doing, what we have become, since we parted. But obviously you have come here for a particular reason tonight. Is it Killian?"

She threw the words like stones into his face, and his eyes rippled with pain.

"Yes. It is Killian. I go to all his concerts."

It took her a moment to absorb that. Killian's father knew who he was, where he was, what he was doing.

"You – you follow him? You spy on him?"

"Kerry, they're public events! I may not have the right to approach him, speak to him, but I do have the right to see him, if only from afar."

"You have no rights. He's my son, mine and my husband's, and if you take one step into our lives I will tell him who you are and what you did. You raped me and you wanted to abort him. I will tell everyone, and destroy you."

Expecting argument, she got only a searching look, and trenchant silence. Some time elapsed before he spoke again, in a low tone that changed the key between them.

"Kerry, we could debate that all night, and miss the concert. So let me simply say that I have been watching Killian for years, from a safe distance, a distance harmful to neither you nor him. I'm a lawyer, and it hasn't been difficult to find out those things I needed to know. Namely, that you were both safe and well."

"Your concern is touching, but rather belated."

"Oh, Kerry! Do you think I'm the same person now?

That I've learned nothing from my mistakes? I made the greatest mistake of my life, when I let you go. By the time I realised that, you had changed too. You were established, successful, and my son was no longer a baby. I needed you, but you no longer needed me."

Astonished, she gazed at him. Darragh de Bruin had made a mistake, he said? What was it, that she heard in his voice? Shame? Sorrow? Humility, even?

"Then what is it you want now? To bask in his glory, is that it? To meet him, and tell him from where he got his music?"

"I want nothing to which I have no right. I played no part in his education, I contributed nothing to his upkeep, and the price I pay today is my silence. Your husband has earned everything, including the right to call my son his son."

"Yes, he has, Darragh. He has made enormous sacrifices for us, and you are not going to undermine them."

Filling with love for Brandon, vibrating with passion, Kerry's voice told Darragh at that moment just how much he had thrown away. Thrown away, never to find again, anywhere, in anyone.

Long since, he had thought the wound healed, the void filled. But as he looked at her, he knew that it was not. That was why he had avoided her, denied her, and sought to remarry. And then, not remarried. She had run away from him, but she had held onto him too, held on like a vice, and beaten him.

God, how bewitching she was, with that light in her eyes! Absorbing her, assessing the woman who had once been his wife, he saw no sign of the naive child, the lost waif; only the elegant, confident being she had become. His gaze fell on her hand, and to his surprise she let him look at it, the short nails, the callused skin, the evidence of a hard life, a toll taken.

He said what he intended to say, and had long needed to say.

"All I ask, Kerry, is your forgiveness. You may not think I've paid, but I have. I have. Over and over . . . Every time I met another woman, I saw your face, felt your skin, heard your voice. I'm happy for you, that you found Brandon, but

I'm ruined for anyone else. I have no other family, and that's why I go to hear Killian. I gave him his genes, if nothing else, and his talent is the only pleasure I have."

She felt it then: all the loss, the loneliness, the fierce pride turned to arid isolation. In his eyes lay nothing but the dusty *brousse* of Senegal.

Senegal! As soon as she thought of it, she could see it: the searing sun, the sparkling water, the milky nights under the shimmering stars. The fun, at first, in that shack smelling of coconuts and gas, fish stew and mosquitoes . . . playing at life, so young, so valiant. A lovely idyll, a bitter memory.

Yet she could not be bitter. It was not in her nature.

"I'm sorry, Darragh. Sorry for you, and for our son, and for the mistakes we made. He has suffered, because of us, and them. I've tried to forget, and if it matters to you, then I can try now to forgive. But that's all I can do."

"It's enough, Kerry. I want more – much more, including Killian. But I gave him away, of my own free will. I'll be in a front row tonight, but I won't be by his side. I've succeeded in my career, but he will have far greater success in his – all the applause, the adulation I once craved for myself. You can share it with him, but I can't. I know that, and I accept it."

She saw that he was telling the truth, and how much it cost him. After almost twenty years, she had won a battle she never knew she was fighting. Defeated by his own rigorous ethics, his own merciless justice, the man she had once loved stood entirely alone. He would not touch Killian, because he could not.

That was why he had never come to them, for them. Not because he hated them, or rejected them. Simply because his honour was greater than his claim.

Quietly, she put her hand on his shoulder.

"You know, Darragh, I can't pretend I care, whatever you may wish tonight, or feel. I no longer love you, or like you, or even think about you. But I do believe you, and have to respect you."

Respect. It was all he had ever wanted.

"Thank you, Kerry. I'm glad you can give me that much. I won't ask for more."

"No. Killian doesn't know who you are, Darragh, and that's how you must leave it. If he ever asks, I will tell him, now that he's old enough, and let him go to you. But then you will have to tell him why we parted. His welfare is my responsibility, but his questions are yours."

Unflinching, he nodded, a captive in the cell of his own design. He was not a broken man, by any means, but under the veneer of success lay a man whose greatest achievement was the son he could never reach, never hold, never bring back. A son who would be loved by everyone, except the father who could show no emotion.

Kerry did not know the effect of her departure on him, that day in Yoff, but she knew it this time, as she left him.

With one sweep of her arm Kerry cleared the dressing room of everyone who stood in it.

"Come on, everybody out. This concert is about to begin, and I want a moment first with my husband and son."

In a flurry they all left, even Zoe with her face full of questions.

"Yes, Yves, even you, *mon chou*."

She puckered her lips to his cheek as he went, and shooed them away until only Brandon remained, with Killian.

"What kept you, Mum? We thought we'd lost you."

"No, darling. You'll never lose me. You're stuck with me for life."

"Who was that man you were talking to?"

"An admirer. Your very first fan."

Thoughtfully, Killian adjusted his cuffs in the mirror.

"I think I know him."

In the glass, their reflected eyes locked together.

"Do you?"

"Yes. I've seen him before. At my concerts. He comes to them all, and sits at the front."

"Well – he must think very highly of you. But it will be more difficult for him to get there in future. After tonight, everyone will want front-row seats."

"But he's been very loyal, ever since I first played in parish halls and little salons. If I knew who he was, I'd see that good tickets were kept for him. But he always comes alone, and leaves on the last note. Did you get his name?"

"No. I never took it."

With a shrug, he turned away from the mirror.

"Oh, well. I suppose I'll find out who he is eventually. But the only people I really want to see in the front row tonight are you and Dad."

He smiled at her, and she smiled back.

"We'll be there. With eyes only for you."

There was a knock at the door, and Brandon looked at his watch.

"Come on, Kerry. Latecomers aren't admitted."

With his arm around her waist, he led her out, and his grip did not loosen as they took their places.

Minutes later, the curtain went up, and their son came on stage.

LIZ RYAN

THE PAST IS TOMORROW

Shivaun Reilly has had enough. Still reeling from the loss of the only family she ever knew, passionately angry at the closure of her beloved hospital, she thinks her heart will break when solid, dependable Ivor – the man she always thought she'd marry – decides to give up his glossy career to follow rugged new paths in Spain.

Shivaun's ever-helpful lodger Alana finds the perfect solution: a job in America as a private nurse, away from all the politics and disappointments. She can't wait to go – and in a pretty New England town, she finds a whole new world of optimism and friendship.

But neither happiness nor unhappiness is that easy to leave behind. Helpful Alana had her own reasons for coming to Shivaun's rescue, and soon, her lies and evasions have led her into trouble. Though Shivaun meets new friends, including a fascinating Irishman, in New England not all of them are what they seem to be. And in Spain, Ivor has begun to re-think his rash decision.

Shivaun discovers both America and some important truths. Truths that are as challenging as they are liberating . . .

'CAPITVATING . . . BRINGS A FRESHNESS AND VERVE TO THE BOY-MEETS-GIRL STORY. THE RYAN TWIST ON FICTIONAL ROMANCE INVESTS THE ROSY GARDEN OF LOVE WITH SOME OF THE SHARPEST THORNS.'
Justine McCarthy, *Irish Independent*

HODDER AND STOUGHTON PAPERBACKS

A selection of bestsellers from Hodder & Stoughton

The Year of Her Life	Liz Ryan	0 340 76878 9	£6.99	☐
The Past is Tomorrow	Liz Ryan	0 340 76876 2	£6.99	☐
A Taste of Freedom	Liz Ryan	0 340 67211 0	£5.99	☐
A Note of Parting	Liz Ryan	0 340 62458 2	£6.99	☐

All Hodder & Stoughton books are available at your local bookshop or newsagent, or can be ordered direct from the publisher. Just tick the titles you want and fill in the form below. Prices and availability subject to change without notice.

Hodder & Stoughton Books, Cash Sales Department, Bookpoint, 39 Milton Park, Abingdon, OXON, OX14 4TD, UK. E-mail address: orders@bookpoint.co.uk. If you have a credit card you may order by telephone – (01235) 400414.

Please enclose a cheque or postal order made payable to Bookpoint Ltd to the value of the cover price and allow the following for postage and packing:
UK & BFPO: £1.00 for the first book, 50p for the second book and 30p for each additional book ordered up to a maximum charge of £3.00.
OVERSEAS & EIRE: £2.00 for the first book, £1.00 for the second book and 50p for each additional book.

Name . . . .

Address . . . .

. . . .

. . . .

If you would prefer to pay by credit card, please complete:
Please debit my Visa / Access / Diner's Club / American Express (delete as applicable) card no:

Signature . . . .

Expiry Date . . . .

If you would NOT like to receive further information on our products please tick the box. ☐